THE COMPLETE SERIES

JAYNE CASTEL

All characters and situations in this publication are fictitious, and any resemblance to living persons is purely coincidental.

The Sisters of Kilbride: The Complete Series, by Jayne Castel

Copyright © 2020 by Jayne Castel. All rights reserved. No part of this publication may be reproduced, stored in a retrieval system, or transmitted in any form or by any means—electronic, mechanical, recording, or otherwise—without the prior written permission of the author.

Published by Winter Mist Press
Cover design by Winter Mist Press
Edited by Tim Burton

Cover photography courtesy of www.shutterstock.com
Map by Jayne Castel
Celtic cross image courtesy of www.pixabay.com

Excerpt from the traditional Scottish song 'These are my mountains.'
http://www.rampantscotland.com/songs/blsongs_these.htm

Visit Jayne's website: www.jaynecastel.com

Historical Romances by Jayne Castel

DARK AGES BRITAIN

The Kingdom of the East Angles series
Dark Under the Cover of Night (Book One)
Nightfall till Daybreak (Book Two)
The Deepening Night (Book Three)
The Kingdom of the East Angles: The Complete Series

The Kingdom of Mercia series
The Breaking Dawn (Book One)
Darkest before Dawn (Book Two)
Dawn of Wolves (Book Three)
The Kingdom of Mercia: The Complete Series

The Kingdom of Northumbria series
The Whispering Wind (Book One)
Wind Song (Book Two)
Lord of the North Wind (Book Three)
The Kingdom of Northumbria: The Complete Series

DARK AGES SCOTLAND

The Warrior Brothers of Skye series
Blood Feud (Book One)
Barbarian Slave (Book Two)
Battle Eagle (Book Three)
The Warrior Brothers of Skye: The Complete Series

The Pict Wars series
Warrior's Heart (Book One)
Warrior's Secret (Book Two)
Warrior's Wrath (Book Three)
The Pict Wars: The Complete Series

Novellas
Winter's Promise

MEDIEVAL SCOTLAND

The Brides of Skye series
The Beast's Bride (Book One)
The Outlaw's Bride (Book Two)
The Rogue's Bride (Book Three)

The Brides of Skye: The Complete Series

The Sisters of Kilbride series
Unforgotten (Book One)
Awoken (Book Two)
Fallen (Book Three)
Claimed (Epilogue novella)

The Immortal Highland Centurions series
Maximus (Book One)
Cassian (Book Two)
Draco (Book Three)
The Laird's Return (Epilogue festive novella)

Stolen Highland Hearts series
Highlander Deceived (Book One)
Highlander Entangled (Book Two)
Highlander Forbidden (Book Three)
Highlander Pledged (Book Four)

Guardians of Alba series
Nessa's Seduction (Book One)
Fyfa's Sacrifice (Book Two)
Breanna's Surrender (Book Three)

Epic Fantasy Romances by Jayne Castel

Light and Darkness series
Ruled by Shadows (Book One)
The Lost Swallow (Book Two)
Path of the Dark (Book Three)
Light and Darkness: The Complete Series

Contents

Unforgotten (Book One) 7

Awoken (Book Two) 193

Fallen (Book Three) 357

Claimed (Bonus novella) 545

Unforgotten

Book One
The Sisters of Kilbride

Jayne Castel

Map

Meminisse sed providere
Remember but look ahead
—MacNichol clan motto

Prologue

I have No Choice

*MacNichol territory,
Isle of Skye, Scotland*

Late summer, 1330 AD

HE WAS LATE.

Annella Fraser should have taken that as a sign, for Gavin MacNichol never kept her waiting. In the three months they had been seeing each other—a long, hot summer that Ella would never forget—Gavin hadn't arrived late once.

Alone in the clearing, Ella started to pace. She couldn't keep still. Butterflies danced in the pit of her belly, and her pulse skittered. She needed to remember to breathe, to calm her excitement.

As she circled the clearing, Ella pulled her linen léine away from her back. She wore only a light woolen kirtle over it, yet the day was humid and she was starting to sweat. The air was heavy, charged. The sky overhead was darkening, and in the distance, she heard the unmistakable rumble of thunder.

Ella's mouth curved in anticipation. She wondered what it would be like to make love to Gavin while the storm raged around them. Her chest tightened, and her lower belly turned molten at the thought.

She stopped pacing and peered through the trees—northeast, in the direction of Scorrybreac Castle.

Where is he?

Worry crept in, dimming Ella's nervous anticipation. Their time together, illicit and stolen, was so precious that neither of them could afford to be late. She wondered what had delayed him. Matters at Scorrybreac perhaps? His father had poor health these days and relied upon his eldest son increasingly.

Ella's breathing hitched. Maybe he wasn't coming this afternoon.

And then she heard it: the snap of twigs and the rustle of undergrowth accompanied by the 'thud' of approaching hoof beats. A smile flowered across Ella's face, and she loosed the breath she'd been holding, the tension flooding from her. She needn't have worried. Gavin had said he would meet her this afternoon, and he'd always been a man of his word.

An instant later a warrior rode into the clearing.

Even now, months after they had started meeting here, Ella's pulse quickened at the sight of him. Tall, broad-shouldered, and strong, the MacNichol chieftain's eldest son had a mane of long dark-blond hair that rippled over his shoulders and warm blue eyes. His face was ruggedly handsome, and whenever he smiled, a deep dimple appeared upon his left cheek.

However, Gavin wasn't smiling now.

Dressed in plaid braies and a loose white léine that was open at the neck, the young man carried an aura of tension about him. His handsome face was strained, and a groove had furrowed between his eyebrows.

Swinging down from the saddle, he deftly tied his stallion up next to where Ella's courser nipped at grass in the clearing. Around them grew a copse of shady birch trees. A burn trickled through the center of the clearing, its banks mossy. This was a secluded place, known only by hunters who ventured into this densely wooded valley that lay a short ride southwest of the MacNichol stronghold of Scorrybreac.

"I was beginning to worry ye weren't coming." The words rushed out of Ella before she had the chance to stem them. She didn't want to appear needy, the kind of anxious lass who clawed at her lover. But his tardiness had concerned her nevertheless.

"I'm sorry, mo leannan." Gavin strode to Ella and pulled her into his arms for a bruising kiss.

My sweetheart. The hunger of his embrace surprised Ella. He wasn't usually so forceful. Though young and eager, Gavin MacNichol had proved to be a gentle lover, something Ella adored. She'd always felt so safe with him.

Even so, the hunger of his kiss excited her. She responded eagerly, wrapping her arms around his neck and going up on tiptoe, pressing her body against his.

When they pulled away, the pair of them were both breathless.

Ella tilted her chin, staring up at him, devouring Gavin's strong jaw, kind eyes, and sensual mouth. Lord, how she'd missed their trysts over the past two weeks. Every moment apart from him had been torture. But at Scorrybreac Castle they had to be wary; Gavin's mother always seemed to be watching. Ella sometimes wondered if the woman suspected something.

Now that she was standing this close, there was no denying the change in Gavin's face. Those blue eyes, the color of a summer's sky, were shadowed.

Ella stiffened. "What is it, love?"

Gavin released a long breath before stepping back and dragging a hand through his unbound hair. "Something's happened, Ella ... we need to talk."

Ella went still. He hadn't given any details away, but she instinctively knew that he brought ill news. Even though he had only just entered his twentieth summer, Gavin MacNichol was a steadying influence, a man of even temper and a ready smile. To see him so on edge, and so obviously upset, made a chill slither down her spine.

"My father," Gavin began, his voice husky. "The healer saw him this morning … he's dying."

The news that clan-chief Iain MacNichol's health had deteriorated didn't come entirely as a shock to Ella. The last time she had seen the clan-chief, he'd been gaunt, his face a sickly-yellow color. Nonetheless, she knew that having the illness confirmed by a healer would have shocked both MacNichol and his kin. "I'm so sorry," she whispered.

Gavin shook his head, his throat bobbing. "My ill news does not stop there," he continued, a rasp to his voice. "There's the matter of my betrothal."

Ella stopped breathing. Over the past three months, the best summer of her life, awareness of his betrothal had cast a constant shadow over her happiness. "What of it?" she finally whispered.

"My parents have insisted that I must honor it," Gavin replied. "They have bidden me wed Innis before Samhain."

Ella stared at him, her lips parting. "But ye promised ye would talk to yer parents … tell them ye would not wed my sister?" Her voice started to rise. She hated its shrillness, but she could not help herself. She began to breathe fast, panic rising within her, buzzing like an enraged swarm of hornets. Her ears started to ring.

Gavin shook his head, his gaze clouding. "It's not as easy as that," he replied. "A betrothal isn't a simple thing to break. And with my father's ill-health, there has never been a right time." He broke off there, his expression turning pained. "Neither of my parents had mentioned the betrothal of late … and I thought it ceased to matter to them." He swallowed hard. "But I was wrong … it does."

"But ye don't love Innis. Do ye?"

Gavin shook his head. "Ye know I don't," he replied softly. "It's ye I want."

"So go to them, tell them how ye feel."

Gavin took a step back from her, shaking his head. "It's too late, Ella. The agreement was writ and signed upon my thirteenth winter: Gavin MacNichol of Scorrybreac shall wed Innis Fraser of Talasgair. I thought it could be broken, but it cannot. I tried to tell my father that my heart lay elsewhere, yet he would not listen." Gavin drew in a sharp breath. "He has made it his dying wish."

For the longest moment, Ella merely stared at him.

She'd strayed into a nightmare. It was as if someone else were having this conversation.

Her elder sister, Innis, was sweet-natured and fair of face—much more so than Ella—but she didn't love Gavin, and he didn't love her.

Ella and Gavin hadn't meant for all of this to happen. Five years earlier, her family had moved from Talasgair—on the western coast of the isle, where the Fraser stronghold lay—to Scorrybreac Castle on the east, so that the eldest daughter could be betrothed to the MacNichol heir.

Ella and Gavin had become friends within the first few days, and then the pair of them had started spending more and more time together as the years passed. Gavin's shrewish mother had always disapproved, but Innis hadn't minded. Ella's elder sister, pious and reserved, preferred to sit at her tapestries or read psalms rather than take walks in the woods or go hunting.

These were pastimes that both Gavin and Ella enjoyed—and so they had started going out together.

It hadn't taken long before a bond had forged between them, although they had only become lovers this summer. Ella had felt guilty at first—Gavin was promised to her sister after all—but the guilt soon passed as passion took hold.

"Ye are breaking my heart," Ella whispered, her voice trembling. "Please don't do this."

Gavin stared back at her, his gaze guttering. "I'm so sorry, mo ghràdh," he whispered, his voice broken. "But I have no choice."

1

Facing the Past

Kilbride Abbey
MacKinnon Territory
Isle of Skye, Scotland

Eighteen years later ...

1348 AD

CHANGE ALWAYS APPEARED in Ella's life when she least expected it.

Fortune's wheel didn't turn on the days when she was ready, like after Yuletide when she prepared herself to face the year ahead. Or after a birth or death—significant events that made her pause and take stock of where she was in life.

No, change arrived at happy moments when she was at peace with the world, or on forgettable days when there was nothing but routine to punctuate the moment of its arrival. Fate liked to sneak in and attack from behind. And for that reason, it always caught her unawares.

Sister Ella was hard at work in the gardens of Kilbride Abbey when the second major turning point of her life came.

It was a breathless afternoon in late summer. It wasn't the kind of weather that Ella liked, for it reminded her of another day many years earlier. A black moment. One she had tried her hardest to forget.

There wasn't the slightest breeze to cool the orderly patchwork of vegetable beds inside the abbey's sturdy walls. The air this afternoon smelled of warm earth and grass, and the heat had brought out the noises of surrounding insects and birdlife. Crickets chirped in the nearby herb beds, while somewhere in the hard blue sky above a skylark trilled. Bees buzzed by, traveling from flower to flower, for the nuns had planted roses and lavender around the perimeter of the garden.

A bumblebee droned by Ella's nose then, as she straightened up and wiped her sweating brow with the back of her wrist. She'd been weeding the onion bed for a long while and was pleased with her progress. She had nearly

15

finished. However, her back was starting to ache. The sun was ferocious this afternoon; she could feel its heat burning into her skin, even through the material of her veil and habit.

"Sister Ella!"

A call drew her attention from the neat lines of onions and leeks that stretched before her toward the eastern wall of the abbey. Ella glanced back over her shoulder at where a small figure, garbed in black, hurried toward her. Sister Leanna's habit swamped her. Like Ella, a white wimple framed her face and a voluminous black habit reached her ankles, in the style of the Cluniac order. The young woman's delicately featured face was flushed, her hazel eyes gleaming with excitement.

Ella rose to her feet, grimacing as her joints protested. She had been crouched over weeding for far too long this afternoon. She wasn't old, not like Sister Magda or Sister Fiona, but at thirty-six winters she found that her body sometimes protested at the demands of life in the order. And after hours of gardening on her knees, now was one such time.

"What is it?" Ella asked. "Did I miss the bell to Vespers again?"

It did happen. Sometimes Ella got so immersed in gardening, so lost in her own contemplation, that she even failed to notice the bells calling the sisters to prayer at regular intervals throughout the day.

Sister Leanna laughed. "No, it's too early for that." A smile curved the novice's mouth. "Ye have a visitor."

Ella went still.

For eighteen years she had resided within the walls of Kilbride, this Cluniac abbey upon the southwestern shores of the Isle of Skye. In all that time, she'd never once had a visitor.

Ella's mouth flattened into a thin line. She didn't welcome the news. A visitor meant someone from her old life, and that life was dead to her now. It had been for nearly two decades.

"Who is it?" Ella forced herself to ask the question.

Suddenly, she didn't feel well. She was sweaty and incredibly thirsty. Not only that, but her forehead now ached dully, the result of spending too many hours out here in the sun.

"A tall man with blond hair. I caught a glimpse of him ... he's handsome." Sister Leanna's smile widened. She'd been at Kilbride just over a year—not long enough for the outside world, and men, to lose their appeal. "I know not his name," Sister Leanna continued, seemingly unaware that Ella had gone rigid. "But Mother Shona bid me fetch ye. He awaits ye in the chapter house."

A wave of nausea swept over Ella.

Tall and handsome with blond hair.

Don't panic, she counseled herself. *That could describe many a man upon the isle.*

Ella swallowed, struggling to keep her face composed. "How old would ye say he is?"

"Mature," Sister Leanna replied with a wave of her hand. "At least yer age, Sister Ella ... possibly older."

Ella's mouth curved into a brittle smile. *Mature*. Had she once viewed anyone over the age of thirty in the same way? Even so, Sister Leanna's last words made Ella's heart start to hammer.

No, it couldn't be.

"The abbess bids ye to come now," Sister Leanna said, her gaze turning questioning. "Are ye well, Sister Ella?" She asked with a frown. "Yer cheeks are flushed."

Ella drew in a deep, steadying breath. "I fear I've taken too much sun," she muttered. Brushing off her dirt-encrusted hands against her skirts, she walked down the path leading between the rows of vegetables, toward the complex of buildings at their back.

Sister Leanna fell in step next to her.

Ella didn't converse. Instead, she fought the tide of panic that rose within her.

He wouldn't come here. He wouldn't dare ... not after all these years.

"It's nearly time for archery practice," Sister Leanna said, breaking the silence. Ella heard the excitement in her voice. "Mother Shona says I am improving swiftly."

It was true. Ella had seen the novice wield a longbow. She had a steady arm and keen eyesight.

"Do ye think she'll let me go out hunting soon?" Sister Leanna asked, impatience tinging her voice. "I want to be able to bring back deer ... to feed the abbey."

"She'll let ye soon enough, I'm sure," Ella murmured, distracted. "When she thinks ye are ready."

Together the two women left the gardens and entered the abbey complex. Like the high walls surrounding them, the buildings of Kilbride were made of a pale grey stone that gleamed in the sunlight.

The tiled roof of the kirk rose above it all, outlined against a cloudless blue sky. Skirting the edge of the kirk, Ella made her way toward the chapter house. On the way, she passed a wide yard. Here, a cluster of nuns were setting up targets while others approached bearing longbows and quivers of arrows.

"There ye are, Sister Leanna," one of the nuns called out. Her name was Sister Coira. She was tall and broad-shouldered with violet eyes framed by dark brows—and she was one of Ella's closest friends here. "Sister Ella ... will ye practice with us?"

"Maybe later," Ella called back, forcing a smile. She wondered if Sister Coira and the others had seen her visitor. If so, Sister Coira gave no sign. She merely smiled back and nodded before turning to the young postulant trotting up behind her with an armload of quivers. "Hand those out please, Sister Mina."

Leaving them to it, Ella walked on.

Gavin MacNichol favored Mother Shona with a smile that he hoped didn't betray his nervousness. "I trust Sister Annella is keeping well?"

It was an inane question, but the silence inside the chapter house—a small building that was used for meetings—was getting to him. The space, which had arched stained-glass windows lining the walls and a vaulted ceiling, had grown uncomfortably silent during the wait.

"The Lord has blessed us with Sister Ella. She is a valued member of our community," the abbess replied, her tone reserved. "Ye will be able to ask after her health face-to-face, for she will be here soon."

Sister Ella.

Even after all these years, he couldn't imagine her living here as a nun, crow-like in austere black robes.

Gavin nodded and resisted the urge to wipe his palms on his braies. He felt as nervous as a lad before his first dance. As civil as the abbess was, he wished she would leave him alone so that he could pace around and rid himself of the nervous energy that pulsed through him.

He could feel his heart hammering against his breastbone, and his breathing had quickened, sounding overly loud in the silence. It felt airless and stuffy inside the chapter house.

The abbess had brought him here so that he could speak to Sister Annella in private.

"May I ask why ye have come here alone?" The abbess asked after a long pause. "It can't be safe to travel without an escort."

Gavin's gaze settled upon Mother Shona. She was barely a handful of years older than him. She had a pleasant face, warm brown eyes, and good skin—but her habit and veil completely covered her hair and robbed her of any femininity. Perhaps, in other circumstances, the woman may have been attractive, but dressed in such a way it was impossible to tell. That was most likely the point. Brides of Christ had no wish to make themselves attractive to men.

"I wished to travel swiftly ... due to the urgency of this matter," Gavin replied. His mouth quirked then. "However, I did narrowly avoid some trouble on the way here ... two men tried to pull me off my horse yesterday, just after I entered MacKinnon territory, but I managed to outrun them."

Holding his gaze, the abbess's expression turned grave. "It never used to be so dangerous to travel the roads of Skye. Ever since the war with the English, the mood has turned here." She paused, her brown eyes shuttering. "Not only that, but I'm afraid the folk of these lands suffer under Duncan MacKinnon's rule."

Gavin raised an eyebrow at her comment. "Lawlessness is a growing problem upon the isle," he replied. "And I did notice that when I crossed into MacKinnon lands, the villages I passed seemed particularly impoverished."

The abbess's lips compressed. "I do not like my nuns to travel unescorted," she said. Her voice was soft although Gavin caught the edge to it. Mother Shona of Kilbride was highly protective of those within these walls. "I allow this only because ye are a clan-chief and because of the nature of the situation."

Gavin nodded. "I understand, Mother Shona ... and I am grateful."

They both fell silent then, and Gavin shifted his gaze to the arched windows to his left. The afternoon sun streamed through the stained glass, creating squares of red, blue, and gold on the paved floor of the chapter house.

Maybe I shouldn't have come here.

The message he bore could have been brought by another. Why then had he made the effort? It was a two-day journey from Scorrybreac Castle. Just like Mother Shona, his kin and clansmen had found it odd that he'd insisted on riding out on his own like this. But it was something he'd felt compelled to do.

Some meetings could not be put off. Some, like this one, were many years overdue.

He'd told himself that the entire journey here. Only, when he'd spied the peaked roof of the abbey's kirk in the distance, standing out against the deep blue of the sea beyond, misgiving had plagued him.

He should have sent a party in his stead, but it was too late now. He was here.

Hearing the soft footfalls of someone approaching outside, Gavin tensed.

He turned his gaze to the door, drawing in a sharp breath as he readied himself to come face-to-face with his past.

The door swung open with a creak, and a nun entered: a small woman cloaked in black.

"Sister Ella," Mother Shona greeted the newcomer, waving her forward. The nun drew close to the abbess and dropped to one knee in front of her. Mother Shona quickly made the sign of the cross and waited till the newcomer had risen to her feet, before she spoke once more. "MacNichol has a message for ye." The abbess's gaze flicked between the two of them. "Are ye happy to speak with him alone, or would ye like me to remain?"

"Thank ye, Mother Shona. Ye may leave us," the nun murmured. Gavin caught his breath. That voice, low and gentle, was exactly as he remembered it.

"Very well ... peace be upon ye both." With a probing glance, first at Gavin, and then at Sister Ella, Mother Shona left the chapter house.

Gavin stared at the figure before him and tried to find a trace of the lass he had once known.

The habit completely obliterated her character. A black veil covered her head, and a snow-white wimple framed a winsome face, while a black habit fell to dusty sandals. A narrow leather belt girded the habit at the waist, where a wooden crucifix hung.

Gavin continued to stare at her. After so many years apart, he drank her in.

It frustrated him that he couldn't see her hair, which he remembered as a soft coppery color. He studied her delicate features. The years had left very little of a mark upon her. The woman's face was perhaps a trifle leaner than he remembered, but she still had the same Cupid's bow mouth, with that sensual upper lip that had once driven him mad with longing. He remembered too her loch-blue eyes, which held a penetrating, intelligent look. Finely drawn eyebrows framed them.

Aye, it was her—and yet it was not.

Once again, Gavin regretted the impulse that had driven him here. He looked into the face of the woman he'd once loved—the woman he had forsaken in order to wed her sister and do his duty.

He realized then that there was a reason why the past was often better left alone.

2
Unchanged

ELLA WAS UNPREPARED for the actual shock of seeing him.

It seemed a lifetime ago—someone else's life—since she'd last set eyes on Gavin MacNichol. She'd told herself that he would look vastly different to how she remembered him. She'd assured herself that he'd have grown old and fat, as his father had as he'd aged.

But he hadn't.

The man who awaited her in the chapter house wasn't so different to the one she'd left behind at Scorrybreac. The years had tempered his boyish good looks, but he still wore his hair long, tied back this afternoon at the nape of his neck. And it was the face of a mature man who looked back at her. Even so, those warm blue eyes were unchanged.

Had he always been this tall and broad? The warrior loomed before her, making Ella painfully aware of her own short stature.

The MacNichol clan-chief was dressed in travel-stained braies and a léine, although to enter the abbey he'd donned a sash of his clan plaid: red lined with green. Dust coated his long leather hunting boots, revealing that despite the humidity in the air this afternoon, it hadn't rained in days.

As if sensing her scrutiny, the man's mouth curved into a smile.

Ella went still. His smile hadn't changed one bit. Gavin's face had roughened with the years, but she'd never forgotten the lazy way his mouth curved when he was amused or the deep dimple that appeared upon his left cheek when he smiled.

"I hope I haven't altered too much," he greeted her, his voice soft and slightly hesitant. "Ye haven't changed at all, Ella."

Her spine stiffened. "Sister Ella," she replied. "Why are ye here, MacNichol?"

Gavin's eyes clouded. Her cool welcome displeased him, but she didn't care about his hurt feelings. She'd ridden from Scorrybreac Castle many years earlier and never looked back. Seeing him again here in the flesh brought up memories that she'd long since buried.

She wanted them kept buried.

"Yer mother is dying," he replied after a pause, all business now. His expression had shuttered. He'd been pleased to see her; she'd seen it in his eyes. But that had been before she'd been offhand with him. Now he wore an aloof mask. "She wishes ye to come to see her at Scorrybreac," he continued. "Before it's too late."

Ella stared back at him. She'd had no contact with either of her parents all these years, although her sister, Innis, had written to her. The last correspondence she'd received had been before her sister's death nearly two years earlier. That letter had been a plea for Ella to visit her. She'd been gravely ill and knew she was dying.

But Ella hadn't gone—she had deliberately stayed away from Scorrybreac. Returning there would have brought back too many memories. She'd grieved for her sister, but she hadn't wanted to face her. Guilt still needled her over cutting contact with Innis, although she didn't want Gavin to see it.

"Ye didn't need to deliver the message in person," Ella replied, folding her arms across her breasts in a protective gesture. "A letter would have sufficed."

His brow furrowed, showing that he'd indeed changed over the years. Once, frowns hadn't come readily to Gavin MacNichol. But she could see the fine lines of care upon his brow now.

"I sent word to ye of yer sister's death," he said after a pause. "Yer parents wished ye to attend her burial, but ye never responded." He then folded his own arms across his broad chest, mirroring her action. "I thought that this time, I would come in person." The challenge in his voice was unmistakable.

That was another difference to the amiable young man she had left behind. There was a hardness to Gavin that had been absent nearly two decades earlier. Ella wasn't surprised. The years had a way of shaping folk, wearing at them like waves upon a cliff. One couldn't go through life without being changed by it—even in a place like Kilbride Abbey, where contact with the outside world was minimal.

"I appreciate ye informing me, but I cannot leave here," Ella said after a pause, dropping her gaze to the flagstone floor. "Ye will have to return home and deliver my apologies. May the merciful Lord watch over my mother."

"As God-fearing as yer mother is, I think she'd prefer *ye* did," Gavin replied. "Why can't ye leave the abbey?"

Ella glanced up, her brow furrowing. She didn't have to explain herself to this man. "The Sisters of Kilbride don't travel," she replied, her tone developing a frosty edge.

"But ye are not cloistered?"

"It doesn't matter. We do God's work best here. The farthest I've traveled in years is Torrin. I can't go to Scorrybreac with ye."

"But the abbess has given her blessing."

Alarm fluttered through Ella. What was Mother Shona doing meddling in her affairs? "She should have asked me first."

Gavin raised his dark-blond eyebrows. "So it was just an excuse," he replied softly. "Ye can come with me, but ye don't want to."

They stared at each other for a few long moments. Tension crackled in the air between them with the weight of so many things unsaid.

After that fateful day of their last meeting in the clearing, events had moved quickly at Scorrybreac Castle. Plans had gotten underway for Gavin and Innis's wedding, while Ella had sent word to Kilbride Abbey, requesting admission as a postulant. As soon as she'd heard back from the abbess, who welcomed her to the abbey, Ella had announced the news to her family. She'd left without saying a word of her plans to Gavin.

"If I don't wish to return to Scorrybreac, ye can hardly blame me." Ella didn't like how sharp her voice now sounded. It wasn't her at all. All the nuns here at Kilbride knew her for her gentleness, soft-spoken ways, and ready laugh. But being in the presence of this man gave Ella a sharpness she didn't usually possess. Every nerve in her body stretched taut.

Those warm blue eyes shadowed. "I understand why ye don't wish to return," Gavin admitted finally. "And that's why I came here in person ... to advise ye that no matter what happened in the past, there are times when ye need to see beyond it. Yer mother is seriously ill, Sister Ella. She was in tears when I left. Would ye deny a dying woman the chance to see her only surviving daughter one last time?"

Ella's hand went to the crucifix that hung at her belt, her fingers clasping around it and squeezing hard. *Lord give me strength.*

He was making her feel like some heartless shrew.

He knew the truth of things when it came to her family. She'd confided in him once, telling him of how Innis had always been the favorite daughter. Her father was a kind but weak man, who easily let himself be ruled by his dominant, blade-tongued wife. Ella's mother had always found fault with her youngest daughter. In fact, ironically, the only thing that Ella had ever done right was to take the veil. Ella had saved her parents from having to pay a dowry. A relief indeed. Their eldest daughter had found the match they desired; Ella didn't matter.

"Ye know how things are between my mother and me," Ella finally managed. "Please don't paint her out to be saintly."

His mouth curved, although there was no humor in his eyes. "I'm not," he replied, his tone clipped. "I'm well aware that ye were always the best of them. If ye return home, don't do it for yer mother. Do it for yerself."

Sister Ella and MacNichol emerged from the chapter house into the soft late afternoon sun.

Clack. Clack. Clack.

"What's that?" Gavin asked.

Shifting her gaze right to the training yard, Ella's body went taut. Archery practice had ended, but a group of nuns were now sparring with quarter-staffs. Sister Coira, who was the best of them save the abbess at wielding the quarter-staff, was taking a group of younger nuns through some drills.

Ella couldn't believe they were being so indiscreet. She'd thought they would have finished their training by now. They rarely had visitors here at the abbey, and as such, the nuns had gone about their daily routines without worrying that an outsider might see their strange ways.

Hadn't the abbess warned them all not to let strangers see them at practice?

Folk fear what they don't understand, the abbess had told Ella once. *It's better that we appear harmless nuns ... that way no one will ever be threatened by us.*

"Nothing," Ella replied lightly, hoping he wouldn't pursue the subject. "There are harvest games in Torrin every year ... perhaps some of the sisters wish to take part."

It was a weak excuse, but the best she could make at short notice.

A small figure swathed in black and white approached them then, preventing Gavin from questioning her further; Mother Shona had mercifully come looking for them. Relief filtered through Ella. She'd begun to think that the abbess had deliberately abandoned her with this man. She still hadn't forgiven the abbess for telling him that she had permission to travel to Scorrybreac. It had made it impossible ultimately to refuse him.

"Is it agreed then?" Mother Shona greeted them briskly. She had a no-nonsense approach to human relations. Often Ella appreciated her directness, but this afternoon it grated on her nerves. The abbess knew about her past, although Ella had never told her the name of the man who'd broken her heart.

Perhaps if she had, Mother Shona would have sent him away.

"Aye," Gavin rumbled. "Thank ye, Mother Shona. Sister Ella has agreed to travel north with me. We will not keep her long. I will return her to ye within two weeks at the latest."

Mother Shona favored him with a smile, although her gaze was guarded. "I appreciate that." The abbess's gaze shifted to Ella then, and her smile faded. "I'm sorry to hear about yer mother. She will be in our prayers while ye are away."

"Thank ye, Mother Shona," Ella replied, lowering her gaze so the abbess wouldn't see the irritation in her eyes. "Ye are most kind to allow me to go to her."

The abbess nodded before shifting her attention back to Gavin. "It's too late in the day for ye to start yer return journey," she said, her tone turning brisk once more. "Ye are welcome to stay within the walls of the abbey tonight. I will have the guest house prepared for ye, and we would be delighted if ye would join us for supper this eve."

Gavin MacNichol smiled back at the abbess, his eyes crinkling at the corners. It was the first unfiltered smile Ella had seen him give since being reunited with him, and despite that she fought the sensation, warmth suffused her. "It would be my pleasure, Mother Shona," he replied.

3
Revelations at Supper

ELLA STEPPED INTO her cell, closing the door firmly behind her.

"Lord have mercy," she muttered, covering her face with her hands. "Why couldn't he stay away?"

But there wasn't any point in agonizing over *why* Gavin MacNichol had ridden two days on his own to reach the abbey, to deliver a message that could easily have been sent by courier. The fact was, he was here—a guest at the abbey. Two of the sisters were preparing the guest house right at this very moment. And later she would have to suffer through a meal in his presence.

Head still in her hands, Ella sank down onto her sleeping pallet. It was narrow, the mattress stuffed with straw, and covered by a linen sheet and rough woolen blankets. As one of the senior nuns here, she had her own cell. The postulants, novices, and younger nuns shared the dormitory across the courtyard, as she once had. This tiny, sparsely-furnished stone chamber was Ella's refuge.

And at a moment like this, she was relieved to be able to shut herself away.

Mother Mary preserve her, it had been a shock to see him again.

She was still reeling from it. Gavin was even more handsome than she remembered. He'd lost the gaucheness of youth and even suited the harder edge he wore these days.

But the last thing Ella wanted was to travel with this man. He hadn't even brought an escort. It was improper for them to travel together, yet the abbess seemed willing to permit it. There had been many times over the years when Mother Shona's open-minded attitude and views had relieved Ella. The abbess made life at Kilbride a joy for the nuns who resided here. Her approach to religion, and to how a woman should behave, was a refreshing change from the ideas that Ella had grown up with.

But the abbess was being too permissive now. Of course, she didn't realize the history that lay between Ella and Gavin.

Maybe I should tell her?

Ella swallowed hard. No—she couldn't do that.

A bell started clanging then, the sound echoing through the abbey.

Vespers.

Ella wasn't in the mood, but she had no choice other than to heave herself off her pallet, straighten her habit and veil, and leave the sanctuary of her cell. Crossing the courtyard outside the nuns' lodgings, she joined the flood of black-robed figures as they all made their way to the kirk.

Around them, the early evening sun had turned the hills gold. As it was late summer, night drew in slowly. After Vespers and supper, there would be time for more chores before Compline. The Sisters of Kilbride were rarely ever idle.

Ella entered the kirk.

As always, the dim interior cast a calming cloak over her. Even on the hottest day, the air in here was cool. Golden-hued light filtered in from high windows, pooling like melted butter on the flagstone floor. Rows of pillars lined the church, leading up to a raised altar, where Mother Shona had already taken her position.

Ella took her place among the orderly rows of nuns that now filled the kirk. Inhaling the heavy scent of incense, Ella sank to her knees, closing her eyes. Although she hadn't been in the mood before, she was now grateful for Vespers. Perhaps the prayers would take her mind off the events of the past hour.

The chanting began. Solemn female voices echoed high into the vaulted ceiling of the kirk, led by Mother Shona in soothing tones. And as Ella joined in the chorus, she felt the afternoon's tension ebb from her. Slowly her shoulders, which had gone rigid, started to relax.

Peace wrapped around her in a soft veil. The ritual always had a calming effect upon her, no matter how upset she was. She loved losing herself in it.

At first, Ella concentrated on the prayers, even though she knew them so well she could have recited the words in her sleep. But as Vespers drew out, her thoughts treacherously returned to Gavin MacNichol.

She didn't want to, but she thought back to their last meeting that day in the woods southwest of Scorrybreac Castle.

What a spoiled, foolish chit she'd once been. How she'd paced so impatiently that afternoon. Gavin had treated her like his queen during their time together. He'd never once made her wait for him, and that day his tardiness had irritated her. But it paled into nothing when he arrived and delivered his devastating news.

Ella swallowed hard as the memories assailed her. She hadn't accepted his decision at first. It seemed impossible he could tell her that he loved her with one breath, and then announce that he was going to honor his betrothal with the next. Her sister was a kind and sweet woman, but Gavin belonged to Ella.

Her feelings on the subject didn't matter though. The longer she'd argued it with him, the more stubborn Gavin became. The discussion he'd had with his father, who'd been gravely ill at the time, had set a resolve in him. Even so, she'd seen the tears glittering in his eyes as he faced her.

No matter how she pleaded, he would not be moved. As the eldest son and heir to the MacNichol lands, he had to think about more than just his own needs. Ella had railed against these words. She hated how self-sacrificing he was being. He believed he was noble, but she thought he was acting like a coward. Their future life, their future happiness, hung in the balance, and he was casting it away as if it meant nothing.

Ella wasn't proud of how she'd behaved that day.

In the end, she'd flown into hysterics. Wracked with sobs, Ella had stumbled over to her horse and gathered the reins before scrambling up onto the saddle.

Her last words to Gavin still rang in her ears and made her cheeks warm with shame. "Ye shall rue the day ye turned yer back on us." She'd choked out the words. "Ye are casting aside something that will never come yer way again."

Ella squeezed her eyes shut. She'd been so fiery, so impassioned. At eighteen, she'd believed that if you wanted something enough, it would be yours. At that age, she believed that love conquered all and that somehow she and Gavin would find a way to overcome the obstacles before them.

But now she knew differently. She'd hoped that after a day or two Gavin might have changed his mind. But he didn't. He'd made his decision, and in that stubborn way of his, he was determined to see it through. Ella was stubborn too.

But in the days that followed, she learned a bitter truth. It didn't matter how much your heart yearned for it—some things were not destined to be yours.

Gavin took a mouthful of venison stew and let out a contented sigh. "This is very good." He looked down at the bowl before him. "Do hunters swap ye meat for vegetables?"

Glancing up, Gavin noted that Ella, who was seated directly across from him, tensed at the question. They sat in the refectory, a rectangular building with a hearth at each end. The abbess and a cluster of senior nuns—some of whom were aged indeed—sat upon a raised platform at one end of the hall, while the others sat at long tables down the center.

"Sometimes hunters barter with us," Mother Shona replied. "But the nuns of this order are highly resourceful, MacNichol. In order to do God's work, we must be strong and healthy. Most of the meat we consume here we have either raised or hunted ourselves."

Gavin observed the abbess with interest. Her tone was pleasant, although with a distant note Gavin had come to expect from her. Ever since stepping inside the walls of Kilbride, he'd felt as if he was intruding on a serene world that had no time for the likes of him. Although the abbess was happy to converse with him, he had the sense that she was distracted, as if his questions were taking her from more important matters.

"I saw some of the nuns at practice with quarter-staffs earlier," he said casually. "They looked to possess some skill."

Catching a glimpse of the black-garbed women swinging staffs at each other had indeed piqued Gavin's interest. Ella had tried to throw him off with a weak excuse, yet he wanted to know more.

"As I said … they were merely practicing for the harvest games in Torrin." Ella interrupted. Her tone was soft, yet there was a pleading undertone as if she wished he would leave the matter alone. Looking her way, Gavin saw that her face had paled.

"An odd skill for a nun to learn though," he continued, shifting his attention back to the abbess. "Don't ye think, Mother Shona?"

The abbess held his gaze, her own steady. "Aye, I suppose, but as I have said … nuns who are strong and healthy do the Lord's work better."

An awkward silence settled at the table. Gavin ripped off a piece of bread and dipped it into his stew, his attention sweeping around him. The nuns all wore composed expressions, their gazes downcast as they focused on their supper. He finished his inspection, focusing upon Ella. She ate slowly, taking small mouthfuls of stew. Only the lines bracketing her mouth belied her tension.

She didn't want him here.

Eventually, it was the abbess who broke the hush. Putting down her spoon, she met Gavin's eye. "Word reached me a few days ago, of the pestilence that has raged through Europe and England," she said fixing him with a level look. "Our sisters on the mainland tell me that it has now moved to Scotland. Have ye heard such news?"

Gavin frowned. He wasn't a fool; Mother Shona had deliberately changed the subject, away from the abbey. "Aye … my clansmen in Lothian have sent word that the plague has now reached Dùn Èideann," he replied before pausing. He was reluctant to go into more detail but sensed the abbess would prefer him to speak frankly. "Whole families have been wiped out … some in less than the space of a day. The illness takes a vile form … a terrible fever, chills, and purple boils appearing over the body."

The abbess's brown eyes shadowed, while around her some of the nuns who'd overheard him dropped their spoons and crossed themselves. "How awful," Mother Shona murmured. "We shall pray for those afflicted … and that this isle may be spared such devastation." Her face took on a determined look. "Of course, the Sisters of Kilbride will do our best to take care of those struck down if it does arrive upon Skye … we will never turn our back on the sick."

"They have no cure for it then?" One of the nuns at the table spoke up. It was the tall one that Gavin had spied leading the quarter-staff training in the yard earlier. She had violet eyes, and she wore a guarded expression.

"Not from what I hear," Gavin replied with a shake of his head. "Word is that ye can catch it by simply breathing the air of those who have the disease."

"Indeed … herbs and medicines seem unable to slow its spread, Sister Coira," the abbess agreed, before her attention flicked back to Gavin. "Sister Coira is our resident healer."

Gavin nodded, looking at the nun in question with fresh eyes. Kilbride Abbey was an interesting place indeed. None of the women residing here were what he'd expected. This was a world where men entered only as guests, and then very rarely. He was in a privileged position indeed to be allowed to visit. In this world, women ruled.

Gavin resumed eating and reached for another piece of bread. The abbess had attempted to distract him from his inquisition about their ways, with her own question about the pestilence, but his general curiosity wasn't yet sated. Eventually, he glanced up and caught the abbess's eye once more. "Mother Shona ... earlier today, ye told me that that the folk of these lands suffer under MacKinnon's rule ... how so?"

Around him, the table went still. He noted then that Ella was watching him closely. Her face was impossible to read, although her blue eyes were narrowed and her mouth compressed into a thin, slightly disapproving line.

She didn't like him asking such a question, but Gavin was curious to know about the goings-on in these lands.

"Duncan MacKinnon makes a poor clan-chief," the abbess admitted, her tone turning guarded.

Next to her, Sister Coira was frowning. The nun stared down at her half-finished bowl of stew, a nerve flickering in her cheek. Gavin was intrigued. MacKinnon was clearly not well-liked here and, having met the man numerous times, Gavin knew why. Duncan was even more unpopular than his brutal father before him had been.

Taking a sip of beer, Gavin shifted his attention back to the abbess. Her expression was shuttered. He realized then that she'd grown wary of him. He was a clan-chief after all, and for all she knew, MacKinnon might have sent him to spy on the abbey. This was the only abbey upon the isle, and it held more power than some of the chieftains here liked.

"I imagine that ye are a very different leader to MacKinnon," Mother Shona continued after a pause. Her tone was still wary, yet, unlike some of the nuns here, who could barely look his way, the abbess met his eye squarely. Men did not intimidate or embarrass her.

Gavin's mouth lifted at the corners. "I do my best," he murmured. "My father always said it wasn't an easy thing to rule, but it was only when I took over as clan-chief that I realized what he truly meant. Everyone with a problem or a grievance comes to yer door. The weight of responsibility can sometimes be a heavy one, although I try to do right by my people."

Ella felt herself growing increasingly more agitated the longer the meal went on.

Gavin MacNichol was in a conversational mood this evening. He didn't seem to care that he was the one doing most of the speaking, or that his questions were unsettling not only Mother Shona but the other nuns as well. Mealtimes were usually passed in silence, with speaking kept to a minimum, but the abbess had relaxed that rule for this evening. However, MacNichol seemed determined to discuss a number of unpleasant subjects.

Ella didn't live in denial; she knew the problems he and Mother Shona discussed were real indeed. When Ella had first come to live here, the nearby villages had been prosperous. But in the last few years, as MacKinnon demanded higher and higher taxes from his people, folk had grown poorer and increasingly desperate. Just two days earlier, when she'd brought vegetables to the local village, she'd seen too many hungry faces and desperate eyes. The Sisters of Kilbride did what they could to help the villagers, but MacKinnon demanded a tithe from them as well, and last winter had ended up being a lean one.

The conversation drifted on, while Ella found her gaze returning to Gavin. She cursed herself for constantly looking his way, but she couldn't help it.

Gavin appeared at ease as he helped himself to another serving of stew and praised its deliciousness once more.

One of the nuns, Old Magda, smiled at his compliment.

Curse ye, Gavin. He'd always related easily to women. That was how it had started between them. They'd become friends first. She'd found him so easy to talk to. He wasn't like other lads. They all seemed boorish compared to him. Gavin engaged a lass's mind, wanting to know her opinions, her thoughts, and her feelings. He hadn't changed.

Eventually, Ella wasn't able to bear it any longer. It was bad enough that this man had reappeared in her life after so many years, and that she would be forced to travel with him tomorrow.

But to listen to the low timbre of his voice was like a knife twisting in her chest.

Ella pushed away her half-eaten bowl of stew and rose to her feet. "Please, excuse me," she murmured, gaze lowered. "But if I am to travel tomorrow, I will need to ready myself."

"Very well, Sister Ella," Mother Shona replied. "We shall see ye later ... at Compline."

Feeling Gavin MacNichol's gaze upon her, but deliberately avoiding his eye, Ella turned and hurried from the refectory.

4

Ready to Depart

ELLA PACKED THE wooden satchel with some clean tunics, a block of lye soap, and a small leather-bound book of psalms.

"Is that all ye are taking with ye?"

Ella glanced over her shoulder to see Sister Leanna watching her, eyes narrowed.

Despite her bleak mood this morning, Ella's mouth curved. She remembered Lady Leanna MacDonald of Sleat arriving upon a palfrey laden with saddlebags, over a year ago now. A mule carrying the rest of her belongings had followed.

That day, the nuns had watched in thinly veiled amusement as a beautiful lass with pale blonde hair, dressed in flowing blue, had dismounted from her palfrey and looked about her with interest. Leanna hadn't any idea of the life that awaited her. She'd believed she would have her own lodgings and space to hang up her colorful array of kirtles and over-gowns. Ella remembered the shock on Leanna's face when she'd set eyes on the dormitory, and her narrow sleeping pallet, for the first time.

"A nun doesn't need to carry much," Ella reminded the younger woman. She patted the coarse material of her habit, her smile turning rueful. "We never have to agonize over what to wear."

Sister Leanna sighed. "I miss the finery of my old life sometimes, ye know," she admitted. "Don't tell anyone though. I'm sure the other sisters would think me frivolous."

"No, they wouldn't," Ella replied. "I felt the same way during my first year here. But after a while, I got used to it. And ye will too."

"Are ye nervous?"

The question made Ella tense. She imagined her displeasure was written all over her face. Sister Leanna hadn't taken supper with them the night before, as being a novice, she dined at the other end of the refectory—but she would have seen Ella depart early.

"It will feel strange to leave Kilbride," Ella replied softly. Of course, that wasn't the real reason for her discomfort, although Sister Leanna wouldn't know any different. "I've had no contact with my parents since I came to live here."

Sister Leanna didn't answer, and slinging the satchel across her chest, Ella turned to her. She saw that the young woman's face was shadowed, unnaturally somber. "I can't imagine having no contact with my kin for that long," she murmured. "I miss my parents so much, sometimes it hurts to breathe."

Ella saw then that Sister Leanna's gaze shone with unshed tears. Something deep inside Ella's chest twisted. How heartless she must seem to the lass. She knew that Sister Leanna was very close to her family. She had confided in her one evening that the real reason for her joining the order was not out of religious fervor. Instead, it had been her father's idea.

MacKinnon had wanted to wed Chieftain MacDonald of Sleat's comely daughter. It had been a drastic move to send her to Kilbride, yet it was the only way they had managed to put MacKinnon off.

Sister Leanna had understood her father's choice, although Ella had seen sadness shadow her hazel eyes at unguarded times—like now.

Stepping close to Sister Leanna, Ella put comforting arms around her. "It does get easier with time," she whispered. As soon as the words left her lips, she realized how little solace they truly gave.

The two women left the cell and walked into the yard beyond. A balmy dawn greeted them. The sun had just risen over the tawny hills to the east, and the air had a sweet smell that promised another hot day ahead.

Ella huffed out a breath. There was so much to do here at the abbey; so much weeding, planting, and harvesting to carry out and oversee. She didn't have time for this trip.

Even so, to change her mind would only cast her in a poor light. All the nuns now knew that her mother was gravely ill. They expected Ella to go to her.

But none of them had ever met Cait Fraser.

Sturdy leather sandals scuffling on the dirt, Ella led the way from the nuns' lodgings to the stables. The abbey kept goats, sheep, fowl, and even a couple of pigs. Despite that the nuns didn't travel much, they also had shaggy ponies, beasts that were native to the Isle, and an old sway-backed donkey.

One of the ponies, a bay gelding named Monadh, awaited her. The beast's name was a beautiful one, meaning 'moorland covered mountain'. However, the pony seemed wide as a barrel and hairy as a Highland cow beside the leggy grey courser that waited next to it. MacNichol had saddled both the mounts and was now ready to depart.

He stood, quietly conversing with Mother Shona. At hearing approaching footfalls, the clan-chief glanced up. His gaze tracked Ella's path across the yard. Just like the day before, the sight of him unnerved her.

Ella inhaled sharply, her hand straying to the crucifix looped through her belt. *Dear Lord, please give me the strength to keep company with this man.*

Approaching the abbess, Ella dropped to one knee before her. "Good morning, Sister Ella," Mother Shona greeted her with a smile, making the sign of the cross. "I'm glad to see ye plan to travel light."

Ella forced a smile. "Aye ... I've taken yer advice to heart." She then glanced over her shoulder to see that a crowd of nuns had gathered behind her, including Sister Leanna.

Ella couldn't fail to note either that some of the sisters weren't looking at her. One or two of the younger ones were, in fact, openly gazing at Gavin MacNichol.

Ella frowned. There was a reason why very few men were admitted to the abbey. MacNichol's presence here was a disruptive one. It was just as well he was leaving.

Oblivious to the stir his presence was creating, Gavin met Ella's eye once more. "A sunny day lies before us," he said pleasantly. "The perfect weather for traveling."

"The perfect weather for sun-stroke too," old Magda called out. "Make sure ye keep out of the noon sun, Sister Ella."

"Worry not ... I shall look after her," Gavin replied to the elderly nun.

Ella tensed, her throat closing as nervousness got the better of her. Despite his self-confidence, she hated the idea of leaving the abbey. These solid stone walls had been her home for so long, she sometimes forgot that there was a world outside it. Panic fluttered up as she considered the two-day journey to Scorrybreac and what awaited her there.

Masking her rising anxiety with a stern look, Ella crossed to her pony. Then, placing her right foot in the stirrup and facing Monadh's head, she mounted side-saddle. It wasn't easy. She hadn't been on horseback for many years. Once she'd been able to spring up into the saddle with ease, but today it was an effort. She hopped up and down, her habit flapping, as she attempted to launch herself upward. All the while, Monadh patiently waited.

Ella felt gazes boring into her as she scrambled in an ungainly fashion onto the pony's back. Breathing hard, she adjusted her skirts and gathered up the reins.

Had Gavin watched that display?

When she chanced a glance his way, she saw that he too had mounted and was mercifully not looking in her direction. Instead, Gavin met Mother Shona's eye, his cheek dimpling as he smiled. "As I said, Mother Shona, we should return no longer than two weeks hence."

The abbess nodded, stepping back from them. "May the Lord's blessings go with ye," she replied her attention shifting to Ella. Their gazes fused, and the abbess's full lips curved. "Make the most of this time with yer kin," she advised softly. "For many of us never get the chance to say goodbye."

Gavin and Ella rode out of Kilbride in silence.

Gavin's mount, a spirited grey mare, didn't like the quiet pace her rider had set this morning. Yet the pony the abbess had loaned Ella had a short stride. It was also grossly fat and would slow their progress north. Gavin didn't mind. He was to have but a short time alone with Ella. It was stolen time, but he wanted to make the most of it.

Nonetheless, he sensed that his companion wished to keep her own counsel this morning. He cast a glance Ella's way to see that she was deliberately staring at the road before her, steadfastly ignoring him.

Watching her, Gavin stifled the urge to fill the silence between them. Ella was probably just nervous, he told himself. Perhaps she would thaw once they got properly underway.

Rolling hills spread out around Kilbride Abbey. As they crested one, Gavin twisted in the saddle and glanced back at the way they'd come. The spire of the kirk pierced the pale sky, a swathe of blue sea behind it. Woodland nestled in the shallow valleys around Kilbride, and to the northwest, Gavin spied delicate wreaths of smoke drifting up into the heavens. He hadn't realized that the village of Torrin lay so close to the abbey.

He had to admit that Kilbride's location—perched just a few furlongs back from a rocky shore, and surrounded by hills and woodland—made it an idyllic spot.

Turning away from the abbey, Gavin focused his attention now on the rutted road before them. They had many furlongs to travel, through the mountainous heart of the isle. In the distance, the shadows of great peaks rose before them—a brutal and sculpted beauty. His lands lay far to the northeastern side of those mountains.

Finally, he shifted his gaze back to the silent figure riding beside him. It was no good—he couldn't ride all the way to Scorrybreac without speaking to this woman.

"It must feel strange," he said, feigning casualness, "to be leaving the abbey after so many years."

Ella did glance his way, briefly. She studied him coldly for an instant before she deliberately shifted her gaze back to her pony's ears. "It does," she replied, her tone as frosty as her expression. "A nun should remain in quiet contemplation. I will not be at ease again until I return to Kilbride."

5
Blades

ELLA WELCOMED THE silence.

After a few attempts at engaging her in conversation, none of which had been welcomed, Gavin had duly given up. The morning stretched before them, and as they traveled northeast, the day gradually grew warmer.

In her heavy habit and undergarments, Ella started to sweat.

The sun beat down on her head, and for the first time in many years, she longed to rip off her stifling wimple and veil for a few moments and let the gentle breeze cool her sweat-soaked scalp. And if she'd been alone, she might have. But with Gavin present, it was the last thing she would do. She'd just have to sweat and bear the heat in stoic silence.

They stopped briefly at noon, on the banks of a glittering burn that flowed over mossy rocks. Ella was glad to take a break. Unused to riding, her backside was already starting to ache.

They were at the feet of the great mountains now. One of them reared directly overhead, tawny red-gold grass rippling in the breeze. This was Beinn na Caillich, the Red Hill, or the Hill of Hag as many local folk knew it.

"Did ye know that a Norwegian Princess was supposed to have been buried at the summit of this mountain?" Gavin said, breaking the silence between them. They sat on two lichen-covered rocks on the edge of the burn, the horse and pony grazing nearby. "Folk say she died of longing for her homeland."

"Aye, I've heard the story," Ella murmured as she helped herself to a slice of cheese. She knew Gavin was only trying to make conversation, but she still felt uncomfortable in his presence. She wished he would leave her to her thoughts.

"There's a cairn of stones up there," Gavin continued. He unstoppered a bladder of water and took a gulp before passing it to her. "I saw it years ago when I went deer hunting in this area with my brother." He twisted, motioning due north, to where the jagged edges of mountains reared into the sky. They were black and red as if fire had scorched them. "I remember the herds of red deer roaming in the narrow vales between these mountains." Gavin's expression turned wistful. "That was a good hunting trip."

Listening to him, Ella felt an odd pang.

How she'd once loved hunting. It wasn't a suitable pastime for a lady, her mother had told her that often enough. *Why can't ye be more like yer sister? Innis behaves as a lady should.* It had been true enough. Ella's elder sister had never spent much time outdoors, except for warm afternoons when she would prune the roses in her mother's garden or collect herbs to dry.

When they were younger, Innis's fair skin had remained milky and unblemished, while every summer Ella's face, neck, and forearms burned dark gold.

Very unladylike, her mother had once scolded.

Thinking back on her sister and mother, Ella stopped chewing. She swallowed her mouthful and took a delicate sip of water, attempting to push back memories of the past into the recesses of her mind where they belonged.

Memories of her mother's shrewish words, and of her gentle sister, made her belly clench. She wondered if Cait Fraser's character had softened with the years.

Stoppering the bladder of water, Ella glanced Gavin's way. "What exactly ails my mother?" she asked.

"She has complained of belly pains for a while now," he replied. "The healer initially thought she had digestion troubles, but over the last year, the pains have grown. They eventually got so bad that yer mother became bedridden. She is very frail and spends her days in agony. The healer has done what he can for her, but I'm afraid she has little time left."

Ella listened quietly. Although she didn't like to hear that her mother suffered, she wasn't afraid of illness or death. Life at the abbey had cured her of such fears. For the last few years, she'd worked alongside Sister Coira. The nun was the healer, not just of the abbey but for all the neighboring villages. Ella had assisted Sister Coira with many patients. The nun dealt with everything, from broken limbs, festering cuts, and fevers, to childbirth and wasting sicknesses that no herb or tincture could heal.

"She will be pleased to see ye," Gavin said when a silence stretched between them. Perhaps seeing Ella's features tighten, he shook his head. "I know that relations between ye were never good in the past." He paused there. "Neither of us have had easy mothers to deal with."

"And how is Lady Maggie?"

Gavin pulled a face. "As outspoken and irascible as always, I'm afraid."

Ella's mouth compressed. Cait Fraser was snobbish and narrow-minded, but Maggie MacNichol was a different type of woman altogether. Strong, proud, with a blade-like intelligence, she was the sort of woman who should have been born a man. She would have made a formidable clan-chief if women had been allowed to gain such positions. Instead, Maggie had always sat in her husband's shadow. However, that had never stopped her from meddling in his affairs, and the affairs of everyone living in Scorrybreac Castle.

"Ye never had much time for her, did ye?" Gavin asked.

Ella lifted her chin, and their gazes fused for an instant. "No," she admitted softly, "but many years had passed since then ... and I'm not the lass I once was."

A hot, gusting wind sprang up as the two travelers resumed their journey once more. Clouds now raced across a pale-blue sky, and all the while, the heat pressed down upon them like a heavy hand.

Gavin's mare walked sedately along, just a few yards before the fat bay pony. She'd finally accepted that this journey would be at a slower pace. Her name was Saorsa—which meant 'freedom' in their tongue—and although she was nearing her tenth year, the horse was as lively as ever.

Gaze shifting around him as he rode, Gavin tried to think of ways to draw Ella into conversation. Despite their brief exchange at noon, Ella had not thawed toward him. Gavin had tried to get her to warm to him numerous times during the afternoon. But when she continued to answer him in short, terse sentences, he got the message and ceased speaking.

The past hung over them both like a heavy storm cloud; the air was charged, crackling with tension. And yet neither of them would address their history directly. Eventually, Gavin intended to bring up the subject with Ella. But so many years had gone by since their last meeting, he wanted to wait a few days first. When they reached Scorrybreac Castle, he would find a way to broach the subject.

Gavin didn't imagine it would change anything. Yet, ever since Innis's death, Ella had been on his mind.

She was lost to him now, but that didn't mean he couldn't try and make amends for the past. He felt that he wouldn't be able to rest, or seek future happiness for himself in any way, unless he mended things between them.

The afternoon stretched on. The days seemed endless this time of year, but gradually, the shadows lengthened, and the afternoon light grew soft and golden.

They were traveling through a vale, its sides studded with rocky boulders, when Saorsa snorted, tossing her head.

The mare sidestepped, and Gavin frowned. Leaning forward, he stroked the horse's neck. "What is it, lass?"

He had barely uttered the words when dark shapes suddenly burst out from behind the boulders and rushed toward them.

Saorsa squealed, rearing up and nearly unseating Gavin in the process. Only years of experience on horseback prevented him from toppling onto the rocky ground.

Behind him, he heard Ella gasp. "Outlaws!"

There were a few of them—twelve that Gavin could see. His gaze swept over the ragged band advancing upon them. They were dirty, barefoot, and wild-eyed.

One man, a lanky fellow with long dark hair and blue eyes, took a step toward Gavin. He carried a hand-axe at his side. "What's this?" he sneered. "A nun and her ... escort?"

Gavin inhaled slowly, considering his next words. "I'm Clan-chief MacNichol," he introduced himself casually as if they weren't surrounded by a group of men brandishing axes, dirks, and sickles. "And I'm escorting Sister Annella here back to Scorrybreac Castle to visit her ailing mother. We're in a hurry, so I'd advise ye to let us pass."

A grin stretched across the outlaw leader's face. It made the leanness of his features even more noticeable. "Did ye hear that, lads? We've netted ourselves a clan-chief. He's bound to carry bags of silver pennies with him."

The man took a threatening step toward Gavin. Saorsa tossed her head and sidestepped once more, but Gavin held her steady. "I'm carrying little coin upon me," Gavin replied, his tone low. "But even if I was, I wouldn't be handing them over to ye." He frowned then. "Stand aside and let us pass."

The man's grin faded, his face twisting. He then spat on the ground. "We'll kill ye and take whatever ye are carrying," he growled. "And then we'll strip yer corpse of those fine clothes ye are wearing."

"That's a decent horse ye are riding too," another man called out. "I could sell her at Dunan market and earn enough silver to feed my family for a full year."

Gavin doubted that, but he wasn't going to argue the detail.

Instead, he drew the claidheamh-mor that hung at his side. He never traveled without his sword. The sun glinted off the folded steel blade.

"I don't want any trouble," Gavin said after a moment when he was sure they'd all had a good look at his sword. "But if ye don't let us pass unmolested, blood is going to be spilled here."

"Aye," the ringleader growled. "Yers ... and the nun's."

And with that, the rabble attacked.

They ran at Gavin and Ella like a pack of howling wolves. Gavin dug his knees in, driving Saorsa forward, blocking their path to Ella. He intercepted the first of them. His blade flashed, whistling through the humid air before it thudded into flesh.

In an instant, the howling turned to screams of fury and pain. And suddenly, Gavin was slashing his way through the fray, fighting for his life.

Panic surged through him—not for his own safety, but for Ella's. Focused on fending off the outlaws, he couldn't make sure none of them had reached his companion.

A man ran at him swinging a vicious-looking scythe. Urging Saorsa forward, Gavin ran his attacker through. He yanked his blade free and glanced over his shoulder then. Ella had been riding a few yards behind him. Apart from her initial gasp of shock, she hadn't made a sound.

And as his gaze fixed upon her, she swung down from her pony's broad back.

Panic surged through Gavin once more.

The Devil's cods ... what's she doing?

She was safer mounted. At least she could attempt to gallop away from the outlaws if Gavin failed to hold them back. Instead, her finely featured face was scrunched up in determination as if she was preparing herself to face them.

The first of the outlaws were past Gavin now, giving the Claidheamh-mor wielding clan-chief a wide berth while they stalked easier prey.

And then Ella moved.

Gavin's breathing caught as she hiked up the skirts of her habit and underskirts, and reached for the knife strapped to her left calf. He caught a glimpse of creamy flesh and a long, pale, shapely leg.

Ella drew the blade and flung it at the nearest man.

It flew through the air, spinning as it went, and embedded in his neck. The outlaw fell with a strangled cry, fingers clawing at the hilt.

Ella reached for a second knife, drawing it from where it was strapped snuggly to her right leg.

Thud.

Then she whipped out another knife from the satchel she wore across her front.

Thud.

Three men lay groaning and whimpering on the ground before her. Three blades embedded into their flesh.

6

Water Under the Bridge

GAVIN STARED, TRANSFIXED. He'd momentarily forgotten his surroundings. Face creased in a ferocious expression, Ella strode up to the nearest man and yanked her knife free from where it had embedded in his shoulder.

"Please," the outlaw whimpered. "Don't kill me."

Ella ignored him.

Meanwhile, Gavin swiveled around to face the remaining outlaws. Fortunately, they had been as surprised as him by the sight of the small knife-throwing nun.

Gavin swung his blade, causing the leader of the rabble to shrink back, his gaze burning.

"I'd abandon this now," Gavin advised him. "Before it's ye who tastes steel."

Gavin glanced right, to see that the other outlaws, who had formerly been advancing toward Ella, had all drawn back. Some of them were now racing away, scrambling over the rocks in their haste to depart.

Snarling a curse, the leader of the band flung himself toward Gavin, his axe hurtling toward Saorsa's neck.

Thud.

A blade hit his upper chest, just below the collarbone. The man gasped and went down like a sack of barley. His mouth gaped, and he struggled to pull the blade free. His blue eyes were now wide with panic, and Gavin realized that he was young, barely more than twenty winters.

It didn't matter though—this man and his followers had attacked them with murderous intent.

Gavin swung down from his mare, drew a dirk from his waist, and slashed the man across the throat. The outlaw's thin body convulsed, his eyes bulging, and then he lay still.

Breathing hard, Gavin glanced over his shoulder at where Ella stood a few yards back. She had retrieved her other knives and was cleaning them on the léine of one of the fallen men. She looked up, and their gazes fused.

The corners of Ella's mouth lifted then, the closest thing she'd given him to a smile since they'd been reunited. "Getting slow in yer old age, MacNichol?" she chided. "He almost had ye."

A small fire burned, a beacon of red and gold in the smothering darkness.

Night had finally fallen, chasing away the smothering heat. Cool air settled in a blanket over the mountains, valleys, and glens of Skye.

Gavin added a gorse branch to the fire, sitting back as sparks shot up into the air. It was a moonless night, and the flames provided the only light in the lonely vale where they'd made camp.

"Do ye think it's safe to let the fire burn so bright?" Ella spoke up. "What with so many outlaws abroad these days ..."

"We'll be fine here," Gavin replied with a shake of his head. "This valley is too remote for outlaws to bother with."

He broke off there, his gaze fixing upon the face of the nun seated opposite him. The firelight played across her creamy skin and darkened her blue eyes. The habit and wimple and veil she wore were hideous, he had to admit. The former shrouded her figure like a sack, while the latter covered her hair and framed her face in a manner that wasn't flattering to any woman.

Even so, Sister Ella of Kilbride made his pulse quicken.

She sat demurely now, her hands folded upon her lap. There was no sign of the blade-wielding assassin who'd taken down three outlaws in quick succession.

Gavin had never seen anything like it.

And yet, as they'd resumed their journey northeast in the aftermath, they'd barely discussed the incident.

Drawing in a slow breath, Gavin decided it was time. "Did ye learn to fight like that at the abbey?" he asked, breaking the long silence that had stretched out between them.

Ella's mouth quirked. That mouth—it didn't belong upon a nun's face. She had full, finely drawn lips. It was an expressive mouth that was made for sin.

Enough.

Gavin pulled himself up with that last thought. He couldn't let his mind drift back to the past. It was another life; they had both been different people then.

"Mother Shona taught me," she admitted.

Gavin raised his eyebrows, inviting her to continue.

"The abbess learned to fight years ago." Ella looked away then, her gaze shifting to the dancing flames. "Our Reverent Mother was once a novice nun at Lismore in Argyle," she continued softly. "But her convent was attacked by brigands. Most of the nuns were raped and murdered, yet she'd been out foraging for herbs and managed to escape."

Ella paused here, her hand straying to the crucifix that hung from her belt. Her fingers closed around it as she continued, "Mother Shona nearly starved, but then she was taken in by a group of men and women who were living wild in the forest ... outlaws too, but not those who'd attacked her convent. They taught her to throw knives, wield a longbow, swing a sword, and hold her own with a quarter-staff. She brought those skills with her to Kilbride. And when she was elected as abbess, she decided that we would learn how to defend ourselves should the need arise."

"She did a fine job of teaching ye," Gavin replied. "I've rarely seen such skill."

Ella inclined her head, acknowledging the compliment.

"I thought nuns took vows that prevented them from using violence against others?" he asked.

"We take three vows: poverty, chastity, and obedience. Nowhere is it writ that we are forbidden from defending ourselves from those who'd do us harm," Ella replied. With her fingertips, she traced the lines of the crucifix she now held upon her palm. "We could refuse to wield blades, but that wouldn't prevent us from dying upon them. How can we serve God then?"

Gavin smiled. He hadn't forgotten how sharp Ella's mind was, or her strength of character. Even so, the years had developed those traits further. He'd never met a woman like her and knew he would never do so again.

"Ye were magnificent this afternoon," he admitted quietly. "God's bones, woman ... ye are wasted as a nun."

Ella stiffened, her gaze narrowing. In an instant, the easy atmosphere at the fireside dissolved and tension settled over their camp.

"Taking the veil and dedicating my life to serving God was the making of me," Ella said after a chill pause. "I do not see it as a waste of a life ... instead, it is the greatest privilege I could have ever received."

Inwardly, Gavin winced. What had possessed him to say those words? Every time he opened his mouth over the last day, he'd managed to offend her. That wasn't hard to do though, for Sister Ella was far pricklier than the lass he'd known nearly two decades earlier.

Guilt lanced through Gavin. *Whose fault is that?*

"Apologies, Ella," he replied, casting her a conciliatory smile. "It was an ill choice of words."

She didn't smile back at him. "*Sister* Ella." Her tone was clipped.

"I handled things badly ... in the past," he said finally, clearing his throat. "If I could have my time again, I'd do things differently."

Gavin remembered that he'd planned to leave this conversation till they arrived at Scorrybreac—but now seemed like the right time.

Ella's face went taut. "I don't want to talk about the past." Her voice turned brittle. "It is dead to me ... I serve the Lord now."

Gavin leaned forward, snaring her gaze with his. "But there are some subjects that should be aired. Our past is like a festering wound; it needs to be lanced or it will only poison yer time at Scorrybreac Castle." When Ella didn't reply, he continued. "I want ye to know that I have lived with regret, every day of my life since that afternoon in the clearing. I hurt ye greatly, and I'm sorry for it."

"It's too late for this, Gavin." The coolness of her voice was a knife to his heart—and yet it was the first time she'd addressed him by his first name since they'd been reunited. "As I said, the past is dead."

Gavin swallowed. "Ye left Scorrybreac so quickly. I never had the chance to say goodbye."

A nerve flickered in her cheek as she stared back at him. "Ye didn't deserve it."

"I did my duty," he replied, his voice heavy, flat. "I never wanted to hurt ye, but I could see no way out of it. As the first-born son, I felt I had responsibilities ... I couldn't disappoint my family."

"Aye, ye could have," she whispered, looking away from him. "It would have cost ye, but ye could have gone against them."

Gavin drew in a sharp breath. At last, there was a crack in her façade; he'd started to wonder if memories of their shared past affected her at all.

"They would have disowned me," he pointed out. "Would ye have wed a pauper?"

"Aye," she replied, her voice barely audible. She still refused to meet his gaze. "It wasn't yer title that interested me."

"Ye say that now, but—"

"Enough." Ella's choked command splintered the night. "Ye made yer choice, MacNichol ... and I made mine. It's water under the bridge now; let us speak no more of it. My life now belongs to Christ."

7

Scorrybreac

THE SIGHT OF Scorrybreac Castle, after so many years, made Ella catch her breath. Drawing up Monadh upon the rise of the last hill before the stronghold, she let her gaze drink the castle in.

So many memories.

And despite the suddenness of her departure, most of them had been pleasant.

When they'd come to live at Scorrybreac, Ella had loved it. The MacNichol clan-chief had been a jolly, red-faced man with a booming laugh, so different from Morgan Fraser, the chieftain of the Frasers of Skye. The inhabitants of Talasgair, the Fraser stronghold, had all minded their chief, for he could be harsh and had a mercurial temper.

She remembered how beautiful she'd thought this castle's setting—perched out on a promontory, cliffs at its back and the Sound of Raasay before it. Scorrybreac's bulk stretched in a long oval, hugging the shore.

It was still as lovely today, with the MacNichol pennant flying from the keep, the sun glittering on the water behind it. Another warm day had followed them north, and the last of the evening sun was setting behind the mountains that thrust up to the west. Soon dusk would settle.

"Is it as ye remember?" MacNichol pulled his grey mare up next to her.

"Aye," Ella replied softly, deliberately not looking his way. She'd avoided eye contact with Gavin all day and had been grateful that he'd had the sense to avoid conversing with her.

Last night's exchange had made them both wary.

Ella's gaze slid over the high granite curtain wall that encircled the stronghold before she took in the thatched roofs of the settlement before it. "The village looks bigger though."

"It has grown in recent years." She caught the edge of pride in his voice. "We've had a number of folk move here from other areas."

They rode into Scorrybreac village, along a wide road that cut through a patchwork of tilled fields. Indeed, the area looked more prosperous than Ella remembered. It didn't surprise her that Gavin ruled well. His father, although a gentle-hearted man, hadn't been cut out for the role of clan-chief. And his shrewish wife had long pressured him to raise the taxes on the folk who farmed their lands.

There were still men and women out, cottars working the land. An elderly man, who'd been reaping barley, leaned on his scythe and raised a hand in greeting.

Gavin waved back.

"They're working late," Ella observed.

"It's the coolest time of day," Gavin replied, "and with the harvest moon almost upon us, the farmers want to reap what they can before the weather turns."

Ella understood that; the weather of their isle could be capricious. This spell of fine weather wouldn't last.

Reaching the guardhouse, they rode up a pebbly incline and under the portcullis. Twin crenelated towers flanked the arched gateway, where the men of the Scorrybreac garrison resided. Spears bristled against the dusky sky overhead, and the gazes of the men taking their turn at the watch tracked their path up the causeway.

The outer bailey within was a hive of activity this eve. Guards were sparring with blunted swords to the right of the guardhouse, their grunts filtering through the warm air, while nearby fowl pecked in the dirt. A group of lads were playing knucklebones on the dusty ground in front of the stables, only to be told off by a stable-hand who was pushing out a barrow of stinking manure.

Ella drew up Monadh once more and looked about her. All was exactly as she remembered. A number of stone buildings flanked the wide space: the stables, armory, stores, and byres. The square stone keep rose to the back, protected by a high stone wall and a second, smaller, guardhouse.

After the quiet of the abbey, Scorrybreac's outer bailey seemed chaotic. At this hour the sisters would have entered the Great Silence, a ritual she'd come to appreciate over the years.

Upon seeing that their chief had returned, the guards sparring with swords ceased their practice and called out to him. Gavin swung down from his mare's back and responded to their greeting with a warmth and familiarity that didn't surprise Ella.

One glance at these men's faces and she could see that Gavin MacNichol was loved by his people.

"Ye took yer time ... I was about to send out a search party."

Ella's gaze shifted to where a tall man with short blond hair strode toward them.

Blair MacNichol, Gavin's younger brother. The family resemblance was startling, although Blair had a heavier stature, a more florid complexion—and his mother's sharp grey eyes.

Gavin snorted, handing his horse's reins to a stable lad while he unfastened the saddlebag he'd brought with him. "I told ye I'd be away a few days."

"Aye, but since ye insisted on traveling alone, I'd assumed ye had been set upon by thieves."

Ella stiffened at these words. She wondered if Gavin would tell his brother what had befallen them on the way here—or would reveal that she carried a number of blades on her person and knew how to throw them.

But moments passed, and Gavin said nothing.

Blair's attention shifted to Ella then, his grey eyes widening. "Lady Annella?"

"Sister Annella now, Blair," Gavin replied.

"Of course." Blair nodded to Ella, his gaze turning wary.

Ella favored him with a subdued smile. She was used to such a response. Her black-robed appearance was a daunting one. Most men no longer saw a nun as a woman—Gavin was the only one who looked at her as if she was.

Checking herself at this thought, Ella swallowed. "Greetings, Blair. I hope ye and yer wife are well?"

"Aye," Blair replied with a nod. "Forbia and I have four strapping lads now ... the eldest has just reached his sixteenth summer."

This news took Ella aback. When she'd left Scorrybreac, Blair and Forbia had only just wed. To think that his eldest son was on the threshold of becoming a man made her feel old.

She glanced over at Gavin, whose face was inscrutable. Did he and Innis have any children? Innis had never spoken of them in her letters, and Gavin hadn't mentioned any on the way here. "Is yer sister still at Scorrybreac?"

Gavin's mouth lifted at the corners. "Aye ... Gordana will be happy to see ye."

Warmth filtered through Ella then. Although Gordana was a few years her elder, she had been close to Gavin's sister when she had lived at the castle. She looked forward to seeing her again.

Aware that a number of curious stares from around the outer bailey were now fixed upon her, Ella shifted her attention back to where the square, dun-colored keep rose to the east.

"Where will I find my mother?" she asked quietly.

"I will take ye to her now," Gavin replied.

"We shall see ye at supper ... Sister Annella?" Blair asked. His grey eyes were narrowed slightly as he continued to watch her with an unnerving intensity that once again reminded Ella of his mother.

Ella was opening her mouth to say that she'd likely be taking all her meals in private when Gavin spoke once more. "Aye ... Sister Ella is a guest here. Of course she will join us in the Great Hall this eve."

Ella's belly tightened at this news, and she drew in a slow breath. Already she felt far too conspicuous here. The last thing she needed was to take a place at the MacNichol clan's table in the Great Hall with kin and retainers all ogling her.

However, as she meekly left Monadh with the stable lad and followed Gavin toward the archway leading through to the inner bailey and the keep, she kept her thoughts to herself.

Gavin walked ahead, ascending a row of granite steps and entering the keep through great oaken doors. Two servants were in the midst of mopping the floor to the entrance hall beyond.

At seeing their clan-chief enter, the lasses straightened up, before curtsying.

"Welcome home, MacNichol," the younger of the two called out.

Gavin cast the lass an easy smile. "Thank ye, Fiona. Don't mind me ... carry on with yer tasks."

Both servants nodded, although they didn't resume their mopping immediately. Instead, their gazes shifted to Ella, curiosity lighting their faces.

Seeing their reactions to her, Ella loosed an inward sigh. She'd have to get used to the stares while she was here it seemed.

Gavin went ahead, leading the way up a spiral stairwell. Picking up her skirts, Ella followed. He didn't try to converse with her, which she was grateful for. She hadn't failed to notice that upon arriving back at Scorrybreac, his manner had altered slightly toward her. A formality had settled, a distant air that she wished he'd adopted during the journey here.

Leaving the stairwell, Gavin strode down a narrow corridor. Despite that it was a bright day out, there were no windows to let in the sunlight in these hallways. Instead, flickering cressets illuminated the damp stone.

Eventually, Gavin drew to a halt outside a large oaken door. He then turned to face Ella, giving her his full attention for the first time since they'd entered the keep. "Yer mother awaits ye within," he said softly. "I will see ye later ... at supper."

8

Blame

CAIT FRASER'S SICKROOM was dark and overly warm. The air smelt musty and slightly sour as if no one ever opened the shutters to let fresh air in.

Ella fought the urge to do just that as she crossed the flagstone floor and took a seat beside the bed. Sister Coira believed that fresh air chased away the dark humors that perpetuated illness. Even so, it wasn't Ella's place to come barging in here and open the window so her mother could watch the rose-hued sunset.

Cait appeared to be asleep, propped up against a mountain of pillows.

Lowering herself onto the stool, Ella took in her mother's frail form. She had never been a big woman, yet the illness that now wracked her body had melted the flesh from her bones, withered her arms to sticks, and caused her cheeks to sink in.

Ella's throat constricted as she watched her mother's face. She barely recognized the woman who had once caused her so much anguish. Cait Fraser didn't look capable of causing anyone trouble these days.

Drawing in a deep breath, Ella reached out, her hand covering her mother's. The skin was cool and papery. "Ma?"

Cait Fraser's eyes flickered open, and for the first time, Ella fully knew the woman before her. Those eyes were a deep blue, the same shade as Ella's.

"Ella?" Her mother's voice held a rasp, yet Ella recognized it.

Her vision blurred as she gently squeezed the frail hand beneath hers. "Aye ... it's me. MacNichol came to fetch me himself from Kilbride."

"Ye look so different in that habit," her mother whispered. Ella could hear the weakness in her voice, the whistle in her lungs with each exhale. Gavin was right, Cait Fraser didn't have much time left. "I barely know ye."

"It's still me," Ella murmured, attempting to raise a smile and failing.

"Aye," her mother croaked. "I see that ... and I am so proud that ye are a Bride of Christ."

Ella didn't reply. Her mother had always been pious. Even now, she wore a small iron crucifix around her neck. The cross lay against the snowy white linen of her night-rail. And as Ella watched, her mother's frail hand reached up to clasp the crucifix. It seemed her faith hadn't lessened with the years. Still, her gaze never left her daughter. Cait's blue eyes gleamed.

"I am glad ye came," her mother said finally, breaking the silence.

The genuine emotion in Cait's voice made Ella's chest start to hurt. Her mother had never before used such a tone with her.

Ella leaned forward, cupping her mother's free hand with both of her own now. "So am I."

"I didn't think ye would … and I wouldn't have blamed ye for it." Cait drew in a whispery breath. "I never treated ye right, Ella … and I'm sorry for it."

Ella swallowed hard. The pain in the center of her chest had now spread up to her throat. Her eyes stung as she blinked back tears.

Mother Mary, please give me strength. She wasn't sure what she'd expected upon her return—perhaps to encounter a mother as haughty and critical as ever—but this soft, broken individual wasn't it.

It ripped a hole in her chest to see her mother so diminished. She almost wished for a tongue-lashing. It would be easier to bear.

"It's all in the past now, Ma," Ella whispered. "Ye should know that I've been very happy at Kilbride. A nun's life suits me well."

"I would have liked to have done God's work," her mother admitted.

"But ye chose to become a wife and mother instead … that too is a good choice."

Cait Fraser huffed, some of her old fire returning for an instant. "I thought so once, but with the years, I found myself wishing I'd made a different choice." She broke off there, recovering her breath. It worried Ella to see that even speaking taxed her mother. "Don't mistake me, I don't regret having ye and yer sister," Cait continued weakly. "It's just that I've always yearned for a simple life that I could dedicate entirely to our Lord."

"Kilbride Abbey would have certainly given ye that," Ella replied softly. "I find myself missing its serenity already."

Cait's mouth curved. "Ye were so spirited once … I was sure ye wouldn't take to such a life." She paused then, her sunken chest rising and falling sharply under her high-necked night-rail. "I was so hard on ye, lass. I favored Innis … and always compared ye to her."

"I know," Ella replied, her voice still soft. "But all of that is forgotten now."

That wasn't entirely true, yet her mother didn't need to hear it. Best to let a dying woman make peace with her past.

"But I was wrong to do so." Some of the fire of old lit in Cait's blue eyes. Her thin fingers wrapped around Ella's, squeezing with surprising strength. "Innis was quiet and biddable, but ye had a spine. I tried to beat it out of ye, to scold it out of ye … but for a long while now, I have regretted my actions. Will ye ever forgive me, lass?"

"Aye, Ma." Tears ran down Ella's cheeks, but she didn't reach up to brush them away.

Their gazes locked and held for a long instant before Cait Fraser's grip tightened around the crucifix she still grasped with her free hand.

"Will ye pray with me, Ella?" she asked, her voice husky.

Ella nodded, smiling through her tears. "Of course I will."

Ella's father was waiting for her when she left her mother's sick room.

Stewart Fraser had gotten broader and greyer in the nearly two decades since they'd last seen each other. His face was even more careworn than Ella remembered, although his hazel eyes were just as kind.

Wordlessly, he enfolded Ella in a bear-hug, and when they drew apart, his eyes were gleaming.

"It is good to see ye, lass," he rumbled. "The years have made ye even bonnier than I remember."

Ella favored her father with a watery smile. "I have missed ye, Da," Ella replied. It was the truth. She'd often railed at her father for allowing his wife to be such a shrew, yet for every harsh word that Cait had rained down upon Ella, Stewart had gifted her three gentle ones.

"Are ye happy, Ella?" he asked softly. "I've often wondered about ye over the years."

"I am content, Da," Ella replied.

A weight appeared to lift from him at her words, and Stewart loosed a sigh. "That is a relief to hear."

Ella's gaze roamed his rugged face. As a younger man, he'd been handsome in that rangy way of the Fraser men: tall and flame-haired. Although he lacked the arrogant bearing of his cousin, Morgan Fraser—the chieftain of the Frasers of Skye. These days his once bright hair had faded to a rusty grey.

"Ma is so frail," Ella murmured, threading her arm through her father's and letting him lead her away down the narrow corridor. Night had just fallen, and cressets now burned upon the pitted stone walls. "I barely recognized her."

"Aye ... she is a changed woman," Stewart replied. "More than just physically ... as I am sure ye noted."

Ella nodded, her throat thickening. "I've never known her so ... soft."

Her father grunted. "Aye ... it's just a pity that it took a fatal illness for her to see clearly."

Ella cast her father a surprised glance. Her mother wasn't the only one to have changed it seemed. She couldn't believe it—her father's tone seemed almost ... critical.

Stewart Fraser let out a heavy sigh, his mouth curving into a tired smile. "I must carry part of the blame too, lass ... for not speaking up when she used to harangue ye. All the same, we are both glad ye have visited her."

Silence fell between them, and when Ella broke it, her voice was heavy with regret. "I should have come earlier, Da. I'm sorry I did not."

"Innis wrote to ye," he replied, his tone guarded now. "We all thought that ye would return when ye heard how ill she was ... but ye never did."

Ella swallowed, guilt thrumming through her. She wished she could tell her father why she'd stayed away. But neither of her parents knew the reason for her taking the veil—and it was too late now to reveal the truth.

It wouldn't change anything even if she was to tell him. It wouldn't erase his disappointment that she hadn't visited her dying sister.

"I regret that, Da," she said softly, a rasp to her voice betraying her churning emotions.

Stewart Fraser halted then and turned to her. Their gazes fused.

"Why didn't ye come?" he asked.

The directness of his question made Ella's breathing hitch. It felt as if someone had grasped her around the throat and was slowly squeezing. Now was her chance to be honest with him. Her father wanted her to speak frankly—and yet she couldn't. She just couldn't.

"We were busy with the harvest at Kilbride," Ella replied, forcing herself not to drop her gaze. "I couldn't get away ... I hadn't realized that Innis was so ill." Her voice trailed off, and when she saw her father's eyes shadow, her chest constricted and a sickly heat washed over her.

He knew she was lying.

9

Lady MacNichol

ELLA HAD HOPED her father would join her for supper in the Great Hall. However, he begged off with the excuse that he took all his meals at his wife's side these days. Ella couldn't criticize him for such devotion; she only wished she could use the same excuse.

She didn't want to dine with the MacNichols.

Entering Scorrybreac's Great Hall, Ella was taken aback by its vast size. Had it always been this big, or was she just used to Kilbride's modest refectory? The hall was long and rectangular-shaped, with a high dais at one end. A stag's head had been mounted over a large stone hearth, and before it sat an oaken table where the MacNichol family took their meals. Pennants made of the clan's plaid—red crossed with lines of blue and green—and a banner of the clan's seal hung above the hearth. The MacNichol seal was a hawk's head, with the clan's motto written in Latin beneath.

Meminisse sed providere: remember but look ahead.

Despite her nervousness, a wry smile tugged at Ella's lips. That motto had meant little to her when she'd lived here as a maid. But at thirty-six winters, those words now struck her.

Indeed, one had to keep focused on the future rather than dwelling on the past—yet the wise never forgot. The events almost two decades earlier had nearly broken her, but she would always keep them in her memory. They would inform her decisions and shape the years to come; they would ensure she never walked the same foolish path ever again.

Rows of MacNichol retainers—the clansmen and women who inhabited the keep—sat at the tables beneath the dais. The roar of voices quietened as she passed. Curious gazes followed Ella, tracking her progress down the aisle between the tables.

Spine straight, Ella passed through them and stepped up onto the dais. She'd come here as soon as she could after spending time with her mother, but it seemed she was late. She inhaled the aroma of rich boar stew and saw that servants had already started serving.

Ella reached the table and looked for somewhere to sit. Her belly clenched when she saw that the only free space was to Gavin MacNichol's left—for he sat at the head of the table—next to his mother.

All conversation at the table stopped when Ella took her seat.

Ella's gaze swept over those seated there. Gavin was favoring her with a soft smile, an expression that made her breathing quicken, while Maggie MacNichol was watching their guest with a narrow-eyed stare. Ella knew many others at the table. Gordana was there, sitting to her mother's left; while Blair, his wife Forbia, and their strapping sons sat farther down the table.

"Ye deigned to join us after all." Maggie MacNichol's first words made Ella start to sweat. If her own mother had been remarkable in her change, this woman was the complete opposite. As a younger woman, the clan-chief's lady had been a striking beauty with straw-gold hair, piercing grey eyes, and a regal presence. Time had not withered her, even though her hair had faded and the years had traced fine lines upon her skin. Maggie still sat as straight as ever, the force of her personality radiating out across the table.

"Apologies, Lady MacNichol," Ella replied, holding her eye. "I spent more time with my mother than expected."

Maggie sniffed at this. "And how is she faring today?"

"She is weak ... I imagine her time draws near."

Lady MacNichol's mouth pursed. "Ye should have come sooner." The woman didn't bother to dilute the accusatory tone of her voice. When Ella didn't reply, Maggie frowned. "Instead, my son had to take time away from the running of Scorrybreac to fetch ye."

"Mother." The warning tone in Gavin's voice caused those seated at the table to go still. Even the circling servants, who were ladling out stew, dishing up dumplings, and pouring goblets of sloe wine, paused in their work. "Sister Ella is our guest. Ye are not to interrogate her."

His mother stiffened, drawing herself up like an enraged cat. At the head of the table, Gavin didn't move. He sat, his posture relaxed, in a high-backed chair. Made out of polished oak, the chair had eagle heads carved into the armrests. Ella remembered the chair well, and how his father's corpulent form had spilled into it. There was nothing corpulent about Gavin though. His long body was hard and muscled, even in repose. He held a bronze goblet in one hand, his gaze hooded as he met his mother's eye.

Ella drew in a breath, waiting for Lady MacNichol to explode. And yet she didn't tear into her son as Ella had expected.

There had been many changes at Scorrybreac over the years it seemed.

Nonetheless, Maggie's mutinous expression warned that the woman had not yet finished saying her piece. She would merely bide her time.

The servants continued to serve supper, many of them not bothering to hide their curiosity at Ella's presence. One or two openly stared. It wasn't every day that a nun sat in Scorrybreac's Great Hall.

Behind the chieftain's table, a young woman, seated upon a stool by the hearth, began playing a harp. The lilting music drifted over the hall, filling Ella with memories.

She had not heard music like this since leaving Scorrybreac. The nuns didn't play musical instruments in the evenings. Innis had played the instrument well. Ella remembered her sister's soft smile then, the look of joy upon her face as her slender fingers danced over the harp strings.

Guilt lanced through Ella at another memory of her sister, causing a warm, sickly sensation to creep over her. Ella's conversation earlier that evening with her father needled at her. Innis had never deliberately done Ella wrong—she'd been hurt and confused by Ella's silence over the years.

If there was one thing she would change, it would be her treatment of her sister.

"It's good to see ye." Gordana leaned forward, catching Ella's eye. "Although I hardly recognize ye in that habit."

Ella smiled back. "Ye look no different to the last time we met."

It was true. Gordana MacNichol was around ten years Ella's senior, but age had not dimmed the pretty lines of her face. Gavin's elder sister wore her white-blonde hair braided down her back, and this eve she had donned a dark-blue kirtle that matched her eyes.

Gordana gave a soft laugh. "If only that were true."

Ella held her gaze for a long moment. In her letters from Innis, Ella had learned that Gordana had lost her husband, Rory, ten winters earlier. He'd fallen in the ice just after Yuletide and cracked his skull. It seemed that his widow had never remarried. Their son had been around four winter's old when Ella had left Scorrybreac. "How is Darron faring these days?" she asked.

Gordana smiled. "As tall as Gavin, if ye can believe it." Pride shone in her eyes as she spoke. "He serves the MacDonalds of Duntulm now ... and is captain of the guard." Gordana paused here, her mouth curving. "And he has just wed ... a lass named Sorcha MacQueen."

Next to her, Lady MacNichol made a choking sound. "The MacQueen chieftain's bastard ... hardly a match to brag about, Gordana."

In an instant, Gordana's face hardened. Her attention snapped to her mother. "My son's happiness means more to me than the parentage of the woman he loves," she said coldly.

Respect filtered through Ella as she glanced from Maggie's haughty face to Gordana's proud one. In the past, neither Gavin nor Gordana had dared to question their mother. Their mother had become even harsher with the years—but it appeared that her offspring had become less tolerant of her sharp tongue.

A servant dished up Ella's supper, and she inhaled the aroma. Mouth filling with saliva, Ella dug her wooden spoon into the stew. She had just taken her first spoonful when Lady MacNichol spoke once more.

However, this time her words were not directed at her daughter.

"I must say ... that habit does nothing for ye, Ella."

"It's *Sister* Ella, mother," Gavin corrected her wearily. "And please, leave our guest be. Her mother is gravely ill, and she has just crossed the isle to see her."

Maggie shrugged as if her son had said something of very little consequence, those grey eyes never leaving Ella.

"As I said … that attire is very unflattering," she continued. "The wimple makes yer face look like a moon. Ye could grow as fat as a sow under all that fabric and no one would be any the wiser."

The urge to laugh bubbled up within Ella. Smothering it, she grabbed her goblet of wine, raised it to her lips, and took a large gulp. "It is lucky then," she replied, her tone deliberately bland, "that the Lord does not judge us on our appearances."

Lady MacNichol's mouth pursed. "Aye … but the rest of us do. Ye resemble a crow in that garb."

Ella didn't reply. Maggie hadn't changed at all. Always a woman to fixate on the appearance and weight of other ladies, she'd never been without a vicious comment for both Ella and Innis in the past. But even Ella's status as a nun didn't stop her.

"Mother." Gavin's voice was rough with anger now. "Enough."

"What?" His mother favored him with a look of mock-innocence. "I was merely making an observation."

"Ye were being rude," he growled back. Gavin leaned forward then, his face hard. "And ye will apologize."

"The Lord is my light and my salvation—whom shall I fear? The Lord is the stronghold of my life—of whom shall I be afraid?"

Ella paused, raising her eyes from the psalm she was reading, to find her mother watching her with an intent expression.

"What is it, Ma … I thought this was one of yer favorites?"

"It is," Cait Fraser replied, her voice whispery. "Ye read it so beautifully to me earlier, but yer heart isn't in it, tonight. Is something amiss, daughter?"

Ella stiffened. She hadn't been aware that her mood had shown so clearly upon her face. "I'm just a little on edge," she admitted, lowering the book of psalms to her lap. "Lady MacNichol was particularly sharp-tongued at supper."

Her mother loosed a sigh, sinking back into the mountain of pillows that propped her up. "That's the only good thing about being laid up here," she murmured. "Avoiding that shrew."

"She appears to have gotten nastier with age," Ella observed before guilt flickered up within her. It wasn't seemly for a nun to gossip about others; nonetheless, she dreaded her next mealtime with Gavin's mother.

"It's bitterness," Cait replied. "Gavin isn't as easy to manipulate as his father was … she feels powerless."

"I will pray for her soul then," Ella replied, flicking through the psalm book. "Perhaps I can find something to combat her ill humor." She paused then, glancing up at her mother. "What about this: Deliver me from mine enemies, Lord. Defend me from them that rise up against me."

Cait gave a weak laugh. "A little harsh I think, Sister Ella."

Ella continued to leaf through the book. "Ah," she said finally, her mouth quirking. "I have just the thing ... from Psalm Ninety-One."

"Go on, read it then." Cait Fraser's eyes flickered shut. Even short conversations appeared to weary her terribly. "I am listening."

"He will cover ye with his wings," Ella began softly, her voice carrying through the silent chamber. "A thousand may fall dead beside you, ten thousand all around you, but ye will not be harmed. Ye will look and see how the wicked are punished."

10

Regrets

CLIMBING THE WORN stone steps, Ella pushed open the heavy oaken door and stepped into a cool, dimly-lit space. Scorrybreac Chapel huddled against the northern wall of the keep, with the curtain wall rearing above it.

The chapel was much smaller than Kilbride kirk, yet she had fond memories of this place. Indeed, it was her refuge now. She'd left her mother sleeping but made the mistake of going to the women's solar afterward. Gavin's mother had been there, surrounded by her ladies, and Ella had soon felt like a fly trapped in a spider's web. She'd had to get away from the pointed looks and whispered comments.

Inhaling the odor of tallow from the banks of guttering candles lining the walls, and the scent of burning incense, Ella made her way across the polished stone floor. She didn't head toward the altar, but to the small shrine located against the left wall. This chapel was a special place, for it had an alcove dedicated to the Virgin Mary.

Kneeling before it, Ella gazed up at the serene face of the statue before her. A woman cloaked in blue gazed down at the swaddled infant in her arms: Mother Mary. The sight of the statue made peace settle over Ella in a comforting blanket. Even before she'd fled to Kilbride, this chapel had been her safe place. Here, it felt as if nothing could touch her.

Innis had loved this chapel too, and Ella's breathing quickened at the memory of her sister kneeling beside her in front of this shrine. Being at Scorrybreac brought back too many memories.

The ones that included her sister were the most painful.

How she'd wanted to hate Innis for wedding the man she'd loved.

She'd barely spoken to her sister after Gavin broke the news to her. In the days while she'd awaited news from Kilbride, Ella had avoided all of her kin for fear that the disappointment and grief that boiled within her would explode if any of them provoked her.

Innis had written to her often at Kilbride, yet she'd never responded to her letters—not once. But her sister hadn't seemed to mind. The messages had continued to arrive, one each month, until the letter that had revealed she was gravely ill. In that missive, her sister had asked something of Ella for the first time since their parting.

She'd requested a visit so that they might see each other one last time before the end.

Ella hadn't replied—and nor had she visited her dying sister.

At the time she'd buried those feelings deep, busied herself in her life at Kilbride. But now, surrounded by so many memories, they resurfaced once more.

Regret twisted in Ella's breast.

"I'm so sorry, Innis," she whispered. "Ye deserved better."

Her vision misted as the pain just under her breastbone built. "I should have come home to say farewell."

Brushing away the tears that now trickled down her face, Ella heaved in a deep breath. She had visited the chapel for solace, yet she should have known that memories would resurface. Innis had been gone for nearly two years—but her presence was still strong in this place.

Removing the crucifix from her belt, Ella entwined her fingers through the beaded wooden necklace and clasped her hands before her. Then, she closed her eyes and began to pray.

Almost immediately a sense of peace settled over her, calming the churning grief and gnawing guilt. All Ella's cares and worries slid away.

Time lost all meaning in the chapel. It was only when Ella's knees started to hurt that she realized she'd been kneeling for a long while. Around her, the tallow candles continued to burn. There was no sign of the priest who oversaw this chapel. He'd likely retired for the night, for it was now growing very late.

It was time for Ella to find her own bed. Servants had taken her satchel up earlier, but she would have to ask one of them to lead her to her lodgings. She'd been too occupied since her arrival at Scorrybreac Castle to seek out her bed-chamber herself.

Wincing, Ella rose to her feet. She rubbed her sore knees and looped her crucifix through her belt.

Despite the grief that had surfaced over her sister, she was glad she'd come to the chapel. Being around so many folk, after years of the peace at Kilbride, had put her on edge. She'd felt overwhelmed, yet her time at prayer and the Virgin's soothing company made her feel stronger—and she knew she'd need strength in the days to come.

She left the chapel, stepping out into the cool night air. Descending the steps, Ella slowed her pace, alarm flickering through her.

She wasn't alone.

Up ahead she spied a man's shadow looming across the cobbles in the light of a flaming torch that was chained to the side of the keep.

Her breathing hitched as Gavin MacNichol stepped into the torchlight.

Ella raised a hand, placing it over her pounding heart. "Heavens," she gasped. "Ye gave me a fright."

"Sorry, I didn't mean to scare ye." The clan-chief stopped and raised his chin to look up at her. "I've been waiting to escort ye to yer lodgings."

Ella stared back at him, the alarm that had just settled rising once more. "Ye don't need to do that ... I can ask a servant."

He inclined his head. "I don't need to, but I'd like to ... if I may?"

Ella tensed. There was no suggestion or flirtatious tone to his words, yet she didn't like them nonetheless. "After our conversation on the journey here, I don't think we have much to say to each other," she said when the silence between them became uncomfortable.

His mouth curved. "I'd like to apologize for my mother's rudeness earlier ... it was inexcusable."

Ella huffed. "Everyone else in this keep has changed somewhat with the years but not Lady MacNichol."

"Ye are mistaken ... my mother has changed. The years have whetted her tongue like a blade. She's even more of a viper than she was when ye lived with us."

Ella raised her eyebrows but didn't respond. Instead, she continued her path down the steps and started across the inner bailey. Gavin walked beside her.

"We shouldn't be alone," she said quietly. "It isn't proper."

"We were alone on the journey here," he pointed out.

"Aye ... but I had no choice about that. Here at Scorrybreac, there are sharp eyes and flapping ears and tongues."

Gavin snorted. "I wouldn't worry about that ... I don't give the gossips in this keep a second thought."

Ella cast Gavin a swift glance. "When we met at Kilbride, I thought ye hadn't altered much with the years ... but I now see ye have."

His eyes gleamed as his gaze met hers. "How so?"

"Ye have a harder edge to ye ... and ye certainly wouldn't have told yer mother off like ye did at supper."

Gavin gave a soft laugh. It was a low, pleasant sound that caused an unexpected warmth to seep across Ella's breast. She'd forgotten his laugh, and how much she'd loved it.

"My mother overstepped ... something she does frequently these days," he replied. "Gordana thinks I should pack her off to live with kin upon the Isle of Raasay. That way, we'd all be rid of her."

"And why don't ye?"

A heavy sigh gusted out of Gavin. "I don't rightly know ... guilt ... a sense of filial duty."

Ella looked away, biting at her bottom lip. *Duty.* He hadn't changed that much after all. An overwhelming sense of responsibility still ruled this man's decisions—his life.

"I take it that ye and Innis never had children?" Ella asked after a long pause. They had skirted around the eastern edge of the inner bailey and were now walking past the high wall that circuited the herb garden, a long rectangular space that hugged the southern flank of the curtain wall.

Glancing Gavin's way, Ella saw tension settle over his face. It was a bold, impertinent question, and had she mulled over it first, Ella probably would never have asked it. As it was, she'd been wondering all day about Gavin's union with Innis. Had they truly been happy together? The question had slipped from her lips before she'd had the chance to stop herself.

"No," he replied, a slightly rough edge to his voice. "We tried for the first few years." He cleared his throat then. "But when Innis's womb didn't quicken, she asked if we could sleep in separate chambers. Once that happened, we never lay together again."

Ella glanced away once more, taking in the news. Years earlier, it might have made her feel vindicated. As it was, she just felt hollow—and a little sad. The guarded edge to his voice warned her from asking anything else. Yet his candor made it hard not to.

"Innis wrote to me often, ye know?" she said finally.

"Aye ... once a moon."

"I read all her letters."

"But ye never responded to any."

There it was, a faint note of accusation in his tone. Ella wasn't surprised or offended. He had every right to think her cruel.

"Innis told me that she was content with ye," she replied, deliberately not responding to his comment. "Was that not the truth?"

A beat of silence followed. "We were happy enough," Gavin replied. There was a heaviness to his voice now as if this conversation was starting to weary him. "Innis and I made good companions, and our friendship deepened over the years. But it was not an ideal match ... we both knew that. Perhaps if we'd had bairns, things might have been different." His voice trailed off there, and Gavin drew to a halt.

Ella stopped next to him, surprised. Turning, she faced him, wilting under the intensity of his gaze. The torchlight that flickered across the inner bailey highlighted the handsome planes of his face, but also the regret in his eyes.

Regret for what? That his union with Innis had been lacking? That he'd wed her in the first place?

"I have no heir," Gavin said, his voice low now, "so my brother or one of my nephews will take my place once I'm gone."

Ella inclined her head, wondering why he was being so frank with her this eve. For the first time since they'd been reunited, she was starting to feel comfortable in his presence. "Does that bother ye?"

"Years ago I thought it might ... but these days I hardly care." His gaze shadowed then, as it held hers. "Maybe it's my punishment for hurting ye, Ella. Perhaps I deserve no better."

11

Saying Too Much

ELLA FOUND GORDANA MacNichol hard at work in the walled garden. Stepping inside the secluded space, Ella inhaled the scents of the last of the summer roses mingled with the strong perfume of lavender.

A few feet away, Gordana stood before a trellis of gillyflowers. She was tying up the stems of the clove-scented, pink and white flowers that grew in large earthen pots, to prevent them from flopping over. Around Gordana spread long beds of rosemary, sage, thyme, chamomile, and myrtle. A large spreading quince tree had been espaliered against the far wall of the garden.

A smile curved Ella's mouth as she took in the scene. How could one *not* smile when standing in such a beautiful spot?

Giving a delicate cough, she moved toward Gordana.

Gavin's sister glanced over her shoulder. Her face had tensed, for she clearly didn't like anyone intruding upon her garden sanctuary.

"Don't mind me," Ella replied, stopping abruptly. "I can leave if ye wish."

Gordana's expression softened. "Stay, Sister Ella ... I thought for a moment that Ma had come to harangue me."

Ella raised an eyebrow before she drew closer. "She does that often?"

"Ye saw her last night. I deliberately break my fast in my chamber to avoid seeing her first thing in the morning. She tends to sour one's mood."

Ella smiled but didn't reply. Indeed, she had been only too happy to enjoy her bannock, smeared with butter and rich thyme honey, in the seclusion of her bed-chamber this morning. She was dreading the noon meal, for Lady MacNichol was likely to be present.

"I'm so sorry about how she spoke to ye yesterday," Gordana continued as the pause lengthened between them. "It was unacceptable."

"It was ... but as ye can see, she hasn't broken me. I didn't come to Scorrybreac for Lady MacNichol."

"How is yer mother this morning?" Gordana asked. Her gaze softened as she spoke.

"Weak ... but glad to have my company," Ella admitted. "I read her psalms earlier. She's sleeping now ... Da says she sleeps often these days."

"Aye." Gordana tied up the last stem of gillyflower and turned to face Ella properly. "She tires easily ... I have visited her often over the past months, but she grows steadily weaker." Gordana hesitated. "I'm glad ye have come."

Ella dropped her gaze, moving over to a seat made from slender willow branches. Arranging the long skirts of her habit, she settled down upon it. "I wouldn't have done," she admitted. "If it hadn't been for yer brother."

Gordana didn't reply. Instead, she too sat down upon the willow seat, her blue eyes settling upon Ella's face in a frank look that Ella recognized. Gavin had the same look.

"Ye should know," Gordana began gently, her face so grave that nervousness suddenly fluttered up within Ella, "that my brother has never forgotten ye."

Ella swallowed and forced herself to hold Gordana's gaze. Of course, Gordana had always been observant; although Ella had never spoken to her of the relationship that she and Gavin had once shared, it appeared that Gordana had guessed at their closeness, unless Gavin had confided in her.

"He has already said as much," Ella replied, her voice tight. "I wish he would keep his feelings to himself. It's too late to voice such sentiments."

Gordana nodded, her gaze clouding. "I feared he'd say something ... when he rode south alone to fetch ye, I suspected he would."

Ella drew in a deep breath, her fingers curling into fists. "I wish ye had managed to dissuade him. All Gavin has done is bring up things that are best left buried."

Sensing Ella's agitation, Gordana reached out and placed a hand over hers. "Perhaps he just wanted to have an opportunity to reconcile." Gordana then favored her with a sad smile. "The mistakes of the past weigh heavily upon my brother's shoulders."

Silence fell between the two women then. It was peaceful in the walled garden, the hush broken only by the buzzing of insects and the faint cries of gulls circling off the coast. The rest of the noise of the busy keep didn't seem to reach them here.

Eventually, smoothing out the wrinkles in her habit, Ella spoke once more. "What of ye, Gordana ... Rory has been gone many years. Why have ye never wed again?"

Gordana's mouth lifted at one corner. "That's another thing Ma has nagged me about over the years." She sighed then, glancing away, a distant look settling upon her face. "After Rory died, I did try to move on ... yet the men who presented themselves to me were awful." She gave a delicate shudder. "The likes of Aonghus Budge of Islay ... ye remember him?"

"Aye." Ella pulled a face. He was a man of her father's age, and although she hadn't seen him in a long while, she remembered him as an overbearing individual with a lecherous gaze. "I understand why ye wouldn't want the likes of him."

"My other suitors weren't much better," Gordana replied. "I kept sending them away ... and eventually what little interest there had been dried up." She turned, meeting Ella's gaze once more. "Truthfully, I am content alone. I have a freedom many women do not."

"Ye could take the veil and come to live at Kilbride?" Ella suggested. "We could do with yer gardening skills."

Gordana snorted. "My lack of piety would make the life of a nun a poor choice for me ... however ..." Her expression turned thoughtful as she studied Ella. "What's it like ... living in a woman's world?"

Ella's mouth curved. "Peaceful ... and structured. We are never idle at Kilbride. There are always chores to be done. I've rarely felt lonely over the years ... the nuns are good company ... most of them at least."

"Ye don't appear to regret yer choice."

"I don't," Ella replied. "If I couldn't have Gavin, I didn't want any man." She broke off abruptly there, having revealed far more than she'd intended. Feeling her cheeks warm, Ella dropped her gaze. "I am content doing the Lord's work."

Gordana didn't reply, although when Ella glanced her way once more, the gleam in the woman's eyes warned her that she had, indeed, said too much.

"A message has come for ye, brother."

Gavin glanced up from where he was going through his ledger of accounts, to see Blair standing in the doorway to his solar, a roll of parchment clutched in his hand.

"Aye?"

Blair approached him, holding out the missive. "It bears the MacKinnon seal," he warned.

Gavin released a heavy breath, replacing the quill he'd been using to scratch out sums, into its pot. "What does Duncan want this time?"

He took the roll of parchment, glancing down at the wax seal bearing the distinctive boar's head with a shin bone in its mouth and the clan motto: *Audentes Fortuna Juvat*: *fortune favors the bold*. Indeed, it was a message from the clan-chief himself. His lips thinning, Gavin broke the seal and unfurled the parchment. His gaze narrowed as he read the message within.

"Well?" Blair asked after a lengthy pause. "What pot of shit is he stirring this time?"

Gavin lowered the parchment and cast his brother a quelling look. Few on this isle loved Duncan MacKinnon, and Blair never held back when it came to voicing his opinion about the man. As clan-chief, Gavin had to be more diplomatic.

"He's on the warpath," Gavin admitted, handing the message to his brother. "Here ... read it for yerself."

Blair took the missive and did just that. A few moments later, he glanced up, his gaze widening. "He's demanding ye *all* meet with him at Dunan?"

"Aye ... in seven days' time. He wants to tackle the lawlessness upon the isle 'once and for all'."

Blair raised an eyebrow at these words.

"This is a discussion we need to have," Gavin reminded him. "Even on our lands, outlaws have become an issue of late." Gavin thought then of a plucky, knife-throwing nun he had accompanied back to Scorrybraec, and a slight smile curved his lips.

"But MacKinnon as host to a meeting? He doesn't get on with the other clan-chiefs and chieftains. Even ye, who can rub along with most folk, can barely stand him."

Gavin's mouth quirked. "Perhaps this is a chance to improve relations upon the isle."

"They won't all come." Blair raised the parchment once more, squinting slightly as he prepared to continue reading it. "MacLeod and Fraser can't be in the same room together … they'll kill each other."

Gavin snorted. His brother had a point there. The last time Malcolm MacLeod and Morgan Fraser had met, it had been on the battlefield. And then when Fraser's eldest son, Lachlann, ran off with MacLeod's youngest daughter, Adaira, relations between the two clans sank to a new low. However, as he'd just pointed out, lawlessness was a problem that now affected them all.

"What's this?" Blair had continued reading. "He wants ye to wed his sister?"

Gavin leaned back in his chair and ran a hand over his face. Suddenly, he felt every one of his thirty-eight years, and more besides. "Aye … it seems so."

Blair lowered the parchment and frowned. "This isn't the first time he's made the offer?"

Gavin shook his head.

"Have ye met Lady Drew MacKinnon?"

"Aye," Gavin replied. "Many years ago … we were both newly wed to others then though. She lost her husband around the time that Innis died."

"And … ye aren't keen on the match?"

"No," Gavin replied, his tone turning curt. "Lady Drew and I wouldn't be suited."

"Why … is she ugly?"

Gavin muttered an oath under his breath. Sometimes Blair had such a simplistic view of the world. He wouldn't have minded if Lady Drew MacKinnon was of humble looks, if her character had been sweet.

"I'm well aware I need to wed again," he said after a heavy pause. "However, I'll not choose a scheming and dominant woman as my bride. Lady Drew reminds me of our mother."

Blair winced, and Gavin saw that his point had been made. Blair wouldn't ask after Lady Drew MacKinnon again. Yet her brother wouldn't be as easy to put off. Duncan MacKinnon didn't like being told 'no'.

"Will ye go to this meeting then?" Blair asked. His brother walked over to the sideboard and poured himself a goblet of wine. He then drained it in two gulps and poured himself another. Like their father before them, Blair MacNichol liked his drink. Even though he'd barely passed his thirty-sixth winter, the color in his cheeks was already high, and he was starting to thicken around the middle.

Watching him, Gavin frowned. If he wasn't careful, he'd suffer the same health problems as their father—the gout and bloated liver that had sent him to an early grave.

"Aye, I'll go," Gavin replied heavily. "The outlaw problem needs addressing. Besides … although MacKinnon isn't my neighbor, I'd rather not make him my enemy."

Across the room, Blair gave a rude snort. "Not yet … anyway."

12

So Soon

ELLA PUT DOWN the book of psalms, her gaze resting upon Cait Fraser's face. Her mother had fallen asleep halfway through the reading. The healer had visited Cait earlier and given her a dose of something strong. Although the herbs dulled the pain, they also made her sleepy.

Rising to her feet, Ella leaned forward and placed a kiss upon her mother's gaunt cheek. The skin was cool and papery beneath her lips. "Sleep well, Ma," she whispered. "I shall see ye tomorrow."

They'd spoken little during this meeting, for fatigue and pain had dulled Cait's senses and she'd preferred to listen rather than converse. Ella could understand why. Her mother's eyes were hollowed with pain.

It was getting late, late enough that Ella could retire for the day without appearing rude. Supper had taken place already. Like all the meals in the Great Hall, this one had simmered with tension. It wasn't only Ella's presence here that caused it, she realized, but the relations between Maggie MacNichol and her three offspring. She seemed to delight in tormenting them, Gavin and Gordana especially.

Still, Maggie would find time—at least once during the meal—to level an insult at Ella. This eve, she had questioned her on life at the abbey before concluding that nuns had spoiled, privileged lives.

Ella sensed the woman's thinly veiled frustration. Maggie had once held a position of power at Scorrybreac. Her husband had been clan-chief, but he had sought her counsel in all things.

Gavin did not.

Ella left her mother's chamber and made her way down the hallway to her own lodgings. Yawning, she let herself into the small yet comfortable room. Although it was still summer, a servant had been in and lit the hearth. In stone keeps like these, the air stayed cool and damp, even on the hottest days. Ella was grateful for the fire. The servants had also brought up fresh water for washing and left linen drying cloths and a large cake of soap.

Picking it up, Ella gave the soap a delicate sniff: rose. A pang went through her. Life at Kilbride didn't allow for such frivolities. None of the nuns used scented soaps or dabbed rosewater behind their ears.

It felt like a forbidden luxury now.

Even so, Ella would still use the soap this evening. She was far from Kilbride—no one would know or care.

Stopping before her bed, Ella began to undress. It always took her a while, for there were a number of layers to peel off. First came the black veil that she wore over her wimple, and then the woolen belt she cinched about her waist, before she unlooped her crucifix and placed it upon a low wooden table next to the bed. She then wriggled out of the habit itself and removed her guimpe, a starched cloth that covered her neck and shoulders. The wimple lifted off afterward. Then, she removed the scapular—an apron that hung from front and back—and pushed down her underskirt, so that she finally stood clad only in a long ankle-length léine.

Ella let out a sigh. At times, during the summer, she felt like she was being smothered under all those layers of fabric.

Reaching up, Ella undid the heavy braid that hung between her shoulders, freeing her long hair. With a sigh, she shook it free. Her scalp had been itching all day; her hair badly needed washing.

Upon her arrival at Kilbride, Ella had prepared herself to have her hair shorn close to her scalp. However, the abbess held a lenient view on the subject, preferring to let all the nuns keep their hair at whatever length they preferred. Instead, she conducted a symbolic ceremony when they took their vows, snipping off just a single lock.

Ella stripped off her léine, shivering in the cool air despite the hearth burning nearby. She moved close to the washbowl and poured water into it, humming to herself as she began to wash. When she had cleaned her body, she bent over and wet her hair before lathering it with soap.

The scent of rose floated over her, and Ella inhaled deeply. It was odd how evocative scents could be. Suddenly, she was sixteen years old again, and full of hope for the life before her. She'd been obsessed with roses at that age. She'd embroidered them on all her mother's cushions, pressed rose petals, taken care of her mother's rose bushes, and made rose-scented water and soap.

Drying herself off, Ella donned her night-rail, a loose robe that she wore for sleeping. With a sigh, she perched on the edge of the bed and gently combed out her long hair. The silence and peace inside her chamber wrapped itself around her. At this hour, all the Sisters of Kilbride would be spending time in contemplative silence. In contrast, Scorrybreac Castle seemed to echo with loud voices and laughter until late in the evening. She'd forgotten just how many folk actually lived here.

She retrieved her crucifix from the side table and knelt at the foot of the bed, hands clasped, as she began her evening prayers.

She usually found it easy to concentrate on the words—but this evening thoughts kept crowding her mind, intruding.

Her conversation with Gordana that morning had haunted her for the rest of the day.

My brother has never forgotten ye.

The solemn look on Gordana's face had made Ella's breathing constrict, as did the sadness that shadowed her eyes with the next words.

Gavin knows all chance with ye is gone.

Now that she was here and had started to mend things with her mother, Ella was relieved she had made the journey to Scorrybreac. Yet there were too many memories in this place. Just walking around the shadowy hallways of the keep brought so much back.

The mistakes of the past weigh heavily upon my brother's shoulders.

Ella heaved a sigh. There had been many times over the years when she'd wondered how Gavin was faring. In the first year, she'd thought of him constantly, especially when—

No. Ella squeezed her eyes shut, her comb snagging on a knot in her hair. She wouldn't think of it. *Not now—not ever again.*

Gavin wasn't the only one who carried a burden, who had been scarred by the past. Ella's wounds went deep, deeper than he realized.

"Ella!" Stewart Fraser's voice boomed through the door, jerking her from a fitful sleep. "Ye need to come quickly."

Heart pounding from being ripped from her slumber, Ella pushed herself up into a sitting position. "What is it, Da?" she called back, her voice croaky with sleep.

"It's yer mother," he replied, "she's in a bad way and is asking for ye."

The edge of panic in his voice roused Ella from her bed. Throwing back the covers, she reached for her habit. "I'm coming," she called back. "I just need to get dressed first."

"There's no time, lass ... she has little time left."

Ella froze and straightened up, her pulse accelerating once more. It was forbidden for others to see a nun in such a state of undress, but what could she do? It took her an age to put on all her layers of clothing.

Dropping her habit back over the chair where she'd draped it before retiring for the night, Ella reached instead for a long robe. She would have preferred something with a hood that covered her unbound hair, yet there wasn't any time to braid it. Instead, she heaved in a deep breath, pulled the robe tightly over her night-rail, and padded, barefoot, toward the door.

Out in the corridor, one look at her father's face and she knew things were bad.

Stewart Fraser looked scared. His rugged face was strained. A nerve flickered under one eye, and his gaze guttered as it met his daughter's. Wordlessly, he reached out and took Ella by the hand, leading her up the shadowy hallway toward Cait Fraser's sickroom.

Ella knew the smell of impending death. She'd attended many patients with Sister Coira and watched the life fade from them as the healer did her best to make them comfortable.

Death had a sweet, cloying odor that made Ella's bile rise.

The healer, an elderly man named Farlan, stepped away from the bed when Ella entered. His gaze widened as he took in Ella's state of undress, yet he said nothing. With a nod, Farlan moved around the bed and leaned close to Ella.

"Her time is near ... shall I call for the priest, or will ye do the last rites?"

Ella swallowed. "I will do them."

Farlan nodded and stepped back. "I will leave ye alone then."

The healer's footfalls whispered across the flagstone floor, and the door thudded shut behind him. Ella glanced over her shoulder, expecting to find her father present. Yet he too had left them alone.

Approaching the bed, Ella's gaze settled upon her mother.

Cait Fraser watched her. The woman's eyes were sunken with pain, her breathing shallow. Her skin was ashen.

"Daughter," she rasped. "Please say the words ... bless me before the end."

Ella swallowed. "Of course, Ma."

The last rites required anointing the forehead of the dying person with oil, yet Ella had none. Instead, she dipped her thumb into a bowl of water that stood on the bedside table and pressed it lightly to her mother's forehead.

"Through this holy anointing," she began softly, "may the Lord in his love and mercy help ye with the grace of the Holy Spirit. May the Lord who frees ye from sin save ye and raise ye up."

Her voice died away, and a smile graced her mother's lips. "Thank ye, lass ... ye were always good, Ella. I'm just sorry I never told ye that."

Ella swallowed once more, in an attempt to dislodge the lump that was making it hard to breathe.

Not now ... not so soon.

Although she didn't like being away from Kilbride, she had wished for more days with her mother before her time came.

She took hold of Cait's thin hand, entwining her fingers through her mother's. "It matters not now," she whispered. "I'm just sorry I came here too late ... I wanted to spend more time with ye."

Her mother gazed up at her. "And I with ye. I have missed ye over the years." Cait's frail fingers tightened around hers. "Are ye truly happy, lass? We didn't all drive ye to a life of misery, did we?"

Ella shook her head, tears trickling down her face now. "Ye didn't drive me to anything. As I have told ye, I am content with this life."

Her mother nodded, her eyes fluttering closed. "That's a relief," she whispered. "Innis blamed herself for ye going away ... and I was sure I'd played a role in it."

"Kilbride was my choice." The words were an effort, for tears now scalded Ella's cheeks. This conversation was tearing her heart out. "I love ye, Ma."

Cait's grip on her hand tightened once more. "And I ye, lass. I wish ..." Cait Fraser broke off there, gasping for breath. "I wish ..."

She never finished her sentence. A heartbeat passed, and then Ella saw the life fade from her mother's face. She'd witnessed such before, the slackening of the muscles and flesh, as the spirit left its mortal shell.

Cait's hand went limp in her daughter's, and she left her last words unsaid.

For a long moment, Ella merely stared down at the woman who'd given her life, the woman she'd resented for so long. One moment Cait had been there with her, the next she'd departed. The suddenness of death was a shocking thing.

A shuddering sob rose up within Ella, a rising wave of grief that had long been held back, like a spring tide behind a seawall. But now that wall was starting to crumble.

Bowing low over the hand she still clasped, Ella began to weep.

13

Laid Bare

ONCE THE GRIEF broke free, it couldn't be stemmed.

For a while, Ella couldn't move. She could only cling to the side of the bed, still clutching her mother's hand as sobs wracked her body.

Years of pain, anger, frustration, and grief broke free with an intensity that felt as if she'd just been physically struck.

It hurt to breathe, to think, to exist.

She wept for all of them. For Innis, who'd never spoken a cross word to her, but whom she'd shunned all those years. For her mother, who had been eaten up with regret for too long. For Gavin, who had done his duty and realized too late what it would cost him—and for herself.

She'd run away to Kilbride, and although she'd found solace and peace there, the fact still remained that she'd used it as a hiding place.

But one couldn't hide forever. Sooner or later the past chased you down. Eighteen years of pain and regret toppled down upon Ella.

Gasping, she released her mother's hand and pushed herself to her feet. Her body trembled from the force of her grief, and the tears that still coursed down her cheeks blinded her.

She needed to be alone, she needed to find a sanctuary where she could let grief consume her.

Ella stumbled to the door, ripped it open, and staggered out into the hallway. Her father was waiting there, his eyes widening in shock at the sight of her.

He took a step forward, reaching for his daughter. "Ella?"

"She's dead," Ella gasped out the words, pain ripping through her chest. "Go to her."

She side-stepped her father's embrace and pushed past him, hurrying down the hallway. Her first instinct was to return to her bed-chamber. Yet that wasn't far enough away. She needed the sanctuary of the chapel. And even if she wasn't dressed, she would go there.

Bare feet slapping on stone, she picked up the skirts of her night-rail and robe and hurried to the spiral stairwell that led down to the bottom level of the keep. It was a foolish thing to do, for tears blinded her, and the heavy material around her legs risked tripping her. But she was too upset to care.

Ella was halfway down the stairwell when she stumbled on the worn stone steps and plunged headlong into the darkness.

A scream ripped from her throat, panic slicing through the blind grief that had sent her running down these steps. In a sickening moment, she realized she was doomed.

And then strong arms caught her.

Gavin had been climbing the steps, on the way to visit Lady Fraser's sickroom, when he'd heard the whisper of bare feet on stone above him. Someone was descending the stairwell—rapidly.

He'd told his nephews off numerous times for sprinting on the stairs. One of the servants had fallen and broken her neck three years earlier, and that had scared all the lads into being more cautious.

But someone wasn't being careful tonight.

A ragged sob reached him and then a long shadow appeared above.

A heartbeat later a frightened cry filled the stairwell, and a woman, encased in flowing white, light copper hair flying behind her, hurtled toward him.

Gavin leaped forward and caught her. However, the force of her fall propelled them both back. Only the fact that Gavin twisted, so that they crashed back against the wall, saved the pair of them from tumbling down the stairs.

"The Devil's cods," Gavin wheezed. The lass had knocked the wind out of him. "That was close."

And then he realized whom he was holding in his arms.

He hadn't recognized her. It had been so many years since he'd seen Ella like this, dressed in a night-rail and robe, her hair tumbling around her shoulders. Holding her soft body in this way, crushed against his chest, made his breathing quicken.

But the desire that arrowed through his groin pulled up sharply when he saw her face.

Tears streamed down Ella's cheeks, her mouth trembled—and her eyes held so much grief, so much pain, that whatever words Gavin was going to speak next died upon his lips.

"Ella," he whispered. "What is it?"

"They're dead," Ella gasped, staring up at him with such a broken expression that it suddenly hurt Gavin to breathe. "Ma is dead ... Innis is dead ... why do I feel like it's all my fault?"

"It's not."

The idea was ridiculous. Who had put such a notion in her head?

"They're gone." The pain in Ella's voice cut Gavin deep. "And I had the chance to put things right, but I didn't ... and now it's too late."

Ella buried her face in Gavin's chest, her shoulders heaving.

Grim-faced, he gathered her against him, lifting her into his arms. Ella didn't resist, for she was sobbing uncontrollably now.

What did Lady Fraser say to her?

He carried Ella up the stairs, back to the floor where her bed-chamber was located. The hallway was empty, the cressets burning low now, for it was well past the witching hour. Most of the keep was asleep, and so had Gavin been before the healer, Farlan, had knocked on his door with the news that Cait Fraser was close to death.

Shouldering open the door to Ella's chamber, Gavin went inside, closing it with his foot behind him. The fire in the hearth had died to glowing embers, although the chamber was warm enough.

Gavin lowered Ella gently to the ground but instantly regretted doing so. He should have carried her over to the bed instead. Letting her down like this made their bodies brush close.

And he felt every curve and contour of her body as he did so.

The Lord strike him down, she felt good. Her body was small yet lush, her breasts soft. He felt their peaks graze down his chest as he set her upon her feet. One of his hands splayed across the small of her back, steadying her. It was an intimate, possessive gesture. In an instant, his groin hardened.

Fighting the lust that pulsed through him, Gavin gently hooked a finger under Ella's chin and raised her face so their gazes met.

"Why do ye blame yerself?" he asked. "No one else does."

Her glittering blue eyes fixed upon him. "It was so hard leaving here," she replied, the words coming out in gasps, for she still fought her grief. "The only way I managed it was to shut myself off from my kin. I was angry at Ma for preferring Innis, and I was furious at Innis for taking ye from me." She let out another soft sob. "I know they're both with God now, but guilt still tears me up inside."

"Enough." He hadn't meant the word to sound so angry, but it did. "No one is to blame for Innis and yer mother's deaths. It's just life, Ella. Cruel, callous life."

She stared up at him, her cheeks wet with tears, and something twisted deep within Gavin's chest. Even when she was a weeping mess, this woman was beautiful. She had a soft, earthy beauty, enhanced by that thick mane of light auburn hair that fell around her shoulders in heavy waves.

When they'd been younger, everyone had said Innis was the prettier of the two—yet for Gavin, Ella had always outshone her sister.

Their gazes fused, and Gavin could suddenly hear the thudding of his own heart.

A heartbeat later he leaned down, cupped her face with both hands, and kissed her.

No previous thought went into the act; if he'd stopped to ponder the decision, he'd never have done it. Yet a need so strong that he felt sick from it rose within him, and before he knew what he was doing, Gavin had reached for her.

And the moment their mouths touched, the last of Gavin's restraint snapped. His lips moved hungrily over hers, his tongue seeking entrance. And when Ella's lips parted for him, he sank into her, lost.

Ella let herself drown in him.

For that instant, the past didn't matter, who they were didn't matter. For that frozen moment in time, they were just a man and a woman. His kiss pushed everything else aside, including her grief.

Ella leaned into Gavin as his lips brushed across hers, as his tongue explored her mouth. Heat throbbed through her, from a fire deep in her belly. Gavin had drawn near so that they were pressed close. The feel of his long, muscular body, the strength and warmth of him, made her want to crawl inside him. The male musk of his skin filling her nostrils was overwhelming, dizzying.

In an instant that one kiss brushed away years of restraint, of denial. And when he gently bit her lower lip before soothing it with his tongue, Ella's body trembled.

Aye, for just a few instants, she gave herself to it. She allowed herself to be greedy, to break her vow of chastity. She let want take over.

But alas, this moment wasn't really frozen in time. Instead, it slid into another and then another, and Ella couldn't deny reality.

She was a nun, he was a clan-chief, and her mother lay dead in her chamber at the end of the hallway. This was wrong on all kinds of levels.

And yet breaking off that kiss and stepping away from him was hard. Even harder than riding away from Scorrybreac all those years earlier. Losing physical contact with Gavin was like tearing off a limb.

Ella's throat ached when she twisted out of his arms and took a few rapid steps back. The space between them now felt like a yawning gulf.

Gavin was watching her; the look of predatory lust upon his face, mixed with tenderness and raw need almost undid her. She didn't want him to look at her that way, and yet at the same time, it was the only thing she'd ever wanted.

She hated herself for needing this man. Even now, all these years later, he had the power to scatter her wits and turn her will into porridge.

She should be outraged at him for taking advantage of her at a weak moment. But she couldn't summon the will. Grief had laid her bare, and she had responded to that kiss as eagerly as he'd given it.

She wouldn't turn her desire for him into a lie. She would just have to live with knowing that this man was her one weakness.

But the incident proved that the two of them couldn't be alone together, ever again.

Ella took another step back and bumped up against the bed. Panic flared. How easy it would be for him to push her back upon the coverlet, tear her flimsy night-rail from her body, and claim her. And to her shame, if he tried, she wasn't sure she'd have the strength of will to stop him.

She wasn't sure she wouldn't welcome it.

Desire crackled between them, their gazes still fused. Gavin's blue eyes had hooded in that look she knew well from the past. He was only just holding himself in check.

Eventually, Ella cleared her throat, breaking the heavy silence. "I think it's best ye go now, Gavin," she whispered.

14

In Ruins

GAVIN CLOSED THE solar door behind him and walked over to the sideboard, where a decanter of wine and a row of goblets sat. His hands shook as he poured himself some wine.

Dolt. Lack-wit. Fool.

He'd made some poor decisions in his life—but kissing Ella when she was in the midst of weeping over the death of her mother was one of his worst. He'd known it was wrong, from the moment he'd cupped Ella's wet cheeks with his hands, and yet he'd been unable to stop himself.

The wine burned down Gavin's throat, warming his belly. But it didn't ease the ache under his breast bone or slow his pounding heart.

Gavin set the goblet down with a thud. Unlike his brother, he couldn't use wine to wash his problems away. It wouldn't matter how much he drank, he'd never stop wanting Ella, never stop aching for her.

Breathing a curse, he stepped forward, leaning his forehead against the cool stone wall next to the sideboard. The chill seeped through his skin, although the pounding in his temples remained.

What a terrible mess he'd made of things.

He'd believed that seeing Ella again would allow him to put things right—so that he could move on with his life. After Innis's death, his clansmen had been putting pressure on him to wed again. There was still time for him to produce an heir. He hadn't been opposed to the idea, yet he'd had the burning need to face Ella again so that he could look forward rather than backward.

That had been a grave error.

Seeing her again had just confirmed that he'd never be able to give his heart to another. Ever.

Gavin squeezed his eyes shut. He hadn't wept in years, but his eyelids burned now. Disappointment, yearning, loneliness—it all churned within him. The force of the emotions made his belly clench, his chest and head ache.

How he wished he could return in time, go back to that day in the clearing eighteen years earlier. He'd have acted differently. He'd have seen beyond the sense of duty that had blinkered him. He'd have broken the betrothal and wed the woman he really loved.

Instead, he'd done what was expected of him, and his life lay in ruins around him as a result.

The fine weather had come to an end.

Long days of shimmering heat and blue skies gave way to grey skies and a chill wind that blew in from the north, ruffling the water of Raasay Sound to the east.

Leaving the chapel, Ella craned her neck up at the sky. Seabirds wheeled and screeched overhead, a sign that the weather was about to become even more unsettled. This was the first day in months that the air had a real bite to it. The warm days of summer were drawing to a close, and autumn was breathing down their necks.

Ella continued on her path through the inner bailey, returning to the keep. On the way, she passed Blair MacNichol, who was overseeing the shoeing of his horse. He waved to Ella as she walked by but didn't attempt to engage her in conversation. Even though she'd been here a few days, Gavin's younger brother's gaze was still wary whenever he looked at her. Likewise, his wife, Forbia, had barely spoken to Ella since her arrival.

They had buried Cait Fraser that morning. The kirk at Scorrybreac had a secluded graveyard behind it. Just a small crowd had come to see Lady Fraser off: Ella, her father, as well as the clan-chief and his closest kin. Ella had remained at her father's side, her hand clasping his in silent support. Father Blayne, the local priest, gave a fine service, and then they had laid Cait to rest.

Ella hadn't wept during the burial. After Gavin's departure from her bedchamber the night before, she had allowed herself to weep softly for a short while longer. Then she'd dried her tears, telling herself that the events of the past days were a test. It was easy enough to serve God within the confines of Kilbride Abbey. But in the world beyond, she'd met challenges at every turn. Stubbornness had filtered over Ella then. She would not fail the Lord. Instead of going back to bed, she'd knelt on the floor by the window and prayed for the rest of the night.

This afternoon, she felt in control again. Her mother was at peace, and now Ella could focus on what lay ahead.

Entering the keep, she asked a passing servant the clan-chief's whereabouts.

"He's in his solar, Sister," the young woman bearing an armload of clean linen informed her.

Spine straight and jaw locked in determination, Ella climbed the stairwell to the second floor and made her way to the double oaken doors that led into the clan-chief's solar. Then she knocked.

"Come in," a male voice reached her through the doors.

Ella drew in a deep breath, steeling herself for the meeting, and pushed the doors open. She stepped into a large chamber with a south-facing window. A great hearth dominated one corner of the room, and deerskins covered the flagstone floor. A large tapestry, showing a group of men at a stag hunt, covered one pitted stone wall.

The clan-chief himself sat at a vast oaken desk, bent over a pile of parchments.

Gavin glanced up as she entered. "Sister Ella," he greeted her, his tone formal although his gaze was shadowed. "Good afternoon ... how are ye faring?"

"Much better, thank ye," she replied. "Ma is at peace now."

Gavin nodded, his expression turning guarded. That was better, how it should have been from the beginning. Ella welcomed this new distance between them.

"I'm sorry to intrude." Ella's gaze dropped to the pile of parchments he appeared to be working his way through. "Ye are busy."

He sighed and leaned back in his chair. "Just accounts that have to be paid ... nothing that cannot wait. How can I be of assistance?"

Ella fought the urge to drop her gaze. Even though his manner was reserved, there was still an intensity to his look that unnerved her. The sooner the pair of them parted ways the better.

"I thank ye for organizing my mother's burial so quickly," she began, her voice low. "But now it is done, I wish to return to Kilbride."

"And ye shall," he replied. "Is tomorrow soon enough for ye?"

His response took Ella aback. She had worried he might try and delay her. Swallowing her surprise, she inclined her head. "No, I will be ready."

"Good." Gavin was watching her steadily now, his expression unreadable. "Ye will be traveling in my company again I'm afraid." He held up a hand to forestall her protest. "But fear not, there will be a company of my men with us. We will be making a detour to Dunan on the way, if ye don't mind?"

Ella frowned. She had a feeling that it wouldn't matter if it did bother her. She was hardly going to say 'no' to a clan-chief, and they both knew it.

Silence stretched out between them for a few moments before Ella spoke. "What business takes ye to Dunan?"

"MacKinnon has called a meeting ... between all the clan-chiefs and chieftains of the isle."

"Really?" Ella's interest was piqued now, and she almost forgot to feel uncomfortable in this man's presence. "Why is that?"

It was an impertinent question and none of her business, yet Ella knew that Gavin wouldn't mind her asking. He'd always spoken frankly to her in the past.

"The unruliness upon the isle gets worse ... as ye and I well know. MacKinnon wants something done about the outlaws and thieves."

Ella pursed her lips, remembering their journey to Scorrybreac. "Is it really that serious ... has Skye turned lawless?"

"Not yet ... things are worse on MacKinnon lands, but throughout the isle folk are restless. A meeting between the clan-chiefs and chieftains is long overdue." Gavin pulled a face. "I just wish MacKinnon wasn't hosting the gathering."

Ella's brow furrowed. Although she'd never met him, she'd heard plenty about Duncan MacKinnon. She also knew that many folk within MacKinnon territory, in which Kilbride sat, loathed him. "Perhaps he'd find it less of a problem controlling those on his land if he didn't rule them with an iron fist," she pointed out. "He increases the taxes every year."

Gavin raised an eyebrow. "I'm sure that'll be pointed out to him during the meeting. Have ye ever been to Dunan before?"

Ella shook her head.

"Well then, ye should find it interesting. The broch sits on the site of an ancient fort. It's a bonny spot ... in a wooded valley."

"How long will we remain there?"

"Not long," he replied, still watching her. "I'm hoping our business should be concluded within a day or two."

Ella left the solar and descended to the ground level of the keep. Despite the grey weather, she knew she'd find Gordana in her garden. She needed to tell her friend that she was leaving.

Frowning, Ella made her way down the spiral stairwell, taking care this time. She wasn't happy about the detour to Dunan. She'd already been away from Kilbride long enough. With the breaking weather, there were fruit and vegetables to be harvested. She needed to be there to oversee the work. Still, part of her was curious to see Dunan, for she'd never visited the MacKinnon stronghold. The other sisters would be full of questions about it when she returned home.

Ella left the keep and stepped outdoors once more. Light drops of rain splattered against her face, brought in by the wind, and in the distance, Ella caught the forbidding rumble of thunder.

Gordana wouldn't be at work in her garden for much longer.

Ella found Gavin's sister on her knees weeding an onion bed when she arrived. Although flowers and herbs filled the garden, Gordana had squeezed a few vegetables into the corners.

"A storm's coming," Ella advised her friend as she settled herself onto the willow seat and watched her work. "Hopefully, it'll spend itself overnight ... I don't fancy traveling in the rain."

Gordana stopped weeding and sat back on her heels, glancing over her shoulder. "Are ye sure ye should leave so soon?" she asked, concern edging her voice. "Ye must still be grieving for yer mother?"

Ella favored her with a brittle smile. She knew that Gordana meant well, yet the last thing she needed was to prolong her visit to Scorrybreac. "God's work calls," she replied. "Gavin and his men are riding to Dunan tomorrow ... and I shall go with them. When they have concluded their meeting there, we will continue on to the abbey." Ella paused, seeing the disappointment filter over Gordana's face. In the days since her arrival, they had struck up their old friendship as if they'd never been apart.

"I will miss ye," Gordana said, her gaze shadowing. "As ye have seen, I spend little time with the other ladies in the keep … but ye and I have always understood each other well."

Ella smiled once more. "Then ye must visit me at Kilbride, Gordana. I know ye aren't interested in taking the veil, but we have a guest house at the abbey, and ye would be welcome whenever ye care to visit."

Gordana's eyes gleamed at this. She rose to her feet and brushed the dirt off her fingers before crossing to the willow seat. Lowering herself down next to Ella, she took hold of her hands, squeezing tightly. "I would love that," she murmured.

15

Unchaste Thoughts

"I WISH YE would stay a little longer, lass." Stewart Fraser squeezed his daughter tightly against him. "I feel like I've hardly seen ye, and now ye are off again … ye are all I have now."

Ella blinked back tears before drawing away. Her father appeared to have aged years over the past few days. Deep lines bracketed his mouth, his expression looked care-worn, and his once-vibrant hair seemed far more grey than red. However, it was the sadness in his eyes that cut Ella to the quick.

"I have to return to Kilbride, Da," she murmured, her voice suddenly choked. "Ye know I must."

He looked so forlorn then that Ella nearly broke down. Blinking rapidly, she stepped close to her pony and checked its girth. Only when she'd mastered herself, did she glance in her father's direction once more.

Stewart still looked bereft. He was gazing at Ella as if he was about to lose her forever.

"Please, Da," Ella whispered. "Ye know I will be alive and well at Kilbride." She drew in a deep breath. "I have invited Lady Gordana to visit … why do ye not join her?"

His expression brightened just a little. "Are men allowed to visit the abbey?"

"Aye … if they're kin," Ella lied. The abbess generally dissuaded the sisters from inviting family to stay. She said that it made transitioning into a nun's life much harder. But she'd make an exception in this case, Ella hoped. After all, Ella had resided for nearly two decades in the abbey without seeing anyone.

A determined look settled upon her father's face then. "I will organize a visit in a few weeks' time … as soon as the harvest is done."

A smile curved Ella's lips. She hadn't expected him to make a date now; he really was keen to spend time with her. Warmth spread through her at this realization. Of course, with everything that had happened, she'd overlooked the fact that her father had missed her all these years.

"Ready to go, Sister Ella?"

The clip-clop of hooves intruded, and Ella tore her gaze from her father to see Gavin approach upon his grey mare, Saorsa. Like the day before, his expression was shuttered. It was hard to believe this was the same man who'd pulled her close and kissed her so passionately.

But, once again, his altered manner came as a relief to Ella. If he'd put up those walls to begin with, neither of them would have ended up in such a compromising position.

Ella nodded before turning her attention back to Stewart Fraser. Her father's eyes glistened as he watched her. Although she'd invited him to visit her at Kilbride, they both knew the truth of it. Her life was dedicated to God—they would see very little of each other in the years to come.

Stepping forward, Ella threw her arms around him one last time.

They started their journey under leaden skies. Storms had raged over the isle during the night, leaving cold, damp weather in their wake. Fortunately, although it was a dull day, no rain fell as Gavin's party left Scorrybreac.

The clan-chief led the way out of the castle, flanked by the captain of the Scorrybreac guard—a heavyset man named Ceard. Ella rode directly behind them while the rest of the party, four MacNichol warriors, brought up the rear.

They passed through the village, hailing folk as they went, before pushing their horses into a brisk trot. Monadh had a short, bouncing gait, but Ella settled into his stride easily. It had been years since she'd ridden, yet the journey here had brought it all back.

Leaving Scorrybreac behind, the party headed south, hugging the coastline. Mid-morning, they crossed into MacLeod territory and skirted the coastal village of Kiltaraglen. Yet they didn't pause, instead continuing on their path across the rolling hills of the eastern coast of Skye. To the west rose the dark shadows of great peaks, ominous against the iron-grey sky.

"It'll rain again," Ceard announced, motioning west. "Those storm clouds over the mountains are headed our way."

Gavin gave a grunt, acknowledging the comment.

Watching the two men, Ella realized that Gavin had hardly spoken since they'd left Scorrybreac. Luckily for him, Ceard wasn't a garrulous man. But after receiving such a brusque response from his clan-chief, the captain didn't make any other attempts at conversation.

Gavin is sore about all of this.

Ella pursed her lips. Of course he was. She wasn't sure what he'd hoped having her return to Scorrybreac would achieve, but she'd wager he hadn't planned on kissing her.

That had been a poor decision.

As was yer reaction to him.

Her conscience wasn't about to let her place all the blame on him. Aye, Gavin had taken liberties he shouldn't have, yet she had melted into his arms like hot tallow; she had parted her lips so he could deepen that kiss.

The memory of it made heat flush across her body.

Stop it. This wouldn't do at all. A nun couldn't have such unchaste thoughts. She needed to stop them before they tormented her further.

"Jesus, Lover of chastity ... Mary, Mother most pure," Ella whispered a prayer that Mother Shona had taught her in her early days at Kilbride, "and Joseph, chaste guardian of the Virgin, to ye I come at this hour, begging ye to plead with God for me. I earnestly wish to be pure in thought, word, and deed in imitation of yer own holy purity."

The other riders were far enough away that no one heard her softly murmured words. Moments passed, and still, Ella didn't feel any more at peace. The melting sensation that thoughts of that kiss had provoked, still lay heavily within the cradle of her hips.

Heaving in a deep breath, she began to whisper another, more strident prayer. "Jesus, bless me with Yer infinite graces, that I may remain in a state of purity. Strengthen my body, spirit, and soul, to continually reflect Yer chastity—"

Up ahead, Gavin twisted in the saddle, his gaze settling upon her. "Did ye say something, Sister Ella?"

"No," Ella replied swiftly, her cheeks flaming. She had taken care to keep her voice low. Surely, he hadn't heard her?

And yet there was a knowing light in his blue eyes that made the heat in her cheeks burn brighter still. He didn't smile; his face was a study in inscrutability. Yet somehow he knew where her thoughts had been, and what her whispered words were in aid of.

Ella dropped her gaze to her hands; they gripped the reins tightly. A moment later she sensed him look away from her, leaving Ella and Monadh alone once more.

Inhaling deeply, Ella promised herself that she'd wait till she was alone in future before murmuring any more prayers.

Gavin knelt next to the fire pit, watching as the tender flames caught alight. It had taken a while, for the wood was slightly damp. However, the tinder he'd brought with him had worked.

It had been a long, tiring day of travel. Heavy sheets of rain had swept in from the west in the afternoon, drenching the party. Thankfully, it had been a short squall, and by the time they made camp for the night, on the edge of a hazel thicket, the skies had cleared once more.

Rising to his feet, Gavin glanced around him. There was no sign of Ella. After rubbing down her pony, she'd disappeared into the woods, possibly to pray. He hoped she hadn't gone far.

His men had put up tents and begun gutting and plucking some grouse they'd just caught. The birds would be spit-roasted over the embers of the fire pit.

"I'm going to collect some more wood," Gavin informed Ceard. "Ye had better get those grouse on to roast soon or we'll all be eating at the witching hour."

Ceard snorted as he sat with a half-plucked grouse upon his knee. "Ye just make sure the fire doesn't go out."

Grinning, Gavin walked off. Ceard could be a curmudgeon at times, but there wasn't anyone he trusted more at Scorrybreac. Not even his brother.

The air inside the hazel thicket was damp and rich with the odor of wet earth and vegetation. Picking up branches and sticks as he went, Gavin surveyed his surroundings. The trees were tightly packed in here. Dusk would settle soon, and he wondered where Ella had gotten to.

Thud. Thud.

Gavin straightened up from retrieving a fallen hazel branch and frowned. *What was that?*

Thud. Thud.

His frown deepened. Following the noise, Gavin walked deeper into the copse. A few yards on, he pushed aside some undergrowth and halted.

Sister Ella had her back to him and was throwing knives at a large tree.

Thud. Thud. Two more blades embedded, side-by-side, in the trunk.

Swathed in black, her head covered by the veil, Ella looked like a deadly shadow come to life in the gloaming.

She moved then, striding over to the trunk, and yanked her six knives, one by one, from their neat row.

Gavin cleared his throat.

Ella whipped around, her face pale and startled. The white wimple framed her face, an austere look that highlighted the delicacy of her features. Yet her hair was now tucked away out of sight.

Gavin's chest ached at the memory of how her hair had felt—fine and soft—tickling his skin and sliding through his fingers. What a terrible thing, to hide such beauty from the world.

"I thought I'd find ye at prayer," Gavin greeted her.

Recovering from her fright, Ella frowned. "What do ye want?"

Gavin dipped his chin to the pile of branches in his arms. "Nothing ... I was out collecting wood and heard a noise." His gaze went to the slender blades that she was now tucking into the belt around her waist. "Please continue ... don't let me interrupt yer practice."

Ella shook her head. "I'm done."

Irritation flowered within Gavin at her frosty welcome. She probably thought he'd planned to seduce her, that he wanted her to break her vows. He'd heard her whispered prayers earlier, and although he'd only caught snatches of the words, he'd known what she was praying for.

She was seeking strength to ward him off. Like he was the Devil and had been sent to tempt her.

Gavin's mouth twisted into a humorless smile at the thought, and he met Ella's eye. "Good," he replied evenly. "Now that ye have finished, ye can help me collect firewood."

"Ye always had a lovely singing voice, Sister Ella … I remember it well."

Ella glanced up from where she'd been staring into the glowing embers of the fire. Ceard sat across from her. A smile softened his usually severe-looking face, and his pale blue eyes were warm.

"Ye do?" she asked, surprised. Of course, Ceard had been at Scorrybreac all those years earlier. He'd been a much younger man then, but already gruff in voice and manner.

"Aye," he replied, looking slightly embarrassed then. "There's nothing I like more than listening to a woman sing."

Next to him, Gavin smiled. "Ye rogue, Ceard … what a charming tongue ye have."

To Ella's increased surprise, Ceard's whiskery cheeks reddened a little as some of the other men around the fire chuckled. However, his gaze remained on Ella. "Will ye not sing for us tonight, Sister Ella?"

Ella stiffened, feeling the weight of many male gazes—Gavin's included—settle upon her. "I only sing hymns these days," she murmured, shifting her attention back to the firepit.

"What of 'These are my mountains?'" Ceard asked. "Do ye remember the words?"

Ella drew in a deep breath. She did. The song—a patriotic ballad—was also one of her father's favorites. At least he didn't want her to sing of love and loss. Finally, she nodded.

Ceard's mouth curved. "Will ye sing it?"

Ella glanced up to see all those gathered around the fire still watching her, their gazes hopeful.

"Go on, Sister Ella," Gavin prompted gently. "Just one song won't hurt."

"Very well," Ella murmured. Drawing herself up, she recalled the tune, wishing that Innis was sitting at her side with her harp to accompany her. Time drew out, and then she began to sing, her voice carrying through the chill night air.

> *"For fame and for fortune I wandered the earth*
>
> *And now I've come back to the land of my birth*
> *I've brought back my treasures but only to find*
> *They're less than the pleasures I first left behind*
>
> *For these are my mountains and this is my glen*
>
> *The braes of my childhood will know me again*
> *No land's ever claimed me tho' far I did roam*
> *For these are my mountains and I'm going home."*

Warmth filtered through Ella as she finished the last verse of the song. All her companions were smiling now, their eyes gleaming with love for their land. The men of Skye were often called away to fight for king and country—but most returned home to this rocky isle where the mountains met the sky.

"That was bonny," Ceard said, his face glowing. "Thank ye, lass."

Across the fire, Ella's gaze fused with Gavin MacNichol's. His clan had inhabited their corner of the isle for a long while, had dug their roots deep into its peaty soil. This land would always be his home—as it would be hers.

16

Duncan MacKinnon

A SMILE SPREAD across Duncan MacKinnon's face as he read the letter.

"Ye look pleased with yerself, brother." His sister's acerbic voice intruded. "Why are ye so smug?"

Duncan glanced up, his gaze meeting Drew's across the table. "That was a letter from Niall MacDonald," he replied. "He will be attending the meeting."

Drew raised finely shaped eyebrows. "That makes all seven of ye?"

"Aye." Duncan's smile grew. "And there was ye telling me not one of them would attend." He favored her with a wolfish grin. "Ye will be pleased to see Gavin MacNichol again."

His sister's answering smile was sly. "I will." She observed him, her expression turning thoughtful. "So this is how ye will finally rid yerself of Craeg, is it?"

Duncan held his sister's eye as he put the missive he'd just received from the chieftain of the MacDonalds of Sleat to one side. "Aye … if all goes to plan."

"How exactly?"

Duncan frowned. He didn't like Drew asking questions, yet his sister had a mind like a whetted blade. "Ours isn't the only territory where brigands attack travelers and outlaws raid villages … they too will want the lawlessness dealt with."

He shifted his attention to the spread of food before him: a large platter of bannocks and pots of butter and honey. Taking a wedge of the large flat cake made with oatmeal and cooked upon an iron griddle, Duncan spread it with a generous amount of butter. He was reaching for the pot of heather honey when he felt someone's gaze upon him.

It wasn't his sister watching him this time, but his wife.

Duncan cast the dark-haired woman seated opposite an irritated look. "What is it, Siusan?"

"When is this meeting?" she asked, her voice low and soft.

Duncan had always liked the sound of Siusan Campbell's voice. Unfortunately, these days it was the *only* thing he did like about her. Since she'd gotten with child, she'd lost her looks. Her body had bloated, her face was blotchy, and her once dark hair had become limp. As soon as her belly had started to swell, he'd lost all desire for her.

"Two days hence," he replied curtly. "Why?"

Siusan put a hand to her swollen belly, shifting in her seat with a grimace. "The bairn is coming soon, husband ... I can feel it."

Duncan shrugged. "And?"

Siusan gave him a pained look. "What if it comes on the day of the meeting?"

Their gazes locked for a long moment, and Duncan's irritation rose. He often felt vexed in Siusan's company these days. She looked at him with those reproachful midnight-blue eyes, and he just wanted to slap her.

A year they'd been wed.

The longest year of Duncan's life.

"Let it," he said before turning his attention back to his bannock, which he drizzled with honey. "I'm sure ye can manage birthing my son on yer own. The healer will be with ye."

Drew let out a soft snigger at this. Duncan glanced up to see his sister eyeing his wife. "It might not be a son," Drew pointed out. "Siusan might bear ye a bonny wee daughter."

"Nonsense," Duncan growled. "The healer is convinced the bairn will be male." The last thing he wanted was a daughter. This broch felt overrun with women as it was. With no brothers, he'd grown up with a dominant mother and blade-tongued sister. He'd had enough of women.

But ye have a brother, a voice chimed in his head. *And he still lives.*

Aye, a bastard. Duncan's brow furrowed as he dwelt on the unsavory fact. *But if this meeting goes to plan, he'll soon be dealt with.*

Bastard brothers aside, the fact remained that Duncan had few male kin still living, which made it all the more important that his wife provided him with a son. Duncan had taken great pains to find himself a submissive wife. However, Siusan wasn't his first choice; the lass he'd really wanted had been taken from him.

His frown deepened. He didn't like reminding himself of that disappointment; it had galled him at the time, and every time he reflected on it, his ire rose anew. Shoving the thought aside, Duncan took a large bite of bannock and chewed vigorously.

Leaning back in his seat, the MacKinnon clan-chief took in the view from his solar window. It was a grey morning, and watery sunlight filtered in. Beyond the window, the wooded sides of Dunan Vale were wreathed in mist. The hottest summer he could ever remember had given way to the inclement weather he was used to.

"Is everything ready for yer guests?" Drew spoke up again.

"Aye," Duncan replied, glancing his sister's way once more. "Or it will be when they arrive."

His sister was delicately buttering a sliver of bannock. Everything about Drew was dainty. She was a small woman with hair the color of peat, smoke-grey eyes, and milk-white skin. These days, Duncan often felt disconcerted when he looked at her; for with the passing of the years, Drew MacKinnon was starting to look more and more like her mother. She had the same cunning face, sharp gaze, and queenly bearing.

A shiver ran down Duncan's spine. He didn't want reminding of that hag. He needed to find a husband for his sister so he could be rid of Drew. MacNichol had been evasive thus far; perhaps Drew would manage to convince the clan-chief if she was able to corner him.

Stuffing the rest of the bannock into his mouth, Duncan brushed the crumbs off his léine and rose to his feet.

"Where are ye going?" Drew demanded, eyebrows arching once more. "Ye only just sat down."

"Ye have reminded me that there are things to be done," he grumbled, grabbing another wedge of bannock from the tray. "I can't sit around yapping with ye two."

Leaving his sister and wife in offended silence, Duncan left the solar.

Bran was waiting for him in the hallway beyond. The coal-black wolfhound leaped to his feet, tail wagging.

"Here, lad." Duncan threw the dog the bannock, which Bran swallowed in one gulp. Then the hound bounded forward, falling into step with his master as Duncan strode along the hallway to the stairs that led down to the lower levels of the broch. Reaching down, the clan-chief ruffled the dog's ears.

Bran was a good dog. Duncan had raised him from a pup, and he preferred the hound's company to anyone else's in the broch.

In the Great Hall, which took up most of the ground floor, Duncan found Ross Campbell, his right-hand and captain of the Dunan Guard, and Carr Broderick, another of his most loyal warriors, seated at one of the long tables with the other men.

"Finish yer bannocks," Duncan barked, approaching the table.

Ross lowered the piece of cake he'd only been able to take a bite from. Raven-haired, with the same midnight-blue eyes as Siusan—Campbell blue— Ross was one of the few at Dunan who weren't cowed by the clan-chief. Duncan had always liked that about him. Ross had fostered here under Duncan's father as a youth but then had stayed on afterward. He'd served Duncan loyally over the past few years, although he could sometimes question him when others wisely knew to hold their tongue.

Ross watched him now, his face impassive, while around him many of the other warriors shot each other nervous looks. "What's the hurry this morning, MacKinnon?" he asked, his voice a low drawl.

"I'm in the mood to go hunting."

More surprised looks were exchanged around the table. Carr, a stocky warrior with pale blond hair cut close to his scalp, frowned. Ross's gaze also narrowed.

"My cousin is due to give birth any day," Ross said after a pause. "Don't ye want to stay close to her?"

Duncan snorted. "No. I want to ride out into the woods and stab a great big boar through the heart. Then I want the beast roasted and pride of place upon the banquet table when my guests arrive."

Silence followed this comment before Ross abandoned the rest of his bannock and rose to his feet. He was a tall man at full height, easily meeting

Duncan's eye—and Duncan towered over most. "They will all attend the gathering then?"

"Aye ... even MacLeod."

Ross grinned, showing his teeth. "He'll want to avail himself of yer fine MacKinnon hospitality."

Laughter echoed around the Great Hall at this comment. Carr grinned, although Duncan barely raised a smile. Campbell was being facetious. Ever since his father's death and his mother's departure for a convent on the mainland, Duncan received few visitors. This was the first time he'd ever extended an invitation of this kind to the other leaders upon the isle.

"He will," Duncan growled. "It's time MacLeod learned that Dunan outshines Dunvegan in every way."

He'd visited the MacLeod stronghold once, years earlier. It was an impressive fortress to be sure, a square stone keep perched upon rocky crags overlooking a loch, but Dunan was more beautiful, and the village that surrounded it was twice the size of the hamlet on the outskirts of Dunvegan.

"I thought ye wanted MacLeod's help?" Ross stepped away from the table and moved toward Duncan. "Ye don't want to anger him ... Malcolm MacLeod isn't a man lightly crossed."

Duncan snorted, making it clear that he cared not if he angered MacLeod. He then turned and strode from the Great Hall, Bran trotting at his heels. He didn't look over his shoulder. He didn't need to, for he knew that Ross, Carr, and the other men would be following as faithfully as his hound.

Leading the way out of the broch, Duncan descended a steep row of steps into a wide bailey. "Saddle our horses," he yelled to one of the lads who was carting fresh hay into the stables. "We're going on a hunt."

Duncan then spun on his heel and found himself eye to eye with the captain of his guard. Ross stared back, unflinching. "MacLeod's held too much clout upon this isle for too long," Duncan growled out the words. "It's time for him to step aside, for younger blood to make the decisions that affect us all."

This time Ross Campbell, wisely, didn't respond.

17

Arrival at Dunan

ELLA'S BREATHING CAUGHT when she spied the broch of Dunan rising out of the mist. Gavin hadn't exaggerated; the MacKinnon stronghold was indeed a majestic sight, especially on an afternoon like this, for mist wreathed the Dunan Vale. It drifted amongst the dark spruce and pine that carpeted the sides of the valley and curled like smoke around the base of the broch, making the fortress look as if it were floating upon a cloud.

"What do ye think?" Gavin's voice intruded, and Ella tore her gaze from the broch to see that he had reined in his mare and now rode alongside her. It was the first time he'd spoken to her all afternoon. They'd exchanged a few brief words at midday, when the party had stopped for a light meal of coarse barley and oaten bread and cheese, but had traveled apart since then.

"Impressive," Ella admitted. "It reminds me of Talasgair."

Gavin's mouth lifted at the corners. "Of course ... I sometimes forget ye are a Fraser."

Indeed, Ella had lived at the Fraser stronghold on the northwestern coast of Skye until she was around thirteen. Despite that many years had passed since she had last seen it, she still remembered the fortress clearly.

Shifting her gaze back to the stone broch looming before her, Ella studied it. "Ye can see it was built on the site of an ancient fort."

"It is," Gavin replied. "Although the MacKinnon clan-chiefs have built up from the base of the tower and raised it much higher than the original. It's now three stories high, whereas the original broch only had one level. The village below is interesting too ... they call it 'the warren', for it's a network of narrow lanes that are easy to get lost in."

Intrigued, Ella continued to observe the approaching stronghold. As they neared it, she spied a high stone wall that ringed both the broch and the village. They clattered over a bridge that spanned the meandering An River and rode toward the North Gate.

Despite the enshrouding mist and poor light levels, there were plenty of folk working the surrounding fields: cottars bent over rows of kale, cabbages, and turnips. There were also a number of huts scattering the edges of the fields, tiny dwellings of stacked stone with sod roofs. Smoke wreathed up from some of the huts, and as she rode past, Ella inhaled the aroma of baking bread and braised onions.

Her belly rumbled in response. It had been a long while since the noon meal, and her appetite was now sharp. Even so, the thought of being a guest at Dunan, where she knew no one, put her on edge.

Once again she felt a pang of homesickness for Kilbride—a place where she knew every face. The abbey also offered her protection from the outside world, which could be so harsh and cruel. Her mother's death had left her feeling exposed, and the incident with Gavin had unnerved her. She was vulnerable away from Kilbride and looked forward to having routine back in her life again.

Not long now, she promised herself, urging Monadh through the gate and into the village beyond. *And I'll be back where I belong.*

"Welcome to Dunan!"

A tall man dressed in black leather strode out to meet them as they dismounted in the bailey before the broch. A leggy wolfhound, with a brindled black coat and a lolling tongue, loped at his heels. Ella stared at the newcomer, tracking his path across the yard.

Duncan MacKinnon ... this must be him.

Ella didn't know what she was expecting, but this wasn't it. Many of the tales that circulated MacKinnon lands portrayed the clan-chief as a depraved beast. Yet the man who embraced Gavin was fine-looking: tall and broad-shouldered with a mane of peat-brown hair, storm-grey eyes, and a ruggedly handsome face. He looked to be around Gavin's age—in his late thirties.

"Good afternoon, MacKinnon," Gavin greeted him. "Am I the first to arrive?"

"Niall MacDonald is here already ... and the rest of them should be here by tomorrow morning." MacKinnon pulled back from Gavin and slapped him across the back. "Leave yer horses with my lads and come up for a cup of mead."

The MacKinnon clan-chief stepped away from Gavin then, his gaze sweeping over the small party that MacNichol had brought with him.

But when he saw Ella, his face froze. "Who's this?" he asked. His bluff tone had completely vanished, and his voice sounded strangely brittle.

Gavin stiffened before taking a step toward Ella. "This is Sister Annella," he replied. "She is a nun at Kilbride and has just been to Scorrybreac to visit her mother. Sadly, the woman has passed away, and I'm now escorting Sister Annella back to the abbey. I hope ye don't mind her staying here?"

MacKinnon continued to stare at Ella, his grey eyes shadowing. When he didn't answer, Gavin cleared his throat. "Can she stay at the broch?"

MacKinnon started slightly before he dragged his gaze from Ella's face and focused on Gavin once more. "What?" he mumbled. "Aye, of course she may." MacKinnon then clicked his fingers, and two stable lads came running. "See to their horses," he barked before flashing Gavin another broad smile, Ella seemingly forgotten. "Follow me."

A woman's wails drifted through the broch, greeting Ella when she entered the Great Hall. A stairwell led off it, climbing up to the higher levels, from where the cries of agony were issuing.

Ella's step faltered, and her gaze swiveled to MacKinnon. "What's that?" She blurted the question out before she could stop herself, dropping the reserved demeanor she'd adopted away from Kilbride.

He frowned, irritated. "It's my wife ... she's giving birth. It's been taking her a while ... she's been wailing for hours now."

"Don't mind us then," Gavin cut in. "Leave us with some mead and go to her."

MacKinnon's frown deepened into a scowl. "Birthing is woman's work," he muttered. "I'll not interfere."

An uncomfortable silence followed before Ella spoke up once more. She knew she should hold her tongue, but the wailing clawed at her. "Do ye want me to go up and see if I can help in any way?" She paused here, aware of the clan-chief's glower. "I have aided births before."

MacKinnon shook his head. "There's no need. My sister and the healer are with her."

Ella's lips parted as she readied herself to argue. A swift warning glance from Gavin stopped her. He was right; she'd only just stepped over the threshold. It wasn't her place.

Even so, the poor woman's piteous cries ripped into Ella, shredding her nerves. She couldn't bear to listen to them and know that she wasn't allowed to help.

They took a seat at the far end of the Great Hall, upon a raised dais. A fire burning in the nearby hearth threw out a blanket of welcome heat. Ella sat down upon a low bench, next to Ceard, while MacKinnon lowered himself into a great oaken chair. Above him, a huge boar's head hung upon the wall. Ella stared at it, taken aback by the beast's size and massive tusks.

Seeing the direction of her gaze, Duncan MacKinnon grinned. "Impressive, isn't he? I brought the rogue down three summers ago ... I've never seen the likes of him since."

"It's certainly a prize," Gavin admitted. His gaze flicked between MacKinnon and Ella, and she saw a wary expression settle over his face. He didn't like the interest that MacKinnon was showing in her; he didn't trust the man.

Ella dropped her gaze then, cursing her outburst earlier. She had done a foolish thing in drawing MacKinnon's attention. *A nun should be serene and silent.*

Servants appeared then, bearing jugs of mead. They filled MacKinnon's cup first before moving on to his guests. Ella shifted restlessly upon the hard wooden bench. The woman's wailing was not as loud here, but she could still hear it.

How could MacKinnon sit there drinking mead when his wife was in so much agony?

A chill slithered down Ella's spine when she dared a glance back at the clan-chief—and immediately regretted it. MacKinnon was watching her under hooded lids: a sensual, brooding look. Maybe the stories about this man had some truth to them.

She'd only spent a few moments in MacKinnon's company, and already she had the urge to bathe in a tub of scalding water and scrub her skin with a hog-bristle brush. Lowering her eyes once more, Ella resolutely ignored his stare.

Around her, the rumble of men's voices filled the hall. Warriors were filtering in after finishing work for the day, and as they settled at long tables, calling out to the serving wenches to bring them drink, Ella realized that she couldn't hear Lady MacKinnon's cries at all now.

She glanced up, her gaze shifting to the stairwell. Perhaps the woman had finally given birth?

Meanwhile, she could hear Gavin making an attempt at conversation with MacKinnon. Gavin's ability to get on with anyone had always impressed her; he was easy company, and although strong-willed, he didn't have that competitive streak many other warriors possessed.

Seated beside the MacKinnon clan-chief, the difference between the two men was striking. Ella chanced a surreptitious look, noting that apart from the fact that they were both tall, muscular, and of a similar age—the similarities ended there.

MacKinnon had a hungry, intense look to him—a restless coiled energy like a trap primed to spring. In contrast, MacNichol was watchful, calm, his blue eyes veiled.

Ella glanced away and raised her cup of mead to her lips.

It was no good denying it—Gavin MacNichol still captivated her.

She'd wanted to hate him all those years ago, she really had, although becoming a nun had made that difficult. Mother Shona had told her that letting hate into her heart was allowing herself to be consumed by darkness. She couldn't serve God while dwelling in the shadows.

The events of the year after their parting had tested her, brought her to breaking point. She had lain upon her pallet at night, weeping herself to sleep. She had railed at him, blamed him for her fate, and missed him with an ache in her breast that felt as if it would make her heart stop.

But it didn't. Time had helped ease her loss, her bitterness, her shame.

Yet despite it all, Ella knew that she could never really hate Gavin. Being back in his company confirmed it. Even when she was sore at him, even when his behavior troubled her, all it took was one look, one smile, and her heart melted.

Mother Mary give me strength. Ella took a gulp of mead, her fingers tightening around the earthen cup. *For just a couple more days.*

18

Reacquainted

A TALL, DARK-HAIRED man walked into the Great Hall, his expression grim. A brown-haired woman dressed in a pine-green kirtle followed him. Her face was pale, her eyes red-rimmed.

Ella didn't know either of the newcomers, yet one look at both their faces and she grew still.

Around her the Great Hall quietened, men and women swiveling around to watch the pair who made their way across the paved floor toward the dais. No one spoke a word. Silence settled like an indrawn breath.

Slowly, Ella shifted her attention to MacKinnon. She'd been making a point of ignoring him while the mead flowed and he'd started regaling Gavin with tales of his hunting exploits. But she looked at him now.

His face was impassive, his grey eyes hooded. When the man and woman neared the dais, he broke the heavy silence. "What news? Has my son entered the world yet?"

The man halted. He was one of the handsomest men Ella had ever set eyes on, with chiseled features and penetrating midnight-blue eyes. He didn't look like the sort of man given to displays of emotion, for there was pride upon his face, and arrogance. Yet his eyes glistened and his throat bobbed before he answered, and when he spoke, there was a rasp to his voice.

"My cousin gave birth to a boy, Duncan," he said softly, "but the bairn was still-born." He broke off there, his gaze fusing with the clan-chief's. "Siusan is dead."

The words fell like an axe-blade in the hall.

Duncan gaped, his fingers clenching around the horn of mead he'd been drinking. "What?"

"The birth was too long." The woman spoke then. She was pretty with sharp grey eyes. Her voice was low and surprisingly strong, despite the haunted look on her face. "She bled out … there was nothing any of us could do."

Another silence fell. This one crackled with tension, like the air before a summer thunderstorm.

Ella's chest constricted, and a wave of dizziness swept over her.

Still-born.
How she wished she'd never come to this place.

She'd never met Lady MacKinnon, yet her heart wept for the woman. Her heart wept for all women who'd died giving birth, for there were far too many of them.

MacKinnon snarled a curse and hurled his horn of mead across the hall. It smacked one of his warriors across the back of the head, drenching him. The man grunted, clutching the back of his skull.

MacKinnon ignored him. "All she had to do was bear me a son—a live one!" The words were savage. The man's voice trembled, not from grief but from rage. "She had but one task, and she failed."

Shock rippled over the Great Hall of Dunan.

In an instant, Ella realized exactly why folk hated Duncan MacKinnon so much. The selfishness, the cruelty, of his words ripped into her. The faces of those surrounding her mirrored Ella's own response.

Gavin's lips parted as he stared at MacKinnon, while the man and woman who'd delivered the news both went stone-faced.

But MacKinnon didn't appear to notice or care. Another tide of obscenities spewed from his mouth, and he launched himself to his feet, shouldering the dark-haired man aside as he strode out of the hall.

Many gazes watched him go. But still, not one person uttered a word.

Gavin escorted Ella from the Great Hall. Together, they ascended the stairwell to the upper levels of the broch.

Ella didn't speak as she climbed the stairs. She wished Gavin hadn't insisted on accompanying her. He should really have remained downstairs with the other chieftains. However, he'd been insistent.

Chieftain Alasdair MacDonald of Duntulm had just arrived. While his pregnant wife had retired to their quarters immediately, Alasdair had taken a seat upon the dais to share a mead with Niall MacDonald of Sleat and Gavin.

After his outburst earlier, MacKinnon hadn't reappeared to join them. It was a relief. Ella wondered if, after his rage had subsided, he'd gone to see his wife.

Reaching the landing to the second floor, Ella turned to Gavin. "I can make my way from here," she murmured. "Ye should return to the Great Hall."

Gavin grimaced. "In truth, I've got no stomach for mead this eve." Studying his face, Ella noted the lines of tension that hadn't been there before their arrival at Dunan. "I'm sorry, Ella," he said softly, taking a step toward her. "I'd known MacKinnon can be a brute ... but his behavior today was inexcusable. Ye didn't need to witness that."

Ella swallowed as the ugly scene flashed before her once more. She'd never forget MacKinnon's angry, red face as he railed at his dead wife: "She had but one task and she failed."

Instead of grief, he'd been filled with rage.
What kind of man behaves that way?
"Is the meeting still going ahead?" she asked when a pause drew out between them. "Surely, Lady MacKinnon's death will prevent it."

Gavin shook his head. "MacKinnon should really delay our talks by a day or two ... but seeing as he's been so eager to discuss matters, I doubt he will."

Ella stared at him, aghast. "But Siusan MacKinnon isn't even buried yet."

Gavin gave her a pained look. "If the meeting is postponed, I will accompany ye back to Kilbride first," he assured her. "With MacKinnon's mood so volatile, I'd prefer ye didn't remain here."

Their gazes held for a long moment, and Ella knew he'd noticed how MacKinnon had stared at her earlier. Yet she didn't bring the incident up, for even recalling the man's stare made her skin crawl.

Ella took a step back. "I should retire now."

"Do ye know the way to yer chamber?" Gavin asked, frowning.

"Aye ... it's the last door on the right."

Gavin nodded, his expression shuttering. "Goodnight then ... I shall see ye tomorrow."

Night settled over Dunan, bringing the encircling mist in closer. Gavin stood at the window of his bed-chamber and looked out over the valley. Tall spruce poked up through the milky fog; it was an eerily beautiful sight, and Gavin might have enjoyed it if his mood had been different.

As it was, he felt on edge.

Ella had suggested that he return to the Great Hall, yet he wasn't in the mood. The scene he'd witnessed earlier had been damning. Even the memory of it made Gavin's ire rise. MacKinnon was a heartless cur. Afterward, Gavin's first instinct was to gather up those of his party and depart from Dunan without a backward glance.

But he'd given his word he'd take part in tomorrow's meeting, and the problems facing their isle needed to be sorted.

Even so, the thought of dealing with MacKinnon the following day, of listening to his demands, made Gavin grind his teeth. Right now, the only thing he wanted to do was smash his fist into the clan-chief's mouth.

The clatter of hooves below drew Gavin's gaze then from the mist-wreathed valley, to the bailey below. A party had arrived, and judging from the booming male voice that echoed against the surrounding stone, it was Malcolm MacLeod.

Gavin relaxed his jaw a little. MacLeod could be bullish, but beneath all his swagger and bluster, the man had a heart. Gavin wasn't sure Duncan MacKinnon did.

He had spoken briefly to Alasdair MacDonald of Duntulm and his wife, Caitrin, after supper. It had been a year since he'd seen them both—but much had changed in their lives since their last meeting.

Caitrin MacDonald.

Despite his bleak mood, Gavin's mouth curved. Just over a year ago now, he'd been one of three suitors all vying for her hand. Ross Campbell, captain of Duntulm Guard, had also been one of them.

Blonde, proud, and recently widowed, Caitrin had been sought after. After losing Innis, Gavin had told himself that it was time to leave the past behind, time to make a fresh start. But when he and the other suitors met with Caitrin at Dunvegan, it had become quickly apparent that the woman's affections lay elsewhere.

She was in love with her dead husband's brother, Alasdair.

They'd both been determined to deny their feelings for each other, but Gavin liked to think he'd played a small role in bringing them together. Once he'd realized that he'd never win Caitrin's heart, he met with Alasdair and forced him to face the truth. The man was deeply in love with Caitrin; Gavin knew the signs and also had to face a few truths himself.

For as lovely as Caitrin was, there was only one woman for him.

Reaching up, Gavin scrubbed his face with the palm of his hand. The Devil take him, he'd miscalculated when he'd thought that seeing Ella again, apologizing to her, would help him move on with his life.

In truth, the opposite had happened.

A soft knock at the door intruded upon his thoughts.

Stiffening, Gavin turned toward it. The hour was late—too much so for visitors.

"Who is it?" he called out.

With a click, the door opened inward, and a slender figure encased in pine-green stepped inside.

Gavin stiffened. "Lady MacKinnon," he addressed her formally, no warmth in his voice. "To what do I owe this visit?"

"With all of today's excitement, we didn't manage to get reacquainted, Gavin." She smiled and shut the door behind her, leaning up against it. "I thought I would rectify that."

Gavin raised an eyebrow. He'd forgotten how bold Drew MacKinnon could be. Of course, she'd been newly wedded the last time they'd seen each other. However, that hadn't stopped her from flirting shamelessly with him—right under her husband's nose.

"This meeting could have waited till tomorrow," Gavin replied, folding his arms across his chest.

Drew's smile became coy. She was comely; Gavin had noticed that years ago. She shared her brother's coloring: pale skin, storm-grey eyes, and peat-brown hair that she had braided and coiled around the crown of her head, revealing a long, slender neck.

However, just like years earlier, her beauty left him cold.

He'd never liked the shrewdness in Drew MacKinnon's eyes, the cunning edge to her smile. She thought she was cleverer than him—than most men—and she could barely conceal her arrogance.

"I know it's late, Gavin," she said, a sultry edge to her voice, "but ye have time to share a cup of wine with me, do ye not?"

Gavin held Drew's gaze, resisting the urge to show her the door. Drew knew he had manners and wouldn't cast her out. At the same time, she was playing a dangerous game. It was not seemly for a widow to be entering a guest's bed-chamber, at any hour.

Silently, Gavin moved to the sideboard, where a jug of bramble wine and a stack of clay cups sat. He then poured some wine and handed Drew a cup, noting that she deliberately brushed her fingers against his as he did so.

Gazing up at his face, Drew took a sip of wine. "Ye grow more handsome with the years, Gavin ... age suits ye."

"Ye look well too," Gavin replied, his tone still cool. Compliments were expected, so he would give them. It was true though; the past decade since he'd seen Drew hadn't aged her at all.

Drew's smile widened, although her gaze remained sharp.

"I'm sorry about yer loss today," Gavin said after a pause. He'd noted that although Duncan hadn't been upset about his wife's death, Drew had been, as had Lady Siusan's cousin, Ross.

Drew's grey eyes guttered. "I can't believe Siusan is gone." She gave a delicate shudder then. "I am glad I've never had to suffer the horror of childbirth." She reached out, placing a hand on Gavin's forearm. "It was horrible."

Gavin went still. The grief in Drew's eyes had been real, although she'd used it to gain closer proximity to him, hoping that he'd comfort her. Exhaling slowly, he took a deliberate step back so that her hand fell away.

"Aye ... it must have been ... especially for Lady MacKinnon. Were ye close?"

Drew held his gaze, her mouth compressing slightly as she realized he hadn't fallen for her ruse. She then nodded. "Siusan was an easy lass to like." She paused there, favoring him with a wry smile. "Unlike some of us."

Finally. For the first time since entering his bed-chamber, Drew MacKinnon had said something that hadn't been carefully thought out beforehand, something that wasn't designed to ensnare him. Something sincere.

Gavin took a gulp of bramble wine; it was delicious—dark and spiced. "Ye are who ye are, Drew," he said finally. The use of her first name made her gaze widen. "As am I." He halted there, letting his words sink in before continuing. "I know ye are looking for a husband, but I'll save ye the effort now by telling ye that I'm not looking for a wife."

Drew stiffened, her eyes narrowing. "That's not what I heard ... ye were keen to wed Lady Caitrin last year, were ye not?"

Gavin smiled, not remotely chastised by her shrewish tone. He was used to women like this, having grown up with a mother that made most men run for cover. "I was," he admitted, "but since then I've changed my mind. I'm not wedding again, Lady Drew ... ye are wasting yer smiles on me."

19

Meeting of the Clans

"I HOPE YE have some solutions for us, MacKinnon." Morgan Fraser's voice echoed across the Great Hall. There was no mistaking the threatening note. "This better not have been a wasted trip."

The chieftain of the Frasers of Skye limped across the floor toward the dais. Watching his approach, Gavin noted that Morgan had aged significantly since he'd seen him last. He'd always been a tall, proud man, although his mane of once flame-red hair was now laced with white, and deep grooves cut into his austere face.

As he approached the dais, Fraser's sharp gaze swept across the table.

Gavin wasn't surprised to see that it froze upon Malcolm MacLeod.

This was the first time that Fraser had met in peace with MacLeod since his wife, Una, had left him for the MacLeod clan-chief a few years earlier. The look on Malcolm MacLeod's face wasn't friendly as he stared his archnemesis down.

Gavin shifted uncomfortably in his seat. Fortunately, both men were unarmed; MacKinnon had wisely insisted upon it for the meeting.

He knew all about the bad blood that existed between the Frasers and the MacLeods, and that the last time these two men had seen each other, it had been in battle. Fraser's rounded posture and limp were the result of a serious wound dealt to him by MacLeod's claidheamh-mor.

"Aye ... although this isn't my problem alone." Seated at the head of the table, MacKinnon watched Fraser with a narrow-eyed stare. Gavin had heard that relations between the MacKinnons and the Frasers hadn't been good either of late—not ideal since they were neighbors. "Take a seat, Fraser."

Morgan Fraser grunted before climbing up onto the dais and taking a seat between Alasdair MacDonald of Duntulm and Niall MacDonald of Sleat, directly opposite Gavin. He acknowledged the others seated at the table with a brusque nod.

Malcolm MacLeod and Brodie MacQueen flanked Gavin. Both men wore formidable expressions. None of the leaders here liked that MacKinnon presided at the head of the table, lording over them all as if he were king of the isle.

Gavin certainly wasn't happy about it. It was clear that this meeting wasn't just about the grievances that MacKinnon wished to air, but about the balance of power upon this isle.

The seven chieftains of Skye rarely met under the same roof. Whether or not the coming years brought war or peace, this meeting would decide it.

The realization put Gavin on edge.

A tense silence settled at the table. The seven men were alone in the Great Hall; even the servants had let them be. Two ewers of wine sat at each end, and seven pewter goblets lined the table.

Fraser poured himself a large goblet of wine and took a gulp. "Come on then," he growled. "Let's talk."

All gazes swiveled to MacKinnon, who was leaning back in his chair, fingers lightly drumming on the table before him. "Did ye all travel here without problems," he began, his voice low. "No encounters with outlaws on the road?"

This comment brought a snort from MacLeod. "No one would dare attack a clan-chief."

"That's not entirely true," Gavin spoke up. "I've been attacked twice of late." He paused here, his gaze shifting to MacKinnon. "Both times on yer lands."

This caused a stir at the table. The men seated there exchanged surprised yet wary glances.

"Exactly," MacKinnon growled. "When even a clan-chief cannot travel unmolested, things are grim indeed."

"The roads to the north have become more dangerous of late," Alasdair MacDonald spoke up. The youngest of the men at the table, Alasdair wore an inscrutable expression. *Clever lad*, Gavin thought. *Don't trust any of them.* Alasdair's gaze swept around the table, a challenge in his blue eyes. "Although we didn't encounter any outlaws on the way here."

"Criminals will always exist," Fraser muttered, taking another gulp of wine. "What are ye going to do, MacKinnon, stamp them all out?"

"Outlaws and cutthroats abound on this isle these days," MacKinnon replied, his dark brows knitting together. "Twice over the last six months, supplies that have come in from the mainland have been attacked."

"What did they rob ye of?" MacQueen, a heavyset man with wild dark hair, spoke up then.

MacKinnon screwed his face up. "The usual … silver, as well as grains and livestock."

"Maybe they were hungry," Niall MacDonald pointed out. He was a tall, lean man of around fifty winters with pale blond hair tied back at his nape. "Ye tax folk too heavily, MacKinnon."

It was a bold statement, and Gavin felt the temperature at the table drop as a result.

MacKinnon met the older man's challenging stare, his own narrowing. Gavin had heard that there was no love lost between these two either. They shared a border and there had been skirmishes between them over the last few years. A rumor also circulated the isle that MacKinnon had wished to wed MacDonald's eldest daughter but had been thwarted.

However, watching the way MacKinnon looked at MacDonald now, the way the muscles flexed in his jaw, Gavin knew that the slight hadn't been forgotten.

"Theft is theft," MacKinnon eventually bit out the words. He then tore his gaze from Niall MacDonald's and let it travel over the other faces at the table. "Brigands must be dealt with."

"And how do ye suggest we do that?" Fraser replied. He was watching MacKinnon with a gleam in his eye.

"We must make an example of them. Those caught should be given a public hanging and left to rot at crossroads."

"And ye think that will stop desperate men?" Niall MacDonald leaned forward, his large hands clenching upon the table before him.

MacKinnon stared back at him. "Aye."

"Lawlessness has become a problem in my lands," MacLeod admitted, shattering the tension. "Cattle rustling has gotten worse, and travelers between Kiltaraglen and Dunvegan were attacked just last week."

"Those men moved onto the north afterward," Alasdair MacDonald added, "they have been caught and imprisoned."

A tense silence followed these words. Gavin studied the young MacDonald chieftain's face, impressed by his impassive delivery.

"Of course, there's a reason why things are so bad in MacKinnon territory," Niall MacDonald said, helping himself to some wine. "And it's not just because ye raise yer taxes higher every year." He paused there, his mouth curving at the scowl upon MacKinnon's face. Meeting the younger man's eye, MacDonald of Sleat raised his goblet to him in a mocking salute. "Yer brother has a score to settle with ye."

Gavin tensed at this news. *His brother?* To Gavin's knowledge, Duncan MacKinnon didn't have one. His only sibling was a younger sister, Drew. Likewise, the other men at the table looked on in surprised silence, their gazes keen.

Niall MacDonald had revealed something of great interest.

"My *bastard* brother, MacDonald," MacKinnon eventually answered, his voice low and hard, "as ye well know."

MacLeod let out a loud, rumbling laugh. He was a big, corpulent man with thick auburn hair and a ruddy complexion. The laugh suited him. "Why doesn't it surprise me that auld Jock MacKinnon spread his seed away from the marital bed."

The words, crude as they were, made some of the men at the table grin—although Fraser didn't look amused. Nothing MacLeod said would please him. Gavin didn't smile either; he could see that MacKinnon was seething.

"My father plowed a whore," MacKinnon bit out the words, "and Craeg was the result."

"Ah, so the bastard has a name." Fraser rubbed his chin, his sharp gaze narrowed. "And what trouble has Craeg *MacKinnon* been causing?"

Duncan MacKinnon's face flushed then—a deep, ugly red like raw liver. Gavin could see he didn't want the likes of Fraser giving his bastard outlaw brother the MacKinnon name. And yet, to react to it would weaken him in the eyes of all present. MacKinnon knew it, and so he held his tongue—barely.

"He leads a band of fugitives," MacKinnon said eventually, his voice hoarse with suppressed wrath. "They move from place to place, hiding in the forests, the mountains, and the vales of my lands as it suits them." MacKinnon's hand grasped the stem of his goblet so tightly that his fingers turned white. "He steals from me ... no one else ... and gives *my* silver and *my* possessions to the poor."

Gavin went still, casting his mind back to the ragged group who'd attacked him and Ella on their way to Scorrybreac. Surely those men hadn't been part of Craeg MacKinnon's band?

"And the people love him for it," Niall MacDonald added with a smirk. "Many wish it was Craeg ruling Dunan, not ye."

MacKinnon's fist slammed down upon the oaken table with such force that wine sloshed over the brim of some of the goblets. His grey eyes glittered as he stared Niall MacDonald down. "So ye say, MacDonald. But I've not heard such tales. How do I know ye are not in league with the bastard? Ye have obstructed me at every turn of late."

Niall MacDonald's face turned thunderous. "Yer brother doesn't need my help," he replied coldly. He leaned forward then, his expression deliberately goading. "Ye are making a mess of things all on yer own. Yer father wasn't much of a clan-chief ... but at least he realized that folk need to eat. He knew that if ye oppress yer own people, eventually they'll rise up against ye ... only now we're *all* paying the price."

Ella studied the rose she was embroidering upon the pillowcase, a pang of homesickness flowering within her. But it wasn't longing for Kilbride this time. Instead, nostalgia for the years of her childhood returned. There were many things about her youth she'd have preferred not to dwell upon, but her love of roses, and the afternoons she'd spent with her mother and sister tending the garden, would always remain among her fondest memories.

"It's a lot of trouble to go to, Sister Annella." Drew MacKinnon's voice made her glance up from the delicate pink rose she'd been embroidering. "For MacNichol to escort ye to Kilbride in person. Why would he do that?"

Ella glanced up, meeting Lady MacKinnon's eye. The woman, who was of a similar age to her, sat opposite, a wooden spindle in one hand, a basket of wool upon her lap.

"He was wed to my sister," she replied. "God rest her soul."

Drew inclined her head. "Ye are a Fraser?"

"Aye."

"I take it that yer hair is flame red under that veil."

Ella smiled. "Not really ... it's more like tarnished copper."

A low laugh answered her. "I've never heard red hair described that way before." Rhona MacKinnon had glanced up from the child's woolen tunic she was knitting.

Ella and Drew weren't alone in the women's solar—a spacious chamber that looked out over the mountains to the west of the broch—for two other women had joined them: Rhona MacKinnon and Caitrin MacDonald. Ella had learned that the women were sisters, both daughters of Malcolm MacLeod.

Ella dropped her gaze, embarrassed at being made the center of attention. "My hair isn't as fiery as yers, I'm afraid, Lady Rhona."

"Ye should see my son, Cailean's, locks," Rhona replied with a chuckle. "Barely a year old and red curls so bright I'll never have to worry about losing him in a crowd when he starts to walk."

Drew MacKinnon's mouth curved at his, although there was little mirth in her gaze. Ella wasn't sure that MacKinnon's sister liked her two companions much. Every comment she'd issued toward them thus far had carried a barb.

Observing her companions, Ella had never seen three women who contrasted each other more. All of them were beauties, although Drew's sharp grey eyes and knowing expression detracted from her loveliness. Caitrin was the only one of them with child. Under her blue kirtle, her belly was noticeably swollen.

The sight of a pregnant woman unnerved Ella slightly, especially after the events of the past day. Caitrin would know of Lady MacKinnon's death; they had buried Siusan in the kirkyard just outside the walls of Dunan shortly after dawn. But Caitrin didn't seem unnerved by the tragic birth; instead, she wore a serene expression as she embroidered a coverlet.

In contrast, Ella was still on edge after the incident. She'd joined the mourners; she'd done so out of respect for she'd never met MacKinnon's wife. The clan-chief had stood, his face stone-hewn, while the priest murmured prayers for the dead woman and her still-born child.

As soon as the priest was done, MacKinnon had turned on his heel and stalked away, his wolf-hound loping along behind him.

Ella had watched him leave, wondering if he grieved for his wife at all.

"Still," Drew MacKinnon shifted her attention back to Ella. "Gavin must be fond of ye if he'd accompany ye to Kilbride himself. After all, he could have just asked one of his men to do it. I have to say ... it all appears a bit unseemly ... a nun traveling alone with a band of men."

The woman was fishing. The intelligence in those grey eyes made Ella wary. Not only that, but the familiar way she said Gavin's name made Ella tense. She seemed to be showing a particular interest in him.

Ella favored her with a demure smile. "Haven't ye heard, Lady MacKinnon? Outlaws infest these lands ... MacNichol is merely concerned for my welfare."

20

Mine

SUPPER THAT EVENING was an awkward affair.

Ella would have preferred to have begged off. She'd spent the afternoon in the small kirk outside the walls of Dunan. It was a tranquil spot, where she'd been able to pray in peace. The priest had then given her a tour of the grounds before she'd retired to her chamber later.

However, a servant had knocked upon her door as the day drew out, advising her that as one of MacKinnon's guests, she was expected to attend supper.

Being seated next to Gavin just made the meal even more awkward. She'd managed to avoid him for most of the day, but sitting between him and Alastair MacDonald, she felt anxiety flutter up under her ribcage.

Gavin was too close. She could feel the heat of his body and smell the spicy scent of his skin. It made her flustered and on edge.

"Are ye enjoying yer stay at Dunan?" Gavin asked lightly. He had just helped himself to a slice of venison pie, after serving Ella first—something which had raised a few eyebrows around the table.

Drew MacKinnon was sitting directly opposite, watching Gavin like a she-wolf stalking her prey.

She's after him. The realization hit Ella then. A strange sensation filtered through her: hot and prickly.

Jealousy.

Mother Mary ... please get me through this. Jealousy was an ugly emotion, one that a Sister of Kilbride didn't entertain. The last time Ella had felt like this, she'd been preparing to leave Scorrybreac while Gavin and Innis's wedding loomed.

Ella swallowed hard and focused on answering Gavin. "Aye," she said softly. "I spent some time in Dunan kirk today ... and Father Athol showed me the crypt where the MacKinnon clan-chiefs are all buried."

Gavin inclined his head, his gaze meeting hers. Ella's breathing quickened. She wished he wouldn't look at her like that, not with so many eyes upon them. He watched her as if she were the only woman alive.

He watched her as if she weren't sitting there shrouded in yards of black cloth.

A memory resurfaced then, one that she had deliberately put away into the deepest vaults of her mind: the pair of them lying under a spreading birch, the dappled sunlight bathing their naked skin. Gavin was propped up on one elbow, his fingertips gently tracing shapes across Ella's breasts and belly. "Ye are so bonny, Ella," he'd whispered. "I shall never tire of gazing upon ye."

Ella blinked. There were many more memories that she kept under lock and key, ones that heated her blood and made her pulse race.

And when Gavin looked at her as he did then, he risked freeing them all.

"How did the meeting go?" she asked, suddenly breathless.

The moment shattered, and Gavin's gaze clouded. "Badly," he murmured. "I was hoping we'd come to some resolution this afternoon, but MacKinnon has insisted we continue discussions tomorrow."

Disappointment lanced through Ella at this news. She'd been hoping to leave Dunan the following day. The atmosphere within the broch smothered her, made her uneasy. She didn't belong here. She needed to return to Kilbride.

"None of ye could agree on things?" Ella asked. She too deliberately kept her voice low. Around them, most folk were deep in conversation. Nonetheless, it was best to avoid being overheard. Especially since they sat near the head of the table, where their host lounged in his oaken chair.

Ella had noticed that MacKinnon appeared in a sour mood this evening. A scowl twisted his handsome face, and he was drinking heavily.

"MacKinnon wants us all to take a harder line with outlaws," Gavin replied, bending closer to her so that he wasn't overheard. That was a mistake, for the heat and scent of him enveloped her, and his breath feathered against the shell of Ella's ear. "He wants them strung up and left to rot at crossroads. But there are also bandits who only target MacKinnon himself, and those men are led by the clan-chief's bastard brother. MacKinnon wants our help to hunt him down."

Ella drew back, eyes widening. "Bastard brother?"

"Aye." Gavin's mouth quirked. "Things are more complex than we all realized—well, most of us anyway."

Ella became aware then of a hard stare boring into her. She glanced across the table to see Drew MacKinnon glaring at her.

"Lady MacKinnon hasn't taken her eyes off us since we sat down," Ella murmured, shifting her attention back to Gavin. "Ye especially."

Gavin's face tightened. "She's a widow ... and looking for a husband."

Ella raised her eyebrows, feigning nonchalance, even as her heart thundered against her breast bone. "And ye are in need of a wife, are ye not?"

Gavin held her gaze. "I was," he said softly. He paused then, silence drawing out between them. "But not anymore."

Heart racing, Ella dragged her attention from Gavin to the slice of venison pie she'd not yet touched. Truthfully, her belly was now in knots. This was a hazardous conversation, although it was her fault for asking him about Lady MacKinnon.

And as she struggled with everything that was forbidden to her, everything she dared not want, she became aware of another gaze upon her.

It wasn't that of Lady Drew, who was now attempting to flirt with her cousin, Taran MacKinnon. The big scarred warrior sat with his wife, Rhona, at the table. The widow wasn't having much luck engaging Taran in conversation, for he answered her in short, curt sentences.

No, the person staring openly at Ella wasn't a woman.

Duncan MacKinnon reclined in his chair, goblet of wine in hand, and stripped her naked with his gaze.

Kneeling by the bed, Ella clasped her hands together and began her evening prayers. It had been a long, exhausting day. She wasn't used to having contact with so many new people or to making idle conversation. Some of the folk she'd met—like Lady Rhona, Lady Caitrin, and their husbands—had been good company. But others had worn upon her. Lady Drew especially.

Ella squeezed her eyes shut, shoving back the sharp dislike that twisted her gut every time she thought about the comely widow. Not only had she succumbed to the sin of lust while away from Kilbride, but now jealousy plagued her.

Inhaling deeply, she began a prayer. "Dear Lord, please free me from all envy and jealousy," she murmured, her voice fervent. "I will only look to ye for all I need. I pray I will be more and more like ye. Conform my mind and thoughts to yer thoughts, Lord."

Ella broke off there, concentrating as she prepared to repeat the prayer.

However, a knock at the door interrupted her.

Rising to her feet, Ella smoothed her habit. It grew late. She couldn't think who could be knocking upon her door at this hour.

Was it Gavin?

A mixture of dread and excitement churned through her then. She hated herself at that moment, for her weakness where he was concerned.

"Aye," she called out. "Who is it?"

The door swung open, and a tall figure stepped inside. Yet it was not a man with dark-blond hair, warm blue eyes, and a boyish smile, who turned her will to porridge.

The man who invaded her space was dark-haired with storm-grey eyes and a wolfish expression.

"Mac ... MacKinnon," Ella stammered, shocked by his presence. "What do ye want?"

It was a rude, direct question. But then, any man who strode into a nun's bed-chamber didn't deserve a polite greeting.

MacKinnon kicked the door shut behind him, the hungry look in his eyes quickening. A grin stretched his lips.

"That's a fine question, Sister Annella ... one I intend to answer."

He advanced upon her. Suddenly, Ella's bed-chamber seemed a cage. There was nowhere to run, nowhere to hide.

Breathing fast, she backed up and found herself pressed against the wall with MacKinnon looming over her.

This close he was overwhelming. He also reeked of wine, and Ella noted that his gaze was glassy. He'd come here on a drunken impulse, one he was likely to regret come morning. She had to convince him to leave.

"Please go," Ella gasped out the words, hating how nervous she sounded. "Ye shouldn't be in here."

"This is my broch," he drawled before reaching out and stroking her cheek. "I decide where I'm permitted to enter." His grin widened. "Ye are a pretty one … too bonny to give yerself to God."

Ella froze, her jaw clenching. His touch made her skin crawl, as did the feral look in his eyes.

"I've always been fascinated with nuns," he continued, oblivious to her reaction, or perhaps not caring. "Ye are forbidden, with yer pious faces and secretive ways … but I know the truth. Behind closed doors, ye are all whores."

Anger started to pulse within Ella's breast, a living thing that wouldn't be quietened. *How dare he?*

MacKinnon stepped closer still, his muscular body pushing her hard against the wall. She felt his arousal pressing against her lower belly and panic surged.

"There's a lass at Kilbride," the clan-chief whispered. "Lady Leanna MacDonald of Sleat … do ye know her?"

The question caught Ella off guard. Her hand was inching down, gathering the material of her habit so that she could reach the knife she always carried strapped to her left calf. But his words stalled her.

"Aye," she replied cautiously. "Why?"

"She was promised to me," MacKinnon growled. His hand slid down Ella's jaw to her neck, before the fingers splayed across her throat. "Before I wed Siusan."

Ella stilled as she remembered the conversation she'd had with Sister Leanna nearly two years earlier. Like Mother Shona and Sister Coira, she knew the reason behind the young woman's arrival at Kilbride. It was to avoid this man.

"That's right." MacKinnon's mouth twisted. "We were to be wed, Lady Leanna and I … but her father came between us." His hand tightened around Ella's throat then. "I want ye to give the lass a message for me. Will ye?"

Ella swallowed. The pressure on her neck was getting uncomfortable, and the look on his face scared her. She wanted to deny him, but she knew to do so would be foolish. "Aye," she whispered.

"Good," MacKinnon murmured. He leaned forward, trailing his lips down Ella's cheek. "Tell Leanna that I'm free to wed again … tell her that I'm coming for her, and that the walls of Kilbride will not stop me from taking what is mine."

Horror bubbled up within Ella. His wife and son had only just been laid to rest. In the space of a day, he'd become a widower, and all he could think about was having Sister Leanna.

Beast.

His fingers tightened around Ella's throat. "Will ye tell her that?"

Ella nodded.

"Say the words, swear ye will tell her," he snarled.

"I swear," Ella rasped. His grip was so tight on her neck she could barely breathe. "I will tell her."

A hungry smile spread across Duncan MacKinnon's face. "That's a good lass. Ye are the biddable sort … I like that." His free hand reached up and grabbed her breast through her habit, squeezing hard. "Ye have a lush body under yer crow's garb too … I like that even more."

The panic that had been simmering within Ella exploded, and she realized with sickening certainty that he was going to rape her—right here against the wall in her bed-chamber—unless she did something to stop him.

Ella moved.

She dropped her weight, dragging him down with her, while her left hand grasped beneath the layers of her habit and underskirts to the knife hidden beneath them. Whipping the blade free, she stabbed him in the chest.

The look of surprise on Duncan MacKinnon's face would have been comical if she hadn't been so scared.

He reeled back, mouth gaping. In an instant, he released his grip on her neck, and Ella slipped past him, making for the door.

But MacKinnon was a warrior. He'd fought in battles and had no doubt taken wounds before. As such, he recovered with frightening swiftness.

Cursing, he yanked the blade free, flinging it away from him. It clattered to the flagstone floor. MacKinnon staggered and lunged for her, blocking Ella's way out.

She needed to reach for another knife, but unlike when she traveled, she only kept one blade on her indoors. The others sat in her satchel beside the bed.

Flying across the room, Ella grabbed a large clay jug full of water.

MacKinnon gripped her around the waist and hauled her back toward him. Ella twisted and hurled the jug at his head.

It smashed across the clan-chief's skull, bringing him down like a charging boar gored by a pike.

Duncan MacKinnon crashed to the floor.

Trembling, Ella stood there a moment, staring down at him.

Dear Lord, preserve me … have I killed him?

No—he was breathing.

A mix of panic and relief swept over Ella. She glanced around her, frozen in place for an instant. She couldn't think what to do. Fear turned her witless, and then as she took in one deep breath and then another, she was able to move.

Heart pounding, she grabbed her satchel and made for the door. She didn't stop to check on MacKinnon on the way, or even to retrieve the blade that lay on the floor behind the unconscious clan-chief. It was too risky. She needed to get out of this chamber, and far from MacKinnon, before he awoke.

21

In the Dead of Night

GAVIN WAS JUST drifting off to sleep when someone shook him awake.

In an instant he lashed out, his fingers fastening around a slender arm. The gasp that followed made the last vestiges of sleep fall away.

"Ella?"

"Aye," she said, her voice tight with pain. "Please let go of me … ye will break my wrist."

In the pale glow of the nearby hearth, Ella's face was pale and taut, her gaze wide with fear.

Gavin abruptly let go of her wrist, and she stepped back, rubbing it gently. "I'm sorry." Gavin ran a hand over his face. "Reflexes, I'm afraid." He observed her once more. She wore her satchel slung across her front, and despite that her habit covered her from head-to-toe, Gavin saw that Ella was trembling. "What's wrong?"

"MacKinnon just attacked me." The words tumbled out of her. "In my bedchamber. I stabbed him and knocked him out with a jug of water … but he's bound to wake up soon. We need to go … now."

For a heartbeat, Gavin merely stared at her—and then fury hammered into him like a sledgehammer to the chest.

With a curse, he swung his legs over the bed and stood up.

And then he froze.

Like most folk, Gavin slept naked.

Ella was staring at him. And as the moment drew out, her gaze slid down the length of him. It was not an innocent gaze, but one that had known carnal desire, the look of a woman capable of great passion.

Yet she didn't utter a word. And as Gavin watched her, Ella's throat bobbed. "Ye should get dressed," she said huskily, a pleading note in her voice.

Gavin drew in a deep breath. Anger pulsed within him; all he could think about was finding MacKinnon and beating him to death. Clothes hardly seemed to matter.

Looking around, Ella spied his braies and léine slung over the back of a chair. She grabbed them and handed them to him, her gaze averted now. However, Gavin saw the pink stain that colored her cheeks.

Gavin took the clothing and started to dress. "That piece of dung," he snarled as he laced his braies and grabbed his boots. "I'm going to rip him apart."

"No!" Ella gasped, rushing forward. "Please, Gavin." She placed her hands upon his bare chest, her sea-blue eyes glistening. "We need to go ... gather Ceard and the others and ride. We must get away from here."

"I'm not leaving without getting my reckoning against that bastard."

"Ye will only make the situation worse."

"I'll make him wish he'd never been born."

"Ye will destroy relations between yer clans ... because of me. I can't let ye do that. It's bad enough that I have to involve ye in my escape."

They stared at each other for a long moment, before he growled a response. "I don't care about that." Gavin reached up, placing his hands upon Ella's shoulders. He could feel the tremors that wracked her. She was terrified. "Did he hurt ye?"

She shook her head. "I stabbed him before he had the chance." Her fingertips splayed across his chest, and she pressed into him. Her touch was a brand upon his skin. Did she have any idea what it did to him?

"I beg ye, Gavin," she gasped. "Leave yer need for reckoning. Take me away from Dunan, away from that man, before it's too late."

The desperation in her voice cut him to the quick. He hated to see her like this. What had MacKinnon said and done to make her so afraid?

"This doesn't end here, Ella," he said, his voice hoarse with the anger that still pulsed in time with his heartbeat. "MacKinnon's not going to get away with this."

She nodded. "And he shouldn't ... but right now, we must go."

They stared at each other for a long moment, and then, reluctantly, Gavin nodded.

A waxing gibbous moon lit the way as the MacNichol party clattered under Dunan's south gate and into the night.

The guards had let Gavin pass without argument. He was a clan-chief after all and had told them that urgent news had reached him by carrier pigeon, calling him back to Scorrybreac.

Ella rode behind Gavin and Ceard. The cool night air kissed her face, and she drew in great lungfuls of it. Never had she been so grateful to leave a place. As beautiful as Dunan was, the broch was rotten at its heart.

The man who ruled it was poison.

Tell Leanna that I'm free to wed again ... tell her that I'm coming for her, and that the walls of Kilbride will not stop me from taking what is mine.

MacKinnon's rasped words echoed in Ella's mind, tormenting her. She'd said nothing of his whispered threat, or of the ugly things he'd said, to Gavin. MacNichol needed reasons *not* to kill MacKinnon. Telling him what had happened in that chamber would have ensured that he murdered the man.

Part of Ella wanted MacKinnon dead. The clan-chief was dangerous; the air inside her bed-chamber had crackled with menace the moment he'd stepped into it. He was twisted, cruel, and manipulative. Nothing good could come from letting such a man live.

Yet she was a nun. For years now the abbess had shown her the way of forgiveness, of peace.

We only use weapons to defend ourselves, Mother Shona had told the sisters sternly during arm's practice. *We never strike out in rage, or for vengeance, for that makes us no better than those who seek to do us harm.*

Ella knew the abbess had spoken true. But more than that, she didn't want Gavin to get into trouble. Even if he were to cut MacKinnon down in righteous rage, the other chiefs weren't likely to see things his way, and nor were MacKinnon's family and retainers.

She wouldn't have Gavin put his own life at risk for her.

Ella didn't glance over her shoulder as she rode, even though she felt the weight of Dunan at her back. With each furlong that Monadh's feathered hooves ate up, the shroud of anxiety that had been smothering her gradually lifted.

Around her, the moon cast its hoary light over a wild, mountainous landscape. They left the dense forest of conifers behind and entered a bare, bleak valley. Great sculpted peaks rose either side, dwarfing the party. Ella was grateful for the moonlight, for without it they would have had difficulty traveling. Even so, Ceard and two other warriors carried flaming torches aloft, illuminating their path further.

None of the MacNichol party spoke as they rode west. Ceard and the two others had been hauled from their beds and told they were leaving. There had been some grumbling in the stables, yet the men had followed his orders anyway.

They understood that if Gavin MacNichol needed to depart urgently in the dead of night, he had good reason.

Ella's attention shifted to Gavin's back, and an image of him standing naked before her in his chamber flashed across her mind.

The Lord strike her down, he'd been magnificent.

His body was long and well-muscled, but it was the body of a mature man, and a number of fine, pale scars traced his torso. The glow from the nearby hearth had kissed his naked, golden skin, and for a long moment, Ella had merely devoured the sight of him.

Shoving the image from her mind, Ella squeezed her eyes shut. She needed to forget she'd ever seen that.

The sight of Kilbride Abbey, silhouetted against the lightening sky, made Ella's vision mist with tears. Relief swamped her, drowning out the fatigue of the past few hours. They had ridden with barely a break all night in order to reach their destination.

The high walls, made of grey local granite, gleamed when the first rays of sun touched them. A chorus of birdsong accompanied the riders as they slowed their mounts to a walk and approached the gates. Drawing near, Ella reflected how well-fortified the abbey was. Mother Shona, having already lived through a brutal attack on her previous abbey, had been determined to keep raiders out; as such, the nuns had hired men from Torrin to dig a deep ditch around the base of the abbey's walls. The walls themselves were around twenty feet high, as were the heavy oak and iron gates that barred their way inside.

Reaching the gates, Ella dismounted and walked to where a heavy iron knocker hung.

She lifted the knocker, letting it fall three times. Touching it was enough for sanctuary, had she been pursued, but Ella would not rest until she was indoors.

None of the party accompanying her spoke as they waited for someone to answer her knocking. Gavin had been worryingly silent on the way here; and whenever Ella glanced his way, she'd seen that he wore an unusually stern expression, his eyes narrowed.

He was angry; she could feel waves of ire emanating from him.

Nerves twisted in her gut as she realized he wasn't going to let this go. Duncan MacKinnon had just made an enemy of clan MacNichol.

And although she knew she wasn't to blame for MacKinnon's behavior, Ella still felt responsible for this turn of events.

If Gavin hadn't brought her with him to Dunan, this would never have happened.

Ella shook her head, irritated by the direction of her thoughts. Life was full of turning points. The Lord's will worked in ways she'd never really understood, despite her many years of prayer and contemplation.

At that moment, a sound of iron scraping against iron echoed through the still morning, and a small window opened around five and a half feet from the ground. A middle-aged woman, with a harassed expression, peered out into the dawn.

"Sister Elspeth," Ella greeted the nun, stepping forward. "Good morning."

Sister Elspeth's gaze widened. "Sister Annella?" Her attention then shifted to the party of men still astride their horses behind her. "Did ye ride through the night to reach us?"

Ella nodded, noting the acerbic edge to the nun's voice. She and Sister Elspeth had never gotten along. Elspeth had just taken her vow of perpetuity when Ella arrived at Kilbride. And after the events of the months that followed, in which Ella lived as a postulant, Sister Elspeth had viewed the young woman with disapproval.

That same censure lay in her eyes now.

An awkward silence fell, and then behind Ella, Gavin cleared his throat. "Are ye going to let us in, Sister?" he asked, irritation edging his voice. "My men have been traveling without rest for hours now. We'd like to stable our mounts and have some beer and bread to break our fast."

Sister Elspeth's mouth pursed, and then she drew back, slamming the iron window shut.

Moments later the clunk of the locks releasing broke the morning's stillness.

Ella didn't bother to remount Monadh. Instead, she led him into the abbey, entering a wide yard, flanked by stables on one side and the guest house on the other.

Before them rose Kilbride kirk, tall and proud, its steep roof standing out against the pale sky. The sight of it made Ella smile.

I'm home.

22

It's Not My Secret to Tell

ELLA'S RELIEF DIDN'T last for long.

Mother Shona met Gavin and Ella in the chapter house, while the rest of the MacNichol party stabled their horses and went to the refectory to eat and drink.

Gavin and Ella would have to wait in order to break their fast.

The abbess listened in silence as Ella recounted the tale of what had befallen her the night before. But, as she had with Gavin, Ella left out MacKinnon's message for Sister Leanna.

Ella wasn't sure exactly why, but instinct told her to keep those details private. She needed to see Sister Leanna herself, for MacKinnon's words alarmed her greatly.

When Ella told of how MacKinnon had shoved her up against the wall and started to grope her, the temperature dropped inside the chapter house.

Gavin's gaze burned, a nerve ticking in one cheek. She'd never seen him like this. Gavin had always been so level-headed, never prone to the explosive temper she'd seen in other men over the years.

Likewise, Mother Shona's brown eyes narrowed, her usually soft-featured face turning hard.

And when Ella told her how she'd stabbed MacKinnon before knocking him out with a blow to the head from a heavy clay jug, the abbess's gaze gleamed.

"We have taught ye well, Sister Ella," she murmured after Ella concluded the tale.

"No, it was *ye* who taught me," Ella replied, a lump rising in her throat. Now that the ordeal was over and she was out of danger, the urge to weep rose up within her. With difficulty, she pushed it down, swallowing hard. "MacKinnon would have raped me if ye hadn't shown me how to wield a blade."

"Sister Ella showed her skill on the journey north too," Gavin said, speaking for the first time since they'd entered the chapter house. His voice held a rough edge to it. "We were set upon by thieves, and she brought a number of them down ... and saved my life."

Mother Shona's eyes widened at this news. However, the woman swiftly recovered. Her gaze, when it settled upon Ella, was grave.

"Ye did what ye had to, Sister Ella," she began softly. "MacKinnon would have raped ye otherwise ... but I'm afraid ye cannot remain at Kilbride now."

The words, even though gently spoken, hit Ella like a backhand across the face. She stepped back from the abbess, her lips parting in shock.

"What?"

The abbess shook her head. Her gaze was shadowed, although she wore a determined expression. With a sinking feeling, Ella realized that the abbess—a woman she had long considered a friend—would no longer protect her.

"But I've taken my vows of perpetuity," Ella continued, her voice rising. "Ye can't cast me out."

"Kilbride sits on MacKinnon lands, Sister Ella," the abbess replied firmly. "We cannot risk turning the clan-chief against us or we will lose his protection. He will seek ye here ... and will demand I hand ye over to him."

"Ye could refuse," Gavin interjected.

The abbess glanced over at the MacNichol clan-chief, her expression hardening. "I could," she replied coolly. "But how would that go for us, do ye think? I have an obligation to the nuns who reside here. I must think of their safety."

Gavin held her gaze. "Ye could hold the abbey ... my men and I will remain here to help ye."

"No!" The word burst out of Ella. Panic curled up through her belly now, making her breathing come in short gasps. "I won't have ye all put yerselves at risk."

Gavin cast Ella a dark look. "I'm tired of hearing ye say that ... I shall decide whether or not a situation is worth risking me and my men over."

Ella held his gaze, her heart hammering now. She felt sick. Her relief at returning to Kilbride had shattered; nowhere seemed safe anymore. She had been innocent to believe MacKinnon wouldn't come after her, wouldn't demand the abbess hand her over.

Of course he would.

I should have killed him.

Ella clenched her hands at her sides. "No," she growled the word. "I will go."

"Sister Ella." Mother Shona stepped forward and reached out, grasping her hands. "If ye leave Kilbride, I don't mean ye to fend for yerself in the wild. Ye will need protection." The abbess cast a look at Gavin then, her expression imploring. "Will ye take her in?"

Gavin's face went taut. "Excuse me?"

Impatience flared in the abbess's eyes. "Will ye wed her?"

It was Gavin's turn to look as if he'd been struck across the face. In the meantime, Ella was so shocked that she couldn't even speak. She merely stared at Mother Shona as if she'd lost her wits.

"I can't wed a *nun*," Gavin finally rasped. "It's forbidden."

"Ella will no longer be part of this order," the abbess countered. "I shall cast her out this very morning."

"For what?" Ella gasped, horrified by the abbess's brutality. All these years at Kilbride, and she'd thought they'd become close friends. Yet now that her precious abbey was threatened, the abbess wanted Ella gone.

Mother Shona shifted her attention back to Ella. "I will tell the other nuns that ye have broken yer vow of chastity ... that ye have fallen in love with MacNichol and gone to live with him as his wife."

A stunned silence followed these words.

Ella tore her hands from the abbess's and drew back from her.

She knows.

Ella had been careful, all those years ago, never to utter a word about the man who'd broken her heart, the man who'd driven her to choose a life of seclusion.

But as she stared at Mother Shona, she realized that perhaps having seen Ella and Gavin interact, the abbess had guessed the truth.

"It's a lie," Gavin said quietly. "Ella hasn't broken any vows."

The abbess ignored him; instead, her attention remained upon Ella. "He doesn't know, does he?"

Ella's breathing hitched, and hot panic surged. She felt as if she were balancing upon a knife-edge with an abyss yawning below her. "Ye are not to say a word, Mother Shona," she said hoarsely. "Ye promised."

"And I will not," the abbess replied, her gaze shadowing, "but ye should ... it is time, Ella."

Ella. Not Sister Ella. Already she was out of the fold; already cast out of the order she'd devoted her life to for so many years.

"What are ye speaking of?" Gavin asked, his voice was low, wary.

Ella didn't look his way; she didn't dare. Instead, she backed up, never taking her gaze from the abbess. Suddenly, her life was falling to pieces before her eyes. Everything she'd worked so hard to hide was about to be exposed. Her life was about to be shattered to pieces.

She couldn't bear it.

With a sob, Ella turned and fled the chapter house.

Gavin watched Ella leave. But instead of following her, he turned to Mother Shona.

Their conversation had both alarmed and confused him. He felt as if he was lagging behind, grasping at snippets of details that meant nothing to him.

He needed some answers.

"I don't understand." Gavin fixed the abbess with a hard stare. "What should Ella tell me?"

Mother Shona dragged in a deep breath. "This is not how it should be told ... by right ye were never to know."

Dread twisted Gavin's gut, although he masked it with a scowl. "Know what?"

The abbess shook her head. "It's not my secret to tell."

Gavin's heart started to pound against his ribs.

Secret?

Their gazes fused for a long moment before Mother Shona exhaled sharply. "Go after Ella and ask her."

Gavin nodded and moved toward the door.

"Wait," the abbess's voice halted him, and he turned to see that she was watching him, sadness etched upon her proud face. "Ye will find her in the graveyard."

Kilbride's graveyard was a small space, encircled by a neatly trimmed hawthorn hedge. Rows of grey headstones thrust out of the grass like small stumpy teeth. At the far end of the yard grew a large shady yew.

And under that tree stood a small robed figure.

Ella's back was to Gavin as he approached. Her shoulders were hunched, revealing her misery.

Gavin slowed his step. He hated to see Ella like this. He'd witnessed her control begin to unravel at Scorrybreac after her mother's death. He couldn't bear to see Ella that upset again.

As he neared her, Gavin saw that Ella stood before a low grassy mound that lay under the spreading branches of the yew.

"Ella?" he said her name softly, hoping that she would not flee.

He wondered if she had even heard him. Ella's head was bowed, her arms folded across her chest in a protective gesture.

Stepping up next to her, Gavin shifted his attention to her profile. Ella's cheeks were wet. She wept silently, her gaze riveted upon the mound at her feet.

"Ella," he whispered. "Please talk to me."

She heard him that time. Ella's eyelids fluttered closed, and she dipped her chin, taking a long, shuddering breath.

"They couldn't give him a gravestone." Her voice was faint, broken. "For he was born out of wedlock."

Gavin went cold. He tore his gaze from Ella's profile to the mound. It was a tiny grave, one that sat apart from the others in the yard. Gavin's throat closed up then, his heart thudding against his breastbone like a battle drum. And when Ella spoke again, he felt as if someone had just driven a blade under his ribs.

"This is our son's resting place, Gavin."

23

Second Chances

IN AN INSTANT, Gavin MacNichol's world tilted.

A son.

It hurt to breathe, hurt to think. For a few long moments, he was lost in a churning sea of pain and regret. And when he finally recovered the power of speech, Gavin's voice didn't sound like his own. It was raw, edged with grief.

"Why did ye never tell me?"

"Ye were wed to my sister by the time I realized I was with bairn," Ella whispered. "My courses have never been that regular ... it was only when I couldn't face my morning bread and beer that I realized something had changed." She paused there. "The healer from Torrin confirmed that my womb had quickened."

Gavin stared at her, his thoughts churning. "And the abbess allowed ye to remain here?"

Ella huffed out a laugh. There was no mirth in it, just sadness. "Aye ... she told me that I could take my vows once the bairn was born, and that if it was a girl she could be brought up as an oblate within the abbey walls."

"And if it was a lad?"

"When the bairn was old enough, we would take him south to the monks upon Iona, where he would be brought up."

Silence fell between them then, broken only by the impatient bleating of goats in the enclosure to the east of the graveyard. They were awaiting milking. Neither Gavin nor Ella paid them any mind.

Gavin didn't speak. Instead, he waited for Ella to tell him the rest of the story. He didn't want to hear it, and yet he knew he had to know every last painful detail.

"It was a hard time for me," Ella said after a long pause. "I carried the bairn uneasily." She dipped her head further, her features growing taut. "I was upset when I arrived at Kilbride ... full of grief, anger ... and fear. The birth was long and painful ... and when the bairn came, he was stillborn." Her voice caught as she said those last words, revealing that although many years had passed, Ella still carried the sorrow within her.

They'd just come from Dunan and the death of both MacKinnon's wife and son. Gavin realized what painful memories it must have brought back for Ella.

Bile rose, stinging the back of Gavin's throat. "I should have been there for ye, Ella," he finally managed. "Ye shouldn't have had to deal with all of that on yer own."

Ella opened her eyes and raised her chin. "Ye made yer choice, Gavin, and I made mine," she replied huskily. "I told myself when I came to Kilbride that I would sever all ties to my old life. I never told anyone here who the father of the bairn was."

"But the abbess—"

"She's a canny woman … she probably guessed when ye came to collect me."

Gavin heaved in a deep, steadying breath. The anguish her news had roused in him was an open wound. He didn't know what to say, what to do. Hunkering down, he placed a hand over the top of the low mound.

"I don't suppose ye gave him a name?" he asked softly.

"The sisters told me not to," she whispered back. "But I ignored their advice. I named him Finn … after my grandfather."

Sorrow rose within Gavin, wreathing up inside him like winter mist. He could not stop it, could not prevent the tears that forced their way out and trickled down his cheeks.

Finn.

He and Innis had never been able to have children. And perhaps if he hadn't abandoned Ella, let her flee Scorrybreac, their son might have lived.

"I'm so sorry," he whispered. But the words weren't enough, and the moment they passed his lips, Gavin regretted them. An apology wouldn't erase the stain of the past, wouldn't change what had befallen Ella. "I want to make amends for this," he continued, his voice ragged now. "I want to ensure that ye never suffer again."

"Enough." A small hand caught his. Ella had crouched down next to him, and she squeezed his hand tightly. "Blaming yerself is useless. I chose to lie with ye … even though I knew ye were promised to my sister … we must both bear responsibility for the past. And we must both let it lie." She paused then. "It's as yer clan motto says: 'Remember but look ahead.' … we should both do that."

Gavin tore his gaze from the grave and met Ella's eye. She too wept. Her blue eyes were red-rimmed, her lovely face strained. And yet there was strength in her; there had always been strength.

"Ella." Gavin swiveled around, catching her hands in his. "The abbess is right … ye need to leave here. MacKinnon will follow us … he will have his men search Kilbride. He will deal with ye harshly if he finds ye. The only way ye will stay safe is under my protection. Let me look after ye, as I should have done years ago." Gavin heaved in a deep breath, holding her gaze firm. "Will ye be my wife?"

Ella stared back at him. After a long moment, her mouth quirked into a watery, melancholy smile. "Years ago I used to imagine what a proposal from ye might be like ... but I never envisioned this ... ye asking me to become yer wife to save me from the hangman's noose."

"Ye think that's why I ask?" Gavin moved toward her then, dropping onto his knees, his grip on her hands tightening. "That I'm doing this out of a sense of obligation?"

Her throat bobbed. "Aren't ye? Ye were always a good man, Gavin ... ye have always sought to do what was right."

Her words cut deep. Yet he deserved them. Indeed, he'd spent his life following the rules his forefathers had set out. He'd lived in fear of disappointing those who'd never had his best interests at heart.

"I'm asking ye to be my wife because I love ye, Ella." The words were soft, barely above a whisper. "I've never stopped loving ye." He broke off there, wishing he was more eloquent, that he could express himself better, but it felt as if an iron band gripped him about the throat and was slowly squeezing. "Fate is giving us a second chance ... and this time I will not turn my back upon it."

Silence fell between them. Ella did not answer; she merely stared back at him, her blue eyes glistening with tears.

Gavin inhaled slowly. He felt ripped apart, close to pleading, yet he prevented himself. "Will ye be my wife, Ella?"

Another pause stretched out, and Gavin felt sure that her silence was damning. It was too late. They'd both gone too far upon their chosen paths to change course now. Ella would leave Kilbride, but not to wed him.

But then Ella offered him a watery smile. It was like watching the sun emerge after a dull day of low cloud and biting wind. Her smile bathed him, soothed his aching soul. "Aye," she whispered. "I will."

Ella paced the chapter house, awaiting the arrival of Sister Leanna and Sister Coira. She was to leave Kilbride in secret, but when Ella had begged Mother Shona to allow her to say goodbye to her two closest friends at the abbey, the abbess had finally relented.

It was to be a hurried farewell, but Ella was relieved she would be permitted to have it.

Leaving Kilbride was unthinkable. She felt as if she'd strayed into a dark dream.

The chapter house door creaked open, and two black-garbed figures appeared: one small and slight, the other tall and broad-shouldered.

"Sister Ella!" The shock in Leanna's voice nearly made Ella smile. "Why aren't ye dressed in yer habit?"

Ella turned to face her friends. She was sure she presented an odd sight indeed. It had been so many years since she had dressed in common-place garb that she felt as if she stood naked before them. The clothes she had arrived at the abbey in had long been given away to the poor. Ella stood before them in far humbler clothing: a plain, ankle-length léine covered with a kirtle made of faded blue plaid, laced across the bodice. Around her shoulders, she wore a threadbare woolen shawl. Her head was uncovered, her hair braided down her back.

"It's just Ella now," she replied, before attempting a smile. She was sure the expression was more of a grimace. "I'm leaving the order."

Both women gaped at her. Sister Coira's lips parted, her violet eyes growing huge. "But how is that possible? Ye have taken yer vows of perpetuity ... they cannot be broken."

Ella sighed. "Apparently, they can if a nun has broken her vows and does not intend to repent for them."

The color drained from Sister Leanna's face at this admission. "Mother Mary," she whispered, aghast, "what have ye done?"

"We returned to Kilbride via Dunan," Ella replied. "There was an ... incident there. Duncan MacKinnon burst into my bed-chamber and tried to rape me. I stabbed him, knocked him out with a jug, and then fled."

Both women stared at her, shock filtering across their faces. Guilt knifed Ella. Mother Shona had told her to keep the story of what had befallen her at Dunan to herself, but Sisters Leanna and Coira were her friends; she wanted them at least to know the truth of things.

Their reactions were interesting, especially Sister Coira's. A shadow moved across her gaze, and a nerve flickered under one eye. She looked almost ... guilty. In contrast, Leanna clenched her jaw, fury tightening her face.

"That filthy bastard," Leanna growled. "I wish ye had gutted him like a pig." The words were shocking coming from one as delicate and sweet-tongued as Sister Leanna. Her sunny disposition and ready smile were what the other sisters were used to seeing—not this fierce, sharp-tongued young woman.

"That's not all," Ella continued. "MacKinnon gave me a message for ye, Sister Leanna. He said to tell ye that he's free to wed again ... he said 'tell her that I'm coming for her'." Ella paused there, hating the words she was having to relay to her friend. "He said that the walls of Kilbride will not stop him from taking what is his."

Silence followed her words. Sister Leanna reached out, grasping Sister Coira's arm for support. "He can't touch me here," she gasped out the words. "Da won't permit it."

"Of course he can't," Sister Coira soothed. However, the nun's gaze now looked haunted, her face strained. "It's just bluster."

"He *will* come looking for me here," Ella interjected. "And that is why I must go ... I just wanted to warn ye first, Sister Leanna. I hope Sister Coira is right, and that it is just an empty threat. In the meantime, ye may want to advise yer father that MacKinnon hasn't given up on taking ye as his wife."

Sister Leanna nodded, determination filtering over her face. "I will do that." She released Sister Coira's arm and stepped forward. "So this is it, Ella ... we are to never see ye again?"

Ella nodded, her throat thickening. "I'm afraid not. Gavin MacNichol has agreed to take me away ... I will wed him."

Sister Coira gasped at this news, drawing close. "What's this?" she demanded. "Ye never said anything about wedding anyone!"

Ella managed a smile then. Her admissions were shocking, and yet she had little time to explain them to her friends. Nonetheless, she would try. "Come and sit down for a few moments." She motioned to the wooden bench below the stained glass windows behind them. "I don't have much time, but ye both deserve to know the truth about me."

24

Don't Look Back

HEARING FOOTFALLS BEHIND him, Gavin turned.

A woman approached. A few feet away, Gavin heard Ceard grunt in surprise, while one of his other men murmured an oath.

Aye, it was like traveling back in time. The woman who held the skirt of her kirtle up as she crossed the dirt yard was no longer eighteen, her blue eyes brimming with excitement, but Annella Fraser still moved with unconscious grace, her head held high. The passing of time hadn't diminished her. There was a strength to her delicate face at thirty-six that had been lacking at eighteen, and a steadiness to her gaze.

Life had battered Ella, but it hadn't broken her. Instead, it had molded her.

She dressed in poor cloth, yet to Gavin she had never looked lovelier. The kirtle had once belonged to a taller, thinner woman than Ella. As such, it was slightly too tight across the bodice, straining against her full breasts, while the skirt dragged upon the ground. Around her shoulders, she wore a shabby blue woolen shawl.

The yard was deserted. All the nuns, save Mother Shona, who followed behind Ella, were in the refectory consuming their noon meal.

Ella was to leave in secret, without a word to anyone except her closest friends. It was harsh, especially after all the years she'd given to the order. Yet Gavin understood why.

Nuns who had taken their perpetual vows didn't just cast aside their habits and leave the order. To be cast out was to leave under a shadow of shame.

Gavin wished he could have spared Ella this. But they couldn't risk lingering at Kilbride. With each passing hour, it became increasingly dangerous for them to remain here—both for Ella and the Sisters of Kilbride.

Approaching Gavin, Ella lifted her chin slightly and met his gaze. She then stopped and drew her threadbare shawl tightly about her as if aware that he and his men were taken aback by her altered appearance.

It must have felt strange, to wear a kirtle again and to go about with her hair uncovered after so many years.

He stared back at her, unspeaking. He wanted to tell her how lovely she was, how the years had barely touched her. Instead, he merely held her gaze. This close, he could see that her eyes were shadowed. Leaving Kilbride was not a happy occasion.

Gavin turned to where Mother Shona drew to a halt at Ella's shoulder. The woman's face was unusually grave.

"Ye will accompany us to Torrin kirk then, Mother Shona?" he asked.

She gave a curt nod. "I must witness yer union."

Next to the abbess, Gavin saw Ella drop her gaze to the dirt. His chest constricted at the sight. This wasn't what he wanted for Ella; she was wedding him out of her own volition, yet at the same time, the union was being forced upon her.

It was either become his wife or leave the abbey without protection. If she did that, it would only be a matter of days before MacKinnon tracked her down. Wedding Gavin would give her shelter and ensure she remained safe, at Scorrybreac.

"We should hurry." The abbess moved to a shaggy grey mare that had been saddled for her. "The sooner ye are wed, the sooner ye can distance yerselves from Kilbride. MacKinnon will be on his way here by now."

Her words were a sobering reminder.

Ella's chin snapped up, her mouth thinning. Without a word, she crossed to where Gavin awaited her. They would ride together. Reaching down, Gavin took her hand. Ella then placed a foot atop his and sprang up before him. As she settled against him, her back pressing against his chest, Gavin's breathing hitched. The feel of her was distracting. Trying to ignore the quickening of his pulse, Gavin gathered the reins.

"Are ye ready?" he asked.

Ella's voice held a rueful note when she replied, "Aye … ye heard Mother Shona. MacKinnon will be here soon enough. Let's go."

Cottars working the fields on the way into Torrin glanced up from their work, gazes alight with curiosity as the party cantered up the potholed road into the village. Ella kept her gaze straight ahead, hoping that she and the abbess were hidden from view by the other riders.

Very little went unnoticed here, which wasn't a good thing, for MacKinnon would likely come to Torrin asking questions after discovering that Ella hadn't returned to Kilbride after all.

Each stride of the leggy courser brought Ella hard up against Gavin. The heat of his body enveloped her, creating sensations that were both pleasant and disturbing. She found herself wanting to lean into him but fought the urge.

Torrin kirk was a small building perched on the edge of a high cliff. The village spread out behind it, a ramshackle collection of stacked-stone cottages with thatched and turf roofs.

The priest came out to meet them, a small bald man with a sharp-featured face.

He wasn't happy about being asked to perform a wedding ceremony at such short notice, yet since the abbess herself requested it of him, he eventually acquiesced.

There was no time for preparations, no time to find a pretty gown or to weave flowers through her hair.

All the same, nervousness fluttered through Ella's belly when she walked up to the altar.

The early afternoon sun filtered in through the kirk's high windows, catching dust motes on the way down. Ella inhaled the familiar odor of tallow and incense, and her nervousness increased.

Just hours ago she'd been a nun. A kirk was a place where she served the Lord, where she knelt and prayed, and found solace from the rest of the world.

She was no longer a Sister of Kilbride, and yet in her heart little had changed. It felt wrong to be standing here with her hair uncovered wearing this ill-fitting kirtle, about to wed the man who'd broken her heart so many years earlier.

Panic gripped her chest. Dragging in a deep breath, Ella did her best to quell it.

Turning, she met the abbess's gaze and shot her a pleading look.

Mother Shona merely favored her with a soft smile, her eyes shadowed.

With a jolt, Ella realized that the abbess was putting herself, and her position, at great risk by helping her.

She was going against the rules of the Cluniac order. A nun who had taken her final vows couldn't leave the order without a lengthy process—one that required seeking permission from the Holy See. And since the Pope resided in faraway Rome, that could potentially take years.

They didn't have years.

The abbess was also about to go against MacKinnon—in order to protect her.

Ella's vision misted.

She would never forget Mother Shona's kindness.

The priest cleared his throat, drawing her attention back to the present. Father Gawen wore a censorious look as he gazed down upon the couple he was to wed. They had given him no details on why the union was to take place today. Nor did they tell the priest that until a few hours ago, Ella had been a Sister of Kilbride.

Even so, Father Gawen's gaze sharpened when it fastened upon Ella. "I recognize yer face," he murmured. "Have we met before?"

Of course, they had, albeit briefly. Ella had seen the priest at spring and harvest fairs in the village over the years, although they had never spoken.

"I think not, Father," she replied, dropping her gaze to the dusty stone pavers that lined the kirk floor.

"Can we start the ceremony now please, Father?" Gavin's voice held a note of impatience. "We have a long road to travel this afternoon."

Father Gawen's mouth thinned at this, although he minded his tongue. Mother Shona had already introduced them as Clan-chief MacNichol and Lady Annella Fraser. As such, the priest was wary of offending Gavin.

"Very well," he replied, his brow furrowing. "Join hands, and we shall begin."

Ella walked out of the kirk with a new identity. No longer was she Sister Ella of Kilbride, or even Lady Annella Fraser. Now, she held the title of Lady Ella MacNichol of Scorrybreac.

Blinking as the bright sunlight assaulted her eyes, Ella glanced around her. There was a magnificent view from the clifftop. To the north, the charcoal peaks of the Black Cuillins stood out against a soft blue sky, whereas a craggy coastline stretched south. The waters of the sea were flat and glassy this afternoon. Out of the sun, the air was cool and the breeze had a nip to it; yet staring out at the view, Ella could have been fooled into thinking that they were still in the midst of summer.

"Ready to go ... Lady MacNichol?"

Ella turned to find Gavin standing behind her. Even tired, anxious, and travel-stained, the sight of him made excitement flicker low in her belly.

Her husband.

As Father Gawen had wound the length of plaid around their joined hands and murmured the words that bound them in wedlock, the reality of the situation had finally sunk in.

She once dreamed of becoming Gavin MacNichol's wife. When she'd been young and foolish, she'd lain in her bed at night imagining the day of their wedding. There would be music—a harpist would play all day—and they would wed in spring when the first of the roses bloomed. She would weave meadow flowers through her unbound hair and wear a wedding gown of shimmering emerald green with matching slippers upon her feet. Their wedding banquet would be a meal that folk would talk about for years to come, with a roasted and stuffed swan as the centerpiece. And that night she and Gavin would make love upon a bed strewn with scented rose petals.

All those dreams seemed to belong to a goose-witted lass now.

None of it mattered one bit.

She was sad that this was how it had turned out. Life wasn't like the songs the traveling minstrels sang. Gavin was a widower, and his late wife had been her sister. No minstrel would sing such a song.

"Aye," Ella replied. "But I would like to say farewell to the abbess first, if I may?"

Gavin nodded, stepping aside to let Mother Shona approach. "I will go and ready the horses."

He walked away, leaving the two women to speak in private.

Mother Shona's eyes gleamed as she moved close to Ella. Wordlessly, she reached out and took hold of Ella's hands, squeezing them tight.

"I'm sorry, lass," she whispered. "I know ye must think I am casting ye out without a thought." Her voice caught then. "But I can think of no other way to save ye. May the Lord watch over ye in the days to come."

"And may God keep ye and the Sisters of Kilbride safe, Mother Shona," Ella replied. "I know why ye must do this … and it is I who must beg forgiveness. I have brought MacKinnon's wrath to Kilbride. Maybe I should have killed him while I had the chance."

Mother Shona shook her head. "No … ye aren't a killer, Ella. Ye hurt him in self-defense, but if ye had taken a knife to his throat while he lay insensible upon the floor, that would make ye a murderer. The other clan-chiefs and chieftains of this isle would put a price upon yer head for such an act."

A shiver passed through Ella at the abbess's words. She was right. This way at least only MacKinnon was after her.

"I'll never be able to return to Kilbride, will I?" she asked softly.

"No, lass … not while MacKinnon still lives." The abbess released her hands and reached up to cup Ella's face. "But don't ye worry about that … it's time for ye to begin a new life, Lady Ella MacNichol. Seize it with both hands and don't look back."

25

Where is she?

MOTHER SHONA, ABBESS of Kilbride, arrived back at the abbey just in time for Vespers. She quickly saw to her pony and strode to the kirk, where the nuns were already gathering for the service.

Reaching the altar, the abbess smoothed sweaty palms upon her habit. She'd been dreading this moment. All the way back from Torrin, she'd gone over the words she would say to the sisters. None of them were adequate.

She couldn't speak the truth. The only way they would accept that Sister Ella had left them was to cast the woman in a dark light, to speak lies about her.

Of course, Sisters Leanna and Coira both knew the truth. Ella had told her that she'd confided in them both. However, she'd sworn them to secrecy.

Reaching up, the abbess's fingers clasped around the heavy iron crucifix that hung about her neck.

Forgive me Lord ... I do this for the greater good. I do this to protect these women.

When the last of the sisters had filed into the kirk and knelt ready to begin Vespers, Mother Shona cleared her throat.

"Before we begin the service, I have ill-tidings to share with ye." The abbess's voice echoed through the quiet kirk. "Sister Annella has left the order."

As expected, a gasp followed this news. Some of the sisters—the younger ones especially—merely gaped at her, while many of the older nuns—those who had been here before Ella's arrival and knew of her sad story—developed hard, pinched expressions.

A few of them, Sister Elspeth for one, had been vocal in their disapproval of Ella when it had been discovered that their new postulant was with child. The fact that the young woman remained tight-lipped as to the identity of the father of the bairn only made the older nuns suspect her further.

Ella had weathered their displeasure and eventually blossomed at Kilbride. Yet the abbess saw vindication flare in Sister Elspeth's eyes now.

"She has broken her vow of chastity," the abbess continued. It was a falsehood, and one that galled her to speak, yet it was a necessary one. "Not only that, but she does not repent … she has wed MacNichol and is now his wife."

Even Sister Elspeth looked shocked. Mother Shona deliberately avoided looking at Sisters Leanna and Coira as she spoke. They alone knew the truth. She'd explained to them why it had to be this way, yet she didn't want to see the disappointment in their faces.

She hoped they understood why she had to do this.

But even if they didn't, it still had to be done. She'd bent many rules since becoming Abbess of Kilbride, had shaped the life here so that the sisters could live to their fullest potential while serving God. But she'd not risk the future unity of this order for one woman.

"It's forbidden to wed!" Sister Magda burst out. The old woman's dark eyes burned as she lurched to her feet, Vespers forgotten. "No priest will agree to it."

"No priest *knowingly* would, Sister Magda," the abbess replied, her voice deliberately calm. "But Sister Ella sinned again by not revealing who she was."

"But the union isn't valid!" Sister Elspeth exploded. She too rose to her feet, hands clenched by her sides. "The woman is a harlot, a fornicator, a—"

"Enough, Sister Elspeth!" Mother Shona's voice, harsh now, cut through the kirk, silencing the nun. This was exactly what she'd hoped to avoid. She'd not have the likes of Sister Elspeth stirring up ill-feeling inside the abbey. "Sister Ella has chosen her path, and I have made my decision. I have cast her from the order."

Silence settled after this proclamation.

It was unheard of, for the abbess to do such a thing. Usually, if a nun broke any of her vows, she was brought back into the fold and taught the error of her ways. Once a nun took her final vows, it was a lifetime's promise. It was a harsh choice indeed, for the abbess to cast her out.

Many of the nuns were watching her now with wary, frightened gazes. Would she do the same thing to them if they ever erred?

Something twisted deep within Mother Shona's chest. Again, she'd hoped to avoid this. All she could believe was that she had committed the lesser of two evils.

"There is something else ye should all know," she said, breaking the heavy silence. "Sister Annella has managed to fall foul of Duncan MacKinnon. I don't know the details, but he tried to force himself upon her … and she fought back and stabbed him. He will come here, looking for her. None of ye are to speak a word about Sister Annella to him."

A beat of shocked silence passed.

"If MacKinnon asks whether ye have seen her, or if ye know where she is, ye are to answer 'nay'." The abbess's voice hardened now. "Is that clear?"

"Aye, Mother Shona." A chorus of cowed female voices answered her.

Guilt had tightened into a hard knot in the base of Mother Shona's belly when she emerged from the kirk. God would punish her for the sins she'd committed today, she was sure of it. Earlier in the day, she'd been so firm in her decision, so sure she was doing the right thing. Yet, seeing the alarm, fear, and wariness on the faces of the women she'd sworn to protect, she realized she'd failed.

Had she done the right thing throwing Ella into Gavin MacNichol's arms?

They'd been lovers once, and judging from the way they still looked at each other, that sentiment hadn't disappeared. Gavin gazed upon Ella in a way that made sadness quicken in the abbess's breast.

Many years earlier, in another life, a man had once looked at her like that.

The moment she'd seen Ella and Gavin together in the chapter house when he'd come to take her back to her dying mother, all the missing pieces in the puzzle that was Sister Ella had fallen into place.

She'd known then that MacNichol was the father of Ella's child.

The sadness that had cloaked Ella during her first months at Kilbride had been painful to see. Each morning, the young woman appeared with a face swollen from weeping while she moved through the day, through prayers and chores, as if she were sleep-walking. And when she'd discovered she was with bairn, she'd been inconsolable.

Mother Shona had asked Ella to tell her the name of the child's father—perhaps he could have helped. But Ella had been vehement in her refusal. The abbess had known then that the young woman bore a secret she would never share with her or the other sisters.

I've given her another chance, the abbess told herself as she stepped outside into the soft evening light. *But a price had to be paid in order to do so.*

The nuns went to wash up for supper, while Mother Shona took a walk in the gardens. She needed to be alone with her thoughts for a short while, to form a plan for the days that lay ahead. It would be a trying time for them all.

Deep in her own cares, the abbess circuited the neatly tended rows of kale and onions. It was only when a voice hailed her that she emerged from the fog of her thoughts.

Sister Firtha was hurrying toward her. The tall, lanky young woman, who was still a novice at the abbey, wore a strained expression, her eyes huge on a lean face.

The abbess stopped walking, turning to meet her.

"Abbess!" Sister Firtha called out once more. "We have visitors ... MacKinnon has just entered the abbey and is demanding to see ye."

Mother Shona walked toward the chapter house, where the visitors had been ushered in. Dread writhed in her belly at the thought of facing Duncan MacKinnon. The few encounters she'd had with the man over the years had troubled her for days afterward.

The clan-chief had a way about him that made all her instincts scream danger.

She'd had trouble with MacKinnon for the last few years. He disliked the influence the abbey wielded over the western edge of his lands. He especially hated how well-loved the Sisters of Kilbride were by the local folk.

It was a love he'd never been able to garner from his own people.

Dragging in a deep breath, and telling herself that a man such as MacKinnon didn't deserve her anxiety, Mother Shona pushed open the chapter door and entered the lofty space.

The clan-chief stood in the center of the flagstone floor, the stained-glass windows behind him. MacKinnon didn't look pleased. His gaze was bloodshot, his expression mutinous, and he held himself gingerly. No doubt, under that mail shirt he wore, the clan-chief's wounded ribs were bound. Two men flanked the clan-chief: one tall and raven-haired with piercing blue eyes, the other heavily muscled with short blond hair and a forbidding expression. Ross Campbell and Carr Broderick—MacKinnon never went anywhere without his two henchmen.

"Where is she?" MacKinnon barked out as she entered. He didn't bother with greetings or preliminaries.

Having expected this, the abbess kept her expression neutral. "Please lower yer tone, MacKinnon ... this is a place of worship."

"Don't obstruct me, woman," MacKinnon growled. "Sister Annella. Bring her to me."

"Sister Ella ... what do ye want with her?"

"I ask the questions here, Mother Shona. Tell me where the nun is."

The abbess held his gaze, her own never wavering. "Ye have made a wasted trip here, I'm afraid. Sister Ella is currently at Scorrybreac Castle, visiting her ill mother. We have been praying for a miracle and that Lady Fraser might live."

"No, she isn't," MacKinnon barked, his dark brows knitting together. He was staring at the abbess with an intensity that made misgiving slither down her spine. "She accompanied MacNichol to Dunan and tried to kill me last night. She then fled ... west."

Mother Shona widened her gaze as she feigned surprise. "Well, she never arrived here," she replied, deliberately keeping her voice low and respectful. "Perhaps she changed course during her journey?"

A muscle bunched in MacKinnon's lantern jaw. He was a handsome man; the abbess had noted that from the first time she'd met him. However, all one needed was a few moments in his company to realize that an attractive exterior hid much that was dark and unsavory. MacKinnon had a shadowed soul, and the abbess wondered if he had been born that way or if life had shaped his unpleasant nature.

"She traveled west," he growled. "To Kilbride."

The abbess inclined her head as if his assertion confused her. "And I can assure ye that she never came here." She paused, her gaze narrowing. "In fact, we have been awaiting her return ... MacNichol promised to return her to Kilbride before now."

MacKinnon stared at her, and danger crackled in the air. His men, Campbell and Broderick, exchanged glances, their expressions veiled. They, like the abbess, were probably wondering what the clan-chief would do next.

When MacKinnon finally spoke, his voice was low and hard. "Ye lie, Mother Shona."

The abbess drew herself up. "How dare ye. I am a servant of God. I do not tell falsehoods."

MacKinnon took a threatening step forward. "Ye forget … this abbey sits upon my land. I rule here, not ye." He paused there, letting his words sink in before he shifted his attention to Ross Campbell. "Search the abbey," he barked. "Find that wee bitch."

26

In Name Only

THEY RODE HARD, cutting north into Fraser lands rather than risk the more direct, faster route home through MacKinnon territory. The day was waning, long shadows stretching across bare hills, when the party reached the tiny hamlet of Frithe nestled in the foothills of the Black Cuillins.

But as small as Frithe was, the village hosted an inn: a low-slung, white-washed building with a thatched roof and a weather-beaten sign revealing a dancing woman with flowing gold hair.

"The Fairy Maid." Perched behind Gavin, Ella squinted in the gloaming so that she could read the inn's name on the sign.

"Aye, the Lochans of the Fair Folk are just a short ride from here," Gavin replied, pulling up his mare, Saorsa.

Ella craned her neck then, looking northwest at where the great shadowy peaks of the Black Cuillins rose above them. She'd visited the Fairy Pools a few times as a child, for they lay in Fraser land and the clan often celebrated weddings at the sacred spot. She remembered rushing water, the serene atmosphere, and a large turquoise pool that she'd bathed in.

If the situation had been different, if she hadn't been running from MacKinnon, fleeing her old identity, she'd have liked to see them again.

'The Fairy Maid' proved to be welcoming lodgings. The elderly couple who kept it directed Gavin and his men to the stables wedged between the two wings that stretched behind the main structure. There, they rubbed down their horses before retiring to the common room and a supper of roast mutton, mashed turnips with butter, and oaten bread.

There were no other travelers in the inn this eve, just two local men playing a game of Ard-ri upon a low table at the far end of the common room. Immersed in their game, the men barely looked up at the newcomers. Ella glanced over to see one of them grin as he moved a white counter close to a small stone figurine, while his opponent scowled. Ard-ri—or High King—was an old game that simulated a Viking raid. The grinning man was about to bring down the Scottish king.

Seated next to Gavin at the long table he shared with her and his men, Ella lowered her chin and whispered a prayer. It was a habit after all her years at

Kilbride, one that she wouldn't lightly cast aside. Once she had given thanks for the food set before them, Ella ate with relish. After everything that had befallen them over the past day, she realized she hadn't eaten anything since leaving Dunan. Likewise, Gavin and his men ate as if they'd been starved for a week, washing down the meal with tankards of ale.

The food was delicious, and Ella focused upon it, happy to let the murmured conversation move around her rather than contribute. She was still reeling after the events of the day.

Ella helped herself to another slice of mutton, and as she did so, her hand brushed Gavin's. Her gaze snapped up, fusing with her husband's. Watching her, Gavin's mouth curved into a smile. Ella stared back, noting that dimple in his cheek that still gave him a boyish look.

"Is the meal to yer liking, Ella?" he asked softly.

"Aye," she replied, smiling back. "I imagine ye had forgotten how I can eat like a horse?"

His smile widened, although those warm blue eyes never wavered from hers. "I've forgotten nothing," he murmured. "Not one detail."

His words made a hot flush creep over her chest.

Not one detail.

Many years may have passed since they'd been lovers, yet they lived a lifetime in that one sultry summer. The memories of it all had tormented Ella when she initially left Scorrybreac. Eventually, with Mother Shona's help, she'd archived all those painful recollections, pushed them so far back into the recesses of her mind that she could barely reach them.

And yet, they were still there—they always would be.

The hours they'd spent in that clearing, laughing, talking, making plans, and exploring each other's bodies under the warmth of the sun.

Ella had told herself that Gavin had forgotten it all, that he'd laid the past to rest when he'd wed Innis.

Yet gazing into Gavin's eyes now, Ella understood that wasn't the case.

The meal concluded with another round of ale, and one by one, the members of the MacNichol party mumbled their excuses and went to find their beds.

Eventually, only Gavin and Ella were left at the table. It wasn't so comfortable there, so they took their ales over to the fireside, settling down into high-backed wooden chairs. The men playing Ard-ri had long since departed for the eve.

"The innkeeper has given us his best room," Gavin informed her, his mouth quirking. "He tells me it looks across his wife's rose garden ... I remember how well ye loved roses."

"I still do," Ella replied.

Gavin took a sip from his tankard, his gaze shifting to the glowing lump of peat in the hearth. "I have asked the innkeeper's wife to make ye up a separate room," he said. His voice was measured as if he was carefully choosing his words. "Worry not, ye don't have to share my bed-chamber."

His words took Ella by surprise.

Of course—tonight was their wedding night. They had not yet consummated their vows. Unless they did so, they would not be officially wed.

The reminder made nervousness flutter up within Ella, like a cage of loosed butterflies. She'd done her best not to think of what the end of the day would bring; truthfully, she'd thought they'd be making camp under the stars rather than finding comfortable lodgings.

"We should share the same room, Gavin," she replied, her fingers tightening around the handle of her tankard. Such bold words made her heart race, yet she forced herself on. "And the same bed."

Gavin went still, his gaze widening.

"We are wed." She rushed out the words before her courage failed her. "And I'd rather it wasn't just in name only."

His blue eyes darkened. "Ye wish to lie with me again … despite everything that has happened?"

The pair of them stared at each other for a long moment. Suddenly, it felt airless in the warm, smoky common room.

When Ella replied, her voice was barely above a whisper. "Aye."

Ella stepped inside the room the innkeeper's wife had prepared for them, and her heart started to race like a hunted deer's.

Indeed, she'd given them a lovely chamber. The rose garden was hidden from view, for the shutters had been bolted closed. Yet a vase of fresh pale pink roses sat on a table in the center of the space, their scent drifting through the warm room. Heavy beams stretched overhead, barely high enough for a tall man like Gavin to stand at full height, yet the white-washed walls gave the chamber a spacious feel. A screen covered one corner of the room, hiding the privy and wash-stand.

However, the sight of a large bed in the far corner, covered with a woad-blue blanket, made dizziness sweep over Ella.

An intoxicating blend of nerves and excitement.

She couldn't believe this was happening. After all these years—she and Gavin were going to lie together again.

The thought terrified her.

Gavin closed the door behind them, lowering the wooden bar so that they were secure inside the chamber.

Ella turned to him. Her heart was pounding so fiercely now that she was starting to feel ill.

It's Gavin, she counseled herself. *Ye know him … why are ye so scared?*

And yet she was. So many years had passed. They'd both changed so much.

As if reading her thoughts, Gavin's expression, which had been serious just moments earlier, softened into a warm smile. "Do ye want to wash up first, or shall I?" He paused then before pulling a face. "I fear I stink like a goat."

"Ye go," Ella replied with an answering smile. She was grateful he was focusing on practical things, not the fact that the pair of them were now wed and standing alone together in their bed-chamber on their wedding night.

With a nod, Gavin threw his cloak over the back of the chair and heeled his boots off. He then loosed his hair from where it had been tied at the nape of his neck. The dark-gold waves fell over his shoulders. Ella watched, mesmerized. She'd always loved Gavin's hair.

Turning from her, Gavin disappeared behind the screen. Moments later Ella heard splashes as he poured water into a bowl for bathing.

She moved over to the fireplace, where the innkeeper's wife had left two earthen cups and a jug of wine. Pouring out both cups, Ella took a large gulp of wine. It was bramble—her favorite. The heat of it pooling in her belly calmed her nerves a little.

Presently, Gavin reappeared. Barefoot and naked from the waist up, the sight of him made Ella's breathing catch as it had that night in Dunan.

The soft firelight bathed his broad chest and the crisp blond curls that covered it. He had a couple of long, thin scars down his left side she hadn't noticed before.

Realizing that she was staring, Ella hastily put down her cup and picked up Gavin's before holding it out to him. "Here," she said. "It's good."

He took the wine with a smile, although his gaze smoldered in a way that told her he'd seen her frank appraisal of him.

Breathing fast, Ella hurried across the room and ducked behind the screen.

Hidden from view, she raised her hands to her cheeks to find them hot. Did Gavin have any idea what he did to her? Over the past two weeks, even a glance from him made her knees go weak.

She felt eighteen years old again, a maid who had never been touched by a man.

After years of wearing so many layers of clothing, disrobing was ridiculously easy tonight. Ella pulled off her snug leather boots and unlaced the kirtle before she reached down and pulled the léine she wore underneath over her head.

Wearing only a thin sleeveless linen shift that reached mid-thigh, she moved over to the washbowl. The water was still warm.

Ella washed deftly in an effort to keep her thoughts from the half-naked man who awaited her on the other side of the screen. It was futile. Her body felt sensitized, every nerve on alert as she dried herself with a cloth and adjusted the shift.

Glancing down at herself, she saw that the garment left little to the imagination. Her breasts, which had grown fuller since she'd carried a bairn, thrust out before her, her hard nipples clearly visible through the thin fabric.

Ella nervously licked her lips, smoothing down the flimsy shift against her thighs.

She felt as if she were standing on the edge of a cliff. Once she jumped there would be no turning back. Aye, she and Gavin were now wed, but it was only when they lay together that their union would be real.

Was she ready for this, for the upheaval taking this step would cause?

Not able to answer the question, for her thoughts were now lost in a churning sea of want, Ella stepped out from behind the screen.

27

Unforgotten

GAVIN WAS STANDING next to the fire, leaning up against the mantlepiece as he cradled his cup of wine. He looked up when Ella emerged, and their gazes locked. Then Gavin's gaze slid from her face, down the length of her body.

Ella watched his lips part, his gaze darken.

Slowly, deliberately, he put down the cup and walked toward her.

Reaching Ella, he lifted a hand and cupped her cheek. "Ye are lovely," he whispered. "Even more so than I remember."

Ella had to smile at that. At eighteen her body and been unblemished and lithe; she didn't think the same still held for her at thirty-six. Yet, his words made warmth flow through her. She was glad he found her attractive, for the mere sight of Gavin made her ache for him.

Ella reached up and cupped her hand over his before she inclined her head so that her mouth slid over his palm. She kissed him there, gently, her eyes fluttering closed as she leaned into the strength of him.

His free hand touched her shoulder then, his fingertips sliding across her skin.

And then, with a groan deep in his throat, Gavin pulled Ella into his arms.

She sank into him, giving herself up to the moment as Gavin tangled his fingers in her hair, drew her head back, and kissed her.

The touch of his lips on hers, the feel of his tongue parting them, unraveled the last of Ella's doubts. Just like back in Scorrybreac, being in his arms, having his mouth on hers, felt right. She'd fought it then, struggled against an impulse that was as natural as breathing, but she didn't need to now.

She was no longer Sister Ella, but Lady Ella MacNichol.

She could give into this.

A soft cry escaped Ella, and she reached out, sliding her palms up his naked chest before she linked her arms around his neck. Pressing herself up against him, she drank Gavin in, her tongue and lips exploring his mouth.

He groaned again, and the sound lit a fire deep within her core.

It was strange how memory erased many tiny details. There was much she remembered about what it was like to lie with Gavin, but that groan—both innately masculine and yet strangely vulnerable—was something she'd forgotten.

His kiss deepened, his hands splaying out across the back of her head.

Ella couldn't get enough of him. She pressed her body against the muscular length of his, and when she felt his shaft—hard and hot—against her belly, excitement rippled through her.

Panting, she drew back from him. Their gazes fused. Gavin's chest now rose and fell sharply. His lips were swollen from their kisses, his eyes hooded with desire. He wore a fierce, hungry expression that sucked the air from Ella's lungs.

How she wanted him. She'd never wanted anything more in her life.

Wordlessly, he reached down and caught the hem of her shift, drawing it upward. Ella helped him, wriggling out of the garment and tossing it aside. Gavin's stare devoured her nakedness. Then he undid his braies and pushed them down, before kicking them away.

Ella let her gaze travel down the length of him, taking in his swollen shaft that thrust up against his belly.

Her breathing caught. He hadn't been aroused that night at Dunan, and yet her gaze had still strayed to his manhood. But she couldn't stop staring at it now. She ached to touch it. She wanted to wrap her mouth and fingers around its strength, as she once had years earlier, and make his groans fill the room.

Before she could, Gavin took Ella by the hand and led her to the bed.

They sank down upon it, coming together with a hunger that took Ella by surprise. Gavin ravaged her mouth now, his big body sliding down the length of hers as his hands explored her. Ella arched up toward him, her own hands tangling in his thick blond hair.

Gavin tore his mouth from hers then, his lips leaving a trail of fire while he kissed his way down her neck to her breasts. As he suckled each one, Ella started to gasp and tremble, her fingers digging into his scalp, urging him on.

And then when he left her breasts and continued his exploration, Ella's gasps turned to groans. His lips, his tongue, his fingers. He knew exactly where to touch, where to stroke, where to lick. Gavin took his time, as if she were a banquet of delicacies he wished to savor.

It was only when Ella started to plead with him that he ceased his delicious torture. Lying spread-eagled on the bed, her body a pool of pulsing, aching need, Ella gazed at him as he rose up between her thighs.

His shaft thrust toward her, and Ella pushed herself up before reaching for it. Her fingers wrapped around the shaft, and she gasped at just how hot and hard it was, the tip swollen and slick with need.

"Ella," Gavin groaned. His voice was raw, a moan escaping when she slid her hand down his shaft's length. She watched Gavin's face, fascinated, while she pleasured him in long, gliding strokes. His eyes closed, a nerve flickering in his cheek. She loved seeing him like this, she loved knowing she was the one to transport him.

Moving closer, she bent over and took him in her mouth.

A low curse echoed through the room. Gavin made a strangled sound in the back of his throat, his body growing taut as she drew him deep into her mouth.

But after a few moments, he caught her by the shoulders, gently pushing her up. Reluctantly, Ella withdrew. She'd been enjoying herself; she'd wanted to bring him to the edge and then watch him topple over it.

She wanted to see Gavin MacNichol lose control.

"I have to be inside ye." He ground out the words, pushing Ella onto her back. "I can't wait any longer." With that, he spread her thighs once more. He then took hold of one knee, lifting it high, and thrust into her.

The movement was swift and brutal—a shock after so many years of abstinence—and yet Ella welcomed it. She cried out, arching up against him. The aching, rippling pleasure of him deep inside her was almost unbearable in its intensity.

"Oh, Gavin," she whimpered. "I don't know … I can't—"

Looming over Ella, he cut off her words with his mouth, kissing her hungrily, his lips bruising hers. And as he kissed her, Gavin started to move inside her—in slow, grinding thrusts.

Ella clutched at his shoulders as he rode her, digging her nails in with each movement. She kissed him back, frenzied now. She wanted to lose herself in this man, to forget the rest of the world existed.

The past ceased to matter, and the future was nothing more than a blank sheet of parchment waiting to be written upon.

The taste of him, the weight and strength of his body as he slammed into her with each thrust, pushed everything else from her mind. In the past, Gavin had been a gentle, sensitive lover, yet there was a tension to him tonight, a fire that consumed them both.

Tonight was a claiming.

He continued his steady rhythm, sweat sliding down his broad back. Gavin tore his mouth from Ella's then and stared into her eyes while he took her. He reached out, entwining their fingers, pushing her hands back against the pillows.

Ella gazed up at him, a deep, aching pleasure building in the cradle of her hips. It was almost too much, too intense to lock eyes with him while he slid in and out of her, driving a little deeper each time.

A wave of fierce tenderness crashed over her, making it hard to breathe. She'd lived apart from Gavin for years, yet the cord between them had never been broken. Giving him up had only made her realize how much she loved him, and bearing him a bairn had served to strengthen that bond. She'd known it was impossible, and that if she let it, her love for Gavin would destroy her. And so, she'd built herself a new life, with a new purpose.

But amongst it all, Gavin had always been there. In her heart he'd lived on, unforgotten.

Gavin sank down upon Ella, his body shaking as he found his release. Her skin against his was sweat-slicked, and he could feel her pulse pounding against the palm of his hand when he laid it upon her breast.

"Mo ghràdh," he murmured, leaning forward and kissing her once more. Ella's full lips were slightly swollen, her cheekbones were flushed, and her eyes gleamed in the lambent glow of the hearth that cast its light across the room.

Gavin wanted to say more, to pour out everything that lay within his heart, but their lovemaking had left him speechless. He could merely lie there, Ella curled in his arms, as they both recovered.

Rolling off Ella, Gavin drew her against his chest. She was a small woman, and he was afraid he might crush her under his weight if he fell asleep on top of her. Nestled against him, Ella lazily stroked the planes of his chest and belly as if committing his body to memory.

A smile curved Gavin's lips, and he bent his head, inhaling the scent of rosewater in her hair. Never had anything felt more right than having her curled up in his arms. Their lovemaking had surprised him, for it had been very different to the past.

During that long, sultry summer, they had both been new to the pleasures of the flesh. They had explored each other's bodies eagerly, yet despite that he'd fallen in love with Ella then, there was always a part of him he kept back when they lay together. He never let go completely.

Tonight, Ella had stripped him bare.

He'd whispered words of love while he'd taken her, worshipped her body with his own. He'd given himself to her without keeping anything back.

As a young man, he hadn't had the courage to do so. That was why he'd been able to give her up all those years ago. That day in the clearing, he'd stepped into the role that had been expected of him: the clan-chief's dutiful first-born son. He'd deliberately shut Ella out.

It had hurt him to upset Ella, but he'd kept telling himself that he was doing the right thing—that his parents and clansmen would appreciate his sacrifice.

Strangely, none of them had seemed to care. Of course, few knew what he'd given up to wed his betrothed.

Gavin stroked Ella's thick hair, his vision misting. "I was a fool to let ye go, Ella," he whispered. "I will never do so again."

In response, she gave a gentle sigh, her small hand splaying over his heart. "I know ye won't," she murmured. "Sometimes life's lessons take us a while to learn ... but I think ye and I understand now."

Gavin's throat thickened. "Ye have always understood," he replied huskily. "It was me with a head as thick as an oak trunk."

Ella huffed a laugh against his chest, one slender leg curling over his hip as she drew him closer to her. "It matters not, love," she whispered. "The past can't be unwritten ... and maybe the Lord had this in store for us all along."

Gavin smiled. "So ye still have yer faith ... despite everything that's happened?"

Ella pulled away slightly, tipping her head back so that their gazes met. Like his, her eyes shone with tears. "I have it *because* of everything that's happened," she replied. "Ye and I were meant to be together, Gavin MacNichol ... and maybe God realizes that too."

28

Weathering the Storm

ELLA STEPPED OUT into the morning and raised her face to the gentle sun that was rising over the mountains to the east. Despite that she and Gavin had managed to sleep later in the night, fatigue pressed down upon her this morning. Her eyes were gritty, her limbs heavy—and yet she'd never felt better.

Last night had been the gateway to a better life, she could feel it in her bones.

"Tired?" Gavin stepped up next to Ella, placing an arm around her shoulders; it was a protective gesture that made warmth filter through her.

Leaning into him, Ella glanced up at her husband's face. "Aye ... but happy."

He smiled, and his eyes crinkled at the corners. "As am I."

They had shared a breakfast of fresh bannock, butter, and honey in the common room, before Gavin's men had gone out to ready the horses. It was now time to continue their journey.

"If we ride hard, we can make it to Scorrybreac by dusk, I reckon," Ceard announced. The older man approached, leading his bay and the clan-chief's grey.

Gavin nodded. "The innkeeper's wife has given us food for the journey ... so there shouldn't be any need to stop at Kiltaraglen on the way."

A tendril of nervousness wafted through Ella at hearing they would reach their destination by day's end. She'd hoped they'd spend the night at Kiltaraglen—a chance for her and Gavin to reacquaint themselves some more, as well as putting off the inevitable.

She didn't want to see the looks of shock, anger, and censure on his kin's faces—or suffer the condemnation that would swiftly follow.

As if sensing her shift in mood, Gavin's arm tightened around Ella's shoulders. "Ye worry about the reception we'll receive, don't ye?"

Ella swallowed before nodding. "Aye ... doesn't it concern ye?"

Not caring that his men now surrounded them and were looking on with interest, Gavin reached out and stroked Ella's face. "We'll weather it, Ella," he said softly. "Just remember, this is nothing compared to what ye have been through."

"But yer mother—"

"Will attempt to slay us with her tongue," he interrupted, his brow furrowing. "But they're just words ... surely ye aren't scared of Maggie MacNichol. Not after facing the likes of Duncan MacKinnon."

Ella snorted. "Lady MacNichol is terrifying, Gavin."

"*Ye* are Lady MacNichol now," he reminded her, a stubborn light gleaming in his eyes. "And my mother will have to accept that."

Ella pondered Gavin's words at dusk that evening as Scorrybreac's bulk hove into view. He was clan-chief, and set in his resolve, but she knew what folk could be like. His marriage would scandalize everyone at Scorrybreac—from the high to the low. News of their union would ripple out from the castle, reaching all corners of Skye within days.

Sooner or later, MacKinnon would hear of it too.

Ella drew in a deep breath, squeezing Gavin's hand. She sat, perched before him, while he held the reins with his right hand, the other arm wrapped around her waist. "Home," she said softly.

"Aye," he replied, his breath feathering against her ear. "Remember what I said ... we'll weather this."

Outlined against a pale pink sky, the castle looked magnificent, as if it would endure forever. Not a breath of wind stirred the MacNichol pennant that hung from one of the keep's towers.

The road leading through Scorrybreac village was empty, for folk had all retired to their cottages for the evening. Smoke rose from the sod roofs, and the smell of overcooked vegetable stew—most likely pottage—wafted across the highway.

Up ahead the men upon the watchtowers had spied them, and the heavy oaken and iron gates opened to receive the clan-chief and his men. They clattered into the outer bailey, which was empty at this hour, and continued on to the inner bailey.

Blair came out to meet them.

As Ella had expected, Gavin's younger brother's eyes widened at the sight of Ella riding with Gavin, dressed in a kirtle and léine instead of a nun's habit. As she was a wedded woman now, Ella had not left her hair unbound. Instead, she'd tamed her pale copper tresses into a long braid and wrapped it around the crown of her head.

"Gavin?" Blair finally spoke. "What's this?"

Turning from helping Ella from the saddle, Gavin met his brother's eye. "I'll save my explanations for when we're all gathered," he replied. His face was enigmatic, his tone even. Yet Ella detected the note of steel beneath; he was already preparing himself for the tempest. "Can ye tell everyone to meet us in the Great Hall?"

A heavy hush settled over the hall when Gavin finished his explanation.

He'd kept the details to a minimum, although Ella had been surprised about his candor relating to MacKinnon. He'd spoken frankly about the clan-chief's behavior, and detailed their escape to Kilbride, before explaining how he and Ella had come to be wed.

He did not speak of their still-born child. Some details were too private to be shared.

When no one broke the silence, Gavin spoke once more.

"Few of ye realize this, but I was in love with Ella years ago ... and wished to break my betrothal to Innis for her," he said, his gaze sweeping over the long table where his kin sat. Many of them stared at him as if he'd just sprouted two heads. Stewart Fraser was in attendance. Ella's father wore a stunned look as if he was having difficulty grasping the clan-chief's explanation. "She fled to Kilbride and took her vows because I broke her heart," Gavin continued. "We now have the chance to start again."

A harsh laugh followed these words. Maggie MacNichol had drawn herself up, her features sharp, her grey eyes flint-hard. "Do ye think yer sordid wee affair was a secret?" Her voice lashed across the table, causing some present to flinch. "We all knew ... that was why yer father insisted ye honor the betrothal. It had nothing to do with his ill health and everything to do with saving yer honor."

Gavin's face went taut. He then shifted his attention to Blair, his gaze questioning.

"It's true," his brother murmured. "We all knew." Across the table, Gordana dropped her gaze to her lap. Watching her, Ella realized that she too had known the full extent of Ella's relationship with Gavin—and yet she'd pretended otherwise.

Ella exhaled slowly. She stood at Gavin's side, yet her legs felt wobbly under her. She wished they were seated. Suddenly, it felt as if the walls were closing in on her. Had they all conspired to keep her and Gavin apart?

"Ye were a headstrong, foolish young man," Maggie MacNichol continued. "Ye had to be reined in. I wouldn't let ye humiliate us and risk our relationship with the Frasers of Skye."

Stewart Fraser's face grew taut at these words, while tension coiled within Ella, tightening with each passing moment. As she'd always known, Maggie MacNichol had dominated her husband's decision-making. She'd never let on, but she'd been set upon keeping the lovers apart.

She was a clever woman too—she understood that if she'd directly opposed Gavin and Ella, they'd have fought her. Instead, she'd used the clan-chief's ill-health and Gavin's sense of duty as her weapons of choice to manipulate him into doing her bidding.

Watching the gleam in the woman's eye, heat kindled in Ella's belly—a slow, pulsing anger. She glanced across at Gavin to see that his expression had turned hard. His eyes were cold as he watched his mother.

"Ye had yer victory, Ma," he said, his tone wintry. "And I congratulate ye for it ... but fortunately, fate has taken a turn. Ella and I are together now, and there's nothing ye can do about it."

"We'll see about that," Maggie MacNichol snarled, drawing herself up further. "It's a crime ye have both committed ... against the church, against decency."

"The abbess cast me from the order," Ella spoke up now. Her voice was low although it trembled with the anger she was now struggling to keep in check. "Gavin and I have committed no crime in wedding."

Gavin's mother glared back at her, not backing down an inch. This woman's viciousness was like standing under a lashing hailstorm. Maggie MacNichol still wielded a lot of influence and power at Scorrybreac. Ella could see from the surrounding faces that many seated upon the dais silently agreed with her. They had to act quickly if they wanted to stem the tide that now rose against them.

"A nun can't cast aside her vows as lightly as that." Her mother-in-law spat out the words. "I'll wager MacKinnon would have something to say about her decision ... as would the Holy See."

Shocked murmuring rippled across the table at these words.

Ella's father's expression had turned thunderous now, although Ella wasn't sure if his anger was aimed at her or Maggie MacNichol. Across from Stewart Fraser, Gordana's face had gone the color of milk, her blue eyes wide as her gaze flicked from her mother to her brother.

Gavin stepped forward then. Leaning down, he placed his palms flat upon the table and fixed his mother with a penetrating stare.

"Mother Shona's decision was good enough for me." His voice was low, with a threatening edge. "I haven't gathered my kin here this eve to gain yer blessing ... but to do ye the courtesy of informing ye that I have taken a new wife. Whether or not ye agree with it means nothing to me ... do ye understand? *Nothing*."

His inflection on the final word made Maggie MacNichol's gaze narrow. However, the woman didn't flinch, didn't back down. Despite that she must have known that her son's temper was hanging by a thread, she held his gaze fearlessly.

"Annella Fraser always held an unhealthy influence upon ye, Gavin," she replied, her own voice brittle with anger. "I fear she has bewitched ye once again." Maggie's gaze shifted to Ella then, her face twisting. "Perhaps the abbess cast her out for she knew that Satan had taken up residence within ye." Her attention flicked to Gavin once more. "Ye have wed the devil's consort, son ... and yer very soul is now in peril."

Shocked gasps followed this pronouncement, although Gavin didn't move. His gaze didn't waver from his mother.

"Hatred and spite are Satan's work." His voice rang across the table, cutting through the whispers and mutters that had followed his mother's words. "There is nothing but goodness within Ella. Ye, on the other hand ..." He paused here as another hush settled over the table. "Ye spread ill-content like the pestilence that is bringing England and the continent beyond to its knees. If anyone is doing the devil's work at Scorrybreac, mother ... it is ye."

29

Vengeance

"SHE'S A VIPER, Gavin," Ella whispered. She leaned into her husband's chest, pressing her hot cheek against his thudding heart. "Yer mother could turn the entire castle against us."

Gavin huffed a soft laugh, although there was little humor in it. She could feel the tension in his body; his pulse was rapid, and he hadn't spoken a word as they'd left the Great Hall and made their way to his solar.

"Do ye remember I told ye that Gordana has advised me to send mother away ... to our kin upon Raasay?" he said finally.

Ella drew back from him, nodding. Gavin's eyes were shadowed although his expression was still thunderous. "Are ye considering it now?"

An angry sigh gusted out of Gavin. He stepped away and dragged a hand through his hair. "Aye, although it pains me. I've always felt an obligation to my family ... Ma knows it ... and as ye have seen, she knows how to exploit it."

Ella frowned. "Aye ... she wields words like a claidheamh-mor."

"She is capable of causing great damage," Gavin admitted. He crossed the solar and poured two goblets of wine. The servants had been in here, and had closed the shutters and added another lump of peat to the fire. A warm golden glow bathed the chamber, highlighting the huge tapestry that hung on the rough stone wall behind them. It depicted a hunting scene in vivid detail. "As ye have just seen ... one under-estimates my mother at their peril. She is a scholar of manipulation. She knows how to read folk ... she always has."

He approached Ella and handed her a goblet. She received it gratefully and took a sip. "All these years and she never let on that she knew about us?"

Gavin shook his head. "She never needed to. She'd gotten what she'd wanted years ago. The knowledge she held was a secret weapon, to be kept in check just in case she needed it in the future." His face shadowed as he spoke these words, making it clear that he was worried.

They looked at each other once more. Ella saw how his gaze guttered and witnessed the tension upon his handsome face. Her ribcage tightened. She didn't want to bring Gavin grief and trouble.

Ella drew in a slow breath before taking another sip of wine. She needed something to soothe her nerves after that scene in the Great Hall. No one besides Maggie MacNichol had said much—although her outburst had been quite enough. Ella had looked around the table, noting that most folk—even Gordana—avoided her eye.

Only her father had met her gaze, his blue eyes gleaming, his face bereft.

"What if yer kin never accept me?" she whispered. Fear lanced through her as she said those words. "Many of them looked as if they agreed with yer mother. Blair had a face like thunder, and his wife looked as if she'd just swallowed a mouthful of vinegar."

"They'll accept ye." The fierceness in Gavin's voice took Ella aback.

"Not with Maggie MacNichol whispering in their ears. When she told them I was in league with the devil, some of the women looked as if they might faint."

Gavin's dark-blond brows knitted together. "My mother has a dangerous tongue, Ella ... I'm well-aware of that now. I also realize that her scheming goes far deeper than I thought." He stepped close to Ella and raised a hand, stroking her cheek with a tenderness that made her breathing catch. Nonetheless, she saw the concern in his eyes, and a glimmer of fear there as well that he tried to hide with his next words. "Worry not, my love. I'm keeping an eye on her from now on. And I will not tolerate my mother meddling in our lives any longer."

Alone, Lady Maggie MacNichol paced the length of her chamber. Heavy skirts hampered her stride, but she paid them no mind. Instead, her thoughts had turned inward.

Annella Fraser has bested me.

Maggie's hands fisted at her sides, squeezing so tightly that the rings encrusting them dug painfully into her palms.

That scheming wee whore always wanted to be Lady of Scorrybreac ... and now she has achieved her goal.

Maggie had never wanted a daughter-in-law, but Innis Fraser had been the ideal choice. Submissive and quiet, the woman had never spoken out of turn, had never challenged Maggie's authority.

Anger thrummed through Maggie, and she paced faster, circling the floor now. Gavin had proved to be a disappointment to her over the years, but she would never forgive him for this. Never.

After Iain had passed away, Maggie had assumed her son would be as easy to dominate as her husband had been.

But, despite that he had given up the woman he'd loved in order to please his family, Gavin had a core of iron she hadn't expected. Shortly after he became clan-chief, Maggie discovered that her son wouldn't let her guide him the way Iain had. He had his own ideas about how Scorrybreac should be ruled, and although he let his mother voice her opinions, he'd argued with her on every point she raised over the years. When he'd lowered the yearly tax for the cottars working his lands, she'd raged at him.

But her anger had washed off Gavin.

Years later, the MacNichol lands thrived. Maggie resented her son for that; she'd hoped he'd fail miserably so that she could sweep in and take control. Unfortunately, Gavin had proved himself highly competent over the past two decades. He'd also won the love and respect of his people—something his father had struggled with over the years.

And he'd developed a thick hide too. Her criticisms, scathing comments, and biting rebukes merely bounced off him these days.

But she'd managed to hit a raw nerve this evening.

When she'd accused his wife of being Satan's minion, Maggie had seen anger flare in his eyes. Finally, she'd discovered her son's weakness. Finally, she had a way to wield power over him.

Maggie stopped pacing as an idea took shape in her head. Her hands slowly unclenched, and she drew in a long, deep breath.

They won't beat me, she vowed, determination filtering over her. She crossed to the table that sat under her shuttered window. *I won't let Annella Fraser remain here as Lady of Scorrybreac. Something has to be done.*

Lowering herself upon her chair, Maggie took a sheet of parchment and smoothed it out before her. Then she reached for her quill and inkpot.

There was only one person upon Skye who would hate Annella Fraser with the passion she did. Only one person who would want to see her fall to the same degree.

Duncan MacKinnon.

The man was a brute. Maggie paused as she dipped her quill into the inkpot. She'd heard that his wife had died in childbirth and had felt a rare pang of sympathy for the dead woman. Men like Duncan MacKinnon made the worst husbands. They had no time for women, besides swiving them or having them wait upon their every need. Maggie had been fortunate in wedding Iain MacNichol, for if she'd been betrothed to a man like Duncan MacKinnon or his boorish father before him, he'd surely have beaten her to death for her sharp tongue and willful character.

Melancholy settled over Maggie MacNichol then, as memories of her dead husband surfaced.

She thought of Iain rarely these days, but sometimes she realized that there was an empty sensation in her breast, a dull ache that revealed she missed him. The early years of their marriage had been good. He'd once been handsome and strong, and she'd been happy to bear him three healthy bairns. But with the years, Iain had taken to eating and drinking to excess. He became slothful and lost interest in Scorrybreac. To compensate, Maggie's tongue grew sharper, her temper shorter, and her will stronger.

With each year after that, the passion she'd once had for her husband gradually burned out.

Even so, there were times, like now, when she missed his booming laugh and gentle gaze. He'd always tempered her sharper edges.

Pushing back the memories that wouldn't serve her now, Maggie lifted the quill from the ink pot, tapped off the excess ink, and began to write.

Scorrybreac's chapel was as cool and peaceful as ever when Ella stepped inside it. The hour grew late, yet a bank of tallow candles still burned against one wall. She was relieved to see that no one else was here. After everything that had happened since their arrival, she needed a few moments to put herself back together.

Crossing to the shrine of the Virgin Mary, Ella let her gaze settle upon the woman's serene face. She then slowly lowered herself to her knees, clasping her hands before her.

"Much has happened since I was last here, Mother Mary," she whispered. "And I beg yer forgiveness if I have done anything to offend the Lord." She broke off here, wondering if it was best to remain in silence rather than pour out her soul. However, the Virgin had always provided her solace in the past. Whenever she visited this shrine, she felt peace settle over her, a sense that everything would work out for the best.

Right now, she welcomed that sensation.

Closing her eyes, Ella bent her head and began to pray.

It was a while later when she finally rose to her feet and dusted off her skirts. It had been wise to visit the chapel, for she felt lighter, not so burdened with worries about what the future held.

Emerging into the cool evening, she was surprised to find her father awaiting her.

In the light of the torch that burned on the wall behind him, Stewart Fraser's face appeared austere, his gaze hooded.

"Good eve, Da," Ella greeted him cautiously. Since her arrival at Scorrybreac, they hadn't had a moment alone together. "How long have ye been waiting out here?"

"A while," he rumbled. "Ye take yer prayers seriously, daughter."

"Ye should have joined me," she replied with a smile. "I'd have welcomed yer company."

Her father shook his head with a grimace. "Yer mother was the pious one ... I've never felt at ease in a kirk."

Their gazes fused then and held, silence falling between them.

"Are ye angry with me, Da?" Ella asked finally.

"No, lass," he replied, weariness creeping into his voice. "Just confused ... I had no idea that ye loved Gavin MacKinnon. I feel a fool for not realizing that was the reason for yer decision to take the veil."

Ella sighed. "Well then, it seems that ye were the only one in this keep who didn't know ... if ye are to believe Maggie MacNichol."

A shadow moved across Stewart Fraser's eyes. "That woman has a poison tongue," he growled. "The things she said to ye today were unacceptable." A muscle bunched in his jaw. "If she continues her slander, I won't be held accountable."

Ella moved close to her father and took his hand, squeezing gently. "Neither will Gavin ... he was still angry when I left him earlier. I fear the time is coming when things with his mother will come to a head."

Her father nodded. "Aye ... it's been brewing for a while now. MacNichol is a good man ... but he's too soft-hearted with those who don't deserve it." His gaze gentled then as he looked upon her, and he covered Ella's hand with his own. "I am glad to see ye both happy together," he murmured. "I saw the way he looks at ye ... the man loves ye."

A soft smile curved Ella's mouth. "Aye, he does."

Duncan MacKinnon hurled the parchment away with a snarled curse.

At the opposite end of the table, Drew lifted her attention from where she was delicately spreading honey over a small wedge of bannock. "Ill-tidings, I take it?" she asked.

Duncan ignored her. "Whore!"

"MacKinnon?" Carr Broderick's rumbled question behind him was edged with censure. Through his haze of rage, Duncan realized that the warrior thought he was hurling insults at his sister. Carr could be ridiculously gallant at times. But, across the table, Drew's sanguine expression didn't change. She knew he wasn't speaking about her.

"That nun who stabbed me." Duncan whirled around, his gaze fixing upon the broad-shouldered man with short pale blond hair who stood by the door to the solar. "She's now Gavin MacNichol's bride."

Duncan heard his sister's sharply indrawn breath across the table, while Carr stared back at him, eyes widening. A few feet away, Ross Campbell, who also flanked the door, muttered an oath.

"That's impossible." Drew's voice was sharp with shock. "She's a nun."

Duncan whipped around, picked up the parchment that had just arrived by pigeon, and shoved it at his sister. "Here!" he barked. "Read it for yerself."

Drew did just that. Her eyes narrowed as she scanned the missive. "This is from Lady MacNichol?"

"Aye," Duncan growled, anger thrumming through him. He watched his sister's face go rigid.

"It says here that the abbess at Kilbride cast Sister Annella out."

"That scheming bitch." Duncan's hands fisted, for he remembered the challenge in the abbess's eyes when she'd given him permission to have his men search the abbey. They had, but had found no sign of Sister Annella. A visit to the nearby village had yielded nothing either. The priest there had denied ever seeing them. "She knew where the nun was ... she helped them run off together."

Drew lowered the parchment. "Lady MacNichol says that the abbess doesn't have permission to cast out a nun who has taken her vows of perpetuity from the order."

"That's right." Duncan leaned back in his chair, the bannock he'd just consumed churning in his belly. "She should have applied to the Holy See ... only the Pope himself can grant such permission."

Drew inclined her head, her gaze shuttering. "So what will ye do?"

Duncan glared back at her, outrage pulsing in his breast. "That woman tried to kill me," he ground out the words. "And I will have my vengeance upon her."

30
Always

"HAVE YE BEEN avoiding me, Gordana?"

Gavin's sister glanced up from her embroidery, guilt filtering across her face. Observing her, Ella's mouth curved. Gordana MacNichol had a gentle heart and an open nature. It wasn't in her character to be cruel to others. All the same, her mother had done an excellent job in making Ella an outcast in Scorrybreac.

In the two weeks since Ella's arrival, barely anyone save Gavin and her father had spoken to her. Even the servants avoided meeting her eye.

It was a drizzly grey morning, hence Gordana was not in her garden. Usually, if she sat in the women's solar, her mother would join her, but Maggie had retired to her bed-chamber after breaking her fast earlier that morning, complaining of a headache.

Ella wanted to make the most of their time alone together to speak frankly.

"I've been occupied of late," Gordana murmured, her gaze dropping to the coverlet she was embroidering with tiny pink roses. "The garden needs a lot of work at the end of the summer."

"I see the folk of Scorrybreac have been preparing for Lughnasadh."

"Aye," Gordana replied, her gaze still downcast. "Let us hope for fine weather tomorrow."

The festival, which marked the start of the harvest season, was one that Ella had always enjoyed when she'd previously lived in Scorrybreac. It had pagan origins, but now nuns and monks all over Scotland would make a pilgrimage to the top of nearby hills on the day of Lughnasadh.

In old times, folk had sacrificed animals and offered up gifts of the first cuttings of grain to the gods. These days though, there was eating, drinking, dancing, music, games, and matchmaking. As a lass, Ella had also enjoyed watching the athletic and sporting contests such as weight-throwing, hurling, and horse racing.

Silence fell while Ella took a seat opposite Gordana. To keep her hands busy, she picked up a spindle and a basket of wool and began to wind wool onto the spindle, teasing out the sticky strands with her fingers.

"Ye always used to make seed cakes for Lughnasadh," Ella said casually, eventually breaking the silence. "Will ye do so this year?"

Gordana shrugged. "I let the younger women do the baking these days."

"Gordana," Ella said gently. "Please look at me."

An uncomfortable pause followed before Gordana complied. Her expression was guarded, her eyes colder than Ella had ever seen them.

"Do ye really believe I have manipulated yer brother?" Ella asked. She decided it was best to get straight to the point. She hadn't been deaf to the rumors that had been circulating the keep of late—no doubt thanks to Maggie. Folk whispered that she was a witch who kept Gavin captive with a vile spell.

It was dangerous talk, for Ella knew what people did to women they suspected of witchcraft. Only her position in Scorrybreac prevented them from stoning her, or worse. Two servant girls had spat on the ground after she passed them outdoors in the inner bailey that morning.

Not for the first time, oily fear pooled in the pit of her belly at the thought that everyone here might turn against her. Gavin was her only ally—and even he couldn't protect her if Maggie MacNichol incited mass hatred.

The rumors were gathering in intensity. Fear gripped Ella by the throat then as she remembered an elderly woman in Talasgair who'd been stoned to death after the locals had accused her of witchcraft. The rumors had to be stamped out.

"I don't know what to think," Gordana replied coolly. "I find it hard to believe that a woman who has dedicated her life to God can just change direction at a moment's notice."

"It wasn't like that," Ella replied quietly. "When I visited Scorrybreac during Ma's illness ... Kilbride was my life ... I couldn't see any other."

"What happened to change things then?"

Ella drew in a steadying breath. She didn't want to talk of the past, of the grief and pain that had nearly torn her to pieces, but if Gordana was ever to be her friend and ally again, she would need to.

"I loved yer brother," she said, her voice barely above a whisper, "and despite that I took my vows and dedicated my life to the Cluniac order, that feeling never went away. Love isn't something ye can just abandon ... although there have been times when I wish I could have."

Ella paused there. She could see she now had Gordana's full attention. The woman had stopped embroidering and was watching Ella steadily. There was no hostility in her gaze, but no warmth either.

"Shortly after I arrived at Kilbride, I realized I was with bairn," Ella continued. "The nuns let me stay on, allowing me to give birth within the abbey, but our son was born dead."

The words sounded barren, spoken so simply. Just a few sentences to encapsulate such pain, such loss. There were no words that would ever explain the grief that had consumed Ella after losing her son. She couldn't even begin to describe it now.

Gordana's gaze widened, the coldness disappearing as her eyes filled with tears. "No, Ella," she whispered. "Why did ye not send word?"

"Ye know why," Ella replied. "Foolishly, I thought our affair had been secret ... Gavin had a new life with Innis, and I didn't want to interfere. Telling him wouldn't change anything."

"Does he know now?"

"Aye ... I have told him everything."

The two women stared at each other for a long moment, before Gordana put aside her embroidery. Ella noted that her hands shook. She then moved to the stool next to Ella and placed her arms around her. "I'm so sorry," she whispered. "Ye must have felt so alone."

Ella swallowed. She didn't want to dwell on those dark days. "I did," she admitted, "but ye must believe me when I tell ye that none of this was planned. I hated leaving Kilbride and given the choice would have stayed there."

Gordana pulled back, her cheeks wet with tears. "Ye didn't want to wed Gavin then?"

Ella snorted. "It's not that ... yer mother talks as if I threw off my habit and ran naked into the sunset with yer brother without a second thought, but the situation was more complicated than that. Gavin agreed to wed me to save me from MacKinnon, and I agreed in order to save the abbess and the other nuns at Kilbride from MacKinnon's wrath." She paused there as she felt her own eyelids start to prickle.

Being with Gavin again, being able to touch him and kiss him, to drift off to sleep in his arms and awake cradled against his chest, made her so happy that she sometimes felt as if her heart would burst. She wasn't sure if she could describe such a feeling without weeping. "What I'm trying to say, is that both Gavin and I wed for other reasons ... but that doesn't alter the fact that we are meant for each other ... I feel as if I'm my best self when I'm at his side."

Gordana offered her a watery smile. "Despite all the tension since ye have returned, I've never seen him look happier. I'm sorry I've been so cold ... Ma has been filling my ears with awful stories about the two of ye over the past days. It's been wearing me down."

Ella smiled back. "So, are we friends again?"

Gordana covered Ella's hand with hers, squeezing hard. "Always."

Gavin went looking for his wife in the afternoon to find her resting in their bed-chamber.

Closing the door gently behind him, he moved across to the bed and sat down next to where Ella lay. She slept upon her side, still fully dressed in the cream-colored léine and dark-blue kirtle she'd donned that morning. However, she'd kicked off her slippers and unbound her hair. The long coppery tresses fell over the pillow in soft waves.

An ache rose in Gavin's chest at the sight of her.

Sleep had erased all the tension from her face; she looked young as a maid again, her full lips parted, her long lashes dark auburn against her smooth cheeks.

The past two weeks had been more difficult than he'd anticipated. His mother had launched a campaign against him and Ella, and had successfully turned most of the keep against them.

None of them were rude to his face, but he saw their expressions, the look in their eyes. He'd also heard the ridiculous yet damaging rumors his mother had spread about Ella being a witch. He'd have laughed them off if he didn't know just how determined his mother could be when thwarted. He'd never seen her so bitter.

The time was coming when he'd have to make a decision about Maggie MacNichol. If she remained at Scorrybreac, she risked causing even greater trouble.

Ella stirred then, her eyelashes fluttering against her cheeks. "Have I slept long?" she murmured, her sea-blue eyes fixing upon him.

"I don't think so," he replied with a smile.

"What have ye been up to?" she asked, covering her mouth as she gave a small yawn. She then propped herself up onto an elbow. This kirtle was low-cut, revealing a deep, creamy cleavage.

"I've spent the afternoon dealing out justice to two men caught stealing cattle," Gavin replied. He reached out, brushing the upper swell of her breast with the back of his hand.

"What happened?"

"Some folk want them hung for the crime." Gavin began to unlace the bodice of her kirtle. "But I've ordered a flogging instead."

"Really?" Ella looked up at him, her gaze veiled, her breathing coming faster now. "Why is that?"

Gavin's mouth curved. "Cattle-rustling is a crime to be sure," he replied. "But I'd rather save hangings for outlaws and cutthroats."

Her gaze shadowed at his words. "It must be difficult to make such decisions."

"It's the lot of a clan-chief, mo ghràdh."

"And I'm sure ye do an admirable job."

He stopped unlacing her kirtle, his hand straying to her cheek. His chest constricted then as a tendril of fear spiraled up within him. He'd done his best to mend the damage his mother had wrought, yet he had seen the baleful looks some within the keep gave his wife when they thought he wasn't looking. "I wish the folk here were more accepting of ye, love. It's been a trying time for ye, and I'm sorry for it."

Ella caught his hand and pressed a soft, sensual kiss to his palm. "As ye said, we shall weather it," she murmured. "Gordana and I have spoken today ... we are friends again."

A little of the tension that had followed Gavin around these days like a heavy mantle eased, as did his fear. "I'm glad," he replied. "Although I always thought my sister too clever to allow my mother to influence her."

"Yer mother is a forceful woman, as ye well know."

"She won't win this ... I promise ye," he replied, his voice hardening.

Ella's mouth curved. "I know."

Gavin pulled her into his arms then, covering her mouth with his. Ella's softness, the perfume of her hair and skin, enveloped his senses, and made the rest of the world—and all its cares—fade. Suddenly, nothing else existed but the two of them upon this rainy late-summer afternoon.

He kissed her hungrily, his lips and tongue exploring her mouth before his hands returned to the laced bodice of her kirtle.

He continued his work, removing the garment before his hands slid down the length of her and caught the hem of her léine.

Ella helped him remove it, wriggling out of the léine and the thin tunic she wore underneath so that she sat naked upon the bed.

Gavin's breathing hitched at the sight of her. He'd looked upon Ella's nakedness many times since their wedding night, and yet it was never enough. His gaze drew it all in: her smooth, shapely limbs; the lush swell of her breasts; the gentle curve of her belly; and the womanly dip of her waist.

Never taking his gaze from her, Gavin rose from the bed and started to undress.

And all the while, Ella watched him. He loved how boldly she did so, her lips parting when he cast aside his léine and began to unlace his braies. A soft sigh escaped her as he stood before her naked—her breathing hitching when her attention traveled down his torso and rested upon his groin.

Lord, how he loved her lustiness, the fact that her passion for him equaled what he felt for her.

They came together with a hunger that made a growl rise in Gavin's throat. Ella wound her arms around his neck, clinging to him as they collapsed upon the bed, mouths devouring, bodies entwining.

Gavin's hands slid down her back, cupping her buttocks. He pulled her hard against him, grinding their hips together. Ella gasped and bit his lower lip, her fingernails raking down his back. She wriggled under him, spreading her legs and arching her pelvis up.

"Please, Gavin," she gasped. "Now ... I want ye, now."

He'd planned to pleasure her for a while, to feast upon her body while she gasped and sighed his name. But Ella's urgency set Gavin's blood aflame, filled him with the ache to possess her.

He kneed her thighs apart and drove into her, groaning as her heat consumed him, as she drew him in.

Ella wrapped her legs around his hips, arching high with each thrust, while Gavin held himself up above her, watching her face transform.

She lost herself in their lovemaking: her cheeks flushed, her lips parted, and her eyes turned dark with passion. Her hair was now in disarray, spread out around her like a cloud. She grasped his biceps, nails digging in with each thrust.

Gavin could feel her core tightening around his shaft, and felt the ripples of her pleasure when she cried out, her body arching back against the bed.

It was too much. He'd wanted to take his time this afternoon, but this coupling was to be wild, fierce. It didn't matter if everyone upon this isle turned against them; they still had each other.

With each thrust, Gavin claimed her. With each thrust, he reminded them both that the promises they'd made to each other would not be broken this time.

Ella was his. She would always be his, and nothing besides death itself would part them.

"Ella!" Gavin gasped and closed his eyes and let go—let everything go. Shuddering, he spilled within her.

31

Bull's Eye

THE SUN CAME out for Lughnasadh. Ella was grateful it did, and pleased for the folk of Scorrybreac too, who had waited all summer for the chance to eat, drink, and enjoy the games.

The festivities took place upon a grassy area behind the village, a space that had not been used for growing food. An old oak grew in one corner, its boughs stretching out like embracing arms. Children played under it, their laughter mingling with the trilling sound of a bone whistle—a merry jig that a few young couples now danced to.

Ella moved through the crowd, her arm looped around Gavin's.

It felt good to be outdoors, away from the whispers and pointed looks inside the keep. The villagers were a merrier lot, too full of high spirits and excitement to bother with staring at the clan-chief and his new wife.

The savory aroma of food wafted across the pasture. A number of village women were dishing out breads and pies. Soon the games would begin in earnest, but before they did, the folk of Scorrybreac wished to fill their bellies.

Ella didn't blame them. The rich smell of venison was making her mouth water.

"Do ye want a pie, love?" Gavin asked, casting Ella a smile.

"Aye, please," she answered quickly. They had eaten simply but well at Kilbride, yet meat pie was not something the nuns got to enjoy, even on feast days.

Gavin's smile widened, and he left her to go and fetch the food.

On her own, Ella tensed a little. She preferred to be at Gavin's side these days, for the hissing and muttered comments ceased when he was about. She'd not told him about the servants spitting at her, for she knew the women would be punished if she did. Even so, the incident had made her wary of folk here. She had kept most of her fears to herself, as she knew Gavin worried for her—all the same, she was happier when her husband was present.

A few yards away, she spotted her father. Stewart Fraser held an untouched mutton pie and was deep in conversation with Gordana MacNichol. Seeing the two of them talking together, the warmth in her father's eyes as he spoke, Ella grew still.

Of course, little more than a decade separated the pair of them in age. Gordana's cheeks were slightly flushed, her gaze bright. Stewart and Gordana had lived under the same roof for years now, but with Cait Fraser's death, something had changed between them—Ella could sense it.

She was considering this change when she spied Maggie MacNichol making her way through the crowd. The sight of her mother-in-law made Ella grow tenser still. Unfortunately, she had to endure the woman at each mealtime in the Great Hall, but she did manage to avoid her at other times.

Yet not today.

Lady MacNichol wore an austere expression. She was dressed in a fine sky-blue kirtle that brought out the golden tones of her hair. Ella could see that Maggie had been a beauty in her youth, and would have still been a handsome woman if she hadn't allowed bitterness in. The harsh lines, creased brow, and compressed lips aged her.

Seeing Ella, Maggie straightened her already stiff posture further. She barked out a command to Gordana, breaking off her conversation with Stewart Fraser. With a murmured apology, Gordana dipped her head and moved to her mother's side. Maggie muttered something to her daughter, her expression severe. She then hauled Gordana right, so that they would avoid walking past her daughter-in-law.

Relief washed over Ella. She didn't mind being avoided. It was infinitely preferable to insults and barbed comments.

Gavin returned then with their pies. His boyish smile made Ella's chest constrict. Sometimes she loved Gavin MacNichol with such fierceness that the emotion scared her. Yet it occurred to her that she was shy when it came to voicing her feelings toward him. She wasn't sure why.

"Thank ye," she murmured, taking the pie he handed her.

"Be careful," he warned. "It's hot."

Moving through the crowd, side-by-side, and gingerly beginning their pies, they took in the surrounding merriment. To one side of where the food and drink was being served, men were setting up a ring for the strength contests, as well as targets for archery and knife-throwing.

Ella finished her pie and brushed crumbs off her fingers, her gaze settling upon the targets.

"Fancy yer chances in the knife-throwing contest?" Gavin asked. There was a teasing note to his voice, for he'd seen the direction of her gaze.

Ella inclined her head. "Ye don't think I'd compete?"

His gaze widened. "Ye would?"

Ella considered it. Doing so would shock everyone, village folk and retainers alike—but what did it matter? She was already unpopular here; why not give folk something real to gossip over? A slow smile spread over her face then. "I would."

Ella drew in a deep breath, her gaze fixing upon the bull's eye target in the distance. She'd made it through the first four rounds, and with each round the targets had been moved back—starting at seven feet and now at sixteen feet.

Only three contestants had reached the final round: Ella, Ceard, and a wiry young warrior named Iver.

A huge crowd had gathered around them now, heads straining forward, while bairns peeked out from between their father's legs and mother's skirts.

By now, all had heard that Lady Ella was competing at knife throwing.

Initially, Ella had weathered some jeering. A few of the warriors had laughed before Gavin stopped them with a glare.

And then, when she made it through the first round, the grins and smothered mirth stopped.

Ella was aware that Maggie MacNichol had pushed her way up to the front of the crowd and was now looking on. Next to her stood Gordana, her cheeks flushed and gaze gleaming. She'd cheered Ella on at the end of each round, only to earn vicious looks from her mother. Ella was pleased to see that Gordana had ignored her mother's glares; their conversation the day before had mended things between them, and it appeared that Gordana had thought on the matter further since then.

Blair and his wife were watching too. Both of them wore bemused expressions.

Catching Gavin's eye, they shared a smile. Then, her husband winked.

Ella turned back to the target, deliberately shutting everyone out as she focused. Around her waist, Ella wore a belt with her throwing knives. She had thrown five during each round: twelve-inch blades with slender wooden handles.

Readying herself to throw, Ella positioned herself with one leg before the other, her weight resting on the leg opposite her throwing arm. She then raised the knife, gripping it by the handle, presenting it at the target. She sighted the target and brought the blade back behind her shoulder.

Around her the crowd hushed. Ella kept her eye on the target, swung the knife in an arcing motion, and released it at the arc's zenith. The knife flew easily from her hand, completing two full spins before it thudded into the target.

A grin spread across Ella's face.

Bull's eye.

It had taken her years to master blade throwing. Every afternoon, before Vespers, Mother Shona had taken her through endless drills.

Let the knife slip easily from yer hand. Do not whip yer wrist. Follow through. Transfer yer weight from the front to the back foot during the throw.

Mother Shona's instructions came back to her as she readied to throw her second blade. She'd been clumsy at first when she'd started with the knives, but the abbess assured her that she had a steady hand and a keen eye.

Forget the other weapons, the abbess had told her. *Make blades yer specialty.*

And she had. When Ella had finally gotten to the point where she knew where her knife would find its mark, a feeling quite unlike any other had filtered through her. She'd never been as good at anything as she was at this. She knew that if she was ever called upon to defend herself, or the other sisters, she wouldn't let them down.

Four more blades hit the target, each within the bull's eye.

Ceard was good, but one of his knives strayed outside the bull's eye line, making Ella the winner.

A roar went up amongst the crowd; men and women cheered while Gavin walked across to Ella, gathered her up in his arms, and kissed her for all to see. The cheering grew louder till it became nothing but a roar in Ella's ears.

Her cheeks were warm when Gavin set her down. His arm curled protectively around her waist as he did so, before he turned to the crowd and raised a hand, signaling that he wished to speak.

The applause died away. "For those of ye who have not yet been acquainted with my wife, I present Lady Ella of Scorrybreac to ye all," he called out, his voice ringing over the hillside. "A woman who stole my heart many years ago, but who has now returned to me ... returned to us all." Gavin paused there, his gaze sweeping over the now-silent crowd of onlookers. "I wish ye to all welcome her into yer hearts, for she is a kind and talented woman who will rule MacNichol lands at my side."

Smiles and applause followed these words, and for the first time since her return to the castle, Ella felt welcome. It warmed her to see friendly gazes upon her. It was a good day to stand before the folk of Scorrybreac. The sun was shining, they had the day off work, and their bellies were full of food and drink. It was easy to accept a newcomer into their midst on a day such as this one; it was easier to like a woman who'd arrived under a cloud of scandal when they could spend the day doing as they pleased.

"What kind of woman throws knives?" A harsh female voice cut through the applause, causing it to die away. All gazes shifted from the clan-chief and his wife to the tall, statuesque figure of Maggie MacNichol, who still stood at the edge of the crowd. Unlike Gordana and Blair, who'd been smiling along with the rest of the onlookers, Ella's mother-in-law's face was pale and taut. Her eyes blazed with fury. "An unnatural woman. Didn't I tell ye all that my husband has wed a consort of the devil?"

A shocked hush followed these words, and Ella felt the cloak of contentment that had briefly settled over her shoulders slough away. Maggie MacNichol would give her no peace, not even today. She was determined to bring her low, and she would use whatever means.

"Mother," Gavin growled. "I warn ye now ... cease talking or ye shall regret it."

Maggie ignored her son. Instead, her gaze was riveted upon Ella. She raised a finger, pointing it at her. "Look upon her ... can ye all not see how she has ensnared my son? She has blinded him with her wiles, but no lady knows how to wield a blade like that. She is unnatural, I tell ye. She is a witch!"

"A bold assertion, my Lady." A loud voice boomed through the crowd before Gavin had the chance to answer. "We shall see if there is any truth in it."

A heartbeat later a portly figure swathed in black, astride a finely bedecked mule, rode into their midst. An iron crucifix gleamed upon the man's breast, and a row of tonsured monks in black habits shuffled on foot after him.

Ella stared, her lips parting as shock rippled through her.

Abbot Camron.

She hadn't seen him in nearly a decade. The abbot had only made one trip to Kilbride in her time there; he and his monks had stayed nearly three months, and all the nuns—including Ella—had been relieved to see him go.

One look at Abbot Camron's high-colored, pugnacious face, and the last shreds of Ella's buoyant mood disintegrated.

There was only one reason why the Abbot of Crossraguel—a Cluniac monastery located in Carrick, southwest Scotland—would be visiting Scorrybreac.

He had been called here.

32

All Lies

"I'M THE MACNICHOL clan-chief." Gavin stepped forward, his brow furrowing. "What brings ye to Scorrybreac ... abbot?"

"Good day, MacNichol." The newcomer inclined his head, acknowledging Gavin. Then with the help of two monks, he dismounted from his mule. The beast—bedecked with bells, silver ornaments, and tassels—snorted as if relieved to be free of its burden. "I am Abbot Camron of Crossraguel Abbey." The newcomer's attention shifted to where Ella stood behind her husband. "Unfortunately, I have been hailed here to deal with an errant nun."

Gavin's frown deepened. "On whose summons?"

"MacKinnon," the abbot replied, his tone haughty. "He advised us that something of great concern to the order had occurred at Kilbride."

"And have ye been to the abbey?"

Abbot Camron's full lips thinned. He didn't enjoy being questioned by the MacNichol clan-chief. Having spent time with the man, Ella knew how the abbot preferred to be in control of any given situation. During his visit to Kilbride, the sisters had ceased their arms training. However, Abbot Camron and Mother Shona had butted heads on a number of occasions; he had disapproved of what he called her 'lenient ways'.

"Not yet," he replied, his tone clipped. "MacKinnon's missive concerned me so much that I was compelled to travel directly here." He paused, his dark eyes now boring into Ella. "And I see that I was right to do so."

His gaze raked down Ella, taking in her knife belt and the target full of blades a few feet away. "What devilry has taken place here?"

Ella folded her arms across her chest and held the abbot's gaze. How fortunate she had been in Mother Shona over the years; the monks who followed Abbot Camron were a cowed lot. They stood now, clustered together, heads bent as if the abbot's very presence made them nervous.

"There hasn't been any devilry," Ella replied. She was surprised how calm, how dispassionate, her voice was. Underneath she could feel her temper starting to simmer, yet she wouldn't let the abbot see it, for he'd only wield it as a weapon against her. "It's simply the day of Lughnasadh, and we are playing games."

"Ye are throwing knives?" the abbot countered, his tone sharpening. "The Lady speaks true." He acknowledged Maggie MacNichol then with an approving nod. "It is unnatural. How is it ye know such a skill?"

Ella stared back at him. She wouldn't tell him of Mother Shona, and of all the skills she'd taught the Sisters of Kilbride over the years. The abbot would suffer a fit of apoplexy if he ever found out—and the abbess would be punished, perhaps even cast from the order.

Ella would never put Mother Shona at risk.

"It is a pastime I have always enjoyed," she answered. "When I was a lass, I used to practice in secret, although the opportunity to do so at Kilbride was obviously limited. I preferred instead to devote my attention to Christ."

"Devote yerself to Christ? The truth is that ye are a wicked woman, Annella Fraser." The abbot's voice became chill. "MacKinnon told me that ye tried to stab him to death, and that ye then fled, fornicated with MacNichol, and forced him to wed ye. Worse still, ye didn't repent yer sins. The Abbess of Kilbride had no choice but to cast yer corrupting influence from the abbey."

"MacKinnon lies." Gavin's voice lashed through the humid afternoon air. "He attacked Ella … he would have raped her if she hadn't defended herself."

Ella stepped forward and placed a hand on Gavin's arm. She appreciated him defending her and shared his outrage. Yet this was a battle she had to fight herself. Their gazes locked and held for a long moment. Ella saw his struggle, noted how his jaw bunched, but he eventually gave a curt nod and held his tongue, allowing Ella to face the abbot on her own.

"MacKinnon entered my bed-chamber at Dunan," she said, her voice low and strong. Nonetheless, it galled her to have spell this all out. "He threatened me and tried to force himself upon me. I did what I had to in order to get away from him. As for the rest of the tale … my husband speaks true. They are all lies. I never broke my vows. After Mother Shona cast me from the order, Gavin MacNichol offered me protection, and I accepted him."

Abbot Camron stared back at her before his lip curled. "Ye were lovers?"

Ella nodded. "Once … many years ago … before I joined the order. But then MacNichol wed my sister, and I took my vows. I did *not* break them."

Her words faded, and the crowd that had grown larger still since the arrival of Abbot Camron and his monks shifted. Many of the faces of those watching the scene unfold looked uncomfortable. Both Gordana and Blair were frowning at the abbot, while Ella's father glared openly at him.

Stewart Fraser's meaty hands were clenched at his side. He looked as if he wished to launch himself at Abbot Camron and pummel his face into a bloody pulp. Anxiety pumped through Ella at the thought. She couldn't let him.

The abbot was enraged. His fury rippled out from him as he drew his bulky figure up, squaring his shoulders. His face had gone the color of a ripe damson, his eyes glittered with the force of his outrage.

"Annella Fraser," he ground out. Ella noted that once again he used her maiden name. He refused to acknowledge her union with Gavin. "Ye are indeed a consort of the devil. This brief interview is all I need to condemn ye as a witch. Such a woman is dangerous and cannot be allowed to live." The abbot broke off there. "Who here has the courage to do the Lord's work? She must be stripped naked and burned at the stake, only then will her wickedness be purged from the earth."

Shocked gasps followed this outburst.

A wave of dizziness washed over Ella, and the world tilted. For a moment, she thought she might faint.

Reaching for Gavin's arm, she clung to him.

The abbot took a menacing step toward her, one hand clasping the crucifix about his neck, while the other pointed at her. "Ye will burn ... only then will yer soul be cleansed."

"Enough!" Gavin stepped in front of Ella, shielding her from the abbot's wrath. "One more poisonous word, and I'll shove yer teeth down yer throat."

"Satan lives within this woman," Abbot Camron continued, ranting now. "She has sinned grievously and will not repent. She must die. She must—"

Gavin didn't utter another warning. Instead, he lunged forward and slugged the abbot in the mouth with his fist.

Abbot Camron staggered back, eyes bulging. His hands went to his mouth, and he stumbled once more, sinking onto his haunches. When he removed his fingers, Ella saw blood leaking from between his lips. It trickled down his chin.

Gavin loomed over him, his right fist still clenched. "As I told ye, abbot, ye are grossly misinformed." The words were spoken in a low, threatening voice. "MacKinnon has filled yer head with lies ... and like the bigot ye are, ye believed every one of them." Gavin paused, letting his words sink in. "But now, it is I who should inform ye that ye are trespassing on my land. And if ye and this murder of crows that follow ye do not depart this instant, I shall have ye stripped and stoned as ye flee ... is that clear?"

The abbot merely stared up at Gavin, his eyes glittering with hate.

"Is ... that ... clear?" Gavin repeated.

Ella watched her husband, shocked by his brutality. She hadn't realized Gavin was capable of such violence. Yet she wasn't sorry he had lashed out. The abbot had spewed ugly words, accusations that could incite an angry mob if not quashed. Gavin knew that, hence his harshness.

He'd told Ella he wouldn't let any harm befall her, and he was now showing her that he'd meant his promise. The abbot and his monks would indeed be stripped and stoned if they didn't obey him.

Slowly, Abbot Camron nodded. Moments passed, and then the abbot heaved himself to his feet. He was trembling, both in fear and rage, while behind him one of his monks started to whimper.

No one said a word as the abbot, with the assistance of three monks, clambered back on his mule. Then he and his flock turned and departed in the direction they'd come, the crowd closing behind them.

A heavy silence settled over the field once they'd gone.

Tearing her gaze from the direction that the abbot had disappeared in, Ella saw that Gavin's expression hadn't softened. Instead, he was glaring at his mother.

Maggie MacNichol's face appeared carven from stone. Her grey eyes were flint-hard as she stared back at her son.

"Ye contacted MacKinnon, Ma," Gavin said, splintering the tension. "Didn't ye?"

His mother's lip curled. "Someone had to."

"And why's that?"

"This business ... ye wedding yer sister-in-law ... a nun ... it's unseemly. Ye have brought our family low, Gavin. Ye have tarnished us all."

Gavin held her gaze. Ella felt the arm she gripped tense. "This ends here, Ma," he said roughly. "Long have I put up with yer venom, but now it risks poisoning us all. Ye would destroy Scorrybreac in yer quest to control it ... to control me."

"Has she fed ye this nonsense?" Maggie countered, casting Ella a look of pure hatred. "This *whore*."

"Ye have insulted Ella for the last time," Gavin cut in. He twisted then, catching Ceard's gaze. The warrior stood on the edge of the crowd with a group of Gavin's most trusted men. "Escort my mother to the Isle of Raasay," he instructed coldly. "Tell my uncle that she is to remain there. I never want to see her at Scorrybreac ever again."

Shock rippled across the crowd. Even Ceard, who was usually unflappable, gaped at the clan-chief.

Ella stared at Gavin as if she were seeing him for the first time. She couldn't believe it. He was sending his mother into exile.

Love for Gavin MacNichol surged through her—the emotion so strong that Ella's breathing hitched. She realized then why she'd held back in expressing how she felt for him. There had been a kernel of fear within her that for all his promises, Gavin might let her down again.

But now he'd proved to her that he never would.

"Ye can't send me away, Gavin." Maggie MacNichol's voice, harsh now, slashed through the shocked chatter, dousing it. "I won't go."

Gavin inclined his head, fixing his mother with a long look. In response, the woman's throat bobbed, her cheeks flushing. It was the first time Ella had ever seen Maggie look unsure of herself. Suddenly, she realized—too late—that she'd pushed her son beyond his limits.

"Let me put it this way," he replied gently. "Ye can either depart from Scorrybreac upon yer palfrey with yer dignity intact ... or I'll have ye hog-tied and thrown over the back of a mule for yer departure. Either way, ye are leaving at first light tomorrow."

33

Fear Not

MOTHER SHONA'S HEART sank when she spied Abbot Camron. The noon meal had just concluded, and the nuns were filing out of the kirk, heading toward their sleeping quarters, where they would rest a while before beginning their afternoon chores.

The sight of the heavy-set figure riding toward her upon a mule, his monks shuffling in his wake, made a heavy sigh rise up within the abbess.

It had taken many days for the atmosphere in the abbey to calm after MacKinnon's disruption. Now, the abbot risked upsetting the sisters again. His visit a decade earlier had been three of the most unpleasant months she'd ever passed. Yet she instinctively knew that his appearance at Kilbride now had nothing to do with paying the abbey a visit.

The abbess halted, watching as the abbot struggled off his long-suffering steed, and turned to her.

"Peace be upon ye, Father," she greeted him with a tight smile. "How unexpected … we did not receive prior word of yer arrival."

"Peace be upon ye, Mother," the abbot mumbled through swollen lips. "That's because I did not send it."

Close up, the abbess saw that Abbot Camron had received a harsh blow to the mouth. His lips were swollen and encrusted with scabs.

"Our Holy Father," she murmured. "Were ye set upon by outlaws?"

"No," the abbot snarled before wincing. Reaching up, he dabbed a handkerchief to his mouth. It came away bloody, for one of the scabs had just split open once more. "Gavin MacNichol, curse him to hell, is responsible."

Shocked murmurs followed these words as the monks, who had halted behind the abbot, started to whisper amongst themselves.

"Silence, ye chattering fools," the abbot growled, dabbing his mouth again. He then shifted his attention fully upon the abbess.

Mother Shona felt herself stiffen under his scrutiny. Abbot Camron had small, dark eyes that reminded her of a bird of prey. They gleamed now as he observed her. "I've just come from Scorrybreac."

"MacKinnon contacted ye?" A heaviness settled over the abbess. She should have realized that the clan-chief would do so; he'd certainly been angry enough when he'd left Kilbride. Surprisingly, no one in Torrin had betrayed them, not even the priest. Nonetheless, the abbess knew he'd learn that Gavin and Ella had wed sooner or later. Skye wasn't large enough for such events to go unnoticed.

"Of course he did!" The abbot spat out the words, his ruddy cheeks deepening in color even further. "As ye should have, Mother Shona."

"I saw no need. I dealt with Sister Annella as I saw fit."

The abbot drew himself up. "Ye take too much upon yerself, abbess. The nun had taken her vows of perpetuity. Ye could not cast her from the order without requesting permission from the Holy See."

The abbess frowned, her irritation rising. "There was no time for that. We live far from Rome, abbot … I had to make a decision, for the welfare of this abbey."

"The Pope will hear of this," the abbot ground out the words, his portly frame vibrating with fury now. "I will write to him … I will inform him of yer arrogance … yer *incompetence*."

Mother Shona let out a long, measured breath. She'd been ready to invite the abbot and his monks in. They all looked hungry and travel-weary. Yet Abbot Camron's threat made her temper flare. After her election, she'd worked hard to strengthen Kilbride over the years; the previous abbess had left it weak and impoverished.

She knew she was unorthodox in her views—and if the abbot knew the full extent of her activities, he'd have written to the Holy See years earlier to demand her removal—but she had always served God faithfully.

"Well, if ye intend to do so, I won't keep ye," she replied crisply. "Good day, abbot … if ye travel hard, ye should make Dunan by nightfall."

Abbot Camron's face stiffened. "We are remaining here overnight."

The abbess made a clicking noise with her tongue before shaking her head. "I'm afraid not. Since ye find me arrogant and incompetent, I feel it wouldn't be right to invite ye into the abbey overnight. Ye should continue on yer journey and find lodgings somewhere that is less offensive to ye. May peace be upon ye."

The abbot's cheeks deepened to puce. Glaring at the abbess, he drew his robes around him, turned, and attempted to mount his mule. The beast sidestepped, the ornaments and bells that adorned it jingling, before it let out an ear-splitting whinny; it wasn't like the sound of a horse, but rather a strangled noise that sounded like someone was sawing wood with a blunt iron saw.

"Help me, ye fools!" The abbot wheezed. An instant later two monks were at his side, helping him into the saddle.

Watching him go, Mother Shona felt a pang of misgiving.

I shouldn't have done that.

Sometimes she forgot she possessed a fiery temper. Life in the order had softened her, as had the passing years, yet the sin of pride occasionally raised its head.

Abbot Camron wasn't a man to make an enemy of. He was haughty and petty. She'd just humiliated him, and he wouldn't forget it easily.

Once the abbot and his monks had disappeared, the abbess heaved a sigh and turned away from the gates.

For years she'd managed to keep the peace here at Kilbride, but a sense of foreboding settled over her now. The incident with Ella had set things in motion that couldn't be stopped. The abbey had two enemies now: MacKinnon and Abbot Camron. She would need to be wary of giving either of those men further offense.

A chill wind whipped through the abbey then, tugging at the abbess's habit and veil. The sky had darkened, and the scent of rain was in the air.

Despite herself, Mother Shona allowed a grim smile to curve her mouth. It looked as if Abbot Camron was about to get a soaking on his way to Dunan.

What a shame.

"Mother Shona." A voice hailed her, and she turned to see a small figure hurry across to her.

"Sister Leanna," Mother Shona greeted the young woman with a frown, waiting while the nun knelt in front of her before she made the sign of the cross to bless her. "Ye shouldn't be outdoors at this hour."

"I know, Mother Shona." Leanna rose to her feet, her gaze pleading. "But I had to speak to ye ... when the other sisters weren't present."

The abbess inclined her head. "What is it, Sister?"

"Sister Ella ... Ella ... brought back a message for me from Dunan," Sister Leanna replied hastily. "She wanted me to warn ye and my father when I was ready."

The abbess tensed at these words but didn't reply. After a brief pause, the novice continued. Her voice was unusually high-pitched, betraying her nervousness. "As ye know, MacKinnon wished to wed me ... but my father was against the match and sent me here so that I would be free of him."

Mother Shona nodded. Niall MacDonald of Sleat had been wise to protect his daughter from MacKinnon. Apart from Sisters Ella and Coira—whom the novice had confided in—they'd decided to keep this news from the other nuns. Sister Leanna was leaving her past behind her, after all.

Sister Leanna's gaze grew haunted. "Ella told me that MacKinnon intends to come for me ... he gave her a message. He says that the walls of Kilbride will not protect me. Sooner or later I will be his wife." The nun paused, dropping her gaze. "When his men searched the abbey for Ella, I hid in the pig sty."

The abbess grew still. Alarm filtered through her. The news shouldn't have surprised her, yet it did. Of course, MacKinnon had wed Siusan Campbell after being thwarted by Niall MacDonald. Unfortunately, he was now free to wed again—and he had not forgotten Lady Leanna.

Troubled, Mother Shona resisted the urge to mutter an ungodly curse. Life had become increasingly difficult of late. She didn't like that MacKinnon had yet another reason to disturb their peace.

"He cannot touch ye here, child," she said finally, hoping that her voice didn't betray the unease that simmered in her breast. "Next year ye shall take yer perpetual vows."

Did she imagine it or did Sister Leanna's hazel eyes shadow at that? Mother Shona knew that coming to live at Kilbride had not been the lass's choice, yet she had adapted well to life here. The abbess had thought she was content in her decision, but maybe she wasn't.

"Yer father would never permit the union," Mother Shona continued. She reached out and placed a comforting hand upon Sister Leanna's arm. "Fear not."

Sister Leanna's chin firmed, and she managed a wan smile. "Thank ye, Mother Shona. I apologize for burdening ye."

"And I'm glad ye shared this news with me," the abbess replied. "Go now and get some rest. We have archery practice this afternoon."

Sister Leanna nodded before turning and hurrying away.

Mother Shona watched her go, misgiving settling upon her.

This was ill-news indeed. She hadn't realized that MacKinnon still wanted the lass. He was a strangely obsessive man; once his mind fixed upon something, he would never give it up. It made her fear him a little.

I need to increase our training sessions, she counseled herself as she turned on her heel and set off across the yard. *The sisters must be ready to defend themselves if the need should arise.*

The abbess entered her hall, a narrow annex that abutted the refectory. Stepping inside the dimly lit space, she felt her shoulders lower, a little of the day's tension draining from her. This was her sanctuary, a quiet space where she could let herself relax. In this place, she wasn't 'Mother Shona', but just merely 'Shona of Lismore'.

Her hall was sparsely furnished, with a desk and chair at one end and a narrow sleeping pallet at the other, shielded from view by a heavy curtain. A large hearth, unlit at this hour, sat alongside one wall, flanked by two high-backed wooden chairs. Mother Shona lowered herself onto one.

A sense of disquiet settled over her, causing her belly to tense and her breathing to quicken. Kilbride had been her life's work. She had poured her passion, her soul, into making it strong, into making the women who lived within its walls independent and learned.

But now, a shadow had fallen over them. Dunan was half a day's ride away, yet it now felt as if MacKinnon lived far too close. There had been times over the years when she'd almost forgotten that the abbey sat on MacKinnon lands—but of late she'd received a sharp reminder.

Difficult times lay ahead, she sensed it in her bones.

Epilogue

Remember But Look Ahead

ELLA SWUNG UP onto the courser's back, a smile spreading across her face. It felt good to sit astride a horse. She knew it wasn't 'ladylike', but she preferred this style. She'd never enjoyed riding sidesaddle.

"Ready?"

Ella turned to see Gavin smiling at her. He'd already mounted Saorsa and was awaiting her. Gavin had gifted her the leggy bay gelding. She'd named the horse Fàd—Peat—for his coat was so dark brown it almost appeared black in certain lights.

Nodding, Ella gathered up the reins. "Let's go."

They clip-clopped out of the inner bailey, through the high stone arch, and into the rectangular-shaped outer bailey beyond. It was a windy morning, and gusts blew straw around the wide space as lads mucked out stables and a servant girl threw grain for the geese and fowl that roamed the outer bailey.

Folk waved as they passed, and both Gavin and Ella acknowledged them. Spying the warmth on the faces of Scorrybreac's retainers, their ready smiles, a sense of belonging settled over Ella.

Maggie MacNichol had departed two days earlier, and the moment she had, it was as if a shadow lifted from Scorrybreac. The woman hadn't gone quietly. Her shrill voice had echoed across the castle and beyond while Ceard and the other warriors escorted her out.

And with Lady MacNichol's departure, the cruel whispers and cold glances ceased. Those women who'd been influenced by Gavin's mother lost their leader. Overnight, their manner toward Ella softened. No longer did the ladies rise from their sewing and embroidery, mutter excuses, and hurry off when Ella approached. No longer did servants sneer and turn their backs upon her.

Of course, everyone had witnessed the ugly scene with Abbot Camron, and the one that followed with Lady MacNichol afterward. They'd seen Ella throw knives during the games and defend herself verbally against the abbot—and they'd seen Gavin's harshness toward those who crossed him, toward those who threatened his wife.

It wasn't a lesson any of them were likely to forget soon.

Ella's attention shifted ahead to where Gavin urged Saorsa on. He'd tied his thick blond hair back at his nape this morning, and a cloak hung from his broad shoulders. The warmth of summer was indeed fading, and as such, both she and Gavin had donned plaid cloaks for their ride. The mantle emphasized the strength and breadth of Gavin's shoulders, his straight yet relaxed posture in the saddle.

Excitement fluttered in the base of Ella's belly at the sight of him. Gavin had always been handsome and charismatic, but ever since Lughnasadh, she'd found him irresistible. It shocked her a little that she'd liked seeing the ruthless edge to his character. He was a fair, kind-hearted man, but he wasn't to be crossed. Her chest constricted then.

Lord, how she adored him.

Up ahead Gavin waved to his brother. Blair was in the midst of shoeing an ill-tempered horse. The beast nipped and kicked at him as he struggled with it. Sweat trickled down Blair's red face when he glanced up and grunted a greeting.

Gavin led the way out of the castle, under the portcullis, and down the causeway to the village. Ella followed close at his heels. Although the wind was cold, she enjoyed the feel of it on her face. They had been riding a few times since their return to Scorrybreac, but this outing was special; this time they were alone. Not even Ceard accompanied them.

As soon as they left Scorrybreac behind, Gavin urged his mare into a swift canter. Ella did the same, and moments later, they were racing southwest over undulating hills toward the thick woodland that filled a shallow inland vale.

The excitement continued to tighten within Ella's belly as she rode. They hadn't spoken of today's destination, yet she knew where Gavin was headed.

They were going to a place where she hadn't set foot in eighteen years—a place where their story had begun.

The clearing in the heart of the copse of birches looked exactly the same. The burn still trickled across mossy rocks. It was as if time had stood still there.

Glancing around her, Ella drew Fàd up. It was sheltered in the glade, the gusting wind hardly seemed to touch them.

Wordlessly, both she and Gavin dismounted, tying their horses up to a coppicing tree.

Picking up her skirts, Ella walked into the center of the clearing, her boots sinking into the carpet of soft moss that grew upon the banks of the burn. And as she stood there, all the memories she'd kept locked up for so many years flooded back.

Her breathing hitched, and when Gavin stepped up beside her, she turned to him, burying her face in his broad chest. In response, Gavin's arms encircled Ella's back, and he drew her close.

"I used to come back to this place sometimes," he murmured into her hair. "When life at Scorrybreac grew wearisome, I'd escape and lose myself in my memories. It made life easier to bear ... the knowledge that ye had once been part of my life."

"I tried not to think of this place," Ella admitted softly. "It was too painful."

"Ye are strong, Ella," he whispered, his fingers wreathing through her hair. "I always knew it."

"And stubborn," she reminded him with a wry smile he couldn't see. "Don't forget that."

His hands still entangled in her hair, Gavin gently pulled Ella's head back so that their gazes met. "I never thought this day would come," he whispered, his eyes gleaming, "that ye and I would stand together in this place again."

"And yet it did." Ella raised a hand and placed it over his heart. She could feel the strong, steady thud of his pulse against her palm. "I want to come back here often, Gavin. I don't want to ever forget the past, or about the fires we had to walk through to reach this point."

"I'll always have regrets," Gavin replied, a shadow passing over his face. "I don't think they will ever leave me."

"Some things we just have to live with," she murmured. "What's important is we learn."

His mouth curved. "*Meminisse sed providere: remember but look ahead.*"

"Aye," she replied softly. "The past is part of us ... as is Finn."

Gavin's gaze guttered at the mention of their son. Although they didn't speak often of the bairn, Ella knew that the loss weighed upon Gavin. She'd seen the devastation on his face when they'd stood in the graveyard together at Kilbride. She'd never planned on revealing her secret to him, but fate had forced her to. And now, although it hurt him to learn of Finn, she was glad she had.

There would be no secrets between them now.

"I love ye, Gavin MacNichol," she whispered, her voice trembling with the force of her feelings. "Every morning, I awake and thank the Lord for being so blessed. I couldn't wish for a better man than ye."

His lips parted at this, and his gaze shone. "I've longed to hear ye say that ye love me," he replied softly. "But I feared ... after everything I put ye through ... that I didn't deserve to hear the words."

"I've always loved ye," she said. Her eyes prickled with tears as she spoke. "I never once stopped."

Silence fell between them then, and when Gavin spoke, his voice was husky. "I want us to have a family. I don't know if it's possible ... but I wish for it nonetheless."

Ella smiled, although the expression was tinged with sadness. The same thought had also been on her mind of late. However, Ella wasn't sure if at thirty-six, she was too old now. Maybe that chance was lost forever. "I don't know if my womb will ever quicken again," she replied, her fingertips sliding down his chest to the hard planes of his belly. "Time will tell ..." Her smile turned wicked then. "But perhaps if we try hard enough, it may come to pass."

Gavin's lips curved, his gaze hooding in that sensual way that never failed to make desire kindle in the cradle of her hips. "If we *try* hard enough?"

Ella's pulse accelerated, and she leaned into him, her mouth grazing the column of his neck. "Let's start today," she murmured. "Right now."

Gavin didn't reply. Instead, with a grin, he scooped Ella up into his arms and carried her under the spreading boughs of an old birch.

The End

From the author

Wow, that was quite a start to the series! Gavin and Ella's story had me in tears more than once during the writing of this novel ... and I hope you enjoyed reading it as much as I loved writing it. I enjoyed exploring the idea that love can blossom from tragedy, and that it's never too late. Gavin and Ella needed their happy ending, and I wanted to give it to them.

Second chance romance is one of my favorite themes, but when you combine it with forbidden love, you get conflict at every turn and a bit of hand-wringing angst!

I've read a few romances that start in a convent or abbey over the years, and many of them portray the heroine trying to escape the confines of a religious life. I didn't want that to be Ella's story. I wanted her to have a strong faith that carries through the whole novel, and I wanted her experience at Kilbride to be a positive one; hence why I created the abbess, Mother Shona (she has her own story, which will be revealed as the series progresses) and her unorthodox ways.

I liked giving the Sisters of Kilbride different fighting skills. Why couldn't nuns learn to defend themselves? They lived in dangerous times, and I wanted to make Kilbride a place where women could flourish.

This story ended up having a lot of 'big' themes, making it far more emotional and heart-wrenching than I'd ever intended. It's also what makes this story so epic and sweeping. It doesn't matter what time period we're born into—people are people, and we all want love and to be loved in return. We all make mistakes, and sometimes we get a chance to put things right.

For those of you who have read my BRIDES OF SKYE series, you will remember that Gavin appeared in Book #3, THE ROGUE'S BRIDE. This story picks up one year after the conclusion of that series, and as such, much of the same historical context applies. Scotland had recently lost a major battle against the English, and as a result, times were tough. Near the start of UNFORGOTTEN, I also mention that the Black Death arrived in Scotland around this time ... more on this in later books in the series!

Kilbride Abbey never existed on the Isle of Skye, so to make it authentic I researched contemporary Cluniac abbeys of the time. Likewise, Dunan (although an actual location on Skye) is entirely a figment of my imagination. I needed a suitable stronghold for the MacKinnons and like to think something similar to Dunan might have existed.

Scorrybreac, however, did exist. It was the MacNichol stronghold although the castle was likely to have been a bit smaller than the one I describe. These days nothing but scattered ruins remain of it.

Of course, anyone who knows about medieval marriage law will realize that I've taken liberties with this novel. The law of 'affinity' existed in medieval times—which prevented widowed men and women from marrying their brother or sister-in-law. Unlike today, once you married into a family, they officially became your 'blood' relatives. The only way around this was to obtain Papal dispensation (a lengthy and costly procedure). Gavin and Ella already break taboos in this story—so I thought they might as well do it in style! Hence, I have allowed them their happy ending, which the church would have otherwise forbidden.

All the clans that I mention in this book (except the Frasers) were actual clans of the time upon the Isle of Skye in the 14th Century. Malcolm MacLeod was a real clan-chief, although all the other chieftains and clan-chiefs (including our hero, Gavin, and the nasty Duncan MacKinnon) are fictitious.

Get ready for Leanna and Ross's story up next—it's an exciting one!

Jayne x

Acknowledgments

Many people deserve thanks for this one. First of all my husband Tim, who edits all my books. We make a great team!

Thanks to Deb, for her help with getting the religious facts right (any errors remaining are entirely mine!).

I'm also immensely grateful to RWNZ (Romance Writers of New Zealand) and especially the Otago/Southland chapter. This organization and its wonderful members have been a constant source of inspiration and encouragement. I attended the RWNZ 2016 conference, and it lit a fire under me. I decided then and there that I would make becoming a full-time author my goal—one that I've now achieved. I don't think I could have done it if I hadn't seen others achieving the same thing!

Awoken

Book Two
The Sisters of Kilbride

Jayne Castel

Map

A misty morning may become a clear day.
—Scottish proverb

Prologue

A Pact with the Devil

Dunan broch
MacKinnon Territory
Isle of Skye, Scotland

Spring, 1349 AD

ROSS STARED AT the clan-chief, shock transforming into incredulity. Surely, he'd misheard? The man he'd served loyally for nearly fifteen years had just ordered him to abduct a nun.

"MacKinnon," he said finally before clearing his throat. "Tell me ye aren't serious about this?"

"I am," Duncan MacKinnon replied. He turned, from where he stood at the window to his solar, and fixed Ross with a gimlet stare that the warrior knew well. "Niall MacDonald is dead. It's time to act."

Ross's gaze shifted from the clan-chief, to the man who stood a few feet away. Red-faced, his leathers caked in mud from the journey, the messenger's chest heaved. He was still out of breath from his flight here from Duncaith and his sprint up the stairs to deliver the message. His name was Aodh, and he was a MacKinnon spy who'd lived among the MacDonalds of Sleat for the past three winters.

The spy's gaze gleamed as it met Ross's. "It's true," he said, his voice raspy from exhaustion. "The chieftain fell from his horse during a stag hunt yesterday ... dashed his brains out on a boulder."

The news left a sour taste in Ross's mouth; he hadn't known Niall MacDonald well, having only met him on a handful of occasions, yet he remembered him as a proud warrior. One who had met a sudden, unfortunate, end.

Ross knew the history between the two chiefs, the rancor that ran deep. MacDonald had thwarted MacKinnon, had prevented him from wedding MacDonald's eldest daughter by sending her to Kilbride to take the veil. Duncan MacKinnon had nursed the grievance like a bruise over the past two years.

"But surely ... she has taken her vows now?" Ross said after a long pause, his attention shifting back to MacKinnon. "The lass is out of yer reach."

Ross watched the clan-chief's face stiffen. At forty winters, Duncan MacKinnon was twelve years his elder. They had known each other a long while, for Ross had come to foster at Dunan at sixteen. He'd served Duncan's father, Jock MacKinnon, first and then remained upon the Isle of Skye once he came of age, to serve Duncan. MacKinnon had treated him well over the years. He'd risen fast in the clan-chief's personal guard, and had no desire to return to Argyll, upon the mainland, where he was the youngest of many sons.

But there were times he wondered if he hadn't signed a pact with the devil when he'd sworn his fealty to this man.

Now was one such time.

"Kilbride sits on my lands," MacKinnon replied, his voice developing a harsh edge. "Leanna won't have taken her vows of perpetuity yet." He halted there, his face screwing up. "But since the abbess lets nuns run off and wed whom they please, I'd say those vows mean very little anyway."

A brittle silence settled over the solar. Of course, MacKinnon was referring to the incident last year, when one of the nuns had left the order to wed the MacNichol clan-chief. It was a sore subject for MacKinnon, for he'd been hunting the woman at the time.

Ross wasn't sure of the details, but the nun—who had accompanied MacNichol to Dunan that summer—had somehow fallen foul of MacKinnon during their stay. MacKinnon's story was that he'd visited Sister Annella's bed-chamber to question her about Lady Leanna, but she'd savagely attacked him, knocking him senseless upon the floor.

MacKinnon had sworn to bring the woman to justice.

The next day MacKinnon and his men had ridden west to Kilbride Abbey, only to find that both Gavin MacNichol and Sister Annella had never arrived there. Or so the abbess said.

Ross wasn't a fool. He knew that MacKinnon hadn't told him the whole tale. He'd seen enough over the years to know that the man he served was far from a saint. However, Ross preferred not to know the details. There were many times when he deliberately ignored things, when he willfully remained ignorant of unsavory facts. He had a good life here at Dunan—and he wasn't about to jeopardize it.

Ross's silence made MacKinnon scowl. "Ye aren't considering defying me, are ye, Campbell?" he growled. "Don't forget who made ye Captain of the Dunan Guard ... before ye came here, ye were nothing."

Ross tensed and took a deep breath to quell his rising temper.

Aye, signing a pact with the devil always came at a price. Sooner or later Satan came to collect. And MacKinnon—the smug bastard—knew that Ross would only oppose him up to a point; his pride prevented him from going further.

"Ye want me to ride in there and just drag the lass away?" Ross asked finally, not bothering to hide the exasperation in his voice. "That will never work ... Mother Shona won't allow it."

MacKinnon smirked. He was a handsome man, with a mane of rich-brown hair, not yet touched by white, and iron-grey eyes. Yet many of his facial expressions tarnished his swarthy good looks. The smirk was one of them.

"Ye are a clever man, Campbell," he replied, crossing the room to a large oaken sideboard where a ewer of wine and cups sat. He poured himself a large measure and slugged it back in three gulps. He then slammed down the cup. Turning to Ross, MacKinnon favored him with a wolfish smile. "I don't care by what means ye get me Lady Leanna MacDonald of Sleat ... only that ye do."

1

The Hunting Trip

Kilbride Abbey
MacKinnon Territory
Isle of Skye, Scotland

A day later ...

THE DOE HADN'T seen her. Oblivious to the hunter that stood on the hill above it, the red deer nipped at grass. The morning sun glistened on the ruddy hues of its coat, and for a moment, Sister Leanna hesitated.

It seemed a pity to strike such a beautiful beast down. The doe was a leggy, graceful creature, with a dished nose and large dark eyes. It grazed in the center of the valley, next to where a burn trickled by.

Inhaling slowly, Leanna drew back the bowstring, sighting her target. She stood side-on, leaning her back against the rough bark of a birch. A light breeze feathered against her face, reminding Leanna that she stood downwind of the deer. The doe had not yet scented her.

However, the deer would not remain so perfectly placed for long. If she didn't shoot soon, she would lose her chance.

Her right arm trembled from strain as she drew the bowstring back farther. Leanna gritted her teeth, strengthening her arm. She'd trained two years for this moment. This was a test, and she wouldn't fail it.

The fletched arrow flew from her bow with a hiss.

A heartbeat later, it thudded into the deer's chest. The animal leaped into the air and then crumpled.

In an instant, Leanna squealed with glee. She then cast aside her bow and bounded down the hillside—difficult to do when hampered by the heavy skirts of her habit.

At the bottom of the vale, the doe was thrashing upon the mossy ground now—it was time to end its suffering. Reaching the deer's side, Leanna drew the knife at her waist. She then knelt behind the doe's neck, bent its head back, and deftly slit its throat.

The struggling immediately ceased.

At the sound of approaching footfalls, Leanna glanced up. Sister Coira hurried toward her, holding up with one hand the long skirts of her habit to quicken her pace. In the other hand, she carried an ash quarter-staff. Tall and lean with unusual violet eyes framed by shapely, dark eyebrows, Coira was garbed head to toe in black—a white wimple framing her face.

"That was deftly done," Coira gasped, recovering her breath as she stopped before the deer. "Where did ye learn to kill like that?"

"My father taught me," Leanna replied with an impish grin, pride filtering over her. "He never had any sons, and since I showed an interest in hunting from an early age, he used to take me with him ... Ma didn't like it though."

Leanna's grin faded. Thinking upon her parents made her chest ache. She missed them terribly, her father especially.

"I should think not," Coira replied with a rueful smile. "Being able to cut an animal's throat like a butcher's daughter is hardly ladylike."

Leanna gave a snort and sat back on her heels. "As soon as I entered womanhood, Ma put a stop to my hunting trips ... but there are some things ye don't forget." She glanced down at the dead deer before her. "What a beautiful doe."

"Aye, it will give us much-needed venison, skin, and tallow. Mother Shona will be well pleased with ye."

Leanna inclined her head. "She meant this hunting trip as a test, ye know?"

Coira nodded. "Ye have practiced with the longbow long enough ... she wanted to see if ye can hunt ... and ye can. I've never seen such a clean shot."

Leanna grinned once more at this. Her friend's praise meant a lot to her. It had been hard adjusting to life as a nun, and she wasn't sure she would ever really get used to it. But Coira, who had been at Kilbride for over a decade, had been at her side through it all. Sister Ella had been supportive of her too—only, Ella had now left the order. The abbey walls still echoed with the whispers of last year's scandal.

Sister Annella was now Lady MacNichol of Scorrybreac. Leanna often thought about her friend and wondered how she was faring. Sometimes she even felt envious of her.

A life completely among women, without the low timbre of male voices, without the roughness and energy of men's company, made her feel flat at times. Many of the sisters at Kilbride appeared to flourish in such an environment, but often Leanna felt stifled by it.

She quashed that sensation now. She loved being out in the forest, stalking deer with Coira. Very soon they would return to the confines of the abbey and the strict routines that dictated life in the Cluniac order. But out here, with the whispering wind, the smell of pine, and the spring sun warm on her face, she was free.

Leanna met Coira's eye then. "I still miss Ella ... don't ye?"

"Every day," the nun replied with a wistful smile.

"I wonder what it would be like to wed a man like Gavin MacNichol," Leanna said before sighing. "He's so handsome."

Coira made a choking sound. "Ye are a nun ... ye shouldn't be thinking about men." Her gaze narrowed then. "Most of them aren't as chivalrous as the MacNichol clan-chief."

Leanna rolled her eyes at Coira's censure. Sometimes her friend talked to her as if she had no idea about the world outside the abbey's walls.

The exchange had introduced tension between them—shattering their earlier camaraderie.

"Come." Coira untied a coil of rope from her belt. "Let's get this deer hitched up to my staff. We'll need to spend the afternoon preparing the carcass. Hopefully, we can get it gutted and skinned by Vespers."

The two nuns made their way through the sun-dappled forest, their feet sinking into the mossy ground. The woods stretched south of Kilbride, down a wide valley. It was the only forest in this corner of Skye, for most of the isle was barren and wind-swept.

Emerging from the trees into softly undulating, grassy hills, Leanna took in the outline of the great mountains to the east, their bulk etched against the blue sky. Beyond the hills to the west, the land sloped down to a rocky coastline. But Kilbride lay directly ahead, a few furlongs north of the forest.

It was slow going with the deer. Coira had hog-tied its fetlocks and hung it from the quarter-staff. They carried each end of the staff upon their shoulders, and the dead weight of the beast was starting to make Leanna's shoulder and back ache. She had grown physically stronger during her time at Kilbride—it was no pampered lady's life here—yet the doe was heavier than it looked.

By the time she spied the pitched roof of Kilbride kirk piercing the sky, Leanna was sweating heavily.

"Can we stop and rest for a moment," she panted as they reached a hazel thicket that encircled the southern and eastern edges of the abbey. "My shoulder can't take much more."

Coira halted before turning to her with a smile. She then lowered the deer onto the ground. "We still need to toughen ye up, I see," she teased.

Leanna huffed. "I'm tough enough."

Running an eye over her friend, she saw that Coira had barely broken into a sweat. The nun was tall and broad-shouldered, and in addition to training the other sisters in archery and use of the quarter-staff, she was also Kilbride's resident healer. Leanna looked up to her—Coira was a formidable woman indeed—yet there was something about her that always remained an enigma.

Coira never spoke of her past.

All Leanna knew was that the nun hailed from Dunan and her family had been farmers. She knew very little else about her.

"I'm not as strong as ye though," Leanna admitted finally, with the playful grin she often used with Coira. "I think I need to haul a few more buckets of water from the well to build up strength in my arms and shoulders."

Coira snorted before picking up the staff once more. "Maybe I need to put ye on log splitting duty for a moon or two. That should give ye arms like a smithy."

Leanna's grin abruptly disappeared. The thought of having bulky, heavily muscled arms like a man revolted her. "Don't ye dare!"

Coira's laugh rang out, the sound echoing through the trees. It was a rare thing to hear the nun show mirth so openly. Sometimes Coira could seem so … severe. But not this afternoon. Like Leanna, her mood had lightened when she was away from the abbey.

Leanna was about to comment on this change, but Coira was already moving forward, and Leanna had to scramble to pick up her end of the staff. Gritting her teeth, she heaved it back onto her aching shoulder, and they resumed their journey.

"How are we supposed to get inside … there's no way we can scale those walls?"

The rumble of Carr Broderick's voice drew Ross's attention from where he'd been observing Kilbride Abbey. His friend, whom he'd brought along on this mission, wore an inscrutable expression, although his gaze was wary.

Like Ross, he hadn't been pleased to be involved in this abduction. But just like Ross, he too wasn't about to cross MacKinnon.

The pair of them were crouched amongst the undergrowth in the hazel thicket to the east of the abbey. They'd been there for at least an hour, and so far neither of them had a plan.

"Aye … ye have a point," Ross murmured. He shifted his attention back to the high walls before him. From the outside, the abbey looked as if it was built to withstand a siege. A deep ditch ringed the base of the outer walls, and heavy oaken and iron gates shielded the complex from the outside world.

If they wanted to enter Kilbride, they would have to do so through those gates—and that would mean announcing their arrival. Locating and then stealing Lady Leanna once they were inside would be close to impossible.

Ross had seen the young woman once before, at a clan gathering. He remembered her as being small, blonde, and delicate-featured. However, all the nuns looked the same shrouded in black, their heads covered by veils.

They'd never find her.

Frustration welled up within Ross, and he dragged his hands through his shaggy hair.

Damn MacKinnon. He'd given him an impossible task.

The clan-chief didn't care what lengths Ross went to in order to retrieve the woman he wished to wed. He'd made his position clear: Ross wasn't to return to Dunan empty-handed.

Muttering a curse under his breath, Ross glanced Carr's way once more. "Maybe we should—"

"Look!" Carr raised a hand, cutting him off mid-sentence. "The abbey has visitors."

Swiveling back toward the gates, Ross's gaze alighted upon a company of men on horseback who'd just emerged from the trees to the south. And as the riders drew near, he saw they wore sashes made of red plaid with green cross-hatching.

The tension that Ross had been holding in his shoulders all day slowly eased. He didn't want the task he'd been assigned, but this development was going to make it so much easier.

"MacDonald men," he whispered before flashing Carr a triumphant grin. "It looks like we won't have to enter the abbey after all ... our quarry is going to come to us."

Carr smiled back. "Good ... let's get the job done and go home. MacKinnon will be waiting."

2

I Must Say Goodbye

AS SHE APPROACHED Kilbride, Leanna was surprised to see the abbey gates open. Usually, the abbess insisted they be kept closed. However, Coira didn't comment on it, and the two nuns entered the wide, dusty yard. Kilbride kirk rose before them, dominating the two wings of buildings that stretched either side.

They carried their prize to a lean-to behind the stables, and Coira strung the doe up by its hind legs. Drawing a knife from her waist, she prepared to gut the beast while Leanna went to fetch pails for the blood and offal. She had just placed the buckets underneath when the scuff of footfalls behind them made her turn.

Mother Shona, Abbess of Kilbride, approached. She was a small woman of middling age, yet she walked with a determined stride. A large iron cross lay upon her breast. This afternoon, her pretty, if a little careworn, face was unusually serious.

"Good day, Mother," Leanna greeted her before hastily dropping onto one knee and bowing her head. Likewise, next to her, Coira sheathed her knife and did the same.

Mother Shona stepped close and hastily waved the sign of the cross. "Rise," she murmured softly, "or ye shall dirty yer habits."

Both Leanna and Coira did as bid.

The abbess's gaze settled upon Leanna then, her brown eyes shadowing. "I'm glad ye have returned earlier than expected," she said. Her tone was gentle, although her expression was now troubled. "For ye have visitors."

Leanna went still.

In her two years at Kilbride, no one had paid her a visit. She had asked for permission a number of times, yet Mother Shona had always refused, telling her that her transition into their world would be made harder if she didn't sever all ties with her old life. Leanna liked the abbess, but she had resented her initially for her refusal.

As such, it came as a shock to know someone had called upon her here.

"Who is it?" Leanna finally asked.

The abbess's features tightened for a heartbeat before she replied. "A group of yer father's men from Duncaith."

Sister Leanna of Kilbride sat upon her sleeping pallet and stared at the floor. She was alone in the dormitory this afternoon. The other nuns who shared these sleeping quarters were still busy with their chores. Sunlight filtered in through a single narrow window at one end of the long rectangular space, pooling on the flagstone floor. Unseeing, Leanna continued to stare at the circle of light.

Her body felt cold, her limbs weak. Time had slowed down; she was painfully aware of the rasp of her own breathing and the dull thud of her pulse.

The MacDonald men had brought ill tidings.

She'd known by the abbess's behavior that something was amiss—and when Leanna had entered the chapter house, she found herself face-to-face with Evan, her father's right-hand.

The grim look upon his face had made dread sweep over her in a chill wave, and when he spoke, Leanna's knees had buckled under her. "Yer father is dead, lass … I am sorry."

It had been a hunting accident. He had fallen from his horse and hit his head. Leanna almost hadn't believed it. Niall MacDonald was an excellent horseman and hunting was in his blood. She couldn't comprehend how he'd met his end doing something he loved.

She couldn't comprehend that she'd never see him again.

When she'd come to live at Kilbride it had been a wrench to leave her father, but he'd still been alive and there had always been the possibility that he'd visit the abbey one day. Still, Leanna had missed him terribly. She'd always been his 'princess', his 'jewel'—she'd spent much of her childhood trailing in his shadow.

Her heart actually ached from the force of the sorrow that now pulsed through her.

Tears trickled down Leanna's face, but she didn't move to brush them away. Instead, she remained seated upon her pallet, like a statue carven from ice.

And yet heat flushed through her as the long moments stretched out. Her hands, which lay upon her lap, balled into fists, her nails biting into her palms. Anger swept over her, warring with the knot of grief that twisted in her breast.

How could God let this happen?

She'd never wanted to take the veil. She'd never felt the 'calling' that many of the other women here had. But she'd wanted to wed Duncan MacKinnon even less. Her father, determined to keep the MacKinnon clan-chief from his first-born daughter, had sent Leanna here. She'd been upset with her father at first; she had felt betrayed. She wasn't interested in dedicating her life to serving God, to giving up all her possessions and any hope of taking a husband and having children. It seemed like a great sacrifice indeed.

Her mother and younger sisters all wept when they heard the news, but Niall MacDonald had been resolved. MacKinnon had developed an obsession with Leanna after meeting her at a gathering between their two clans the previous summer. Her few conversations with him had left her shaken and him determined to have her. He wouldn't let it go.

Leanna squeezed her eyes shut, but still, the tears flowed, burning down her cheeks. The ache in her chest increased, and she raised a hand, rubbing at her breast bone with her knuckles.

Her father had been a good man. He'd deserved to live to an old age.

Leanna clenched her jaw so tightly that pain lanced through her ears. Indeed, there was no fairness, no justice at all in this life—when men like Duncan MacKinnon lived and her father died.

The door to the dormitory creaked open, causing Leanna to snap out of her grief-induced trance. Sister Coira had come to check on her. The nun's violet eyes were shadowed with concern, her proud face taut. She approached Leanna without a word before settling down upon the pallet next to her.

Still silent, Coira reached out, placing her hands over Leanna's.

Leanna's breathing hitched, a sob escaping. It was easier to cope, easier to keep a leash on her sorrow when she was alone. But in the face of Coira's kindness, she crumbled.

Leaning into her friend's shoulder, she wept.

Coira didn't speak. Instead, she merely sat and held her, and Leanna gave herself up to the sorrow that swept over her in a tempest.

Eventually, her sobbing ceased, and she moved back from Coira. Drawing in a shaky breath, Leanna wiped at her wet cheeks with the sleeve of her habit. "I can't believe he's actually gone ... it all seems like a dark dream."

"I'm not surprised," Coira replied softly. "He died so suddenly ... may the Lord rest his soul."

Leanna looked up, her gaze meeting Coira's for the first time since she had broken down. Her father had been a God-fearing man. Part of him had been proud to gift his eldest daughter to the abbey. She hoped that Coira was right, that he was at peace now, and that God was watching over him. Her throat constricted as tears welled once more.

It was no good—she couldn't see the positive in this. The two years she'd spent at Kilbride had not given her the same faith her father had.

"We should go to the kirk and pray for him," Coira said after a pause. "Do ye feel strong enough to do so?"

Leanna swallowed hard. "I can't, Sister Coira. My father's men are waiting for me. I'm supposed to be in here gathering my things. They're preparing Da for burial in Duncaith and awaiting my arrival."

Coira's gaze widened. "Ye are going away?"

Leanna nodded. "Just for a couple of days ... Ma wishes me to be there when they bury him."

"Has Mother Shona agreed to this?"

Something in Coira's voice made Leanna tense. "Aye," she replied warily. "Although she isn't happy about it ... ye don't look pleased either?"

Coira sat back, expelling a long breath as she did so. "It's not a good idea for nuns to leave the abbey," she said, holding Leanna's eye steadily. "Look what happened to Sister Ella."

A strange thrill went through Leanna at these words, momentarily overshadowing her grief. How she'd been jealous of Ella's new life as wife to Gavin MacNichol—a man as kind-hearted and strong as he was handsome.

"I won't be away for long," she replied, shoving aside the sensation. Resolve caused her spine to straighten and her shoulders to square, even as the loss felt like a kick to the chest. "I have to go ... I must say goodbye to my father."

A group of nuns had gathered in the yard before the kirk when Leanna finally emerged from the dormitory. She carried little with her, just a leather satchel slung across her front.

Many of the sisters wore sad expressions, their gazes full of empathy. However, there were some, such as Sister Elspeth, who looked disapproving. The older woman folded her arms across a flat bosom and fixed Leanna with a stern stare.

Leanna ignored her. Sister Elspeth had never been a friend of hers. More often than not, the nun wore a sour look as if the whole world offended her. She'd disliked Sister Ella, and as Leanna had been close to her, she had also received Sister Elspeth's jaundiced eye.

"Ye are yet a novice," Sister Elspeth greeted her. "It is not seemly for ye to go riding off ... with a company of *men*." The nun spoke that last word with clear distaste. Her gaze shifted then, to the group of horses that were being saddled outside the stables near the gates. "A sister with true devotion to the Lord would remain here."

The nuns flanking Sister Elspeth started nodding in agreement. News of Leanna's imminent departure had caused quite a stir it appeared.

Leanna regarded Sister Elspeth coldly. Heat flashed across her chest as anger surged once more. She didn't care what this sour-faced witch thought of her, and she didn't care if every last one of the nuns here questioned her faith.

Right now, she needed to be at home in Duncaith.

She wanted to see her mother and sisters again, to lay her father's body to rest. She had no patience for this woman's judgment, and she was about to tell her so in very blunt terms when Mother Shona's voice interrupted them. "That's enough, Sister Elspeth."

A small figure glided through the crowd of nuns. They parted to allow the abbess to approach, and Sister Elspeth hurriedly stepped back, her mouth compressing.

"Sister Leanna grieves for her father's sudden death ... we shall not make this parting more difficult for her."

Mother Shona stopped before Leanna, meeting her eye.

Wordlessly, Leanna dropped to one knee, waiting while the abbess blessed her. When she rose to her feet, Leanna met Mother Shona's eye, and guilt twisted in her breast. Unlike Sister Elspeth, the abbess had only ever treated her well.

Leanna averted her gaze. She should really feel more gratitude for all that Mother Shona had done for her. Leanna's life at Kilbride was much better than many folk living upon this isle could hope for. She worked hard, but she always had food to fill her belly and a warm fire to keep the winter's chill at bay. She had company and a bed of her own.

Leanna knew she should be grateful, yet at that moment, she couldn't wait to be away from Kilbride. It suddenly felt as if the walls were closing in on her. The shock of her father's death had ripped something from her, torn away all pretense.

The truth was that she wasn't completely happy here.

The tightness in Leanna's chest increased as panic now wormed its way up. She couldn't leave the order. In just a couple of months, she would be expected to take her vows of perpetuity. Suddenly, she felt as if she were standing in a dark dungeon watching the doors slowly close before her. Soon, she'd be trapped here forever.

Maybe this trip back to Duncaith, seeing her family again, would make her appreciate Kilbride more. Her mother was prone to whining, and her sisters bickered constantly.

Probably, she would miss the peace of this abbey.

She certainly hoped so—for she wasn't sure what she'd do if the opposite occurred. What if she never wanted to come back here?

After a long pause, Leanna raised her gaze once more, meeting the abbess's eye. "Thank ye for allowing this journey, Mother Shona," she murmured, forcing down her simmering panic. "I won't linger at Duncaith. As soon as father has been buried, I will return." She inwardly cringed as she said these words, sure her voice would betray her.

The abbess nodded, her gaze holding Leanna's fast. "Take these days to reflect, Sister Leanna," she said softly.

Shame filtered over Leanna then, causing her cheeks to warm. Like the other sisters here, she hated to disappoint Mother Shona. The woman wasn't like any other she'd met. Gently spoken and kind-hearted, the abbess also possessed a will of iron.

Mother Shona had a shadowy past, and after being elected as abbess, she'd revealed that she knew how to wield a knife, a sword, a longbow, and a quarter-staff. Her time living rough on the mainland years earlier had given her a set of unusual skills. Unlike most women, the abbess could also defend herself with her bare hands if need be.

With outlaws and bands of starving men roaming the barren hills of Skye, and news of a terrible pestilence now ravaging the mainland, Mother Shona had warned them that there might come a time soon when they would need to defend these walls from outsiders.

Leanna was grateful that she'd learned to wield a longbow and defend herself if a man grabbed her. Who knew what the future would bring—even Kilbride Abbey couldn't keep the world at bay forever. And yet, at that moment, Leanna just wanted to return to Duncaith and take back the old life she'd been forced to give up.

Leanna revealed none of what lay in her heart to the abbess. She felt too ashamed. "I will reflect, Mother Shona," she agreed, lowering her gaze.

"May the Lord grant ye a safe journey," Mother Shona said. "Go now … the day is waning, and ye have much ground to cover."

Leanna nodded and stepped back. As she moved toward the stables, she cast a glance right, at where Coira stood. The older woman's expression was veiled this afternoon, and Leanna wondered if she was upset with her for going away.

Meeting the nun's eye, Leanna offered her a weak smile. "Peace be with ye, Sister Coira … I shall see ye soon."

However, her friend merely nodded.

3
Leanna's Savior

ROSS CAMPBELL WATCHED the party leave Kilbride Abbey. Gaze narrowed, he tracked the five riders that trotted through the gates and onto the narrow, rutted path that led south through the hazel thicket.

Shifting position, Ross stretched out his left leg, which had gone numb. It had been an uncomfortable wait.

"And here they are … finally."

Carr Broderick's whispered comment made a grim smile curve Ross's lips. His companion, who crouched next to him in the undergrowth, had been impatient during their wait.

Four riders had entered Kilbride, and five departed. One of them was a small woman swathed in black, who rode side-saddle upon a sturdy grey pony.

"Lady Leanna MacDonald of Sleat," Ross murmured. "We finally have ye."

"Are ye sure it's her?" Carr grumbled. "All the nuns look the same to me in their crow's garb."

"I'd wager ye all my savings that's her," Ross replied. "It's one of the sisters we saw earlier."

Indeed, shortly after the arrival of the MacDonald party, Ross and Carr had spied two nuns also approach from the south. Hauling a dead deer between them, they'd made an incongruous pair—one tall and broad-shouldered, the other much shorter. The smaller of the two nuns also carried a long bow and quiver of arrows slung across her back. The sight had intrigued Ross.

He'd no idea that the Sisters of Kilbride hunted their own deer.

No doubt, MacKinnon would be interested to learn so. It appeared that these nuns were not as helpless as one might think.

Rising to his feet, Ross brushed the dirt off his braies. "Come on … let's fetch the horses."

Wordlessly, Carr nodded, and the pair of them shifted back into the heart of the hazel thicket, where their coursers awaited. Untying the horses and tightening their girths, the men swung up onto their backs. Then they set off south, following the MacDonald party.

Despite her chest-crushing sorrow, Leanna felt better the moment she left Kilbride Abbey. Riding across the hills of Skye eased the warring emotions within her. Panic, shame, guilt, and anger—each of them sought to dominate. But out here in the open, she could outrun them.

Evan and the three warriors accompanying him weren't men prone to prattle. Leanna was grateful for that, although it meant that shortly after leaving the abbey, she retreated into her own thoughts.

And when she did so, memories of her father returned.

She could still envisage him, seated in his carven chair by the hearth at Duncaith, his white-blond hair spilling over his shoulders, his hazel eyes twinkling with amusement as he listened to his wife lamenting how tiresome it was to have five daughters.

Leanna's throat constricted, and a sob welled up deep in her chest. Choking it down, she blinked rapidly as her vision blurred. She was riding blind, but the pony was docile and merely plodded after Evan's leggy courser, happy to follow.

Her father really was gone. She'd never see him again.

How would she feel upon arriving at Duncaith again? How could she bear to step back inside the broch and not see him? It would seem empty and cold without Niall MacDonald.

Life was empty and cold without her father.

A wind blew in from the west, bringing with it the salty whisper of the sea. They were just out of sight of the coast here, although as they entered the woodland, the rich smell of vegetation and damp peaty earth dominated.

Golden afternoon sunlight filtered through the canopy of trees, and birds twittered, but Leanna scarcely paid her surroundings any notice. Instead, grief shrouded her, blocking out the rest of the world.

The afternoon drew out, and eventually, they left the wooded valley behind and rode out across windswept hills. Huge mountains rose to the east, their smooth sides turning red and gold as the setting sun caught them. Finally, Leanna emerged from her fog of despair, her gaze alighting on the majesty of the mountains. This isle was so beautiful that it could take your breath away.

And yet a heavy sensation settled in the pit of Leanna's belly as she gazed upon the peaks. *Da loved these mountains.*

A keen hunter, Niall MacDonald had led a number of hunting parties into the steep, wooded valleys at the base of those peaks, where great stags were known to roam. And in the end, his love of hunting had been his demise.

Eyes stinging as fresh tears surfaced, Leanna swallowed hard. Closing her eyes, she whispered a soft prayer for her father's soul.

The light was fading when Evan drew the party up. "We won't reach Duncaith before dark," he announced, dismounting his horse. "It's best we make camp here overnight."

They had reached a stand of pines that grew in the mountains dividing MacKinnon and MacDonald lands. With the setting sun, the air had grown cool, and the scent of pine resin filled the narrow valley where they halted.

It had been a long while since Leanna had slept out under the stars. Not since before she had entered womanhood. The thought made the ache of sorrow in her breast ease just a little; a night out in the wild would bring her closer to her father. It also gave her time to compose herself before seeing her mother and sisters once more. She slid down from her pony's back, her sandaled feet sinking into a bed of pine needles.

Leading the shaggy grey mare over to a tree, she tied it up and unsaddled it. Then she broke off a piece of pine from an overhead branch and began to rub the pony down in long, smooth strokes.

"I see ye haven't forgotten yer upbringing, Sister Leanna," Evan observed from behind her. "Yer father taught ye how to look after horses well."

Leanna glanced over her shoulder to see the man watching her, a smile softening his hawkish features.

"Aye," she replied, her throat thickening as other memories surfaced. "When I was a lass, I wished to sleep in the stables with the horses ... until Ma forbade me."

Evan's smile widened. "Ye were a wild lass." He paused then, his expression sobering. "Although I see the past two years have tempered ye."

Leanna looked away, her fingers clenching around the prickly pine. "They have," she replied softly.

Evan might have replied then—and their conversation may have lasted a while longer—but Leanna was never to know.

The snap of a twig underneath a heavy tread made Evan swivel around, his gaze sweeping their surroundings. He then drew his claidheamh-mor, the great broadsword that hung at his waist.

Around him, the three other warriors had also grown still. Wordlessly, Evan motioned to his companions. A moment later they left their horses, drew their own weapons, and formed a protective semi-circle around Leanna.

Heart pounding, she tried to peer around her escort. Her skin suddenly prickled with awareness. There was someone out there, hiding in the trees, watching them.

The unmistakable twang of a bow string cut through the gloaming.

Thud.

In front of Leanna, Evan grunted.

Thud.

He then staggered forward before he turned.

Horror rose in a cold, sickly wave within Leanna when she saw an arrow protruding from his throat and another arrow embedded in his chest. Evan went down on his knees. His gaze seized upon Leanna, and he wheezed, "Run!"

Leanna dropped the pine and glanced around frantically, her breathing now coming in panicked gasps. Although she hadn't yet seen their attackers, she realized they were now surrounded. Where did he expect her to go?

Outlaws.

They were under attack, yet Leanna couldn't see anyone.

Arrows flew across the small clearing. The horses squealed in fright, pulling at their tethers.

Another man went down in front of her, his cry echoing through the trees.

Heart pounding, Leanna dropped to a crouch and edged back against the tree trunk. She carried no weapons on her. Unlike Sister Ella who'd never gone anywhere without a few blades strapped to her person, Leanna didn't carry her longbow with her usually. The only item that hung from her belt was her crucifix, and that wasn't going to help her now.

Shapes burst out from the undergrowth. A group of around half a dozen men dressed in soiled braies and léines. To Leanna's shock, she recognized the tattered sashes some of the men wore: a deep red crisscrossed with pine green.

It was the plaid of her own people—the MacDonalds of Sleat.

A wave of dizziness swept over Leanna.

These outlaws, who were cutting down MacDonald men, had once served her father.

That's impossible. Niall MacDonald's men were loyal. They didn't desert the clan and attack travelers. And yet, there was no mistaking the plaid.

An agonized grunt split the air, as another of her escorts went down, stabbed through the chest with a dirk.

Leanna reached up, clutching her throat as panic clamped its iron grip around her windpipe. She had to do something, or she'd be on her own out here—soon an arrow would find her too. Weakness flooded through her, and for a moment, she thought she might faint.

Move or ye are going to die—or worse. Somehow, she had the presence of mind to drop to her hands and knees and scramble forward to where Evan lay. His pale blue eyes stared at her sightlessly, even as his limbs twitched.

Bile rose in the back of Leanna's throat, yet she forced it down. With trembling hands, she drew the dirk from Evan's belt and turned—just in time—to see one of the outlaws bearing down upon her.

He was a huge man with unkempt auburn hair and a feral expression. The MacDonald sash he wore across his chest was dirty and threadbare, yet recognizable.

"It's a prize we have here," the outlaw called out to his companions as he advanced toward Leanna. He leered at her, the sword he held gleaming dark with blood. "I'm having her first, lads."

Terror sliced through Leanna, ice-cold and paralyzing. She never knew fear could be like this, so utterly immobilizing. For a heartbeat she merely stared at the outlaw, freezing like a frightened fawn—and then she remembered Mother Shona's advice when she'd been showing the novice nuns how to fend off a man with their hands.

Let them come to ye. Many men don't believe a small woman can do them harm. Wait for them to get close, and then strike.

The outlaw reached out a meaty arm, grabbing for her, and Leanna slashed at him with the dirk. She'd held the weapon against her skirts, concealed. He hadn't seen it.

The blade cut into his forearm, and the man bellowed, reeling back as if he'd just discovered an adder sleeping in the grass.

"Whore!" he snarled. Blood poured down his arm, but he appeared not to notice. Instead, there was a murderous glint in his eye. "Ye are going to regret that."

Leanna scrambled back, her pulse thundering in her ears. Her defense had been clumsy. She should have gone for somewhere more vulnerable than his arm, but her nerves had gotten the better of her.

A wave of dizziness rose once more, surging like a spring tide, and black spots suddenly appeared in Leanna's field of vision. He was going to hurt her, and there was nothing she could do about it.

But instead of lunging at her, the outlaw gasped, his big body going rigid. And then, as Leanna watched with horrified fascination, he keeled over.

Someone had saved her—had one of Evan's men survived the attack?

However, she didn't recognize the man standing behind him.

As the outlaw fell, the stranger withdrew the dirk blade he'd shoved under his ribs.

Tall, dark-haired, and with chiseled good looks, Leanna's savior straightened up and met her eye. And then, to her surprise, his mouth curved into an arrogant smile. "Looks like we arrived just in time, eh ... Lady Leanna?"

4

We Mean Ye No Harm

LEANNA SWALLOWED HARD. "*Sister* Leanna ... but how do ye know my name?"

The newcomer's smile widened, but he didn't answer her. Instead, he glanced right, his gaze narrowing. "Are we done here, Carr?"

"Aye." A broad, heavily muscled man with short blond hair emerged from the bushes. He carried a dirk—its blade dripping with blood. "They're all dead."

"How many of them?"

"Six."

Leanna's savior's smile widened. "Two against six ... we haven't lost our touch, I see."

The man's companion snorted. "We had some assistance ... it appears this lass isn't completely helpless." His attention then shifted to where Leanna still crouched on the ground a few yards away. "Is Lady Leanna hurt?"

"I don't think so." The dark-haired warrior replied, his gaze returning to Leanna. "She's quick with a knife. I'll grant her that."

The man named Carr frowned.

A tense silence fell in the clearing. Around them lay the bodies of the four men who'd accompanied Leanna south. And now that Leanna could divert her attention from the big auburn-haired man who'd attacked her, she spied the corpses of some of the outlaws around the fringes of the glade.

"Who are ye?" Leanna finally managed. Still clenching her dirk in a death grip, she rose to her feet.

The dark-haired man's smile faded. "Just travelers, milady."

"But how do ye know my name?"

"Ye were traveling south with a MacDonald escort ... most folk in these parts know that MacDonald of Sleat's eldest daughter is a nun."

Leanna's gaze narrowed, and she took a step back. "Do they?"

"Ye can lower the blade, milady," The man's companion rumbled. "We mean ye no harm."

"Aye ... so why don't ye put away yer dirks?"

The two men shared looks before they both did as bid. The dark-haired man then moved toward her, arms raised. "As ye can see, I'm unarmed now."

Leanna's fingers flexed around the handle of the dirk. She knew this man had saved her life, yet something felt 'wrong' about this rescue. As she studied his face, she realized that she'd seen the man somewhere before—however, the context eluded her.

"What's yer name?" she asked, still holding her weapon aloft.

The warrior paused, his head inclining as a smile curved his lips once more.

Mother Mary save me, he is handsome. The thought rose unbidden. It was true though; this close, the chiseled lines of the man's face drew clear in the gloaming. He possessed moody good looks: a firm, well-defined jaw shadowed in stubble, with a slight cleft in the chin, and dark eyebrows winging above penetrating midnight blue eyes. A mane of wavy black hair that fell just short of the shoulders framed his face.

"Ross Campbell at yer service," he replied. "And my companion here is Carr Broderick."

Leanna went still as she suddenly realized where she'd seen him in the past. "I remember ye," she murmured. "Ye were at the MacKinnon and MacDonald clan gathering two years ago."

That comment wiped the arrogant smile off his face. "I was," he admitted, wary now.

Leanna's pulse accelerated as she finally placed him. "Ye stood at Duncan MacKinnon's side … ye serve him."

"I do … please lower that blade, milady."

Leanna backed up farther, heart hammering now. "What do ye want with me?"

Ross Campbell heaved a sigh. She could see he was tiring of her defiance, yet Leanna didn't care. Her instincts were on alert now; it seemed that there had been more than just a band of outlaws tracking their progress south.

"If ye keep waving that dirk around, ye will only risk injury to yerself," he said lowering his tone as if talking to a frightened filly. He took a cautious step toward her, and then another. "Put it down. Ye are coming with us now."

"Get away from me," Leanna snarled. Terror pulsed through her. She swiped the blade between them, warning him off. "I'm more than capable of defending myself, and I'm certainly not going anywhere with ye."

She didn't know what these two warriors had in mind, but any men who served MacKinnon weren't friends of hers.

Ross Campbell moved then—so swiftly that Leanna barely registered it. One moment he'd been standing a few yards distant, the next he was right before her. He caught her wrist in an iron grip.

Leanna cried out, struggling against him. "Unhand me!"

"Take her knife, Carr," Campbell instructed coolly. "And bind her wrists." The big blond man stepped close and wrested the dirk from Leanna's clutching fingers. She gave a wail as he did so—that weapon was the only thing she had left. The only thing between her and capture.

They took her north, away from the pine clearing strewn with bodies, and into the heart of the mountains. Night had settled over the world, a waxing half-moon rising into the inky sky, when the party of three stopped in a rocky gorge and made camp for the night.

Fighting nausea, Leanna tried to get down off her grey pony—not an easy task when her hands were bound. However, she didn't want either of her captors touching her.

She was halfway down when she realized the ground was rushing up to meet her. Unfortunately, she couldn't put out her hands to break her fall.

Leanna cried out—and then a pair of strong arms fastened around her, catching her.

"Easy there." Campbell set her down upon the ground. "Ye will do yerself an injury if ye aren't careful."

"Bastard," she snarled. His touch wasn't rough, yet it made her clench her jaw all the same. "If ye hadn't bound my hands, I could have dismounted without yer help."

Campbell huffed a soft laugh. "Nice try, milady. But we can't take any chances with MacKinnon's prize, can we?"

Leanna made a choking sound in the back of her throat as fury gripped her. "Loathsome worm! Ye will burn in hell for this!"

Campbell merely raised a dark eyebrow in reply, whereas behind him, Broderick barked a laugh. "Looks like MacKinnon's fallen for a feisty one."

Broderick set a small fire going while Campbell saw to the horses. Meanwhile, Leanna sat in stony silence on a rock a few feet away.

Neither man conversed with her. In fact, they appeared to have little interest in her at all.

Leanna glared at Campbell's back as he unsaddled one of the horses. "We shouldn't have left Evan and the others like that," she said finally. She knew her voice had a high, querulous edge, but she didn't care. "They were charged with protecting me ... they deserve a proper burial. My father would have given them one."

Campbell glanced over his shoulder at her, his dark brows drawing together. "There wasn't time for that." He paused then, watching her for a heartbeat. "They're dead now anyway ... whatever becomes of their corpses now, it won't matter to them."

The harshness of this comment made Leanna's heart start to hammer against her ribs. "Evan was one of my father's most loyal warriors." She gasped out the words. "He deserves better."

Campbell turned away. "He probably does."

Heat exploded within Leanna, spiraling up from her belly. Anger felt good—it chased away fear and sorrow, it made her feel strong. When she finally spoke again, her voice had a raw, harsh edge. "So, MacKinnon sent ye to fetch me ... to steal me away?"

"Aye."

"He wishes to wed me, I take it?" Even as she said the words, Leanna's already racing pulse sped up to a gallop. She couldn't believe MacKinnon had stooped to this; it was unthinkable.

"I believe that's his plan, milady."

"Stop addressing me as 'milady'," Leanna snarled, panic causing her temper to fray. "In case ye hadn't noticed, I am a *Sister* of Kilbride." She drew in a sharp breath, in an attempt to master the wobble in her voice, before continuing. "I won't wed him."

Ross Campbell turned to face her properly this time. Strangely, he didn't answer her. His dark-blue gaze was veiled.

Leanna drew herself up, outrage bolstering her courage. "I'm a *nun*," she spat out the word as if speaking to a halfwit. "I have taken vows."

Campbell's mouth compressed. "Ye are yet a novice. Ye have done nothing that cannot be undone."

Leanna stared at him, shocked by his callousness. "If those outlaws hadn't attacked us, ye would have killed my escort, wouldn't ye?"

"Aye … but fortunately it didn't come to that," he replied. Did she imagine it or had his gaze shadowed slightly at her accusation?

"Ye are MacKinnon's hound," Leanna snarled. "What ye are doing is wrong. Have ye no will of yer own?" When he didn't reply, she balled her hands at her sides. "My uncle Bard will be enraged when he hears of this … he'll rip out yer guts!"

Campbell didn't give her the satisfaction of a reply. He merely bestowed her with a withering look, before he gave her his back once more and resumed unsaddling his horse.

"The lass has some spirit," Carr murmured, poking the glowing embers of the fire pit with a stick. "Unfortunately for her."

Ross glanced up and frowned before he looked across the fire at where Lady Leanna slept. The woman had curled up into a ball, and Ross had lain his cloak over her. Her face peeked out; illuminated by the fire's glow, the nun looked young and vulnerable in slumber. It had been a tense evening. They'd attempted to share their supper of dried meat and bread with their captive, but she'd refused to eat anything.

"Aye … MacKinnon likes his women biddable," Ross replied, deliberately keeping his voice low lest they wake Leanna.

"I don't understand it really," Carr said, his expression genuinely puzzled. "Is meekness that attractive?"

Ross's mouth quirked. "What? Ye would prefer a shrew … like Drew MacKinnon?" The comment had been deliberately aimed. The two men had known each other many years, having arrived at Dunan at about the same time—long enough for Ross to have caught Carr staring at MacKinnon's blade-tongued sister on more than occasion.

He'd expected Carr to look embarrassed, yet he merely shrugged. "Lady Drew is a survivor," he replied, his expression unreadable.

Disappointed at Carr's lack of reaction, Ross glanced back at their captive's sleeping face. "Let's hope Lady Leanna is," he said softly. "MacKinnon's not easy on his wives."

As soon as the words were out, Ross regretted them. Although he and Carr were friends, he was still wary of being too open with him. Both of them were the youngest sons from large families. Both had been set on carving a new life for themselves elsewhere. MacKinnon had given them the future they'd craved—and as such their loyalty was primarily to him, not each other.

However, Carr didn't appear irritated by the veiled criticism of the clan-chief. Instead, he raised a blond eyebrow. "I take it ye speak of yer cousin?"

Ross nodded. As always, his mood shadowed when he thought of Siusan. She'd deserved so much better than the life she'd been given. Wed to MacKinnon, Siusan had died the previous summer. An exhausting pregnancy culminated in a grueling birth that had claimed the lives of mother and bairn.

"She was gentle and quiet ... an ideal match for MacKinnon," Ross said finally. "But I didn't like how his manner cooled toward her as soon as he got her with child ... or that he started frequenting whores again."

Carr frowned at this, although he didn't contradict him. They both knew it was the truth.

"I liked even less how he raged when she died ... how he blamed her," Ross continued.

Silence followed this admission, and when Carr frowned, Ross knew he'd gone too far.

"It was grief," Carr replied, a warning edge in his voice now. "Her death came as a shock to him, that's all."

Ross didn't reply. His tongue was too loose as it was tonight—if he kept talking. he was going to land himself in trouble. Nonetheless, he didn't share Carr's conviction.

5

Trapped

LEANNA AWOKE TO a pain in her side and a breeze feathering across her face. For a moment, she merely lay there, disoriented. For a blissful instant, the events of the last day eluded her, and then they hit her with the force of a charging boar.

Her father's death.
Her journey back to Duncaith.
The attack.
Her capture by MacKinnon's men.

Leanna sucked in a pained breath and clenched her eyes shut. Maybe if she tried hard enough, she could go back to sleep, return to oblivion. But such wishes were useless. She was awake now, and the weight of sorrow settled upon her breast once more.

Stifling a groan, Leanna sat up and rubbed her flank. Somehow, she'd rolled over onto a sharp stone during the night. It had dug into her while she slept. However, she welcomed the pain—it distracted her from the fog of hopelessness that now rose around her.

A few yards away, Carr Broderick was saddling the horses while Ross Campbell kicked dirt over the ashes of last night's fire.

Meeting her eye, Campbell favored her with a cool smile. "Ready to go?"

He reached out a hand then, offering it to her.

Leanna ignored his hand. Instead, she glowered at him and pushed herself to her feet. They'd released the bonds on her wrists while she slept, and she wondered whether they'd bind her again. She guessed they would refrain from doing so. It wouldn't look good—bringing her into Dunan as a prisoner.

"I need some time alone," she informed him, shoving her grief behind an icy tone. And when Campbell gave her an incredulous look, she compressed her lips. "I need to relieve myself ... and then I must conduct my morning prayers."

"No prayers this morning," Campbell replied, his expression irritatingly neutral. "But ye can empty yer bladder before we leave." His gaze flicked to his companion. "Carr ... can ye accompany her?"

"I'm saddling the horses," the warrior grumbled.

"I'll finish them off ... go on. Nature calls Sister Leanna."

Balling her hands at her sides, Leanna tensed as her temper flared. How dare this cur mock her?

"Come on then, Sister." Broderick left the horses and approached her. "There's a boulder behind ye ... let's visit it."

Ross turned from tightening the pony's girth, to see Carr and Lady Leanna emerge. As often, his friend's expression was impossible to read, while Leanna's face, framed by that austere white wimple, was stony. Grief strained her delicate features; she was doing her best to hide it, but the cracks were showing.

"Let's get going," he greeted them. "Dunan isn't far ... if we ride hard, we can reach it by noon. Ye'll feel better once ye arrive at the broch, milady—ye'll see." In truth, Ross thought it highly unlikely, but telling her so wasn't going to help things.

"I told ye ... I can't go anywhere until I've completed my morning prayers," Leanna countered, folding her arms over her breasts.

Ross suppressed a sigh. He should have anticipated this; the lass was spoiled and used to getting her own way. "And I told ye that we don't have time. Ye'll just have to conduct yer prayers on horseback."

To his surprise, Leanna marched up to him. Tilting her chin, she fixed him with an imperious stare. Not for the first time, Ross was struck by the loveliness of her face. The shapeless habit and enveloping veil and wimple did her looks no favors, yet there was no denying this woman was a beauty.

No wonder MacKinnon fell for her.

She had smooth, milky skin; large, expressive, hazel eyes; and a small, lush mouth. He remembered her from that gathering two years earlier—under that veil her hair was a pale ash-blonde, like her father's.

"Ye won't get away with this."

Ross couldn't help smirking. "I think ye'll find that we already have."

"My father wanted to protect me from MacKinnon for a reason," she countered, high spots of color appearing upon those creamy cheeks.

Ross snorted. "Aye, there's never been much love between the MacKinnons and the MacDonalds."

"This isn't about feuding. Would ye want to wed yer daughter to Duncan MacKinnon?" she demanded, her voice growing husky. This close, Ross could see the tell-tale gleam in her eyes, the tension in her shoulders. Sorrow vibrated off her, as did fear, and Ross's smirk disappeared. Her defiance was a shield, and a brittle one at that. The lass was close to breaking.

Silence fell. Ross inhaled deeply in an effort to ease the unexpected tightening in his chest. Since taking Lady Leanna prisoner, he'd put up a barrier of his own. Yet at that moment, he realized he pitied her.

He hadn't wanted to take on this distasteful task—and neither had Carr—but orders were orders.

MacKinnon wanted her. And Duncan MacKinnon never gave up once he set his will upon something. Ross knew the man he served was flawed—but who wasn't? Ross deliberately didn't examine his own soul too deeply, for he too had a darker side. Ambition had driven him for years now. All he'd ever wanted was to make something of himself, to rise from being a callow youth without purpose or pride. MacKinnon had given him something his own father never had—respect. And for that, Ross was prepared to turn a blind eye to some things.

This situation was becoming more of a challenge than he'd anticipated. But he couldn't let his comely captive get to him.

Shoving aside the urge to empathize with Leanna, Ross deliberately hardened himself against her. "Yer father dishonored MacKinnon by refusing a betrothal between ye both," he said finally, injecting a callous drawl into his voice. "MacKinnon believes that ye belong to him, Lady Leanna … and if ye are unhappy with his decision, *he* is the one ye need to discuss it with."

The morning passed swiftly—far too swiftly. A chill wind blew in from the north, a reminder that although spring had come to the Isle of Skye, the last of winter's chill still lingered.

Bleak, carven peaks rose above the party of three, their bulk dwarfing the travelers. The landscape of this isle often awed Leanna. However, this morning, it depressed her. This morning, the mountains reminded her how little control she now had over her fate.

It occurred to her then that this was merely a continuation of the powerlessness she'd felt until now. She hadn't wanted to take the veil, but her father had given her no option. Her choice of husband wouldn't have been up to her either, even if she hadn't wed MacKinnon. And now that her father was gone—the only barrier between MacKinnon and his desires—another man had merely taken her by force.

And these two warriors, who followed MacKinnon so loyally, didn't see anything wrong with that.

Once again, fury writhed up within Leanna. She welcomed its heat, which cut through the chill of sorrow and made her feel stronger.

She knew it was a man's world—but her time at Kilbride had taught her a few things. Mother Shona was strong and independent. The abbess bowed to no man, and Leanna wanted to follow her lead.

At the same time though, she was no fool. MacKinnon's reputation as a brute preceded him. He wouldn't hesitate to raise a hand to her. She wouldn't be able to rail at him the way she had with Campbell.

Her pulse accelerated then as resolve flowered within her. She couldn't give up yet; she had to try and get her captors to see sense.

Her father had once told her that every man had his price.

Casting a glance in Ross Campbell's direction, Leanna studied his proud profile. "It doesn't have to be this way," she said, breaking the silence between them. "If it's silver ye want, my kin can give it to ye. Take me to Duncaith instead of Dunan, and I'll see to it that my uncle pays ye and yer friend handsomely. Ye could leave Skye … become yer own masters."

Campbell's attention swiveled to her, his dark brows drawing together in surprise. Ahead of them, Broderick twisted in the saddle, his own expression incredulous. Clearly, neither of them had expected such an offer.

"This isn't about silver," Campbell replied after a pause.

Leanna's fingers clenched around the reins. "Ye follow MacKinnon willingly?"

"Aye."

"But he's a beast!"

Broderick had already turned from them, his attention focused on the road ahead. However, Campbell watched her for a few moments more, his gaze shuttered. His lips parted as if he was about to answer her before he closed his mouth. A muscle feathered in his jaw. Then he looked away, making it clear the conversation was over.

Leanna glared at him, her throat closing up. No, she'd been mistaken. Neither of these men would help her.

They approached Dunan through a densely wooded vale. Dark spruce and pine carpeted the hills, and a meandering watercourse, the River An, cut its way west to east along the valley. They'd made even better time than Campbell had predicted; Leanna guessed that it was not yet noon.

Leanna's gaze focused on the bulk of what had once been an ancient round-tower, turned into the MacKinnon broch over generations. The broch rose high, over-shadowing its encircling walls, and the village spread out around its base.

Her belly clenched at the sight.

Leanna had been here once before when she'd been a child. Despite that the sun was shining, the broch appeared a gloomy, oppressive place as it loomed in the distance. Leanna's gaze slid from the broch to the tightly-packed rooftops beneath it. That would be 'The Warren', a network of fetid alleyways in the village. She and one of her sisters had sneaked out to catch a glimpse of the taverns and brothels there—and had both received a scolding from their mother upon their return to the keep. Dunan was far different to the wind-swept broch of Duncaith, which perched on the edge of a loch, and the clusters of shepherds' huts that encircled it.

Leanna straightened in the saddle, her breathing now coming in short, shallow gasps. She couldn't believe this was happening. Right now, she should be with her kin at Duncaith, not here.

Ma will be wondering where I am. How long before Uncle Bard sends out riders to look for us?

The thought of the grim scene they would find in the forest glade made her feel queasy. Evan had been a good man, and he'd died protecting her.

She felt as if she'd strayed into a night terror—one there was no waking from.

They rode into Dunan along a road flanked by fields. This river valley was fertile indeed, and the spring greens grew riotously. Men and women, weeding in amongst the vegetables, glanced up at hearing the tattoo of hoofbeats. Their gazes widened in curiosity at the sight of two of the clan-chief's men accompanying a nun.

Leanna's fingers clenched around the reins. The urge to cry out to them for help reared up within her. She could throw herself off the pony and run to those strangers, begging them to assist her. She opened her mouth to cry for help, yet the words choked in her throat.

All she'd achieve would be utter humiliation. These folk wouldn't help her. Just like Campbell and Broderick, they'd merely throw her to the hungry wolf who waited for her in his lair.

Calm yerself. Leanna sucked in a deep breath, and then another, to quell her clawing panic. *Hysteria isn't going to help ye now. Ye need to think.*

Leanna knew she wasn't goose-witted, yet fear could easily render her foolish. She needed to master her feelings, bide her time, and look for a chance to make her escape. She'd observe her surroundings and scrutinize every person she met, searching for someone who might help her.

Even so, as the high dun-colored walls of Dunan rose before her, swallowing the sky, Leanna found it hard to cling to hope. Right now, it felt as if she was riding into her tomb.

6

We Must Make the Best of Things

DUNCAN MACKINNON WAS exactly as Leanna remembered him. Tall and handsome with wavy peat-brown hair and slate-grey eyes, he cut a striking figure. The clan-chief wore braies of the muted red, green, and blue MacKinnon plaid; hunting boots; and a black léine open at the neck.

MacKinnon strode into the solar, a leggy charcoal-colored wolfhound at his heel—and upon spying Leanna, the man stopped dead in his tracks. His dog sat down next to him, its heavy tail thumping upon the flagstone floor.

The clan-chief's gaze swept over her, devouring her. His eyes hooded in a way that made Leanna suppress a shiver of dread. He'd looked at her that way at the clan gathering: a charged sexual look that had stripped her naked before him.

Yet his stare was even more intense today, and his lips parted, his broad chest rising and falling in excitement. His voice, when he eventually spoke, was husky. "Lady Leanna ... how pleased I am to see ye."

Leanna swallowed the lump that had risen in her throat. "Does this mean I am a guest here, MacKinnon?" she asked, deliberately keeping her tone low and gentle. "Am I free to leave whenever I wish?"

Duncan MacKinnon watched her for a heartbeat before smiling. It was a hungry smile that revealed perfect white teeth. "No, mo chridhe," he murmured. "Ye have come to Dunan for good."

Leanna inhaled deeply, clenching her fists against her thighs. *My heart.* He addressed her like a lover, even though she'd never once said a word to encourage him.

Nausea rose within Leanna, and she took an unconscious step back. She'd told herself that she'd master her fear—but panic, as wild as a trapped bird, wheeled within her. The urge to explode into hysterics, to plead, weep, and even try to flee, all vied for dominance within Leanna.

"I don't want to be here," she said, her voice trembling slightly. "Please let me return to the abbey."

MacKinnon ignored her; instead, his iron-grey gaze flicked to his two henchmen. Campbell and Broderick stood silently, flanking their captive. "Ye have done well," he said, his mouth lifting at the corners. "I knew ye wouldn't disappoint me."

"Did ye not hear me?" The words burst out of Leanna. She hated being ignored. "Ye can't keep me here against my will!"

MacKinnon smirked, his gaze focusing on Campbell. "Was she difficult to find?"

"Not really," Campbell replied, his voice as impassive as his face. "Her father's men came to fetch her for the burial. We merely followed. However, a group of outlaws attacked her party, before we had a chance to catch up with them."

MacKinnon's smirk faded at this news. "Outlaws?"

Ross Campbell nodded. "Not the men ye are looking for … but a band of ragged men bearing MacDonald colors. All of them are now dead."

The clan-chief appeared to relax at this news. "Good," he grunted. "How fitting though … that men who once served Niall MacDonald would attack his own warriors." MacKinnon's attention swiveled back to Leanna. "Yer father self-righteously blamed me for the problems with outlaws I've been having of late. However, it seems he too has made enemies of his own people."

The urge to argue, to defend her father, reared up within Leanna, but she choked it back. MacKinnon was trying to provoke her, yet she wouldn't rise to the bait. If he chose to ignore her whenever it suited him, she could play the same game.

As such, she remained in stony silence.

MacKinnon's mouth curved. "Nothing to say, eh?" he murmured. "That's good. A woman should know when to hold her tongue."

Heat flushed through Leanna, as did the urge to spit at him. Once again, she restrained herself. She sensed that a fight was exactly what he wanted.

His gaze raked over her once more. "As lovely as ye are in that habit, the time has come for ye to cast it aside. We will be wed before the sun sets today." MacKinnon glanced to where Carr Broderick stood, a still figure carven from stone. "Fetch the priest."

Broderick gave a brisk nod and left the solar without a backward glance, the door thudding shut behind him.

Leanna watched him go, her heart racing. Events were moving so swiftly now; it was impossible to keep up. She couldn't imagine being MacKinnon's wife by nightfall, and yet that fate was now rushing toward her.

MacKinnon moved to the mantelpiece and retrieved something. He then approached her, holding out his hand. A beautiful scotch thistle brooch, set around a large piece of amber, gleamed up to her.

It was exquisite, and if her father had gifted her such a piece of jewelry, Leanna would have squealed with joy.

However, the sight made her belly clench and caused a sickly sensation to wash over her.

"Something pretty for my lovely bride-to-be," MacKinnon murmured, his voice developing a crooning edge. "Make sure ye wear it from now on." The clan-chief then turned to Campbell. "Take my betrothed to Drew … and see that she is given more ladylike attire. She will then join us for the noon meal."

"This kirtle will suit ye well, Lady Leanna … it will go with the flecks of green in yer eyes."

A slender woman with regal bearing approached Leanna. Dressed in a fitting dove-grey kirtle, her thick brown hair piled up onto her head, Drew MacKinnon had her brother's grey eyes. It was hard to tell her age, for her skin was smooth and unlined. Yet there was a knowingness in the woman's gaze, a shrewdness, that made Leanna guess Drew MacKinnon had seen her thirty-fifth winter at least.

Her voice, as she held up the pine-green kirtle for Leanna's inspection, was faintly mocking.

Leanna took the kirtle without a word, her fingers digging into the soft fabric. She had to admit, it was beautifully made. It was ironic really. How often had she dreamed of being able to dress again in one of the kirtles she had once worn? She hated her heavy, shapeless habit, and yet at that moment, she wanted to clasp it to her. Suddenly, she wanted to wear it for the rest of her life.

Lady Drew's gaze met hers then, and Leanna swore the woman's eyes twinkled.

"Does my plight amuse ye?" Leanna asked, anger sweeping up from her belly.

MacKinnon's sister inclined her head. "Not in the slightest. But we must make the best of things, mustn't we?"

"I don't want to make the best of things. I want to go back to Kilbride."

Drew huffed out a breath and turned, retrieving a soft léine from the bed. It was a beautiful garment, a warm butter-yellow in color. The old Leanna, the one who had delighted in each new kirtle and shawl, would have reached for it, would have marveled over the fine needlework. However, Sister Leanna viewed the léine as if it were a serpent about to strike.

"Kilbride is lost to ye, my dear," Drew murmured, passing her the long shift dress. "It's best ye don't dwell upon it." She motioned to the screen behind them. "Ye can change there. Let me know if ye need any help."

Leanna didn't move. Holding the garments, which smelled of lavender, she merely stared at Drew MacKinnon. Rage simmered, and despite that it was cool inside the chamber, sweat beaded her skin.

"So ye think forcing a woman to wed against her will is right?" she managed finally.

Drew held her gaze, her mouth lifting at the edges in a smile that didn't reach her eyes. "I didn't choose my husband either. Few high-born women get to."

"Yer brother can't just take me like this … there will be consequences."

Drew's smile turned hard. "From whom? Yer father?"

Silence fell in the chamber then. A narrow window was open, allowing a crisp breeze to filter inside. Somewhere beyond, Leanna could hear faint children's laughter.

How she longed to go back in time, to those days when she had been under her parents' care, those days when she had believed that nothing could touch her, or those she loved.

"My husband wasn't a bad man," Drew said after a weighty silence. "But he was an interminable bore ... and his touch made my skin crawl. He was older than my own father, yet I was still bid to wed him."

Leanna clenched her jaw. "Is that supposed to give me solace?"

Drew gave a soft laugh. "I'm just trying to make ye see that for women like us, life has few choices. Ye have to use yer wits to rise above it."

Long moments passed, and Leanna didn't move. With one hand, she reached down and clutched at her habit's heavy skirt. "I can't take this off," she choked out the words. "I'm a Bride of Christ."

Leanna's breathing constricted as she finished speaking. How many times over the past year had she thought enviously of Ella and her new life as Lady of Scorrybreac? She'd noticed how attractive Gavin MacNichol was during his visits to Kilbride, and had even lain awake a few nights imagining what it would be like to undress for a man like that.

She flushed hot with shame now at the memory. Maybe this was God's way of punishing her for those fantasies. Did she even deserve to wear this habit?

As if reading her thoughts, Lady Drew made a scoffing sound in the back of her throat. "A nun's life is behind ye now, Leanna." Her voice developed a warning edge. "And if ye don't remove that habit willingly, my brother will only rip it off ye."

7

Years I have Waited

ROSS SHIFTED IMPATIENTLY, his gaze going to the closed door. Leanna had disappeared in there earlier and had not yet re-emerged. Folk would be amassing downstairs in the Great Hall for the noon meal by now. At this rate, MacKinnon's bride-to-be would make her entrance late.

It was quiet in the hallway—a narrow, windowless space lit only by a row of flickering cressets upon the damp walls. Ross didn't like being forced to wait; naturally impatient, he preferred to be kept occupied.

Especially today.

Not for the first time, he silently cursed the man he served. He hadn't expected MacKinnon to give Leanna the chance to refuse him—yet his callousness toward her had made Ross's hackles rise nonetheless.

Her wishes meant nothing to him.

Or to ye, he reminded himself. Leanna had already pleaded with him and Broderick. There was little point in him being angry with MacKinnon for ignoring the woman. Ross knew he was no better.

As they'd stood before the clan-chief in the solar, Ross had braced himself for an ugly scene. Leanna had come close to losing control. He'd seen the pallor of her face, the horror in those wide hazel eyes. When MacKinnon had sent Carr off to fetch the priest, she'd trembled like a reed in the wind. Yet she'd managed to rein in her panic, perhaps sensing that MacKinnon had been goading her deliberately.

Ye know who he is, a traitorous voice whispered to him then. *After what ye saw Siusan go through, would ye want yer sister wed to MacKinnon?*

Ross shoved his niggling conscience aside, irritated by the intrusion. His opinion on all of this mattered not. He'd been given a task, and he'd completed it. His only loyalty here was to the man he served.

The creak of hinges roused Ross from his brooding, and he turned to see a woman emerge from the chamber.

Ross's breathing caught.

Sister Leanna of Kilbride had disappeared, and Lady Leanna MacDonald of Sleat stood in her place: an elegant young woman with a slender yet womanly figure encased in flowing green. But it was her hair that caught his attention. Ash-blonde and lustrous, it fell in waves over her shoulders. The brooch MacKinnon had gifted her earlier had been pinned to her breast.

Leanna halted before him, and Ross was vaguely aware of Drew emerging from the chamber behind her.

"What do ye think, Campbell?" Drew asked with a sly smile. "She is a vision, is she not?"

Aware that he was staring, Ross caught himself before clearing his throat. "I ... thought nuns cut off their hair," he said finally, only to inwardly kick himself. *Ye sound like a lack-wit.*

"Not all nuns do," Leanna replied, her bleak tone at odds with her beauty. "When I took my vows as a novice, the abbess requested only a lock of my hair." She paused then, her delicate features tensing. "I swore that no one would look upon my hair again."

Drew huffed impatiently. "Enough of this, Leanna ... those days are over, remember? If ye are clever, ye'll make good use of yer fair face and nubile body from now on."

That comment earned Drew a frosty look. "Do ye think that's all I've got to offer the world? I've got wits as sharp as any man."

Drew's mouth curved, her grey eyes twinkling. "Aye ... sharper I'd say. But the world doesn't care how clever ye are, lass ... and my brother certainly won't."

Ross stepped forward and offered Leanna his arm. "We've delayed long enough, milady. It's time for ye to join MacKinnon in the Great Hall. He will be waiting for ye."

Leanna met his eye then, and a long look passed between them. Ross knew he shouldn't hold her gaze so, that nothing good would come from staring at a woman meant for the man he served. However, he couldn't stop himself.

Neither could he miss the desolation he saw in the depths of Leanna's eyes.

"What a bonny sight." Duncan MacKinnon leaned back upon his carven chair, his gaze raking Leanna from head to toe. "My sister has done quite a job with ye ... it was certainly worth the wait."

His gaze settled upon the brooch pinned to her breast, and a lazy smile stretched his mouth. "I knew that brooch would suit ye."

Leanna crossed the Great Hall toward the MacKinnon clan-chief, one arm linked through Ross Campbell's. Each step felt as if she were nearing the steps to the gallows. She was aware of every gaze in the hall upon her, tracking her progress across the floor.

They walked between rows of long tables toward a raised dais at the far end. MacKinnon sat at the head of the table. A huge boar's head reared above him: a ferocious-looking beast with a wiry black coat and great yellow tusks. A few retainers sat at the table with the clan-chief, although three places near him had been left free.

"It's quite a transformation, isn't it?" Drew quipped as she swept up onto the dais and took her seat. "Out of that awful black habit, most women look more attractive."

MacKinnon smirked at that, although his gaze never left Leanna.

Wordlessly, she stepped up onto the raised platform and was guided by Campbell to the seat next to MacKinnon. The clan-chief's right-hand then sat down on Leanna's other side.

MacKinnon leaned back in his chair and clicked his fingers. The sound splintered the hush of anticipation inside the hall, and a horde of servants descended bearing platters of food and ewers of ale and wine.

Leanna's gaze slid over the platters of roast fowl and braised kale and onions, and the baskets of oaten bread that the servants placed before her.

"Bramble wine, milady?" A lass asked timidly.

Leanna nodded. She hadn't drunk wine since arriving at the abbey, for they usually took ale with their meals, but right now she longed for something to take the edge off her nerves, off the panic that boiled within her, threatening to burst free at any moment.

She was relieved to see that the serving wench filled her goblet to the brim. Leanna raised it to her lips and took a large gulp, welcoming the heat as the liquid slid down her throat to her belly.

At this point, she'd grasp at what she could to keep her nerve.

The rumble of voices, which had ceased when had entered the Great Hall, resumed once more. The retainers and warriors present turned their attention from Leanna to their meals, and she let out a long exhale in relief.

However, there was one person present who'd not stopped staring at her since she'd entered the hall.

MacKinnon still reclined in his chair, ignoring the spread of food before him. Instead, he watched her under hooded lids, one hand loosely clasping the stem of his goblet.

"Years I have waited for this, Lady Leanna," he murmured. "Like a skittish doe, ye have eluded me ... but no longer. Tonight we shall be man and wife."

The wine she'd just swallowed rose, stinging the back of Leanna's throat. Those words sounded like a dire threat. She couldn't bear the thought of becoming MacKinnon's wife, of having to endure his touch. He was handsome to be sure, but his looks left her cold. The thought of his hands upon her naked flesh, of having her maidenhead stolen by him, made nausea surge once more.

Leanna swallowed hard, dropping her gaze to the empty platter before her. Woodenly, she helped herself to some roast fowl. It gave her something to do. However, she wasn't sure she would be able to eat anything. Right now, it felt as if a stone sat in her belly.

Picking up a knife, she began to push the food around her plate. And all the while, she was aware of MacKinnon's heated gaze upon her.

Stop staring at me. Her fingers clenched around the knife. How she wished she was good with a blade, like Sister Ella. She should have been able to fend off Campbell and Broderick in that clearing. She'd made a mess of defending herself.

"Are ye sure ye wish to wed so soon, brother?" Drew asked, breaking the silence at their end of the table. Leanna glanced up to see that Drew was regarding MacKinnon with her usual look—something between amusement and derision. "If ye wait a day or two, I can have the seamstress adjust a gown and get the cooks to prepare a feast worthy of the occasion."

MacKinnon pursed his lips, making it clear what he thought of his sister's offer. "Such trappings don't matter to me," he replied. "Lady Leanna will be wed in the pretty kirtle ye have gifted her, and we shall have a feast tomorrow with whatever the cooks can prepare in time." He paused there, his gaze narrowing. "I have waited long enough for this day."

Drew raised finely arched eyebrows before she helped herself to a slice of bread. "Very well ... I will instruct the kitchen."

"See that ye do."

"So, it matters not that I'm not willing?" Leanna realized she was shaking as she choked out the words, but she couldn't hold her tongue any longer. She hated the way MacKinnon and his sister discussed her fate like she wasn't even present. Ignoring Drew's warning glance, Leanna gripped the table edge and leaned toward MacKinnon, meeting his gaze squarely for the first time since her arrival at Dunan. "I'm a chieftain's daughter ... ye have no right to wed me without my consent."

MacKinnon held her gaze, and to her ire, a slow smile stretched his lips. "Ye are mine, Lady Leanna," he drawled, holding his goblet up to her in a mocking salute. "Ye might be a chieftain's daughter, but I'm a *clan-chief* ... yer father should never have defied me."

Quivering from the force of the outrage that now pulsed through her, Leanna continued to glare at MacKinnon. Vitriol bubbled up within her. She was a hair's breadth from losing her hard-won control.

She'd told herself she needed to be wise. She needed to rein in her temper and use it to her advantage when the opportunity arose, yet she was beginning to realize there wouldn't be any such occasion.

But at that moment, MacKinnon's attention shifted right, shattering the tension, toward the Great Hall's entrance. Leanna's gaze followed his, and she spied a well-built warrior with short blond hair entering the space. Carr Broderick wore a grim expression upon his face as he strode toward the dais.

"Ye took yer time," MacKinnon greeted the warrior with a frown. "How long does a man need to fetch the priest?"

"Father Athol isn't in Dunan at present," Broderick replied, drawing to a halt before them. "I searched for him everywhere before discovering that he's gone to visit the sick in Kyleakin. He will be back tomorrow."

Relief slammed into Leanna, dousing her fury. The sensation was so strong that she almost gasped. However, MacKinnon glowered at this news. "What the devil's he doing there?" he growled. "I don't want him bringing the pestilence back to Dunan."

A murmur of worried voices followed these words, echoing through the Great Hall. Those at the table shared confused looks, and even Drew lost her smirk.

Leanna swallowed, a chill flowering through her belly. She wondered how many here had heard of the plague. She only knew of it because Sister Coira had mentioned the sickness a few times over the past months. The nun, who was also Kilbride's healer, had gleaned snippets of news from the odd traveler to Torrin who brought word about the goings-on beyond their secluded corner of the world.

Until now the terrible pestilence that had brought Europe and England to its knees had seemed like something far off, something that wouldn't touch this remote isle. But this news changed everything. Now, not only had it reached Scotland, but it had crossed the water and appeared upon their shores.

"I'm sure Father Athol won't take any unnecessary risks," Drew said finally. The unusually subdued note to her voice betrayed her own nervousness. "And once he returns, he will perform the wedding ceremony as ye wish … ye will just have to wait a day, that's all."

MacKinnon cut his sister a dark look, and Drew wisely dropped her gaze, refraining from making further comment.

Leanna stared down at her platter of untouched food. The news about the plague was unsettling to be sure, but right now she had more pressing issues to deal with. Unexpectedly, these ill-tidings had brought her a reprieve.

She now had time to figure out how she was going to escape this union.

8

Ye Have No Heart

LEANNA CLIMBED THE stairs, her pulse accelerating with each step. A stay of execution, albeit a short one. One more night out of MacKinnon's clutches. Nerves clenched her belly, and by the time she reached the second-floor landing, her heart was beating so hard she could feel it in her ears.

Ross Campbell walked two steps behind her, accompanying her to the chamber where she would be lodged until the following day. They walked down the hallway in silence, although Leanna was aware of the man's gaze boring into her back. He'd said little during the noon meal, and when he'd escorted her from the hall afterward, his face had been an enigmatic mask, his gaze shuttered.

His lack of reaction made her already racing heart beat faster. Anger quickened like a stoked furnace in the pit of her belly. How could he be so heartless? How could he let MacKinnon away with this? She wanted to rail at him, tell him once again that he was no better than a hound, but desperation overrode the instinct.

Without allies here, she was doomed.

"Yer bed-chamber is up ahead, milady," Campbell said, breaking the tense silence. "The last door on the right."

Stopping before the door, Leanna turned to him. They were alone in the hallway. This was the only chance she'd get to ask Campbell for help. She was grasping at shadows, she knew it. After all, this was the man who'd crossed MacKinnon territory to abduct her.

"Ross," she said softly, meeting his eye. "Please help me."

The slight quaver in her voice alarmed her; it wasn't feigned.

The warrior had stopped before her. His dark-blue gaze narrowed at her use of his first name. However, he didn't answer her plea.

Clinging on to her courage, Leanna took a step closer to him. "Ye can't let this happen."

Ross Campbell's beautifully molded lips flattened into a grim line. "Ye shouldn't be saying such to me, milady. It's best if ye go into yer chamber now."

Pain flowered under Leanna's breastbone, and her mouth went dry. Instead of obeying him, she took another step closer, her clenched hands rising to the broad wall of his chest.

Her knuckles pressed against his leather vest, yet he didn't move, didn't reach up to remove her hands. There had to be a beating heart inside there. He had to see how much danger she was in.

"I can't keep silent any longer, Ross," she said. It choked her to plead before this man, yet she pushed on. "We have time now that the priest is delayed. Help me leave this place ... don't let this wedding take place. *Please!*"

"Leanna." Did she imagine the husky edge to his voice? He took hold of her hands and pulled them from his chest, his fingers tightening over hers. "Stop this talk. Ye aren't helping yerself. Dunan is yer home now."

"But my kin don't even know what's become of me." Her voice rose as desperation clawed at her throat. "My mother will think I'm dead. She'll be going mad with worry."

A shadow moved in those midnight blue eyes. Up close, she noted that he had long dark eyelashes and that he smelt of leather and warm male. However, his expression had turned grim, his firm grip on her hands tightening.

"As soon as ye are wed, I shall send word to Duncaith, if ye wish ... so they know ye still live," he replied, his tone gruff. "But ye must stop resisting this. It'll only make things worse for ye."

"No!" The word exploded from her. "Wedding MacKinnon will be the end of me ... why can't ye see that?"

"Enough." His voice was strained now. "I can't do anything more for ye ... ye know that."

A sob rose within Leanna, despair bubbling up. She twisted her hands free of his grip, clawing at him. "Ye are a merciless bastard, Campbell," she gasped. "No better than the beast ye serve. May ye rot in hell for aiding him!"

She managed to rake him across the face, her nails leaving a red welt down one cheek before he caught her by the wrists and pushed her back against the door. Breathing hard, Ross Campbell struggled to hold Leanna still.

The last remnants of restraint had gone from her now. She fought like a woman possessed, twisting in his grasp as she attempted to knee him in the cods. "Devil's spawn," she shrieked. "Ye have no heart."

Finally, the only way he could still her struggles was to press his body flush against hers. Arms pinned to her sides, Leanna continued to writhe, her vision blurring as despair consumed her. It was all over. She was completely alone here.

It had been a foolish, desperate move to ask this man for help. But now she had just made the situation worse for herself.

"God's bones, woman," Ross muttered through clenched teeth. "Halt yer struggles before ye hurt yerself."

Panting, Leanna sank against the door. She stared up at Ross to see that their faces were now only inches apart.

A flush had crept across Ross's cheekbones, a muscle ticked in his jaw, and his blue eyes had darkened nearly to black. He looked angry—and upset.

"This won't help, Leanna," he rasped. "Even if I wanted to, I cannot aid ye."

Leanna didn't answer. She merely stared up at him, her throat aching. The back of her eyes prickled as tears welled, yet she kept them back. She wouldn't weep in front of this man. She became aware then that their bodies were pressed hard together. She could feel the long, lean length of his body, the heat of him enveloping her. His closeness made her breathing quicken.

Leanna started to tremble. Suddenly, she bitterly regretted asking Ross Campbell for help. She wished only to be gone from his presence, to shut herself away.

"Then ye condemn me to death," she replied, her voice barely above a whisper. "Let go of me, Campbell. I will do as bid now."

His gaze narrowed further, yet after a long moment, he released her wrists and stepped back. A chill rushed in between them.

Dragging in a deep breath, she moved toward the door. Then, with one last look, she turned away and let herself into her bed-chamber.

Ross Campbell stood in the hallway, watching the door thud shut.

His heart thundered in his chest, his breathing coming in short gasps.

What had just happened?

He knew Leanna was desperate, but he hadn't expected her to lose control like that. Her behavior had angered him, and yet at the same time, her despair had stabbed him through the heart like a dirk blade. She had fought him without any thought to her own wellbeing, desperation turning her frenzied.

He didn't blame her. In the space of a day, she'd lost her father, seen her escort murdered, and been ripped away from the security of her old life—and now she was about to be forced to wed a man she despised.

She'd asked for his help, and he'd refused her.

Ross breathed a curse under his breath. *She'd have me risk my whole life for her.*

There were some paths he'd never take—even if a beautiful, grief-stricken woman pleaded with him.

Ross bolted the door from the outside—as MacKinnon had instructed. He then stepped back and raked a hand through his hair. He'd known this whole business was ill-fated. MacKinnon thought he could bend this woman to his will, but even after just one day in her company, Ross realized he wouldn't.

Instead, Duncan MacKinnon would just break Lady Leanna.

Ross turned and walked away down the hallway—and as he did so, he heard the muffled sound of sobbing.

"What happened to ye?" Carr frowned, peering at the scratch upon Ross's cheek. "Looks like ye had a fight with a she-cat."

Ross huffed a humorless laugh, lowering himself to the bench seat and reaching for the flagon of ale between them. They sat in the guard's hall, a rectangular space upon the ground floor of Dunan's guardhouse. At this hour there were a few men seated around the space, although none occupied this table but Carr and Ross, giving them a rare moment of solitude.

"Lady Leanna gave her opinion of me," he said, pouring himself a tall cup of ale.

Carr raised fair eyebrows, his grey-blue eyes widening. "She attacked ye?"

Ross nodded. "When I accompanied the lady to her bed-chamber, she flew into hysterics ... and begged me to save her."

This comment caused Carr to raise his eyebrows higher still. "And of course, ye refused?"

"Aye." Reaching up, Ross traced a finger down the raised welt upon his cheek. It still stung. "Can't say I blame her though ... not after everything we've put her through."

Carr raised his own tankard of ale to his lips and took a measured sip. "Careful, Ross ... sounds to me like ye are growing sympathetic toward the lass."

Ross tensed at his friend's observation. The scene with Leanna had rattled him. The fear in those wide hazel eyes, the desperation in her voice. He'd been tempted to reveal his concerns to Carr. But something in his friend's voice warned him from doing so.

Aye, they were close and would always watch each other's backs. Yet their first loyalty was always to the man they served—Ross would do well to remember that. Checking his impulse to confide in Carr, he took a deep draft of ale.

There are some thoughts a man should keep to himself.

9

Not a Happy Woman

"I WANT THE hunt for my brother intensified." Duncan MacKinnon's voice cut through the dew-laden air. Riding at the clan-chief's side, Ross glanced across at him. MacKinnon wore an expression he knew well: a look that was a blend of anger and dogged determination. They'd been out early, stalking deer in the valleys to the south of Dunan. MacKinnon had been quiet earlier as they'd ridden out in the predawn hush.

Ross realized now that he'd been brooding, and their lack of success at bringing down a deer had worsened his mood. The gibbet they passed on the roadside, where a dead brigand hung by the neck, had spurred MacKinnon to speak up.

"How exactly?" Ross asked, looking away from the grisly sight. A crow sat upon the corpse's shoulder and was pecking at its rotting flesh. "We're doing everything we can … and all the other chieftains and clan-chiefs have been keeping an eye out for him."

"Aye, but he's still on my lands … I know it in my gut," MacKinnon growled back. "MacLeod and Fraser both report that the outlaw problem has lessened of late in their territories … but it hasn't in mine. Neither of them has a bastard brother intent on ruining them. I don't care if ye have to get the entire Dunan Guard out combing the land … I want ye to find him."

Ross frowned, considering the clan-chief's orders. The two men rode side-by-side, leading the hunting party east along the road into Dunan. The broch rose before them—a dark, solid mass in the midst of the wreathing river mist.

As much as he sympathized with MacKinnon about his brother, Ross had been silently impressed by the outlaw over the years. He was as cunning as a stoat and elusive as a wraith. Time and time again, he'd attacked the clan-chief's supply wagons and couriers before disappearing into the wilderness.

Ross had led the search for 'Craeg the Bastard'—the result of the old clan-chief's dalliance with a whore—over the years, but he'd never been able to get close to him. MacKinnon knew that he already had men out searching for the outlaw band, but it clearly wasn't good enough.

"As soon as yer wedding has passed, I shall widen the search," Ross said finally.

"Aye, see that ye do. I want Craeg's neck in a noose by summer's end."

The veiled threat in MacKinnon's voice caused Ross to tense. Glancing over his shoulder, his gaze briefly met Carr's. He could see by his friend's pursed lips that he'd overheard the short exchange.

Like Ross, Carr knew that capturing the outlaw leader was no easy task—if it had been, they'd have accomplished it already. MacKinnon had made himself unpopular throughout the territory due to his harsh treatment of folk and increasingly high taxes. As such, locals were uncooperative with Ross and his men—and had even gone as far as to harbor outlaws.

A heavy sensation settled in Ross's chest when he turned back and urged his courser toward the North Gate—Dunan's main entrance. MacKinnon's threat was a blunt reminder that it didn't matter that he was the clan-chief's right-hand and Captain of The Dunan Guard. His position here was still precarious.

Duncan MacKinnon had reminded him that as he'd had the power to raise Ross up, he could bring him low just as easily.

"Ye are fortunate, milady ... the apple blossom is particularly beautiful this year ... it looks lovely in yer hair."

The servant's high-pitched chatter echoed through the bed-chamber, yet Leanna ignored it. She sat still, her gaze focused on the opposite wall while Tyra fussed over her hair.

"And that gown suits yer coloring ... it used to belong to Lady Siusan, ye know. The seamstress didn't need to adjust it much, as ye are of a similar build. I do believe Lady Siusan wore this same dress to her wedding."

Leanna swallowed. *Wonderful ... they're dressing me in the dead wife's wedding gown.* The pressure under her breastbone increased, the sensation feeling as if a giant hand were gripping her ribcage. With any luck, it would stop her heart before the ceremony took place.

"Enough prattle, Tyra. Lady Leanna doesn't need to hear all that." A cool female voice interjected.

Leanna tore her attention from the wall, to where Drew MacKinnon stood in the open doorway. As always, the widow looked impeccable in a dark blue gown that suited the rich brown of her hair. Her tresses were swept up into an immaculate coil. She had a regal way of carrying herself, an elegance that Leanna hadn't seen in anyone else. It made her feel gauche and bumbling in comparison.

She wished she had Drew MacKinnon's composure, her strength. Somehow, the woman had lived under the same roof as Duncan MacKinnon all these years and hadn't been broken by him.

That's because she's as heartless as he is.

The women's gazes met and held for an instant. "Tyra is right though," Drew said with a small smile. "Ye are lovely. I'm glad we had the extra time to dress ye properly. My brother will be delighted."

A sickly lump rose in Leanna's throat. She didn't want to delight MacKinnon. The thought of standing at his side in the kirk made her belly roil. She wasn't sure she could endure this.

"So, the priest has returned?" she asked finally, hating the slight tremor in her voice that betrayed her fear.

Drew nodded. "Aye … Father Athol is readying himself as we speak."

"Has he told ye of Kyleakin … of the sickness?" Tyra asked, her chirpiness fading.

Drew frowned. "He tells me that things are grim there," she admitted. "A handful of folk died during his visit … he administered their last rites."

"Did he speak of how the sick are afflicted?"

Drew's mouth flattened. "No … and I didn't ask."

"I was speaking to a cloth merchant at market yesterday." Tyra's voice developed a shrill edge as she continued. "He's come from the mainland, where smoke stains the sky each night from dozens of funeral pyres. He says the illness is punishment from God. We are all wicked and must pay for our sins." The handmaid glanced at Leanna then, her eyes wide. "Ye are a nun, Lady Leanna … do ye not agree?"

"I … I don't know," Leanna stammered. "I don't think that God wishes for—"

"Enough," Drew cut in, her tone sharp now. "Lady Leanna isn't a nun anymore, Tyra. Please don't ask her such things."

The handmaid flushed. "MacKinnon should close the gates to travelers, milady. In my opinion, the priest shouldn't have come back to Dunan. We cannot let the sick infect us here."

Drew snorted. "I saw Father Athol earlier, and he seemed perfectly healthy to me." Her tone was hard, yet worry now shadowed Drew's grey eyes. "Ye are not to run off and start frightening folk, Tyra … is that clear?"

The maid lowered her gaze, jaw clenching. "Aye, milady."

Drew's attention then returned to Leanna. She smiled, although the expression had a brittle quality to it. "The ceremony will take place at noon," she informed her briskly, returning to the wedding. "And a feast and dancing will follow."

Leanna didn't reply. Instead, her gaze dropped to her slippered feet. How she had once loved attending weddings. She'd adored the gaiety, and the chance to dine on rich food and dance the evening away with handsome young men.

After today, she would never see these occasions in the same way.

"Yer betrothed is not a happy woman." Drew's voice made Duncan MacKinnon open his eyes. He reclined upon a chair in his solar while his manservant shaved his chin with a blade. Hume, a lean man with thinning dark hair and a nervous manner, but a steady hand, always did an excellent job of shaving him. Letting the servant scrape off the last of the stubble, MacKinnon took the cloth he passed him and dried himself off.

"And why should that concern me?"

"It doesn't have to at all," his sister replied. She'd entered the solar and taken a seat, uninvited, by the hearth. Despite that it was a mild spring morning outdoors, a lump of peat glowed there. Even during the hottest days of summer, the damp stone of Dunan broch always held a chill. "But how content will ye be, wedding a lass who isn't willing?"

Duncan snorted before waving to Hume that they were done. Picking up the bowl of water and retrieving the drying cloth, the man left with a nod.

Once they were alone, he fixed his sister with a level look. "Extremely content ... I've wanted Leanna MacDonald for years. I care not if she's willing." His mouth curved then. "If I'm honest, it adds to the excitement."

Drew stared back at him. She was adept at hiding her feelings; she always had been. Even when he'd bullied her during their childhood, she'd been tough. He'd used to pinch her under the table during mealtimes, but she'd never squawked, never let on to their parents. She was the hardiest person he'd ever met, and yet in those cool grey eyes, he saw something this morning.

Was it disgust?

"She's not like Siusan," Drew said after a lengthy pause. Once again, her voice was cool, expressionless. She spoke as if she cared little about the subject matter, and yet the very fact that she'd brought it up was telling; it told Duncan that his sister wasn't as cold as she liked the world to believe. "Yer last wife was quiet and compliant. Lady Leanna isn't like that ... she will fight ye."

A grin stretched across Duncan's face. Bending down, he ruffled Bran's ears. The wolfhound lazed upon the deerskin rug before the hearth. "Then I will enjoy breaking her."

10

Fight to the Last

LEANNA STEPPED OUT of her chamber to find both Ross Campbell and Carr Broderick awaiting her. Campbell wore a sash of his clan's plaid—green and blue crisscrossed with charcoal—while Broderick, who hailed from Éire, had donned the MacKinnon colors for this special occasion.

Swallowing hard, Leanna noted that her mouth tasted sour. Despite that she'd spent all morning trying to stave off her fear, the sight of the men who'd escort her up the aisle of the kirk made the full reality of the situation hit her.

Broderick wore a stony expression, while Campbell was frowning. However, his gaze was hooded and angled at a point beyond her right shoulder. Ross was deliberately avoiding her eye. Both warriors carried dirks and claidheamh-mors at their sides. She had no chance of escaping them.

Wordlessly, she made her way down the hallway toward the stairwell, where Drew MacKinnon waited.

MacKinnon's sister watched her approach, her expression keen. Her gaze then slid past Leanna to the men following her, and her mouth quirked. "MacKinnon colors suit ye, Broderick."

"Not as well as the blue of yer kirtle looks well on ye, milady," the warrior replied gruffly.

Drew's smile widened. "What's this … a compliment? I never thought I'd see the day."

Broderick didn't respond to this teasing comment, but this didn't seem to bother Drew. Still smiling, MacKinnon's sister turned away. She then led the way down the stairs without another word.

Leanna had no choice but to follow her.

The journey down to the ground level of the broch, and out through the bailey below to the South Gate, seemed to be over all too quickly. Unlike the exit near the stables, which led down through the surrounding village to the fort's North Gate, this way out was for the clan-chief's use only. The walk took them around the back of the broch, across a cobbled yard, and under a stone arch. Before Leanna knew it, they were walking through the kirkyard toward a pitch roofed stone building.

The sight of the cross at the roof's peak, silhouetted against the blue sky, made Leanna's belly twist. How she wished she was back at Kilbride with Mother Shona, Sister Coira, and the other nuns. She'd even welcome Sister Elspeth's acid tongue.

To think that she'd once chafed at the confines of the abbey.

Right this moment she'd give anything to be back there. She'd never again complain about the heavy habit that made her skin itch in the summer. She'd never bother about the numerous prayers every day, or the hours of back-breaking work looking after the fields and the livestock within the abbey walls.

Mother Shona will be worrying about me ... and so will Coira. The thought rose unbidden, and Leanna's throat thickened. Coira hadn't wanted her to leave Kilbride. She should have heeded her friend's advice.

The kirk doors were open, and Leanna entered the building behind Drew MacKinnon to find that rows of retainers and clansmen packed the low bench seats on either side of the narrow aisle. And standing at the foot of the altar, at the far end, was Duncan MacKinnon.

Her already knotted stomach tightened further. This man's behavior was reprehensible. There had been no betrothal—she had never been promised to him.

Once again, MacKinnon cut a handsome figure dressed in chamois braies, a fine snowy white léine, and his clan sash. His brown hair fell in smooth waves almost to his shoulders, and his lantern jaw had been freshly shaved.

He tracked her progress down the aisle, while behind him a dark-robed figure also waited: Father Athol.

Leanna tore her attention from MacKinnon and focused upon the man who'd wed them.

The priest looked to be around a decade older than MacKinnon. He was a tall, lean man with a stern face and dark eyes. A large iron crucifix hung about his neck, glinting in the hallowed light of the guttering banks of candles behind him.

As she neared the altar, Leanna started to feel sick. Her skin under her wedding garments felt clammy, and her legs trembled. Her ears started to ring, and she wondered if she might faint.

Up ahead, Drew stepped neatly to one side, allowing Leanna to draw close.

Heart pounding, Leanna stopped next to MacKinnon. She dared glance back then, at where Campbell and Broderick now moved to take their places in the wings, Campbell at MacKinnon's right-hand, and Broderick next to the clan-chief's sister. Ross Campbell's face was a blank mask.

Look at him, she thought bitterly. *He's partially responsible for this mess, and he can't even look me in the eye.*

"Are ye ready?" Father Athol's low voice echoed through the kirk.

"Aye, Father," MacKinnon replied. Leanna heard the tension in his voice, the excitement. "Begin the ceremony."

Leanna turned back to the altar, her pulse tripling when she saw the priest approach them, a ribbon of MacKinnon plaid in hand. "Take each other's hands, please," he said quietly.

Benevolent Lord, please save me ... this can't be happening.

Never had she prayed so fervently. The night before she'd prayed beside her bed until her knees throbbed. She'd promised to be especially diligent in her devotion if only He would return her to Kilbride. However, God wasn't about to save her it seemed.

Leanna stared at the ribbon as if it were a serpent about to sink its fangs into her. She didn't want to touch his hand, to be bound to him forever. Tearing her gaze from the plaid, Leanna looked at the priest once more.

This close, she could see that his eyes were the color of peat. They were kind eyes.

Leanna's pulse started to gallop, sweat now trickling down her back. She couldn't do this; she wouldn't stand here meekly, like a sacrificial lamb, before MacKinnon and his retainers, and pretend she was happy about this union.

With Father Athol's absence from Dunan, she'd been given a little time and now it had run out. Arguing hadn't worked, and neither had pleading.

Leanna's hands balled into fists at her sides.

She had no other choice. She'd now throw herself upon the mercy of the priest.

"No!" Her choked cry echoed through the now silent kirk. "I won't take his hand ... I won't wed him." Leanna's gaze snared the priest's, holding him fast. "This wedding is a crime, Father ... I am a Bride of Christ and am being forced against my will."

Shocked gasps and murmurs rippled through the kirk, yet Leanna didn't take her gaze from the priest. She watched his face stiffen, his gaze widen, and realized with a jolt that he hadn't known.

A nerve ticked under one eye as he slowly shifted his attention to MacKinnon. The clan-chief stood, stone still next to Leanna. She hadn't looked his way, hadn't dared to.

"This woman is a *nun*?" Father Athol asked, his voice rising.

"She *was* a novice at Kilbride," MacKinnon replied, his tone hardening. "But as ye can see, she isn't now."

"He abducted me!" Leanna gasped, the words rushing out of her. She had an audience at last—a kirk full of people who needed to know what a villain this man was. Maybe they were ignorant of all of this? Perhaps they'd turn against him once they knew? "He brought me to Dunan by force."

Father Athol went still, and his dark brows knitted together. "Is this the truth, MacKinnon?"

"Of course not," MacKinnon replied. "The woman lies ... she is merely nervous ... pay her no attention."

Leanna did tear her attention from the priest then and stared at MacKinnon. He stood there calmly, a faint smile upon his lips. However, those grey eyes of his were wintry. She'd angered him, although he was doing an admirable job of hiding it.

Father Athol cleared his throat, obviously uncomfortable. "But ... if this woman is a nun, ye cannot wed her."

"I told ye, Father ... she was merely a novice. It was her father's will that we should wed. I am merely carrying out his wishes."

"Filthy liar!" Leanna's temper exploded. Fury pounded against her ribs. Suddenly, she didn't care what happened to her. "How dare ye use my father's death as a shield? My father hated ye ... he sent me to Kilbride so that I may *avoid* being wed to ye ... and the moment ye heard he was dead, ye sent yer men after me."

She swiveled around, meeting the priest's stunned gaze once more. "Please, Father ... ye must believe me. Send word to Mother Shona at Kilbride, she will confirm what I have just told ye." She dropped to her knees before him then, clasping her hands before her. "Please don't wed me to this man."

A brittle silence descended upon the kirk. All the whispering and muttering ceased, and suddenly the only thing Leanna could hear was the rasp of her own breathing. She'd taken this as far as she could now—she'd placed her fate in the priest's hands.

Father Athol stared down at her, and she saw the conflict upon his face. "This is indeed wrong, lass," he said finally, his voice held a rasp of outrage. He hastily made the sign of the cross. "I cannot allow this union to take place." He looked over at where the clan-chief had not yet moved. "I apologize, MacKinnon, but I won't sanction this union. Ye must send this woman back to Kilbride Abbey where she belongs."

Hope jolted through Leanna at these words. Like the parting of the clouds after days of rain, sunlight filtered into her dark world. Finally, someone saw the madness of all of this and was willing to help her. The tension that had wound itself into a tight knot within her released. She was saved.

It took MacKinnon a while to answer, so long in fact that Leanna dared to look his way.

He stood, hands by his sides, his face carven from granite, and when he finally spoke, there was a rasp to his voice. "I must have misheard ye, Father. Surely, ye are not refusing me?"

The priest nodded, his shoulders squaring as resolve settled upon him. "I am ... this wedding cannot take place," he replied. His hand reached up, his fingers curling over the crucifix around his neck. "It is against God's will ... against what is right."

"And that's yer final word on the subject?"

"Aye ... I am sorry."

"Not as much as I am."

And then, Duncan MacKinnon moved.

One moment he was standing there, staring at the priest—and the next he drew the dirk at his hip, leaped forward, and sank his blade into Father Athol's belly.

11

His Word is Law

THE PRIEST'S SCREAM echoed through the kirk.

Father Athol reeled back, but MacKinnon went after him. And to Leanna's horror, he yanked his dirk from the man's belly and stabbed him thrice more—once to the belly, once to the chest, and then to the neck.

The priest crumpled, and this time MacKinnon let him fall. And as the man lay dying at his feet, the clan-chief kicked him in the ribs.

Leanna stared, her breath choking. A wave of dizziness slammed into her. She couldn't believe what she'd just witnessed. She'd known MacKinnon was a brute, yet she'd never imagined he'd murder a priest. Frozen to the spot, she merely gaped at him while he stepped down from the raised platform before the altar. Crimson splattered his pristine white léine, and he clutched the bloodied dirk in one hand.

"I need another priest," MacKinnon barked, turning his attention to where Carr Broderick stood next to Drew MacKinnon. Like Leanna, the pair of them stood frozen after the clan-chief's vicious display. "Go find me one, Broderick."

A long silence followed, and when Broderick replied, his voice held a wary tone. "There are no other priests nearby ... I will have to travel to the Frasers and bring one from there."

"I don't care where ye get him," MacKinnon snarled. "Just find me another man of the cloth and drag the bastard here."

Black spots danced before Leanna's eyes, her dizziness intensifying. Digging her fingernails into her palms, she tore her attention from the clan-chief, her gaze sweeping over the rows of retainers who'd just witnessed this appalling scene. Many of them appeared pale and shaken. For the first time since meeting her, Leanna saw that Drew MacKinnon's face was strained and her gaze haunted. Across from Drew, Ross Campbell's face had gone rigid with shock.

Campbell met Leanna's eye for the first time since she'd entered the kirk. A long look passed between them.

"Please," Leanna whispered, her voice breaking. "Help me."

"Silence, woman." MacKinnon's voice lashed across the aisle, and she cringed. His face had gone red, the veins on his neck standing out. "Or I'll take my hand to ye." His attention then swiveled to Campbell, his grey eyes hard.

The warrior stared back.

The moment stretched out, before MacKinnon's lip curled. The stare was a challenge. He was defying Campbell to intervene on her behalf—yet Ross didn't. Satisfied his servant still knew his place, the clan-chief swiveled, gesturing to two warriors standing a few yards away. "Clean up this mess." MacKinnon glanced back at his right-hand, his gaze dismissive. "Campbell ... take my betrothed back to her chamber."

Leanna walked stiffly out of the kirk at Ross Campbell's side. She couldn't fail to notice that he kept a tight hold upon her arm.

Stepping outside, the warmth of the sun bathed Leanna's face, calming her racing heart. But her body still trembled in the aftermath of what she'd just witnessed.

The clan-chief had just cut down a priest in cold blood.

"MacKinnon will burn in hell for what he's just done," she hissed to her escort as he propelled her down the path toward the north gate.

"Most likely," Campbell replied, his voice flat.

Leanna glanced his way to see that the warrior was staring straight ahead, his handsome face set in hard lines. He looked furious—but it was most likely with her.

"How could ye let him kill Father Athol?" she demanded, her voice rising.

"I didn't expect MacKinnon to do that," Campbell growled. "None of us did."

"At least the priest stood up to him!"

"Aye." Campbell glanced her way, his dark eyebrows knitted together in a deep scowl. "And the man bled out on his own altar for the trouble. Athol was a fool ... he should have done as he was told."

"Just like ye?" Leanna snarled back, a hot tide of fury sweeping over her. "Just like everyone else in this broch?"

"MacKinnon rules here," Campbell countered. "His word is law."

"Ye are all scared of him."

Campbell's grip on her arm tightened just a fraction, the only sign that her words affected him.

"Ye are as bad as he is." Leanna struggled against his grip. They'd entered the fort and were circuiting the edge of the bailey toward the broch's entrance. "A man without a conscience ... without a moral compass!"

Campbell continued to hold his tongue. Ignoring her struggles, he hauled Leanna up the steps and into the broch. And although she continued to berate and insult him, all the way to her bed-chamber, he refused to engage with her.

His face—the last thing she saw before he slammed the door shut—was grim, his dark-blue eyes narrowed.

Leanna stared at the closed door, her breathing hitching. Once again, she was wasting her time. Campbell had seen MacKinnon's behavior in the kirk, and yet he still stood by him. That was all the proof she needed that the man had no integrity at all.

Alone in the bed-chamber, Leanna wrapped her arms around her chest, in an attempt to stave off the panic that now clasped long fingers about her throat and slowly squeezed.

There was no escape from this cell. She'd heard Campbell bolt the door after he'd shut her in, and the single window was too high and narrow for her to see out of, let alone climb through.

With trembling hands, she reached up and unfastened the brooch at her breast—MacKinnon's gift. Drew had made her wear it for the ceremony. Bitterness flooded her mouth, and she flung the offending object across the chamber. It thudded against the wall, yet to her disappointment, the brooch didn't shatter.

Just like the beast who was intent on wedding her, she couldn't rid herself of it that easily.

Tears welled then, blurring her vision and making her throat cramp. When they'd brought her to Dunan, she had thought this nightmare couldn't get any worse—and yet with each moment, she felt as if she were passing through Dante's nine circles of hell, with each level being worse than the last.

"Ye do realize that no priest is going to want to replace Father Athol ... not once they discover what happened to him."

"What do I care?" Duncan MacKinnon drained his wine goblet and set it down on the window-sill with a thud.

"Dunan needs a priest, Duncan ... if ye slay them, this broch will get a reputation as a Godless place."

MacKinnon turned from the window, his gaze settling upon his sister's proud face. The woman had followed him, uninvited, into his solar, and now proceeded to lecture him.

"What's this?" he murmured. "I thought ye had no time for religion? Didn't our mother sour ye of it, as she did me?"

Drew's mouth pursed. "I'm not interested in spending hours on my knees praying for forgiveness, if that's what ye mean? However, Father Athol did much good here. The folk of Dunan loved him. They will be upset about this."

Duncan's mouth twisted into a sneer. Scooping up his goblet, he strode to the sideboard and poured himself another.

A few yards away, sitting before the glowing hearth, Bran whined. The wolfhound had picked up on its master's dangerous mood and was giving him a wide berth. However, Drew wasn't being so prudent.

"I care not what the folk of Dunan think," he said after he'd taken another gulp of wine. "They should take this as a lesson ... of what happens to those who defy me."

Drew moved a few hesitant steps toward him. Closer up, he could see the strain on her face; usually, his sister appeared ageless, but today he could see the fine lines around her mouth and eyes. "Leanna will never bend to yer will," she said after a pause. "If ye wed her, it will mean misery for ye both ... surely ye can see that?"

Duncan drained his second wine and set the goblet down upon the sideboard. He then approached his sister, looming over her.

"Ye have gotten mouthy of late, Drew ... it begins to vex me."

Drew raised her chin, angling her head up so that she held his gaze. "I have always vexed ye," she reminded him with an arch look. "But in the past, ye have sometimes heeded my counsel."

"Have I?" Duncan looked his sister up and down dismissively. "Ye think yerself cunning and adept at manipulating men ... yet ye couldn't get Gavin MacNichol to do yer bidding, could ye?"

Drew's mouth thinned, her eyes narrowing. MacKinnon knew he'd hit a raw nerve there, for his sister had been taken with the MacNichol clan-chief and shocked to learn he'd wed another. However, when Drew replied, her voice was controlled. "MacNichol was in love with someone else," she pointed out coldly. "But that'll never be yer problem, Duncan. Ye are incapable of love. Ye are incapable of caring for anyone besides that damn dog of yers."

Ross climbed the steps to the broch, barely acknowledging the guard who greeted him near the doors. His mood was dark and tension had settled upon his neck and shoulders. He'd gone looking for Carr, but his friend had already departed for Talasgair upon a swift courser.

It would take him at least two days before he returned with a priest to do MacKinnon's bidding. And in the meantime, the only person Ross trusted was absent from the broch.

Perhaps it was for the best—in Ross's current state of mind, Carr wasn't the ideal audience. He'd already been too frank with him of late.

Inside the broch, he crossed the entrance hall, and was about to enter the Great Hall beyond, when a figure on the stairs caught his eye.

Lady Drew MacKinnon halted, her slender frame tensing.

Ross's gaze immediately went to the angry red swelling upon her left cheekbone. However, the lady didn't lift a hand to it. Her grey eyes glittered as she watched him. "Campbell," she greeted him coolly. "Join me in my solar, please ... I wish to speak to ye."

12

He's Gone Too Far

ROSS FOLLOWED LADY Drew into the women's solar.

The chamber stood in stark contrast to the clan-chief's. The latter was a purely masculine space, with a stag's head mounted above the hearth, deerskins covering the cold flagstone floor, and tapestries of battles upon the wall. But the women's solar—not a room he usually frequented—smelled of drying herbs. Soft embroidered cushions dotted the room, and sheepskin rugs covered the floor. A great loom, with a half-finished tapestry upon it, sat by the open window.

Lady Drew, her back ramrod straight, walked to a low table, where she poured herself a goblet of wine. Ross noted that her hands were trembling slightly. He tensed, surprised; he'd never seen MacKinnon's sister lack composure. The woman had the warmth and vulnerability of iron. And yet, this afternoon, there were serious cracks in the façade.

Lady Drew was upset, and she wasn't trying to hide it.

"Wine?" she asked, her voice huskier than usual.

"Aye," he replied, grateful for the offer. The events at noon still unsettled him, perhaps wine would push the images of Father Athol bleeding to death before the altar to the back of his mind.

Drew handed him a goblet before motioning to one of the high-backed chairs before the hearth. "Please ... sit down."

Ross did as bid, although he couldn't relax. It was highly unusual to be invited into the women's solar with a woman alone—widow or not.

He'd known Drew MacKinnon a long while. She was nearly a decade his elder and had wed not long after his arrival at Dunan. Even as a younger woman, she'd been a force to be reckoned with though—blade tongued and sharp-witted. Her much older husband hadn't known what to do with her. It wasn't entirely a surprise that she'd remained a widow since his demise.

Drew took the chair opposite. She sat stiff and tense, her fingers wrapped around her goblet, although she didn't drink from it. Her gaze never left Ross, as if she was silently taking his measure. And when she finally spoke, Drew's voice was softer than he'd ever known it. "He's gone too far this time."

Silence drew out between them then. Ross wasn't sure how to respond. His first instinct was that this was a trap. MacKinnon was testing his loyalty. Duncan and Drew had always been close, and in the past, she'd been as unfailingly faithful to her brother as Ross had been.

He had to be careful around her. She could still be talking to him on her brother's behalf. Ross had seen the look in the clan-chief's eye when he'd stared him down earlier. MacKinnon had been challenging him, and perhaps he wasn't yet done.

Her words were shocking, traitorous. No one in this broch spoke out openly against Duncan MacKinnon. No one.

"How far do we follow him?" Drew asked when Ross didn't speak. "We both hated it when he raged at Siusan for dying in childbirth, and I'm sure ye heard about how he attempted to rape that nun last year? Aye, we're both willing to let him wed a woman against her will … but murdering a priest? When do any of us say that he's crossed a line that can never be uncrossed?"

Once again, Ross wasn't sure how to respond. He'd spent the last fifteen years serving this family, and being asked to give such a frank opinion unsettled him. Instead, he raised a hand, touching his left cheek as he continued to hold Drew's gaze. "He did that, I take it?"

Drew's mouth pursed. "He used to hit me when we were bairns, ye know … but once we grew up, he never lifted a hand to me … until today." She drew in a deep breath then, her jaw firming. "*Today* will be the last time."

Ross held her gaze, impressed by her iron will, her strength. He knew that she meant her words, yet he wasn't sure how she expected him to respond to her admission.

He decided to make light of it. "What are ye saying?" he asked, lifting an eyebrow. "That ye will hold yer tongue around him in future … no matter how he provokes ye?"

Drew's nostrils flared, her eyes turning flint grey as she stared him down. "Duncan has reasons for being the way he is," she replied, her tone clipped. "Our parents were … harsh … but I'm done making excuses for my brother."

Ross caught the bitter edge to her voice. "Why are ye telling me all this?" he asked, frowning.

They continued to watch each other, and Ross's wariness grew. He'd never trusted Drew MacKinnon, and she'd given him little reason till now.

"I saw the way ye looked at Lady Leanna today in the kirk," Drew said, her voice softening. "Ye sympathize with her."

Ross grew still. "Aye," he admitted reluctantly, "but that doesn't mean I'll act on it."

Drew inclined her head, mouth quirking. "I've watched ye over the years, Ross … and must admit there have been times when I've thought ye as immoral as my brother. But of late I see ye have a sense of right and wrong after all."

A man without a conscience … without a moral compass.

Ross's mouth soured as Leanna's accusing words rang in his head, mocking him.

"Maybe I'm no better than him," Ross replied, his tone cooling. "I've put up with things others would not."

"As has Broderick ... as have I," Drew murmured. "But that doesn't make any of us black-hearted ... yet. We are entangled in his web, but there's still time to untangle ourselves."

Ross's fingers clenched around the stem of the goblet he'd not yet touched. A cold, hard stone settled in the pit of his belly. This conversation was now steering itself into dangerous waters indeed. "What do ye want of me, Lady Drew?"

Drew took a dainty sip of wine before swirling the goblet, her expression serious now. "Nothing stays the same," she began, holding his gaze. "Ye might think yer position is secure at Dunan, but it's only as safe as the mind of the man who rules these lands. How sane do ye think my brother is? How long before he starts a feud with the MacDonalds or the Frasers? How long before he raises taxes so high that folk rise up against him?"

Ross didn't answer, although he took her point.

"Change is afoot," Drew continued, her voice low and determined. "Soon ... the balance of power in this broch is going to shift." Her gaze narrowed then as it snared his once more. "I need to know that when it does, ye will be my ally ... not his."

I need a plan. Unable to sit, or rest, Leanna paced the confines of her bedchamber. *I won't give up.*

After Campbell had locked her inside the chamber, despair had visited Leanna for a spell. She'd thrown herself down upon her narrow bed and wept until she felt sick from it. But after the storm of tears had passed, a strange calm had settled upon her.

She was young and strong and had her wits about her. She wasn't beaten yet.

Today had been a setback, and yet at the same time a reprieve. By rights, she should have now been MacKinnon's wife and cringing in their marital bed. But since Carr Broderick had ridden to the Frasers in search of a priest, she'd been given another couple of days' breathing space at least.

Escape would be impossible without assistance. Leanna's mouth compressed as she swiveled on her heel and completed another circuit of the chamber. MacKinnon had everyone in this broch leashed by duty and fear; she couldn't rely on any of them for help.

It was likely then, that the only way she'd get free of MacKinnon was if she killed him.

Leanna halted in her tracks, a chill shivering through her.

How she wished that Sister Ella—now Lady Ella MacNichol of Scorrybreac—had ended MacKinnon's life when she'd had the chance. Ella had been a guest at Dunan when MacKinnon had forced his way into her bedchamber and tried to rape her. He'd also left a message for Leanna—a warning that one way or another he would have her.

At the time, Leanna had believed his threat to be an empty one, yet she now realized that MacKinnon didn't bluster. He'd meant every word.

Ella had managed to escape him, by drawing a knife and stabbing him with it. She'd then hit him over the head with a jug, knocking him unconscious before fleeing Dunan.

Leanna inhaled deeply, smoothing sweaty palms upon the skirts of her kirtle. Of course, if Ella had killed him, she'd have been hunted down as a criminal. Even wedding Gavin MacNichol wouldn't have saved her from the noose.

No—it was just as well that Ella hadn't killed him.

Leanna would do it instead.

A thrill of fear trembled through her.

How she wished she had a bow and arrow. She was an excellent shot with the weapon—although a longbow wouldn't be that practical right now. Still, she'd learned other skills at Kilbride. The abbess had taught her how to wield a quarter-staff, wriggle out of a man's grip, and handle a knife—albeit clumsily. She wasn't as confident with any of those skills as she was with a longbow, but she wouldn't give up.

Exhaling sharply, Leanna looked about the chamber. There was nothing here she could use as a weapon. The servant who'd just brought her supper had deliberately not left her a knife. Her hair was loose, so she had no pins she could stab him with either.

There will be something I can use, she thought, sitting down upon the bed. There would be another wedding ceremony and after that a feast. If she was clever and quick, she'd have the opportunity to take something as a weapon.

And when she was alone with MacKinnon, she'd use it.

Leanna's heart started to pound.

She'd been timid when that outlaw had attacked her in the clearing. She'd panicked, and as such had completely disregarded Mother Shona's advice about letting your attacker get close enough before striking for a vulnerable spot.

But next time she'd be ready.

Ye shall hang for killing a clan-chief.

Aye. A humorless smile curved Leanna's lips then. *But at least I won't have to suffer his touch.*

13

Long Have I Awaited This Moment

DUNCAN MACKINNON REFILLED his goblet before frowning. The ewer was empty. He needed more wine. Luckily, he'd bid his manservant bring up a few ewers that evening after supper, and so he heaved himself out of his chair, staggered over to the sideboard, and fetched another jug. Then, settling down before the fire, his long legs stretched out before him and crossed at the ankle, Duncan resumed drinking.

The Lord knew how much wine he'd consumed since that disaster of a wedding ceremony, but, like his father before him, Duncan could handle his drink. Rage had boiled within him after he'd cut Father Athol down, a fury that sought an outlet.

Striking his mouthy sister across the face had helped, a little, but even though the wine had blunted the sharpest edges of his anger, the rage was still there, simmering like a cauldron of stew.

He hadn't been this angry since his useless wife had died in childbirth.

Having Lady Leanna MacDonald wasn't as easy as he'd thought. He'd fantasized about this moment a while now. He'd imagined wedding the object of his desire and ripping her wedding gown from her nubile young body afterward. In his fantasies, he hadn't cared if she was willing or not—and the fact that she was so set against their union excited him—but he hadn't expected to be thwarted like this.

That damn priest.

He'd never liked Father Athol. The man had been respected at Dunan, but he was always sticking his nose in where it wasn't wanted. He'd had no business traveling to Kyleakin to bless the plague-ridden, and he'd certainly had no business refusing to perform the ceremony. The man's haughtiness had been his undoing.

He'd deserved a blade in his belly.

Even so, Duncan was now without a priest, and he needed one if he was to wed Lady Leanna.

Damn the wedding ceremony, damn all of these rules.

Fury kindled once more, racing through Duncan's veins. He'd planned to bed Leanna tonight, and now he was being forced to wait. His groin ached, and his body was restless.

Duncan clenched his jaw. *I need to plow a woman.*

He wasn't used to being thwarted, and if he hadn't been determined to wed Leanna, he'd have had her by now.

Maybe I should go to The Goat and Goose, he thought dully, taking another gulp of wine. It was his favorite brothel. The whores there were always accommodating, although these days there weren't any that really took his fancy. There hadn't been for many years, not since the delectable Coira.

Duncan's eyes closed as he lost himself in memories. Coira—tall, dark-haired, and sultry. How he'd reveled in her long-limbed body and full breasts. How he'd enjoyed reducing her to a trembling wreck upon the bed, those startling violet eyes huge with fear. Her disappearance from the brothel a decade earlier had soured the place for him. Duncan had looked for her, but the woman appeared to have simply disappeared. He often wondered what had become of her.

Shoving aside memories that still rankled, Duncan decided against visiting *The Goat and Goose* tonight. Despite that Coira's ghost tantalized him, the only woman he burned for these days was Lady Leanna.

He remembered spying her for the first time at the clan gathering between the MacKinnons and the MacDonalds of Sleat, over two years earlier. It had been a bright summer's day, and she'd been wearing a robin's egg blue kirtle, her long pale hair tumbling down her back.

Entranced, Duncan had watched Leanna dance with the other maids, her laughter drifting over the glen—a sound he infinitely preferred to the wail of the highland pipe.

He'd decided then and there that he'd one day have her as his wife—no woman but Lady Leanna would do. And despite all the trouble the woman had caused him of late, he still felt the same way.

Leanna was lying upon her bed, staring up at the rafters, when she heard the thud and rattle of her door being unbolted.

In an instant, she sprang into a sitting position, heart pounding. It was late, almost at the witching hour. Who would dare enter her bed-chamber at this time of night?

To her surprise, a wiry man with a permanently downcast gaze entered. Leanna went still as she recognized him. She'd seen him attend on MacKinnon a few times since her arrival at Dunan. His name was Hume—and he was the clan-chief's manservant. "What's the meaning of this?" she demanded, fear turning her hostile.

"I'm sorry to bother ye at this hour, milady," the man murmured with a low bow, gaze still averted. "But ye must get dressed and come with me."

Leanna's breathing caught in her throat. "Why? Where are we going?"

"Please don't ask any questions of me, milady," the servant replied. His voice quavered nervously. "Just dress quickly in yer nun's habit and come with me. I will wait outside while ye ready yerself."

As quickly as he'd appeared, the manservant vanished, the door shutting with a gentle thud behind him.

Leanna got to her feet, her pulse racing.

Why did he want her to dress in her nun's habit? Was this an escape? Had she been wrong about not having any allies here? That was the only explanation she could find to this bizarre request.

Hope fluttered up within her. She'd prayed fervently before retiring for the night—maybe the Lord was indeed answering her prayers. It looked like this nightmare was about to end.

Leanna moved over to the chair, where her black habit and underclothes still draped. With a trembling hand, she reached for them.

"Where are we going?" Leanna's whispered question echoed loudly in the silent corridor. She had dressed as bid and was now following Hume along the hallway.

"Hush, milady ... it's best we do not speak," he replied, his tone gruff now.

Of course, Leanna chided herself. *We must be quiet.* If they were making an escape, she should hold her tongue. However, now that she was dressed and following the manservant, a strange misgiving had settled over her.

Something about this felt wrong.

Hume hadn't met her eye once. And his furtive, guilty manner put her on edge. She tried to tell herself that he was merely nervous, for he was going against his master in order to aid her escape, yet that assurance couldn't smother her instincts.

Why would he help me?

Halfway along the hallway, they stopped before a large oaken door. Leanna frowned. She didn't know this door—it didn't lead to the clan-chief's solar at least. Perhaps this was the chamber of the person who was helping her.

Hope speared through Leanna once more. Was this Lady Drew's bedchamber?

The servant pushed open the door and motioned for her to enter before him. "Go on, milady ... ye are expected."

Leanna moved forward, her gaze sweeping the interior of the space as she did so. It was indeed a bed-chamber, although one far bigger than her own. However, the moment she stepped inside, Leanna realized that it didn't belong to a woman.

This was a purely masculine space, sparsely decorated save one deerskin upon the floor. A huge bed dominated the room, covered in dark furs and blankets.

Leanna's throat closed, her blood suddenly roaring in her ears. *This isn't Drew MacKinnon's room ... but her brother's.*

Leanna turned to leave, but at that moment, the door slammed shut behind her. Grappling with the handle, she found it locked.

Heart galloping now, she turned, back pressed against the door, and watched as a tall, broad-shouldered figure stepped out of the shadows in the corner of the chamber.

Stripped to the waist and barefoot, clad in nothing but a pair of braies, Duncan MacKinnon moved unsteadily toward her, a wolfish smile stretching his face.

"Good eve, mo chridhe," he murmured. "Long have I awaited this moment."

14

Obsession

ROSS KNEW HE should probably retire for the night. However, as he sat in the Great Hall of Dunan, staring down at the tankard of ale he'd barely touched, he realized he wasn't sleepy at all. His conversation with Lady Drew earlier had merely stoked the fires of unease within him, turning his mood strangely inward. He wasn't a man given to lengthy brooding, yet the events of late had started to make him question everything.

A rot had set in at Dunan, long before Lady Leanna had arrived here. It had begun years ago, Ross realized, from the moment Duncan MacKinnon had taken over from his father. Old Jock MacKinnon had been a brutish man, yet he'd known how to rule these lands, and unlike his son, he hadn't carried the torments of hell inside him.

After she'd asked him to shift allegiance to her, Lady Drew had told him a few things about her brother's past. Her story had put Ross on edge, for it bore an eerie similarity to his own unhappy upbringing—although he was grateful not to have had a mother like theirs.

Neave Campbell was a meek woman who was incapable of dominating others, but apparently, MacKinnon's mother used to beat and shame Duncan as a bairn—his only crime being that he was born a lad. She'd been angry that she'd wed a harsh, unloving man, who made no secret of the whores he kept—and she'd taken that fury out upon her young son.

MacKinnon carried a hatred within him, a need to prove himself to the world that drove each decision.

Ross traced a knot of wood upon the table before him with a fingertip. He'd reached great heights here at Dunan, yet he had the sinking feeling it was all about to come to an end.

Lady Drew was right. He wasn't sure how much longer he could stomach serving MacKinnon. How much longer could he stand by without lifting a finger to help those the man hurt?

Ross's thoughts shifted to Lady Leanna then. She'd accused him of being a rogue, a man without morals or decency. At the time, he'd brushed her insults aside, but somehow they'd wormed their way under his shield and cut deep all the same.

With a jolt, he realized that Leanna's good opinion of him mattered.

Like the man he served, Ross's childhood had shaped him. His brutal father and bullying brothers had made him tough, determined, and ruthless. But if he continued on this path, would he end up like MacKinnon?

Ross muttered a curse and ran a hand over his face. What a mess this all was.

"Campbell ... what are ye doing up?"

Ross glanced up to see a wiry figure standing a few feet away. Hume, MacKinnon's manservant, twitched like a nervous hare, his dark eyes flitting around the hall nervously. A few of MacKinnon's warriors slept in here, their gentle snores lifting up to the rafters.

"I could ask ye the same question," Campbell replied, his gaze narrowing.

"MacKinnon called for me," the manservant muttered, his thin hands clenching and unclenching at his sides, "and so I did his bidding ... I *always* do his bidding."

Something in the man's voice made Campbell tense.

Wordlessly, he rose to his feet, took Hume by the arm, and led him from the hall. In the entrance room beyond, he turned to him. The light of the burning cressets around them illuminated the lines of strain upon the older man's thin face. Hume's mouth trembled. Something was definitely amiss with him.

"What is the matter?" Ross demanded. "Ye look as if ye have seen a wraith."

"I've done a terrible thing," Hume replied, his voice turning querulous now. "The Lord will send me straight to hell."

Ross stilled, his breathing slowing. "What, Hume? Speak plainly."

The manservant's gaze fused with his. "MacKinnon bid me fetch Lady Leanna ... and so I did. She is now alone with him in his bed-chamber."

"Let me leave." Leanna backed up against the door, her breathing coming in short gasps as she struggled to contain the panic that welled within her. "We shouldn't be alone like this."

Duncan MacKinnon drew closer, his smile widening further. "This will be our secret then ... none but us and my manservant can know. Hume is loyal though ... he will not tell a soul."

Leanna fumbled for the door handle, but once again it didn't budge.

"There's no point in doing that, my sweeting," MacKinnon said, the crooning note to his voice deepening. "Hume bolted it from the outside ... he will only open it again when I call for him. Ye are trapped inside here with me."

Leanna's breath started coming in panicked gasps at this news, and she darted sideways as he closed in on her.

Just like the day before when he'd stabbed Father Athol, MacKinnon struck fast, grabbing her by the arms and slamming her up against the wall. He then pressed himself up against Leanna, grinding his hips hard against hers.

The rigid length of his arousal stabbed against Leanna's belly, and a wave of dizzying nausea swept over her.

For a moment, the ragged sound of her breathing and the thrashing of her heartbeat almost deafened her.

Merciful Lord, this can't be happening.

And yet it was. MacKinnon had her trapped against him, and he intended to rape her. He'd tired of waiting for a priest to bind them; he'd merely take what he wanted tonight.

MacKinnon leaned forward then, his hot mouth searing her cheek. She smelt the reek of wine on his breath and realized then why he'd appeared so unsteady upon his feet.

The man was rotten drunk.

"I've dreamed of this moment," he rasped, his rough hands groping her through her habit. "I have dreamed of taking ye like this."

Leanna struggled against him, yet he held her fast, his hips grinding into her even harder. One hand went to her breasts, kneading them like bread dough, while the other grabbed her backside, squeezing hard. Revulsion shivered through Leanna, although MacKinnon clearly thought her reaction was caused by lust, for he gave a soft chuckle.

"Aye ... that's right, mo chridhe ... I knew ye would like it rough. Ye nuns appear cold and sexless, but underneath that habit, ye are all sluts."

Leanna's skin crawled now. She froze in his grip, her heart beating so hard it felt as if it would burst from her chest.

"I like a woman in a habit," he murmured, pushing down her wimple so that he could ravage her neck. "My favorite whore used to dress up as a nun for my pleasure ... I used to enjoy ripping her habit off her, as I will ye."

Through the fog of terror, Leanna remembered the hot way his gaze had raked over her when she'd stood before him in her nun's clothing. She also recalled how he'd attempted to rape Ella during her visit to Dunan the year before. Did a nun's attire arouse him?

He started to whisper things then—ugly, frightening things that made Leanna draw in short, rasping breaths—descriptions of all the acts he was going to perform on her, and the things he would make her do. They were things that would hurt her, things she hadn't even realized that men and women did together.

Leanna drew in a deep breath, preparing to let out a blood-curdling yell for help, but at the last moment, she hesitated.

She had no allies in this broch. Who would come to her aid?

Leanna couldn't rely on anyone else but herself. At the abbey, she'd been taught what to do if a man ever tried to force himself upon her. Trying to fight him off was ill-advised as men were stronger and would always win in a struggle. She had to go for his most vulnerable areas: eyes, throat, belly, or groin.

However, if she was to manage to hurt him, she needed to get MacKinnon to lower his guard first.

Leanna shivered again—not hard to do, for bile surged up her throat now, making it difficult not to gag. He'd hitched her skirts up, and his hands were roughly exploring underneath, his thigh forcing her legs apart.

"Ye like this, don't ye?" MacKinnon growled. He leaned back and gazed down. His eyes were now glittering slits of desire. "I'm going to plow ye here ... up against the wall."

This was Leanna's moment. In order to meet her eye, he'd shifted back from her, just a little, and when he released her with one hand—reaching down to unlace his straining braies—she made her move.

Gathering every bit of her strength—all her loathing and fear—she brought her knee up and slammed it into his cods. And as she did so, Leanna brought up her arms, linking them around his neck, to give herself purchase.

MacKinnon's face froze, his eyes rolling back in his head. With a wheeze of pain, the clan-chief let go of her and reeled away, but Leanna held on tight. Drawing her knee back, she drove it upwards again, into his groin a second time.

She had to make sure she hurt him, ensure he stayed down long enough for her to somehow escape this chamber.

MacKinnon's roar echoed through the room, and when Leanna did release him, falling back against the wall, he crumpled forward onto his knees, clutching at his injured cods. His face had gone milk-white, and he began to retch. However, his grey eyes blazed with fury.

Heart racing wildly now, Leanna edged along the wall, toward where a ceremonial shield hung upon the damp, pitted stone. Maybe she could slam him over the head with it.

MacKinnon spat out a vile curse and lunged for her. But the movement cost him, and he collapsed upon the floor, bent over his damaged bollocks. "Bitch," he howled. "I'll beat ye bloody for that!"

Leanna edged farther toward the shield, and had almost reached it, when the door to the clan-chief's bed-chamber crashed open.

Ross Campbell appeared in the doorway, a drawn dirk in his hand.

15

Allies

ROSS WASN'T SURE what he'd expected to see when he burst into MacKinnon's bed-chamber. He'd tried not to imagine how far things had already gone after Hume told him what had transpired. After sending the manservant on his way, he'd leaped for the stairs, taking them two steps at a time till he reached the second-floor landing.

He hoped Lady Leanna had managed to fend the man off, or that MacKinnon wasn't too eager, and had decided to take his time.

However, he certainly hadn't expected to be greeted with this sight.

Duncan MacKinnon lay on his side, curled over as he clutched at his cods. In between gagging and groans of agony, the clan-chief snarled abuse at the small woman pressed against the wall a few feet away.

Lady Leanna, dressed in her nun's habit, was edging toward the great shield that hung upon the wall above the hearth. Ross realized her intent, but also knew that she'd never be able to lift the shield. It had been made for someone twice her size.

"Lady Leanna, stay where ye are," he barked.

Two strides took him into the chamber, and up to where his master sprawled. "Campbell!" MacKinnon wheezed, his eyes glittering with pain. "Get her."

Ignoring him, Ross circled behind the clan-chief and slammed a booted foot between his shoulder blades, pushing him flat onto the ground.

MacKinnon cried out, as the movement aggravated the injury to his groin.

Ross frowned. Although it was late and most folk within the broch slumbered in their beds, MacKinnon was likely to attract attention if he kept making this much noise. Fortunately, Hume wasn't going to come to his master's aid tonight; after lightening his conscience, the man-servant had stared at Ross with the eyes of a condemned man. They both knew what such a betrayal of the clan-chief's trust meant. Ross had told him to go, to get as far away from Dunan as he could—and, without another word, Hume fled into the night.

Lowering himself, Ross shifted his boot and pressed a knee between MacKinnon's shoulder blades instead. Then he held his dirk to the clan-chief's cheek. "Keep silent," he instructed coldly, "or this might accidentally slip."

He could feel the fury vibrating through MacKinnon's body. The man was tough; he was in terrible pain from the blow Lady Leanna had clearly dealt him to the cods, and yet he could still focus enough to pay attention to his surroundings.

Ross glanced up, catching Lady Leanna's eye for the first time since he'd entered the bed-chamber. "Take off yer veil and wimple," he ordered.

For a moment, Leanna merely stared at him. Her wide hazel eyes were green in the light of the glowing hearth next to her, and her face was ashen. She watched him, frozen in place, as if she wasn't sure why he was here and what he meant to do.

Ross would have thought it was obvious.

"Go on!" he said, his tone sharpening. "We don't have time to waste here."

Leanna's mouth thinned, but she did as bid, pulling off her black veil and the white wimple that she wore underneath. Beneath the layers of fabric, her long pale hair hung in a braid down her back.

"What now?" she asked, her voice chill.

"Rip the wimple in half and gag him with it."

Leanna's eyes widened at this, as the realization that he really was here to help her sank in. Jaw clenching, she tugged at the wimple. The garment was well made, and it took her a few moments before a tearing sound filled the chamber. Once she'd ripped the wimple, she rolled one half into a thick strip, which she then held out to Ross.

"Ye do it," he replied, jerking his chin down to where he still held the flat of the dirk blade against MacKinnon's cheek. "I'll make sure he behaves himself."

Face set in determination, Leanna approached. Her manner was wary, as if she neared a seething hornet's nest, yet she didn't waver.

"Ye will pay for this, Campbell," MacKinnon wheezed, his eyes wild, his face contorted. "I'll hunt ye down like a dog."

Ross ignored him, his gaze fixed upon Leanna. "Do it."

Moments later MacKinnon's mouth was firmly gagged.

"Bind his ankles with the other half," Ross instructed, "and pass me the veil."

This time she obeyed without hesitation. Meanwhile, his knee still pressed firmly between MacKinnon's heaving shoulder blades, Ross straightened up. He used his dirk to cut the veil into strips, and with them, he bound the clan-chief's wrists behind him. He then secured the binding on MacKinnon's ankles with it—once the man recovered from his blow to the groin, he'd find a way to free himself of his bonds. However, Ross wanted to ensure it took him a while to do so.

Rising to his feet, Ross gazed down at the man he'd followed loyally for the past decade, a man he'd sworn fealty to. He'd pledged his life to serving MacKinnon, and now he hadn't just broken that pledge, but he'd openly betrayed him.

Ross had imagined that he'd feel a terrible weight of guilt at doing such a thing, but he did not.

The only emotion he felt right now was a seething anger in his gut as he stared down at MacKinnon, trussed like a Yuletide capon. The man writhed against his bonds, his movements frenzied, his eyes wild.

The urge to kick him to death reared within Ross, his rage a dark beast that screamed to be unleashed.

Controlling the impulse, Ross took a step back from the clan-chief. He wouldn't do it. Unlike the man he served, he didn't have that streak of latent cruelty. He could be ruthless when necessary, but he knew when to draw the line.

Ross's mouth compressed at the irony of it. *Perhaps ye have a moral compass after all.*

He turned to Lady Leanna then. She was staring at him as if he'd just sprouted another head.

"I'll get ye a cloak, and then we must leave Dunan." He made for the doorway. "Come on."

Leanna edged past MacKinnon. Her heart still hammered, and she felt sick with nerves, yet the relief at seeing the clan-chief trussed upon the ground made her knees wobble.

She deliberately avoided his wild gaze, for she knew it would be murderous. Instead, she wordlessly followed Ross Campbell to the door. His appearance in the chamber shocked her. When he'd first burst into the room, brandishing a dirk, she'd thought he'd come to help MacKinnon.

A moment later he'd surprised her by coming to her aid instead.

She didn't understand his behavior or entirely trust it, but there was no time to question him. For the moment, he was her ally, and she would do as he asked if it meant getting free of Dunan.

Stepping out into the hall, she pulled the chamber door closed behind her. However, she saw that Campbell had halted a few feet away, his gaze trained farther down the hall.

Leanna's attention followed his, and she froze.

A few yards away stood a woman. Dressed in a night-rail, with a long shawl pulled tight around her shoulders, Drew MacKinnon stared at them.

It was then that Leanna saw the angry red swelling upon the woman's left cheekbone. Her long brown hair was unbound tonight, giving her a softer, more vulnerable look.

Long, tense moments passed, and Leanna held her breath, waiting for MacKinnon's sister to explode, to yell out and bring the guards running. Yet she did not.

Instead, Lady Drew met Campbell's eye, and a strange look passed between them. "Take the South Gate and leave via the kirk yard," she murmured, her voice barely above a whisper. "There are fewer guards there ... it's safer."

Campbell gave a curt nod.

Drew MacKinnon's gaze shifted then to the closed door of the clan-chief's bed-chamber.

"He's alive," Campbell said softly. "I've tied him up ... so he won't cause any trouble for the time being."

Lady Drew's head inclined, her mouth lifting at the corners.

"Lady Leanna needs a cloak," Campbell continued.

MacKinnon's sister favored him with a cool smile. "Then I shall fetch her one of mine."

They slipped out of the broch and into the bailey below, before making their way to the stables. Cloak clutched close, Leanna watched as Campbell saddled a leggy courser with deft movements. He didn't look her way while he worked, yet she stared him down nonetheless.

She didn't understand why he was helping her—not when he'd refused her earlier. It made no sense to her at all. Her mind felt tied up in knots of confusion. Even Lady Drew had turned into an ally in the end.

Images from her encounter with MacKinnon assailed her then, and she shuddered. With the door bolted from the outside and only a cumbersome shield as a weapon, she'd have had little chance of getting away from him.

What would have happened if Campbell hadn't burst in?

Her savior finished saddling his mount and turned to Leanna, motioning her over. Without a word, she sprang up onto the saddle, brushing aside the hand he held out to assist her. She was grateful that he'd appeared when he did, but after what she'd just endured, she wished for no man's touch tonight.

She could still feel MacKinnon's hand on her, roughly kneading and groping her flesh. She wished to bathe in scalding water and scrub her skin raw, but that ritual would have to wait.

If her dismissal bothered him, Campbell showed no sign. Instead, he merely took hold of the reins and led the horse from the stables.

The moon nearly full overhead, they made their way around the base of the broch toward the South Gate. The clip-clop of the courser's hooves upon the cobbles sounded obscenely loud in the night's quiet, and with each yard, Leanna grew tenser. To calm herself, she heaved in deep breaths. The cool night air, laced with the scent of pine and peat-smoke, relaxed her just a little.

She didn't understand how Campbell was going to get them out of the broch. He was MacKinnon's right-hand, but that didn't mean the guards at the gate were going to let him pass, especially with her.

Yet the warrior didn't appear remotely worried. He walked with a long, confident stride, his gaze sweeping his surroundings. Leanna did note though, that his free hand rested upon the pommel of his sword. He was ready for trouble.

Up ahead, hove the South Gate. The guard tower on this side of the broch was much smaller, and the gate was half the size of the one to the north—only wide enough to let through one horseman at a time.

Two leather-clad figures bearing spears stood before the closed gate. They watched the travelers approach, light from the nearby burning braziers highlighting their wary faces.

"Campbell." One of them greeted MacKinnon's right-hand. "What are ye doing? Isn't that MacKinnon's lass?"

"Sorry about this, Glen." The scrape of steel echoed through the night as Campbell drew his claidheamh-mor in one fluid gesture. "But ye and Clyde are going to have to step aside."

A heartbeat later the point of that gleaming broad-sword was pressed against the guard's heart.

The warrior—a young man with heavy-lidded dark eyes—swallowed hard. "Ye will swing for this, Campbell."

"That may be … but not tonight. Drop yer spears … both of ye."

Glen did as bid, the weapon thudding to the ground. However, next to him, Clyde didn't budge.

"Drop it." There was steel in Campbell's voice as he drew a dirk with his free hand. "Or after I skewer Glen's heart, I'll cut yers out."

The menace in his voice was so real that Leanna shivered. She believed him—and so did Clyde, for he lowered his spear to the ground a moment later.

"Good lad," Campbell said softly, motioning to the guard house to their left. "Now move along."

Both young men glared at Campbell, their eyes bulging with outrage, yet they did as bid. He was their superior after all, Captain of The Dunan Guard, although tonight would be his last in the role, and this his last order.

"If ye make a squeak before we are through the gate and on our way, I'll personally come back here and cut yer throats … don't doubt I will," Campbell told the men as they filed inside the narrow space that was furnished only with a couple of low stools and a lantern.

Both guards remained stonily silent, and the moment they were inside the gate house, Campbell swung the door shut and bolted it. He then went to the wooden gate and heaved up the iron bar that kept it locked.

He shoved open the gate with a shoulder before going to where Leanna and the horse still waited a few yards back. Wordlessly, she shifted back in the saddle, giving him space to mount, and then he swung up in front of her.

"Hold on," he said, his tone grim. "This will be a wild ride."

Reluctantly, Leanna did as bid, wrapping her arms around his waist. Then Campbell gathered the reins, and they bounded forward, through the gate and into the night.

16

Not the Best of Men

THEY RODE SWIFTLY down the moonlit valley, the outlines of great spruce and pines rearing overhead, and the thunder of the horse's hooves in their ears.

Leanna clung on, her jaw clenched, while the courser stretched into a full gallop. It was risky to ride this fast at night, but they were fortunate, as this stretch of road was good and the moon lit their way. Campbell had clearly chosen the fastest horse in the stable, for the beast ran as if pursued by hounds.

Which they soon would be.

Leanna's ears strained for the baying of dogs, the shouts of men, or the tattoo of pursuing hoof beats, but she could hear nothing over the pounding of her heart.

She couldn't believe she was actually free—that Ross Campbell and Drew MacKinnon had risked their own lives to help her.

Hopefully, the clan-chief would never know that Lady Drew had assisted their escape from Dunan. She had been careful to keep her vice low in the hallway and had fetched Leanna a traveling cloak without any fuss before disappearing into her quarters.

As they waited for Lady Drew to fetch the cloak, Campbell had whispered that Leanna actually had Hume to thank for her escape. MacKinnon's man-servant had betrayed his master. Fortunately, Hume had been wise enough to run for his life after doing so.

The chill night air bit against Leanna's cheeks, despite that she had pulled the cowl of her cloak over her face. Bowing her head, she found herself leaning in to the man seated before her.

The warmth and strength of Ross Campbell's back became her anchor during their flight, and although she'd initially been reluctant to wrap her arms around his waist, Leanna now clung to him as if he were a lone rock in a stormy sea—her only chance of survival.

The horror of her near-rape was ebbing now, MacKinnon's hold slipping with each furlong they traveled west. The threat had been real, and even now the memory of his hot breath on her cheek, his rough hands upon her body, made Leanna's pulse race.

She'd directed every bit of strength she possessed into kneeing him twice in the groin. She'd have shoved his cods up into his throat if she could have. Still, she knew she'd inflicted injury upon him. Even if someone freed him before dawn, he'd be able to do little—and he certainly wouldn't be able to ride a horse in the state he was in.

A tight smile stretched Leanna's lips.

I wish Mother Shona could have seen that. She also wished Sister Coira had been present. Her friend was skilled at defending herself with her hands.

Leanna's eyes stung as a wave of homesickness swept over her. It wasn't for Duncaith, but for Kilbride Abbey and the women who'd become her family over the past two years.

She'd felt restricted by her life in the order, but now that her world was in chaos, she longed for its safety, its simplicity.

Leanna stiffened against Ross Campbell's back as a thought took hold. Leaning forward farther still, she spoke for the first time since they'd galloped from Dunan.

"Where are ye taking me?" When he didn't answer immediately, Leanna pushed on. "To Kilbride?"

"No," he replied, the word gruff. "MacKinnon will look for ye at the abbey … ye won't be safe there."

Leanna tensed for a moment before she realized he was right. As fierce as the abbess and her nuns were, they couldn't protect her from MacKinnon and his men.

"Where then?"

"Duncaith," he replied. "I'm taking ye home."

Leanna caught her breath before she spoke once more. "But won't MacKinnon search for me there as well?"

"Aye … but I'm hoping yer kin can protect ye, hide ye. MacKinnon would have to declare war upon the MacDonalds of Sleat and storm their broch to get ye back … an act that might go ill for him."

Leanna considered these words. He was likely right, and as she thought about returning to her family, a warmth grew in the pit of her belly.

"Why are ye doing this?" she asked after a brief pause. "I don't understand."

Campbell's voice held a note of censure when he replied. "This is not the time for such a conversation, Lady Leanna."

She stiffened. "Why not?"

A tense silence stretched between them, before he spoke once more, his voice strained. "Ask me again in the morning … and I will answer ye."

They didn't halt until the rosy blush of dawn crept across the eastern horizon. As soon as the sky lightened sufficiently, Campbell turned his horse from the road and took them across country. They rode through stands of spruce, the heavy resinous scent of the trees lacing the dewy morning air.

Eventually, Campbell drew the tired courser to a halt near a trickling mountain burn. Without a word to Leanna, he swung down from the saddle before helping her to the ground. And unlike the last time he'd helped her down, Leanna didn't resist. However, this time her hands weren't bound. Only a couple of days had passed since then, and yet to Leanna, it felt as if weeks had gone by.

If Ross remembered the incident, he didn't say. Instead, he turned his attention to the horse, loosening the girth, and murmuring soothing words to the beast as he led it over to the stream for a brief drink.

Their mount had done a valiant job of taking them a great distance from the walls of Dunan, yet it would have to carry them farther, and Campbell clearly wanted to ensure that the courser lasted the distance.

Leading the horse over to a grassy spot where it could graze for a short while, Campbell eventually turned to Leanna.

It was the first time their gazes had met all night, and the impact of it made Leanna grow still. Back in Dunan, Ross Campbell's expression had often been aloof, his gaze shuttered. Yet there was no veil over his face this morning.

His features were strained, yet his eyes were the most intense she'd ever seen them.

Leanna's pulse accelerated as the stare drew out. Eventually, she swallowed, before licking her lips. He was starting to make her feel nervous. "What is it?" she finally asked huskily.

His mouth quirked. "I owe ye an explanation, do I not? Ye wish to know why I freed ye? Why I've put a price on my own head as well?"

Leanna didn't answer. She merely stared at him, awaiting his answer.

After a drawn-out moment, Campbell sighed and raked a hand through his shaggy dark hair. He had beautiful hair—as black and shiny as a raven's wing, it fell in soft waves around his face. "I don't claim to be the best of men, Lady Leanna," he said, still holding her gaze. "But I'm not a beast either ... I couldn't have lived with myself if I'd let MacKinnon force himself on ye, and then make ye his wife."

Leanna frowned. "I asked ye for help before, and ye didn't give it ... I still don't understand what changed?" She watched him closely then, noting the way those midnight blue eyes shadowed, the tension that rippled along his chiseled jaw.

Campbell favored her with another wry smile. "As I said before, I'm not the best of men."

Heat kindled in Leanna's belly at these words as her anger rose. That explanation wasn't good enough. "MacKinnon is a brute," she said, suppressing a shudder at even uttering the man's name. "How can ye follow someone so black-hearted?"

Campbell's smile faded, and she watched his gaze shutter. "We come from different worlds, milady ... I wouldn't expect ye to understand my motives."

Leanna folded her arms across her chest. "Well, explain them to me, and we shall see."

Campbell inclined his head, his gaze narrowing. "When ye grow up among brutes, a man like MacKinnon seems no worse."

Leanna frowned in response. "Go on."

"I'm the youngest son of Iver Campbell ... he's not a man many would dare cross," he replied. Tension rippled off him now, the cloak of arrogance he usually wore sloughing away. "Growing up, I was terrified of him ... we all were. He beat my mother, and he thrashed me and my brothers and sister. Dogs cowered whenever he came near. It was a harsh environment, and my elder brothers grew up as hard as their father, while my sister, Una, found herself a husband and fled our broch as soon as she was of age." Campbell paused, his mouth twisting. "Una's a survivor. She's now on her second marriage ... to the MacLeod clan-chief here on Skye. But like me, she's avoided any trips *home*."

"Was it really that bad?" Leanna asked, her tone still guarded.

"Aye ... it was," he replied, his voice flat now. "As the youngest bairn, I bore the brunt of my brothers' bullying. When I had twelve winters, one of them tried to drown me after I bested him at Ard-ri. Da beat him so badly for it that Doug lost sight in one eye. Life in the broch became even harsher for me after that ... and when I got the chance to foster on the Isle of Skye upon my sixteenth winter, I grabbed it with both hands."

Ross Campbell halted there. Reaching out, he tore off a stem of pine from the tree next to him and began to shred it. His handsome face was now pale and strained. Leanna could see that the words cost him; he was not used to revealing himself before someone like this. He didn't like to divulge his unhappy past.

An uncomfortable silence settled between them, and Campbell's gaze shifted to the pine he was pulling to pieces. "Ye grew up in a loving environment, Lady Leanna ... and yer father went to great lengths to protect ye. My father wouldn't have done the same for his daughter." He glanced up then and met her eye once more. "When I arrived at Dunan, I found a place where I was wanted, appreciated. If I'd stayed with my kin, I'd have amounted to nothing, yet here I quickly rose in the ranks, and when Duncan MacKinnon became clan-chief, he made me Captain of The Dunan Guard. I grew up being told I was worth nothing ... but MacKinnon changed all that."

Leanna watched Campbell, and a little of the heat in her belly cooled. She wanted to rage at him, to vent the fury she still held within at her abduction and treatment over the past few days. And yet, seeing the vulnerability upon his face, she couldn't muster the stinging words she longed to hurl at him.

He was right. Until her abduction, she'd never known cruelty and brutality. She'd grown up in a brash, yet loving, family, and then had entered the safe confines of Kilbride Abbey.

She had no idea what it was like to feel unwanted, unloved.

Looking at Ross Campbell, she imagined he was a few years older than her—in his late twenties perhaps—and yet his eyes belonged to a much older man. She wondered if he'd ever been in love, had ever made himself vulnerable to anyone. She had the suspicion he hadn't.

"So ye could no longer pretend that yer master wasn't the devil?" she asked finally.

Ross huffed a bitter laugh. "Aye ... there comes a time in every man's life when he must decide what he stands for." He cast aside the now naked sprig of pine and stepped toward her. "Last night I decided that time had come."

17

What Do Ye Stand For?

"AND WHAT DO ye stand for, Ross Campbell?"

The question was bold, and yet Leanna felt compelled to ask it. This conversation had changed things between them. Until now, she'd merely seen him as MacKinnon's henchman. She hadn't given even a passing thought to the events that had made Campbell into the man he was, hadn't cared. But now she did.

And try as she might to deny it, Ross Campbell fascinated her. He had from their first meeting in that clearing. There were layers to him that made her want to dig deeper.

His mouth lifted at the corners. "I'm not rightly sure … all I know is that from the moment I agreed to ride to Kilbride and abduct ye, my conscience has not given me an instant of peace. With each passing day, as MacKinnon's behavior worsened, I have felt as if I am traveling into a land that I have no wish to explore. I knew that if I journeyed much farther into it, I'd be lost forever."

He took a few steps closer, and suddenly he was towering over her. Leanna didn't shrink back though. Even when she'd been a captive at Dunan, Ross Campbell's presence had never intimidated her.

"I owe ye an apology, Lady Leanna. Because of me, ye did not attend yer father's burial, and have been frightened and abused."

The directness of his admission threw Leanna. She tilted her chin up, something that was necessary to meet his eye. Heat flowered out from the center of her chest as the moment drew out.

She didn't know how to respond. Warmth crept up her neck now, and she realized that his proximity, and the fierceness upon his face, flustered her. She'd had little to do with men of late and was suddenly aware of him in a way she hadn't been before.

Likewise, *he* seemed to be affected by the moment. His eyes darkened, and his throat bobbed. He looked like he wanted to speak, and yet he didn't.

Instead, slowly, almost hesitantly, he reached out, the back of his hand brushing her cheek. Leanna caught her breath yet didn't step out of his reach, didn't shrink away. That feather-light touch set her pulse racing.

After MacKinnon's brutal treatment the night before, she'd flinched away from contact with Campbell during their escape. Yet as the soft light of dawn filtered over them, and a sky lark warbled above, something shifted within her.

Honesty had a way of shattering reserve.

"Ye are lovely, Leanna MacDonald," he said, his voice turning husky. "Lovelier than men like MacKinnon, or myself, deserve. Ye were meant to be treasured. I vow I shall get ye to safety, no matter what it costs me."

His knuckles feathered across Leanna's cheek once more, before he dropped his hand and stepped back from her.

Cold air rushed in between them, and for an instant disappointment lanced through Leanna. She wasn't sure exactly why her heart suddenly felt as if it was shrinking.

Surely, she hadn't expected him to kiss her? After everything that had transpired between them, that would have been an enormous breach of trust. And yet as Ross Campbell stepped away, their gazes still holding, she felt strangely bereft.

His words had surprised her. She had no idea how to respond to them, and so she held her tongue. Truthfully, she felt out of her depth.

"Come on." Campbell crossed to the courser and gathered the reins. "We have rested here long enough. MacKinnon is likely to be on our trail by now … but if we ride hard, we can make Duncaith by sundown."

Ross's mood was oddly dark as he guided the horse to the top of the wooded slope. They wound their way down the other side, their pace slowed, for the courser had to pick its way through clumps of bracken. It was rough country for travel and would slow their progress southwest into MacDonald territory. However, this route was necessary.

MacKinnon would send men ahead along all roads out of Dunan. Cross-country was now the only way to travel.

Ross's brooding was not due to their situation though, as serious as it was, but more to do with himself.

Leanna had asked honesty of him, yet he felt as if he'd revealed too much. He'd bled out in front of her, giving her details of his past that he'd not revealed to any other soul. His near-drowning was a memory that he preferred not to dwell on. His brother Doug was a man cast in his father's mold. After losing sight in one eye as the result of nearly killing Ross, he hadn't been sorry. Instead, Ross had become his enemy.

He hadn't scripted any of his responses to Leanna and had been unprepared for how raw his answers had been. He wasn't sure what had possessed him to draw close to her, and to have the audacity to reach out and stroke her face—twice. He was lucky she hadn't slapped him for his trouble.

After what he'd made the lass endure, he deserved no less.

Aye, he'd more or less ripped himself open when he'd told her why he'd come to her aid, and then apologized, but it didn't make him feel any better.

Words were easy. He would show Leanna how sorry he was by taking care of her, by ensuring she reached her kin safely. He would die before letting MacKinnon capture her again.

Ross's belly knotted at this realization, and he frowned, trying to push aside the discomforting sensation. After years of hard-won self-control, he felt as if his life was unraveling before his very eyes.

There had been security in his old existence, but this new path was carrying him into the wilds, literally and figuratively. He wasn't sure he was going to emerge unscathed.

At the bottom of the valley ran a shallow burn. They splashed through it and then turned, following the water-course southwest. Wooded hills rose either side, at the feet of huge sculpted mountains that reared up. In order to catch a glimpse of the pale sky, Ross had to crane his neck right back. And when he did, he saw an eagle circling, its screech echoing through the valley.

"Do ye know where we are?" Leanna asked, breaking the tense silence between them.

"Roughly enough," he replied. "I've hunted stags in these valleys before ... if I'm right, this vale lies around half a league north of MacDonald territory."

"Won't MacKinnon just follow us onto my father's land?" He could hear the tension in her voice, the worry. Like him, she knew the chase had not ended. Just because they couldn't hear dogs baying at their heels didn't mean that MacKinnon wasn't tracking them down.

"Of course he will," Ross replied. "He'll be desperate ... and with yer father dead, he's bolder than before."

"My uncle, Bard, will be chieftain now," she reminded him. "He's probably still got men looking for me ... and he's got no more love of MacKinnon than my father had."

"Good to hear ... with any luck we'll cross yer uncle's path. That way he can set his dogs on MacKinnon and send him back to his own lands."

"What will ye do, Ross ... once ye have delivered me to my kin?"

Ross didn't answer immediately. Her abrupt change of subject and the use of his first name threw him. Few called him 'Ross' these days besides Carr. At Dunan he was simply known as 'Campbell'. And, in truth, he'd given little thought to the future.

"I don't know," he replied, deciding that he might as well be honest. "I'll tackle that once ye are safe at Duncaith."

"Ye won't return to yer kin on the mainland?"

Ross snorted. "Ye heard the sorry tale of my upbringing ... would ye?"

"But there must be other Campbells throughout Scotland?"

"Aye ... but none that I like well enough to impose upon." Ross paused there. "Maybe I shall go to the capital."

"What will ye do there?"

"I hear that a man named Edward Balliol has laid claim to the Scottish throne. Perhaps I shall join his guard and make a name for myself there instead." Even as he said these words, they depressed Ross. All his life he'd been ambitious, had fought to climb up through the ranks so that he might lead men instead of merely follow them. Suddenly, he was exhausted at the thought. He patted the leather pouch he wore under his vest. "Or since I carry a purse of silver—all my wages over the past decade—maybe I'll just find myself a wife in some sleepy backwater and make a living as a farmer."

Leanna went quiet for a spell after this admission, and when she spoke once more, her tone was reserved, slightly shy. "And do ye wish for a wife, Ross?"

An unexpected smile stretched across Ross's face. "Aye ... I have even wooed a few ladies in the past years but to no avail."

"Really ... who?"

He could hear the curiosity in her voice, and his smile widened.

"Lady Caitrin MacLeod for one," he replied. "After she was widowed, her father became desperate to find his daughter another match. I was one of three suitors who traveled to Dunvegan to vie for her hand ... but in the end, she chose none of us."

"I heard she wed her dead husband's brother," Leanna replied. "There were whispers about it all over the isle afterward ... I'm surprised ye were one of her spurned suitors?"

Although he knew Leanna couldn't see his face, Ross raised an eyebrow. "And why's that?"

"Ye are a handsome man ... I can't imagine a woman resisting yer charms."

Ross actually laughed at that, the sound rumbling across his chest. It felt good to laugh after such a fraught night; it lightened his heart. "Not all women think as ye do, Lady Leanna. But fear not, my pride is intact. Lady Caitrin cast me aside in favor of Alasdair MacDonald ... a man she secretly loved. And I'm now glad she did."

"And why's that?"

Ross's smile faded, and his mood suddenly sobered. "Because if I'd wed Lady Caitrin, my path would likely have taken me away from Dunan. Ye and I might never have met."

As soon as the words were out, he regretted them. What was it about Leanna that made truth pour from him like an unstoppered barrel of mead? They'd been having a light-hearted exchange, something that was sorely needed after their conversation at dawn, but he'd just ruined it.

Leanna's arms were loosely looped around his waist, yet he felt the tension in them nonetheless. She fell silent and didn't question him further about Lady Caitrin. It had all happened nearly two years ago now. Ross had been in a position to look for a wife, and when MacLeod had sent word throughout the isle that his lovely widowed daughter sought a new husband, he'd thought to try his luck.

However, he hadn't been at Dunvegan long when he'd realized that Caitrin's heart was already spoken for.

The tense silence between Ross and Leanna drew out, and Ross was considering how best to break it when the snap of a twig underfoot tore him from his thoughts. His chin jerked up, his instincts suddenly on the alert. The courser snorted, its nostrils flaring. Ross's ears hadn't deceived him; the horse had heard it too.

"What's wrong?" Leanna asked, her voice low and tense. "Is there—"

She never got to complete her sentence, for, at that moment, figures emerged from the trees around them. Ross drew up the courser, his gaze swiveling left and right.

A circle of leather-clad men emerged from the shadowy undergrowth, drawn longbows at the ready.

18

The Outlaw

LEANNA FROZE AGAINST Ross, her arms instinctively tightening around his midriff.

Mother Mary, where did all these men come from?

Ross had obviously heard something, a moment before they'd emerged from the trees, yet it had come too late. They were now surrounded by a band of outlaws. Even if Ross was to draw the claidheamh-mor at his waist and swing for them, he'd be cut down before he ever reached his first victim.

Wisely, Ross did no such thing.

Instead, he sat still and watchful, as yet more men emerged from the thickets of pines that surrounded the banks of the burn. Silent in leather hunting boots, the men approached.

At a glance, Leanna saw they were very different to the men who'd attacked her party on the way to her father's burial. Those had been a much smaller, ragged band that had possessed an aura of desperation.

The men encircling them now didn't appear desperate. Most of them looked well-fed, and all were dressed in hunting leathers. They wielded longbows, carried dirks, and had swords strapped to their sides.

Leanna's pulse quickened. *Who are they?*

At that moment, as if answering her silent question, a tall, broad-shouldered figure emerged from the trees.

Unlike the others, this outlaw didn't wield a bow. A claidheamh-mor hung by his side, the scabbard knocking against his leg as he walked, yet he didn't draw it.

Leanna stared at the newcomer. A prickle of recognition flared, and for an instant, she stopped breathing, ice settling in the pit of her belly.

Duncan MacKinnon.

But as the man drew closer, she realized that although he bore a striking resemblance to the clan-chief, it was not him.

Even so, the similarity made nausea roil in her belly.

Just like MacKinnon, the man was tall—although he was possibly even bigger, broader, and more muscular than the clan-chief. He had the same ruggedly handsome face, while his rich-brown hair was longer and wilder.

But what really set them apart was the thin white scar that slashed vertically from his temple to cheek, only an inch from his left eye.

Leanna swallowed hard as realization dawned. She'd heard about this man—all of Skye had by now. Even the walls of Kilbride couldn't stop the rumors.

This was 'Craeg the Bastard', the outlaw leader who'd spent the last decade living in the territory's forgotten places—and all the while causing problems for Duncan MacKinnon. He'd drawn the angry and disillusioned to him, and regularly stole from MacKinnon's coffers, attacking supply wagons and tax collectors.

Leanna stared at the outlaw, fear and fascination warring within her. Meeting her gaze, the man's sensual mouth curved. "Do ye know me?"

"Aye," she whispered. "I think I do."

"Craeg MacKinnon," Ross murmured, his tone flat. "So, this is where you've been hiding."

The big man inclined his head, gaze narrowing. "MacKinnon, eh? I suppose it's a better name than 'Craeg the Bastard'."

Ross huffed a laugh at this, although Leanna could feel the coiled tension in his body; his back muscles were taut.

Silence stretched out then, broken only by the whisper of the wind, the chatter of the burn behind them, and a lonely eagle's screech high above. The bowmen surrounding them didn't lower their weapons, and Craeg the Bastard's face didn't show a hint of friendliness.

When he broke the brittle hush, his voice was hard. "It seems fitting ... since ye know my name ... that I should know yer identities as well."

Ross shifted in the saddle, and Leanna wondered if he would lie. Although she had no wish to tell this outlaw who she was, she knew to spin him a tale wouldn't end well for either of them. There was a sharp intelligence to this man's looks. He would sniff out a falsehood easily.

"I am Ross Campbell, and my companion is Lady Leanna MacDonald of Sleat," Ross said after a lengthy pause.

The outlaw leader's big body tensed. "Campbell ... I know that name." His gaze speared Ross. "Ye are MacKinnon's right hand."

"I *was*."

Craeg's jaw flexed, before his attention shifted from Leanna to Ross, his gaze narrowing. "Why are ye out here in the wilderness?"

"We're riding to Duncaith," Ross replied, his tone flat, guarded.

The outlaw's dark brows rose. "There's a good road from Dunan to Duncaith ... is there a reason why we find ye in this forgotten valley?"

Ross didn't answer, and a stubborn silence drew out. Leanna sensed he had given up being cooperative; the conversation might take an ill turn if someone didn't intervene.

"We're on the same side," she gasped, the words spilling out of her. "Ross and I are running from MacKinnon. He wishes to wed me against my will. Campbell helped me escape Dunan ... and we're riding across country to avoid capture."

As she'd expected, her words caused a stir. A deep groove formed between the outlaw leader's brows. The surrounding men shared glances while Ross muttered a curse under his breath. "Ye should have left the talking to me, milady."

Leanna stiffened. "This isn't the time for stubbornness," she replied under her breath. "We need help."

A few yards away, Craeg stared at her, surprise etched upon his handsome face. "I take it my *brother* will be hot on yer heels?" he asked finally.

"Aye," Ross growled. "And I suggest ye let us continue on our way so that we all might avoid him."

Craeg reached up a hand and rubbed his clean-shaven jaw. "Duncaith won't save ye from MacKinnon's wrath," he replied, his gaze meeting Ross's. "Take it from one who's spent years eluding him. The best place to hide from the clan-chief is in the forgotten corners of his own lands."

Ross stiffened. "Aye ... how is it that ye have managed to evade capture for so long?"

Craeg watched them for a heartbeat before a smile stretched across his face. "I learned how to meld with the shadows, Campbell ... and I can show ye too." He glanced around at the bowmen, who stood like statues, their weapons still drawn. "Lower yer bows, lads ... these two aren't our captives, but our guests."

Slowly, cautiously, the men did as bid.

"Ye should have let me speak on our behalf," Ross murmured as he turned his horse and followed the outlaw band through the trees. "The less these people know about us the better."

"I was just trying to stop a fight," Leanna muttered between clenched teeth.

Panic fluttered up under her ribcage then as Craeg fell into step beside them. The Lord preserve her, he looked so much like his brother.

She just hoped he was as different from Duncan MacKinnon as folk said—or they were riding into even more trouble.

Craeg the Bastard glanced at the claidheamh-mor that hung at Ross's side. "That's a fine blade. Where did ye get it?"

"My father's smith fashioned it for me," Ross replied, his tone guarded.

The outlaw reached out, drawing the broadsword up so that the top half slid from the scabbard. He then peered at the blade he'd just revealed. "There's writing inscribed here ... what does it mean?"

"*Ne Obliviscaris*. It's the Campbell motto ... Forget Not."

Craeg's mouth quirked. "A good creed ... and one I also live by."

Ross snorted. "Yer brother has a long memory too, and never forgets a slight."

To Leanna's surprise, the outlaw grinned at that. "Aye ... that's why he's provided me such sport over the years. I enjoy poking the adder with a stick."

Ross snorted in response. "Ye had better be wary of the serpent's fangs then."

19

Offering Hospitality

THE OUTLAWS LED them away, south of the burn, and into a densely packed wall of pine trees.

With each furlong deeper into the wilderness, Leanna grew tenser. She wasn't sure they'd made the right decision by accepting the outlaws' hospitality. Could they really trust Craeg the Bastard?

Maybe I shouldn't have been so open with him?

She could feel the tension in Ross's body as they traveled farther and farther into the heart of the forest. She didn't need to see his face to know that he wasn't comfortable.

Eventually, the land grew too rough and stony, the undergrowth too thick, to continue on horseback. They dismounted, and Ross led his horse after them, following the outlaws in silence now.

They walked for a long while, pushing through bracken and brambles, traveling through a press of trees so dense that they blocked out the sky. The land gradually grew rougher and steeper still, and Leanna realized that they were hard against the feet of the mountains now—a wild, lonely place where men rarely ventured.

The perfect spot to hide.

Emerging from between two prickly spruce, Leanna finally stepped out into a clearing—and there before her spread the outlaw camp.

It was a shock, stepping out of the cool silence of the forest and into a bustling village. A wall of noise hit Leanna: the rise and fall of voices, the clang and hiss of iron being forged, the bleat of goats, and the squawk of fowl.

One glance told her that these folk had lived here a while. Squat huts nestled amongst the trees like large brown toadstools, smoke rising from their sod roofs. This wasn't just a male environment. Women and children moved about the clearing before the trees, while a mountain stream trickled by.

As they approached, one of the women glanced up from where she was washing clothes in the stream, her gaze widening when she spied the other outlaws and their captives. The woman wasn't dressed in a kirtle, but in braies and a leather vest—a sight that disconcerted Leanna. The outlaw woman's pretty features tightened, and she rose to her feet, leaving the pile of sodden washing upon the stone where she'd been scrubbing it.

"Who's this?" she asked, moving toward them.

"We have guests, Fenella," Craeg greeted her. "Go and ready a hut for them."

The woman's gaze narrowed, and her hands went to her hips. She was a comely woman who looked to be in her early thirties, with a wild mane of dark-gold hair. "What have ye gone and done, Craeg?"

The outlaw leader snorted a laugh. "Nothing. These two are fleeing Duncan MacKinnon ... so I thought we could offer them some hospitality."

The woman, Fenella, went still at this, her gaze sweeping from Craeg to Ross and Leanna. Her blue eyes turned hard, suspicious. "Why would ye bring them here?"

"It's the safest corner of these lands, Fen."

The woman's expression darkened further. "It won't be if ye let strangers know where we're hiding."

Craeg waved away her comment. "Worry not ... these two have good reason to remain hidden." He motioned to Leanna. "Meet my brother's bride-to-be ... Lady Leanna of Sleat. It appears she doesn't want to wed him."

His introduction didn't thaw Fenella's eyes. If anything, her gaze grew colder. "And who's this?" she asked, pointing to Leanna's companion.

Craeg grinned. "Meet Ross Campbell ... the Captain of The Dunan Guard and MacKinnon's right-hand."

These words caused the outlaw woman to draw in a sharp breath. Likewise, around her folk turned to stare. Mutters and whispered comments followed.

The fine hair on the back of Leanna's neck prickled. Those gazes weren't friendly.

"Stop glaring, Fen." A huge man with thick red hair stepped up next to the outlaw leader. A longbow and quiver hung from his back. "Campbell has left MacKinnon's employment." The fire-haired outlaw glanced at Ross then, a thoughtful expression upon his face. "He might be able to give us some helpful details regarding his former master."

Next to Leanna, Ross frowned. Such things hadn't been discussed.

"Even so, ye shouldn't have brought them here, Gunn," Fenella scolded. "Have the pair of ye lost yer wits?"

"Listen to yer man," Craeg spoke up. He was still smiling although Leanna glimpsed a flicker of irritation in his gaze. "Go on ... get our guests' lodgings ready for them."

Fenella clamped her mouth shut, yet her blue eyes still gleamed with annoyance. This time though, she didn't argue. Instead, she turned on her heel and stalked off to do his bidding.

Craeg turned to Leanna and Ross. "Apologies for the frosty welcome ... folk here are wary of outsiders."

"For good reason," the red-haired outlaw added. "Bringing the wrong person into our midst could spell our doom."

Craeg raised a dark eyebrow, a silent gesture that told the outlaw he was well aware of that. "Come ... I'll show ye where to tether yer horse," he said to Ross. "And after that, the pair of ye can join me for an ale in my hut."

Carr Broderick rode into Dunan just as the last rays of sun burnished the wooded hills surrounding the broch. His horse was lathered, and the priest he'd brought from Talasgair was pinch-faced with exhaustion, yet they'd made good time.

Hooves clattering on the cobbles, the two horses entered the bailey and headed toward the stable complex against the western walls.

Carr drew up his mount before the stables and swung down from the saddle, throwing the reins to a lad who'd emerged to greet him. Usually, he liked to see to his horse himself—and this courser definitely deserved a generous nosebag of oats—but the clan-chief would be waiting.

Likewise, the priest dismounted. Father Crannog winced as he rubbed his posterior and glanced around him. He was a portly man with a gleaming bald pate and a sharp gaze. This eve, he looked tired and vaguely irritated.

Carr had deliberately not told the priest the truth about what had happened to Father Athol. As far as Father Crannog knew, the man had choked on a fishbone and died. Carr didn't like keeping the news from him, but he risked the priest refusing to come with him otherwise.

The image of Father Athol crumpling to the ground in front of the altar, while MacKinnon stabbed the life out him, flashed before Carr then. A chill feathered down the back of his nape. Any man capable of murdering a priest in cold blood had to be watched.

And yet, Carr couldn't turn his back on MacKinnon. He'd pledged fealty to him at the age of sixteen, had knelt on one knee before him and promised that he'd serve the MacKinnon clan-chief for the rest of his life.

Carr Broderick wasn't a man who broke his promises.

"Take me to the clan-chief then," Father Crannog muttered. "We'd better not keep the man waiting a moment longer than he has to."

There was no mistaking the acerbity in his tone. He resented MacKinnon demanding his presence here.

"This way," Carr grunted. With a nod to the stable lad, he strode across the bailey, heading toward the steep stone steps that led up to the great doors.

He had nearly reached them when a figure swathed in grey appeared in the doorway above.

Lady Drew MacKinnon had come out to meet him.

Carr's step slowed at the sight of her. The lady now descended the steps, and so he waited at the bottom for her. An elegant figure, her brown hair piled up high upon her head, Lady Drew captured Carr's eye as she always did—as she always had.

Carr had been barely old enough to grow his first whiskers when he'd arrived at Dunan, and ever since that day, he'd been fascinated by

MacKinnon's sister. Not that it mattered to her. To Lady Drew, he was nothing more than her brother's servant—a cur that rushed to do his bidding. As he had this time too.

But today something was different about Lady Drew. When she neared him, Carr saw that she bore a raised red welt upon her left cheek.

He went still. "Lady Drew ... what has happened here?"

"Much, I'm afraid," she replied. MacKinnon's sister glided down the stairs, stopping before she reached the bottom step so that their gazes were level. For a moment, she merely held his eye.

"Yer face ... what—"

Lady Drew waved his concerns away with an impatient hand. "My brother had enough of my viper's tongue ... but unfortunately that's not the worst of it. Ye should know that Campbell has run off with Lady Leanna ... Duncan is incensed."

Carr stared at her, struggling to take the words in. The knowledge that MacKinnon had dared raise a hand to his sister made ice-cold rage seep through his belly. Carr wasn't a man quick to anger, yet right now he could have shoved the clan-chief's teeth down his throat.

But he couldn't focus on that. Instead, a chill washed over his body at the lady's news about Ross and Lady Leanna. He merely stared at her stupidly, wondering if he'd misheard.

"What do ye mean?" he finally managed. "Surely, Ross couldn't have—"

"He did," Lady Drew cut him off, irritated now. "And not only that, but he interrupted Duncan when he was about to force himself upon Lady Leanna." Her glance flicked to where Father Crannog stood silently behind Carr. "Duncan grew overly impatient and sought to consummate the union before the wedding ceremony could take place."

Lady Drew's voice was carefully impassive, yet her grey eyes carried a flinty look that Carr knew well—the lady was displeased and rightly so.

Carr's chest constricted. This entire situation was a colossal mess, one that he was ashamed to be part of.

"What now then?" he asked, his voice flattening. Suddenly, he just felt weary and heart sore. He couldn't believe that Ross had betrayed them like this. He'd just signed his own death writ. MacKinnon would never stop hunting him for stealing his bride away.

"My brother awaits ye in his solar," Lady Drew replied. "Ye had better go to him before his temper sours further." Her attention flicked back to the priest. "Apologies for this, Father," she said coolly, "but it looks as if ye will be a guest in Dunan for longer than ye planned. My brother has to catch his bride before the wedding can take place."

Carr entered the solar to find the clan-chief seated by the window. One glance at the man and Carr could see he was in pain. His face was ashen and strained, and he sat awkwardly. MacKinnon's wolfhound curled at his feet, for once ignored by its master.

Once again, Carr tried to make sense of what had happened. Lady Drew hadn't given him any more details about the incident. He would need to question her about it later.

Warmth settled in the pit of Carr's belly at the thought. Despite the circumstances, he welcomed any opportunity to converse with MacKinnon's sister. He lived for those rare moments.

"I have brought the priest," Carr greeted him, "although I hear that we are too late ... yer betrothed is gone?"

"Aye," MacKinnon growled. "But she's not gone for good ... she will be found again. I have men out hunting for them. They won't get away."

The words were spoken with such venom—such naked hate—that whatever words Carr might have replied with died upon his lips.

"Why did ye not ride after them yerself?" he asked finally.

"I'm injured, ye lackwit," MacKinnon snarled. "Although rest assured, as soon as I am well enough, I shall search every last corner of Skye till I find them."

Carr observed MacKinnon keenly then, his gaze traveling over the man's muscular form. Apart from the pallor and tension upon his face, MacKinnon didn't appear injured. However, instinct told him it was wise not to question the clan-chief further. He was in an evil mood as it was.

"When will ye be ready to travel?" Carr asked finally.

"If the men don't return with Campbell and Lady Leanna by tomorrow eve, we shall ride out in search of them." The clan-chief paused there, his grey eyes narrowing into glittering slits as he glared at Carr. "Ye and Campbell are as thick as thieves ... did ye know that he had sympathies for Lady Leanna?"

Carr started, taken aback by the question. Yet he did take a moment to consider it. He knew Ross had been unsettled by the events of late at Dunan, and Carr sensed he'd started to question his loyalty. But at the same time, Carr knew his friend was ambitious. He couldn't imagine what had driven Ross to behave as he did. And so, he answered honestly, "No, this is as much of a shock to me as it is to ye."

Craeg the Bastard's hut was a humble dwelling. Low beams hung overhead, making it difficult for tall men like the outlaw leader or Ross to stand fully upright. Deerskins covered the floor, and a fur hanging divided the sleeping area at the back from the hearth. Craeg clearly often welcomed folk to his hearth, for half a dozen low stools sat around the fire, where a lump of peat glowed.

Taking a seat upon one of the stools, Craeg reached for a clay bottle and pulled out the wooden stopper. He then poured out three wooden cups and passed two of them to his companions.

Ross and Leanna had sat down opposite him.

Fingers tightening around his cup, Ross took a tentative sip. The ale was good, refreshing after a long, exhausting journey. Yet it didn't relax him.

It was difficult to relax when Duncan MacKinnon's double was sitting before him.

Cool moss-green eyes—refreshingly very different from the clan-chief's—rested upon him, assessing him. Ross knew the outlaw leader was taking his measure and attempting to judge whether or not he could really trust him.

But Ross was doing the same.

He hadn't wanted to come here, and yet this camp was probably the safest place upon the isle for them right now.

Guests of a man who'd long learned how to hide in plain sight.

Are we really guests?

The outlaw leader seemed friendly enough, although Ross had difficulty trusting his ready smile. Especially, since until a day ago, Ross's life would have been forfeit if he'd wandered into this camp.

He'd seen the glares, the muttered comments, as they'd led their horse to the enclosure on the southern side of the village. Craeg might have welcomed them here, but others within the settlement didn't.

"I get the sense that there is more to yer tale than ye have spoken of so far," Craeg said finally, breaking the heavy silence.

Ross shared a look with Leanna then. Of course there was. The question was—how much did they share with this stranger?

"The first thing I'm curious to know, is how ye ended up at Dunan at all, Lady Leanna. Surely, yer father wouldn't want ye wed to MacKinnon?"

Leanna inhaled slowly, her throat bobbing. "He didn't ... but then my father is dead now so he has little say on the matter."

Craeg's gaze widened. Of course, he was isolated here. He didn't know.

"Niall MacDonald of Sleat died in a hunting accident a few days ago," Ross said quietly. This wasn't a pleasant tale, but since Craeg was likely to get the details out of them sooner or later, he decided the man might as well hear the story from him. "Ye are right ... he denied MacKinnon when he asked for Lady Leanna's hand years ago ... and to make sure yer brother never got his hands on her, he put his daughter in Kilbride Abbey."

Craeg took a gulp of ale and gave an incredulous shake of his head. "This tale gets more intriguing by the moment ... go on."

Ross did. He told the story plainly, baldly even—and he deliberately didn't look Leanna's way as he did so.

The facts didn't make him look good at all.

The outlaw leader didn't interrupt him, he merely listened, until the point when Ross described what had happened in the kirk—how MacKinnon had slain Father Athol.

Craeg sucked in a sharp breath, his eyes shadowing. "During my years in Dunan, Father Athol was one of the few who showed me any kindness," he said, a rasp to his voice.

"MacKinnon cut him down without hesitation," Ross replied, watching the outlaw leader's face harden. "But that shouldn't come as a surprise ... ye know what he's capable of."

A dangerous look flickered in Craeg the Bastard's eyes. Ross realized then that despite his friendly manner, this man wasn't one lightly crossed. Ross had heard of Craeg's origins. He knew that the man had plenty of reasons to hate his half-brother.

But now Ross had just given him another.

20

Awoken

CRAEG WAS STANDING on the edge of the village, taking his turn at the watch, when he heard the heavy tread of men approaching behind him. Twisting around, he peered through the gloaming to spy two familiar figures: one hulking with wild red hair; the other older and dark-haired, dressed in dusty hunting leathers, and carrying a slight limp.

Gunn and Brochan.

"I hear we've got visitors?" the latter greeted Craeg.

The outlaw leader inclined his head, noting the brusqueness of Brochan's tone. He'd known the man for years—in fact, it was Brochan who'd taught him how to use his fists properly, swing a broad-sword, and wield a longbow—but sometimes he thought his friend forgot that Craeg was in charge here.

"Aye ... Gunn has told ye who they are?" he replied, his tone non-committal.

Brochan halted, folding his arms across his chest. "He has ... MacKinnon's right-hand is now our guest."

Next to Brochan, Gunn rolled his eyes. "I've told him that Campbell is no longer MacKinnon's man, but he won't take my word."

"Well ye will just have to take mine," Craeg said with a smile. "Did ye have any luck with yer hunt by the way?"

Brochan shook his head. "The hinds eluded me today." The older man's weathered features tensed then. "This is a wasted opportunity, ye know?"

"What is?"

"Ye have never been in such a strong bargaining position with MacKinnon. Those two would be worth all our weights in silver." Brochan's eyes gleamed. "Think of all the good ye could do ... all the folk who could buy food for their families with that coin."

Craeg's smile faded. "Ye think I should ransom our visitors?"

Brochan nodded, while beside him Gunn shifted uncomfortably, his bluff features tightening. "That's a cracked idea."

Brochan cut Gunn a sharp look. "Is it? Ye have two people that MacKinnon wants to get his hands on. This time, ye can really hit him where it hurts."

"And if he discovers the location of this village as a result?" Craeg was scowling now. Gunn was right; Brochan's idea was mad. He clearly hadn't thought the details through.

"If ye handled this right, he wouldn't."

"Campbell and Lady Leanna are our guests," Craeg reminded him, with a shake of his head that made his opinion clear. "We won't be ransoming them, and I certainly wouldn't risk any of yer lives to go and treat with him."

"I'd do it," Brochan countered. His face wore a strained expression now, his fingers flexing at his sides. "I'd love to see MacKinnon's face when he hears the news."

Craeg knew that the outlaw bore MacKinnon as much hate as he did. Many years earlier, Brochan had been a member of The Dunan Guard, but had been cast out after he'd dared contradict the young clan-chief. Duncan MacKinnon had beaten Brochan so badly for the slight that he still walked with a limp as a result.

Brochan wanted to avenge himself upon MacKinnon, but his need for reckoning had clearly clouded his judgment.

"No ye won't ... no one will," Craeg hit back, his anger rising. "Put this wild idea of yers to bed, Brochan ... there will be no blackmailing."

It was dark inside the hut, the only light streaming in through the smoke hole in the roof. A small lump of peat burned in the hearth, warming the damp air. Nonetheless, it was cool this evening.

Leanna shifted uncomfortably, arranging herself upon the fur next to the hearth. The hut was empty except for the furs covering the dirt floor. The air smelled dusty and stale as if this hut wasn't used often. After sharing two cups of ale with the outlaw leader, Craeg had brought them here.

His final words, as he'd gestured them inside, had made worry knot Leanna's belly. "There are a few folk here who don't welcome yer presence ... for yer own safety, I suggest ye stay out of sight till dawn. I'll get someone to bring ye supper."

Seeing Leanna's frown, the outlaw leader had favored her with a reassuring smile. "Fret not, Lady Leanna ... ye will be safe here. I just want folk to get used to yer presence, that's all."

He'd meant his words to soothe her, but after his departure, she found it difficult to relax.

Glancing across the space, Leanna's attention settled upon Ross.

He hadn't spoken since they'd entered the hut, and in the murky light, she saw that his expression was grim, his gaze shuttered.

"Ye are worried, aren't ye?" she asked finally. "Ye don't trust them either."

He shrugged, his gaze shifting to the flames dancing in the hearth.

"Maybe we shouldn't have come here," Leanna said, plucking at a stray thread on her cloak.

Ross's attention flicked up, and he frowned. "I can't help thinking that we're safer here than anywhere else right now."

"So why the furrowed brow?"

"Because ye wouldn't be in this mess if it weren't for me."

Leanna huffed. "If ye hadn't abducted me, MacKinnon would have just sent someone else to do it."

"Aye ... but I've known for some time the kind of man he is, and I ignored my gut. Ye aren't out of danger yet. MacKinnon will never let this go."

Leanna swallowed a lump in her throat at these words. She wanted to dispute them, yet she knew that Ross was right. Duncan MacKinnon had a madness within him where she was concerned, and he wouldn't take Ross's betrayal lightly either. She imagined his rage and shivered.

"Are ye cold?" Ross asked.

Leanna shook her head.

"Here." He shrugged off his traveling cloak and handed it to her.

Leanna's lips parted to tell him that her shiver had been due to dread, not the chill. She was already wearing Lady Drew's cloak, and it wasn't that cold in here. However, her fear of MacKinnon wasn't something she felt like discussing right now, so she took the cloak without argument.

And as she did, their fingers brushed.

Ross's face tensed, and she heard his sharp intake of breath. Their gazes locked for an instant, and then Leanna drew back, averting her gaze.

Why was her heart suddenly beating so quickly?

Wrapping the woolen cloak about her, Leanna attempted to settle her racing pulse. After a few moments, she glanced Ross's way once more and saw that he was staring moodily down at the fire before him.

"Ross," she began softly. "Before the outlaws appeared, ye said something ... that ye were glad ye hadn't wed Lady Caitrin ... or ye wouldn't have met me."

He glanced up, and for the first time since entering the hut, his mouth curved into a wry smile. "Ye remember that, do ye?"

"Aye." Leanna's already thudding heart started to beat wildly then, and she suddenly regretted speaking so frankly. She wasn't sure why she'd even brought it up. Was it out of vanity? Did she need to hear sweet words from a man who'd willingly abducted her? She now felt more than a little foolish and out of her depth in this conversation.

Ross glanced away, his mouth pursing. "Aye, Leanna ... as ye have probably realized, I didn't help ye flee out of purely unselfish motives." He broke off there, a muscle feathering in his jaw. "I'd like to say that I've assisted ye because I couldn't bear to see a woman in distress ... but ye already know that I'm not a saint. The truth is that I couldn't bear the thought of MacKinnon having ye, ruining ye. Somehow, ye have touched me, awoken something I thought never existed within me."

Leanna's breathing stilled, heat flooding across her chest. Surely, she was hearing things? When she didn't reply to his comment, Ross looked up and met her eye. He then gave a bitter laugh. "I know ... ye didn't think yer opinion of me could get any lower?"

"Ye care for me?" The question was bald, direct—and necessary. It suddenly felt close and airless inside the hut, and under two cloaks, Leanna was starting to sweat.

Ross's throat bobbed. "Aye."

Their gazes continued to hold. Time drew out, and the tension between them grew so taut that Leanna suddenly realized she was trembling. What was wrong with her? She was aware then that although she was entering her twenty-first summer, she'd led a sheltered life, protected by her father and then by the high walls of Kilbride Abbey. She knew little about the world or men.

Ross Campbell wasn't like the men she'd grown up among. He'd already told her of his harsh upbringing, of his drive to better himself. In order to rise to Captain of The Dunan Guard, he'd developed a hard shell—one that she'd somehow managed to penetrate.

But even so, she didn't know how to handle a man like this, or what to say to him.

All she knew was that as he silently moved toward her, she couldn't take her gaze from him. An ache rose under her breastbone, a longing for something she didn't even understand.

And then he was on his knees before her, and his hands were cupping her face. She felt the roughness of the callouses upon his palms against her skin, yet his touch was gentle.

A heartbeat later, he kissed her.

Like his hands, the kiss was soft, as if she was fragile and might shatter. His lips brushed hers, once, twice—testing to see if she'd recoil from his touch.

Heart now thundering, Leanna closed her eyes and leaned into him.

With a swiftly indrawn breath, Ross's mouth covered hers, and when his tongue gently parted her lips, she welcomed it. The heat of him, the taste of him, consumed her. He kissed her softly, yet deeply, with a tenderness she'd never have expected from the likes of Ross Campbell.

Still cupping her face, he angled it back slightly, so that he could deepen the kiss further. A groan rose in Leanna's throat as he did so and, shyly, she stroked his tongue with her own. She had no idea how to do this. One of her father's men had kissed her once—a stolen moment in a stairwell at Duncaith. It had been quick and hard, and had crushed her lips against her teeth. But Ross's embrace was nothing like that—it was melting, coaxing, and Leanna's welling groan finally escaped her.

Her body melted, and her lower belly suddenly felt incredibly alive as if a fire had kindled there.

Breathing hard, Ross drew back.

His gaze was hooded, his eyes almost black in the dimness. Despite the gentleness of his touch, his expression was taut, almost feral. He looked dangerous, and a strange thrill shivered through Leanna in response.

She should be scared of him—especially after her ordeal with MacKinnon the night before—and yet the moment he'd cupped her face with his hands, the opposite had occurred.

She might have roused tender feelings in him that had caused him to throw away his future in order to help her, but his kiss had awoken something wild within her too.

Recklessness surged through Leanna, and the aliveness in her lower belly deepened to an ache. Lord, how she wanted him to kiss her again.

"I shouldn't have done that." Ross's voice, low and sensual, held a husky edge that made Leanna's breathing quicken further. "Not after what ye have suffered of late."

"I am well, Ross," she replied softly. "MacKinnon frightened me … but I stopped him before he managed to inflict any harm." Her mouth curved into a hard smile. "Lucky for me, he was rotten with drink … it made him careless."

Ross managed a half-smile, although his gaze was still dark and fathomless. "It was a brave thing ye did."

Leanna's smile widened. "Aye … I did Mother Shona proud." Seeing the confusion that filtered across his face at these words, Leanna realized that, like most folk upon the Isle of Skye, he had no idea what the Sisters of Kilbride practiced behind the sheltering confines of their abbey. "The abbess teaches all the nuns how to defend themselves," she explained. "Once we learn the basics, we get to choose a specialty … mine is archery."

Ross sat back on his heels, his mouth quirking. "Before ye left Kilbride, Carr and I watched ye and another nun returning from a hunt," he admitted. "I remember the longbow and quiver of arrows ye carried upon yer back."

"Ye were there?" Leanna's body tensed at this news, her smile slipping.

"Aye," Ross ran a hand through his hair, his gaze shadowing. "I'd seen yer father's men arrive and knew it would be only a matter of time before ye departed with them."

Silence fell between them, and the tender, sensual mood shattered. Although he hadn't intended them that way, Ross's words were another sharp reminder of how this mess had all started—and the role he'd played in it.

Leanna tensed. She remembered Ross's arrogance when he'd captured her. It was hard to believe the man before her was the one who'd abducted her—yet he was.

"I told ye I shouldn't have kissed ye," Ross said as he moved farther back from her. The regret in his voice cut into Leanna. "We may overlook the history between us for a few moments … but it can never be forgotten."

21

The Weight of the World

AS DUSK SETTLED over the camp, the outlaw woman named Fenella brought them some food. The wooden door to the hut creaked open, bringing with it the fading light outdoors, and she entered.

Fenella carried an oil lamp with her, which she set upon the ground before a tray of bannock and hard cheese. Moving away, the outlaw motioned to the clay bottle on the tray. "There is ale to slake yer thirst," she said, her tone guarded.

Leanna offered the woman a tentative smile. After the kiss she and Ross had shared, she'd been on edge. They'd spoken little since, yet seeing this woman reminded Leanna that she'd revealed herself to be strong-willed and independent of thought earlier in the day—the sort of woman Leanna usually got on with well. "Thank ye, Fenella."

The woman stiffened, her gaze meeting Leanna's. However, she didn't return the smile.

Emboldened nevertheless, Leanna pressed on. "I appreciate the hospitality ... worry not, we won't stay long."

"I hope not, Lady MacDonald," Fenella replied, her tone chill. "We don't want yer kind here."

The words were a slap across the face. Leanna's shock must have shown upon her face, for a grim expression settled upon Fenella's. "I have no love for either MacKinnon *or* MacDonald," she continued. "My Da served yer father ... and when he was injured in a skirmish with cattle rustlers, Niall MacDonald cast him out of his guard. A lame warrior was no good to him ... my family nearly starved as a result."

Heat rushed through Leanna. "I don't believe it ... my father would never treat one of his men so."

Fenella's pretty face turned hard. "Whether or not ye believe it matters not to me ... it happened." She shifted toward the open door. "Enjoy yer supper."

The door shut with a dull thud, leaving Leanna and Ross alone once more. Only this time, the glow of the oil lantern illuminated the interior of the hut, revealing that there was, in fact, a screen in one corner, which would no doubt have a chamber pot behind it.

After a moment, Ross moved over to the tray, picked it up, and set it down between them. He then folded his long legs into a cross-legged position and tore off a piece of bread.

Leanna didn't move. The outlaw woman's words had upset her. She'd been hungry earlier, but now her appetite had just died.

Tearing her attention from the closed door, Leanna glanced over at Ross to find him watching her. He was chewing a mouthful of bread, his expression guarded.

"Don't mind her," he said once he'd swallowed his mouthful. "Bitterness makes a person speak harshly."

"She lies," Leanna replied stiffly. "My father would never behave in such a callous manner."

Ross raised an eyebrow. "I met MacDonald a few times ... and would say he possessed a much better character than MacKinnon does. All the same, a man must have an edge of brutality to him if he wishes to rule. He managed a vast tract of land and would have made enemies over the years."

Leanna's spine went rigid, and she glared at Ross. "His people loved him!"

Ross inclined his head. "What a short memory ye have. Do ye not recall the sashes worn by those outlaws who attacked yer father's party?" When Leanna didn't reply, he continued. "It was *MacDonald* plaid."

The truth of his words tasted bitter in Leanna's mouth, yet she couldn't argue with him over it. She'd seen their sashes. They were deserters from her father's guard.

Tears pricked the back of her eyes then, and she lowered her gaze to where her hands clasped before her upon her lap. "I've always believed those on MacDonald lands were happy," she said softly.

Ross didn't reply, and when Leanna finally glanced up, she saw that he wore a weary expression. "We both have lived in worlds of relative privilege, Leanna," he said softly. "I might have suffered numerous beatings during my childhood, but I never knew what it was like to go hungry, to go without shoes or a warm cloak in the winter. There are folk upon this isle who have known too much hardship to warm to the likes of us."

The brutality of his words made Leanna flinch. "Do I really seem so foolish?" she asked after a pause, her throat thickening. "So spoiled?"

"No," he replied softly. "But ye are part of a class that has made Craeg the Bastard's band loved throughout southern Skye."

Leanna cocked her head. "Ye sound as if ye admire them?"

He laughed. "Maybe I do. It takes a brave man to go against those who rule ... this band is known for taking MacKinnon's silver and giving it to those who'd starve otherwise."

Leanna's mouth curved. "I'd wager he's furious about that."

"Aye ... MacKinnon's face went the color of a turnip when he first discovered that his bastard brother was stealing his supplies and coin, and handing them over to the poor." Ross halted there, his expression turning thoughtful. "Craeg knows he's on borrowed time, for the clan-chief will hunt him down one day ... but he doesn't seem to care."

"Ye respect him, don't ye?"

Ross shrugged. "Aye ... and I envy him a little. He's free. He serves no man but himself."

Listening to Ross, Leanna caught the wistful note in his voice. He was a complex individual, she realized. When she'd first met him, she'd thought him ruthless and arrogant, but the past day had revealed that there was far more to Ross Campbell than met the eye. Leaving Dunan had freed something within him, and she got the feeling that he never spoke this frankly to anyone.

Not for the first time, she felt drawn to him. Warmth spread through her abdomen, and her breathing quickened as she watched him under slightly lowered lids. She forgot what Fenella had said about her father. Suddenly, the world shrank to this hut and the man who sat before her.

She wanted to tell him how much he fascinated her, how she longed for him to kiss her again—yet she wisely held her tongue. She was untutored in many things, but she knew when it was wise to avoid a subject.

Instead, Leanna reached for the bread and tore a piece off for herself.

Ross unstoppered the bottle of ale and poured it into two wooden cups. Taking a sip, he found his attention returning—once more—to the comely young woman seated just a few feet away.

The air was now close and stuffy inside the hut, and so she'd shed both cloaks, revealing the dark habit she wore beneath. However, without her wimple and veil, she didn't appear a nun. The braid that hung down her back was messy, and strands of pale blonde hair had come free, curling prettily around her face.

It was hard not to stare at her, for his gaze not to settle upon her small, lush mouth.

That kiss had been a mistake. He wasn't sure what madness had taken him to move close to her and cup her face with his hands. He'd been possessed by a need that had consumed him for a short while. Fortunately though, he'd managed to break free from it.

Even so, the memory of how she'd tasted, the tentative exploration of her tongue gliding against his, made Ross's groin start to ache.

She was so innocent, and yet so beguiling. He wished she hadn't welcomed his kiss; better that she'd slapped him for his forwardness. Instead, she'd leaned into him, and when she'd let out that soft groan, the beast had stirred within him.

God strike him down; he'd wanted to take her right there.

Ross's fingers tightened around the cup. What a mess all of this was. Fortune had not been smiling upon him of late, and if he ever ended up back in Dunan, MacKinnon would rip him to pieces.

Ross's mouth thinned. He wasn't afraid of the clan-chief, but he feared for Lady Leanna if MacKinnon managed to get her back. His punishment upon her would be terrible, and a chill rippled through him at the thought of the lengths that Duncan MacKinnon might stoop to in order to exact his reckoning.

In stealing Leanna away, he'd possibly just made things worse for her.

And yet, she'd already taken an axe to the tree, so to speak, by attacking the clan-chief. Without his help, she'd have never gotten free of the chamber.

"Ye look as if ye carry the weight of the world upon yer shoulders." Leanna's soft voice roused him from his brooding. "Why do ye scowl so?"

Ross glanced up and met her gaze. "Just bitter thoughts that aren't worth sharing," he replied.

"Not still blaming yerself are ye?"

Ross shrugged. "And if I am?"

"Ye are wasting yer energy, Ross," Leanna replied finally. Her voice was soft, yet there was a strength to it. Despite the precariousness of her situation, she wasn't afraid. "There is little point in brooding over what is done." Ross stiffened at her bluntness, but Leanna was not yet finished. She brushed crumbs off her habit, her gaze fusing with his. "The last few days have taught me much," she continued, her tone firm, resolute, "and many things have become clear to me. The first is that I am not suited to be a nun. When we first fled Dunan, I hoped ye would take me back to Kilbride … to a place where I'd always felt safe … but I now realize that whatever happens in the future, I shall never return there."

Ross's gaze widened. "Really?"

Leanna nodded. "I made a poor nun. My heart was never really in it. I only agreed to go to Kilbride to save myself from wedding MacKinnon … and to please my father."

Ross stared at her. God's bones, this woman fascinated him. She had such a soft, feminine appearance, and yet a will of iron lay beneath it. No wonder Leanna had chafed at the restrictions of religious life.

Leanna drew herself up, although, at the same time, her face grew strained. She glanced away, suddenly nervous. "We can't stay here forever," she murmured, still not meeting his eye. "Sooner or later we'll have to move on … and MacKinnon will be waiting for us."

Ross nodded, a weary sensation settling over him. Of course, she was right.

Leanna's chin snapped up then, her eyes gleaming. She had the look of a woman who'd just made an important decision. "I want to forget MacKinnon's touch. Life is so short, Ross … I want to know what it's like to give myself to a man I desire." She broke off there, her breast heaving with the force of the emotions roiling within her. However, when she finished speaking, her voice was steady. "I want to lie with ye."

22

What Ye Wish

ROSS STARED AT Leanna. There were few moments in life when he was lost for words—but now was one of them. He couldn't believe that this young woman, this lady, had just told him that she wished to give her maidenhead to him.

"Lady Leanna," he began, the huskiness in his voice betraying his shock. He needed to step back from Leanna. The connection between them was strong, and had been growing ever since their departure from Dunan, but he had to put a stop to things before they spiraled out of control. "Ye don't know what ye ask."

"Please call me 'Leanna'," she replied, lifting her chin. "I haven't been a 'lady' for a while now ... I forfeited that title when I entered Kilbride, and I don't want it back."

Ross frowned. "But ye *are* a lady ... and I won't take advantage of ye."

Leanna gave a huff of frustration. She then picked up the tray and shoved it to one side, shifting closer to him. A faint flush now stained her cheeks. To Ross, she'd never looked so alluring, but he still fought the urge to reach for her.

"Ye wouldn't be taking advantage if I give myself to ye willingly," she pointed out. "I'm tired of letting other people dictate my behavior. All my life I've done as I've been told ... and look where it's gotten me? Today, just once, I want to be in control of what happens to me." She broke off there, her hazel eyes luminous as she stared at him. "Do ye not want me, Ross?"

Satan's cod's—he couldn't believe she'd asked him that.

"Of course, I want ye," he growled. "What man wouldn't? Ye are lovely."

"Then lie with me."

Ross muttered a curse before dragging a hand over his face. "There are some things ye can never take back, Leanna. Yer maidenhead is one of them."

"And what do I care about that?" she snapped, her ire rising now. "Would ye prefer I gave it to MacKinnon ... is he more worthy than ye?"

Ross went still. Of course he didn't want MacKinnon to have her—he'd made his opinion on that very clear. Even so, after everything that had transpired, this felt wrong. "I'm not a humble man," he said, his voice hardening as he made one last attempt to keep Leanna at arm's length, "but even I know when I'm not worthy of something. After what I did ... I don't deserve to lie with ye."

Leanna moved closer to him, one small hand resting upon his knee. "Let me decide that." Her breathing caught then, her fingers tentatively sliding up his thigh. "Cast yer conscience aside, Ross. Just like my maidenhead, it is meaningless now."

Heart pounding, Ross caught her hand just as it neared his aching groin. "Ye don't know what ye ask," he repeated, a rasp to his voice.

"I do."

He stared into her eyes and realized that despite her innocence, there was a wisdom in Leanna that transcended age and experience. She didn't know how to behave, or what to expect from coupling with a man, yet she was honest in her desire for him.

He could see it in the way her pupils dilated at his nearness and the sharp rise and fall of her chest.

Suddenly, Ross was tired of fighting this, tired of punishing himself for all the mistakes he'd made.

Leanna spoke the truth—neither of them knew what the coming days would bring. These moments alone might be all they'd have.

His pulse was racing so fast now that Ross was starting to feel a little sick. Still grasping Leanna's hand, he reached forward with his free one and traced his fingers down her cheek.

It was no good—he wasn't made of stone. A man could only deny himself up to a certain point.

"Ye are the bonniest thing I've ever seen," he murmured, "and I will give ye all of me this night ... I will worship yer body with my own if that is what ye wish."

He watched Leanna swallow, her lips parting.

Ross's hand slid down from her cheek, following the graceful line of her neck. He then reached behind her, gently taking hold of her braid. In a deft movement, he removed the leather strip binding it, before he gently unwound the plait, weaving his fingers sensually into the fine softness of her hair.

He heard her breathing quicken further, and then he leaned forward, tracing his lips down her cheek to her neck. There, he inhaled the sweetness of her skin. Leanna's answering sigh made his already aching shaft stiffen to the point of pain. Did she have any idea what she did to him? His hand released hers and delved into her pale-blonde mane, his fingers spanning across the back of her scalp.

And then he tore his lips from her neck and covered her mouth with his.

Earlier, when he'd kissed her, Ross had gone gently. He knew what she'd narrowly avoided at MacKinnon's hands and hadn't wanted to frighten her. She responded eagerly to his kiss now, but even so, he still held back. He wanted to ravage her mouth with his, yet he kept the kiss tender and achingly sensual.

However, when Leanna's tongue tangled with his and she let out a soft moan, he had to keep a tight leash on his self-control.

Take it slowly ... don't frighten her.

He felt her hands upon his chest then, exploring its breadth. He wore a leather vest with a black léine underneath, and when one of her hands passed over his heart, he was sure she'd be able to feel it pounding against her palm.

Gently, Leanna bit his bottom lip.

Lust slammed into Ross, hot and aching, and with a moan of his own, he hauled her onto his lap, so that she now sat astride him. It was no good—when she did things like that, he couldn't think straight.

His kisses deepened now, as his hands slid down her back to her buttocks. It was difficult to feel her contours under all the layers of clothing she wore. It appeared that the habit was merely the top layer—and underneath there were other skirts and tunics—all designed to protect a nun's modesty no doubt.

But there was no modesty to this lass. She pressed her high, round breasts against the wall of his chest and wriggled against his groin, her moans of pleasure intensifying as the kissing drew out.

And then she began to unlace his vest.

Breathing hard, Ross broke off the kiss and leaned back, allowing her to complete her task. He then raised his arms so that she could strip off his léine.

Naked to the waist, he closed his eyes as her hands explored the planes of his chest. He could hear the excited catch of her breath and felt the slight tremble in the fingers that slid over his skin.

He could hardly bear it.

And yet, he didn't open his eyes—he merely let her touch him.

Moments later her touch drew back, and Ross's eyes flickered open to see that Leanna was untying her belt. She tossed it away before grasping the heavy material of her habit and pulling it over her head. Underneath, she wore another tunic and an overskirt, as well as a long linen léine. Leanna started to tug at them, a soft cry of frustration issuing from her.

Ross's mouth curved. He liked to see her so eager, so instinctive.

"Here," he murmured, stilling her struggles with his hand. "Let me help."

Taking her gently by the hips, he slid her back off his lap before stripping off her skirt. An instant later he took the hem of her léine and slowly drew it up, over the supple length of her body.

And as, inch by inch, her smooth, creamy skin revealed itself to him, his groin started to throb.

He'd never seen anything lovelier.

She was slender, yet her body was soft, with just enough curve to give her a womanly rather than girlish appearance. Her breasts were small, round, and high, yet with large rose-pink nipples that made Ross's mouth water.

Without thinking upon his actions, he drew her toward him on her knees, his mouth feasting upon her nipples.

Leanna's soft answering cry, and the way she dug her fingers into his scalp, urging him on, dissolved the last of Ross's self-restraint.

He knew he should leave this young woman be, but he was acting on instinct now. He couldn't stop touching her. His hands squeezed her pert bottom before traveling up her smooth back. Her nakedness excited him to the point of madness.

The beast rose within him once more, yet he shoved it down. He couldn't lose control, or he might frighten her. He wanted this to be a good experience for Leanna. After everything she'd been through of late, and everything that waited in the days to come, she deserved a night of tenderness.

But it cost him to hold back.

His breathing came in ragged gasps as he lay her down on her back upon the fur. Lord, his heart was beating so fast, it felt as if it would break free of his chest.

Leanna gazed up at him, her hazel eyes wide and trusting. Her lush lips were parted, her breasts heaving. Their swollen tips thrust up toward him, tempting him further.

With a soft curse, Ross leaned over her, covering Leanna's mouth with his. She reached up, her small hands grasping his shoulders while their kiss deepened. Pulse thundering in his ears now, Ross then kissed his way down her neck and began a slow exploration of her body.

He'd promised Leanna that he'd worship her body with his, and he wanted to make good on one vow at least. He wanted to make them both forget, for just one night, everything that threatened them.

He loved how responsive she was, how she arched against his seeking mouth, how she made soft mewing sounds of pleasure when his tongue explored her—and how she shuddered and gasped as time drew out. A fine mist of sweat covered her bare skin, and she was panting when he finally rose above her once more and positioned himself between her parted thighs.

Pale hair fanned about her, Leanna stared up at Ross. The look upon her face was so raw, her gaze dark with lust, that he bit back a growl. Her gaze slid down his naked midriff, to where he now unlaced his braies.

And when he took his shaft in hand, her eyes grew wide, and she stifled a shocked gasp. Ross knew he was well-endowed, and glancing down at his swollen rod, he realized that the sight possibly intimidated her.

"Will this hurt?" she asked, a tremble in her voice.

"Perhaps ... a little," he replied. Truthfully, he wasn't sure how Leanna would respond, for he'd never bedded a virgin before. He'd heard that a woman's first time could be painful, and he'd do his best to be gentle. Still, he couldn't make any assurances—this was new to him as well. "Worry not ... I will go slowly."

Holding himself up above Leanna, Ross slid gently into her, inch by inch.

Heavens, she was wet. It took all his self-control not to plunge into her. His body trembled from restraint as he slid into her deeper still. She was tight, and he felt a barrier to his penetration and halted.

Breathing hard, they both locked eyes.

"Shall I stop?" he rasped. He wasn't sure he'd be able to, actually, but he had to ask. He didn't want to frighten her.

Fortunately, Leanna shook her head. Her cheeks were flushed now, and she wriggled experimentally against him, her gaze widening further. "Don't stop." She moaned the words, and wrapped her legs around his hips, drawing him against her. "Please, Ross ... please."

With a groan, Ross sank into her, pushing past the barrier of her maidenhead.

He felt her tense, her legs tightening their grip around him. Staring into Leanna's eyes, he watched pain shadow their depths. Long moments passed, and then her hold upon him eased slightly.

A heartbeat later she undulated her hips against his, the movement tentative yet instinctual. The feel of her tight heat contracting against his shaft made a low, animalistic groan escape Ross. Coupling had never felt this good. Never.

Slowly, he started to move inside her.

And as he did so, his gaze fused with Leanna's once more, and her mouth curved into a sensual smile. "Ah," she breathed, her voice full of sultry promise. "I understand now what all the fuss is about."

23

In the Shadows

THEY LAY TOGETHER in silence for a long while after coupling. Ross had rolled off Leanna, taking her with him so that she rested against his chest. He must have dozed off, for the rise of his ribcage slowed and deepened.

But Leanna didn't sleep.

How could she when the most magical event of her life had just occurred?

To think she could have missed out on experiencing this? If she'd remained at Kilbride, she would never have known Ross's touch. And worse still, if she'd become MacKinnon's wife, she would have equated brutality with lust.

Whatever happens now, I'm content.

But was she? Ross had shown her another world, one she didn't want to leave just yet. It had been her first time, and he'd gone slowly and gently in an effort to make her comfortable. It had hurt, yet the pain had been fleeting.

The way he'd moved inside her, and the sensations that had followed, had been a revelation. She'd hadn't realized her body was capable of giving her such feeling. Afterward, pleasure had built in aching, rippling waves that made her groan and sigh. She knew they'd just scratched the surface though, that there was so much more pleasure to be experienced—that something wondrous lay just out of reach. She'd felt as if she'd arched toward it, brushed it with her fingertips.

She wanted to fall into Ross, to spiral through oblivion with him.

But as she rested against his naked chest, her throat tightened while sadness rose within. They were running out of time. Leanna squeezed her eyes closed pushing back tears. Tonight was a frozen moment, something magical that neither of them had counted on.

With the rising of the dawn, the enchantment would shatter and time would march on. If MacKinnon ever caught up with them, there was a real chance that she would never lie with Ross Campbell ever again.

The thought made an ache rise under Leanna's breastbone. Life could be so cruel—to show her something so wondrous and then to rip it from her would be more than she could bear. And yet some things were out of her control.

"Ye have a visitor, MacKinnon."

Duncan jerked up his head and glared blearily at where Broderick stood in the doorway to his solar. The clan-chief had fallen asleep upon his high-backed chair before the hearth. "At this hour?" he rasped. It was late, the middle of the night in fact. He should be slumbering in his bed, not receiving visitors. Who the devil would disturb him now?

Broderick nodded, his face giving nothing away.

"Well ... tell whoever it is that I'll see them in the morning."

"Ye will want to see this man," Broderick replied, his manner as phlegmatic as ever. "He is known to us all ... and brings word from yer brother."

Duncan went still, the last vestiges of sleep sloughing off him. "My *bastard* brother?" he snarled.

"Craeg has taken Campbell and Lady Leanna prisoner," Broderick replied, ignoring the correction. "Yer visitor is one of his band. He comes bearing terms."

At Duncan's feet, Bran stirred. The wolfhound gave a soft whine as it picked up on the tension that suddenly rippled through the chamber. For once, Duncan didn't reach out to ruffle the dog's ears. Instead, his attention was wholly upon the warrior who'd taken Ross Campbell's place as his right-hand. He wasn't as fond of Broderick as he had been of Campbell; the man was as difficult to read as a granite boulder.

"Show him in then."

With a nod, Broderick stepped back and jerked his chin to someone who stood just out of sight.

A heartbeat later, a tall man with greying dark hair, sharp features, and a hard gaze stepped forward. Clad in well-fitting hunting leathers, the newcomer stared him down as he entered.

Likewise, Duncan glared back, a chill seeping through him.

Him.

MacKinnon rose to his full height before the fire, while at his feet Bran started to growl low in his throat. The dog had sensed the animosity between the two men, the tension that flooded the solar.

His brother's emissary was unarmed, yet he carried himself with the calm self-assurance of a man who didn't need a weapon to feel confident.

"Brochan," Duncan murmured. "I thought ye were dead?"

The outlaw grinned, although his eyes were hostile. He was around a decade older than Duncan, his leathery, tanned skin crisscrossed with fine lines. "Aye ... ye did yer best, MacKinnon ... but I lived and found a place at Craeg the Bastard's side instead."

Brochan came to a halt in the center of the solar. Broderick and four other warriors stood behind him, awaiting the clan-chief's command.

Duncan MacKinnon observed the outlaw, and as he did so, the chill faded and heat stirred in his belly. His hands, which hung at his sides, slowly clenched and unclenched.

So Craeg had abducted Lady Leanna—and had sent this cur to deliver his terms?

Hatred coiled within him, with such strength that his gut hurt.

I should have made sure Craeg and Brochan died all those years ago ... why did I not?

He'd been foolish back then. He'd been sure both men would die from their injuries, but clearly, his arrogance had gotten the better of him. It had been a gross miscalculation, for instead Craeg had grown strong over the years and amassed a loyal following.

Men like Brochan—who'd die for him, if necessary.

Duncan clenched his jaw so tightly that pain arrowed through his right ear. Brochan was a fool to come here alone and try to blackmail him, and Craeg was reckless to have sent him here.

The outlaw would have a nasty end. But first, Duncan would get the details he needed from him.

Craeg was kneeling by the burn, splashing water across his face, when Gunn approached. The morning sun had just broken through the mist, and around him, the trees chattered and trilled with the dawn chorus.

"Brochan has disappeared," the warrior announced.

Craeg sat back on his heels and blinked water out of his eyes. He then glanced up at the big man. His face was creased with concern.

Craeg made an impatient noise in the back of his throat. Reaching for a rough cloth, he rose to his feet and dried his face. "He's probably just gone hunting."

Gunn folded brawny arms across his barrel chest. "He left his longbow and arrows behind ... and told no one he was leaving."

Craeg went still, a heavy sensation settling in the pit of his gut. "He wouldn't."

"Wouldn't he?"

"But I forbade it."

"Ye know Brochan doesn't take well to being told 'no'." Gunn was scowling now. "He was angry after ye denied him yesterday. I heard him complaining at the fireside later."

Craeg rose to his feet, anger coiling within him. "Everyone else would agree that his plan was reckless."

"Aye ... but when he talked of all the silver our guests would buy us, some of them looked half-convinced."

Craeg gave a snort of disgust. Coin. It had a corrupting influence on everyone, even those who'd sworn to use it for good. "So he left alone?"

"Looks like it ... no one else is missing."

Craeg raked a hand through his already disheveled hair and growled a curse. "That idiot will bring hell down upon us."

"If ye could go anywhere, live anywhere, where would it be?"

Leanna's question shattered the companionable silence within the hut. A new day had dawned, and Fenella had brought them food to break their fast. The outlaw wore a grim expression and had thumped the tray down without a word before departing. However, she'd left the door open, allowing the fresh dawn air to filter in. Outdoors, Leanna glimpsed a pale, misty morning.

Ross put down the wedge of bannock he'd been buttering and met her gaze, his mouth lifting at the edges. "I don't rightly know ... it's not a question I've ever asked myself."

"But if ye could?"

There was a restlessness within Leanna as she asked the question, a need to 'know' this man. Time was running out; she could feel it slipping through her fingers like fine grains of sand. She needed something to cling on to, something to remember.

Ross considered the question. In the soft morning light filtering into the hut, his face was achingly handsome. He wore a whimsical, almost boyish expression, the dawn sun glowing upon the dark waves of his hair.

His dark léine lay open at the neck, revealing a light covering of crisp, dark curls. Leanna's lower belly clenched with desire as she remembered how she'd run her hands over his chest the night before, how she'd traced the contours of his chest with her lips.

How she wanted to do that again.

"I once believed I wanted to rule a broch of my own," Ross replied finally. "I wanted lands and a loyal following of warriors like my father ... but I'm not sure I desire that anymore." He paused then, his gaze swiveling to the view outdoors, where cloaked figures moved by. "Many of my clansmen are farmers ... sometimes I imagine having land and sheep, fertile fields, and a home that I built with my own hands."

Ross glanced back, and their gazes met. The look that passed between them was so intense that Leanna suddenly forgot to breathe. "All my life I've striven for what was never worth having," he said huskily. "Meeting ye has made me realize just how empty it's all been. If I could go anywhere, I would take a boat to some forgotten isle with ye, Leanna, and build a new life there for ourselves ... away from the noise and strife of the rest of the world."

Warmth filtered through her at these words. "Then that is what we should do," she murmured.

Their gazes held, and she watched his throat bob and his dark eyes glisten with sudden emotion. "I promise ye that if we survive the coming days, we will," he replied.

24

Betrayal

"CRAEG ASKS THAT ye both join us for the noon meal."

Seated upon a mossy log, where she'd been making a wildflower posy, Leanna glanced up.

Fenella stood before her, hands on hips, her gaze narrowed. The woman's attention slid down to the stalks of heather, bluebells, and primroses upon Leanna's lap. Her mouth thinned, and Leanna's cheeks warmed in response. No doubt the woman thought her a witless goose of a woman. Making a posy seemed like a frivolous act, but since the entire camp had appeared busy this morning, she'd gone looking for something to keep her busy. After breaking their fast at dawn, both she and Ross had been at a loose end.

They'd passed most of the morning talking. She'd told him of her childhood, her time at Kilbride, and about the things she missed about Duncaith.

Likewise, Ross had talked of his past. She already knew his childhood hadn't been pleasant, but there had been light-hearted moments. As a wee lad, he'd collected frogs, which he used to frighten his mother and sister with. He'd been close to his uncle, who'd died in battle when Ross had been around twelve, and the man had taught him how to hunt, how to shear a sheep, and how to shoe a horse. After his death, Ross had felt alone amongst a family that didn't understand him.

Ross now sat a few feet behind her, sharpening the blade of his claidheamh-mor with a small whetstone he'd brought with him.

"He's remembered we're here, has he?" Ross asked, a rueful note to his voice. "I imagined he might have some questions for me?"

Leanna tensed. They'd discussed that very subject over their bannocks earlier. Ross was sure that Craeg hadn't let them stay in the outlaw village purely out of generosity. He was bound to want something from them.

"Craeg's been ... preoccupied this morning," Fenella replied coolly. "But now, if I can drag ye away from yer tasks." She cast Leanna another pointed look. "He wishes ye to join us."

Cheeks burning, Leanna put aside her posy. Upon her arrival here, she'd thought she might warm to Fenella, but she was hurriedly revising her opinion of her. Leanna twisted around then to see that Ross had risen to his feet. He winced as he stretched out his long back.

She too got up, dusting off her skirts, and they followed Fenella through the village. It was a murky day. The light levels were low; a morning mist had given way to overcast skies.

Around them, the outlaw village bustled with a surprising amount of industry. Women were bringing in the washing, and children were tending oatcakes over a nearby fire pit; while at another, two men turned haunches of venison over the glowing coals.

Leanna's belly growled as the delicious aroma of roasting meat wafted over her.

It was then that she noted there was more to the busyness than just the day-to-day routines of the settlement. A group of women sat near one of the fires, deftly fletching arrows and fastening on iron tips. The odor of hot iron drifted through the village, as did the clang of a smith's hammer. Men strode past, carrying spears and dirks.

Leanna's belly tightened. It looked as if they were preparing for war.

Glancing at Fenella, she saw that the woman wore a scowl. She clearly wasn't happy about something. Leanna had thought it was likely their presence here that was bothering her, but now she suspected there was something else.

At the heart of the outlaw settlement was a large central fire pit, where a haunch of venison was being sliced up and served onto wooden platters. A scattering of men sat around it.

The nervousness in Leanna's gut fluttered like a cage of butterflies when she saw they were all armed.

Craeg sat among them, as did the red-haired outlaw, Gunn. Craeg's expression was shuttered as he raised a hand and beckoned Leanna and Ross over, motioning for them to sit down at his side.

Sharing a wary glance with Ross, Leanna did as bid. However, tension rippled through her. It didn't matter how she steeled herself, every time she set eyes on the outlaw leader, her breathing constricted. At first glance, he looked so much like his half-brother. But as his green eyes settled upon her, her pulse calmed.

This isn't Duncan MacKinnon, she assured herself.

"I hope ye are finding yer lodgings comfortable enough?" he asked.

Leanna nodded, while next to her, Ross let out a non-committal grunt.

Craeg grinned at their responses. "It's not as fine as ye are both used to, I'd warrant."

Leanna stiffened. Did Craeg think her as spoiled and haughty as Fenella did?

Seated before the glowing embers, she reached out and warmed her fingers. It was hard to believe they were in the midst of spring, for the air this high in the mountains had a definite nip to it.

Taking the platter of venison the outlaws were passing around, Leanna helped herself to a slice. She then gave the platter to Ross, who did the same. However, his gaze was focused on Craeg.

"Something is up?" he murmured. "Yesterday this was a lost mountain village, yet today it looks like ye are preparing for a siege. Why's that?"

The outlaw leader inclined his head. "Observant aren't ye, Campbell?"

"Call it more of a survival instinct."

Craeg smiled at that, although Leanna noted the expression was strained. "The situation has changed," he said after a moment. "It appears that one of my men may have done something ... stupid."

Leanna swallowed the mouthful of venison she'd been chewing, her pulse quickening. The wary look in the man's eyes warned her she wasn't going to like what he was about to tell them.

"Last night, the man in question, suggested we ransom the pair of ye to MacKinnon," Craeg continued.

Leanna sucked in a breath, and even though she didn't look his way, Leanna felt Ross tense. "And?" he asked warily.

"Of course, I dismissed the idea," Craeg replied, frowning. "But now Brochan's disappeared. We believe he's gone to Dunan."

A beat of stunned silence followed, and then Ross spoke, his voice low and rough with anger. "Ye have betrayed us."

Craeg shook his head. "We haven't done anything of the sort. I don't even know if that's where Brochan has gone, but we're taking precautions nonetheless. I've put more men on the watch and sent out scouts farther down the valley. They'll let us know if anyone approaches." He paused then. A muscle flexed in his jaw, betraying his tension. "I didn't sanction this, Campbell ... and I will do all I can to keep ye and Lady Leanna safe."

Leanna shifted her attention from the outlaw leader and focused on Ross. His face was pale and taut, his midnight blue eyes darkened to black. With a jolt, she realized he was struggling to rein in his temper.

Casting aside the piece of meat he'd been eating, Ross got to his feet. "We can't stay here," he announced roughly. "Yer man has put Lady Leanna at risk. We need to go now."

Silence settled around the fireside. No one touched their food now or sipped from the skins of ale they'd been passing around. Instead, the men and women seated there watched Ross with strained expressions.

"Aye ... maybe that's for the best," Craeg admitted finally. "If Brochan has indeed gone to MacKinnon, he'll likely get the whereabouts of this camp out of him eventually. Ye should leave and get a head-start on him."

Around them, outlaws exchanged glances. Next to Gunn, Fenella frowned. "Maybe we should also think about packing up and going?" she suggested. "Ye have no idea how many men MacKinnon has in his guard."

All gazes shifted to Ross then, and Leanna's breathing quickened. Of course, he'd know.

"There will be at least eighty of them," Ross replied coolly. "Possibly more if MacKinnon empties out The Dunan Guard."

This news made Leanna start to sweat. She glanced around her. He was right. They had to go.

However, for the moment, Ross's attention was focused on the outlaw leader.

Craeg's gaze shadowed. His lips parted, as he prepared himself to question Ross once more.

However, a shout behind them forestalled him.

"We're under attack!"

The group around the fire scattered. One moment they were seated there, watching the exchange between their leader and Ross, the next, men and women were rolling to their feet and lunging for weapons.

A heartbeat later cries echoed through the settlement.

A young man sprinted toward them, face flushed with panic. Craeg, who was already up on his feet and had drawn his sword, met him.

"It's MacKinnon!" the lad announced, eyes wide with panic. "He's found us."

Craeg spat out a curse, his expression turning savage. "Why haven't the scouts alerted us?"

"They'll be dead." Ross drew his own claidheamh-mor, his expression fierce now. "As will yer foolish friend. Ye of all people should know that ye under-estimate Duncan MacKinnon at yer peril."

25

Lethal

CRAEG'S GAZE CUT to Ross, his moss-green eyes darkening to jade. Gunn had stepped up to the outlaw leader's side while, behind him, Fenella had shouldered a quiver of arrows and taken a longbow that one of the outlaws passed her.

I need a bow too. The thought rose unbidden before Leanna dismissed it. Her body trembled, and her heart raced; she wasn't sure she could think straight right now, let alone wield a weapon.

Instinctively, Leanna stepped close to Ross and reached for him, her fingers curling around his forearm.

"The guard has at least twenty bowmen," Ross spoke up then, his gaze spearing Craeg's. "All the others will have claidheamh-mors."

"All of them?" Gunn interrupted them, alarmed.

"MacKinnon has always invested heavily in The Dunan Guard," Ross replied, his mouth twisting. "Most of them will be wearing mail shirts as well."

Craeg's face turned grim at this news. "Will MacKinnon be leading them?"

"After the injury Leanna dealt him, I'd say not," Ross replied. "He'll be there though ... watching at the rear."

Something feral moved across Craeg's face. Watching him, Leanna realized that the man wanted MacKinnon to be there. He wanted a chance to have his reckoning upon him.

Spitting out another curse, Craeg then sprang into action, shouting orders at the panicked men and women who scrambled around him. The low timbre of his voice echoed across the valley, and Leanna noted that his commands had a calming effect on the band. The alarm quietened, and instead, the outlaws gathered their weapons and fanned out around the perimeter of the village.

Moments later the twang of bow-strings releasing cut through the gloaming. MacKinnon's men had initially kept to the shadows, hiding amongst the trees. But now, as they loosed their arrows, they advanced upon the settlement itself.

Ross glanced around, his features tightening. "They've got us surrounded," he murmured. This comment earned him a sharp glance from Craeg, to which Ross answered. "Aye ... it's his preferred method of ambush."

Craeg's gaze flicked from Ross to Leanna. "Ye need to go now," he said roughly. "While ye still can."

The outlaw turned then, dismissing them, his attention upon the figures that approached from the perimeter of the village. Many of his men had already engaged the attackers. The whistle of flying arrows and the clang of blades clashing split the misty air.

Leanna watched the outlaw leader stride off to join the others, and then she took an instinctive step closer to Ross. "What now?" she gasped.

An arrow flew past and embedded into the door frame of a nearby hut. Leanna tensed, fighting the urge to cower. She felt so exposed out here. Fletched arrows peppered the air now.

"Ye heard the man," Ross grunted. "It's time to leave. Come on."

Together they edged back from the fire pit, gazes scanning their surroundings. There was fighting on all sides, it seemed, and shouts and cries rang out over the valley.

Fear clutched at Leanna's chest, and her legs trembled under her. She didn't know how men coped with battle. She felt as if she might lose her wits if someone ran at her swinging a broad-sword.

However, Ross remained calm, focused, his gaze flicking left and right. A few yards to their right, they came upon their first fallen outlaw. A young man with an arrow through his neck.

There was nothing they could do for him so they kept moving, heading toward the northern edge of the village. Ten more yards in, and they found themselves on the edge of a pitched battle. Men flailed and stabbed at each other.

Leanna's legs wobbled once more, threatening to give way as terror seized her. She dug her heels into the ground, yet Ross towed her forward as if she weighed nothing.

"I need to find ye a weapon to defend yerself," he said, his voice tight with tension.

He cut down a man who'd broken through the outlaw lines and lunged toward him, before they reached the prone figure of an outlaw woman. A discarded longbow lay upon the ground next to her.

Ross grasped it and passed the weapon to Leanna, before he pulled out the quiver of arrows from beneath the woman's body and looped it over Leanna's shoulder.

Their gazes fused for an instant, and then he flashed her a hard smile.

"Time to put yer skills to use, m'eudail."

My darling.

The endearment cut through the horror of the attack, just for an instant, and then Ross was swinging away and raising his sword to fend off another of MacKinnon's men.

They would know him, Leanna realized, for until a day ago he'd been Captain of The Dunan Guard.

And yet Ross didn't hesitate to bring the man down, slicing him across the neck. The warrior crumpled to the dirt, blood pumping from the wound, his body convulsing.

Leanna's heart started to pound at the sight, and she swallowed down bile.

Ross moved back from the fallen warrior, his attention shifting around them. "The fighting's too thick here," he observed. "We need to find another way out." He glanced Leanna's way. "Draw an arrow and follow me."

With trembling fingers, Leanna did as bid.

She suddenly wished she hadn't boasted to him of her skill with a bow. It was true that she'd spent most of the last two years training, and that she had a good aim. But that was when she was calm and focused.

Not when she felt sick with fear.

Nonetheless, she wasn't going to admit such to Ross. He needed her support, and she would have to give it.

Leanna notched the arrow into the longbow and hurried after Ross, retracing their footsteps toward the center of the village.

And when they returned there, they discovered chaos.

The fighting from the east had shifted in, and Craeg was now facing the MacKinnon warriors on the edge of the clearing that marked the heart of the settlement.

Upon spying the fighting, Ross breathed a curse.

As they'd expected, things were going ill for the outlaws.

"We should keep going," Leanna whispered. She glanced south, at the steep wooded hillside that backed onto the village. Surely there would be fewer MacKinnon men up there. If they ran now, no one would see.

Ross glanced over his shoulder, following the direction of her gaze.

She could see he was torn. He wanted to run, but something prevented him.

Spitting out another curse, he shook his head. "Not yet ... ye stay here and try to pick off as many of The Dunan Guard as ye can with yer bow." He managed a harsh smile then. "Be careful of yer aim though."

With that, Ross turned and strode off toward the skirmish.

Panic grasped Leanna by the throat as she watched him go.

What's he doing?

They needed to flee, but instead, he'd decided to join the outlaws. Stepping up to Craeg's side, Ross swung his sword at a huge MacKinnon warrior who bore down upon them.

Terror welled within Leanna.

Mother Mary, we're all doomed.

Leanna gulped in a breath, and then another, in an effort to quell the fear that now pumped through her.

Part of her just wanted to turn on her heel and run—and yet she didn't. She couldn't abandon Ross, not when he was acting so bravely.

She had to help as well.

Inhaling deeply, Leanna positioned herself side-on to the fracas and lifted her longbow. She drew it taut and raised the arrow so that it was in line with her eye. It was difficult to get a clear shot, for both sides were engaged now, yet she bided her time.

Breathe.

She exhaled slowly, before drawing in another breath. Then, she held it and awaited her chance.

A heartbeat later, it presented itself.

One of the MacKinnon warriors staggered back, after deflecting a blow from Craeg. For just an instant, Leanna had a clear line of sight.

She loosed her arrow.

Thud. It embedded at the base of the warrior's neck. He choked, his free hand clutching at the fletched arrow.

Craeg glanced her way, his gaze widening when he saw who had fired upon his opponent. Then he inclined his head in a gesture of silent thanks before wheeling around to face his next attacker.

Leanna notched another arrow and raised her bow once more. After firing upon the first of the MacKinnon warriors, a strange calm had settled over her. Before loosing that arrow, she'd been so scared her hands had shaken. Yet they were steady now, and her gaze narrowed as she sought out another of The Dunan Guard to bring down.

A tall man clad in leather with the MacKinnon sash proudly displayed across his chest burst through the fighting. He bore a massive claidheamh-mor—a weapon that had to be wielded two-handed, one that few women would be strong enough to use.

However, a woman wielding a longbow could be just as lethal.

A tight smile curved Leanna's mouth as she sighted her next target.

Perhaps the longbow wasn't such a useless skill after all.

26

On the Run

SWEAT SLID DOWN Leanna's back, trickling between her shoulder blades. Ignoring the ache in her upper arms and shoulders, she notched yet another arrow and sighted her next target.

However, as she did so, she realized that the fighting was drawing nearer. The outlaws were doing a valiant job of defending the village, yet inch by inch, MacKinnon's men were tightening the noose.

Ross fought at Craeg's shoulder, while a few yards away, Gunn swung a heavy axe at his assailants. All three men were sweat-soaked and blood-splattered, yet they didn't let down their guard, not for an instant.

It mattered not though—for eventually they were forced back.

Not shifting her gaze from the fracas, Leanna drew away a few yards. Her quiver was almost empty. Soon, she would have to go in search of more arrows.

Hopelessness rose up within her—a chill, sickly feeling. It punctured the calm that had enabled her to bring down a handful of MacKinnon's men.

She'd helped slow the tide, but she couldn't stem it completely. There were just too many of them.

And then, as she notched her last arrow, she saw Craeg stagger.

An arrow had just hit his left flank.

The outlaw swore savagely and swung his blade at the warrior he'd just engaged. The pain of the arrow hit seemed to galvanize him, for he brought the man down an instant later with a savage cut to his groin.

Clutching the wound to his left side, where the arrow now protruded, Craeg turned to Ross.

"Run, Campbell," he rasped. "I'll focus on taking what's left of my people to safety … but ye need to get Lady Leanna away from here."

Ross, who'd just bested a pike-wielding warrior, turned to him. His gaze widened when he saw Craeg was wounded. "Ye need help," he replied.

"And I'll get it," Craeg countered before he favored Ross with a savage grin. "Thank ye both for coming to our aid. Now get out of here before ye end up skewered on a claidheamh-mor." The outlaw leader glanced Leanna's way then, just as she loosed her last arrow.

The warrior with the pike wasn't dead. He'd staggered to his feet behind Ross and was drawing his dirk. The arrow thudded into his breast, and he crumpled with a cry.

Craeg shook his head in wry bemusement as if he found it hard to believe she possessed such skill with a bow. "Go now, milady … ye won't get another chance."

Ross didn't need further urging. With a nod at the outlaw leader, he strode past him toward Leanna. She tossed her empty quiver and now useless longbow aside as he approached.

Meanwhile, Craeg turned away to focus on the fight once more.

Leanna's last glimpse of Craeg was of a tall, dark-haired figure, flashing his sword as he lunged forward to meet his next opponent.

They fled through the cluster of tightly-packed dwellings toward the southern edge of the village.

Ross's breathing was coming in sharp gasps now. The fighting had drained him, but he couldn't afford to rest yet. He wouldn't do so until he'd gotten Leanna to safety.

Craeg's situation concerned him. He knew as well as the outlaw leader that they were on the losing side of the battle. Shortly, Craeg would need to retreat with what was left of his band, or they'd all be slaughtered.

Ross and Leanna had to run now.

The fighting was sporadic at the southern fringes, and they managed to avoid it by ducking behind some store huts and edging their way out. Poised on the perimeter of the village, they shared a look, before Ross took hold of Leanna's hand.

"Are ye ready?" he whispered. "Once we run, don't look back."

Leanna gazed back at him. Her face was pale and taut, yet her small mouth had flattened into a determined line, and her eyes were narrowed. She hadn't lied when she'd told him she knew how to wield a longbow; Ross had rarely seen such a true aim. It was dangerous to fire upon a skirmish like that, as you risked hitting an ally, yet Leanna had impeccable timing.

Ross squeezed Leanna's hand once, and then he sprang forward, away from the cover of the storehouses. They made a dash for the dark wall of pines. It was a dull afternoon, but they'd have a few more hours of daylight to flee in before darkness would slow their progress. Even so, Ross didn't know this part of the isle well. He was taking Leanna into rough, uneven terrain, but he had no choice.

It was either that or face Duncan MacKinnon.

The thought of what that bastard would do to Leanna made Ross clench his jaw and lengthen his stride. He didn't care what happened to him; he could handle it. However, MacKinnon's revenge upon Leanna if he caught her would be terrible—slower and less bloody most likely, but ultimately much worse.

They reached the trees, and immediately the heady scent of pine resin enveloped them. A mattress of soft pine needles lay underfoot, masking the noise of their footfalls. Behind them, shouts and cries echoed high into the valley.

Ross's belly twisted at the sounds. The fighting was not yet done. He wondered if any of the outlaws would survive the attack.

Tightening his grip on Leanna's hand, Ross sprinted on, weaving in and out of the tightly-packed pines. Branches snatched at his limbs, and prickly pine needles clawed at his face, yet he didn't slow his stride. He needed to get Leanna to safety. Right now, he could think about nothing else.

Leanna didn't know how she kept running. Each breath was ripped from her lungs, which now felt as if they were on fire. Her legs wobbled underneath her, making her stumble.

Shortly after escaping the village, the land rose steeply, and the way grew steadily rougher. Boulders rose from the rocky ground, and the trees became sparser.

They were climbing a mountainside now, yet they couldn't halt to rest, not yet.

She had no idea if they were being pursued or not; she couldn't hear anything over the pounding of her own heart and the roar of blood in her ears.

Soon they were climbing their way over mossy rocks and through stunted pines.

Eventually, the rocks gave way to shale, and they started to slip and slide.

"We need to continue south," Ross panted. "Maybe there's a pass down the other side of the mountain."

Leanna didn't answer. She lacked the breath to do so. She was gasping now, exhaustion making her feel sick.

After a while, the shadows lengthened and the light started to fade. However, Leanna and Ross didn't halt.

Not speaking, the pair of them edged south, often slipping and stumbling on the shale, which moved like quicksand underfoot. This high up, the air had a bite to it, despite that spring was now fully upon the isle.

Leanna was grateful for the nippy breeze that feathered across her heated cheeks. The heavy fabric of her habit, underskirts, and léine caught at her legs as she scrambled after Ross, hampering her movement. He'd let go of her hand a long while back, once they were clear of the outlaw village.

It was silent up here, and no sounds of the fighting they'd left behind echoed up from the valley far below. It was an ominous quiet, and Leanna wondered what it meant.

As she traveled, Leanna's thoughts often returned to the people they'd left behind. Craeg had made a mistake in giving them shelter. His offer had been well-meant, but he hadn't thought how some members of his band might react to having her and Ross among them.

His friend's rash and foolish act had cost them all dearly.

The image of Craeg continuing to fight, even with an arrow sticking out of his side, made a cold knot form in Leanna's belly. The man was brave, but would it be enough? Would MacKinnon slaughter them all?

Leanna shoved the thought aside, her heart pumping now.

We're not safe yet, either, Leanna reminded herself as she wiped the sweat from her eyes.

She knew she wouldn't be until she was far from the Isle of Skye. While she remained here, she'd always have the threat of MacKinnon hanging over her like a great shadow, dimming any happiness.

Ross was supposed to bring her home to Duncaith, and they were certainly heading in the right direction to do so. However, she knew she couldn't do that to her kin.

With MacKinnon hot on the trail, and incensed now, Leanna realized that she and Ross would need to change their plan. Her uncle would be forced to protect her—and doing so would launch the MacDonalds of Sleat into a full-scale feud with MacKinnon.

I can't do that to them.

Leanna swallowed as the thought of never seeing her mother and sisters again thickened her throat. Of course, as a nun at Kilbride, she'd already struggled with that realization. But once she'd decided she wouldn't return to the abbey, a kernel of hope had taken seed in her breast—the hope that she'd be able to live at Duncaith amongst those who loved her.

But MacKinnon's reach was long. She wouldn't be safe from him, even there.

Where would I go instead?

Leanna's feet slid out from under her then, and she pitched forward onto the steep slope.

Muttering a curse under her breath, she pushed the question aside. Now wasn't the time to start planning the future. She was getting ahead of herself.

Now was all about survival.

She and Ross had to somehow get across these mountains and into MacDonald land. They had to lose themselves in the wilderness. Once they were far enough away from MacKinnon, she could start focusing on what lay ahead.

But, for the moment, she had to focus on putting one foot in front of the other.

27

Till the Last Breath

ROSS KNELT AT the edge of the stream and splashed ice-cold water over his heated face. It was so chill that it took his breath away—yet it was just what he needed. The cold cut through the fog of exhaustion that dragged at his limbs.

They'd now traversed the mountains. The rest of the journey would, hopefully, be easier.

Sitting back upon his haunches, Ross glanced over his shoulder at where a small figure lay upon her back, spread-eagled upon the mossy bank. Leanna's face was flushed, and her breast heaved. Her pale hair spread out in a cloud around her.

Night had long fallen, although a full moon cast its friendly light over the world, illuminating Leanna's exhausted features.

"Are ye well?" he croaked. It was a foolish question really, for she'd just thrown up from exhaustion, but he wanted to make sure that it was only tiredness that ailed her and nothing else.

"I'll live," she rasped back. "I think." With a groan, Leanna rolled onto her side, her gaze fusing with his. "Do ye think we've outrun them?"

"For the moment."

Ross had turned back to the stream and was splashing more water on his face. Gasping, he shook his head and felt a little more of the fatigue slough away. He needed to keep a clear head; he needed to think.

"We're in MacDonald lands now, Leanna," he said after a pause, glancing her way once more. "We need to decide which way to go."

A pause followed these words, and he saw a shadow move across her hazel eyes. He realized then that the gravity of their situation had finally settled upon her. She knew there was no going back to Duncaith.

He'd feared he'd have to explain that to her, but he saw he had no need to. Leanna understood.

"He'll never stop hunting me," she whispered. Her eyes gleamed as tears rose. "If I go home, it'll only bring his wrath down upon my uncle ... and I won't do that to them." She paused then, a groove forming between her eyes.

"I know war is a way of life for this isle, but I'll not be the cause of another blood feud. I need to leave Skye."

Ross's mouth quirked. "Aye ... we both do."

She watched him, her expression turning pensive. "Will ye help me, Ross?"

He turned from the stream and shifted over to Leanna's side. She rose up onto her knees to meet him. He placed his hands upon her shoulders, seizing her gaze with his. Then he leaned forward.

They were so close, their breaths mingled.

Ross was surprised to discover that his heart was racing. "I will remain by yer side till the last breath leaves me," he murmured, his voice husky now. "We shall find a boat that will take us away from here, and search for a quiet corner of Scotland where we can make a life together."

Leanna's eyes grew wide at these words, but Ross rushed on. He had to keep speaking before his courage failed him. He'd never felt like this before: an overwhelming, chest-crushing need to protect this woman, to remain at her side.

"I love ye, Lady Leanna MacDonald of Sleat," he continued. "And if ye will do me the honor of becoming my wife, we shall be wed as soon as we reach safety."

Leanna stared at him, her rosebud lips parting at the shock of his admission.

Ross didn't blame her; frankly, he couldn't believe what he'd just said. It hadn't been rehearsed. He'd simply acted on instinct, and without realizing it, he'd just revealed what lay in his heart.

And now that the words were out there, he felt strangely unburdened.

They'd been growing in him for a while now, he realized—since long before he made the decision to help Leanna escape Dunan.

But he'd understand if she spurned him. Circumstances had thrown them together, and she'd given herself willingly to him. That didn't mean, however, that she wanted to become his wife.

Long moments passed, and then a soft smile curved Leanna's lips. "It would be my honor," she whispered.

Surprise and then joy flowered within Ross, a fierce warmth that exploded under his breastbone and spread up to his throat and down to his belly. Wordlessly, he drew her to him, his mouth slanting hungrily over hers. Leanna responded eagerly, her arms linking around his neck as she drew him against her. She kissed him back, her lips parting and her tongue sliding against his.

A low groan escaped Ross, and it was with great effort that he eventually broke the kiss and shifted back from her. "I could easily lose myself in ye," he told her, watching as Leanna's eyes darkened with desire, "but we're not out of danger yet."

She nodded, although the limpid look in her eyes still tempted him. She had no idea how much he wanted her; it took every ounce of his willpower not to throw her back onto that mossy bank, spread those creamy thighs, and sink deep into her velvet heat.

Ross's groin started to ache at the thought.

Mercifully, Leanna moved away from him then, severing eye contact. He watched her rise to her feet and brush off her skirts. When she spoke, her voice held a husky edge that made Ross's breathing catch. "So, we need to head to the coast … and find ourselves a boat."

"And we will," Ross replied, not moving, "but we need to catch our breaths a while longer … or neither of us will make it there. Rest while ye can, my love."

Leanna nodded, before sinking back down onto the mossy ground with a soft sigh of relief.

"Kyleakin would be the best choice of port," Ross murmured. His gaze shifted back toward the way they'd come. Although he couldn't see in the darkness, he knew that the wall of rugged mountains they'd passed through thrust up from the valley floor. "But I'd rather not travel back onto MacKinnon lands … or retrace our steps."

Leanna shuddered. "Me neither." She met his eye then. "There's a village on the south coast called 'Knock'. I visited it once with Da … merchants often bring their boats ashore there, with supplies from the mainland. We could find passage at the port."

Ross nodded, the tension within him loosening slightly at this news. The truth was that, not being a native of Skye, he didn't know this side of the isle well at all. He was glad that Leanna did.

"How far is it from here?" he asked.

Leanna glanced around, her face screwing up as she tried to get her bearings. "My father used to go stag hunting in the mountains we just crossed," she murmured finally. "They're around half a day's ride from Duncaith … which means we are nearly a day's journey on foot to Knock."

"Right then." Ross lay back on the bank, his gaze taking in the wide swathe of starry sky above. "We'll rest a little longer and then head for the coast." Fatigue lay upon him in a heavy blanket, and his leg muscles ached. His body cried out for sleep, yet it wouldn't be getting any—not yet. They had to keep moving. Even at Knock, they wouldn't be safe.

MacKinnon would be stalking them, and many of his men would be on horseback. Night provided some protection from their hunters. But, as soon as dawn broke, he and Leanna would have to watch their backs.

He turned his head, his attention settling once more upon his companion, and saw that she was watching him, her gaze resolute. Yet a gentle smile lay upon her lips. Warmth filtered through Ross once more. Despite everything, the lass could actually smile. He adored her resilience; it was something he'd noted from the first day of their acquaintance.

Lady Leanna was a survivor.

Duncan MacKinnon drew his courser to a halt, his gaze sweeping right and left. They'd rejoined the rutted highway that led into MacDonald lands and had now reached a crossroads.

A weather-beaten gibbet marked the intersection of three roads. A gruesome spectacle hung from the noose—the rotting corpse of what had once been a man.

Duncan's attention rested upon the body for a few moments, before his mouth thinned. An outlaw, most likely. In other circumstances, it would have pleased him to see that the MacDonalds were taking the lawlessness upon this isle as seriously as he was.

However, this morning, there was only one thing he cared about—one thing that consumed his thoughts.

Behind him, the sun rose over the edge of the mountains into the eastern sky, burning away the morning mist. MacKinnon felt sunlight warm his back as he twisted in the saddle and fixed Carr Broderick with a gimlet stare.

The warrior stared back at him, unflinching. Broderick's face, however, was strained with fatigue and blood-splattered. They'd overtaken the village eventually, but MacKinnon's bastard brother had somehow disappeared.

Duncan had searched the dead, but Craeg hadn't been among them.

Worse still, Leanna and Campbell had also escaped.

"We need to widen our search," Duncan informed his right-hand. "Ye take a group south and patrol the coast … while I go to Duncaith."

Broderick frowned. "Do ye really think she'd go home?"

"Aye," Duncan growled. "She'll think the walls of Duncaith will shield her from me … but they won't. Nothing will."

"And if she's not there?"

"Then I'll ride to Kilbride."

Broderick took this news in, before nodding. "And yer brother?"

Duncan's face screwed up at the mention of the outlaw leader. He then leaned forward and spat upon the road. Craeg had been a fool to try and blackmail him. Did he really think Duncan was ever going to negotiate? Brochan had lasted the night. The outlaw's arrogance had endured for a while, and Duncan had feared the man would hold his tongue—but before he'd died, he'd gasped the name of the valley where the outlaw camp lay.

"I heard Craeg took an arrow," Duncan said after a pause. "He won't last long."

Broderick didn't reply to that. They both knew injuring Craeg wasn't enough. The bastard had survived terrible injuries once—he was capable of doing so again.

MacKinnon wouldn't rest until he saw his half-brother dead.

His gaze returned to the decaying corpse hanging from the gibbet. Crows had picked out its eyes, and the mouth gaped horrifyingly.

I swear that will be Craeg's fate, Duncan promised himself. *One day that bastard will swing.*

28

Temptress

THEY REACHED THE village of Knock late in the day. The shadows had grown long, and a warm breeze blew in from the south, ruffling the water, as Leanna and Ross crested the last hill.

Halting upon the brow, Leanna held up her hand, to shield her eyes from the low sun, and took in the settlement below.

Knock was larger than she remembered—a sprawl of stacked-stone cottages with sod roofs that hugged the edge of a wide sound. A row of boats bobbed against a wooden pier. Squinting, Leanna could make out a promontory on the southern edge of the village, where the ruins of an old Pictish round-tower stood.

Arable fields spread up the hillside behind Knock. Folk worked tirelessly there with hoes and spades.

"At last." The words gusted out of Leanna, and with them, she felt the day's exhaustion hit her with its full force. Her legs wobbled under her, her whole body ached, and her head spun from hunger. She glanced then at Ross and saw her own tiredness and strain reflected in his face.

Despite his exhaustion though, he was smiling.

"What now?" Leanna asked. She was so tired she could barely think. Even though only around two furlongs lay between them and their destination now, it felt like a huge distance. She'd truly reached the limits of her endurance.

"First we find a merchant who'll be happy to take us with him at dawn," Ross replied, "and then we find lodgings for the night."

Leanna nodded. Her heart sank at the thought of scouring the village for someone who'd help them before she'd had the chance to fill her belly. However, she knew he was right. That had to be their priority.

Slowly, they made their way down the hill between the fields of produce and into the village.

On the waterfront, they found a tavern. A white-washed building, *The Drover's Inn* was filled with local farmers, fishermen, and a couple of merchants. One of them was northbound and had no space upon his vessel anyway, while the other was from Barra, a small isle to the southwest of Skye. Once every few months, he brought wool to trade from his island.

"I'm heading back tomorrow, at dawn," the man told them as they sat near the hearth with him, cradling tankards of ale in their hands. "Is that soon enough for ye?"

Leanna suppressed a grin of excitement. Barra was a goodly distance by boat from Skye. She'd heard it was a windswept isle of sandy beaches, moor-covered hills, and ancient standing stones. It was as good a place as any to start afresh.

"That will suit us well," Ross replied with a smile. He then dug into his vest and produced two silver pennies. "For yer trouble."

The merchant offered him a toothless grin in reply before he took the coins. "No trouble at all. Meet me at the docks just before sun up ... I like to make an early start."

"As do we," Ross assured him.

The Drover's Inn rented out rooms to travelers, but Ross and Leanna didn't lodge there. Ross pointed out that the inn would be the first place MacKinnon would look if he arrived at the port—they needed to find somewhere more discreet.

A few questions with locals sent them to the home of an elderly couple who were happy to let travelers stay in the tiny annex behind their cottage. Located upon the southwestern fringe of the village, the cottage sat amongst a sprawling garden.

Their hosts were welcoming, inviting Ross and Leanna to share supper at their table.

Despite that she was now weak with hunger, the invitation made Leanna nervous. She didn't want to answer any awkward questions about her identity. Tonight, they posed as a wedded couple traveling by the names Fergus and Greer, Fortunately, as it turned out, their hosts weren't of a nosey disposition. Luckily too, without her veil and wimple, and crucifix hanging from her belt, Leanna no longer appeared a nun. Instead, it looked as if she wore an unflattering dark-colored, ankle-length tunic.

Their hosts served up a delicious mutton stew that had been simmering over the stove all day, accompanied by fluffy oaten dumplings.

Leanna stifled a groan as she took her first mouthful. She didn't know whether it was just her hunger—but stew and dumplings had never tasted so good.

After supper, the old woman, Inghean, wrapped them up some bread and cheese for the following day. Ross had informed her that they would be leaving before dawn, and she didn't want them to travel with empty bellies.

"Ned will bring ye hot water to bathe with," Inghean said when they eventually rose from the table. The warmth of the nearby hearth was making it difficult for Leanna to keep her eyes open. She hadn't slept the night before, and fatigue had now well and truly caught up with her. "I've left some drying cloths and soap for ye, as well," the old woman added.

Thanking Inghean for her hospitality, Ross and Leanna retired to the annex.

It was a tiny space, with a low, sloping ceiling, but Inghean took care of it well. Lavender scented the air from bunches of the herb that hung from the rafters. The floor and bedding were clean, and a small hearth burned in one corner. Ned followed them in, bearing a large bowl of hot water, which he placed upon a washstand in one corner behind a narrow wooden screen.

Then, bidding them both goodnight, the old man left the annex, closing the door behind him.

Leanna turned to Ross, to find him watching her, a gentle—if tired—smile curving his lips.

"Do ye want to wash first?" he asked.

Leanna nodded. In truth, she was so exhausted all she wanted to do was collapse onto the bed fully clothed and fall into a deep slumber. However, she also longed to bathe, as she hadn't done so since fleeing Dunan.

Ducking behind the screen, she deftly removed her habit, underskirts, and léine, before she picked up the cake of soap and began to wash. It felt strange to be standing naked, just a few feet away from Ross. They had lain together, had explored each other's bodies, but she suddenly felt shy around him.

The scent of lavender wafted through the annex, and Leanna breathed it in with a sigh of pleasure. Lavender would forever remind her of her mother. Sadness filtered over her with the thought.

I'll never see her again.

But it was just as well—this way her mother would be kept safe. Their hosts here didn't know her real identity, a secret which would hopefully ensure their safety too.

Returning to her ablutions, Leanna quickly washed her hair before wrapping it up in a drying cloth. Then, dressed only in her ankle-length léine, she emerged from behind the screen.

Ross was reclining on the bed. He'd stripped off his boots, léine, and vest, and wore only his braies. However, he'd fallen asleep while waiting for her.

Leanna halted before the bed, her gaze devouring him. The first time she'd set eyes on him, she'd been struck by his beauty—and she was again now. His expression was softer in repose, younger.

Leaning over the bed, Leanna gently shook him. "Sorry, Ross … it's yer turn."

His eyes flickered open, their midnight blue depths focusing upon her. "Did I fall asleep?" he croaked.

"Aye," Leanna replied with a smile. "Go on … before the water cools."

With a pained groan, he rolled off the bed, cast her a rueful look, and padded behind the screen. Moments later Leanna heard splashes as he started to wash.

Drying her hair as best she could, Leanna hung up the linen cloth over the back of a chair. Then, yawning, she stretched out upon the bed. The straw-filled mattress was surprisingly firm and comfortable, the linen soft. It felt as if she was lying upon a cloud.

The moment Leanna's head hit the pillow, her eyes fluttered shut, and sleep took her.

She awoke much later, rising from sleep like a swimmer emerging from deep water. Softness and comfort surrounded her, yet she was aware of a strong, warm male body pressed against her back—and of a hand that lazily stroked her thigh.

Leanna stirred with a soft moan.

"Are ye awake, mo leannan?" Ross murmured, his breath feathering against her ear.

Leanna gave a slow, languorous stretch. "I am now ... what time is it?"

"Very late ... we've both been asleep for a while."

"I don't even remember ye coming to bed."

"That's because ye were snoring away when I'd finished washing."

Leanna stiffened. "I don't snore."

His soft laugh made pleasure shiver down her neck. "Aye, ye do ... just softly. Don't worry, I like it."

Leanna rolled over to face him. "I *don't* snore."

He was grinning now. "Ye do ... like a wee pup." He reached out then, his fingers tracing the line of her hip and thigh through the thin material of her léine. "An adorable sound."

Leanna glared at him a moment longer before the sensation of his warm hand distracted her. His touch glided over her hip, and up to the dip of her waist. She was aware then, that Ross was naked. The fire behind him had died to glowing embers, casting a soft red light over his skin.

Leanna's pulse accelerated, and her mouth went dry. "Lord ... ye are a feast for the eyes," she murmured, boldly letting her gaze travel down the length of him.

"Am I?" he asked, a laugh in his voice.

Leanna raised an eyebrow. Surely, he was trawling for compliments now. "I imagine women have told ye that?"

"One or two, perhaps," he replied softly, "but such an observation from ye means much more."

Leanna gave a snort. "Ye are insufferably arrogant."

His grin softened. "Hopefully, ye don't find that too off-putting?"

"Luckily for ye, I don't," Leanna replied. Reaching out, she traced her fingertips down his chest to the toned muscles of his belly. Her breath caught when she noted how his shaft hardened in response, and without hesitating, or questioning her bold behavior, she reached down and took him in hand.

Ross gasped. "Gently now, mo leannan." He reached down then and guided her hand, showing her how to fist him, how to glide her hand up and down the length of his shaft, increasing the pressure just slightly beneath the swollen tip. And when Leanna had mastered the action, he rolled onto his back with a groan. His eyes shut, and a nerve flickered in his cheek. "That's right," he breathed.

Watching him, Leanna felt heat pool in her loins, and the sensitive skin between her thighs started to ache. She loved seeing him like this, loved having this much control over his pleasure.

After a few more lazy strokes, she released his shaft and sat up.

Ross's eyes flickered open, and he watched her under hooded lids as she wriggled out of her léine.

"Ye are lovely," he murmured, his hot gaze raking down the length of her. "A fae maiden all of my own."

Leanna flushed at the compliment.

Ross reached out and pulled her close, positioning Leanna so that she sat astride him. Her breathing quickened then, for she felt his erection pressed hard up against her. She wriggled against him, and he gasped. "Temptress."

Gazing down at him, Leanna undulated her hips once more, this time eliciting a deep groan. A thrill went through her. She loved this.

Ross started to stroke her then, his hands sliding up her thighs to her buttocks, back, and then belly. And all the while, Leanna rubbed herself up against him, a delicious heat building in the cradle of her belly.

"Lean forward, my love," he whispered. "Kiss me."

She did as bid, her mouth capturing his. They kissed hungrily, a tangle of lips and tongues, and then Ross's hands fastened upon her hips, lifting her up and settling her onto his engorged shaft.

The feeling of him penetrating her made a cry rise within Leanna. She'd enjoyed their first coupling, but she'd been a maid, and it had hurt at first. This time was different—there was no pain, just aching pleasure. She sank onto him, taking him in fully as their kisses deepened.

Then, still holding her hips, Ross started to rock her against him.

Leanna gasped into his mouth as delight shivered through her loins. With a groan of his own, Ross tore his lips from hers and greedily feasted upon her breasts, suckling them hard.

Writhing against him, Leanna started to experiment, lifting herself up so that she could slide down the full length of him. The sensation that movement caused made her quiver, and made Ross groan into her breasts.

Again, she lifted herself up, and again she slid down his hard rod, impaling herself to the root.

Ross threw his head back then, growling a curse.

She began to ride Ross, bringing him deeper inside her with each thrust of her hips, before heat and a deep throbbing pleasure exploded in her core. Leanna arched back, her cry filling the annex.

A heartbeat later Ross thrust up against her, his shout joining hers as he too found his release.

Pulse racing, her body slick with sweat, Leanna collapsed against him.

Heat pulsed through her, a wildness that she'd never known possessing her. She wanted to claim this man, wanted to brand herself upon his skin. Maybe if she did, she could chase away all the things that threatened their happiness.

29

A Long Time Dead

THEY WERE AT the dock before sunrise, as instructed. The rest of Knock still slumbered as two figures moved down the waterfront, hand-in-hand. The moon had long since set, and the faint glow upon the eastern horizon warned that dawn was very close to breaking.

Leanna squeezed Ross's hand, scanning her surroundings nervously as she walked. Initially, upon leaving the annex, she'd been wary of the darkness. However, now that her eyes had gotten used to it, she could make out her surroundings with more ease.

Apart from the gentle lapping of the water against the dock, the morning was eerily silent. It was too early even for the dawn chorus.

They arrived at the merchant's birlinn to find the man already there and loading the boat up with supplies. The birlinn was a wooden vessel common to Skye and the surrounding isles. The boat, which could be sailed or rowed, had a small furled sail and a streamlined look—hailing back to its Viking origins—and was made of thin wooden planks of pine.

"Good to see ye both managed to rise so early," the merchant observed. "Help me with the last of these crates, and we'll be off."

No sooner had the merchant spoken when a gruff male voice—younger and deeper than the merchant's—intruded. "Going somewhere?"

Leanna went still. She knew that voice.

A moment later, a broad-shouldered figure with close-cropped blond hair stepped out of the shadows on the dock behind them.

Leanna's heart started to race. *Carr Broderick.*

Somehow, MacKinnon had found them.

Ross gently squeezed the hand he still held, warning her to keep quiet and calm. Of course, he knew Broderick much better than she did—he would have to handle this.

"Aye, Carr," Ross replied, his voice soft in the pre-dawn hush. "We're leaving Skye for good."

"MacKinnon might have something to say about that." Broderick stepped closer, and as the first glimmers of sun lightened the morning behind him,

Leanna saw his face clearly. He had handsome, if austere, features that were set in a hard expression. However, his eyes were troubled.

"Is he here?" Ross asked, his tone unchanging.

"No ... he's gone to Duncaith."

A brief silence followed these words. Leanna's gaze slid down Broderick's burly form to the sword that hung at his side. Interestingly, he hadn't yet drawn it.

"And the rest of yer men?" Ross asked. "Surely, ye aren't searching for us alone."

"I sent them ahead, to look farther down the coast," Broderick replied, his voice giving nothing away. "I had a feeling ye would be at the docks this morning."

Although Leanna didn't glance his way, she sensed Ross's smile. "Ye know me well."

"I thought I did ... until a couple of days ago."

"Don't tell me ye wouldn't have done the same thing," Ross replied, his tone hardening just a little. "We both knew MacKinnon had gone too far ... we should never have abducted Leanna."

"And yet we did," Broderick countered. "And unlike ye, I continue to serve him."

"Ye saw MacKinnon slay Father Athol," Ross said quietly. "Do ye think if any of us displeased him, he wouldn't have done the same to us? We were both living on borrowed time at Dunan. I had to make a decision."

"And ye have, it seems." There was an edge to Broderick's voice then that Leanna couldn't quite isolate. Anger or wry humor, she couldn't be sure.

Silence fell upon the docks. Leanna glanced askance at the merchant. The older man stood upon the deck of his birlinn, gaze narrowed while he observed the unfolding scene.

"I love Leanna," Ross said finally, his voice low and steady, "and I'll die before I see her back in MacKinnon's clutches."

Leanna's chest tightened at these words. Suddenly, she found it hard to draw breath. Ross had told her how he felt, but to hear him publicly announce it confirmed that he'd meant what he'd said.

Carr Broderick's grey-blue eyes widened, before his mouth quirked. "Ross Campbell in love ... never thought I'd see it."

"Neither did I ... but the past few days have changed me."

"Ye have given everything up," Broderick replied, his tone pensive now. "Everything ye sweated blood to achieve."

"Leanna is worth the sacrifice."

"But ye have nothing other than the clothes on yer back."

"I have some coin I've managed to save over the years." Ross patted the pouch he kept tucked away inside his vest. "It'll be enough to get us started."

Broderick huffed a deep breath and folded his arms across his broad chest. "So, ye think I'm going to let ye go, do ye?"

Ross held his friend's eye, his head cocking slightly. "Ye sent yer men ahead for a reason ... ye wanted to speak to me alone. Ye didn't want MacKinnon or the others knowing ye had found me."

Broderick's mouth thinned at this, and Leanna realized with a jolt that Ross was right. His friend was conflicted; she could see the battle he was waging with himself in his shadowed eyes.

"Damn ye, Ross," he growled finally. "Do ye realize the position ye have put me in?"

Ross nodded. "I'd hoped to spare ye this."

"Does this mean we're going now?" the merchant spoke up. His gravelly voice held a wary edge. "Sorry to intrude, lads ... but the sun's rising, and I'd prefer to be on my way."

Broderick frowned at this, his attention never wavering from Ross. "Where are ye headed?"

"It's best ye don't know, Carr," Ross replied softly. "For yer own good ... and ours."

A bitter smile twisted Broderick's face. "Afraid that MacKinnon might try and torture it from me?"

"Aye," Ross replied, not smiling back. "Ye know as well as I what he's capable of."

Broderick's smile faded, and a muscle bunched in his jaw. Leanna wondered what part he'd played in the torture of Brochan.

Silence fell once more, and then the warrior nodded. "So be it, Ross ... I never saw ye here." He stepped forward, reaching out an arm. "Ye might as well enjoy this happiness while it lasts ... for ye are a long time dead."

Relief washed over Leanna, turning her knees weak under her. Slowly, she let out the breath she'd been holding. She couldn't believe it—he was letting them leave.

Ross's face relaxed for the first time since Carr Broderick had stepped out of the shadows. He moved toward the warrior and clasped Broderick's arm with his, before pulling him into a bear hug. "Go well, my friend," he murmured. "I will never forget this."

The high walls of Kilbride rose against the washed-out morning sky, the peaked roof of its kirk piercing the heavens. Eyes upon his destination, Duncan MacKinnon slowed his courser to a brisk trot. His men fanned out behind him. The jangling of iron bits, the thud of hoofbeats, and the creak of leather intruded upon the quiet of the dawn.

However, Duncan didn't pay the sunrise any mind—for his attention was wholly upon the abbey. Fury churned in his gut, making it ache dully. The pain had been there ever since they'd departed from Duncaith the evening before.

Leanna and Ross weren't there.

The new chieftain of the MacDonalds of Sleat had given him a frosty welcome, yet MacKinnon hadn't cared. He'd ridden into the bailey, swung down from his mount, and demanded that MacDonald hand over the fugitives.

Bard MacDonald had stridden out to meet him, white-lipped with rage. They'd nearly come to blows out there in the bailey, in front of warriors and servants—yet at the end of the altercation, Duncan had been forced to accept that Leanna and Ross had not fled to Duncaith as he'd thought.

MacDonald had been hostile, but there'd been no lie in his eyes. Instead, Duncan had seen concern for his niece.

He wasn't harboring her.

So that left Kilbride—the only stone yet unturned. Duncan had sent Broderick out to cover the south coast, but part of the clan-chief still believed that Leanna and Ross would have sought out the safety of allies.

The abbess of Kilbride had already shown herself to be a liar—the woman had willingly hidden knowledge of Annella Fraser and Gavin MacNichol just under a year earlier.

She'd looked him in the eye and told him they'd never returned to Kilbride. But MacKinnon had *known* she was lying.

If the woman tried the same this time, he'd cut out her tongue.

"Mother Shona!" An excited young female voice intruded, drawing the abbess out of the book she was reading.

With a sigh, the abbess glanced up. This time of the morning was Mother Shona's quiet time—one of the few moments of the day when she could sit and relax. Lauds, morning mass, and the first meal of the day had all been completed, and she had a brief respite before the daily chapter meeting.

Seated upon a chair in her hall, she'd been immersed in a history about the kings of Scotland, and had just been reading about King Duncan the Second, who'd ruled Scotland over three hundred years earlier—a military man who hadn't been skilled in the art of peace-weaving. Mother Shona had been musing what a pity it was that Scotland no longer had a strong ruler to stand against the English when she'd been interrupted.

"What is it?" she called out.

"We have visitors, Mother Shona ... MacKinnon is here!"

The abbess closed her book with a snap and rose to her feet. Two days after Sister Leanna's departure for Duncaith, she'd received word that the nun's escort had been attacked on its journey south. Sister Leanna had disappeared, and there'd been no news of her since.

Placing the book on the mantelpiece, Mother Shona picked up her skirts and hurried toward the door.

Outside she found Sister Firtha—a young novice—waiting for her. The nun's pale blue eyes were wide, and she was shifting nervously from foot to foot. Without thinking, she dropped onto one knee, as was the custom when approaching the abbess.

Distracted, Mother Shona hastily made the sign of the cross and moved past her. "Where is he?"

"MacKinnon's standing before the kirk, Mother Shona," the novice gasped, clambering to her feet. "And he's in a foul temper."

The abbess clenched her jaw. "Of course he is."

30

No Stone Unturned

DUNCAN MACKINNON STOOD, legs akimbo and his hands folded across his chest, watching Mother Shona approach.

The abbess straightened her spine, her own gaze narrowing to match his hard stare. She was glad that she'd had the foresight to briefly return to her hall and strap on some knives to her person before coming out to meet him.

She'd never trusted MacKinnon, and of late her relationship with the clan-chief had gone from strained to acrimonious.

One look at his face, and she knew he'd journeyed here to confront her.

His men hung back from MacKinnon, forming a horse-shoe behind him. However, the abbess could see they were all at the ready, hands lightly resting upon the pommel of their swords.

At the foot of the kirk steps, a group of nuns had clustered. Mother Shona's gaze swept over them, and she was relieved to see that Sister Coira was among the group. The nun was taller than her companions and stood at the back of the crowd.

It reassured the abbess to spy Coira there; the nun was one of her most able fighters. Should this conversation go ill, she'd need Coira's assistance.

"Where is she, abbess?" MacKinnon's voice lashed through the cool morning air. "I know ye are hiding Lady Leanna."

Mother Shona didn't reply. Instead, she stopped a few yards back from MacKinnon and eyed him coldly.

"Answer me, woman," MacKinnon snarled, his right hand straying to the pommel of his sword, "before I make ye."

Surreptitiously, Mother Shona's own right hand moved to the hilt of the knife she kept secreted in a special fold in the skirts of her habit.

Cold anger pulsed through her, and her senses sharpened.

"Don't threaten me, MacKinnon," she replied, her own voice cutting. "Ye should know that *Sister* Leanna departed Kilbride a week ago now and never returned. The last I heard of her, the MacDonald party bound for Duncaith had been attacked and Sister Leanna taken." She paused there, her gaze never leaving his. "Did ye have any part in that?"

MacKinnon scowled. "None of yer business."

"It is my business if ye turn up on my doorstep accusing me of hiding a nun who rightfully belongs here." Rage pulsed in time with Mother Shona's heartbeat now. She hadn't been this angry in years, not since she'd been in her twenties and running wild with a band of outlaws who'd taken her in after her convent had been destroyed. The years had tamed her, as had her role as abbess. Yet the same woman, the same fire, lay dormant underneath. "I'd wager that ye killed the MacDonald warriors and stole Sister Leanna away. What happened? Did she escape?"

A nerve flickered under MacKinnon's left eye, and Mother Shona saw that she'd driven straight to the truth of things.

"Sister Leanna is no fool," she continued, her voice icy now. "If she managed to flee from ye, the last place she'd come would be here. I hope for her sake that she's left these shores."

Silence settled in the yard, one charged with menace. MacKinnon's fingers closed over the hilt of his claidheamh-mor—as did Mother Shona's over the handle of her dirk.

I'm ready for ye.

However, as the moments stretched out, good sense prevailed. MacKinnon had ridden here enraged; it would take little to unleash the beast. If the situation here unraveled, there would be no going back.

The abbess realized that her aggression was putting all the sisters within these walls at risk. If MacKinnon attacked her, she'd defend herself. Until then, she needed to keep her temper tethered.

"But I can see that ye do not believe me," she said finally, her voice chill. "Go then ... search the abbey ... leave no stone unturned. Ye will see that I do not lie."

Duncan's fingers clenched around the hilt of his sword.

Fury churned in his already aching gut, and the urge to cut Mother Shona down became unbearable.

The woman's arrogance, her impertinence, would have to be dealt with.

He'd never encountered such a strong woman; even his own mother hadn't held a man's eye with such fierceness.

Her utter lack of fear perplexed him. Was her faith in God so strong that she wasn't afraid of death?

"I *will* search this place," he growled finally, barely able to prevent himself from drawing his claidheamh-mor and lunging for her. "And if I discover ye have been hiding Lady Leanna and Ross Campbell ... my wrath will be terrible."

The abbess's brown eyes widened at that. With a jolt, Duncan realized that it wasn't his threat that had shocked her, but his revelation.

She didn't know about Campbell.

Maybe she's telling the truth.

Duncan brushed the suspicion aside and turned to his men. "Search the abbey," he barked, "every corner of it."

As MacKinnon turned from issuing the order, his gaze swept over the gaggle of black-robed nuns gathered before the kirk. As always, the sight of a woman robed in a habit made his pulse race, cutting through his vile temper.

Many of the nuns here were young, their faces—framed by white wimples and dark veils—comely.

And then Duncan saw a face he recognized.

Standing at the back of the group was a tall woman with distinctive violet eyes and patrician features. She stood proud, broad shoulders back, and watched his band with a look of open dislike.

Duncan's breathing caught. *It can't be.* MacKinnon hadn't looked upon that face in about a decade.

Coira?

He'd always wondered what had become of her. And here she was at Kilbride, just half a day's ride out from Dunan. All these years, and she'd been right under his nose.

Duncan stared at her, willing the woman to meet his eye.

But then the nun stepped back, turned away, and climbed the steps of the kirk. The moment shattered. Blinking, Duncan shifted his attention back to where Mother Shona was watching him, her gaze flint-hard.

It wasn't her. He forced himself to focus on the present. *Whores don't become nuns.*

Shoving aside memories of the past, MacKinnon met the abbess's eye. "I think I'll begin my search with yer quarters," he said, injecting menace into every word. "Lead the way, Mother Shona."

A chill wind whipped across the water, filling the birlinn's single sail and carrying the travelers southwest toward the isle of Barra.

Leanna and Ross did their best to keep out of the merchant's way as he moved about the boat, trimming the sail. The older man conversed little, clearly used to his own company. They sat upon a narrow wooden plank amidships, surrounded by sacks of grain and crates of vegetables that the merchant had traded for wool, while the salt-laced wind caught at their hair and clothing.

Ross wrapped an arm around Leanna's shoulders, and she leaned into him, sighing at the warmth and strength of his chest.

"How close was that earlier?" she asked, speaking for the first time since they'd set sail. "With Broderick?"

Ross gave a soft laugh, the sound barely audible as the wind whipped it away, although she felt the rumble in his chest. "Things weren't as dangerous as they seemed ... Carr and I have known each other since we were both fosterlings at Dunan."

"He could still have betrayed ye though?"

"Aye." Ross's face grew serious as he considered her words. "But he didn't. I suppose he just had to know why I behaved as I did ... maybe he also wanted to say goodbye."

"And ye told him that ye loved me." Leanna's voice caught as she spoke. The words he'd said still rippled like a wake behind a boat in her mind. "That ye would protect me from MacKinnon no matter the cost."

"And I meant it," Ross replied, a rasp to his voice now. "It wasn't for his benefit, Leanna. I know this has come upon me suddenly, but life can be like that sometimes. It was like I was waiting ... somehow ... and when I met ye, everything started to change."

"I feel the same way," Leanna breathed. She drew back and tilted her chin so that she could meet his eye. "I love ye too, Ross ... I've just been afraid to say it."

His mouth quirked, and he lifted a hand, his fingers brushing a lock of hair back from her face. "Afraid?"

"Aye ... ye see me like no one ever has. I love ye so much that my heart aches from the force of it ... and that scares me a little." She raised her hand, her fingertips tracing the strong line of his stubbled jaw. "Wherever ye go, Ross, I shall follow. I don't want any future that doesn't have ye in it."

His midnight blue eyes gleamed at these words, and Ross cleared his throat before he answered. "I can't give ye the life of a lady, even if I wish I could."

Leanna made a dismissive sound in the back of her throat. "As if I care about that."

"Ye don't mind that I will likely become a farmer ... and ye a farmer's wife?"

"No."

His face grew serious then. "Ye don't mind living in a one-room hut, spending yer days at toil? Sometimes love isn't enough, Leanna. I don't want ye to regret this."

Leanna's mouth curved. He looked genuinely worried, and she realized that he really wanted the best for her.

"Ye forget," she murmured, gazing up into his eyes, "that I gave up the life of a 'lady' when I took the veil. I learned what hard work was at Kilbride, and I learned how to be resourceful. I'm not afraid to get my hands dirty, or of toil. If it means that I get to spend my life with ye, I welcome it."

31

True Freedom

BARE GREEN HILLS greeted Leanna and Ross when the birlinn slid into port at Bàgh a' Chaisteil—Castlebay. On the way, they sailed past a great fortress perched upon a tiny island.

"That's Kisimul Castle," the merchant informed them. "The home of Clan MacNeil."

Leanna gazed up at the castle as they slid by, awed by its high curtain wall. It was late in the day, and the sun had given the grey stone a golden hue. Likewise, the light gilded the rows of fishing vessels that hugged the port beyond. A huddle of white-washed houses clustered around the shore, and when she turned her attention from the castle, Leanna caught a glimpse of silver-sand beaches.

She caught her breath, turning to the merchant. "It's beautiful."

The old man chuckled. "Aye, lass … it's home."

As they drew near the docks, Leanna inhaled the familiar odor of smoking herrings. Excitement fluttered in the base of her belly then. The isle of Barra was indeed remote and small, yet the idea of making a new life here filled her with joy. She glanced over at Ross and saw that he was smiling, his gaze taking in his surroundings.

Once they'd docked, Ross helped Leanna out of the birlinn, before he assisted the merchant with unloading his supplies.

"We'll be needing lodgings for the night," Ross said when he'd heaved out the last crate and set it down upon the dock, "any suggestions?"

The merchant laughed. "There's only one inn in town … the *Fisherman's Rest*. Just walk down the waterfront, ye'll find it quick enough." The man's gaze flicked to Leanna then, and his expression grew soft. "I wish ye both all the best for yer new life upon the isle," he said. "And if ye should ever need assistance, just come down here and ask for 'auld Alban'."

"We appreciate that," Ross replied with a warm smile. "But for now, I just have one final request." He paused there, the smile turning into a grin as he met Leanna's eye. "Can ye tell us where we can find ourselves a priest?"

It was a blustery morning when Ross and Leanna walked out of Bàgh a' Chaisteil. Gulls swooped low, their cries echoing over the hills. Side-by-side, the two travelers slogged their way up the first hill out of the port, heading east.

"Are ye sure there isn't a road we should be taking?" Leanna puffed when they crested the first hill.

"No path leads to where we're headed," Ross replied with a grin. "Our cottage is a morning's walk across the hills from Bàgh a' Chaisteil."

Excitement lanced through Ross as he said those words. They'd been on Barra two days, but already it had started to feel like home. Upon their arrival, he'd made initial inquiries and discovered a small-holding was available that had once belonged to an elderly farmer.

Ross had taken a boat across to Kisimul Castle and met with the MacNeil chieftain. He'd given a fresh false identity, calling himself Roger Murray of Atholl. However, MacNeil—a distracted man of middling years—hadn't shown much curiosity in him. He'd been more interested in gaining a tenant for his land. Ross had paid him a decade's worth of savings in order to secure the plot. It was nearly everything he had, but it was what he wanted to spend his coin on.

And now, he and his wife were traveling to their new home.

Wife.

Warmth seeped through Ross, and he glanced over at Leanna's flushed face. Two evenings previous, after their arrival upon the isle, a priest had wed them. He still couldn't believe his good fortune. Every morning since, he'd woken up and lain there watching Leanna sleep.

He would do everything he could to give his wife a good future.

The small-holding came with a flock of sheep and arable fields that had been left fallow since the tenant's death. A neighboring farmer had been looking after the land while MacNeil looked for a new tenant, but the chieftain had sent word ahead that they were to expect Roger Murray and his wife, Elsa.

It was a slow journey east, for both Ross and Leanna carried weighty leather packs filled with provisions. However, the cool wind on their faces was refreshing, and the warm sun on their backs reminded them both that summer had arrived. It was a good time to start afresh.

"How many sheep do we have?" Leanna asked, taking Ross's hand when he helped her across a stream.

"Nearly two-dozen," he replied, "and a few lambs."

"And ye know how to look after them?"

Ross could hear the skepticism in her voice and smiled. He didn't blame her really; after all, he was a warrior from a high-born family. What did he know of sheep farming?

"Aye ... as I told ye ... my uncle farmed sheep," he replied. "He taught me how to raise them, shear them ... and butcher them." He grinned at Leanna then. "Worry not, wife ... we won't starve."

She huffed. "I wasn't worried about that. I'm a good enough cook ... at Kilbride, my bannocks were reputed to be the tastiest."

Ross laughed. "Good to hear." He sobered then, glancing at Leanna once more. "Did ye send word to the abbess yesterday?"

Leanna nodded, meeting his eye. "Aye ... I sent missives with a boat bound for Skye ... both to Kilbride and my uncle." She paused there, perhaps catching how he suddenly tensed. "Worry not, I didn't tell them we're on Barra or reveal our new names here ... it's just that I wanted my kin and the abbess to know that I am alive and well. I'd hate for them to worry."

Ross digested this before the tension eased from his shoulders. He knew Leanna would have been prudent; he just didn't want to put their new life in jeopardy in any way.

Barra was far enough away from Skye to start afresh, yet if MacKinnon heard of their location, he could find a way to reach them, even here. Ross could understand why she'd wanted to let those she cared about know that she still lived, but even so, they had to be wary.

"As long as we remain hidden, I'm content," he said finally. "Fortunately for us, MacNeil has few dealings with MacKinnon so there should be little risk of anyone recognizing us here."

"It seems a friendly isle," Leanna replied, her tone pensive. "The folk have been welcoming so far."

Ross smiled at this. "Aye ... although I'm glad that we left town today ... in such a small place, the locals soon start to gossip or ask too many probing questions."

Leanna nodded. "Aye ... the innkeeper's wife is a terrible busybody. She wanted to know who our kin are ... and why we've settled upon Barra when we have no family here." At Ross's alarmed look, she smiled. "Don't worry, I spun her a tale."

Ross raked a hand through his hair as he crested yet another hill. Beyond lay a rumpled blanket of moorland, framed by blue sky. "I suppose our presence here has caused a stir," he admitted. "It's only natural upon an isle as small as Barra."

They walked on, traveling across bare hills interspersed with shallow valleys and the odd trickling creek. Sheep grazed in the distance, and a briny sea breeze cooled their faces.

Ross found it hard not to smile as he walked; it was a good day to be alive.

He couldn't believe how different he felt. It was as if a great weight had been lifted from him—one he hadn't even realized he'd been carrying. It was strange really; his whole life he'd been so ambitious. He'd thought he wanted to rise up through the ranks as warrior, to earn the coveted place at a clan-chief's side. But shortly after Leanna came into his life, his priorities had started to shift. He'd resisted it at first—for the feelings that arose within him had gone against everything he valued—but now that he'd finally surrendered to it, he felt almost reborn.

Everything was simpler now. Suddenly, all he wanted was to build a future with the woman he loved, have a family, and make his small-holding thrive. No longer would he feel compelled to do the bidding of a man he should never have sworn allegiance to.

On this fine morning, as he walked toward his new home, he tasted true freedom.

The sun was high in the sky when they reached their destination at last. Breathing hard, after climbing the last—and very steep—hill, Leanna halted beside her husband. Before them sat a low-slung stacked-stone cottage with a thatched roof in dire need of repair. A crumbling stone wall and overgrown garden surrounded the dwelling. A chorus of bleating greeted them from a flock of woolly white sheep grazing upon the hillside behind the cottage.

Looking upon the dwelling, a slow smile spread across Leanna's face.

"I'm sorry it's so small ... I know it's not what ye are used to." The worry in Ross's voice made her tear her attention from the untamed garden. He was watching her, his brow furrowed.

"I've already told ye," she replied with a shake of her head. "My days as a 'lady' are long gone. My time at Kilbride toughened me up."

"But I hadn't realized the cottage would be so run down."

Leanna snorted before she reached out and clasped his hand in hers. "It's perfect, Ross ... and I can't wait to make it our own."

"This is for the abbess." The messenger, a harried-looking man in travel-stained leathers, handed Sister Coira a small roll of parchment, sealed with wax. "Can ye make sure she receives it?"

Coira nodded, taking the scroll. "I will take it to her now ... thank ye ... may peace be with ye."

"And ye, Sister." The man, who stood at the abbey gates, ducked his head before moving back over to his horse and swinging up into the saddle.

Coira watched him move off, urging his lathered mount south. Then her gaze shifted to the furled message in her hand. She wondered whom it was from.

Turning from the gates, Coira walked across the yard, under the deep shadow of the kirk, toward the abbess's hall. It was just after the noon meal, a quiet time when all the nuns rested for a short while before beginning their afternoon chores. The day was sticky and windless, the first hot day of summer, and while her sisters rested upon their sleeping pallets, Coira had decided to go into the woods and collect herbs for her healing poultices and potions. Gathering herbs usually put her in a good mood, but she felt strangely restless today. Upon her return to the abbey, she'd been considering going into the kirk to pray, when the messenger had arrived.

Life at Kilbride felt increasingly lonely of late. The two women she'd been closest to here—Sister Ella and Sister Leanna—had both left the abbey. Coira liked to think of herself as self-sufficient; she'd certainly been at Kilbride long enough to be able to endure solitude, yet she'd found herself often thinking of her friends.

She'd heard that Ella was well. Word had arrived from Scorrybreac just a couple of weeks earlier that Ella was with child—happy news indeed, especially after the tragedies that had marked her early years. But no one had heard a word from Leanna. After the party escorting her to Duncaith had been ambushed, she'd simply disappeared.

And as far as Coira knew, MacKinnon's search for her had been unsuccessful.

Coira raised a hand and knocked briskly on the door to the abbess's hall, suppressing a shudder as an image of Duncan MacKinnon's face surfaced.

He'd visited Kilbride a handful of times over the years, and she'd always managed to keep out of sight. But the last time, she knew he'd seen her—and she thought she'd seen recognition flicker in those iron-grey eyes.

She hoped that wasn't the case.

While MacKinnon and his men had searched the abbey, she'd remained in the kirk, silently praying before the altar. She'd heard heavy footfalls as men entered and searched the alcoves nearby—yet none of the warriors spoke to her.

Tension had slowly ebbed from Coira at that—maybe MacKinnon hadn't recognized her after all. Nonetheless, she'd have to be more careful in future.

"Enter." Mother Shona's voice, soft yet firm, filtered out into the humid air.

Coira pushed the door open and walked into the cool, lofty space beyond. The abbess's hall was a long space divided in two by a heavy hanging that shrouded the sleeping quarters from the living area. It was a clean, simply furnished space with a scrubbed flagstone floor, a small wooden desk, and a hearth flanked by two high-backed chairs. Mother Shona sat upon one, a heavy leather-bound book upon her knee.

"A message has come for ye, Mother." Coira crossed the floor to the abbess and handed her the scroll before lowering herself on one knee so that Mother Shona could bless her.

Once the abbess had done so, she rose to her feet and turned to go.

"Please stay, Sister Coira," the abbess said with a smile, gesturing to the chair opposite. "Let's see who has written to us."

Coira did as bid, settling into the chair without comment. She wasn't a 'chatty' woman, and fortunately Mother Shona seemed to appreciate nuns who didn't feel the need to fill a silence with conversation. Even so, as the abbess began to undo the scroll, her gaze settled upon Coira—and she frowned.

"Is something amiss, Sister ... ye have seemed a little distracted of late."

Coira tensed. She sometimes forgot just how perceptive the abbess was; she missed very little and was highly attuned to the moods of those living within the walls of Kilbride.

"Nothing's wrong," Coira replied with a weak smile. Although the abbess was the only one here who knew most of the truth about Coira's past, she'd never confided in Mother Shona about her history with Duncan MacKinnon—

and didn't intend to. Some things could never be spoken about. "I suppose I just worry for Sister Leanna."

Mother Shona's gaze clouded, and she nodded. "As do I."

Unfurling the missive and scanning it, the abbess's expression suddenly cleared. "What a happy coincidence, Sister. This letter is from Leanna ... she is well and—" The abbess broke off there as her brown eyes grew wide. She glanced up then, her gaze spearing Coira's. "She's married."

Epilogue

Breathless

The Isle of Barra, Scotland

One month later ...

LEANNA LEANED OVER the pot, brow furrowing in concentration while she sprinkled some fresh rosemary in. The mutton stew had been simmering since dawn, and a rich meaty aroma filled the interior of the cottage. It was nearly ready to serve.

Stepping back from the hearth, Leanna wiped her arm over her sweating brow. The air was smoky and close inside the dwelling despite that she had opened both the small windows.

Golden summer light filtered into the one-room space, and for a moment, Leanna paused, taking in her surroundings.

The cottage had been a mess when they'd first arrived—the roof had needed fixing, and rodents and cobwebs filled the filthy interior. After a couple of days, Leanna had scoured it clean and set about making it comfortable to live in.

Ross had repaired the gaps in the roof, and Leanna had gotten to work filling their shelves with stores and drying bunches of herbs, which scented the once musty air.

A heavy blanket curtained off the living space from the stuffed straw mattress where she and Ross slept. However, Leanna had drawn back the curtain this morning to air the bed.

Leanna's breathing quickened a little when her gaze rested upon the mattress. Her days were long and tiring, yet every evening excitement curled in the pit of her belly in anticipation of retiring for the night with her husband. One month since their wedding, and she was still discovering carnal desire, still delighting in new ways to be pleasured and give pleasure.

And every morning when she awoke and looked upon her husband's face, joy filtered through her, along with a sense of belonging she'd never before experienced.

Letting out a contented sigh, Leanna wiped her hands upon the apron that covered the plain brown kirtle she wore and walked outdoors.

The garden was another thing that she'd transformed over the past moon. When they'd arrived here, it had been overgrown, a wild tangle of herbs and vegetables, many of which had simply self-seeded in the wrong places.

There, in one corner grew the apple tree sapling she'd planted in honor of her father. Ross had brought it back one day after a trip to market. The tree was getting a foothold in the stony soil this year, but next summer she hoped it would bear fruit. There were also two older apple trees growing on the slope behind the cottage, which would hopefully pollinate it.

The rest of the garden was slowly taking shape.

Remembering Ella's advice—for her friend was a gifted gardener and had been in charge of Kilbride's vast vegetable plots—Leanna had worked systematically. She'd started at the southern corner of the garden and worked her way to the north. Beds of woody herbs, such as rosemary, sage, and thyme now grew separate from the leafier plants, such as parsley and mint. Leanna was also growing beds of kale, cabbages, carrots, and onions, and she had just put in a small turnip crop.

Ross had kept her company through most of her work, as he spent days fixing the crumbling wall that encircled the cottage. This morning though, he'd been out with the dogs, moving the sheep to another pasture. He was due back any time now.

Walking along the path, between beds of lavender, Leanna smiled at the feel of the sun bathing her face. It had been a warm start to the summer, and although it could get windy upon the isle of Barra, she loved the wide skies here. Upon Skye, you were never far from soaring mountains that always reminded you of how small and insignificant you were. Barra had a more intimate feel.

As she reached the gate, Leanna swung her gaze right and caught sight of a tall, dark-haired figure striding over the hill toward her. Two shepherd dogs ran at his heels—stocky, hairy beasts with long bushy tails. Their names were Moss and Yarrow, a brother and sister of the same litter from a nearby farm. Fortunately for Ross, their former owner had done most of the work training them.

Raising a hand to show that she'd seen him, Leanna walked through the gate to meet her husband.

Her gaze devoured him as he approached.

Black shoulder-length hair blowing in the wind, his skin lightly tanned after their spell of good weather, Ross wore a loose brown léine, unlaced at the neck, and tan braies. These days he carried a crook rather than a claidheamh-mor, and the tension that had once sharpened his handsome features had gone.

Ross's mouth curved into a wide smile, and Leanna's belly somersaulted. He still had no idea how devastating his smile could be.

"That stew smells incredible," he greeted her. "I sniffed it before I crested the last hill."

"It should be," Leanna replied with an answering grin, "I've been tending it long enough."

The dogs bounded up then, tongues lolling and tails wagging. They pushed at Leanna's legs, but she ignored them for a moment, her gaze entirely fixed upon Ross.

Likewise, his attention never left her. Stepping close, he clasped Leanna around the waist and pulled her into his embrace, his mouth covering hers.

When he ended the kiss, they were both breathless.

"Did ye have a good morning?" Leanna asked, trailing her hand down his chest. She could feel the heat of his skin through the léine's thin material. "I hope the sheep behaved themselves."

"They're a scatty bunch," he replied with a snort, "but Moss and Yarrow know how to handle them." He glanced down at where the two shepherd dogs were now seated at his side, tails thumping on the ground. He reached down and ruffled the hounds' ears. "Without their help, I'd be running myself ragged over the hills of Barra."

Leanna laughed at the image. Sheep were notoriously nervy and foolish creatures that could often test a herder's patience. She'd thought Ross might find them irritating, but the opposite was true. He was at his happiest when he returned from spending the morning with them.

"How are their fleeces growing?" Leanna asked. She was aware that lamb's wool was a valuable commodity. They would shear the sheep next spring, and it would hopefully bring them in some extra silver. Until then, they had to gain the supplies they needed by bartering meat and vegetables. Ross still had a little silver left, but they preferred to keep it in reserve, for the long winter ahead.

"It's decent wool," Ross replied. "Although a little harsher than the breeds on the mainland … it's the meat that'll get us the most coin though."

Leanna nodded before she stepped to Ross's side and linked her arm through his. Together they headed toward the gate. "Speaking of meat … that stew ye can smell is ready now."

As they stepped into the garden, Ross paused and surveyed his surroundings. "This space is unrecognizable, love," he said softly. "I can't believe what ye have achieved in just one moon."

Leanna flashed him a grin, pleased by the compliment. "I told ye I was resourceful … I'm not some decorative lass, only fit for embroidering and bearing bairns."

Ross grinned back. "I shouldn't have doubted ye." He sobered then, turning to Leanna and taking her hands. Meanwhile, the dogs ran ahead before flopping down next to the entrance to the cottage, where Leanna had left them out two large shin bones. "It occurred to me this morning just how isolated our life here is … ye don't feel lonely, do ye?"

"Sometimes," Leanna admitted. She liked to be honest with Ross; it wasn't in her nature to hold back how she felt. "I didn't really enjoy being a nun … but the thing I miss about Kilbride is the female company." She cast him a wry look. "Women like to talk while they work … sometimes I find myself chattering to the plants as I garden."

Ross's lips quirked at her admission. "Now that we're settled here, I think it's time we started to socialize more with the locals. I saw Fergus MacNeil this morning ... he and his wife have invited us to supper next week, if ye are keen?"

A smile flowered across Leanna's face at this suggestion. Fergus MacNeil—a second cousin to the MacNeil chieftain—was the farmer who'd looked after these lands before their arrival. Leanna had met his young wife shortly after they'd moved in. She'd seemed like a sweet, if shy, woman, and Leanna was pleased that she'd extended the hand of friendship to them.

"I'd like that," she replied. "It's important that we make ourselves part of the community here."

Ross's expression turned serious. "Aye, but we must still be careful."

"I know ye are wise to keep our real identities secret," Leanna replied. "But we can't live like fugitives forever. We have to start trusting folk ... once winter comes, we might need their help."

"Ye are right, mo ghràdh." Ross favored her with a lopsided smile. "How did I find myself such a wise woman?"

Leanna snorted at his teasing before giving him a playful slap on the arm. "Fortune was shining upon ye indeed, ye rogue."

Ross stepped close, his expression softening. He reached out and cupped her face with his. "I mean it, love."

He leaned in, brushing his lips softly over hers. Heat spiraled up from Leanna's belly. She inhaled the musk of his skin, overlaid with the smell of leather and the oily taint of sheep's wool. Her eyes fluttered shut, and she leaned into him. The kiss deepened, and Leanna reached out, her hands exploring the solid breadth of his shoulders.

Eventually, she drew back, breaking off the kiss. Once again, his touch left her breathless, wanting. Ross's eyes had darkened in a look she knew well. One more embrace and he'd scoop her into his arms and carry her off to bed. And as much as she wanted him to do that, she had an afternoon of chores waiting for her—they both did.

"Come on," she said softly, taking Ross by the hand. "I don't want that stew to burn."

"It can keep," he growled before he pulled her against him once more. "This can't."

The End

From the author

I hope you enjoyed Ross and Leanna's dramatic, high-action story of redemption and new beginnings. Initially, I'd planned this book to be all about the heroine's 'awakening' to passion, but (as often happens with my stories), it turned out to be about Ross's awakening just as much—if not more!

Many of my books are about difficult choices—and Ross has an important one to make. We are often a product of our upbringing, and since I had to give Ross a decent reason for following the likes of MacKinnon, I deliberately made his childhood a difficult one, so that we understand his ambitious streak and dogged loyalty to the vile Duncan MacKinnon. I love a good 'reformed rogue' story (who doesn't have a soft spot for bad boys?), so Ross was a fascinating character to write. In contrast to Gavin MacNichol from Book #1, Ross has a bit of growing to do—fortunately, Leanna helps him with that.

I realize you've probably got your knives out for MacKinnon (he's a revolting individual, I know!), but since he's the arch-villain of the whole series, I have to keep him alive for a while longer. Bear with me—his downfall will be worth the wait!

MacKinnon's behavior in the book was unforgivable. Rape—attempted or otherwise—isn't easy to write about. And even though I have Leanna taking control in that scene, it made her romance with Ross harder to write.

Unlike UNFORGOTTEN, this novel doesn't spend much time at Kilbride Abbey. However, expect to return there for Book #3, as Coira and Craeg's story will unfold around the goings-on at Kilbride. I'm so excited to share the final book in this series with you—if you thought AWOKEN was dramatic, FALLEN is going to blow your mind!

Jayne x

Fallen

Book Three
The Sisters of Kilbride

Jayne Castel

Map

*Death leaves a heartache no one can heal,
Love leaves a memory no one can steal."
—From an Irish headstone*

Prologue

I Will Die First

*Dunan broch
MacKinnon territory,
Isle of Skye, Scotland*

Winter, 1338 AD

COIRA LAY UPON the bed and thought about the best way to kill him.

She could lunge for his dirk.

Or she could reach for the heavy iron poker lying next to the hearth.

This was her chance, and yet she didn't take it. She'd swing for murdering a clan-chief anyway—so it was just as well that she lacked the courage to act upon her thoughts.

The young man in question—Duncan MacKinnon—was getting dressed a few feet away, whistling a smug tune as he laced his braies and reached for his léine. Now that his lust had been slaked, he had no use for her.

Coira watched him go through his usual routine, hate cramping her belly. Every part of her body hurt.

She lay naked on her side, resisting the urge to curl up into a tight ball—resisting the urge to whimper. Instead, she breathed shallowly. Her gaze never left the tall, broad-shouldered figure who pulled on his léine—a loose shirt laced at the throat—before buckling on his belt.

He was handsome, yet she'd soon learned that the clan-chief's good looks hid much that was rotten beneath.

Running a hand through his short brown hair, MacKinnon then fixed her with his storm-grey gaze, and an arrogant smile quirked his mouth.

"That was a delight," he drawled. He then circuited the big bed, to where he'd heeled off his boots earlier in a hurry to disrobe so that he could plow his favorite whore. As he passed her, MacKinnon slapped Coira's naked bottom. "Ye always give a man good sport, don't ye?"

Drawing in a slow, measured breath, Coira squeezed her eyes shut. Rage, hot and prickly, rose up within her. Hate thundered in her breast; her heart pounded painfully against her ribs. She took one deep breath, and then another. Her fingers clutched at the tangled sheets upon which she lay.

She didn't answer him. And she knew he wouldn't care.

MacKinnon didn't visit her for conversation.

She listened to the scuffing sounds while he pulled on his boots and then his heavy tread as he left the chamber, the door thudding shut behind him.

After that, she heard the creak of the floorboards while the clan-chief walked across the landing and descended the stairs to the lower levels of *The Goat and Goose*, Dunan's most popular brothel.

Still lying upon the bed, Coira squeezed her eyes shut even tighter. A tear managed to escape nonetheless, trickling down her temple and onto the sheet beneath. However, it wasn't a tear of despair, but of fury.

Today, on this bleak winter's morning, she'd had enough.

I will never suffer that man's touch again, she vowed. *I will die first.*

Slowly, she opened her eyes and pushed herself up into a sitting position. Glancing down at herself, Coira tensed when she saw the raised red welts on her breasts, belly, and thighs. As usual, he'd been rough—pummeling, squeezing, and pinching her body as he rutted her.

Coira rose to her feet, swaying slightly as her head spun from the pain that knifed between her thighs. Out of all the men who visited this brothel, MacKinnon was the one she dreaded the most. Few of the customers were gentle, but the clan-chief delighted in hurting her, in humiliating her. Trembling, Coira wrapped her arms around her torso. This time had been one of the worst.

Her gaze dropped then to where a rumpled, dark robe lay pooled at the foot of the bed.

A nun's habit. It was one of MacKinnon's peculiarities. Part of what got him really excited was for her to dress up as a nun. He went into a frenzy at the sight of it, his gaze gleaming with lust when he ripped the habit off her.

Coira had no idea why such a guise excited him. But she preferred not to delve into Duncan MacKinnon's motivations. She didn't want to think about the man at all.

Bile rose in her throat, and she swallowed hard.

It's time. I'll not suffer this life any longer.

Moving stiffly, for each step pained her, she walked to a corner of the chamber and pushed back the heavy curtain, to reveal a washbowl and a collection of kirtles hanging against the stone wall. The gowns mocked her, like brightly colored butterflies.

She got to keep little of the coin she earned at *The Goat and Goose*, but Maude, the woman who ran this place, liked her lasses to be dressed well. The brothel had a reputation, and the old woman wanted her whores to do her proud.

Coira flushed hot then, and she thought of how she would have liked to take an iron poker to Maude as well as MacKinnon. The woman knew what a beast he was, but she didn't care. In the three years Coira had worked in this place, Maude had never shown her the slightest softness, sympathy, or consideration. She was merely a body, to be sold for silver.

Her feelings didn't matter.

The desire to reach out, tear those kirtles down, and rip them to shreds with her bare hands flooded through Coira. However, she fought the urge.

Now wasn't the time for revenge. She had to get out of here.

She hobbled over to the washbasin and cleaned herself as quickly as she could manage. All the while, her teeth ground with pain. The water came away bloodied, but she preferred not to examine what MacKinnon had done. There would be time for that later. Once she had washed, Coira reached for a dun-brown léine and the plainest of all the kirtles—a gown of jade green. She donned the léine first, an ankle-length tunic that fell softly over her bruised body. The kirtle went on next, lacing up over her aching breasts. It hurt to pull on her leather ankle boots, but she would need them for what lay ahead.

Finally dressed, Coira then sank to her knees in the corner of the alcove. Using the handle of her hairbrush, she pried up a loose floorboard. Underneath was all the wealth she possessed. Three years of awful work and only four silver pennies shone dully up at her.

But it was better than nothing.

Amongst the pennies, something else gleamed: a small silver ring, tarnished with age. Coira's throat thickened at the sight of the item of jewelry; it was the only link she now had with her parents. The ring had belonged to her mother, and Coira would have worn it if she wasn't afraid of Maude. The woman was worse than a magpie.

Coira reached down and picked up the ring, her vision blurring as memories of her mother surfaced. She'd been so wise and strong—and taken too young. Coira slid the ring upon her right hand, her fingers curling into a fist.

Today, she'd remember her mother as she took back her freedom.

Retrieving the pennies, Coira replaced the floorboard and rose to her feet. She then took a heavy woolen cloak from its peg behind the door and left the bed-chamber.

It was a loathsome place, for although it was her home, and where she slept each night, the room had never been Coira's sanctuary. It was the place where men used her—day in, day out. Sometimes it felt as if the walls were closing in.

Out on the landing, Coira paused a moment. Three other closed doors surrounded her, and behind the nearest one, she could hear a man's groans as he took his pleasure, followed by a woman's giggle.

Coira's throat closed. She never wanted to hear those sounds again.

On trembling limbs, she descended the rickety wooden staircase. Her bed-chamber lay upon the top floor of the brothel, and she passed two other levels on the way down to the common room. On the way there, she heard further sounds of coupling—cries, grunts, and groans. The noises, which had been commonplace for so long now, made her pulse race once more. *The Goat and Goose* would forever haunt her nightmares.

Maude was downstairs, presiding over the busy common room. A few men reclined in chairs around the fire, tankards in hand. A girl, not yet old enough to service customers, circled the room with a jug of ale, while an older lass perched on one of the men's knees.

Hot male gazes raked over Coira as she stepped onto the sawdust-strewn floor.

"Where do ye think ye are going, lassie?" Maude barked. A portly woman with a florid face, Maude's low-cut kirtle showed off a fleshy cleavage. She'd once worked as a whore in her younger years, but these days the woman ran this brothel. Maude had a mane of thick blonde hair, now laced with silver, and small, sharp green eyes that missed nothing. That jade gaze narrowed now as it swept over Coira's cloaked form. "I have another customer for ye."

Maude motioned toward a hulking man in the corner who was watching Coira with a hungry stare. A chill slithered down Coira's spine, and suddenly it was difficult to breathe, difficult to swallow.

I have to get out of here.

Meeting Maude's gaze, she forced herself to speak calmly. "I've just seen MacKinnon." Coira paused there, her gaze holding the older woman's. Maude knew that she was in no fit state to see other customers directly after the clan-chief had visited her. She hoped she wouldn't need to spell it out, especially in front of the common room full of men. A squeal intruded then, as the whore wriggled on a customer's lap. Her name was Greer, a foolish goose of a girl who had only recently joined the brothel. The man had a hand down the front of her kirtle and was groping roughly.

Coira's legs started to tremble then, and she was glad that the long skirts and cloak hid her fear.

"I'm off to see the herb-wife," she continued, "for a poultice."

Maude's mouth thinned, her eyes narrowing further. Coira thought that she might refuse her, that her lust for silver would be too great. But then she gave Coira a brisk nod. "Hurry up then. As ye can see, we're run off our feet this morning."

Coira nodded back, relief crashing over her. All she cared about was getting out.

A biting wind gusted down the fetid alley outside the brothel. It bit into the exposed skin of Coira's face and dug through the layers of clothing she wore. Glancing up at the sky, she noted that it was grey and stormy. Bad weather was on its way. It wasn't a good day to travel, but she would do so nonetheless.

It hurt her to hurry her stride, to make her way hastily out of 'The Warren'—the tightly-packed network of alleyways of Dunan. Above it all rose the grey bulk of the broch, threatening against the stormy sky. MacKinnon's lair.

Reaching the busy market square before the North Gate, Coira worked quickly. She bought herself some oatcakes and cheese for the journey, and then made her way toward the gate itself, where she joined the trickle of travelers out onto the road beyond.

The wind was harsh beyond the fortress, battering the high stone walls that surrounded Dunan and tugging viciously at Coira's cloak. Despite the chill morning and the dank smell of an approaching storm in the air, cottars still worked the fields around the MacKinnon stronghold. This time of the year, many of the fields lay fallow, but it was a time to enrich the soil, to dig in compost, and there were plenty of hardy greens, such as kale and cabbages, which grew all year round.

Coira hesitated only a moment in front of the gate before she turned left and took the road that circuited Dunan. She'd already made her decision about which direction she was headed in: west. North would take her into MacLeod lands and to the port village of Kiltaraglen. But there was nothing there for her but a life just like the one she was fleeing—and she had no intention of ever working in a brothel again.

Instead, she took the road that headed into the depths of the wooded vale behind Dunan. Tall, dark pines spread up the hillsides, their pungent scent lacing the chill air. This road would take her to the wild western shore of Skye, and the only place upon this isle that could give her sanctuary.

Kilbride Abbey.

Warmth spread through Coira's belly at the thought of her destination and the safety that awaited her there.

It was an irony really after she'd worn a habit for MacKinnon's pleasure just a short while earlier. She was not pious and hadn't been brought up in a god-fearing family. Her parents had died when she was barely ten winters old, both from a deadly fever that had raged through the isle one winter. They'd left her an orphan, and for a while, every day had been a struggle against starvation. Finally, desperation had brought her to Maude's door. She'd been taken in, first as a servant, and then, when she grew into womanhood, as a whore.

After what she'd endured during her twenty winters, she found it hard to believe in God. If such a force existed, it was cruel indeed and cared nothing for her happiness.

But the abbey wasn't just a place where pious women could live in contemplation. It was a sanctuary from a world that was both harsh and cruel. Coira had heard that the abbess of Kilbride was compassionate, and that she'd given many women shelter and a new start.

Drawing her cloak close against the howling wind, which now had spots of rain in it, Coira lowered her head and walked toward the mountains. And as she did so, she touched the small silver ring upon her right hand, tracing its intricate decorations with a fingertip.

The ring gave her strength; it made her feel as if her mother was watching over her.

For the first time in years, Coira looked toward the future with hope.

Ten and a half years later ...

1

Uncanny

*The village of Torrin
MacKinnon territory,
Isle of Skye, Scotland*

Summer, 1349 AD

"DO YE THINK I have the plague?"

The old man's raspy voice filled the smoky cottage, and Coira heard the note of fear in it.

Straightening up from where she'd been mashing herbs together with a small wooden pestle and mortar—creating a comfrey poultice that she would rub upon his chest—Coira met his eye. "Ye have the grippe, Colin ... and it's settled upon yer lungs. But it's not anything more serious."

"But how do ye know?" The farmer's voice rose as he pushed himself up against the mound of wool-stuffed pillows.

"The pestilence has not yet reached this corner of Skye," Coira replied evenly. "And the symptoms are different to what ails ye."

Over the past year, Coira had heard tales from travelers and visitors to the abbey about the dreaded sickness, some of them conflicting. However, she didn't want to frighten her patient with the details.

"But what *are* the symptoms?" Colin pressed.

Coira heaved a sigh. "Chills and weakness of the limbs ... and terrible cramps to the belly," she murmured, "and then, as the illness takes hold, dark pustules appear on the body."

As expected, Colin visibly blanched at this description. Coira had to admit that the symptoms did sound ghastly; she'd been on the lookout for them ever since the plague—which had wreaked havoc over Europe, England, and Scotland—had crossed the water to the Isle of Skye.

She was as sure as she could be that no one in Torrin had yet shown signs of it.

"Even so," Coira continued when Colin didn't respond, clearly cowed, "we must take care that yer lungs do not worsen. I will spread this salve upon yer chest, and ye must drink a special tea that will help clear the mucus and lessen the aching in yer limbs."

Colin nodded, meek now that he'd been assured he was not infected with the plague.

Coira worked deftly, administering the salve and then wrapping the old man's chest. Behind them, his wife fussed over a pot of what smelled like mutton stew over the hearth.

"It's nearly time for the noon meal, Sister," the old woman said as Coira started packing her things away in her basket. "Will ye not join us?"

Coira flashed her a grateful smile and picked up her staff, which she'd leaned against the wall. "Thank ye for the offer, Alma, but I can't stay … a few chores await me at the abbey before I can sit down to eat."

It was true. She'd noticed her supply of herbs was getting low. She'd need to gather some more in the abbey's sprawling gardens before joining the other nuns in the refectory for the noon meal.

Leaving the stone cottage, Coira stepped out into a narrow dirt street. The air was soft, cool, and damp—a balm after the reek of peat smoke indoors. The smoke wasn't good for old Colin's lungs either, but like most folk in the village, he lived in a one-room dwelling that gave him no respite from it.

Coira hitched her basket against her hip and made her way through the cluster of dwellings, heading south. Torrin perched near the edge of a cliff-face, with a small kirk presiding over it and arable fields to the back. In the decade she'd lived here, Coira had gotten to know the locals well. They were hard-working and generous with what they had, if a little small-minded and superstitious at times. She'd done her best to tend their ailments and had grown fond of many of them.

A gentle smile curved Coira's mouth as she left the village and took the narrow road down the hillside. A shallow wooded vale lay before her, and in its midst sat the high stone walls of Kilbride. From this vantage point, she had a wide view of the surrounding landscape. A rugged coast stretched south, to where a green headland jutted out into the sea; and although she didn't bother to look over her shoulder, she knew that the charcoal shadow of the Black Cuillins, Skye's most dominant mountain range, rose to the north. To the east, the bulk of other great mountains thrust up into a veil of low cloud. This was a mountainous isle, and Coira had grown very fond of this corner of it.

Kilbride felt like a world away from the hardship she'd known as a child and young woman. She felt safe here, protected.

A soft summer rain started to fall as she walked, a cool mist that kissed Coira's skin. She inclined her face up to it, closing her eyes a moment. Over the years, she'd gotten used to having her head covered by a wimple and veil, but her face was still exposed to the elements.

The road led her down the hillside, in amongst copses of birch and hazel, before the high walls of Kilbride loomed in front of her. The peaked roof of the kirk rose above it all.

Despite that Kilbride Abbey was a place of sanctuary, of peace and worship, its austere appearance made it off-putting. The abbess had increased this unwelcoming air by employing men from Torrin to dig deep ditches around the base of the walls, making them even harder to scale should anyone dare. Huge gates, made of iron and oak, barred Coira's way—although as she approached, she noted that they were ajar and a black-robed figure awaited her.

Drawing nearer, Coira recognized the nun as Sister Mina: a novice who was due to take her vows of perpetuity that autumn. She had a sensitive face and wide grey eyes that were huge this morning.

As Coira drew near, Sister Mina rushed forward to meet her. "Sister Coira! Ye must come immediately!" the young woman gasped.

Coira abruptly halted, tension rippling through her. "What is it ... what's happened?"

"There's a man here ... he's badly injured ... and is delirious with fever."

Coira frowned, snapping into her role as healer. "Where is he?"

"We've taken him to the infirmary," Sister Mina replied, her slender hands clasping before her. "He's in a bad way."

Coira gave a sharp nod and moved past the novice. "I shall go to him now."

Not looking to see if Sister Mina followed her, Coira strode across the wide yard that stretched out inside the gates. Before her rose the steepled kirk, while the various outbuildings—dormitories, the abbess's hall, the chapterhouse, guest lodgings, the refectory, the kitchen, and storehouses—flanked it on either side. Her long legs ate up the ground, and moments later she heard the patter of Sister Mina's sandaled feet as she attempted to keep up with her.

The infirmary was a narrow, low-slung building made of stone that sat behind the kirk. There was room inside for six sleeping pallets. One of the older nuns had recently been laid up there for a while after suffering a fall, but she'd just returned to her usual lodgings, leaving the infirmary empty once more.

Only now, Coira had a new patient.

Two tiny windows let in pale light, illuminating the tall figure sprawled upon the pallet in the far corner. Even as she approached him, Coira could see from the sharp rise and fall of the man's chest that he was suffering.

However, when she drew up before the bed, and her gaze alighted upon his face, Coira forgot all about the reason she was here.

She froze, a cold sensation creeping out from her belly and numbing her limbs.

That face. It was as if a ghost had just risen up before her.

"Sister Coira?" Sister Mina had stopped next to her. "Is something wrong?"

Coira didn't answer. She couldn't. Her attention didn't waver from the man who lay before her, eyes closed, his handsome face gleaming with sweat.

"He was conscious when we brought him in," the novice said after a few moments, perhaps thinking that Coira was merely shocked by his state. "But he's worsened since then."

Coira was grateful he wasn't awake. The last thing she wanted was those iron-grey eyes to open and stare up at her.

And yet, as the initial shock faded, Coira realized that maybe she was mistaken.

This wasn't the man who'd caused her to wake up in a cold sweat at night for the first couple of years after she left Dunan. This wasn't the beast who'd hurt her, humiliated her.

Aye, the lines of this man's face were similar to those of Duncan MacKinnon's. Yet his hair was shaggier, wilder than the clan-chief's, and his physique more heavily muscled.

She'd also last seen MacKinnon only a moon earlier, when he'd arrived at the abbey looking for Lady Leanna—the novice he'd abducted and then lost. She didn't remember the clan-chief sporting a long, thin scar that slashed vertically from his temple to cheek, just missing his left eye. It was an old scar, silvered with age.

Coira exhaled slowly. This wasn't Duncan MacKinnon—although the resemblance was uncanny.

"Did he give his name?" she asked finally, surprised at the slight tremor in her voice. Even after all these years, MacKinnon could still rattle her.

"None that I heard," Sister Mina replied. "We found him alone … sprawled on the ground before the gates. He was muttering, but most of it was incoherent. I think Mother Shona managed to get some sense out of the man before we carried him in here, but I didn't hear what passed between them."

Coira nodded, only then daring to move closer to her patient. Setting down her basket, she lowered herself onto a stool beside the pallet.

That's how they'd found her too—over a decade ago. Her flight from Dunan hadn't gone well. A few hours after fleeing the stronghold, a winter storm had blown in, bringing with it sleet and a freezing wind that had chilled her to the marrow. She'd plowed on though, leaving the road and scrambling cross-country to avoid anyone who might be searching for her. Night had fallen swiftly, and she'd been forced to find shelter, crouching shivering under the lee of a boulder while the wind screamed across the exposed landscape. The next morning, she'd awoken with an aching body and a fever—and by the time she reached the abbey, she'd been staggering. It was the abbess herself who'd found her crumpled before the gates.

"Ye said he was injured?" she murmured, running her practiced gaze down the length of his strong body. He was clad in a leather vest and plaid braies wet with sweat.

"Aye … there's a festering wound to his left flank. I checked under his vest, but it's all bandaged up."

Coira nodded before reaching down and deftly unlacing the vest. As the novice had said, a bandage had been wrapped around his chest. It was filthy, and Coira could see a dark stain on the left-hand side. Drawing a knife from her belt, she carefully cut away the bandage.

A putrid stench immediately filled the infirmary.

Mother Mary preserve him … this doesn't look good.

Behind her, Sister Mina made a gagging sound, before she muttered something incoherent under her breath.

Stifling the urge to clap a hand over her mouth, Coira straightened up. "Open the windows," she ordered, "and fetch me some vinegar, a clean cloth, and a bowl of hot water … quick as ye can."

Grateful to have an excuse to flee the stench of rotting flesh, Sister Mina did as bid, leaving Coira alone with her patient.

Staring down at the wound upon the man's left flank, Coira's mouth pursed. It looked to her as if the man had sustained a battle wound—an arrow most likely. The offending item had been removed, but looking at the red, swollen sore, and the pus leaking out of it, she knew the wound had soured. Angry red lines now stretched out from the injury, a bad sign indeed, as was the fever that had brought the man to his unconscious state.

She'd have to work hard if he was to be saved.

2
Taking Risks

COIRA ROSE TO her feet and stretched her aching back. She'd lost track of time, of how long she'd been bent over the injured man, cleaning and then dressing his wound. She'd missed the noon meal, and Sister Mina had come and gone with steaming bowls of water, clean cloths, and bandages as the afternoon slipped by. But now she was done.

Heaving a sigh, Coira glanced down at the man's sleeping face. He was still fevered and had started to twitch and thrash about. However, his wound was now clean. She'd do her best to dress it regularly, but the rest was up to him.

She wondered if her care had come too late.

Covering her patient up with a light blanket, Coira left the infirmary. Outside, a misty rain continued to fall and a low mantle of cloud had settled over the abbey, closing them in. Sister Mina approached, a slight figure through the gloom, carrying a pile of clean linen.

"Is it done?" the novice asked, her gaze flicking over Coira's shoulder to the closed door of the infirmary. "Will he live?"

"It's too early to tell," Coira replied, her voice heavy with fatigue. "The next day will be crucial. If his fever rages, then he may lose the fight." She massaged a tense muscle in her shoulder then. "I'm starving … is it time for supper yet?"

"Not for a while, although I'm sure ye can get some bread and cheese in the kitchens," Sister Mina replied. "But before ye do, ye had better go and see Mother Shona. She's asked that ye pay her a visit once the patient is tended to."

Coira nodded. However, she wished she could have gotten herself something to eat first. She felt light-headed from hunger. "Very well, I'll go to her now," she replied. "Please stay with him for a while … fetch me if his state worsens."

Coira found the abbess in her hall. At this time of day, Mother Shona often shut herself away for a period of study and quiet contemplation, while the nuns took an opportunity to rest before the last of the afternoon chores and Vespers.

Mother Shona was seated in a high-backed chair by the hearth, where a lump of peat glowed. She motioned for Coira to enter.

Crossing the floor, Coira lowered herself onto one knee before the abbess. Mother Shona then made the sign of the cross above Coira's bent head. Once she'd blessed her, the abbess gestured to the seat opposite. "How is he?" she asked without preamble.

"Very ill," Coira replied. "I removed a splinter of wood from an arrow wound to his left flank, which had caused the problem ... it should have been attended to long before today."

Mother Shona nodded, her brown eyes shadowing. She was a small woman with a deceptively gentle demeanor that belied the steel underneath. Around twenty years Coira's senior, the abbess was the strongest person Coira had ever known. Thanks to her, Coira had grown hardy, both in body and spirit. She had learned to defend herself and had found solace in her life as a Bride of Christ.

"Did he speak to ye?" the abbess finally asked.

Coira shook her head. "He was in a fevered sleep when I attended him ... and remains in one."

"He was delirious when we found him earlier," Mother Shona replied, her expression still veiled, "but I managed to glean his name."

Coira frowned. "Sister Mina told me ye all didn't know his identity?"

"I decided some news is best not shared," the abbess replied with a wry glint in her eye. "The name 'Craeg the Bastard' is not one to be bandied about in these parts."

Coira went still, the cold, fluttery feeling she'd experienced upon entering the infirmary at noon returning.

"No wonder I recognized him," she whispered.

The abbess's face turned stern. "I'm surprised the others didn't. The similarity is striking."

For a moment, the two women merely watched each other. The intense look upon the abbess's face made Coira tense. Sometimes she swore the woman could read minds. Mother Shona was the only soul in the abbey who knew her history, knew that she'd fled the life of a whore. However, she didn't know the whole story—that Coira had run from Duncan MacKinnon's brutality.

She didn't know that Coira's heart had nearly stopped when she'd set eyes upon her patient.

"I heard there was a skirmish ... to the south ... around a month ago ... between MacKinnon and outlaws," Coira said, breaking the brittle silence between them. "The outlaw leader has likely been carrying the wound since then."

Mother Shona shook her head. "It's a miracle he still lives."

Coira let out a long exhale. "Aye ... but it's a risk having him here. There's a price on that man's head that would tempt many. If MacKinnon ever discovers him here, all of us are in jeopardy."

"I'm aware of that," the abbess replied. Her voice was unusually weary. "But he came to us out of desperation. We couldn't turn him away."

Of course they couldn't. Coira had never refused to tend anyone, and had been pleased to hear that MacKinnon's bastard brother was causing the clan-chief so much trouble of late.

However, keeping him at Kilbride was another matter. Here, he risked bringing the wolf to their door.

"So, what should we do?" Coira asked, almost dreading the answer.

"We will keep him here, out of sight." The abbess now adopted a determined expression that Coira knew well. "Unfortunately, news of an injured man's arrival has already spread through the abbey, but no one beyond its walls knows he's here, yet. If he survives his injuries, as soon as he's able, he will have to leave."

Coira nodded. Mother Shona's decision didn't surprise her. Neither of them was going to turn an injured man away, and yet the sooner they rid themselves of Craeg the Bastard, the better.

After supper, Coira discovered that she couldn't settle. She'd filled her belly with bread, cheese, and onion broth; slaked her thirst with a cup of ale; and tried to rest—but she found that she was full of nervous energy.

Instead, she decided to practice with her quarter-staff.

Having MacKinnon's half-brother here at Kilbride had put her on edge. It didn't matter how much she steeled herself before visiting Craeg, every time she set eyes on the man the likeness between him and MacKinnon made a shiver slide down her spine.

However, unlike the clan-chief, Craeg was loved rather than reviled by the people of this territory. There were a number of stories about this man that had almost become folklore upon Skye. Despite that he was a criminal, Craeg had recently become a savior figure for the folk here, the only one who'd stand up against the clan-chief's iron fist. His behavior was audacious and foolhardy to the extreme. He boldly attacked supply wagons, couriers, and even MacKinnon's own men, stealing food and silver, most of which he gave away to the poor. MacKinnon had been hunting him for a while now, but Craeg always seemed to slip free of his net.

Maybe this time he wasn't going to be so fortunate.

Outdoors in the misty gloaming, Coira noted that tension had turned the muscles in her neck and shoulders into planks of wood. The evening chores had been done and Compline completed, and the abbey had just entered the Great Silence—a period of quiet reflection during which the nuns did not converse until after Mass the following morning.

The Great Silence was actually Coira's favorite time of day. And usually at this hour, she was happy to rest upon her sleeping pallet—but not this evening. Returning briefly to her tiny cell in the building next to the dormitories, Coira retrieved her quarter-staff—a six-foot stave fashioned of ash with pointed iron tips.

This was her weapon of choice.

Upon arriving at the abbey, it hadn't taken Coira long to realize that all wasn't as it seemed. Aye, the abbess was a pious woman who took her service to God very seriously, and expected the nuns to do the same, but she was also an enigma. Like Coira, she appeared a woman who kept secrets.

Even so, Mother Shona had revealed some of her past to the nuns. Over the years Coira discovered that the abbess had once been a novice in a convent in Lismore upon the mainland. One summer, brigands attacked the convent, raping and slaughtering any nuns they found there before burning it to the ground. Shona had been spared that day, for she'd been out collecting herbs when the attack had taken place. Terrified, she'd fled into the forest, and had been on the verge of starving when a group of outlaws found her and took her into their fold.

Coira wasn't sure what had happened afterward, for this was the part where the abbess had been vague, but it appeared that the outlaws had taught the young nun how to defend herself. Eventually, she'd left the band and traveled to the Isle of Skye, where she'd entered Kilbride Abbey. Years later, when she was elected as abbess, Mother Shona had determined that the nuns under her care would always be able to defend themselves, and had set about teaching them all skills that were highly unusual for a nun—abilities that she'd kept secret from her fellow sisters for years.

Over the years, Coira had learned to fire a bow and arrow, throw a knife, handle herself with a sword, and defend herself with her hands if the need arose.

But wielding the quarter-staff—a weapon that could be as dangerous as a sword—was the skill she'd focused on. Coira carried it with her whenever she left Kilbride's walls, which was often because she needed to collect particular healing herbs in the woods and attend to the sick and injured beyond. To the folk beyond here, it looked as if she carried a staff to help her walk upon the uneven terrain, but the Sisters of Kilbride knew differently.

Coira was lethal with a quarter-staff.

She walked to the wide yard before the shadow of the kirk now and stood for a few moments, legs planted hip-width apart as she centered herself.

Around her, it felt as if the mist had closed in further still. The oil lamp that Coira had brought, and placed down on the ground a few yards behind her, only illuminated a limited space. She couldn't even see the surrounding walls of the abbey. It mattered not though; she could still practice, even in the fog.

Swinging the quarter-staff around in an arc, Coira started through a series of drills. She could have done them in her sleep, for they were movements that she taught all the young nuns who'd entered the abbey after her. These days, she and Mother Shona shared the duty of training the others.

The wooden stave whistled and swooshed through the air as she spun it around. She shifted stance then, holding the staff two-handed—attacking, feinting, and parrying as if an opponent stood before her.

She went through the drills, again and again, her mind completely focused. For a short while, the rest of the world receded. Her past ceased to exist, and all the problems that had plagued the abbey of late disappeared as well. She'd lost two friends recently, both of whom had been very dear to her. Coira knew that a woman who dedicated herself to serving Christ shouldn't cling on to earthly relationships, but she'd been very close to Sisters Ella and Leanna.

Fortunately, both women were still alive. However, due to extreme circumstances, they'd left the abbey for new lives. And although Coira kept herself busy at Kilbride, she sometimes felt an ache in her chest whenever she thought of Ella and Leanna. Without them here, she sometimes felt very alone.

Finally, the sweat pouring down her face and back, Coira finished her practice. She was breathing hard, yet the tension had now eased from her neck and shoulders, and the muscles felt loose.

I needed that, she thought as she turned, retrieved her oil lamp, and headed toward the nun's quarters. Yet halfway there, she halted. She'd intended to return to her cell, where she'd retire for the evening. But something prevented her.

Instead, she turned and made her way around the back of the complex, to where the infirmary stood, shrouded in mist.

Her patient would be alone.

She couldn't leave him like that—not tonight. Not when his life hung by a thread.

With a heavy sigh, Coira entered the infirmary. It was dimly lit by the glow of the hearth at one end and a flickering oil lamp on the low table next to the only occupied bed.

Craeg the Bastard lay sprawled upon his back, his breathing deep and even as he slept. He wasn't thrashing now, which could be a good or bad sign, depending on how his body was responding. Lamp aloft, Coira approached the sleeping pallet and peered down at his bandaged midriff. They'd removed his vest, leaving him naked from the waist up. Examining the bandage, she was pleased to see there hadn't been much seepage—that there was no telltale yellow stain from pus. That was a positive sign.

Satisfied that she had done all she could for the moment, Coira set down her lamp and pulled up a high-backed wooden chair next to the bed. With a sigh, she sank down onto it and clasped her hands before her.

All she could do now was pray.

3

Just a Man

CRAEG AWOKE TO a dull throbbing pain in his side and a raging thirst.

He opened his eyes slowly, for although the room in which he lay was dimly lit, his eyes still stung from the candlelight.

For a few moments, his vision was cloudy and blurred, and then his surroundings sharpened into focus.

And the first thing he saw was an angel standing over him.

A woman with a face that looked as if it had been sculpted by the hand of the master: strong patrician features, and high cheekbones, with a full, beautifully drawn mouth. But the thing that really caught his attention was her eyes. They were an unusual color—violet—and framed by dark arched eyebrows. Truly, he'd never seen such beauty.

An instant later though, he realized he was not looking up into the face of an angel, but a nun. Those angelic features were framed by an austere white wimple and a black veil. She was tall and broad-shouldered for a woman, and her body was shrouded in a heavy black habit, girded at the waist with a leather belt, where a small wooden crucifix hung.

A jolt of surprise made Craeg catch his breath.

He wasn't dead and being attended by one of heaven's angels after all—although in retrospect, after the life he'd lived, he was much more likely to have been sent to the depths of hell—but very much alive.

Craeg tried to remember how he'd gotten here. He could remember telling Gunn and Farlan to return to the others before he'd finished the journey to Kilbride on his own. He also recalled staggering through the trees, to where the austere walls of Kilbride Abbey rose in an impenetrable barrier against the outside world. He'd barely made it to the gates, and hadn't had the energy to reach for the heavy iron knocker to alert them to his presence. Instead, pain, fever, and crushing fatigue had slammed into him like a charging boar, and he'd collapsed upon the dirt before the gates. An instant later, darkness had taken him.

Staring down at him, the nun's lovely face tightened a little. Those unusual violet eyes widened.

"I'm so thirsty," Craeg croaked. "I can't swallow."

With a brisk nod, the nun moved away and returned an instant later at his side with a wooden cup. Craeg found he was propped up on a mound of pillows, and as such, when the nun raised the cup to his lips, he was able to take a sip, and then another, without choking. The ale that she fed him was watery, yet it tasted like the sweetest mead to his parched mouth and throat. He could have gulped it down, but since he knew it would only make him ill, he prevented himself.

With a sigh of relief, Craeg sank back against the pillows. Then, dreading what he might see, he lowered his chin to look down at his left flank.

Unlike the last time he'd seen it, when the bandage had been filthy, stained with blood and pus, and stinking like the devil's toenails, it now looked clean, although the dull throb set his teeth on edge.

"How is the wound?" he asked dreading the answer. Craeg knew he'd been a fool to leave it as long as he had; the last month had been fraught as he and his band had narrowly escaped capture again and again. There had been no time to think about himself. A chill settled in his belly as he remembered just how awful the wound looked last time he had dared uncover the bandage.

"Much better than it was," she replied. Her voice was as lovely as her face. It had a low, husky quality to it, and its timbre soothed him. "The souring came from a splinter of wood that hadn't been removed." She paused here, those startling eyes narrowing. "From an arrow, I take it?"

Craeg nodded. "I took the wound around a moon ago, and it started to trouble me a few days later." He halted there, his eyes closing as he braced himself for bad news.

"Don't look so worried," the nun continued, her tone rueful. "Ye might live yet, outlaw."

His gaze snapped open. "I might?"

She nodded, the edges of her sensual mouth lifting in the barest hint of a smile. "Last night was the most dangerous time, and ye passed it. Now, if I can keep the wound clean, and help it to heal, ye will live and continue to be a thorn in yer brother's side."

Her dry sense of humor made Craeg smile. "I see ye know who I am?"

The nun nodded, breaking eye contact with him. She then took the wooden cup from him and set it down on the table next to the pallet.

"The people of this territory have much to thank ye for," she said, her voice soft now as she started to sort through what appeared to be a basket of herbs. "Last winter ye gave silver to the folk of Torrin after MacKinnon robbed them. They'd have starved otherwise. Because of ye and yer band, they have hope."

Her words, strangely, made warmth spread out from the center of Craeg's chest.

He knew that many folk living upon MacKinnon lands saw him as some kind of savior figure, but he never spent much time dwelling upon the fact.

The truth of it was less pretty.

He didn't do this for them, but for himself. Revenge fed him, drove him—it was his beer and bread. However, he prevented himself from telling the nun this. Despite that he'd only just met her, he realized that he wanted this stranger to think well of him. Odd really, but he did.

"I need to take a look at that wound," the nun informed him, her tone changing from warm to cool in an instant. It was almost as if she realized the conversation had become too familiar. She was now trying to distance herself from him.

"Go on then," Craeg replied.

He fell silent, observing as she approached once more and deftly cut away his bandage. He noticed as she did so that she had beautiful hands with long, nimble fingers. When she had removed the bandage, he forced himself to look upon the wound.

It still wasn't a pretty sight. The flesh around the wound was badly swollen, although the red lines that had scared him into making the journey here had started to fade a little. Thank the Lord that the wound no longer stank. It was red and angry looking, but there was no pus, and it no longer had a putrid appearance.

The nun bent close, her cool fingertips gently prodding the inflamed skin around the injury. She then glanced up, and their gazes fused for an instant. "I'm going to have to wash it again," she informed him. "It's going to hurt."

He nodded, steeling himself. "I'm ready."

She hadn't been lying. When the vinegar poured over the wound, red-hot pain exploded down his left flank. Craeg gritted his teeth, his hands clenching by his sides as he bit back a groan. The first jolt of pain receded, followed by waves of burning agony that seemed to pulse in time with his heartbeat.

"Sorry about this," she murmured, meeting his eye once more. Craeg saw that she meant it to, for her gaze was now shadowed. "The vinegar removes the evil humors."

Craeg nodded, not trusting himself to speak. He'd taken a few wounds over the years, but even the one on his face hadn't hurt as much as this did. He didn't want to embarrass himself over it though, so he kept his jaw clamped shut.

"I'm curious," the nun said as she continued her torturous work. "How is it that ye and yer band have eluded MacKinnon for so long? I'd have thought there were only so many places ye can hide."

She was trying to distract him, he realized. All the same, Craeg appreciated the gesture.

"The heart of MacKinnon lands is a wild place," he replied through clenched teeth. "There are many hidden corners where few men have set foot ... I have discovered them."

"The people of this land must truly love ye," she replied with a shake of her head. "But don't ye worry all the same that one of them might betray ye?"

Despite the red-hot agony that pulsed down his left side, Craeg's body tensed. One of his men already had, barely a month earlier. However, this wasn't the time to discuss it.

"Not really," he grunted. "MacKinnon has done a fine job of making himself the most hated man upon Skye."

"He has," she agreed, "but silver has a way of making folk forget such things."

Their gazes met, and he saw the keen intelligence in those violet eyes. An instant later the nun rose to her feet and wiped her hands upon a damp cloth.

"That's done for now," she said with a half-smile. "Ye did well."

Somehow Craeg managed a wan smile of his own. "Aye, thanks to ye distracting me. I'd tell ye that ye have the gentlest touch this side of the Black Cuillins... but I'd be lying. I've never been in so much pain."

Her mouth curved then into a proper smile, and if Craeg had thought the nun was beautiful before, she was positively radiant now. That smile illuminated her face like winter sun emerging through a bank of frozen fog. For a moment, Craeg merely stared at her, entranced. Eventually, when he spoke, his voice had a slight husk to it. "So as ye will know, my name is Craeg. May I know yers?"

The nun's smile faded, although her eyes were still warm. "I am Sister Coira," she replied.

Coira stepped out of the infirmary into the misty dawn and raised an unsteady hand to the center of her chest. As she suspected, her heart was racing.

Mother Mary ... it's like looking upon MacKinnon's twin.

The man had been civil and respectful in his manner, so different to the clan-chief. But it didn't matter that Craeg wasn't his brother, he still unnerved her. The similarity in their looks was eerie—although she'd noted a few differences.

Firstly, his eyes. She'd expected them to be grey, like Duncan MacKinnon's. But the eyes that stared back at her this morning were a deep moss green—as different from MacKinnon's as mid-winter was to mid-summer. Even shadowed with pain, there had been wry humor and a large dose of arrogance in them, which wasn't surprising. She hadn't met a warrior who wasn't arrogant.

His voice was markedly different to MacKinnon's as well. It was much lower and deeper. Just like his eyes, the outlaw's voice held a warmth that the clan-chief's had always lacked.

And yet, standing outside the infirmary, Coira struggled to regain her equilibrium.

She wished there was another healer in the abbey—another nun who could help him besides her.

Goose, Coira chided herself. *He's just a man. Ignore who he is and treat him like any other.* She walked away from the infirmary, and toward the refectory where bread and beer would be served to break the nuns' fast.

Truthfully, she had no appetite. She usually enjoyed all her meals, for she worked hard and was rarely idle during the day. But this morning, her encounter with the outlaw had left her shaken.

Her only solace was that she didn't think the man had picked up on her reaction to him. He was in too much pain.

Lost in brooding thoughts, Coira circuited the complex, and was about to join the flood of nuns who were entering the refectory, when the clang of iron echoed across the yard.

Coira's step faltered. Someone was at the gates and had just let the knocker fall.

Kilbride had visitors.

Glancing around her, she saw that a few of the other nuns had halted, including Sister Elspeth, one of the older women who'd been here long before Coira arrived at the abbey. The nun wore an expression of constant disapproval, her small mouth pursed, her eyes narrowed. She drew herself up now, irritation vibrating through her thin body, and when she spoke, her voice held a querulous edge. "Who dares bother us at this hour?"

Coira didn't reply, as she realized the question was probably rhetorical. With a huff of irritation, Sister Elspeth picked up the long skirts of her habit and hurried across the dirt yard toward the gates. Without thinking, Coira fell in behind her.

Once she reached the gates, Sister Elspeth drew open the small window that sat at eye height. Coira couldn't see what the older nun was looking at, but judging by the way Sister Elspeth went rigid, she hadn't liked what lay beyond.

"Who is it?" Coira whispered.

Sister Elspeth ignored her. Instead, she stepped back and started unbolting the gates. "Help me, would ye?" she snapped.

Irritated at having orders barked at her, Coira reluctantly stepped forward and aided Sister Elspeth. Together, they gripped one of the heavy wooden and iron gates and hauled it back.

A thin, milky mist breathed in, its tendrils twisting like crone's hair. A jingling sound filtered through the damp air then, and a harsh command cut through the dawn. "Open the gates ... I have business with the abbess!"

Coira's breathing slowed. *The Saints preserve us ... I know that voice.*

She peered through the fog, where shadowy figures now emerged. The nearest was a lanky, round-shouldered figure: a monk garbed in black who'd just knocked upon the gates. Behind him clustered a group of his fellow monks, who suddenly parted to admit a heavyset figure atop a pony.

Only, it wasn't a pony but a mule. The creature was bedecked in bells, ornaments, and tassels; the bells tinkling as the burdened beast swayed forward. The man astride it wore a truculent, pinched expression as if his arse pained him.

Coira heaved in a deep, steadying breath, even as her belly dropped.

Father Camron.

The Abbot of Crossraguel was paying them another visit.

4

Thwarted

*Dunan broch
MacKinnon territory
Isle of Skye*

DUNCAN MACKINNON SLAMMED the goblet down upon the table, his gaze fixed on the blond man standing at the foot of the dais. "This isn't good enough, Broderick ... the bastard can't have disappeared into thin air!"

A tense silence settled upon the Great Hall of Dunan—retainers and kin swiveled in their seats, their attention settling upon their clan-chief. Everyone was halfway through their noon meal of blood sausage, braised leeks, and hefty loaves of oaten bread when MacKinnon's right-hand, Carr Broderick, had entered the hall.

MacKinnon glared down at the warrior, irritated that his outburst hadn't moved the man at all. His rugged face was set in an unreadable expression. Although not overly tall, Broderick made up for it in breadth and strength; his stocky frame was pure muscle. His close-cropped blond hair just added to his severe, unyielding appearance.

"We've combed yer lands over and over again," Broderick said when the silence between them started to crackle with tension. Like his expression, his voice gave nothing away. "There's no sign of the outlaws."

"But I saw my bastard brother take an arrow in the side," Duncan exploded. "He'll be injured ... he won't have gone far."

"Maybe he's dead?" A cool female voice interjected then, and MacKinnon swung his gaze left to where a dainty woman with rich brown hair piled up onto the crown of her head had just spoken. Undaunted by her brother's outburst, Drew MacKinnon's sharp grey-eyed gaze met his. "Have ye not considered that?"

"I'll not believe Craeg's dead till I see his rotting corpse with my own eyes," Duncan snarled back.

"Lady Drew has a point," Broderick rumbled. "That might be why we can't find him ... he's buried under six feet of dirt somewhere."

Broderick hadn't moved from his position. He waited before the raised platform at the end of the Great Hall, where the clan-chief and his kin took their meals. The warrior stood, legs akimbo, in an arrogant stance that grated upon MacKinnon. His previous right-hand, Ross Campbell, had been an arrogant man too, but he'd also been clever with words, and had known how to ease a tense situation or offer explanations that would appease MacKinnon.

Carr Broderick was charmless and disarmingly blunt at times. Duncan watched the warrior, gaze narrowed. Campbell's betrayal had made the clan-chief wary of the men who served him. He knew the two men had been friends, and initially, after Campbell had run off with the woman Duncan had planned to wed, Lady Leanna, the clan-chief had suspected Broderick of somehow aiding them. However, the man had been off fetching a priest for the marriage ceremony when the incident occurred.

MacKinnon's attention shifted back to his sister. He didn't trust her either. Drew swore that on the night Campbell and Lady Leanna escaped the broch, she'd heard nothing. Duncan didn't fully believe her at the time—and he still suspected she was hiding something. However, he had no proof against her.

The memory of that humiliating night still burned within him, and his chest constricted whenever he recalled it. He'd underestimated Leanna it seemed, and shouldn't have drunk so much wine before attempting to claim her. She'd been cowering against the wall as he explored her lithe body, and then she'd kneed him in the cods—twice.

The wee bitch had put every ounce of her strength into the attack too. In the days that followed, Duncan had wondered if he'd ever father another child; although Dunan's healer had assured him there had been no lasting damage.

He'd been curled up on the floor, retching from the pain, when Campbell burst into the bed-chamber. He'd trussed Duncan up like a capon, and then the pair of them had fled, locking him inside the room.

"I repeat," MacKinnon growled, shoving aside the memories that made him break out in a cold sweat. "Until I see my bastard brother's body, I'll not believe he's dead." He leaned back in his carven chair then, drawing a deep breath as he sought to master the rage that made his pulse thunder in his ears.

Wisely, Drew didn't argue the point with him. Dismissing her, he pinned Broderick with a hard stare. "Ye have already failed me once ... if ye let Craeg slip through the net, I won't give ye another chance to redeem yerself."

The threat fell heavily in the silence. Everyone in the hall had stopped eating now and was watching their clan-chief.

Broderick stared back at him, and although his expression was still inscrutable, Duncan saw his gaze narrow slightly. The hardening of his jaw also betrayed him; like Ross Campbell before him, Carr Broderick was a proud man. He didn't like being threatened.

MacKinnon didn't care—he was done with being thwarted.

Raising a hand, he dismissed the Captain of the Dunan Guard before clicking his fingers, holding his goblet aloft to be refilled.

A young woman appeared at his elbow. She was a shy, dark-haired lass—one of his cousins—of plain face and with a figure so slender that MacKinnon found her sexless. A pity really, for he was in the mood for some bed sport.

The lass filled his goblet and scurried away, gaze averted. Duncan ignored her. Leaning back in his chair, he took a large gulp of sloe wine and retreated into his own thoughts.

And as often when he withdrew from others, his mind went to Lady Leanna MacDonald.

The pounding in his ears increased. How he'd wanted the woman—ever since he'd first set eyes upon her at a gathering between the MacKinnon and MacDonald clans. Her father had thwarted him, but after his sudden death in a hunting accident, Duncan had wasted no time in tearing Leanna from Kilbride Abbey, where she'd been living as a novice nun.

Things should have gone his way then. Campbell and Broderick delivered her to Dunan, but fate had turned against him. MacKinnon couldn't believe she'd managed to escape, or that Ross Campbell had betrayed him. Where had Campbell taken her? He'd even dispatched men to the mainland to look for her when his search upon Skye was fruitless. He'd sent word to all the clan-chiefs and chieftains upon the isle, along with thinly veiled threats of what he'd do to any who dared harbor her, but none had responded to him.

Over a month on, Leanna still dominated his thoughts, as did fantasies of what he'd do if he ever caught her.

Duncan took another gulp of wine, welcoming its heat as the rich liquid slid down his throat. He was drinking too much these days, yet he found that it was the only thing that took the edge off his rage. He hadn't lain with a woman since that disastrous attempt with Leanna. It was time to break the curse she'd cast upon him.

Setting down his goblet, the clan-chief shoved back his chair and rose to his feet. Next to him, Drew stopped eating, her gaze swiveling to his untouched platter and then to his face.

"Does the food displease ye?" she asked.

"I'm not hungry."

"I thought blood sausage was yer favorite?" Drew continued, her dark brows drawing together. "Ye hardly eat at all these days … ye will be nothing but skin and bone soon if ye don't take care."

Heat flushed across Duncan's face as irritation surged. "Stop nagging, sister," he snarled. However, as he stepped off the dais and strode across the floor of the hall, past long tables where his retainers still ate and drank, he reflected that, indeed, his clothing was starting to hang on him these days. His need for vengeance had become an obsession; it had narrowed his world. He'd lost his taste for food.

He was having trouble accepting that Leanna was lost to him, but he wouldn't give up on seeing his brother swing from a gibbet. Once Craeg was caught, the world would return to normal.

Bran, his faithful wolfhound, leaped down from where he'd been sitting under the table upon the dais and fell in behind Duncan. The dog loped at his heel as the clan-chief strode across the broch's wide entrance hall and descended the steep steps to the bailey below.

The wolfhound was the only occupant of the broch who didn't irritate Duncan on a daily basis. But of late he hadn't paid the dog the attention he usually did. Bran didn't appear to care though—he merely trotted after his master, his ever-present shadow.

MacKinnon left the bailey through a high stone arch and made his way into the streets below. Without even thinking about his direction, his feet carried him toward 'The Warren', a squalid tangle of alleyways in the lower village.

Duncan hadn't walked this way in a while. Of late, what with the threat of pestilence, and everything else, he'd been preoccupied. After Leanna's brutal attack, his cods had taken a while to heal. Yet the ache in his bollocks now had to be satisfied. It would also relieve the tension within him, distract him from his own thoughts for a short while.

The Goat and Goose was a high, narrow building made of pitted grey stone that loomed over a shadowy lane. The air outside the brothel reeked of stale piss, but Duncan paid it no mind. *The Goat and Goose* had the best whores on the isle, and Old Maude always did her best to ensure the clan-chief left satisfied.

Stepping inside the common room, Duncan left behind the squalor of 'The Warren' and entered a softly lit space. Pine and herbs scented the air, from the soft mattress of sawdust underfoot, and flickering cressets of oil perfumed with rosemary and lavender lined the walls. Yet underneath it all, the faint odor of stale sweat pervaded—it always did here. There weren't many customers present at this hour, and as such, the whores who lolled on chairs near the glowing hearth all snapped to attention at the clan-chief's arrival.

"MacKinnon!" Maude, blowsy and busty with a mane of greying blonde hair pinned up into an elaborate tangle upon her head, swept in from nowhere. The woman brought with her a wake of rose perfume—a scent MacKinnon would always associate with this brothel. "We have missed ye."

"I've been busy," he replied, his tone deliberately cold. Duncan wasn't here to indulge in idle chatter.

Maude favored him with a sly smile. The woman was sharper than most, and she'd sensed his mood. "Would ye like the usual?"

"Aye." Duncan lowered himself down into a chair one of the whores had just vacated and took the goblet of wine the serving lass passed him. "But give me a different girl this time … the last one didn't please me."

A shadow passed over Maude's face. This was ill news indeed, for she lived to please the clan-chief. "Of course," she replied hastily. "If ye would give me a few moments to organize things for ye?"

Duncan nodded curtly. He didn't mind waiting, just as long as he got the whore he wanted. Indeed, the last time he'd visited *The Goat and Goose*, he'd ended up with a lusty, over-eager whore who'd tried to wrench his braies off him and suck his rod. He preferred women who let him take control—and if he glimpsed fear in their eyes all the better.

That last thought brought another woman to mind—one he'd thought of often over the years.

Coira.

Every time he stepped into this brothel, he felt a pang of longing for her. His obsession with Lady Leanna had distracted him over the last few years, but Coira was always there, a shadow from his past. And Duncan's recent visit to Kilbride Abbey had brought her back into his thoughts.

He was sure he'd seen her there.

It was true that the black habits and veils the nuns wore made them difficult to tell apart, yet he'd never seen anyone with eyes the color of Coira's—violet. And that nun, long-limbed and broad-shouldered, who'd stood at the back of the group while he'd confronted the abbess about Leanna's whereabouts, had violet eyes.

She'd also watched him with contempt and fear upon her lovely face.

It could be her.

One day, MacKinnon intended to go back to Kilbride Abbey—and when he did, he'd investigate.

A whore shouldn't be hiding in the guise of a nun anyway. A smile curved Duncan's mouth then as he remembered the games he used to play with Coira. If that woman had, indeed, been her, it was a real irony.

"More wine?" The serving lass drew near him once again, and with a jolt, Duncan realized that he'd drained his drink without even realizing it.

He nodded and held out the goblet for her to fill. As he did so, he noticed that the lass didn't look well. A light sheen of sweat covered her thin face, and the hand that poured the wine trembled slightly. When she moved away, the girl hunched as if her belly was in pain.

She was a plain-looking wench, Duncan observed, and on the brink of womanhood. He certainly wouldn't be asking for her to warm his bed.

"MacKinnon ... if ye are ready?" Maude descended the stairwell from the upper levels. "Yer woman awaits ... upon the top floor ... last room on the right."

Duncan nodded before draining his new goblet of wine in a few gulps. He then rose to his feet and shoved it at the pale-faced serving lass. Without a word, he strode past Maude and climbed the stairs to the upper levels. As he went, he heard Maude's voice, harsh now that the customer was out of sight. "Stand up straight, Fiona ... what's wrong with ye today!"

Reaching the top floor, Duncan strode toward his destination. His belly tightened in anticipation, the ache in his groin intensifying as he imagined what awaited him.

He strode along the narrow hallway, the wooden floor creaking underfoot, till he was before the last room on the right. Then, he tore the door open and stepped through the threshold.

A small lass, barely old enough to be called a woman, sat perched upon the bed. She watched him, blue eyes huge upon a winsome, heart-shaped face. A black habit and veil swathed her slender form.

Duncan halted, his gaze drinking her in. A moment later, a delighted smile stretched his face. Maude had done well indeed; he could smell this lass's fear.

Still grinning, he kicked the door shut behind him.

5

Happy Endings

"I TOLD YE I would return." Father Camron picked up his spoon and viewed the bowl of stew before him with thinly veiled distaste. "I warned ye that yer behavior would be investigated, Mother."

Heat rose in the pit of Coira's belly as she listened to these words, and her fingers clenched around her own spoon. She couldn't believe this man's arrogance, his presumption.

However, at the head of the table, Mother Shona appeared unruffled by the abbot's inflammatory words. "Ye are always welcome here, Father," she said, meeting his eye. "We have nothing to hide."

Coira's pulse accelerated, and she quelled the urge to exchange glances with the other nuns at the table.

They all knew that statement was a lie.

There was much Father Camron didn't know—much he couldn't know. If there was anyone in the outside world they had to protect themselves against, it was this man. The abbess had confided in Coira that Gavin MacNichol had offended the abbot's pride when he'd gone to Scorrybreac to corner Ella about leaving the order. To compound matters, when Father Camron had arrived at Kilbride, he'd not gotten the welcome he'd expected. Mother Shona had let her temper get the better of her for once, and had given him further offense.

She would be regretting those rash words now.

Father Camron was a man who nursed grievances like a bruise. He never forgot a slight.

"I have informed the Pope about the goings-on here," the abbot continued, undaunted by the abbess's sanguine reaction. "MacKinnon sent word to me that yet another of yer nuns has left the order … this is highly irregular."

Mother Shona inclined her head, favoring the abbot with a long-suffering look. "Did he also tell ye the reason for Sister Leanna's departure?"

The abbot's blank look told them all that the clan-chief had not.

"Sister Leanna's father died, and she was going to his burial when MacKinnon's men abducted her." The abbot's face tensed at this, his dark gaze narrowing, yet Mother Shona pressed on. "He took a novice nun against her will back to Dunan, where he planned to wed her. Sister Leanna managed to escape, and we haven't heard from her since." The abbess paused there, letting her words sink in. "I can assure ye, we had nothing to do with her disappearance. It saddens me greatly that we have lost such a devoted sister."

Father Camron watched the abbess, high spots of color appearing upon his already florid cheeks. "MacKinnon said none of this to me."

Mother Shona's expression grew grave. "That doesn't surprise me. He wouldn't wish to cast himself in a poor light."

Coira watched the abbot's heavy jaw tighten, although he held his tongue this time. This news clearly shocked him, and she could see he was debating whether to believe the abbess or not.

With a suppressed sigh, Coira dropped her gaze to her half-full bowl of stew.

The man's company was tiresome at best.

A few years ago, Father Camron had spent three months at the abbey. But during that stay, he'd been a guest, not an inquisitor. And at that time, the relationship between the abbey and the MacKinnon clan-chief hadn't deteriorated to this level. A heavy sensation settled in the pit of Coira's belly, dulling her appetite.

She'd joined the order to embrace a life of peace, stability, and order—but the chaos of the outside world was always clawing at the door, seeking a way in.

Craeg watched the nun climb up onto a stool and peg a heavy woolen curtain to the rafters. The thick material blocked out the pale light filtering in from the infirmary's tiny windows and the glow of the hearth. His stuffy corner of the building was now illuminated only by a guttering candle.

"What are ye doing, Sister?" he asked. The weakness of his voice both shocked and irritated him. It didn't sound like it belonged to him. He wasn't used to feeling this physically feeble either.

Finishing her task, Sister Coira stepped down from the stool and turned to him. Her expression was carefully composed, those startling eyes shuttered. "There's a price on yer head," she said, her voice low. "And as such, I'm taking precautions."

"Surely, no one is likely to see me in here," he pointed out.

"The abbey has visitors at the moment," the nun informed him coolly, "and we don't know how long they'll stay."

A fluttery sensation rose in Craeg's gut. The way she'd said the word 'visitors' immediately made his hackles rise; years of living as a fugitive had honed his instincts. Craeg attempted to push himself up off his nest of pillows. "I should go," he grunted. "My band will be wondering what's become of me, and I don't want to put ye and the others here at risk." An instant later a wave of sickly pain crashed over him. Sweating, Craeg sank back down onto the pillows. "Maybe not … just … yet. Looks like ye might have to put up with me a bit longer."

Sister Coira's mouth compressed as she eyed him. "Aye, ye are in no fit state to be going anywhere."

"These visitors," he wheezed. "Who are they?"

The nun's gaze met his. "The Abbot of Crossraguel Abbey ... he's here to investigate the abbess's conduct."

Craeg frowned as he struggled to focus on her words. The pain in his side was starting to subside although his body still quivered in its memory. "Really? What has she done to warrant that?"

Sister Coira let out a slow exhale, and he sensed her wariness around him. However, he wasn't about to push her. If she didn't want to speak openly, he understood. "There have been a few ... incidents ... here over the past year," Sister Coira admitted finally. She folded her arms across her chest then, an unconscious defensive gesture. "Two nuns have left the order in ... questionable circumstances."

Craeg cocked his head. "Now I'm curious."

"Aye, well some things are best not discussed."

The clipped tone of her voice didn't put him off. Instead, it merely intrigued him further. "Ye can't just leave it there."

Her gaze narrowed. "Can't I?"

They watched each other for a long moment, and Craeg suddenly became acutely aware of every detail of the woman standing before him. The voluminous black habit she wore, along with the veil and wimple that shrouded everything except her face, did their best to cancel out her femininity. And yet he saw beyond the austerity of her clothing. She was tall, which he liked, and the generous swell of her breasts was evident despite the heavy material of the habit.

But it was her face that drew him in. The blend of strength, vulnerability, and sensuality in her features.

What a pity she's a nun, he mused. Life had been a fight for survival of late, and there had been no time for women. Yet he'd never met one that intrigued him like this Sister of Kilbride did.

"Around a month ago, I met a young woman who claimed she'd been a nun here at Kilbride," he said finally, shattering his silent appreciation. "Her name was Leanna."

Sister Coira's lips parted, her gaze widening. "Where did ye see her?"

"She was fleeing Dunan ... with the aid of Ross Campbell," Craeg replied, his gaze steady as it continued to hold hers. "They entered the valley not far from where my band camped, and we hosted them for a night." He paused there, aware that her expression had turned stern. Craeg made a face. "Worry not, I didn't take them prisoner ... although I made an error of judgment during their stay that cost me dearly." His chest constricted then as he remembered the mess Brochan had made. He should have seen that coming. "One of my men tried to use Leanna and Ross to blackmail my brother ... and everything went to hell."

Sister Coira didn't answer him, although her face now wore a wintry expression. Craeg knew he wasn't giving a good account of his band, yet he forced himself on. Nonetheless, it was an effort to keep eye contact. His throat thickened as he continued. "The man, Brochan, under-estimated my brother—we all did. Before he killed Brochan, MacKinnon tortured him ... and discovered where we were hiding."

Craeg dragged a shaky hand through his hair and sank back into the nest of pillows behind him. "Ross and Leanna helped us defend our camp when MacKinnon's men attacked, but it wasn't enough to save us. Many of my band fell that day, and I took the arrow that landed me here."

Sister Coira was watching him, her gaze shuttered. Craeg thought she might comment, but when she didn't, he pushed on, concluding his tale. "When the fight turned against us, I told Ross and Leanna to run. I hope they managed to elude MacKinnon."

He stopped speaking then, his eyes flickering shut. Their conversation, short though it was, had drained him, the weight of guilt settling over him. Brochan had been one of his closest friends. Aye, he'd acted foolishly, but that didn't make Craeg feel any less to blame for his end.

"They're safe," Sister Coira said finally. "Mother Shona received a letter around two weeks ago. We don't know where they are now ... but they've left Skye and made a new life together."

Craeg's eyes snapped open, and a little of the heaviness lifted. "That's good," he replied, his mouth rising at the corners into a half-smile. "Ye could see Campbell was in love with the lass. At least life has happy endings for some of us."

It was her turn to incline her head then, her gaze questioning. "Aye," the nun murmured, favoring him with a rare smile that was tinged with sadness. "Leanna wasn't suited to be a nun. Her father sent her to Kilbride only in order to protect her from yer brother; her heart was never in it. I miss her all the same though."

Again, Craeg felt a pull toward the woman before him. What a contradiction she was: at once strong and capable, yet with a softness, a vulnerability, just beneath the surface.

"What about ye, Sister Coira?" he asked finally. "Why did ye take the veil?"

The moment he asked the question, Craeg realized he'd overstepped. It was like watching a door slam shut between them. Sister Coira took an abrupt step back, her jaw tightening and a shadow passing over her eyes.

"I came here for a better life," she replied, her tone clipped. With that, the nun turned, pushed aside the curtain, and departed the alcove, leaving Craeg with his own company.

6

Sickness

DREW MACKINNON STEPPED out of her bed-chamber and closed the door firmly behind her. Leaning up against it, she inhaled deeply, a chill seeping through her. Behind her, she could hear the rumble of the healer's voice and the weak sounds of his patient's reply.

Mother Mary, save us.

Drew clenched her eyes shut and wished she was a pious woman. Her mother had tried to instill religious fervor within her years earlier, but the hours spent kneeling on the stone floor of the kirk, praying for forgiveness for her numerous sins, hadn't made the slightest difference. If anything, it had made Drew rebel further.

But a strong faith would be welcome now.

"Lady Drew?" A gruff male voice intruded. Drew's eyes snapped open, and she glanced left to where Carr Broderick had halted. He was watching her, his grey-blue eyes clouded with concern. "Are ye unwell?"

Swallowing, Drew shook her head. "No … but my handmaid, Tyra, is." She paused there before forcing the words out. "The healer thinks she has the plague."

Plague. The word hung between them like a death sentence.

Broderick's features tightened. "Is he sure?"

"The signs are there." Bile stung the back of Drew's throat. "Her fingertips have blackened, and she has swellings under her arms and at her groin."

Did she imagine it, or did Broderick's face pale at this description? The symptoms of the sickness that was now sweeping across Scotland were clear enough.

There could be no doubt.

"How is he treating her?" he asked, the rough edge to the warrior's voice betraying his alarm.

Drew screwed up her face. "In the usual fashion … not that it seems to do much good. Blood-letting and a tonic of vinegar and heather honey. He's rubbed raw onion over the swellings on her skin … the chamber reeks of it."

Their gazes fused then and held for a long moment. It was unusual for Drew to interact with her brother's right-hand in such a fashion. She and Carr

Broderick had lived under the same roof for over fifteen years now, but until recently their paths rarely crossed. However, with Ross Campbell's disappearance, Broderick had taken on his role as Captain of the Dunan Guard. These days, the warrior was never far from her brother's side.

"I should go and inform Duncan," she said, breaking the tense silence between them. "It's the first sickness inside the broch … he will want to know."

"I will tell him, milady," Broderick replied with a brusque nod.

The tension that had turned Drew's shoulders to stone eased just a little. She'd been avoiding her brother recently and had taken to having most of her meals alone in her solar. It wasn't like her to shrink from confrontation—but she needed time to think, to plan.

Of late, Duncan had become not only a danger to himself, but to the MacKinnon clan. Ross Campbell had been her only ally here—and just hours before she'd helped him flee Dunan, he'd agreed to support her if she ever made a move against her brother.

Campbell was no good to her now though. She didn't even know if he still lived. And with his absence, she was truly alone here.

She could ask Carr Broderick for help, but the man was an unknown quantity. It appeared his loyalty to her brother was unshakable. She couldn't confide in him.

"I shall go and inform the servants then," Drew said, injecting a brisk note into her voice. She needed to get ahold of herself. Fear of the sickness wouldn't help any of them. The number of cases inside Dunan village was rising sharply with each passing day—it had only been a matter of time before someone within the broch fell ill.

And now that it had happened, they'd have to deal with it.

"Very good, milady," Broderick replied. The usual impassive mask the man wore had slipped back into place. You would never have thought the news about the sickness had alarmed him. Drew admired the man's self-control, his strength.

Watching him turn and stride off down the hallway in search of her brother, Drew inhaled slowly and wiped her damp palms upon the skirts of her kirtle.

Aye, they'd all have to be strong in the face of what lay ahead.

Carr Broderick was sweating as he stood before MacKinnon—a chill sweat that made his skin crawl. Dread ran its cold fingertip down his spine, causing his pulse to slow. Yet he kept his reaction to Lady Drew's news hidden under a mask it had taken him years to master.

He wasn't the only one shaken by news that the sickness had entered the broch. In all the time he'd served the MacKinnons, he'd never seen Lady Drew scared. Yet, the pallor upon her lovely face, the alarm in those iron-grey eyes, had made him want to reach for her, enfold her in his arms.

Something he would never do.

Lady Drew was likely to scratch his eyes out if he ever attempted such a thing.

Nonetheless, he'd noted the slight tremor of her body, the way her throat had bobbed as she swallowed. She was alarmed, and she was right to be. The devil had entered their home. How many of them would survive his visit?

A scowl split Duncan MacKinnon's forehead once Broderick had delivered his news. The clan-chief sat before the hearth, a goblet of wine in hand, his wolfhound, Bran, curled at his feet.

"If the maid is ill, I don't want her in my broch," he growled, his voice slurring slightly. It was still an hour or two till the noon meal, yet MacKinnon was clearly not on his first sup of wine. Ever since Lady Leanna's disappearance, MacKinnon seemed always to have a goblet of wine in hand—a habit that had turned his already mercurial temper into something even more dangerous.

Carr chose his words very carefully around the clan-chief these days.

"But the healer is attending her," he ventured. "Surely, it's dangerous to move the lass?"

"Get her out of my broch," MacKinnon ground out. He rose unsteadily to his feet, stepped over his sleeping hound, and stumbled to the sideboard, where he helped himself to another goblet of wine. "And burn her bedding ... that is my final word. Don't argue with me, Broderick."

Silence filled the clan-chief's solar. The window was open, revealing a monochrome sky beyond. A breeze, chill for this time of year, blew inside causing the lump of peat in the hearth to glow bright red. However, the draft couldn't mask the stale odor of wine and sweat that emanated from the clan-chief.

Carr studied MacKinnon as he returned to his place by the hearth and sank back down in his chair. Of late, his master's state of mind had started to concern him. MacKinnon had always liked to drink, but there was a recklessness to his behavior in the past days, a bleakness in his gaze that worried Carr.

Ross was the clever one, he mused. *He got out while he could.*

No one here knew that he'd caught up with Ross Campbell and Lady Leanna in Knock, a fishing village on Skye's south coast, where they'd been about to board a merchant's birlinn. He'd confronted Ross, but had let him leave all the same.

Today, he wished he'd gone with him.

He wondered what MacKinnon would do if he knew. Most likely lunge for his dirk before plunging it into Carr's belly. If the clan-chief ever discovered what he had done, his life would be forfeit.

"How long are ye going to stand there, gawping at me?" MacKinnon eventually growled. "Instead of bothering me with ill news, how about some good tidings instead?" He swirled the wine in his goblet, his grey eyes narrowing as he fixed Carr with a glare. "How goes the search for Craeg the Bastard?"

Carr returned the clan-chief's stare. "I have half the Dunan Guard out searching for him now, MacKinnon," he replied. "We have redoubled our efforts, especially along the borders and coast. He may be trying to leave Skye."

A muscle ticked on MacKinnon's jaw at this admission. Of course, as much as his half-brother had caused him trouble over the years, the clan-chief didn't want him to move on. Instead, he wanted the man caught.

A heavy sensation settled upon Carr then, like two large hands had just fastened over his shoulders and were pushing him into the floor. He would never admit as much to MacKinnon, but he held out little hope of finding the outlaw leader, or his band of followers. In all the years they had caused strife here, MacKinnon had only been able to get close to them a couple of times.

They were ghosts, appearing and disappearing at will.

Some of the folk of this land actually believed that the outlaws were Fair Folk who disappeared into fairy mounds at dusk. However, Carr knew better. He'd seen the village hidden deep within that lost valley. After the skirmish with the band a month earlier, he'd searched the ruins of the camp, and had been surprised to see how settled they'd been there. He'd discovered a forge, store huts full of food, and fields full of crops on the southern slopes of the valley.

They weren't supernatural beings; they were just very good at hiding.

"The Bastard mustn't slip through our net," MacKinnon said, his voice rough now. "I want ye to bring him to me in chains."

Duncan MacKinnon shifted in his chair and stared moodily down at his goblet of wine. The rich liquid gleamed darkly up at him, but after Carr's visit, he'd lost his taste for it. He'd sent his right-hand on his way and was grateful to be left alone in the solar once more.

But, of course, that left him alone with his thoughts. And they were bleak these days.

Muttering a curse, Duncan ran a tired hand over his face. Fatigue pulled him down, making his limbs feel leaden and his body ache. He was only forty winters old, so why did he suddenly feel like an old man?

With a sigh, he set his goblet aside on the stone edge of the hearth, and leaned down, ruffling Bran's ears. The charcoal grey brindled wolfhound stirred from its sleep and sat up, pushing against his leg.

Warmth rushed through Duncan, and he let the hound lick his hand.

No matter what happened in his life, despite his many disappointments and betrayals, he could always rely on Bran. Dogs were uncomplicated. No matter what he did, Bran would remain at his side.

Heaving himself up out of his chair, Duncan walked unsteadily to the open window of the solar. There, he braced himself against the stone ledge, closing his eyes for a few moments as his head spun. He'd consumed too much wine on an empty stomach. A foolish thing to do.

I must stop drinking so much. With everything he had to deal with at the moment, he needed a clear head. He needed to be strong. And that also meant that he had to start eating properly again.

Duncan opened his eyes. He would make sure he cleared his platter at the noon meal today. He would also resume his afternoon swordplay sessions with Carr. At his age, he couldn't afford to let his physical condition slip.

The clan-chief's gaze swiveled then to the view beyond his window. He spied industry in the bailey below: men shoeing horses, and servants carrying barrels of ale and sacks of grain into the broch. Beyond, the roofs of Dunan village itself rose. Outside the walls, stark against the jade pinewood, he saw smoke rising in a dark column.

A lump rose in Duncan's throat at the sight of it.

Funeral pyres.

Just after daybreak, he'd been returning from a ride out with his hounds when he'd seen the folk of Dunan carrying the dead out of the fortress.

There had been a dozen of them, and he'd heard that at least another dozen were gravely ill in 'The Warren'. The sickness now had Dunan in its grip, and he was powerless to stop it.

The pressure in Duncan's throat increased, clamping down and making it hard to breathe. This stronghold belonged to him, and the lives within it were his responsibility.

Yet for the first time since he had assumed the role as clan-chief of the MacKinnons, Duncan wished the charge had fallen to someone else.

7
Unnatural Behavior

ONE DAY SLID into the next, and Coira grew increasingly jittery and on edge.

Kilbride felt overrun with men.

Coira didn't like it. Her past had left her with a distrust of males. The best thing about coming to live at Kilbride had been the ability to thrive in a female environment. She didn't need to be wary of her companions here or drop her gaze in fear of inadvertently enticing a man. She didn't need to lock her door at night, scared that some drunken letch might stumble in and collapse on top of her. It had happened once at *The Goat and Goose*. But here, Mother Shona ruled. And she was a woman who taught others to be strong. She'd given Coira skills that made her feel as if she was taking back just a little control over a world that had nearly destroyed her.

One evening, as the shadows lengthened and a chill breeze blew in from the sea, Coira decided that she needed to relieve some tension, to forget about the worries that plagued her.

It was bad enough that they were harboring a fugitive—although Coira had slowly relaxed in Craeg's presence over the past days—but they now had Father Camron and his flock to contend with. The mere sight of the abbot's self-righteous face put her teeth on edge.

She'd deliberately avoided practicing with her quarter-staff since Father Camron's arrival. However, this evening Coira decided to take a calculated risk and find a private spot away from prying eyes.

Retrieving the stave from her cell, she made her way to the eastern edge of the abbey grounds, to a secluded area where a small orchard of apple and pear trees grew on the far side of the vegetable plots.

The trees were in full leaf now, the first tiny bulbs of fruit just making an appearance.

Carrying her staff loosely at her side, Coira entered the orchard. A little of the strain within her unknotted, and she deepened her breathing, letting the stress of the past few days release.

In the midst of the orchard, in a small clearing, she halted. There, she began to go through her drills. Immediately, as the staff whistled through the air, Coira started to feel better. The physical exertion eased the tightness in her chest and loosened the rigid muscles in her neck, back, and shoulders. She hadn't realized she'd been so tense.

Sweat trickled down Coira's back between her shoulder blades as she went through her drills again and again—thrusting, spinning, and blocking with her staff. Her blood pulsed in her ears, her breathing now coming in gasps. She had almost reached the limits of her endurance, and was about to stop, when she heard stifled gasps behind her.

Whipping around, Coira's gaze settled upon two black-robed figures standing but a handful of yards away.

Ice slithered down her sweaty back, and her fingers clenched around the staff.

Two young monks, their smooth faces slack with shock, gaped at her. It was almost comical, for the pair stared as if they'd just seen her sprout horns and a forked tail. A heartbeat passed, and then another—and a sickening sensation clawed up Coira's throat from her belly.

How was she going to explain this to Father Camron?

"This is unnatural behavior."

The abbot's voice boomed through the chapter house, making the stained glass windows that lined one side of the small building vibrate.

Eyes downcast, her gaze fixed upon the flagstone floor, Coira wondered how Mother Shona was going to respond. She'd barely been able to meet the woman's gaze since being called in here. Guilt compressed Coira's chest, and she started to sweat. Not from exertion this time but dread.

"Sister Coira has a different background to most of the nuns here," the abbess finally replied. To Coira's surprise, the woman's voice was serene. Raising her chin, she shifted her attention to where Mother Shona stood, facing the abbot. Hands clasped before her, the crucifix about her neck glinting in the light of the surrounding banks of tallow candles, the abbess appeared unruffled. "Before coming to live with us, she had to fend for herself. She developed skills that most women do not."

The abbess's attention shifted then to Coira. "I have told ye, child. Ye are safe here. There is no need to keep up such ungodly skills."

"I am sorry, Mother." Coira dropped to one knee before the abbess, allowing her to make the sign of the cross above her. "With all the talk of pestilence and outlaws, I grew fearful for our safety here. I wish only to protect the abbey should evil men attack us."

Coira's contrition wasn't feigned. She was truly sorry for putting Mother Shona in this position. She would apologize properly later though when the abbot wasn't present.

"Foolish, presumptuous woman." Father Camron's harsh voice slammed into her. It grated like a rusty saw. "How dare ye take matters into yer own hands? Have ye not learned to trust in God? Ye have no need to take up arms ... not if yer faith is strong enough." His face twisted then. "Ye are no better than that *witch*, Annella MacNichol. I saw how she wielded knives. Such skill is unnatural in a woman!"

Tearing her gaze from the abbess, and remaining upon one knee, Coira forced herself to look at the abbot. His high-colored face had gone the shade of boiled beet. His dark eyes blazed, and his heavy jaw was locked in rage. Wisely, she did not contradict him. Instead, she swallowed what little pride she had left, clasped her hands before her, and bent her head. "I am sorry, Father. I should know better. Please forgive me for my sin. Please forgive me for my lack of trust."

A brittle silence settled in the chapter house. The three of them were alone in here. A small mercy at least; Coira was spared an audience to witness her humiliation. Even so, her belly clenched and indignation pulsed like an ember under her breastbone. Her faith was strong these days. Mother Shona had taught them that a nun could do the Lord's work while learning how to defend herself. There was no shame in it, and it galled her to apologize to the abbot.

It had been years since she'd knelt before a man, and she hated the feeling.

When the abbot spoke again, his voice hadn't softened. "It is not entirely yer fault, Sister. Mother Shona has clearly been too lenient with ye over the years." His attention shifted to the abbess, his gaze narrowing. "This transgression should never have happened. Ye should take a rod to this nun for her behavior."

Coira's breathing hitched. The heat that pulsed within her now threatened to ignite into a raging furnace. She couldn't believe the abbot would suggest such a thing, and yet she shouldn't have been surprised. Just the night before, she'd seen him smack one of his monks around the ear for accidentally spilling some ale during supper.

Shifting her attention back to the abbess, Coira saw, for the first time, Mother Shona's calm splinter. Her jaw tensed, and she frowned. "There will be no violence here, Father. I have never lifted a hand to any of the nuns here. And I never will."

Father Camron snorted. "Well, I have no such qualms, Mother. Find me a good stick, a rod of willow will do nicely, and I will see to this nun for ye." He glanced back at Coira, his dark eyes gleaming. "I'll teach her a lesson she won't forget."

"I repeat, Father, there will be no violence at Kilbride." The steel in Mother Shona's voice was evident now. She was done holding back her irritation with this man. Coira tensed at this realization. The last thing she wanted was for Mother Shona to lose her temper with the abbot. He could make life very difficult for them all if he so chose.

Witnessing the stand-off between the pair, a hollow sensation lodged itself in the pit of Coira's belly. Mother Shona wasn't going to back down—and from the look on the abbot's face, neither was he.

"Sister Coira knew harsh treatment before coming to live here." Mother Shona's voice was low and firm, although the hard edge was still there. "I vowed that she would only ever know kindness within these walls."

Coira's throat thickened at these words. It was true; the abbess had always treated her with respect.

However, Mother Shona hadn't yet finished. "The Sisters of Kilbride entrust me with their well-being. I will not betray that trust," she continued, her gaze never wavering from the abbot. "Sister Coira will spend the night praying before the altar in the kirk for her transgression. That will be sufficient punishment."

"That's not enough," Father Camron countered, a vein now pulsing in his temple. "Ye need to set an example!"

Mother Shona folded her arms across her chest, her chin lifting as she eyeballed her adversary. "And I am," she said, her tone hardening. "If one of my flock strays, they will be guided back to the fold. My methods differ from yers, Father, but in the end, we both serve our Lord the best we can. That's all that matters."

Coira welcomed the solitude and peace inside the kirk. A night here was supposed to be her penance, yet part of her actually looked forward to it.

After supper and Compline, the abbey entered the Great Silence. Usually, she'd have gone to the infirmary to tend to her patient, but the abbess had insisted that she was to go to the kirk immediately to begin her prayers. As such, Coira had sent Sister Mina to attend to Craeg in her stead. The nun would bring the man some gruel and bread, and check that his fever hadn't returned.

Coira would visit him again in the morning.

A frown marred her brow when she thought about her patient. With each passing day, his presence here grew riskier for them all. Craeg kept insisting he should leave, and yet he still wasn't well enough to do so. Coira hoped Sister Mina would be careful when she went to the infirmary.

Strangely, she felt a little envious that the novice would get to spend time with Craeg this evening, would hear of his escapades with his band of outlaws. She liked hearing his stories, but tonight she'd do penance instead.

Kneeling upon the stone floor of the kirk, Coira winced. The flagstones were ice-cold. Despite that the warmer months were now upon them, the air inside the kirk was chill, and it remained so even on the hottest days in summer.

It was going to be a cold, uncomfortable night.

She had no cushion to protect her knees from the cold stone, and after a short while, her kneecaps began to ache, numbness creeping up her thighs. But, hands clasped before her, Coira didn't move. Head bowed, she murmured prayers of penance, asking the Lord for forgiveness for her sins.

However, she didn't ask forgiveness for practicing with her quarter-staff—only that she'd let selfishness blind her to the risk she was taking.

She was truly sorry about that. Sorry too that she'd compromised Mother Shona.

Slowly, the tension ebbed out of her. As always, when she prayed in the kirk, Coira felt God's presence settle upon her like a warm, comforting blanket. She hadn't been devout before entering the abbey, but the kindness she'd found here had made her change her views.

The evening stretched on, and eventually, the witching hour approached. Twice Coira heard someone enter the kirk. The first time, it was a gentle presence, and although Coira didn't look up from her prayers, she sensed that it was Mother Shona, checking in on her. The second visitor arrived much later, at the time of night when the world seemed to hold its breath. The heavy scuff of sandaled feet on stone approaching from behind warned her that it was not the abbess or any of the other nuns.

A man approached.

Coira's spine stiffened, her body growing taut. Even after all these years, her instincts were honed around men. After over a decade now, she still didn't trust them. It couldn't be Craeg, for the man was barely able to rise from his sickbed. No, she knew, without even glancing up, who her visitor was.

Father Camron.

The footsteps halted behind her, and she heard the rasp of a man's breathing. When he spoke, his voice was barely above a whisper. "Ye are a wicked woman, Sister Coira. Don't think yer averted gaze, and yer feeble apologies, have fooled me. I see through it all."

Coira's mouth went dry, her heart hammering against her ribs. Wisely, she kept her gaze downcast, her hands clasped tightly in prayer. She squeezed her eyes shut and continued to murmur her prayer. "Please, Lord, forgive us our trespasses, as we forgive those who trespass against us, and lead us not into temptation, but deliver us from evil."

"Empty words," the abbot murmured. "But lucky for ye, the abbess guards ye all with the fierceness of a mother hen." She heard the whisper of his feet on stone as he moved closer still. Coira's skin prickled, her breathing accelerating.

If he touches me, I'll defend myself.

"But be warned." His voice lowered further still. "I'm watching ye."

8

Until My Last Breath

"I WAS HOPING to see ye, Sister," Craeg greeted Coira with a smile when she pulled aside the hanging and stepped inside the alcove. However, an instant later, his expression grew serious. "Ye look as if ye haven't slept?"

Coira huffed and let the hanging fall behind her. "I haven't."

The air was close in here. She didn't like it. Coira believed that the sick should have free-flowing air around them, for it chased away ill humors. But it was too risky to set this patient up near the window. One of Father Camron's monks could peek into the infirmary at any time. The hanging wouldn't keep prying eyes at bay forever, but it was the best she could do in the meantime.

Stiffly, for her knees ached with each step, Coira made her way toward the sleeping pallet. In one hand she carried a bowl of warm water, in the other her basket of healing herbs.

Observing her patient, Coira was pleased to see that color had returned to Craeg's cheeks. A sheen of sweat no longer covered his skin, and his eyes weren't fever bright as they had been. He sat, propped up on a nest of pillows.

The man exuded an impatient energy—Coira could see he wasn't the type used to being forced to stay still.

"I sometimes have trouble sleeping too," he admitted with a boyish grin. "Maybe it's the result of a guilty conscience."

"I sleep like a bairn," Coira replied, arching an eyebrow. "It wasn't restlessness that caused my sleepless night. I transgressed yesterday, and so had to spend the night praying as penance."

His gaze widened. "A nun who doesn't follow the rules ... I'm intrigued."

"The abbot wasn't," Coira answered, breaking eye contact as she set the basket down on the end of the bed. "How are ye feeling?"

Craeg didn't answer right away, and Coira eventually glanced up, frustrated that he wasn't letting her change the subject. She was tired and irritable. She didn't want to discuss herself. Their gazes held for a long moment before his smile faded. "Much better, I guess. My side doesn't hurt as much as it did. Can I go now?" She caught the restlessness in his voice.

Coira frowned. "It depends on how yer wound is faring."

"Take a look at it then." Craeg sank back against the pillows and pushed down the coverlet covering his bare torso.

After a moment's hesitation, Coira moved close to him. Even injured and weakened, this man had a strong physical presence. His chest was broad and heavily muscled, with a light dusting of dark hair across it that narrowed to a thin strip at his belly. And that strip then disappeared under the waistband of his breeches.

Coira hurriedly averted her gaze. It wouldn't do for a nun to stare at a man's groin, even if it was clothed.

Stepping forward, she removed Craeg's bandage with deft, practiced ease. Observing the wound to his flank, Coira relaxed a little. She had packed the arrow hole with a poultice of woundwort, and it had done its work beautifully, withdrawing the evil humors from the flesh. The wound no longer festered, and it was beginning to heal.

Coira glanced up, catching Craeg's eye once more. "It looks like it is mending well."

Craeg's mouth lifted at the corners. "Thanks to ye."

Coira smiled. This man had a warmth and charisma that was hard to resist. No wonder he had inspired a band of loyal followers—men and women who lived as fugitives simply because they believed in him.

I'd believe in him too.

Catching herself, Coira straightened up.

Mother Mary, what a foolish thought.

Coira set her jaw and began to clean the wound. Fatigue had clearly turned her witless this morning. She then reached for her basket and extracted a small wooden pestle and mortar. "I need to mix up some more woundwort," she murmured. "Just to make sure the injury doesn't sour again."

"I should leave," Craeg said after a pause. "My band is waiting for me ... if I don't reappear soon, they will think I have died here."

Coira glanced up to find him watching her, his expression shuttered. "Ye are gaining strength," she replied, holding his gaze, "but ideally ye should rest for another day or two before moving on."

A muscle bunched in his jaw. "I don't have a day or two. My brother still hunts me ... I can't stay here."

"I'm aware of that ... but if ye leave before ye are ready, all my work will be undone."

Silence fell between them for a long moment, before Coira moved to the small table next to the bed and lowered herself onto a stool; it was hard not to groan as she did so. Her knees felt as if they belonged to a crone this morning. Trying to ignore her aching back and legs, she transferred a handful of fresh herbs to her mortar. She then began to mash them.

"The hatred between ye and MacKinnon," she said finally, as the hush drew out between them. "It runs deep?"

He huffed a bitter laugh. "Aye ... deeper than most realize."

"Clan-chiefs sire bastard bairns all the time," Coira pointed out as she continued to mash the woundwort into a paste.

"Aye, but few threaten the order of things," Craeg replied, his voice lowering. Coira could tell from his tone that he didn't want to continue this conversation. But, glancing up at him, Coira's interest blossomed further.

"How so?" she asked.

Craeg's face tensed, and Coira instantly regretted the question. What was she doing interrogating the man anyway? It was best she knew as little about him as possible, best that she healed him and then got rid of him.

"I see ye know of my origins," he said, a wry tone creeping into his voice.

Coira nodded. These days, few folk in this territory didn't know that Craeg was the result of Jock MacKinnon plowing a whore. The story had often been told at *The Goat and Goose* during Coira's time in the brothel. Years earlier, Craeg's mother was said to have worked there before succumbing to consumption.

"I grew up in a brothel," he said, glancing away. Did she imagine it, or did he seem embarrassed by this admission? "While Ma worked, it was my job to clear tables, empty hearths, and run errands for the woman who ran the place."

Coira tensed. *Maude.* "Were ye ill-treated there?" she asked softly.

Craeg's mouth twisted, although he shook his head. "Not particularly ... I was seen more like an annoying hound that gets under everyone's feet. Although as I grew into a strapping lad, I had my uses. It became my role to throw out any patrons who became violent or mouthy. Maude—the woman in charge—kept me on, even after Ma died ... and that's how I met my brother."

Coira stopped mashing the woundwort, her breathing slowing. She hadn't heard this part of the story.

"Our father continued to visit *The Goat and Goose*, even after Ma died," Craeg continued. His gaze looked past her now as if he were no longer seeing his surroundings but his old life. "And one day he brought Duncan along ... so that his son might bed his first woman." Craeg paused there, his gaze snapping back to the present. He favored Coira with a harsh smile. "It was hate at first sight."

"He knew who ye were?"

"Aye ... everyone in Dunan did."

Coira swallowed hard before picking up the mortar and carrying it over to Craeg. Perched on the edge of the straw-stuffed mattress, she began packing his cleaned wound with the paste. She wished now that she hadn't been so curious about Craeg's past. Even the mention of Duncan MacKinnon made a chill shiver down her spine.

"Our father didn't help matters," Craeg continued, a bitter note in his voice. "He acknowledged who I was ... in front of Duncan ... deliberately provoking him."

Coira's chin raised, her gaze narrowing. "Why would he do that?"

"He wanted his son—his *legitimate* son—to prove himself, I guess. He wished to see if Duncan would be threatened by me ... and he was." Craeg paused there, his eyelids fluttering closed, his face going into spasm. Coira knew that although she was trying to be gentle, she was hurting him as she applied the salve.

"It's all right, I'm almost done here," she murmured.

Craeg nodded, and she saw that sweat had beaded upon his forehead. She didn't know how the man thought he was going to get up and walk out of here today. His injury, and the sickness that had followed, had seriously weakened him.

"We fought once, in the brothel," Craeg said finally, his voice rough with pain. He continued to keep his eyes shut, his big body tense while Coira completed her ministrations. "He was rough with one of the lasses, and she was in tears. I confronted him downstairs, and he attacked me." A smile curved Craeg's mouth then, unexpectedly. "I split his lip, blackened his eye, and sent him away." The mirth faded as quickly as it had appeared. "And that was when the tide turned against me.

"Until then, I'd been liked in Dunan ... but as the months passed, the mood changed. Vendors refused to serve me at market, women spat at me when I passed them on the street, and when business slowed at *The Goat and Goose*, I was blamed. I'd just passed my sixteenth winter when I found myself living rough, sleeping in alleyways and begging for crumbs. No one in Dunan would give me a job."

Coira sucked in a breath. She knew what hardship was, what it was like to look hunger in the eye. The outlaw didn't realize how much she understood what he'd gone through. "Why didn't ye leave?" she asked finally.

Craeg's eyes opened, and for a moment, their gazes fused. "I eventually decided that I would," he replied softly, "on the day my father died, I realized that there was no future for me in Dunan. Duncan, who was eighteen at the time, would become clan-chief, and what little protection I'd had from him would be gone. But that last night, as I scrabbled for scraps of bread to feed me on the journey I planned to take north into MacLeod lands, Duncan and a group of his friends found me."

Craeg paused there, scrubbing his face with his fist. Coira realized then that this was a tale he rarely shared with anyone. Even though it had happened a long time ago, it clearly still pained him to dredge up the memories.

"One against six isn't good odds," Craeg said, his tone wry now. "They beat me bloody, and then Duncan drew his dirk and slashed me across the face with it." Craeg reached up, a fingertip tracing the fine white scar that ran from his temple to his cheek, skirting his left eye. "They then dumped me in the river outside Dunan and left me for dead."

"But ye didn't die," Coira finished the story for him. "And ye have plagued Duncan MacKinnon ever since."

Craeg flashed her a hard smile, his gaze gleaming. "Aye ... and I will continue to do so until I draw my last breath."

Craeg watched the nun pack up her supplies. Her movements were deft and purposeful, matching the resolute expression upon her face.

He drank her in.

He'd missed her last night. When one of the other nuns had tended to him, he'd been disappointed. As much as he hated to admit it, Sister Coira had gotten under his skin.

Why else would he have been so candid with her?

He rarely spoke of his past. Telling the tale of how his half-brother had nearly killed him still left a sting of humiliation in its wake. That humiliation had fueled his need for vengeance, and he felt it again now.

He liked the way Sister Coira listened to him, the understanding and compassion in those lovely eyes. She lived a sheltered existence here behind the walls of Kilbride, yet he'd sensed that she grasped exactly how difficult his upbringing had been. There had been no shock in her eyes when he'd spoken of his quest for revenge.

Somehow, she understood.

Ye shouldn't be lusting after a nun, his conscience needled him as he continued to observe Sister Coira. She had almost finished tidying up and would soon leave him alone. *Ye shall go straight to hell.*

A grim smile stretched Craeg's lips then. Luckily for him, he wasn't a pious man. As a lad, he'd regularly gone to the kirk to pray. Father Athol had been good to him, had given him soup and bread when his mother was too busy to feed him. Yet despite the priest's best efforts, Craeg had never embraced God. Maybe he'd seen too much ugliness already, even as a lad.

"Sister Coira," he said finally when she picked up her basket and moved toward the hanging that separated his dark space from the rest of the infirmary. "Would ye stay with me a while longer?"

She halted and turned to him, her eyes widening. "I shouldn't really," she murmured, favoring him with a half-smile. "I have chores to do."

"Just for a wee while?" he replied, returning her smile. He knew he could be charming when he wanted, although Sister Coira seemed immune. "I've spent too much time alone of late … it sends my thoughts to dark places."

Her expression softened at this, and her gaze shadowed. Once again, he got the feeling that she understood him better than anyone ever had. How was that possible?

"Very well," Sister Coira said softly, setting the basket down on the end of the bed and moving toward the stool. "I suppose I can spare a little time."

9
Ships in the Fog

"CRAEG CAN'T REMAIN here."

The tension in Mother Shona's voice made Coira glance up from the psalm she'd been reading. The abbess closed the leather-bound history volume perched upon her knee. She then fixed Coira with a level look.

"It's been over a week … he has to go."

Coira let out a soft sigh. "He's still weak, Mother."

"That may be, but the abbot is showing no signs of leaving. Just this morning, he informed me that he wishes to inspect all the buildings within the abbey to ensure 'good practices' are being upheld."

Coira's belly tightened at this news. "How long before he or his monks venture into the infirmary?"

"Exactly." The abbess's small frame bristled with indignation, her brown eyes hard, and her jaw tight. Her outrage at Father Camron's interference was palpable. The two women sat in the abbess's hall. It was a cool, grey afternoon, and Vespers was approaching. Often, Mother Shona spent this time alone, but over the past few days, she'd asked Coira to join her.

Coira wondered if it was to keep her out of trouble, and out of the abbot's way.

"I'm sorry about that incident … with the quarter-staff," Coira said after a pause. She hadn't properly apologized to the abbess about that, although she'd meant to. "It was a foolish thing to do. I wasn't thinking."

The abbess sighed, leaning back in her chair. Her gaze shifted to where a single lump of peat glowed in the hearth. It was proving to be a cool summer, and without a fire burning, the air inside the hall would have been unpleasantly chill and damp. "I don't blame ye, Sister … it's hard to break a routine ye are used to. But unfortunately, Camron is sniffing around like a hound on the scent, looking for anything that will damn me." Her gaze shadowed. "And sooner or later, he shall find it."

Alarm fluttered up under Coira's ribcage. It was unlike the abbess to sound so defeated. "No, he won't," she said firmly. "He will stay on a few months, like he did last time, and leave Kilbride empty-handed." She shut the book of psalms with a 'snap'. "Ye are right ... even if he still has some healing to do, the outlaw has to leave. I will see to it this evening."

Mother Shona fixed her with a wary look. "Be careful, Sister. The abbot's monks hide in shadows and listen at open windows and doorways. If ye will take Craeg out of here tonight, ye must wait until well after the witching hour."

"Make sure to leave the gates ajar," Coira replied with a nod, her pulse accelerating as she contemplated just how careful they'd have to be. There was only one way in or out of the abbey. "We will have to leave quickly."

"I will ask Sisters Mina and Firtha to keep watch on the gates tonight," the abbess replied, her brown eyes narrowing. "They will let ye know when it is safe."

The two women watched each other for a long moment, and Coira noted the lines of strain on the abbess's face—lines that hadn't been there a year earlier. The troubles with Ella and Leanna had taken their toll upon her.

A chill settled in the pit of Coira's belly then, a foreboding. For years, Mother Shona had managed to keep the rest of the world at bay. Kilbride had grown strong and prosperous under her guidance, and they'd been able to help the folk of this corner of the isle as a result.

But now, the defenses that the abbess had built were starting to crumble. Mother Shona knew it, and Coira felt it too—the sensation that control was slowly slipping through their fingers.

The future of this abbey now teetered upon the edge of a blade, and it would take very little to topple them all off it.

※

The wind moaned and sighed against the stone walls of the infirmary, and made the roof creak. The noise was reassuring, for Coira had worried that it would be a still evening, one of those nights when the slightest noise traveled. Even so, the waiting was stretching her nerves to breaking point.

Restless, Coira shifted upon the uncomfortable stool and spared a glance at the man who sat upon the edge of the sleeping pallet.

Clad in the cleaned vest and braies he'd arrived in, but with a new woolen cloak about his broad shoulders, Craeg was dressed and ready to go.

He looked as on edge as Coira felt, his hands clenching and unclenching, his jaw tense.

"How much longer?" he asked finally, his voice a harsh whisper.

"Sister Mina will arrive soon," she replied, hoping that would be the case. "We wanted to wait until we were sure *everyone* was abed."

"But surely no one is awake at this hour?"

Coira huffed. "Ye would be surprised ... the abbot and his monks like to keep us all on our toes."

Craeg frowned at this news. "He's determined to find something to discredit the abbess, I take it?"

"Aye ... and that's why ye must go tonight."

They fell silent again while the wind continued to whine and rattle. Over the past days, the silences between Coira and Craeg had often been companionable. After he'd told her the brutal story of exactly why he hated his half-brother, Coira had felt an odd kinship toward the outlaw.

He had no idea of her own history with MacKinnon, or of her past at all, but knowing that they'd once lived under the same roof—albeit during different timeframes—made her feel as if this man understood her a little.

His mother had been a whore, after all.

A lump rose in Coira's throat, her body flushing hot and then cold. Even after a decade away from the brothel, a sickly sensation still swept over her whenever she thought about her previous life.

Will I ever outrun the memories?

Coira's breathing started to come in short, fast breaths as her chest tightened. She wanted to run right now. It was torture to sit and wait like this. Time inched forward, and just when Coira decided she would have to get up and start pacing the cramped space of the alcove, she heard a gentle thud of the door.

"Sister Coira?" Sister Mina's voice reached them, low and urgent. "It is time."

Wordlessly, Coira rose to her feet, took the quarter-staff that she'd rested against the wall, and motioned to Craeg. He stood up, his attention shifting to the weapon she held loosely at her side. His gaze widened questioningly, for he hadn't noticed it till now, but Coira ignored him.

It was best he didn't know Kilbride's secrets.

Pushing aside the hanging, Coira led the way into the main space of the infirmary. Sister Mina awaited them by the door, a small figure outlined against the shadows. They followed her outside into a blustery night, shutting the door quietly behind them.

The wind had a bite to it, cold for mid-summer, and clouds raced across a mottled sky. A waxing half-moon hung above, casting the world below in a silvery light.

Coira pulled her cloak close and followed Sister Mina's slender silhouette around the back of the kirk. They hugged the shadows, the sound of their footfalls masked by the whistling wind. Although Coira didn't glance behind her, she sensed that Craeg was following at her heel, no more than three paces behind.

She didn't need to worry about him being careless or noisy. The man was used to making himself one with the darkness, to traveling unseen.

Skirting the edge of the complex of buildings that spread out around the kirk, the three of them avoided the shortest route to the gates, which would have taken them into the open across a wide dirt yard. Instead, Sister Mina took them the long way, past the graveyard and the fowl coop, before they edged along, under the shadow of the high stone wall that encircled the abbey.

Sister Firtha, a lanky young woman who'd just recently taken her vows of perpetuity, awaited them at the gates. Swathed in a slate-grey cloak, the nun blended in perfectly with the darkness. When she stepped forward to greet them, Coira's step faltered, her heart leaping in her chest.

Placing a hand over her thudding heart, Coira nodded to Sister Firtha. Without a word, Sisters Firtha and Mina both went to the gates—high slabs of oak and iron. From a distance, the gates appeared closed, yet this close, and now that her eyes had adjusted to the darkness, Coira realized that they were indeed ajar. The two nuns hauled them open, creating a gap of around two feet.

Coira and Craeg squeezed through it. As she crept away and scanned her surroundings, Coira heard a soft creak as the nuns pushed the gates closed once more. They'd leave them ajar ready for her return, hopefully sooner rather than later.

Still not speaking, she led Craeg east, into the hazel wood that flanked the abbey. Earlier that evening he'd told her that direction was the closest to where he was headed. Craeg had been careful not to reveal any detail about the location of the new outlaw camp.

She supposed he was being tightlipped for her benefit, not just for his. If she didn't know where he and his band were hiding, she couldn't betray them, even under duress.

As soon as they entered the woods, a little of the tension that had coiled tight within Coira eased. They were outside the abbey walls now at least, and she was confident that no one had seen them leave. Father Camron would now be none the wiser that they'd been harboring a wanted criminal inside the walls.

It was beautiful amongst the trees, with the moonlight frosting them. Coira rarely walked in the woodland after dark, and despite the roar of the wind through the branches, the peace settled over her, soothing her jangled nerves.

Behind her, she heard Craeg's heavy tread and the whisper of his breathing. He walked close now, so she slowed her stride, mindful that he'd been bed-ridden for the past week.

"How are ye feeling?" she murmured, slowing further so that he drew up alongside.

"A bit weak, but well enough," he replied in a voice that warned her from inquiring further. Of course, his injury would be paining him, but he was stubborn and he wouldn't tell her that.

Ye need to stop fussing, Coira reminded herself. *He's no longer yer patient.*

No, he wasn't, but she worried for him nonetheless. An odd sort of friendship had struck up between them in the past days, and she'd found herself looking forward to her trips to the infirmary. Despite that he couldn't linger at Kilbride, she knew Craeg shouldn't be up and about this soon, not after being so ill.

They continued walking, side-by-side now, the wind tugging at their cloaks, until they reached a small glade. They were around ten furlongs east of the abbey, and here the land sloped upwards. If they were to keep walking in the same direction, the trees would soon give way to foothills. And then shortly after that, they would stand under the shadow of great mountains.

Craeg halted in the midst of the glade and turned to Coira.

Moonlight filtered in, highlighting his face in sharp angles. However, his eyes were dark as his gaze settled upon hers. "This is where our paths diverge," he said softly. "It's not safe for ye to travel any farther, Coira."

The intimacy in the way he spoke her name made Coira catch her breath. She'd never thought her name a beautiful one, but it was when *he* said it. Warmth spread across her chest, and she was glad the darkness hid the blush she was sure now stained her cheeks. "It's *Sister* Coira," she managed finally, her voice higher than usual.

"Aye ... it is." He stepped closer to her, dipping his chin just a little so that he could continue to hold her gaze. "Ye saved my life ... and I will never forget it. Ye are an angel."

An angel.

Coira's breathing quickened as if she'd just been running. The low timbre of his voice, the sensuality of it, made her struggle to catch her breath. For the first time, his nearness, the heat of his body, caused her to feel light-headed.

What was the man doing? It almost seemed as if he was trying to seduce her.

"I am a healer," she finally managed, cursing the sudden huskiness in her voice. "I wasn't going to let ye die, was I?"

"No." There was a smile in his voice now, a masculine self-confidence that was both attractive and irritating. And yet she wasn't cowed by him. For years, she'd been afraid of men—any man. The first few farmers from Torrin she'd tended had terrified her; big men with rough voices and hot stares. She'd been sure they'd take liberties, and yet they hadn't.

Craeg was taller and stronger than her. He was a warrior used to living rough, and he shared the same blood as a man who'd used and tormented her. But he wasn't Duncan MacKinnon. The past days had made that evident.

He stepped even closer to her then, and suddenly she realized that they were standing little more than a hand-span apart. Coira lifted her chin, holding his eye.

She heaved in a steadying breath. The air seemed to have been sucked out of the clearing, and her surroundings disappeared. The roar of the wind, the chill of the night air, the rich smell of damp earth and vegetation—all of it faded. Craeg dominated her senses.

"Ye and I are but ships passing each other in the fog," Craeg said softly, his voice husky now, "but know this, Sister Coira ... if things were different. If I wasn't a fugitive, and if ye weren't a Bride of Christ, I would do all I could to make ye mine." His hand reached up and, gently, his knuckles brushed her cheek. Coira stopped breathing, stopped thinking. "I've never met a woman like ye," he concluded softly, "and I doubt I will again."

10

Unrepentant

I WOULD DO all I could to make ye mine.

Craeg's words whispered to Coira, mocked her, all the way back to Kilbride. She strode out briskly, cheeks burning, yet his voice, rough with longing, still followed her.

I've never met a woman like ye, and I doubt I will again.

They were bold words, charming words, and yet they had drawn a web around Coira. And she'd been ensnared by them. Once he'd finished speaking, they'd stared at each other for a long, drawn-out moment—and then he'd stepped back from her, dropping his hand and breaking the spell.

Clutching her staff so hard her knuckles ached, Coira had spun on her heel and taken off back the way she'd come.

They're just words. Aye, but words had power. Hadn't Coira been her most frightened when Duncan MacKinnon loomed over her, whispering cruel, hateful things?

Why hadn't she seen this coming? All these days Craeg had been her patient and she hadn't realized that he'd developed feelings for her. Coira hadn't encouraged him. She'd treated him as she did all those who needed her help—but that hadn't prevented him from seeing her as a woman.

Looking back, she now saw the signs. The way his gaze often lingered upon her face, the intense way he watched her, and the warmth of his smiles.

How could I have been so blind?

It was improper, both she and Craeg knew it. A man didn't say things like that to a nun, and a nun wouldn't tolerate it. She should have reviled him, should have made the sign of the cross and warded him off like the devil. But instead, she'd turned tail and fled.

Coira's breathing came in ragged gasps. Despite the cool wind whipping against her face, the blush that had started in her cheeks had now spread over her entire torso, pooling in her lower belly.

"Dear Lord," she murmured, horrified by her body's betrayal, "please forgive me." She couldn't believe how swiftly she'd responded to Craeg, how she'd leaned into him as he spoke. For an instant, she'd longed for him to dip his head and capture her lips with his. She'd wanted to tangle her fingers in his wild, dark hair, to plunge her tongue into his mouth and—

Stop it!

Coira clenched her jaw so fiercely that pain darted through her left ear. This was wrong, all of it. When she returned to the abbey, she'd spend the night praying on the floor of her cell. She'd do anything to send these lustful thoughts back to whence they'd come.

She hurriedly retraced her steps back to the abbey, and when the high walls of Kilbride loomed before her, Coira sucked in a deep, relieved breath. Despite all the dangers around them, the abbey was still her refuge, still the place where she could shut out the rest of the world.

Pushing the gates open wide enough so that she could slip through, Coira re-entered the abbey. As she'd expected, both Sisters Firtha and Mina had retired to the dormitory for the night. The yard before the kirk was empty, and no cloaked figures waited in the shadows around it.

Coira pushed the gates shut, but didn't risk bolting them. She didn't like leaving the abbey gates unlocked, but even in the wind, the noise would travel. She would just have to hope that no one slipped in.

Heaving a deep breath, Coira edged her way right, past the stables and the guest lodgings—where the abbot and his monks would be slumbering—toward the low-slung complex of buildings that were the dormitories, and the cells belonging to the more senior nuns. And since Coira had lived at Kilbride for many years now, she was considered one of them.

Coira's chest tightened in anticipation at being able to close the door on the world for a few short hours, to be able to put herself back together again and make sense of her jumbled thoughts and emotions.

She'd almost reached the entrance to the lodgings when a man's voice, rough and accusing, cut through the chill night air. "Stop right there."

Light blazed behind her, and Coira abruptly came to a halt. Her heart then started pounding. Without turning, she knew that Father Camron stood at her back and that he was carrying a torch.

"Turn around," he ordered sharply. "Let me see yer face."

"The nun is unrepentant. This time, she must be punished."

Father Camron's voice boomed through the abbess's hall, echoing off the stone walls. Standing a few feet back, her gaze bleary, for she'd just been torn from sleep, Mother Shona winced. "There's no need to bellow, Father," she said wearily. "None of us are hard of hearing."

"I caught her, Mother," the abbot continued, barely lowering his tone. "With that staff of hers. And look at her … she's wearing a cloak. The nun has clearly been outside the abbey walls!"

Coira said nothing, although she didn't take her gaze off the abbot's face. His dark eyes gleamed, and his cheeks were flushed. He could barely contain his glee at catching her.

"Was she practicing with the quarter-staff again, Father?" Mother Shona asked with a long-suffering tone that Coira knew well. It was one she used with the likes of Sister Elspeth when the nun came to her telling tales about the 'misconduct' of other sisters.

"No." A little of the abbot's glee ebbed from his face. "But that matters not ... the point is, Sister Coira has no godly reason to leave the abbey at night." His attention swiveled to Coira then, his gaze pinning her to the spot. "What were ye doing?"

"I have trouble sleeping, Father," Coira replied, her voice frosty as she fought anger. It was rising within her like a springtide, and it took all her effort to choke it down. "So I took a walk in the hazel wood. I didn't go far ... and I took my staff with me, for the ground is uneven and I didn't want to trip in the dark."

The abbot gave a loud snort, his broad chest expanding with the force of his disbelief. The large iron crucifix he wore gleamed in the light of the cressets burning upon the surrounding walls. "Ye must take us both for fools, Sister Coira. Ye were out consorting with men, weren't ye? Ye were *fornicating*!"

"Father!" Mother Shona gasped. "How dare ye suggest such a thing?"

"I dare because it is the truth!"

"But ye have no proof."

"I don't need any ... not when I caught her returning from outside the walls." Father Camron rounded on Coira before taking a menacing step toward her. "This time, ye will be flogged ... and I shall wield the rod."

"No, she won't—and *ye* won't." The abbess's voice cut in, flint-hard now. Glancing Mother Shona's way, Coira saw that the last vestiges of sleepiness had disappeared from her face. The abbess's eyes had turned dark and hard, and her nostrils flared.

Coira's belly dropped in response. In all the years she'd lived at Kilbride, she'd never seen Mother Shona look so angry.

"If ye dare take a rod to anyone here, I shall rip it from yer hands and use it upon ye," the abbess said, her voice tight with the force of the rage she was barely keeping in check. "Ye are a guest here, Father. Remember that."

The abbot pulled himself up short, his broad chest expanding even further. His eyes bulged, and he began to breathe noisily, in short, rasping breaths. "I am an *inquisitor*, Mother," he growled. "I can do what I wish."

Mother Shona drew herself up, eyeballing him without the slightest trace of fear. "No ... ye can't." Her voice had turned icy now. Watching her, Coira's breathing caught. How she admired the abbess. Although small in stature, she wasn't afraid to stand up to men. That day Mother Shona had stood her ground against MacKinnon, Coira had been frightened for her. But now watching her face-off against the abbot, her small hands balling into fists at her sides, Coira felt nothing but respect for the woman.

How she wished she was that brave.

It hurt to kneel upon the hard stone floor of the kirk—especially since the bruising upon Coira's knees had only just healed. But it was preferable to a flogging so she bore the pain in silence.

Dawn wasn't far off; she sensed its approach. The interior of the kirk was beginning to lighten as the sky outside the high narrow windows turned from black to indigo.

Closing her eyes, Coira swayed. Fatigue pressed down upon her. She was so tired she could have happily stretched out upon these icy flagstones and gone to sleep.

But instead, she was praying to atone for her misbehavior.

The words of the prayers blurred into each other now, for tiredness had muddled her thoughts. Instead, the abbot's words intruded.

Ye were fornicating!

If the accusation hadn't been so serious, she'd have laughed at its ridiculousness. After what she'd suffered at the hands of men in the past, sneaking out to copulate with one was the last thing she desired.

However, the abbot didn't know of her past—and if he had, he'd likely have just used it against her.

The argument had escalated after Mother Shona had thwarted the abbot. He'd bellowed and threatened, yet the abbess had stood firm.

In the end, he'd turned and stormed from the abbess's hall, leaving a hollow silence in his wake.

Coira's legs had weakened with relief at the sound of the door slamming shut, yet she knew it was but a brief reprieve. Father Camron would be out for her blood now.

At least Craeg got away.

Coira's fingers, clasped together in prayer, curled into each other. Since returning to the abbey, she'd done her best not to think about the outlaw. Having to deal with the abbot had been a distraction, as had her cold and discomfort as she knelt on the floor of the kirk.

But with this last thought, her shields came down.

Suddenly, she was back there in that dark, windy glade, staring up into his eyes. His face had been beautiful in the moonlight, had seemed carven from marble, yet his touch—feather-light and reverent—had been warm.

His touch had lit a fire within her. Coira's return to the abbey had banked it momentarily, but now that Craeg crept back into her thoughts, it flared once more.

How she'd wanted him to kiss her. How her fingertips had ached to touch him, to trace that thin silver scar on his face.

A lump rose in Coira's throat, and it hurt to swallow. The abbot would have her flayed for such thoughts. Maybe he wasn't that wrong about her after all.

A nun shouldn't desire a man's touch.

A burning sensation rose behind Coira's closed eyelids, and she squeezed them even tighter shut, forcing back tears. She hadn't wept in years, had thought she'd forgotten how.

This wasn't any good. She couldn't continue like this—as soon as she could, Coira would seek the abbess's counsel. Mother Shona would teach her how to overcome this weakness.

She has to.

11

A Fiery Dawn

IT TOOK CRAEG longer than he'd expected to reach his camp.

His injury had weakened him on a deeper level than he'd realized. Aye, he could walk, yet he seemed to have lost his stamina. It was as if the soured wound and the terrible fever that followed had both sapped him of strength.

As such, he found himself needing to rest numerous times during the journey inland, especially once the land steepened. The woods gave way to scrub-covered hills, and then stony slopes.

The wind whipped against Craeg as he climbed, cooling his heated cheeks. Yet it wasn't enough to keep exhaustion at bay.

Panting, he stopped halfway up the mountainside and lowered himself onto a rock to rest. He reached inside the small leather pack the nuns had given him and withdrew a bladder of beer before taking a few gulps. The liquid revived him, yet his limbs felt as if they were weighted down with boulders.

Once he got to safety, he'd have to spend a few days resting up. He was no use to his people in this state—as weak as a newborn lamb.

Seated there upon the mountainside, staring up at the windy sky, where the clouds chased each other over the glowing face of the moon, Craeg enjoyed a rare moment of solitude. A lot of responsibility had rested upon his shoulders of late. Despite the attack on their old camp earlier in the summer, his followers had swollen in number once more.

Folk throughout MacKinnon territory had heard about the skirmish, and many men—farmers and shepherds mostly—had left their families to join his cause.

Craeg's jaw tensed as he dwelled upon just how much these men trusted him.

He wouldn't let them down. Until now, he'd been content to make his half-brother's life difficult. It had been enough to rob from him, to inconvenience him. But the situation had shifted. MacKinnon had tortured and murdered Craeg's friend. His guard had killed a number of Craeg's followers.

It had been personal before, a grudge that followed Craeg like his shadow. But now the need for vengeance burned like an ulcer in his gut.

I'm going to bring him down.

An idea formed in his mind then—one that would require a huge risk. He'd never be able to get to his half-brother behind Dunan's high walls. Instead, he needed to draw him out.

Craeg's mouth thinned. This time, when Duncan MacKinnon went looking for the outlaws, he'd be ready for him.

Heaving himself up off the rock, Craeg stifled a groan. Sister Coira had bound his side tightly for the journey and given him instructions on how to look after the healing wound once he returned to camp. However, he now realized why she'd looked concerned as she'd secured the bandage one last time. It was too early for him to be exerting himself like this.

It didn't matter though. Sometimes circumstance was against you. Every day he lingered at Kilbride increased the risk of his discovery by that visiting abbot.

Craeg moved off, gingerly picking his way up the slope. The going was harder now, and his boots slipped on loose shale. Nonetheless, he pushed himself forward. He needed to reach the camp by dawn.

Yet as he walked, his thoughts returned to the woman who'd saved his life. The nun who'd risked much on his behalf.

Coira.

How lovely her face had been in that clearing, her proud features bathed in the soft glow of the moon. For a few instants, he'd forgotten that she wore a habit under that cloak, that a veil and wimple framed her face.

He'd forgotten she was a nun.

He wasn't sure where his declaration had come from. He certainly hadn't planned to say anything so inappropriate. The past days, he felt as if he'd strayed into a strange dream.

He and Sister Coira had spent many hours together, and during that time a connection between them had been forged. Those expressive eyes were filled with wisdom and understanding and often shadowed by a sadness that only served to intrigue him further.

Lord, how he'd wanted to kiss her in that glade.

He couldn't believe he'd had the audacity to touch her face. A man didn't *touch* a nun.

And yet, he wanted to do much more than that.

Reaching up, Craeg scrubbed his hand across his face. He needed to stop these thoughts. It was hard enough scaling this mountainside as it was, without a pole in his breeches.

Ye don't make life easy for yerself, do ye? Craeg's mouth twisted. All the women living upon this isle, and the only one he wanted was a Sister of Kilbride. A foolish wish indeed. It was just as well he had other, more urgent, matters to draw his attention now.

The sooner he forgot about Sister Coira, the better.

Dawn was breaking behind the dark bulk of the mountains when Craeg reached his destination. It was a fiery daybreak, a foreboding one.

Climbing the last slope, this one so steep that he had to virtually claw his way up on his hands and knees, Craeg's mouth thinned.

A Blood Dawn.

The ancient people of this isle had believed such a dawn was an ill-omen, a harbinger of death and destruction. These days, folk were just as superstitious of such a red sky.

Misgiving feathered in the pit of Craeg's belly. Over the last few months, all his neatly laid plans had unraveled. MacKinnon had closed in on him. He couldn't hide forever, and neither could the men and women who followed him. It was definitely time to meet his half-brother in battle.

Breathing hard, Craeg reached the top of the slope and paused. A group of men, leather-clad and bearing drawn swords, awaited him. He wagered the scouts had been observing his journey up the mountainside. Two of them broke away from the group and approached him.

"I knew it was ye." One of the men, a huge warrior with wild red hair, stepped forward, sheathing his claidheamh-mor. "Although ye climb like a woman … we started to take bets on whether ye would make it by sun up."

Craeg snorted. It was hard not to pant like a winded carthorse. Holding his flank, he favored his friend with a tight smile. "Ye try climbing a mountain with a hole in yer side."

Gunn's gaze narrowed. "How's the wound?"

"Healing. The nuns at Kilbride managed to stop the festering … and the fever lifted."

"Ye have been away for days." The second man also put away his broadsword. Tall and rangy, with a lean, sharp-featured face, Farlan was at least a decade younger than Gunn and Craeg. "We were beginning to think we'd lost ye."

"Ye almost did," Craeg grunted. "Come on. Leave the others to keep watch and follow me. We'll continue this back at camp. I need to eat something, or I'm going to keel over."

The three men left the mountainside and slithered down a pebbly slope into a narrow ravine. The rock walls of the gorge were so steep that Craeg had to crane his head to see the sky. The heavens looked ablaze now, and Craeg's mouth thinned.

Blood Dawn indeed.

It had been a while since Craeg had left this place, and the ravine was busier than he remembered. It seemed that even more folk had joined them. Word of mouth traveled fast, even among the sparsely populated villages of Skye. Men, with a few women and children among them, were shaking out their bedding and breaking their fast.

A smile stretched Craeg's face as he remembered Sister Coira questioning him about the loyalty of those following him. He took great risks letting the folk of this territory learn of his hiding places. He had to if he wanted to rally more fighters to his side. And yet, till now, none but Brochan had betrayed him. As he'd pointed out to Coira, he wasn't the only one who bore a deep hatred for Duncan MacKinnon.

The rise and fall of voices broke the morning hush, echoing off the surrounding stone, as did the clang of metal. Men sharpened blades as they waited for their bannocks to fry upon iron griddles, and a forge had been built against the valley wall. Craeg passed the smithy hard at work, hammering out glowing splinters of iron that would be fashioned into arrow-tips.

Craeg's smile widened at the sight of such industry. It pleased him to know that his people hadn't been idle in his absence. Although he hadn't announced his plan to face MacKinnon in battle, they had anticipated him.

The folk of this land wanted rid of the oppressive clan-chief as much as he did.

Breathing in the scent of frying bannock, Craeg's empty belly let out a loud growl. There were few things he liked better in the morning than a freshly baked bannock smothered in butter and honey.

At the heart of the ravine, he came upon a large fire pit. A tall woman with curling blonde hair stood over an iron griddle and was flipping a circular cake over. Her attention focused upon her task, she didn't see the three men approach.

"Morning, Fen," Craeg greeted her with a tired smile. He lowered himself down onto a boulder, suppressing a groan as he did so.

God's bones, he felt eighty winters old this morning.

Fen—Fenella—glanced up, her blue eyes widening as her gaze settled upon him. "Craeg! We thought ye were dead."

"I didn't," Gunn interrupted, before seating himself next to Craeg.

Fenella ignored her man, her attention remaining on Craeg. "How are ye feeling?"

"Hungry," Craeg grunted. "How about some bannock?"

"Healed, I see," she replied not bothering to hide a wry tone. "Thinking of yer stomach, as usual?"

Craeg ignored the jibe and instead waited while she cut the bannock into hearty wedges, before smearing it with yellow butter and heather honey.

Watching her, Craeg's mouth filled with saliva. If she didn't hand over a slice of bannock soon, he'd have to beg.

When she did, Craeg flashed Fenella a wide smile.

The first bite nearly made him groan in pleasure. The wedge of bannock was gone moments later, and Craeg had his platter out for another.

"Didn't they feed ye at the abbey?" Fenella asked, dishing Craeg up another two slices.

"Aye ... but no one makes bannocks like ye, Fen," he replied.

"Still haven't lost yer charming tongue I see." Fenella's voice was stern although she was smiling.

"No ... I'd have to be extremely under the weather for that to happen."

Next to Craeg, Gunn snorted. "Stop flattering my woman and tell us what happened ... I take it the nuns won't tell anyone ye were at the abbey?"

The question sobered Craeg. Finishing his third wedge of bannock, he brushed crumbs off his braies. He then met Gunn's eye.

"They kept me hidden ... although things got difficult when the abbey had visitors."

Gunn inclined his head. "MacKinnon?"

"No ... a meddling abbot sent to investigate the abbess."

"Ye know, I've heard rumors about the Sisters of Kilbride," Gunn said, his expression turning thoughtful. "Three men from Torrin arrived yesterday.

One of them said that he once spied the nuns sparring with blunted swords. One of his companions added that he'd seen them bring down deer with longbows in the woods."

Craeg went still at this news. He remembered then the iron-tipped quarter-staff that Coira carried. He also recalled how skillfully Lady Leanna had wielded a longbow when she and Ross Campbell had helped defend the outlaw camp earlier in the summer.

"After everything I've seen of late, I'd believe such tales," he murmured. "There's something odd about that abbey."

His companions digested this news before Farlan spoke up. "Ye will note that our numbers have swelled in yer absence, Craeg."

Craeg nodded, meeting the warrior's eye. "The tide is turning against MacKinnon now ... fear of the sickness has made folk take action. Life was hard enough here as it was, thanks to him."

"We hear that things are getting worse in Dunan," Fenella said quietly. "A man arriving from there yesterday said that they're burning the dead outside the walls."

A chill settled over Craeg at this news. The Grim Reaper had indeed come to Skye. Things were looking bleak for them all, and yet in times like these, folk looked for a savior.

He turned to Gunn then. "How are our coffers looking?"

His friend smiled. "Healthy ... we still have a bag of silver left over from the last raid at Kyleakin."

"Good," Craeg grunted. "See that it's distributed in as many villages as possible in the coming days ... make sure everyone knows the silver came from MacKinnon's purse." He paused then, his gaze sweeping over the faces of his companions. "That raid was our last though. I've had plenty of time to think while I was laid up. I'm done hiding in the shadows. The men who've joined us don't want to rob MacKinnon ... they want to fight him. The hour has arrived for us to bring my brother down."

12

Distracting Thoughts

"FOLK ARE STARTING to flee Dunan, brother," Drew's voice, tense and sharp-edged this morning, made Duncan MacKinnon glance up from buttering a wedge of bannock. "They are saying ye have abandoned them."

The challenge in his sister's tone was evident, and the clan-chief heaved in a slow, steadying breath. He hadn't seen much of Drew lately, although this morning, she'd honored him with her presence in his solar while he broke his fast.

"I haven't," he sneered. "But the good Lord has."

"A group of flagellants have taken up residence in the market square," Drew continued. "Did ye realize?"

MacKinnon scowled. His sister's acerbic tone was starting to grate upon him, although her news came as a surprise. "No," he admitted.

Across the table, Drew put down her knife. Those storm-grey eyes narrowed. "They've taken to beating each other with long leather straps studded with sharp pieces of iron … they do it three times a day as a display of penance and punishment for our sins."

Duncan snorted. "Best of luck to them."

"They are saying that our clan-chief is depraved and immoral … that God is punishing Dunan for his wickedness."

A heavy sensation settled across Duncan's chest then, and his belly closed. He'd been enjoying his morning bannocks until this conversation. To cover up the chill of dread that now crawled up his spine, he reached for a cup of milk and took a measured sip.

Nonsense, all of it.

His mother had turned him against religion many years earlier. Every time she'd beaten him, she'd shrieked that he was full of sin and that God would one day punish him for it.

A sudden dropping sensation in his belly made Duncan's fingers tighten around his cup. "And what do ye think, Drew?" he asked finally, meeting her eye. "Do ye blame me as well?"

The woman's boldness made him itch to take his fist to her face. He'd done so before when she'd overstepped, and she'd minded her tongue for a while afterward. However, now that nearly two months had passed since that incident, Drew had grown viper-tongued and critical once more.

His sister's mouth pursed, and he watched her slender shoulders tense as danger crackled between them. "Of course not, Duncan," she replied, her voice as cold as her gaze. "But I thought it worth bringing to yer attention … this outbreak could well put yer position here in danger."

MacKinnon peered down at the horse's hoof, a scowl marring his brow. "Damn the beast … it's got an abscess."

Carr leaned forward, at where the clan-chief still held his stallion's fetlock between his knees. Pus oozed from the horn of the sole. "Aye," he muttered. "That's why he's been favoring his near forequarter."

"Favoring?" MacKinnon replied with a snort. "Curaidh is as lame as a club-footed peasant."

As if hearing his master's appraisal, the huge bay courser snorted. Curaidh—Warrior—had been the clan-chief's mount for the past five years. True to its name, the horse was tough. It hadn't foundered once, but this morning, it had limped its way out into the yard.

MacKinnon would have to take another horse out hunting.

The clan-chief released Curaidh's fetlock and straightened up. He then gave the stallion an affectionate slap on the shoulder. Watching him, Carr marveled how the clan-chief was always gentler with animals than with his own kind.

Bran sat a few feet away. The wolfhound waited expectantly, ears pricked. MacKinnon always took the dog out hunting.

"See to this, would ye, Broderick," MacKinnon said, meeting Carr's eye. "I'll saddle another horse and ride out."

Carr nodded. He wouldn't be joining MacKinnon and the others on the hunt. Not that he cared. With half of Dunan ill at the present, he found it difficult to relax and enjoy such pursuits. Tyra, Lady Drew's hand-maid, had died two days earlier, and the situation was so bad in the village now that folk were starting to panic.

MacKinnon continued to watch him, his gaze narrowing as if he had somehow read his right-hand's thoughts. "Have any of the other servants within the broch sickened?" he asked.

Carr's spine stiffened. He hadn't been looking forward to this question—although he'd known MacKinnon would ask it eventually. There was only so long the clan-chief could ignore the worsening situation. "Aye," he admitted softly. "Two of the scullery maids and a stable hand."

MacKinnon broke eye contact then, his gaze swinging around the yard, at where two lads were cleaning tack in the misty morning light. "Get all of them out of the broch," he said, his voice tight. "And if anyone else falls ill, ye are to tell me immediately. Is that clear?"

Carr nodded, heaviness settling in his gut. Lady Drew wouldn't be pleased—she'd told Carr not to bring up the sickness with her brother. She'd known about the three servants who'd fallen ill over the last day, and she'd called Dunan's healer to tend to them.

However, Carr had just let her secret slip.

The clan-chief's gaze settled upon one of the stable lads. "Brice ... saddle me another horse."

"Aye, MacKinnon." The youth dropped the stirrup he'd been polishing and darted back into the stables.

MacKinnon swung around to Carr, a deep frown marring his brow now, his lips parting. Drawing in a deep breath, Carr readied himself for the sharp edge of his master's tongue once more.

However, the arrival of a man on horseback, clattering into the bailey under the stone arch that led down into the village and the North Gate, forestalled the clan-chief.

Both men watched the newcomer approach. He was a heavyset man of around forty winters, clad in a sweat-stained, dusty léine and braies. Red-faced, the man rode upon a swaybacked beast that was lathered from the journey, its thin sides heaving.

"MacKinnon?" The stranger greeted them, his gaze settling upon the clan-chief.

"Aye, who are ye?" MacKinnon barked.

"My name is Gowan," the man replied, his voice rough with fatigue. "I'm a smithy from Torrin." He paused there, his throat bobbing. "Ye have sent out word that anyone with news of Craeg the Bastard will be paid ten silver pennies?"

"Aye," MacKinnon growled, "and any man delivering him to me will be paid out his weight in silver."

Gowan's rugged face tensed. "I don't have the outlaw ... but I have news of him. Yesterday afternoon, I spied the Bastard and a group of his men in the woods east of Kilbride."

Silence settled upon the yard.

"How many of them?" MacKinnon asked, his voice sharp now.

"It was hard to tell ... their numbers were many though."

Something dark and feral moved in Duncan MacKinnon's eyes. Slowly, he turned to Carr, his face taut, eager. "Ready the guard ... we ride out within the hour."

Carr nodded and stepped back, preparing himself to do the clan-chief's bidding. However, MacKinnon hadn't finished yet. "Ye will remain here, as steward of Dunan, until my return."

Carr halted, tensing. "Why?"

"My sister's been meddling in my affairs too much of late," MacKinnon growled. "I don't want her in charge of the broch while I'm gone."

Carr's breathing slowed. "MacKinnon," he began, making sure to keep his tone low and respectful. "I'm captain of yer guard ... ye will need me if ye are to face yer brother."

"My *bastard* brother," MacKinnon snarled. "How many times must I correct ye, man?" He paused there, his mouth thinning into a hard line. "I can captain my own warriors, Broderick. Ye are more useful to me here. Get the sick out of my broch and keep an eye on my sister. I expect a full report on her behavior when I get back ... ye had better not keep anything else from me."

A dog's soft whine behind them drew the clan-chief's attention then. Bran stood, tail wagging, impatient to ride out.

Favoring his hound with a tight smile, MacKinnon shook his head. "Not this time, lad," he murmured, his tone gentling. "Best ye remain here too. Keep my seat warm while I'm gone."

"Mother Shona ... may I speak with ye for a few moments?" Coira halted before the abbess and lowered herself onto one knee. She'd found Mother Shona in the tiny herb garden behind the kitchens, a rambling space filled with profusions of rosemary, sage, mint, and parsley—as well as a number of healing herbs that Coira used in her poultices and salves.

"Of course, Sister Coira," the abbess replied with a smile. The tension in Mother Shona's expression betrayed her. She made the sign of the cross above Coira and waited while she rose to her feet.

"Lavender?" Coira asked, peering into the basket.

The abbess's smile turned rueful. "I've had trouble sleeping of late ... I thought the scent of lavender might help."

Coira's own mouth curved. "Aye ... it should. My mother always said lavender soothed the soul."

Mother Shona huffed a brittle laugh. "Mine could do with some soothing. The abbot's presence here grates upon my nerves, I'm afraid ... no amount of prayer lessens my desire to slap his impudent face."

Coira's mouth quirked at the abbess's frankness. It was reassuring that Mother Shona also struggled with her baser instincts. It would make it easier to tell her what was on her mind.

"Mother," she began hesitantly. "May I be frank?"

The abbess inclined her head. "Always."

"I too have been a little on edge of late, although I must confess that the abbot's presence here only plays a small part." Coira paused, suddenly unsure how to phrase the rest. It felt strange, frightening, to expose her thoughts to anyone, even the abbess. Coira was used to keeping all her feelings under lock and key. "Craeg ... the outlaw's ... stay here unbalanced me."

Mother Shona's eyes narrowed, her expression sharpening. "We've all been worried that MacKinnon might somehow track him here," she replied softly.

Coira shook her head. "It's not that ... I mean ... I don't want MacKinnon here ... and I'd never turn someone who needed my help away. It's just that ..." Coira broke off there once more. The Lord give her strength, this was harder than she'd anticipated. "Since Craeg left, I have found myself plagued by ... distracting thoughts."

The abbess went still at this admission, her brown eyes widening. Moments passed, and with each one, Coira's throat tightened further.

I've made a mistake in being so open. Maybe she shouldn't have confided in Mother Shona.

However, when the abbess spoke, her voice was gentle. "Ye are attracted to him?"

Coira nodded, feeling even more wretched than before.

Mother Shona let out a soft sigh. "Come, Sister Coira. Let us sit together for a few moments."

The abbess led Coira over to the low wooden bench on the far side of the herb garden. Nestled up against a wall festooned with flowering honeysuckle, it was a sheltered, welcoming spot bathed in sunlight. Even so, Coira started to sweat as she took a seat. Inhaling the sweet scent, Coira waited for the interrogation to begin.

"Please don't look so grim, Sister," the abbess said with a sigh. "I'm not going to condemn ye."

Coira, who had been staring down at her folded hands upon her lap, glanced up. "Ye should," she replied, her voice rising. "A Bride of Christ mustn't fall prey to lust."

A soft smile curved the abbess's mouth. "The vow of chastity is perhaps the hardest one for many nuns," she replied.

Coira's jaw clenched. "But it shouldn't be for me," she countered, hating the bitterness she heard in her own voice. "Ye alone know I spent years in a brothel, being used and abused by men. I should hate them."

"So ye mean to say that ye have never before felt desire?" Mother Shona asked, surprise lacing her voice.

Coira shook her head, her gaze dropping once more. She twisted her fingers together, a sour taste flooding her mouth. "Would ye, in such circumstances?"

It was an impertinent question, but tension had given Coira a sharper tongue than usual. Moments passed, and she braced herself for a chastisement from the abbess. However, none came.

"I imagine some ... who have been in the same position as ye ... do feel desire," Mother Shona said. She spoke slowly as if choosing each word with care. "There will be women who will never leave the brothel ... even if they have the opportunity to do so. Few would take the risk ye did in order to make a new start."

Coira continued to stare down at her entwined fingers, her throat thickening. The abbess was right. There were a number of women she knew would always remain at *The Goat and Goose*. Some didn't appear to dislike the life, and one or two actually seemed to enjoy servicing patrons. Others grew insensitive to the life over the years. These women had frightened Coira, for when she'd looked into their eyes, they'd been empty. She suppressed a shudder at the memory. She'd feared that she too would end up like that if she stayed.

"Aye, a nun should cast off all earthly desires ... and that includes carnal sin," the abbess continued when the silence between them drew out. "But that does not mean that most of us don't struggle with the vow from time to time."

Coira's chin snapped up. She twisted around so that she faced the abbess squarely. "Have ye?"

Mother Shona smiled. "Ye know that my life hasn't always been as sheltered as it is now."

Of course, the abbess had barely escaped being raped and murdered when her convent on the mainland had been set upon by brigands. But there had always been a gap in her story. Mother Shona was always vague about the time she'd spent with outlaws before her arrival on the Isle of Skye. All Coira knew was that they'd taught her how to wield weapons.

"I have known carnal pleasure," Mother Shona said finally, her words so bald that Coira resisted the urge to flinch. "I have known what it is to love a man ... and to lose him."

Coira stared at her, taking in the abbess's finely boned face. The older woman looked sad.

Mother Shona's gaze shadowed, and she sighed. "As ye know ... after I fled from those brigands, I would have surely starved if a group of outlaws hadn't found me," she continued. "They became my family for a time." The abbess's mouth lifted at the corners then. "A man named Aaron led the band. He was charismatic, strong, and so arrogant that just being near him robbed me of coherent thought. The moment he took me in, I knew that I was in trouble."

Coira made a surprised sound at this, but Mother Shona pushed on. "During my time with the outlaws, I simply became Shona, a wild young woman who ran with the wolves. And after the first summer had passed, Aaron and I became lovers." The abbess halted there. She met Coira's eye once more, her gaze gleaming. "I was never happier than when I was with him. We had a hard life, but an exciting one. I never lost my faith though ... my prayers were always sacred to me ... and he knew what I'd given up to remain with him."

The abbess paused then, her expression changing. Her eyes developed a faraway look, as she lost herself in memories. "Scotland was immersed in dangerous times during those years; we were engaged in a violent struggle against the English. Soon enough, there was an uprising, and our band got dragged into it." Mother Shona's eyes fluttered shut then. "I lost him in the battle that crushed Scottish hope. A few of us survived, but sadly Aaron didn't."

Mother Shona inhaled sharply, her shoulders squaring. "Without Aaron, living as a fugitive lost its appeal. I decided that I would take the veil once more. But this time I traveled to a far-flung corner of Scotland where I could leave my past safely behind me." The abbess shifted her attention back to Coira then, and she gave a wry smile. "Ye see, Sister. Ye are not the only one with a weakness for handsome rogues."

For a few moments, Coira was at a loss as to how to respond. When she did, her voice was subdued. "It must have been hard to go back to a nun's life after all that."

"It was ... at first," the abbess admitted. "But then I realized that it's much easier to take a vow of chastity when ye know exactly what it is ye are giving up. I felt very lucky with Aaron. We had four years together ... years that I will forever cherish. But because of that, I was able to give myself wholeheartedly to serving God." Mother Shona's gaze grew intense then. "What I'm trying to say ... is that what ye felt for Craeg was natural. Ye are a woman, and he is a man ... and men like him are difficult to resist. Take what ye felt for him, cherish it, and put it somewhere safe within yer heart. It is part of who ye are now, but don't use it as a stick to beat yerself with. Such self-blame will only make ye miserable ... and how can ye do the Lord's work then?"

Coira gazed back at Mother Shona. Once again, she had no idea how to respond. The abbess had completely floored her. This woman's wisdom had always been an anchoring force in the abbey, and it was no different now.

A little of the guilt that had formed a hard knot in Coira's chest unraveled. Mother Shona was right; she needed to find a way to make peace with her conscience.

Silence stretched between the two women, and when Coira eventually broke it, her voice was subdued. "There's something else, Mother ... something I have never told ye."

The abbess frowned, and Coira dropped her gaze to her lap, nervousness fluttering in her belly. There was a good reason why she'd never spoken of this to a soul. However, she might never have the opportunity to confide in Mother Shona like this again. She had to tell her everything.

Clearing her throat, Coira forced herself to look up and met the abbess's eye. "Ye know of my past," she murmured. "But I've never told ye about the man who is the real reason I fled to Kilbride ... the man who nearly broke me."

13

The Odds are Against Them

"CRAEG, WAKE UP."

Gunn's rough voice jerked Craeg from a fitful slumber. Sprawled out upon a fur in his tent—a lean-to that had been built up against the rocky side of the ravine—he'd been dreaming. It had been a pleasant dream. He'd been back at Kilbride again, and Sister Coira had been leaning over him, her cool fingertips tracing lines across his naked chest.

However, Gunn brought him rudely back to the present, and the vision of lovely Coira evaporated like morning mist.

"Satan's cods, Gunn. What is it?" Craeg pushed himself up into a sitting position and scrubbed a hand over his face. His heart was racing after being torn from a deep sleep. He felt disoriented in the aftermath.

"Sorry to wake ye," Gunn replied, not sounding sorry in the least. "But we've got a problem, and I thought ye would want to know."

The last of sleep sloughed away, and suddenly Craeg was alert. "What's wrong?"

"The two men from Dunan who joined our ranks a few days ago are both unwell," he replied, his voice flattening. "I'm no healer, but I think it's the sickness."

A chill settled in the pit of Craeg's gut at this news, seeping outward. It was as if he'd just stepped, waist-deep, into a freezing loch. "Where are they?"

"We've isolated them from the rest of the camp in a tent at the end of the ravine," Gunn replied. "Ye had best come and see for yerself."

Craeg walked through the camp, aware of the anxious gazes that tracked his progress. Unlike when he'd returned here from Kilbride, there were no cheery waves and relieved smiles. News of the two sick men had spread through the ravine—faster than any illness could.

If he was honest, Craeg didn't want to go anywhere near the men from Dunan.

He'd been awaiting the arrival of the pestilence for a while now, and the chill the news had given him had not yet abated. But he couldn't show fear or weakness in front of his people. Every man, woman, and child here was his responsibility. They had all come here to aid him, and he wouldn't turn his back on them.

Until this morning, things had been progressing well for the outlaws. Craeg had deliberately been taking his men out on patrols and letting locals catch glimpses of him. One of them was sure to bring word to MacKinnon.

The pungent, woody aroma of burning sage greeted Craeg as he approached the long tent pitched in the shadow of an overhang. Someone had lit burning pots of herbs outside the door. Sage was said to chase away the dark humors that caused sickness. However, right at that moment, Craeg didn't set much store in its ability to ward off the pestilence.

Fenella stood outside, waiting for him, and when Craeg halted before the entrance to the tent, he met her eye. "How bad is it?"

"They both have terrible pains to the belly and are racked with chills. I'm told these are the first signs," she murmured, her blue eyes shadowed.

Craeg set his jaw. *Great.* "I should speak to them," he said, hoping the reluctance didn't show in his voice.

"Don't get too close," Fenella warned. "They've developed coughs as well."

Craeg set his jaw. Fenella's words weren't making him feel any better—yet he'd never been one to shy away from unpleasant tasks, and so he ducked his head and entered the tent.

A single brazier lit the cramped interior, although the fug of peat-smoke couldn't mask the sour odor of illness.

Two figures lay on either side of the brazier, their bodies covered with blankets.

Craeg's gaze swept from the face of one man to the other. They were both awake, both staring at him with fever-bright eyes, their faces taut with fear and pain.

"I'm sorry, Craeg," one of them, the youngest of the two, croaked. "We didn't mean to ... but I fear we've brought the sickness here."

"Ye have had contact with it at Dunan?" Craeg asked, fighting the urge to retreat from the tent.

"Aye," the man rasped. "I served in the Dunan Guard ... but when some of the other warriors fell ill, I panicked."

Craeg went still. "Ye served MacKinnon?"

The man nodded. "Long have I wanted to join ye ... to help the folk of this land rise up against him. With the sickness rife in Dunan, I took my chance."

Craeg held the man's desperate gaze, not sure whether to be angry, flattered, or exasperated. Right now, he felt all three emotions. After a pause, he shifted his attention to the second man in the tent. He was a hulking fellow, the sort that would have been useful in a fight if he hadn't been so ill.

"Are ye from the Dunan Guard as well?" he asked.

The man shook his head. "I'm a weaponsmith," he said, his weak voice at odds with his powerful frame. "I lost my family to the sickness ... and when it didn't touch me, I thought that perhaps God had spared me." The man halted before taking in a labored breath. "It seems I was wrong."

Stepping out of the tent, Craeg sucked in a deep breath. He was grateful for the steadying aroma of burning sage, and that Fenella and Gunn were both waiting outside for him. Gunn had an arm around Fenella's shoulders, and the pair of them wore somber expressions. Craeg's breathing slowed. God knew how much contact these two had already had with the sick men.

They might be infected ... and so might I now.

A prickly feeling rose up within Craeg then. Gunn and Fenella had been with him from the beginning. They were family to him.

"Does anyone recover from the plague?" Craeg finally asked, dreading the answer.

Gunn shrugged, his expression unusually helpless. Next to him, Fenella's full lips flattened. "From what I hear, it spares some folk," she replied, a husky edge to her voice "... but few who develop the sickness appear to live through it."

Bile stung the back of Craeg's throat. *Not what I was hoping to hear.*

Inhaling deeply once more, Craeg shoved the slithering chill of fear aside; it was the last thing he needed now. Instead, he had to look for a solution. Perhaps there was some way these men could be cured. They needed a healer—a skilled one.

Coira. He didn't like the idea of putting her at risk, yet without her skills, these men would most certainly die.

Craeg raked a hand through his hair and met Gunn's eye. "Get Farlan ... he's the fastest rider amongst us. I need him to deliver a message to Kilbride."

Coira straightened up, her gaze traveling over the girl's slender form, to her flushed face. Lying upon a stuffed straw pallet, the girl wore nothing but a sleeveless shift. "My belly hurts terribly," the lass groaned. "Make the pain go away, Sister."

Coira's breathing grew shallow, her chest tightening as she met the girl's panicked gaze. She was only eight winters old; she didn't understand what was happening to her. "I shall give ye some hemlock juice," Coira murmured. "Hopefully, it will ease yer pain a little."

The lass favored her with a tremulous, grateful smile, and Coira's throat started to ache in response. Hemlock juice would only dull the pain, but it would not provide a cure.

It had only taken Coira a few moments alone with this girl and her mother, who was also poorly, to ascertain that the scourge had reached them. Both mother and daughter were at early stages, for there were no signs of swellings at the armpit or groin—the 'plague boils' that were said to form on the skin as the illness progressed. However, they both had a hacking cough, stomach pains, and chills, and they were both horribly weak.

Also, Coira had noted that they had inflamed flea bites upon their arms, a sign that both mystified and confused her.

A few feet away, the mother started to cough, the sound muffled by the bundle of cloth she now pressed against her mouth. Coira had insisted they both did that, the moment she entered the dwelling.

She knew little about this illness, although she realized that most healers would try to fight it by bleeding the patient and rubbing certain herbs upon the skin. Coira—like her mother before her—wasn't an advocate of bleeding. In her view, it merely weakened the patient.

With little news of the plague to aid her, she was forced to use her intuition now. Her mother had been a gifted herb-wife. She'd once told Coira that many illnesses were passed from one person to another by bodily fluid, or by breathing in the same tainted air as the afflicted.

It made sense then that if a patient had a cough, one should keep their distance. These were the first cases in Torrin, and Coira wanted to stop the illness from spreading.

Emerging from the cottage, Coira found Sister Mina waiting with a heavyset man. The farmer was pale and wild-eyed, and he didn't look at Coira, but past her, toward the open doorway.

"Where have yer kin been of late?" Coira asked, pulling the door shut behind her.

"My wife went to visit her sister a few days ago," the farmer answered. "She lives in a village near Dunan."

Coira frowned. This was what she'd been afraid of. Of course, folk traveled, and when they did, they inadvertently brought the sickness home with them.

"Can ye do anything for them, Sister?" The farmer asked, desperation in his voice now.

"I've made them as comfortable as I can," she replied softly. "But I'm afraid I can do nothing more for the moment."

The farmer's gaze guttered, his jaw clenching. "I feel so useless," he ground the words out.

"Attend to yer wife and daughter," Coira answered, "but do not venture into the village or have contact with the other folk here. Ye must ensure the sickness doesn't spread. I will make sure food is brought to ye."

The farmer stared at her, his gaze hardening. He didn't want such advice. It didn't help his plight; it only prevented others from falling ill. But that wouldn't aid his wife and daughter, nor him if he was to sicken.

Coira swallowed. How she wanted to give assurances—to tell him she had all the answers. Her throat aching, she nodded to Sister Mina, indicating that they should go. She then glanced back at the farmer. "I will visit again tomorrow," she promised.

Heart heavy, Coira started back in the direction of the abbey. The farmer's cottage lay on the southern outskirts of Torrin, apart from the other houses. That was a good thing, for if they could isolate the sickness, perhaps they could halt its spread.

The weight in her chest only increased, however, as she followed the path through fields of kale. Coira had taken precautions when entering the cottage and been careful not to touch her patients directly. When she returned to the abbey, she would scrub her hands with lye soap, but there was still a chance she could fall sick too.

Coira set her jaw. *I can't ... the people here need me.*

Ironically, that was often the fate of healers—dying from the same illness as those they sought to heal.

Forcing herself not to dwell on that possibility, Coira glanced up at the darkening mackerel sky. It was growing late in the day. The afternoon was odd, without the slightest breath of a breeze to stir the humid air. She didn't like this kind of weather; it put her on edge.

"Will they die?" Sister Mina asked finally, breaking the silence between them. They were halfway back to the abbey now, the high walls outlined against the sky.

"The odds are against them," Coira admitted. "I will not lie to ye. And I fear that this is just the beginning of things."

She glanced left at the novice, expecting to see fear upon her face. Yet Sister Mina's gaze was steady, and although she was a little pale, she looked resolute. Not for the first time, Coira was pleased that she had Sister Mina to assist her. Panic wouldn't do them any good now. She needed someone with a cool head at her side.

However, Sister Mina didn't speak again, and Coira withdrew into her own thoughts. They continued in silence and, a short while later, re-entered the abbey.

To Coira's surprise, she found the yard in front of the kirk filled with men and horses. Rough male voices and laughter echoed over the grounds, shattering Kilbride's tranquility.

And then Coira saw that the warriors—for they carried claidheamh-mors at their sides—wore sashes of a familiar green and red plaid.

MacKinnon.

14

Breaking Bread

"THIS IS POOR man's fare, Mother Shona." MacKinnon's voice rumbled across the table where the abbess and her senior nuns—Coira among them—ate quietly.

"I apologize for the frugality, MacKinnon," the abbess replied, her voice toneless. "But we live simply at Kilbride ... as the Lord would wish."

"Aye ... but ye have important guests."

"If ye had sent word that ye were planning to stay at Kilbride, we would have made preparations," Mother Shona replied gently.

MacKinnon snorted, and Coira started to sweat.

Years had passed since she'd been this physically near him, but the man could still instill terror in her.

It wasn't Coira the clan-chief sat next to this evening, but Sister Magda, at the far end of the dais. The sisters and their guests—the clan-chief and the abbot—lined the long table upon the raised platform at the end of the refectory. Yet, even so, MacKinnon's presence dominated the space. Coira had deliberately avoided looking in his direction since taking her seat.

The devil is sitting at my table.

Bile bit at the back of Coira's throat. Gaze downcast, she tried to ignore the crawling sensation that now covered her arms and chest, and the horror that made it hard to breathe.

MacKinnon is breaking bread with me.

As guests at the abbey, the abbess had been obliged to invite MacKinnon to eat with them, while extra tables and benches for his men had been dragged into the refectory. The warriors' voices echoed loudly in what was usually a tranquil space. The other nuns and the monks were seated a few feet away, hunched over their bowls of stew, faces pale and pinched.

Coira didn't blame them. MacKinnon and his men brought an atmosphere of aggression into what was usually a silent, peaceful time of day.

This evening the odious company had killed Coira's appetite for her supper of mutton, leek, and carrot stew served with coarse oaten bread.

Opposite Coira, Sister Elspeth wore a sour expression as she helped herself to some bread. She disapproved of any man setting foot inside the abbey—yet now there were so many of them that they far outnumbered the women here. The abbot was forced to share the guest lodgings with the clan-chief, while the monks had shifted over to the dormitories with the nuns—something that Sister Elspeth was still fuming over. Meanwhile, MacKinnon's men would sleep in the byre and stable complex.

You couldn't go three paces without spying a man inside the abbey now. It had put all the sisters, including Coira, on edge.

"How long do ye plan to remain at Kilbride, MacKinnon?" Sister Elspeth's sharp voice lashed across the table. Coira, who'd just taken a tentative mouthful of stew, nearly choked. The nun had drawn herself up and was staring down the table at the clan-chief. Her thin body vibrated with outrage—an emotion that she clearly could no longer suppress.

Long moments passed, and when MacKinnon didn't answer, Coira chanced a look in his direction.

She immediately wished she hadn't.

Heavens preserve her, he and Craeg looked so alike. They had the same arrogant bearing, chiseled jaw, and brooding good looks. The shape of their mouths and noses were identical.

A hard knot clenched in Coira's breast, her pulse speeding up, as she stared at him. Fortunately, he wasn't looking in her direction. Instead, he watched Sister Elspeth, his expression shuttered.

However, those eyes—iron-grey—weren't Craeg's. MacKinnon was thinner than she remembered, his shoulders lacking the outlaw's breadth, his face bordering on gaunt. His dark hair, although the same peat-brown as Craeg's, was cut much shorter.

And no scar disfigured his face.

Coira's heart calmed just a little. No, they weren't identical. And when MacKinnon spoke once more, the gulf between the two brothers widened further.

"As long as it takes, Sister." His mouth twisted into a sneer. "Why ... do ye disapprove of our presence here?"

"I'm sure Sister Elspeth is merely curious," Mother Shona cut in smoothly. "We aren't used to having so many visitors, and do wonder at the reason for yer arrival ... especially with so many of yer guard."

MacKinnon shifted his attention from Sister Elspeth, who was now scowling, to the abbess. "Word has reached me that Craeg the Bastard and his band are sheltering near Kilbride," he replied. "I'm here to find him."

Coira flushed hot and then cold. She lowered her spoon, her heart now hammering against her ribs.

No one at the table spoke. However, Father Camron wore a shrewd expression, his gaze flicking from MacKinnon to the abbess.

"Have ye seen any of the outlaws?" MacKinnon asked after a pause, his attention never leaving the abbess. His voice had lowered, and Coira shivered. It was a tone she knew well, one that screamed 'danger'.

Mother Shona didn't react. Her face remained a mask of serenity, her eyes guileless. "No, we have not."

"Are ye sure?"

"We live sheltered lives inside these walls," the abbess replied, her voice as steady as her gaze. "The outlaws could well be nearby, and we wouldn't know. However, none of the sisters have reported seeing anyone suspicious."

"And yet a man from Torrin tells me that he has seen them ... in the woods no more than ten furlongs from Kilbride's walls."

"As I said ... we are sheltered here."

Silence fell once more at the table, tension vibrating through the air. MacKinnon still stared the abbess down although Coira noted how the muscles in his jaw flexed. He was angry and suspected that Mother Shona was hiding something.

The knot in Coira's breast clenched tighter. He suspected right—and if he ever discovered the truth, it would be over for all of them.

Long moments passed, and then MacKinnon's attention shifted to the abbot. "Father Camron ... how long have ye been visiting the abbey?"

"Nearly two weeks now," the abbot replied, helping himself to a cup of ale.

"And ye have not seen anything to arouse yer suspicions?"

Coira's breathing hitched, her heart now racing so fast she started to feel dizzy. Suddenly, she wanted to dive under the table and cower there like a beaten dog. She felt exposed seated at the same table as MacKinnon—and was grateful that he hadn't yet noticed her presence at the far end of the dais.

But the abbot had long been looking for an opportunity to cause trouble—and now it had arrived.

Father Camron's mouth curved into a small, wintry smile, an expression that did not warm his dark eyes. "I'm here in the role of inquisitor ... did ye not know, MacKinnon?"

The clan-chief raised a dark eyebrow. "And why's that?"

The abbot raised his cup to his lips and took a leisurely sip, aware that all eyes were now upon him. For the first time since the meal had begun, the abbess's serene mask was slipping. Tension now bracketed her mouth, and her gaze had narrowed.

"Of course, ye know about the two nuns who have *mysteriously* left the order of late," the abbot continued.

"Aye ... ye know I do." The words were uttered roughly, a sign that MacKinnon's patience was thinning.

Coira wondered then whether the abbot would dare raise the issue of MacKinnon's own part in Leanna's disappearance.

Her fingers clenched around her spoon. Father Camron was playing a game, and from the glint in his eyes, she knew he was enjoying it. For the first time since arriving at Kilbride, he felt in control.

"The Pope takes a dim view of such things," he said after a pause, clearly deciding to steer clear of the clan-chief's poor behavior. "I have written to him, and he has given me permission to investigate Mother Shona."

MacKinnon inclined his head. "And have ye found any condemning evidence?"

Feeling a gaze upon her, Coira glanced over to where Sister Elspeth was watching her. Of course, all of the nuns knew about her run-ins with the abbot. And the warning glint in the older nun's eye told Coira that Sister Elspeth knew Camron was going to drop her right in it.

Coira's spine tensed. There was nothing she could say or do; she was trapped.

"The abbess is far too lenient with her nuns," the abbot drawled, favoring Mother Shona with a quick, nasty smile. "She allows them to practice with weapons ... to take witching hour walks outside the abbey walls with no explanation."

And then, Father Camron looked straight at Coira.

The world stopped, and it felt as if, for an instant, so did Coira's heart.

All gazes at the table swiveled to her—including MacKinnon's.

And when he looked at Coira, his expression froze. Until this moment he'd been so intent on his conversation with the abbot and abbess that he'd barely paid any attention to the senior nuns seated around the table.

But he did now.

MacKinnon and Coira's gazes fused. The years rolled back, and suddenly Coira was cringing upon a soiled bed at *The Goat and Goose*, watching as MacKinnon loomed over her.

Despite that the air was close inside the refectory, Coira's limbs started to tremble as if she'd just caught a chill.

"How many of the nuns have behaved this way?" MacKinnon asked. His voice was soft now, barely above a whisper.

"Just this one." Father Camron's tone was jubilant. "Sister Coira." He paused a moment before adding. "Although I suspect there are others who are just as *deviant*."

MacKinnon ignored the abbot's last comment, his attention never wavering. "Sister Coira."

"Aye ... two of my monks found her practicing with a quarter-staff in the orchard over a week ago. She wields it like a man." The disgust in the abbot's voice was evident, yet MacKinnon continued to ignore him. "And I suspect her of *fornication*."

An unpleasant smile twisted the clan-chief's lips. His gaze then shifted to Mother Shona. "I need to question this nun," he drawled. "Alone."

Coira's breathing choked off, sweat now trickling down between her breasts. *Mother Mary, No.*

The abbess scowled, her face growing taut as she cast a worried look at Coira. "Why?"

MacKinnon inclined his head, his gaze narrowing. "If she has been outside the abbey walls at night, she may have had contact with the outlaws."

Mother Shona drew herself up. "If ye have any questions for Sister Coira, ye can ask her here."

A heavy beat of silence passed, and then MacKinnon leaned forward, his gaze snaring the abbess's. "I think ye misunderstand, Mother Shona," he said coldly. "That wasn't a request ... but a command."

15

No Way Back

COIRA WALKED INTO the chapter house on trembling legs.

She couldn't believe Mother Shona was allowing this meeting to take place, that she was letting MacKinnon bully her. The abbess knew the full story about Coira's past—of her history with the clan-chief.

But, unlike the abbot, MacKinnon wasn't a man you defied.

MacKinnon's threat had hung over the air, like the heavy pause between a lightning flash and a thunderclap. They'd all sensed the danger, and when Mother Shona had dropped her gaze, giving her silent assent, Coira had felt as if the walls of the refectory were suddenly closing in on her.

The same sensation assaulted her now, as she walked into the chapter house. Deliberately, she left the door open behind her, but even so, the usually lofty ceiling and large windows seemed oppressive this evening. Outside, it was still light—for night fell very late this time of year—and as such the banks of candles that lined the walls hadn't been lit.

In the center of the space, MacKinnon awaited her.

He stood still, legs akimbo, hands hanging loosely at his sides. Yet his gaze tracked her every step across the floor.

Pulse throbbing in her ears, Coira halted a few feet back from him. She was relieved that her long skirts hid her shaking legs, and she clasped her hands together in front of her so that he wouldn't see how they trembled.

"My last visit ... I knew it was ye," he greeted her, his voice a low rumble.

Coira forced herself to meet his eye. "I wasn't sure ye recognized me," she admitted. The steadiness of her voice surprised her. One thing her experiences over the years had taught her was self-control, it seemed.

MacKinnon favored her with a sharp smile. "I wasn't sure, I admit ... for one nun looks much like another ... but few women have eyes like yers. Ye are a difficult woman to forget, Coira."

The intimacy in his voice made her skin crawl. Acid stung the back of her throat, yet Coira swallowed it down. She needed to keep a leash on her fear; if he saw it, things would only go worse for her.

MacKinnon took a step closer, his gaze raking over her. "Aye ... ye are still comely ... especially in that habit ye wear." His smile widened to a grin then.

"And all the 'Hail Marys' in the world can't cancel out who ye were ... *what* ye still are."

Coira remained silent, even if his words made her nostrils flare. Lord, this man knew how to wield words like blades; he always had. Deliberately, she didn't answer him, didn't deny his comment.

MacKinnon's gaze hooded. "So ye go for walks at night, do ye Coira?" He stepped closer still. They now stood little more than three feet apart, and it took all Coira's will not to shrink back from him.

"Sometimes," she admitted. "I'm the healer here at Kilbride ... some woodland herbs have to be collected at night."

He snorted. "That's a weak excuse ... I thought ye were cleverer than that. Ye are still a whore at heart, aren't ye? I'd wager ye sneak out at the witching hour to spread yer legs for outlaws."

His words were a slap across the face, and Coira started to sweat with the effort it was taking her not to react. Unfortunately though, Duncan MacKinnon wasn't yet done. "Have ye serviced my bastard brother yet?"

Nausea swamped Coira. She'd not done anything to be ashamed of with Craeg, and yet MacKinnon's words made her feel dirty.

"I haven't seen any of the outlaws," she lied, her voice husky with the effort it was taking not to turn tail and bolt from the chapter house. "And if that's all ye want to know, our conversation is at an end."

"No, it isn't." MacKinnon closed the gap between them, and suddenly he was looming over her, invading her space.

Coira went rigid. Her arms dropped to her sides, and her fingers curled into her palms, the nails digging in. Her heart was pounding so fast that she was sure he'd be able to hear it.

"I've missed ye, Coira," he murmured, his voice lowering. It was an intimate tone, a lover's voice. "And seeing ye again has reminded me how much I enjoyed our time together."

"I didn't," she bit out the words. "I hated every moment."

His eyebrows raised, and then he gave her a slow smile. "Good."

Coira backed away from him. Once again, the walls were closing in on her. His closeness was a stranglehold. However, his hand shot out, his fingers closing roughly over her upper arm and halting her.

"When I'm done with the outlaws, I'm coming for ye, Coira," he growled, "and if ye give me any trouble, I will have my men butcher every last nun within these walls. Is that clear?"

Coira's breathing came in short, rasping gasps, her body now shaking uncontrollably. "Ye are a beast, MacKinnon," she replied, choking out the words. "Curse yer soul to eternal damnation."

He grinned at her, his gaze gleaming. "It's too late for that." His grip tightened, his fingers biting into her flesh. "I'm done being thwarted. Ready yerself to leave Kilbride ... prepare for a life as my whore at Dunan."

MacKinnon let go of her then and stepped back, his chest heaving. The lust on his face made Coira's belly roil. Clamping her jaw shut, she staggered back from him. Her hands fisted at her sides.

Enough. If he dared reach for her again, she'd break his jaw.

But MacKinnon didn't. Having delivered his terms, he favored her with one last lingering look before turning on his heel and striding from the chapter house.

A hollow silence, broken only by the rasp of Coira's breathing, settled over the space. For a few moments, she merely stood there, body coiled. She'd almost wanted him to grab her so that she could unleash the fury she'd smothered for over a decade. But he hadn't given her the chance.

Once again, MacKinnon had bested her.

A sob splintered the air. Had she just made that wretched sound? Trembling, Coira wrapped her arms about her torso and staggered over to the narrow bench seat that ran around the perimeter of the floor. She sank down onto it and squeezed her eyes shut as terror pulsed through her.

He won't have me again. The vow was a silent scream inside her head.

The abbey had become a prison.

It seemed that everywhere Coira turned there was a man wearing MacKinnon plaid, leering at her. She was sure she was imagining the lecherous looks, and yet she couldn't help fear that the clan-chief had told his men about her past, of who she'd been before taking the veil.

The morning following the clan-chief's arrival was misty and cool. Coira and Sister Mina escaped the confines of the abbey with a trip to Torrin to tend on the sick farmer's wife and daughter. Although it was a relief to be free of Kilbride, the visit didn't provide Coira any solace. Her patients' conditions had worsened—they both had swellings under their armpits and their bodies were wracked with fever—and the farmer had grown more agitated.

"Ye must be able to do something?" His voice rose as he loomed over Coira when she emerged from the dwelling. "They're going to die."

Coira faced the farmer down, her belly twisting when she saw the grief in his eyes. "I've done all I can think of … but they're not responding to the herbs that usually bring down a fever. I'm sorry. I can do nothing but pray for them."

Her words were heartfelt, and yet they felt hollow. The farmer didn't want them. The man's face grew hard. "Useless," he rasped, as he turned away from her. "What good is yer God to me now?"

"It's not yer fault," Sister Mina murmured as they left the cottage behind and stepped onto the path that would take them back to Kilbride. "Deep down, Bred knows that."

Coira heaved a sigh, putting away the scarf she'd tied around her mouth and nose when dealing with the patients. Her mother had often covered her face when tending those she thought infectious, although it hadn't stopped her from succumbing to a terrible fever sickness that had swept through Dunan and the outlying settlements one winter. It likely wasn't going to protect Coira much either, yet she had to do what she could to keep herself healthy.

"I know," she replied, her heart heavy. "I wish I could have given him hope ... but it would be a false one."

"So they really will die?"

"Aye."

Sister Mina's grey eyes clouded, but she didn't comment further. There wasn't really anything one could say to that.

The two nuns had walked another few yards when a man suddenly stepped out onto the path before them. Tall and lean, with a sharp-featured face, the stranger wore dusty leathers and carried a longbow and quiver over his back.

Sister Mina cried out, fumbling at her belt for the knife she always carried. Meanwhile, Coira dropped her healer's basket and brought up her quarter-staff; she gripped it two-handed, barring him from approaching further.

The man halted. His gaze widened, flicking between Coira and Sister Mina, even as his mouth quirked. "Fighting nuns ... now I've seen it all."

Coira gritted her teeth. She'd had enough of the arrogance of men. One more jibe and she'd jab him in the cods with the pointed iron end of her staff.

As if reading the fierce expression on her face, the stranger's face grew serious, and he raised his hands, palms facing outward, above him. "I mean ye no harm." His attention flicked from where Sister Mina now held her knife at hip level, blade pointed toward him, back to her companion.

"Are ye Sister Coira?"

Coira scowled. A long moment passed before she nodded.

The man let out a gusting breath that she guessed was relief. "Just as well ... I've not been able to get near the abbey gates to ask for ye."

"MacKinnon's here," Sister Mina spoke up.

"So I've gleaned," the stranger replied, his gaze never leaving Coira.

"Who are ye?" Coira demanded, her temper fraying.

"My name's Farlan ... I'm part of Craeg's band. He sent me here." The outlaw paused, his lean face tensing. "Two of our men are sick ... we think it's the plague but have no healer to attend them. Craeg asks that ye visit them."

Coira stiffened. "The sickness is here now too ... I've just come from a mother and daughter afflicted with it. They'll likely die ... as will yer men." The words were harsh, and yet Coira's nerves had been stretched to breaking point of late. She didn't have it in her to soften her answer.

However, Farlan didn't appear offended. He continued to hold her gaze, his own steady. "All the same, Craeg has asked for ye ... will ye come?"

It was on the tip of her tongue to refuse, to send the outlaw away with a sharp reprimand.

But then a strange sensation settled over Coira—one that made her pause.

She looked away from him, her gaze settling upon the grey stone walls of Kilbride in the distance.

For years, the abbey had been her refuge from the world, but not anymore. Her past had finally caught up with her. If she returned to her life amongst the sisters, it would only be a matter of time before MacKinnon made her choose: her life or theirs.

Coira glanced over at Sister Mina. The nun still had her knife raised, her young face screwed up in consternation as she glared at the outlaw. "Ye go on ahead, Sister," Coira said softly.

Sister Mina's attention snapped to her. "Ye are going?"

Coira nodded, her belly fluttering as she did so.

If ye do this, there's no way back.

But did she actually want to go back? For years she'd lived contentedly as a nun, yet in the past days, something had shifted within her. A restlessness had surfaced, a yearning that would not be quietened.

Craeg had been the catalyst. The hours she'd spent in his company while he'd been recovering, and then that intense exchange in the moonlit clearing, had ignited something inside her. She wasn't sure what the future held, but the urge to go to him grew with each passing moment.

She wouldn't ignore it.

"But ye can't go alone ... I'm coming with ye."

"Ye can't, Sister," Coira replied with a shake of her head. "I've gotten myself into trouble with both the abbot and MacKinnon now. This will be one step too far. If I go to the outlaws, I won't be able to return to the abbey ... and so neither will ye."

Sister Mina stared at her, realization dawning. "Ye are leaving the order?"

Coira favored the young woman with a soft smile. There was so much she wanted to say to Sister Mina; her chest felt tight with the need to unburden herself. Yet she held herself back. "It seems that way, doesn't it?"

Silence fell, and then Farlan cleared his throat. "Sorry to interrupt, but if we linger out here in the open much longer, someone's going to see me. We need to go now."

Still holding Sister Mina's eye, Coira gave a curt nod. "I'm ready."

The novice's eyes gleamed, and she started to blink rapidly. "This isn't right. Ye mustn't leave."

"I'm afraid, I must," Coira replied, her throat tensing. The determination in her voice surprised her, as did an overwhelming sense of relief. She didn't actually want to return to Kilbride. "Peace be with ye, Sister Mina. Please tell the others I've gone to collect herbs and will be back later."

Sister Mina's throat bobbed. She lowered her blade and resheathed it at her waist. "Peace be with ye, Sister. Worry not, I will not betray ye," she murmured.

Coira forced a smile. "Thank ye."

She then lowered her quarter-staff, picked up her basket and looped it over one arm, and followed Farlan into the trees without a backward glance.

Hidden in a clump of bracken, the watcher observed the two nuns part ways.

He saw Sister Coira follow the man into the woods, while Sister Mina continued on her way along the path leading down the hillside toward the abbey.

Heart racing, Brother Ian rose to his feet and dusted off his habit. He'd shadowed the healer for days now, watching and waiting for her to transgress once more. Following someone without being spotted was a challenging task, but the monk was small and slight, and could easily make himself invisible if he so wished.

Secretly, he'd begun to question Father Camron's fixation with this nun—until now.

Excitement fluttered in Brother Ian's belly. The abbot was right. The nun did fraternize with outlaws. He'd seen it with his own eyes.

Drawing his robes close, the young monk crept away through the bracken.

16

Yer Luck Has Run Out

COIRA FOLLOWED THE outlaw and wondered if she had taken leave of her senses. The heady rush of resolve that had made her turn her back on Kilbride was now ebbing, and she was starting to doubt her decision.

There's still time. Ye can turn around and flee back to the abbey. Back to MacKinnon.

The thought made her keep walking, although her heart leaped with each step. The people she was traveling to help were those who'd risen up against the clan-chief, those who would one day bring him down.

She wanted to be part of that. She'd gladly help those who rebelled against a clan-chief who over-taxed his people, who controlled these lands by terrifying folk into submission. His time was coming to an end, and she would join the rebellion against him.

Heat spread across Coira's chest, recklessness catching fire in her veins. Suddenly, she knew in her bones that she'd made the right decision.

The time had come to act.

Reaching into the small leather pouch upon her belt, Coira's fingers curled around a silver ring. After arriving at Kilbride, she'd been forced to remove the ring from her right hand, and had instead donned a fine gold band when she'd taken her vows—a new ring that marked her as a Bride of Christ. But she had always kept her mother's ring close, even though she knew she really shouldn't. It was the only thing she had left from her past—the only link to her parents.

And although she still donned her habit, the desire to wear the old ring once more swept over Coira.

Removing the gold band, she put it away in the pouch and slipped her mother's ring onto her right hand. A smile spread across her face.

Once again, instinct had taken over, and she would follow where it led.

Farlan took her to a glade where a saddled horse awaited them. Wordlessly, he untied the gelding and tightened its girth, before he sprang up onto the saddle. Reaching down, he helped Coira up behind him.

To keep her seat, she squeezed with her thighs as the outlaw urged the horse into a bouncing trot and then a jolting canter.

Moments later they were flying through the trees, heading east.

Duncan MacKinnon stirred the turnip and kale pottage around the earthen bowl before him.

Stew ... again.

Maybe that was why his appetite was poor today. Did these nuns eat anything else but stew and coarse bread?

Putting down his spoon, Duncan reached for his cup of ale and took a sip. He didn't feel himself. He'd awoken feeling listless and hadn't broken his fast with a plate of bannocks as he usually did. Now the sight of food made him feel queasy, and his belly had developed a faint ache.

He hoped the mutton stew he'd eaten the day before hadn't made him sick.

Next to him, Father Camron spooned great mouthfuls of stew into his mouth. Heavyset with an appetite of three men, the abbot certainly hadn't complained of the fare at Kilbride. However, he was obviously used to eating this way.

Gaze drifting around the table, Duncan searched for Sister Coira. He knew that she took her meals with the senior nuns at the abbess's table, yet he hadn't seen her enter the refectory.

And there was an empty space at the table.

He glanced over at the abbess to find Mother Shona watching him. Duncan frowned at her. "Where's Sister Coira?"

"There are sick villagers in Torrin," the abbess replied, her voice cool. "Sister Coira has gone to attend them."

Across from Mother Shona, Father Camron stopped shoveling stew into his mouth. Straightening up, he wiped his lips with the back of his hand. "Ye should forbid her to do so, Mother." His dark brows knotted together as he frowned. "Do ye want the plague entering the abbey?"

The abbess glanced over at the abbot, her mouth pursing. In the day he'd been here, Duncan had seen the woman grow increasingly tense. "The abbey has an important role," she replied, her tone sharpening. "We will not abandon the folk of these lands."

MacKinnon snorted, drawing her gaze once more. "From what I hear, there is no cure for the sickness ... Sister Coira is wasting her time."

His belly tightened then as he considered that the nun might fall ill and die. He had plans for the lovely Coira—the last thing he wanted was to lose her again.

Ye don't want to catch the pestilence off her either, he reminded himself.

"MacKinnon is right," Father Camron added with a cold smile. "A nun's place is here ... serving the Lord in prayer."

"A nun's place is helping others ... as Christ taught us," Mother Shona replied crisply. "Sister Coira is a gifted healer. Even if she can't cure folk, she can ensure their last hours are as comfortable as possible … and bring comfort to their families."

The abbot's smile twisted. "A lot of good that'll do."

Mother Shona's brown eyes glinted, and she inhaled sharply. Her lips parted as she readied herself to reply to the abbot. However, the arrival of a monk at their table forestalled her.

The monk was young—small and slender as a lass. His dark hair was cropped short, the crown tonsured. And even though heavy dark robes swathed his small body, MacKinnon could see that the monk was quivering with excitement.

"Father Camron!" The monk dropped to one knee next to the abbot, his voice high and breathless. "I have news."

The abbot swiveled, his face creasing into a scowl. "Not *here*, Brother Ian," he snapped. "Come … we'll talk outside."

Father Camron made to rise from the table, but MacKinnon reached out and caught the sleeve of his robe, restraining him.

"Yer friend looks excited," he murmured. "I think we'd all like to hear his news."

The abbot's throat bobbed, his gaze darting from Duncan to the abbess. Mother Shona was watching him with a furrowed brow. "This is private," he muttered.

"Ye are on my land, Father," MacKinnon warned him with a tight smile. "And as such, I will hear what this man has to say." The clan-chief shifted his attention to the monk. The excitement had ebbed from his lean face, and he now wore a hunted expression. No doubt, this transgression would earn him a beating from the abbot later.

Father Camron sank back down onto the bench seat, defeated. "Very well," he growled. "Tell us then, Brother Ian."

"The nun … Sister Coira … I saw her on the path back from Torrin, Father. She was talking with a man. And then she left with him."

Duncan went still, his tender belly clenching further. "Describe him."

The monk's gaze flicked between the abbot and clan-chief before he swallowed hard. "Tall and lanky with dark hair … he was clad in hunting leathers and carried a longbow."

MacKinnon sucked in a breath. *An outlaw*. "Why didn't ye follow them?"

The monk's gaze widened. "Father Camron told me to return to him if Sister Coira did anything suspicious."

Heat exploded in Duncan's chest, creeping up his neck in a sensation he knew well; he was having trouble keeping a leash on his temper. "Lackwit," he growled. "What good is this news, if we don't know where they went?"

Brother Ian licked his lips, his gaze darting now. The abbot hadn't uttered a word, although his face had turned red. Indeed, the monk was going to get a thrashing the moment he got him alone. "Maybe the other nun knows," he finally replied, his voice strangled.

Duncan scowled, his hands fisting as he prepared himself to lash out at this clod-head. "*Other* nun?"

"Aye … she was with Sister Coira at the time, but she returned to the abbey afterward." The monk's thin cheeks flushed while the words poured from him. He then swiveled around, his gaze searching the sea of faces beneath the dais. The nuns, monks, and warriors seated there had all stopped eating and were watching the scene unfold. "There!" he gasped, pointing. "There she is!"

MacKinnon's gaze followed his and settled upon a young nun seated at the far side of the refectory. Large grey eyes stared back at him, and the lass cringed under the weight of his stare. The clan-chief pushed himself up from his seat and slowly beckoned to the nun. "Come here," he growled.

"We've picked up their trail ... they're heading east."

The warrior panted the words, pulling his horse up in the yard before MacKinnon.

Duncan nodded, his jaw clenching. Frustration pulsed through him. It had taken much longer than he'd have liked to get the information out of that novice. She'd looked young and easily cowed, yet the wee bitch had kept her mouth shut initially. It was only when Duncan twisted her arm to breaking point behind her back that she'd gasped out the details he needed, tears of pain streaming down her face.

Two of his bastard brother's men were sick—the outlaw was taking Coira to their camp.

"Track them as far as ye can," Duncan growled. "I want to know the location of their hide-out."

"And then?" The warrior asked. Tall and blond with a broad face, the man's name was Keith MacKinnon—a distant cousin to the clan-chief. In Carr's absence, he was now MacKinnon's second. However, unlike Carr Broderick, Keith lacked initiative. He didn't do anything unless Duncan barked an order at him.

"Get back here, and we'll pay them a visit," Duncan snarled back. "Go!"

He watched Keith ride out of the yard, dust boiling up under his horse's hooves, and listened as his second cousin bawled orders at the other members of the Dunan Guard waiting outside the walls.

Reaching up, Duncan raked both hands through his hair. He was aware then that the listlessness that had afflicted him since rising that morning had grown. His limbs felt heavy and achy, and despite the cool, cloudy afternoon, he was sweating.

It's the strain of all of this, he told himself. *It's getting to me.*

Tension coiled within him, longing for release. For years he'd hunted his half-brother, and for years Craeg had eluded him. However, the game of cat and mouse was coming to an end.

"Not long now, Bastard," he muttered. "Yer luck has run out."

17

I Will Do What I Can

FEET SLIPPING ON the loose shale, Coira made her way down the bank into the ravine. Below her lay a narrow valley floor, shadowed either side with high stone walls. The smoke from numerous cook fires drifted up to greet her, as did the aroma of roasting venison. The murmur of voices and the wail of a bairn somewhere in the ravine echoed off the damp rock.

Coira's breath caught. Just how many people were packed in here? She'd heard that over the past month many folk had rallied to the outlaws' side, but she hadn't expected to see such a crowd.

Farlan walked ahead, booted feet slithering on the steep bank. They'd both dismounted his horse, and he now led the beast.

"How long have ye been camped here?" she called out.

"Nearly a moon now," he replied, not looking her way.

They continued down the ravine. Curious gazes settled upon her, and Coira knew she must cut an unusual figure: a tall nun with a basket of herbs in one hand and a quarter-staff in the other. Many of the faces of the men, women, and children watching her were strained, their gazes worried.

News of the sick men was clearly common-knowledge throughout the camp.

Farlan led her down the length of the valley, past clumps of hide tents and fires where MacKinnon's deer spit-roasted over embers. Coira's mouth watered at the aroma, reminding her that she hadn't eaten since dawn.

Eventually, as the ravine narrowed to a point and the rocky sides, studded with clinging outcrops of pine, reared overhead, Coira spied this band's leader.

A man she'd never expected to set eyes upon again.

Coira's breathing quickened, and her heart started to drum against her ribs. It was hard not to remember the intensity of the last words he'd said to her, and how she'd fled like a frightened deer into the night afterward. She'd never thought it was possible to be both frightened and captivated at the same time.

Seeing him again brought it all back.

Craeg stood before a single large tent, muscular arms folded across his broad chest. He wore a sleeveless leather vest and leather breeches that molded to his body. His wild dark hair was unbound, stirring gently in the light breeze that whispered through the gorge. His moss-green eyes were fixed upon her, tracking her steps as she drew near.

Mother Mary, give me strength. Coira needed to keep her composure. She was here to help the sick, not for a reunion with Craeg. Awkwardness warred with the urge to rush to him.

With a jolt, she realized just how much she'd missed the outlaw in the past days. He'd only been in her life a short while, but she already felt a bond with him that went beyond the friendship they'd forged as patient and healer.

Craeg stepped forward to greet her. Behind him stood a huge man with a mane of red hair—he was a striking individual, yet Coira had been so focused on Craeg, she hadn't even noticed him. Another figure, an older woman with greying dark hair and a careworn face, ventured forth.

The grim look on the red-haired outlaw's face made her belly tighten.

"Thank ye for coming, Sister Coira." The formality in Craeg's voice caused Coira to tense. His face was a study in composure. Had he forgotten the things he'd said to her in that clearing? Of course, he'd called for her help, not for any other reason.

"Peace be with ye, Craeg," Coira answered, dipping her gaze. Once again, shyness was getting the better of her.

"It's good to see ye," he said, breaking the awkward silence between them. "I—"

"MacKinnon's at Kilbride, Craeg," Farlan interrupted from behind Coira.

She glanced back up to see that Craeg had gone still, his expression suddenly hawkish.

"It's true," Coira murmured. "He's brought the Dunan Guard with him … someone in Torrin has betrayed ye, after all, it seems."

Craeg's mouth stretched into a humorless smile. "Aye … I was hoping they would."

Coira frowned. "Excuse me? Ye told me the folk of this land were loyal to ye. Why would ye want one of them to inform on ye?"

"I wanted to draw MacKinnon out," Craeg replied, his smile widening. "So we can face each other at last."

"But didn't ye already do that … earlier in the summer?"

Craeg snorted. "That was an ambush, not a fair fight. This time we're ready for him."

Judging from the gleam in Craeg's eye, he couldn't wait to face his half-brother.

"Victory in battle will feel hollow indeed if yer band sickens and dies," she said crisply, her attention shifting to the tent behind him. "Are yer men in there?"

Craeg nodded, his expression sobering.

"One of them is in a bad way." The older woman added softly. "I don't think he's got much time left."

"My woman, Fenella, has taken ill too." The red-haired outlaw spoke up behind Craeg. "Will ye take a look at her as well?"

Coira met the man's gaze. "Of course, I will."

Setting down her staff, she withdrew her scarf from her basket and began to tie it around her mouth and nose.

"What are ye doing?" Farlan asked, suspicion edging his voice as he watched her preparations.

"Just taking precautions," Coira replied. She glanced Craeg's way then. "Ye must keep folk away from those who have taken sick."

He nodded, his handsome face taut with concern now. "Fenella has been looking after the sick men." He motioned to the man and woman behind him. "As have Gunn, Flora, and I."

Coira drew in a deep, steadying breath. "Then all three of ye are at risk as well." She shifted her attention to where Farlan stood a few yards behind her. "Keep back from this area ... and warn the others to do the same."

The young man nodded, his brow furrowing. He then glanced over at Craeg, awaiting his confirmation.

"Do as she says," Craeg said. His voice was cool, calm. She was grateful that he wasn't letting fear of the sickness, which could turn folk witless, dominate his decision-making. "Let the others know that MacKinnon is at Kilbride ... and that we'll be riding out to meet him first thing tomorrow."

Coira caught her breath and turned back to Craeg, to find him observing her. His mouth then lifted at the corners. "Aye, that's tomorrow's plan ... but tonight we focus on other matters," he said quietly. "Since we're already at risk of getting sick, consider me and Flora yer assistants."

Coira's own mouth curved, although he wouldn't see that under the scarf that protected her face. "There's no point in ye taking risks though ... keep yer distance from those afflicted unless absolutely necessary."

He nodded, stepping aside to let Coira past. "Is there anything ye need?"

"A bowl of steaming hot water and a cake of lye soap would help."

"I'll see to it," Flora spoke up. She shot Coira a quick, grateful smile, before hurrying off to fetch the water.

Heaving a deep breath, Coira walked forward and ducked through the entrance into the tent.

One glance at the two men within and Coira knew they were both past her help.

The man lying to the left of the brazier certainly was—he was dead, eyes staring up at the roof of the tent, his mouth twisted in a grimace of pain.

Coira swallowed hard as dread trailed its icy fingers down her spine.

I don't know how to stop this.

She'd always felt confident in her skills, yet she was seriously out of her depth here. Nothing she'd learned from her mother, or from the last decade working as a healer, could prepare her for this moment. She had no idea how to proceed.

"Sister." A weak, raspy voice interrupted her.

The man lying to the right of the brazier was still alive, although barely so. He stared up at Coira, his gaze glassy. "Help me."

Coira swallowed hard. "Aye," she whispered, reaching with shaking hands for a small clay bottle of hemlock juice inside her basket. "I will do what I can."

Night fell over the ravine, a misty day giving way to a damp, cool night.

Craeg crouched before the fire pit and nudged the embers with a stick before adding a gorse branch. A moment later, a shower of bright sparks and tongues of flame shot up into the darkness.

Shifting his attention from the fire, Craeg's gaze settled upon Gunn. His friend sat cross-legged opposite him. The warrior's eyes were desolate, his face seeming carven from stone.

Fenella was his life, his soul. And now she was gravely ill.

Sister Coira was still with her.

Craeg studied Gunn a moment, his chest tightening. They'd spoken little as the last rays of daylight had seeped from the world—there wasn't much either of them could say. Both of them risked falling sick too. It was just a matter of waiting to see.

Strangely, Craeg wasn't worried for himself. He'd long ago overcome a fear of death. He'd been reckless with his own life too many times to be afraid of losing it. Instead, the thought of losing Fenella and Gunn filled him with a sense of despair so powerful that it hurt to breathe.

And underneath it all, guilt plagued him over Coira. He shouldn't have called her here. In doing so, he'd put her life at risk as well.

Fate was a cruel bitch. They were so close to bringing MacKinnon down. But if this pestilence dug its claws in and ripped through his band of followers, it would be a hollow victory indeed. It was poor timing, and yet the moment had been coming for a long while now. He wouldn't turn away from it, and neither would those who followed him.

Gunn glanced up then, his eyes hollowed in the firelight. He seemed to have aged a decade in the past few hours. "Dawn can't come soon enough," he said roughly. "I'm looking forward to giving MacKinnon's men a taste of my blade."

"Ye don't have to join us," Craeg replied. "If ye wish to remain here with Fen, I'll understand."

Gunn shook his head, his expression turning vehement. "Fen wants me to fight tomorrow. I'll not stay behind."

Craeg nodded. He certainly wasn't going to argue with Gunn when he was in this mood.

He was aware then of a dark-robed figure appearing from the small tent where Fenella was laid up. Coira had finally joined them.

Both men turned to her, watching as she approached the fire and pulled off the scarf that covered the lower half of her face. Her expression was tense, her lovely eyes hollowed with fatigue.

Once again, guilt arrowed through Craeg's gut. When he'd seen her earlier, for the first time since she'd helped him escape, his pulse had quickened. Heat had then flowered across his chest, obliterating the gnawing worry the sickness had brought.

He'd devoured the sight of her, and for just a few moments, had forgotten why he'd called her to his side. All that mattered was that Coira was with him.

He hadn't lied. He was happy to see her again—happier than Coira realized.

"How is she?" Gunn asked, his voice hoarse with worry.

Coira met his gaze steadily. "She's worsening ... I'm sorry."

Gunn's face went taut. "Do none of yer herbs and potions work?"

Coira's expression shadowed. "I've given her something for the fever, which should slow the sickness's progress," she replied softly.

"Join us at the fire," Craeg spoke up, motioning to the hunk of bread and cheese that sat on an oiled cloth beside him. "I've kept some food back for ye."

Coira nodded, relief suffusing her face. She crossed to him and lowered herself to the ground with a stifled groan.

Craeg looked at her sharply, concern knotting his belly. "Are ye unwell?"

She shook her head. "No ... just exhausted." She paused there, looking about her. "Do ye have some water and soap? I need to wash my hands."

"The water's cold," Craeg said, rising to his feet. "Will that do?"

"Aye, well enough. Thank ye."

Craeg brought the bowl and soap to the fireside, handing them to her. He watched as Coira washed her hands and then devoured her supper.

"Are yer men ready to face MacKinnon tomorrow in battle?" Coira asked finally, brushing the crumbs off her habit. Her tone was guarded, and she avoided his eye. He wondered if she thought him rash.

"Aye ... they've been ready for weeks now," he replied. "And with the sickness in the camp, it will give them something else to think about."

"The men are eager to fight," Gunn spoke up, his jaw set, his gaze gleaming. "As am I. If the pestilence is going to take us ... we want to see MacKinnon go down first."

Coira glanced up before her gaze flicked between the two men. Her mouth compressed. Craeg sensed she wanted to say something but was holding herself back. Moments passed, and then her attention settled upon him. "How is yer wound?"

Craeg smiled. "Healing well ... thanks to ye."

Coira stared back at him, her cheeks growing pink. The nun's blush intrigued Craeg. Everything about Coira fascinated him.

She cleared her throat. "If ye are set on going into battle tomorrow ... I should take a look at it."

"What ... now?"

"Can we go to yer tent?" she asked, the blush upon her cheeks deepening. "I have something to ask of ye."

18

Broken

COIRA FOLLOWED CRAEG into his tent, her heart hammering. Wiping damp palms on the skirts of her habit, she attempted to steady her nerves.

Calm down.

She hadn't expected to be this anxious, but the thing she needed to ask Craeg made her feel as if she were climbing the steps to the gallows.

What if he denies me?

She hoped he wouldn't, for her hopes rested upon his consent. If she never intended to return to Kilbride, she needed to carve another role for herself among these people.

It was a conversation that couldn't wait.

Craeg's tent was a lean-to built against the ravine wall. It was small and furnished only with a single fur on the floor and a brazier in the center, where a lump of peat glowed.

The outlaw leader turned to Coira, and suddenly the tent felt cramped and airless. His presence sucked the air out of the smoky interior. Craeg's height and breadth made her feel tiny in comparison. Her thoughts suddenly scattered.

Concentrate, she chided herself. *Ye must focus.*

"What did ye want to speak to me of?" he asked with a slow smile. It was a purely masculine expression and a reminder that Craeg hadn't forgotten what he'd said to her back in that moonlit glade.

Neither had Coira, but that wasn't why she'd asked for a moment alone with him.

She swallowed. "I will get to that in a moment," she replied. "First ... let me take a look at yer side."

Craeg hesitated, as he continued to watch her intently. He was probably wondering what was amiss with her. However, he didn't argue. Not shifting his focus from her, he began to unlace his vest. He then shrugged it off.

The sight of his naked chest was distracting. She'd seen his nude torso before, yet this time it made Coira's breathing grow shallow, an ache forming just under her breast bone.

Forcing herself to focus, she stepped toward him, set down her basket, and deftly unwrapped the light bandage he wore. Then, bending close, she examined the injury to his left flank.

It was healing beautifully—better than she'd expected. The scab that had formed was dry, and there was no unpleasant smell issuing from it.

"Ye are tough," she admitted, drawing back from him. "Such a wound would have killed many men."

Craeg's mouth curved, his eyes gleaming. "Aye ... so I'm healthy enough to swing a sword tomorrow?"

Coira nodded. His proximity was making it hard for her to keep her thoughts netted. The heat of his body was like a furnace, and the warm, spicy scent of his skin made a strange yearning rise within her belly. "Make sure ye bind the injury well first though ... or ye risk splitting it open again."

Reaching for a clean bandage, she wrapped it around his torso, and as she did so, she became increasingly aware of his nearness and the gentle whisper of both their breathing.

The words that he'd said that night returned to her, taunting her. She'd not remind him of that incident. Yet she knew he was watching her, waiting for her to speak.

Coira finished her task and stepped back from him. "Ye can put yer vest back on now," she said, cursing the huskiness in her voice. She couldn't let herself get distracted. He looked like he wanted to kiss her, and although part of her yearned for it, her heart suddenly shrank at the thought.

She'd made this journey partly because of him, but the situation was starting to feel too real, too intense. Coira realized then that she wasn't ready to take the next step, whatever that was.

Craeg did as bid, but as he laced up the vest, his mouth quirked. His eyes darkened as he gazed upon her. "Out with it then ... what do ye wish to ask?"

Coira heaved in a deep breath. When he looked at her like that, it was nearly impossible to form a coherent thought. Yet now he'd given her an opening, she wasn't going to waste the opportunity. "Would ye let me remain here?" she asked, the words rushing out of her. "With yer band?"

Craeg's eyes widened, a smile creasing his face. "Of course, Coira." He reached forward then, clasping her hands with his. "So ye have left the order?"

Coira nodded. "I must," she whispered. She was tempted to leave it at that, but her thudding heart warned her that she couldn't. Craeg needed to hear this story—even if the truth repelled him. She was tired of carrying around her dark secrets. The urge to bare her soul to him was too great.

Coira's breathing caught. "It's MacKinnon," she gasped the hated name. "He's after me."

Craeg went still, dangerously so. The joy in his eyes faded, as did his smile. All trace of good humor leached from his face. "Why?"

Dear Lord, please have mercy on me. This was her chance to lie, to cover up a past that she wished belonged to someone else. But she wouldn't. She'd tell the truth.

"Do ye remember when ye told me about yer upbringing in Dunan?" she asked finally, forcing herself to keep looking at him.

"Aye," he replied, his tone wary.

"Well." She cleared her throat then. Lord, this was harder than she'd expected. "I didn't tell ye at the time, but I know *The Goat and Goose* well ... for I ... I worked there for a time."

His green eyes grew wide at this admission before they shadowed. In their depths, she saw sympathy, and a hard knot formed in her belly in response. She doubted he'd look so compassionate when he heard the next part of her story.

"I arrived around a year after ye left," Coira pressed on. She lifted her chin then as she continued. "I was yer brother's favorite whore."

Craeg's sharply indrawn breath filled the tent. He drew back as if she'd just struck him, although he didn't release her hands. Coira swallowed hard. It was as she'd feared, and yet she forced herself to continue. He might as well know everything.

"My parents were cottars who worked the land near Dunan. They died suddenly, and then I fell on hard times. I was still young when Maude took me on as a serving lass ... but when I entered womanhood, I was expected to service the men who visited the brothel—or be cast out onto the street again." Coira sucked in a deep breath, noting that Craeg's face had gone taut. "MacKinnon took a liking to me ... and then started asking for me each visit."

Coira broke off there. Saying the words aloud made her feel ill. Surely, Craeg would be revolted by her once he heard it all.

"He liked me to dress up as a nun ... and then he'd rip off my habit and use me." Her voice, raw now, choked off. Suddenly, it was too difficult to continue.

"Coira," Craeg breathed her name, his voice raw. "Mo chridhe ... did he hurt ye?"

My heart. How could he even call her that? Didn't the truth disgust him?

"Aye ... he used his fists on me ... did vile things to me," she whispered. "And finally, one day, I couldn't stand it any longer. I fled Dunan to Kilbride ... and started a new life." She halted, sucking in a deep breath. "But MacKinnon knows where I am now, and he has given me an ultimatum: return with him to Dunan or he'll slaughter everyone at the abbey."

A hollow silence filled the tent as her voice died away. Coira's belly twisted. It occurred to her then that she might have already put the sisters' lives in danger. Had her act in running away made MacKinnon turn on Mother Shona and the other nuns? Had he already taken his revenge?

Coira clenched her jaw, her gaze remaining upon the fur beneath her feet. She couldn't bear the thought.

Craeg didn't answer immediately, yet when he did his voice was barely above a whisper. "No one should have to endure what ye did," he said, his grip upon her hands tightening as he spoke. "*No one.*"

Coira lifted her chin and forced herself to meet his eye. She expected to see disgust written upon his face, yet she didn't. His face was taut, and a turmoil of emotions in his eyes had changed them from moss-green to dark jade. But there was no revulsion.

Suddenly, Coira felt as if she were standing naked before him. "Will ye still let me stay with yer band?" she asked softly. She needed to bring the conversation back to safer ground. "As ye can see ... I can't go back to the abbey."

Silence stretched between them, and finally, Craeg broke it. "Do ye remember what I said to ye that night ... the night I left Kilbride?"

Coira's pulse started to gallop. *Dear Lord*. This wasn't the time to bring that up. However, when she didn't answer, he continued.

"I said that if things were different, I'd do everything in my power to make ye mine."

"Stop, Craeg," Coira gasped. She tried to pull her hands free, yet he held her fast. "Things aren't different ... they're *worse*. How can ye even say that ... after what I've just told ye?"

He scowled. "None of what happened to ye was yer fault. I care not about yer past. My own isn't a rosy tale as ye well know."

Coira shook her head. Her belly now churned. Her eyes burned, and it felt as if an iron band was squeezing her throat. "But I'm broken," she whispered.

His eyes shadowed, and he stepped closer to her. He then lifted one of her hands to his lips. The kiss he bestowed upon the back of her hand was feather-light, reverent. "So am I, Coira," he said, a rasp to his voice. "Why don't we heal together?"

19

Let Me Have Mine

I'M GOING TO enjoy killing him.

Cold, splintering rage pounded through Craeg as he watched Coira leave the tent. Whispering a curse, he raked his hands through his hair. The urge to storm out of this ravine, go straight to Kilbride, and rip Duncan MacKinnon's heart out almost overwhelmed him. The look on her face as she'd recounted that tale, the shadows in those beautiful eyes, would haunt him forever.

Cursing once more, Craeg scrubbed his face with his fist. An edgy, twitchy sensation swept through him. His hands clenched and unclenched as he imagined them around Duncan MacKinnon's throat—as he squeezed the life out of him.

The man had to die, and he would enjoy ending his cruel, perverted life. MacKinnon scorched anyone he came in contact with. Tomorrow couldn't come soon enough.

Heart hammering, Craeg left his tent and made his way back to the far end of the ravine.

Gunn still sat by the fire, staring sightlessly into the dancing flames, whereas Coira was nowhere to be seen.

"Have ye seen Coira?" he asked his friend.

Gunn glanced up, his gaze struggling to focus. "She's gone back in to attend Fen."

At that moment, a slight figure emerged from the larger of the two tents, where the two men had been tended. Flora—a woman who'd lost her husband earlier that summer when MacKinnon raided their camp—was pale and tense.

"They're both dead now," she announced, her voice flat. "There was nothing to be done."

Craeg nodded, his already racing pulse quickening further. The lives of all the souls in this ravine were his responsibility. If the sickness took more of them, he'd feel to blame.

The bodies of the dead men would have to be burned, but there would be no time for that tomorrow. They would have to wait.

Craeg's hands fisted. Battle had to come first. He had to have his reckoning against his brother—especially now that he'd discovered what Coira had suffered at MacKinnon's hands. He'd make him suffer before the end, and how he'd enjoy doing so.

Events were set in motion now; they couldn't have turned back even if they'd wanted to. MacKinnon was after him too.

Craeg knew his brother wouldn't have wasted any time in sending out scouts; it was likely he'd discovered their hiding place by now. Craeg would need to leave a group of warriors behind to protect the camp, and he'd make sure the war party left a little earlier than planned, just in case MacKinnon decided to launch a dawn raid.

A few feet away, Gunn's face twisted. "It will take Fen too," he said, his voice hoarse with grief. "My bonny love."

Flora's chin trembled at these heart-wrenching words, while Craeg swallowed hard.

He wanted to reassure his friend, to tell him that maybe Coira would find a way to save her. Yet he wouldn't lie to Gunn. He wouldn't lie to himself either.

"Dear Lord of Mercy, send out yer words to heal."

Coira's whispered words blended with the rasp of Fenella's breathing in the tent. Kneeling before the fur on which the sick woman lay, her hands clasped in prayer, Coira squeezed her eyes shut. "Please send yer healing words to yer servant. In the name of Jesus, drive out all infirmity and sickness from this woman's body."

The words, murmured in desperation, poured out of Coira. She'd donned her scarf over her lower face to re-enter the tent but noted immediately that Fenella's condition had worsened.

The lumps that had formed under her armpits had grown. They were now red and angry-looking. Her skin had gone a pasty color, highlighting a strange rash upon her lower arms. Just like the farmer's wife and daughter in Torrin, it looked as if Fenella had been bitten by fleas. The woman's breathing had become labored.

If she continues this way, she won't last the night.

Coira squeezed her eyes shut. She couldn't let despair in; she couldn't lose hope. "Dear Lord," she continued with dogged determination. "I ask ye to turn this weakness into strength, this suffering into compassion, sorrow into joy, and pain into comfort. Let this woman be filled with patience and joy in yer presence as she waits for yer healing touch."

Drawing in a ragged breath, Coira opened her eyes. The prayer had calmed her, focused her. She'd been close to tears when she left Craeg's tent, and the urge to find a shadowed corner where she could seek refuge and weep had almost been overwhelming. His gentle words had nearly unraveled her.

However, she couldn't indulge in tears—not when she had the sick to attend.

Fenella needed her.

Coira lowered her clasped hands, her gaze sweeping over the woman's body. She was clad in a sweat-soaked linen tunic, and although she'd been conscious when Coira entered the tent, she appeared to have entered a strange delirium now. Her limbs twitched and shivered, and she uttered soft, piteous groans.

Watching her, Coira searched her mind for every last bit of healing knowledge her mother had imparted upon her.

How I wish ye were here, Ma, she thought. *I could do with yer wisdom right now.*

Indeed, her mother had been bold and fearless in her skills; never afraid to go against common wisdom if she thought it would save a patient.

Coira's gaze settled upon those horrid swellings under Fenella's armpits. The two men from Dunan had shown the same symptoms. She'd heard about these 'plague boils' and how they appeared during the latter stages of the illness. However, no one had said how a healer dealt with them.

Shifting closer, Coira peered at one of the boils. It reminded her of a large abscess.

How would she treat such a thing usually?

I'd lance it.

Coira's belly twisted at the thought of touching the vile swellings. However, as she continued to stare at the swelling, an idea took form in her mind.

Her pulse quickened then, and she rose to her feet. Emerging from the tent, she found Craeg, Gunn, and Flora seated around the fire, their faces grim.

Craeg glanced up, his gaze meeting hers. His lips parted as he readied himself to speak, but Coira forestalled him. "Can ye get me a pair of leather gloves?"

His eyes widened, while both Gunn and Flora turned to stare at her. "Aye … the smithy will have some … why do—"

"I also need a small, long-bladed knife," she continued. "And some vinegar."

Gunn drew a boning knife from a sheath on his thigh. "Will this do?"

Coira nodded. Meanwhile, Craeg had risen to his feet. "I'll go and get those gloves and vinegar."

Coira swallowed down nausea and held the knife steady.

The gloves Craeg had found for her were too big, making her movements clumsy; yet it was a necessary precaution. She'd not lance these boils without protecting her hands.

She'd cleaned the blade by holding it in the flames till it glowed red. Now she held a small earthen bowl under the boil she was about to lance, ready to catch whatever fluid escaped.

Clenching her jaw, Coira sliced the knife into the boil. Pus and blood burst forth, and her belly roiled. Fighting a gag, she continued her work, cutting open the swelling so that it emptied completely.

Revolting.

Coira had never seen a boil like it. She just hoped that lancing them in this way wouldn't send her patient's body into shock. Once the first had been lanced, she moved onto the second boil—and once that too had emptied, she doused both with the vinegar Craeg had given her.

Her mother had always used vinegar on lanced ulcers and boils, swearing that it prevented them from festering. Coira too had noted how effective it was.

Fenella, who'd been insensible during the entire process, moaned. Sweat slicked her face, and her body still trembled from the chills that wracked her.

Sitting back on her heels, Coira let out the breath she hadn't even realized she'd been holding. No wonder she was starting to feel light-headed. The drained plague boils weren't a nice sight, but they were definitely less sinister-looking than how they'd looked previously.

Gathering up her things, Coira left the tent.

Gunn was standing outside, waiting for her. "Did it work?" he asked. The man's face was haggard with worry, his gaze gleaming.

Coira stripped off the gloves, dropping them onto the ground next to the tent's entrance. "It's too early to tell," she admitted softly. "But what I've done has not worsened her condition." She straightened up and met Gunn's eye. "If she survives the night, ye may have cause to hope."

Heading in the direction of the fireside, Coira removed her scarf and tucked it away in her healer's basket. Her limbs felt heavy, and her temples ached. She wasn't sure what the time was, but she sensed it was growing late.

"We all need to sleep ... like everyone else in this camp," she murmured, her gaze sweeping around at her companions. "There's nothing more any of us can do for the moment."

Craeg nodded, rising from the fireside. "Very well ... I'll be in my tent if anyone needs me." His voice was subdued as well, his gaze shuttered.

Watching him, Coira wondered if he was brooding about what she'd told him earlier. She hadn't expected such kindness, such compassion, from him. It had unbalanced her. She knew his hatred for Duncan MacKinnon ran deep, and she wondered if she'd just added fuel to the fire.

A strange hush had settled over the camp, now that most of the folk here had retired for the night. However, it was a watchful, tense silence, for they all knew what the dawn would bring.

Craeg needed to rest, and Coira wanted to let him retire to his tent, yet she needed to ask something else of him tonight.

"Craeg," she called to him as he turned to go.

The outlaw leader swiveled around. "Aye?"

Coira faced him, her gaze steady. "When ye and yer men ride out to face MacKinnon tomorrow, I want to go with ye."

Craeg tensed. "War isn't for women," he replied, his tone terse now. "Ye will be safer here."

"I can fight," Coira replied, scowling. "All Sisters of Kilbride know how to wield a weapon."

A muscle flexed in Craeg's jaw. Coira was aware that Gunn's gaze was boring into her back, yet she deliberately kept her attention upon the man who stood between her and her wishes.

"As ye all might have guessed, the quarter-staff I carry isn't to help me walk," she continued. "Mother Shona taught me how to do harm with it."

"That may be so," Craeg replied after a pause. "But being able to wield a weapon, and facing a screaming warrior bearing down up ye with a claidheamh-mor is another."

Coira raised her chin, her own jaw tensing. "I'm aware of that."

Their gazes fused. A battle of wills ensued. Although she appreciated Craeg's empathy earlier, she'd not be ordered around by him now.

"Ye are needed here, to tend Fen," Gunn spoke up from behind her, his voice wary.

"Flora will be able to look after her," Coira replied, her gaze still fixed upon Craeg. "I've done all I can for the time being."

Silence settled over the fireside. "I won't get in yer way," Coira continued, stubbornness settling within her. She'd argue this with Craeg all night if he wished. "But ye will have yer vengeance tomorrow. Let me have mine."

20

No Going Back

"MACKINNON ... ARE YE unwell?"

Duncan MacKinnon's head snapped up at the abbess's inquiry.

No, he wasn't. His head hurt. His body ached. And it felt like someone had just taken a stick to him. Not only that, but he was sweating as if he sat next to a roaring fire. Although it was a cool morning, the air heavy with mist, it felt the hottest day of the year to him. There was no doubt about it, he was getting sick. Yet he wasn't about to admit his frailty—not to this bloody woman.

"I'm fine," he rasped and returned his attention to where he was tightening his horse's girth.

"So ye know the location of the outlaw camp?" she asked.

Duncan shot her a hard look. He was grateful she'd changed the subject, but the gleam in the abbess's eyes made him suspicious of her. Mother Shona was taking far too much interest in his affairs. Indeed, Keith and the others had returned with news that they'd tracked the outlaw and nun into the mountains. They'd taken refuge in a hidden ravine.

Still, it mattered not if she knew his intent this morning.

"Aye," he growled. "They're hiding out in the mountains east of Kilbride ... and we're heading there to slaughter them."

The abbess appeared to flinch at the brutality of his words, and despite that he felt like death warmed up, MacKinnon managed a grim smile. This pious woman, with her peaceful ways, paled at such violent talk.

He held her gaze for a moment, darkness stirring within him. He hadn't been making idle threats to Coira. He'd meant it when he'd told her that he'd butcher the abbess and her flock of nuns if Coira didn't return to Dunan with him.

But Coira had still defied him. Right now, she was with his bastard brother.

Duncan's already aching belly, twisted. *Anyone but him. She'll pay for disobeying me.*

When he'd dealt with his brother, and his ragged band, Duncan would return to this abbey and slit this annoying woman's throat. Then he'd torch this place.

As if glimpsing the violence in his eyes, the abbess drew back and made the sign of the cross before her.

"Peace be with ye, MacKinnon," she murmured, her voice cowed.

Duncan flashed her a harsh smile. "Aye ... it will be."

He swung up onto his horse's back and twisted in the saddle, noting that the rest of his men had also mounted and were awaiting his orders.

A wave of nausea washed over Duncan then, and he clutched the pommel of the saddle. *Satan's cods, I feel wretched.* Fear slithered in the pit of his belly, cold and clammy. *Is it the plague?*

No—he wouldn't entertain the thought. He'd merely eaten something that had made him ill.

"We ride!" He called out, gathering his reins. Turning his horse on its haunches, he urged it toward the open gates.

Mother Shona watched the clan-chief and his men empty out of the yard. One moment the space had been filled with men and horses—the next she stood alone, listening to the drum of hoofbeats as they galloped east.

Murmuring a prayer, she crossed herself once more.

The good Lord protect me ... that man is evil.

She'd never looked into someone's eyes and feared for her life like she just had. She'd seen his intent, as clear as if he'd spoken the words.

He planned to kill her.

Heart drumming against her ribs, Mother Shona wiped her damp palms on her skirts, her gaze still upon the open gate where the clan-chief had just departed.

MacKinnon was sick. He could deny it all he wanted, yet the pallor of his face, the sheen of sweat upon his skin, and the way he moved as if he'd suddenly aged overnight told a different tale. The sickness had dug its claws into him.

Still, the knowledge didn't make him any less dangerous. He wasn't ill enough to be prevented from spilling blood today.

A chill feathered down Mother Shona's nape. Until now, Kilbride had been a sanctuary against the sickness, yet MacKinnon had brought it here. How many of them would fall ill because of him?

The abbess clenched her jaw, her gaze still upon the empty gateway. She recalled the things Sister Coira had told her, of how MacKinnon had tormented her.

No wonder she's run off. The very sight of the clan-chief must have turned Sister Coira's stomach. Mother Shona's breathing hitched. *Satan rules this land ... and he must be stopped.*

A cool feeling of resolve settled over the abbess then, drilling in the marrow of her bones. MacKinnon's rule of terror would end today, and she would sacrifice her life, if need be, to see it done.

She tore her attention from the gateway and swept her gaze around, taking in the peaceful surroundings of Kilbride. This place had been her home for so long, but it wouldn't be for much longer.

Everything was changing. Father Camron's campaign against her would never end. Even without MacKinnon threatening the abbey, the sanctuary that she'd worked so hard to protect would soon be no more.

That being the case, she'd do what she could to help Craeg and his men bring MacKinnon down.

Turning on her heel, she glanced about her. It was early, just after dawn. She and the sisters had just finished Lauds, the prayer dedicated to recounting the eternal light bestowed on the world by the Risen Christ.

The monks were now at prayer in the kirk. As soon as the nuns exited, the abbot and his monks had filed inside. Father Camron insisted on conducting his own dawn service, in which the nuns were not welcome.

Spying a small figure across the yard, hurrying toward the refectory, Mother Shona called out. "Sister Mina."

The novice halted and turned to her. After the awful scene the day before, in which MacKinnon had strode across the refectory, hauled Sister Mina from her seat, and twisted her arm behind her back, she was surprised not to see the young woman's face gaunt and strained. MacKinnon had come close to breaking her arm. Yet the novice wore a composed, if wary, expression this morning.

She expected a rebuke from the abbess—although none had been forthcoming the day before.

"Come, Sister ... help me. We must bar the doors," Mother Shona instructed, striding toward the kirk. "Now!"

Thankfully, although Sister Mina's gaze drew wide at the instruction, the novice didn't question her. A heartbeat later the nun joined her, and they ascended the stone steps to the kirk. There was a heavy iron bar inside the building, in case the nuns ever had to barricade themselves inside during an attack. However, there was also a bar on the outside—one that Mother Shona had never used, until today.

Halting before the closed oaken doors, the abbess listened. Inside, she could hear the low rumble of the abbot's voice.

Mother Shona's mouth thinned. *There's no going back after this.*

Father Camron was looking for something to condemn her for—and she was about to give him an excellent reason. However, this man's meddling could no longer be borne.

For what she planned to do now, he had to be kept out of the way.

Together, the two women lifted the heavy bar and slid it through the iron handles, locking the doors together. Fortunately, there was no other exit from the kirk, for the narrow windows were too high to reach.

Father Camron and his monks were now trapped inside.

Turning to Sister Mina, the abbess saw the novice's gaze was gleaming with excitement. Although she hadn't yet explained her plan, the young woman knew that something was afoot.

"Gather the others. Tell them to don their winter woolen leggings, and collect their weapons and bring them to the stables," she ordered, her voice sharp with purpose. "No time must be wasted."

"Where are we going, Mother?" Sister Mina asked. She was already moving away, intent on doing the abbess's bidding.

"MacKinnon plans to carry out a massacre today," Mother Shona replied. "We must stop him."

Sister Mina's step faltered, her eyes growing huge. "We're going to fight the clan-chief?" The novice's voice trembled, betraying her fear. Mother Shona didn't blame her. Sister Mina hadn't been at Kilbride long and hadn't spent as long as the abbess preparing for this day.

But many of the others had. This was the day they'd all hoped would never come.

"Hurry, Sister," the abbess instructed sharply. "Time is against us."

Dawn had barely touched the edge of the ravine as Craeg strode through the ranks of his men. Shouldering quivers of arrows and pinewood shields, their faces were grim, their gazes glinting with purpose.

Craeg met their gazes, his chest constricting as both pride and trepidation filled him.

These men trusted him.

They'd put their lives in his hands—he couldn't fail them.

"We leave shortly," he shouted, his voice echoing about the rumble of conversation. "Ready yerselves." It wasn't a rousing speech, but there would be time enough for that on the battlefield.

Approaching the far end of the ravine, Craeg tensed, preparing himself for the worst. No word of Fenella had reached him for the remainder of the night. He'd slept fitfully and awoken in the pre-dawn, exhausted.

Had Fen died overnight and no one told him? A heavy weight pressed down upon Craeg's breastbone at the thought of losing Fenella; she and Gunn had been with him since the beginning. They were the family he'd always longed for. The fear in Gunn's eyes the night before had been a dirk-blade to Craeg's guts.

He hated to see his friend suffer like this.

Gunn stood before the smoking ruins of last night's fire, his face hewn from stone as he prepared himself for battle. He'd donned a mail shirt and was attempting to lace leather bracers about his forearms.

"Here." Craeg stopped before him. "I'll help ye with that."

"Fen usually does this," Gunn replied softly.

"How is she?" Craeg asked, deftly drawing the laces tight, fastening the leather bracer.

"Still alive."

"Her condition has steadied overnight." A woman's voice intruded then. "And her fever has lowered a little."

Craeg's chin snapped up, his hands stilling.

A woman he barely recognized stood a few feet away.

Coira had removed her habit and dressed in men's clothing: leather breeches, hunting boots, a léine that reached mid-thigh, and a brown vest. The only concession to her former attire was the small wooden crucifix that hung about her neck.

For a moment, Craeg merely stared.

He'd spent far too much time in the past days dreaming what Coira's hair looked like. He'd imagined it would be dark, and it was. Yet it wasn't shorn against her scalp as he'd expected. Instead, it hung in a dark glossy braid over one shoulder.

"She's the same size as Fen," Gunn spoke up when the silence stretched out. "So she might as well borrow some of her clothes. The woman can't go into battle in long skirts, can she?"

Craeg tore his gaze from Coira and saw that his friend now wore a tight smile.

Still speechless, Craeg glanced back at Coira. She seemed taller, leaner, and younger dressed like that.

"Coira." The strangled edge to his voice drew him up sharply. "What weapons do ye have?"

"Just this and a knife," she replied coolly, holding up the quarter-staff with her right hand and slapping the blade strapped to her thigh with the other. "I need nothing else."

Watching her, Craeg's pulse quickened. Coira appeared transformed. The woman's self-confidence stunned him; she wasn't putting on a brave face. He could see the steely determination in her eyes.

Craeg shifted his attention back to Gunn's bracers. Quickly he finished lacing them, and then he stepped back, turning to face Coira.

"I need to speak to ye," he said firmly.

Her eyebrows arched, her gaze turning wary. "Now?"

"Aye ... follow me."

Craeg walked past the two tents, leading the way to the farthest edge of the ravine, where a thin stream of water trickled down the rock face. The air here was misty and smelled of moss. The light of the braziers and torches down the ravine barely reached here—as such, Coira's face was heavily shadowed when he turned to face her.

"Craeg," she began, her voice husky. "I don't think we should—"

"I know this isn't the time or place for this," he cut in. He was aware of the tension in his own voice, yet he pressed on. "But since we're about to depart for battle, I think there are a few things that need to be said."

21

Remember

COIRA'S JAW FIRMED, although her gaze was suddenly wary. "Go on then."

"The first thing ye need to know is that *nothing* about yer past bothers me," he continued. Her lips parted as she prepared to argue with him, but Craeg pressed on. "Ye forget ... I've seen it all. I was *born* in a brothel ... my mother was a whore. I know what happens there, how many of the women are forced into that life." He paused and drew in a steadying breath. "I also know that Duncan MacKinnon is a pig. He took his perversions, his hatred for women, and made them yer burden. I vow that he'll pay for that."

Coira's throat bobbed, although when she replied, her voice was firm. "We'll *both* make him pay, Craeg," she murmured.

"Aye," Craeg replied, vehement now. "Ye too want reckoning ... I understand that." He took a step closer to her, half expecting her to back away, but instead, Coira held her ground. "Once he's dead ... once ye trust men again ... ye will heal."

She swallowed, her gaze gleaming now as tears threatened.

Craeg's throat thickened. He didn't want to make her weep, but the words inside him had to be spoken. "Time moves against us now," he said, softening his tone. "I don't want to go into battle without knowing what it's like to kiss ye."

Her chest heaved, and even though they weren't touching, Craeg felt the tension emanating off her.

"I'm still a nun," she finally managed the words, although her voice sounded choked.

Craeg's mouth curved. "Not dressed like that, ye aren't."

"A habit doesn't make a woman a nun ... but the vows she takes."

"Aye." He moved closer still to her, unable to stop himself. "But ye have left the order, have ye not?" He raised a hand then and brushed the back of his knuckles across her cheek—as he had that night in that moonlit glade. How he'd longed to kiss her back then, and the yearning had not lessened. It had grown to a hunger that now dominated every waking thought.

He felt her tremble, heard the whisper of her quickened breathing. She was fighting the hunger too—he knew it.

Heat pulsed between them, as did an ocean of things unsaid. Words were pointless now though. There were too many reasons why he shouldn't be touching her, shouldn't want her with his body and soul. But none of them would stop him now.

With a stifled groan, Craeg cupped her face with his hands and leaned in, his lips brushing hers. It was a tentative kiss, feather-light. He didn't want to startle her or force this moment.

Craeg brushed his lips across Coira's once more, giving her the chance to pull away, yet she didn't. And when a soft, breathy sigh escaped her, Craeg covered Coira's mouth with his.

Coira had never been kissed before.

The men who'd frequented *The Goat and Goose* didn't kiss the whores. There wasn't any tenderness, any intimacy, in what had passed between her and the men she'd once serviced. They'd disrobed, rutted her, tossed her a coin, and left.

This was completely new to Coira, and when Craeg's lips first touched hers, a dizzying wave of panic rose up within her. He was crossing her boundaries, smashing down the walls that had kept her safe over the years.

But she didn't shrink away.

Despite the blood roaring in her ears, her wildly beating pulse, she forced down her fear. His lips brushed hers once again, and the need she'd been fighting for days now ignited within her like dry kindling to a naked flame.

His lips were soft, and the heat of his body, the spicy male scent of his skin, sucked the breath from her. She couldn't help it; a sigh of need escaped her.

And that was when everything changed.

His mouth slanted over hers, firmer now, and his tongue gently parted her lips.

Aching want swept over Coira, along with a desperation that shoved any lingering fear aside.

He tasted better than the first apple wine of the autumn, better than fresh bread or heather honey. He smelled like summer rain, like crushed grass, like oiled leather. He was life, death, and eternity all in one kiss.

A cry rose in Coira's throat, smothered by his gently exploring lips, his masterful tongue. She heard her quarter-staff thud to the ground, slipping from nerveless fingers. Not caring, she leaned into him, her tongue tentatively stroking his.

Craeg groaned, deep in his throat, his hands sliding down from her face to her shoulders. He drew her against him, gathering her into his arms as his kisses deepened.

Coira was lost. Her hands came up, her fingertips tracing his jaw, his neck—resting in the hollow between his collarbones, where his pulse raced. She couldn't believe she'd lived her whole life till now without this.

His body, pressed against the length of hers, was strong, warm, and exciting beyond measure. Her fingers ached to strip away the clothing that lay between them. She longed to know what his naked flesh felt like pressed up against hers. Hot desire flooded through her, dizzying in its intensity.

It was Craeg who eventually ended the kiss. His breathing came in ragged pants, his eyes gleaming, when he pulled back. His face was taut, his expression feral.

Their gazes fused as the first glimmers of early dawn filtered into this dark corner of the ravine.

"Whatever comes to pass today," he said, a rasp in his voice, "I want ye to know that the shadow MacKinnon has cast over ye will soon lift. Please remember that, Coira." He reached up, stroking her lower lip with the pad of his thumb.

A lump rose in Coira's throat, making it hard to swallow, to breathe, and to speak. His voice was a balm, his touch an anchor. Suddenly, she dared believe he was right. How she wanted to believe that.

She sought his hands with hers, their fingers entangling. Finally, she nodded.

Carr Broderick stood on the walls and watched a damp, misty dawn rise over Dunan.

The village beneath him, still cast in night's long shadow, was eerily quiet. Usually at this hour, he could see smoke rising from stacked stone chimneys, could smell the aroma of baking bannock.

But this morning, it was as if ghosts inhabited Dunan.

Even before MacKinnon had ridden out with his men, folk had started to flee the fort, hurrying out into the hills with rolled blankets and packs upon their backs. But in the three days since the clan-chief had departed, so had the bulk of the village's residents.

The streets were now deserted, the markets closed. Sickness had come to Dunan, and its people had sought sanctuary elsewhere. Carr's gaze narrowed at this observation. Of course, they'd just taken the sickness with them, and would likely spread it.

The fortress at Carr's back was also empty. The broch of Dunan hadn't been spared. Most of the servants who hadn't sickened had run off.

Carr heaved in a deep breath and turned, making his way along the narrow walkway to the steep stone steps leading down to the bailey. A grim sight awaited him there: a row of bodies covered by sacking. Three of the stable lads and one of the cooks lay under there. Carr and the few remaining members of the Dunan Guard would have to burn them later in the day.

A knot tightened under Carr's ribcage. He'd been spared so far—but how much longer would it be before he fell ill? He lived day-to-day now, with the Grim Reaper breathing down his neck. Sooner or later, he expected to feel the Reaper's cold touch.

Entering the broch, Carr went first to the kitchens. The only soul there was a lass—the only one of the kitchen staff remaining—frying a large round cake upon a griddle. Carr shouldn't have been surprised really. Kenzie was a tough wee thing and doggedly loyal to MacKinnon.

She glanced up when he entered and favored Carr with a tired smile. "The bannock is ready if ye are hungry?"

"Thank ye, Kenzie," he replied, not returning the smile. His mood was too dark this morning to make the effort. No word of MacKinnon had returned to Dunan. Carr wondered if the clan-chief had indeed managed to track his bastard brother down, and if so, what the outcome had been.

"I'll take some up for Lady Drew first," he added.

Kenzie nodded, relief suffusing her face. There weren't any servants left now to carry out such tasks. Working quickly, she flipped the bannock onto a platter before slicing it up into wedges. She then added earthen pots of butter and honey before lifting up the tray and handing it to Carr. "I'm sorry ye have to be saddled with such tasks, Broderick," she murmured, offering him another smile.

Carr suspected that the young kitchen wench had developed an affection for him of late—feelings which had intensified as the inhabitants of the broch slowly dwindled. Carr had given her little encouragement, yet that did not dim her interest.

"I don't mind," he answered, returning her smile now. It was the truth. Bringing Lady Drew some food to break her fast was merely an excuse to see her. The only good thing to come from this sickness was that he now interacted with Lady Drew far more often than he had in the past.

Climbing the stairs, he made his way to her solar. He knocked on the door.

"Enter," a soft voice called out.

Carr pushed open the door with his elbow and made his way in.

Lady Drew was seated by the fire, a thick shawl about her shoulders. Carr's step faltered a little at the sight of her. It was rare to see MacKinnon's sister with her hair unbound. Long and wavy, and the color of peat, it tumbled over her shoulders.

Drew's grey eyes widened at the sight of him. "Oh … it's ye, Broderick … I thought it was Kenzie."

"She's busy downstairs," he replied with an apologetic shrug. "Ye shall have to make do with me, milady."

He moved to the center of the solar and set the tray down upon a table.

"I'm quite at a loss, ye know," she said, her tone rueful. "I'm used to having servants fuss around me in the morning … it looks like I'll have to dress myself and put up my own hair."

Carr huffed a laugh at this pronouncement. "I would offer to help, but …"

Drew snorted, before she rose to her feet, drawing the shawl tight. "I'm sure I'll manage. God's bones, Broderick … it's cold in here. Could ye put some more peat on the fire?"

Carr nodded and went to do as bid. However, he personally found the chamber warm and a little stuffy. He couldn't see how she could feel a chill. "I was going to open a window," he said, "but I take it ye would prefer I didn't?"

"Please don't," she replied, moving over to the table. "Come and join me at the table instead … I take it the lass didn't expect me to eat all these bannocks?"

After attending to the fire, Carr returned to the table and took a seat opposite Drew. He waited until she had helped herself to a bannock before he did the same.

Being able to sit at the same table as the woman he longed for was both an unexpected pleasure and a torture—but he'd not deny her.

Spreading some butter upon his wedge of bannock, Carr glanced up, his gaze fixing upon her. This close, he saw her heart-shaped face was pale.

Carr went still. "Lady Drew," he said softly. "Are ye well?"

She nodded, her mouth tightening in annoyance. "Of course ... don't fuss."

Carr watched her, his gaze narrowing. Her sharp tongue didn't bother him. However, her well-being did. Without asking permission, he rose from the table and crossed to her, placing his hand upon her forehead.

It was the first time he'd ever touched the woman he served.

The move was bold, and in other circumstances, he wouldn't have dared. But today was different.

"Broderick!" she gasped, twisting away from him. "What the devil are ye doing?"

Carr withdrew his hand, dread twisting under his ribcage. Her brow was burning hot, the skin clammy.

Their gazes fused then, and whatever admonishments she'd been about to utter died upon her lips when she saw the look on his face.

22

Face-to-Face

DUNCAN REINED IN his horse and watched the riders approach, before frowning. He'd sent scouts ahead, to keep an eye on the outlaws, but they'd returned sooner than he'd expected.

"They're on the move," Keith greeted him. The blond man's face was flushed. He'd ridden hard to reach the clan-chief as quickly as possible. "The outlaws are traveling west … toward us."

"How far away are they?" Duncan barked, trying to ignore the chills that wracked his body and the cough that tickled the back of his throat.

Curse them all, he felt terrible.

Keith MacKinnon's gaze settled upon the clan-chief, and his pale blue eyes narrowed. Duncan could tell by the way his face tensed that he didn't look good. However, the man was wise enough not to comment upon it.

"Around twenty furlongs distant," Keith replied. "Our paths will cross before noon."

This news made MacKinnon scowl. He hadn't expected his bastard brother to ride out to meet him—at least not so soon. He'd wanted Craeg's scouts to spot them and scurry back to their hiding place before chaos and panic ensued. Duncan clenched his jaw; it mattered not. The sooner they clashed the better.

"Did someone let them know we were coming?" One of Duncan's men asked behind him, echoing the clan-chief's own thoughts.

"Who cares," Duncan growled. "The Bastard has saved us all a long ride." His gaze swept right to left, taking in the wide valley they'd pulled up in. Behind him stretched woodland, whereas broom and gorse dotted the slopes of the valley below. "We make our stand here."

They'd been marching for over an hour when the sky above cleared and the sun appeared. Warmth filtered over Coira, and she raised her face to it.

This was the first time in a decade that the sun had shone upon her naked head. She felt strange, lighter, walking without being shrouded by her veil. The sensation had been discomforting at first—she'd felt naked without her habit. It had been her shield for so long. When she'd warn it, men ceased to see her as a woman. But ever since she'd appeared before the outlaws in Fenella's clothing, the world looked upon her differently.

"Can ye really use that quarter-staff?" Farlan's question made Coira lower her face from the sun's gentle caress and glance right. The outlaw walked beside her in the long column that snaked down the mountainside.

Coira's mouth curved in her first real smile in days. "Do ye want a demonstration? I can knock ye flat on yer back, if ye would like?"

Farlan raised his hands, dark eyes glinting. "No need for that ... save yer aggression for MacKinnon's lot."

Coira's smile faded. "I intend to."

"So ... the rest of the nuns at Kilbride ... are they like ye? Can they fight?"

"Aye."

"Why?"

"Mother Shona taught us. Before she came to Skye, she had a hard life. When she was elected as abbess, she decided that the Sisters of Kilbride should be able to defend themselves if the need ever arose."

Farlan gave a low whistle. "And there was me thinking nuns were useless."

Coira's gaze narrowed. "The Lord's work is never 'useless'. Kilbride is the reason the people of Torrin haven't starved over the past years. MacKinnon always raids their stores in autumn."

"So ye have been helping folk?"

"Aye, when we can. It's just one of the reasons why MacKinnon has always disliked us."

Farlan frowned. "And the other reasons?"

The young man was sharp—too sharp. Coira might have confided in Craeg, but she wasn't about to do the same with Farlan. She liked him well enough, yet he asked too many questions.

Coira glanced away then, her gaze traveling down the column to where Craeg strode next to Gunn. The red-haired warrior was easy to spot in a group, and he was never far from the outlaw leader.

Warmth settled in the cradle of Coira's hips, radiating out.

If she'd been alone, she'd have raised her fingers to her lips, allowing the memory of that kiss to flood through her. However, under Farlan's penetrating gaze, she prevented herself.

That kiss had shifted her world. Everything was different in the aftermath. She felt desire for a man—a man that didn't turn her stomach, a man that didn't want to pay her so she'd spread her legs, a man who treated her as if she were something precious, something to be cherished.

A pressure built in her chest as she thought about Craeg, recalled the tenderness in his eyes and the fierceness upon his face as he stared down at her at dawn.

The shadow MacKinnon has cast over ye will soon lift.

He'd said those words with such conviction that she'd believed him. For the first time, she actually had hope. It was something she'd searched for at Kilbride, yet despite her strong faith, she'd never truly found it.

Not until Craeg entered her life.

A soft laugh drew her from her reverie. Coira glanced back at Farlan to find him still watching her, a knowing grin upon his lips. "Ye wouldn't be the first woman to fall for him," he said with a shake of his head. "Craeg wields charm like a blade."

A chill stole over Coira at these words. He made Craeg's behavior seem contrived, practiced—as if he'd put on a show for her. Perhaps Farlan saw the alarm on her face, for his grin abruptly faded. "Sorry, poor choice of words. I could do with some lessons in charm myself. No wonder the lasses prefer Craeg."

Coira huffed a laugh, although underneath it she was now wary of Farlan. "Aye ... one day ye will cut yerself on that sharp tongue of yers, Farlan."

He offered her a sheepish smile. "I think I just have."

The two bands met just as the sun reached its zenith in the sky.

Craeg, who walked ahead of his men, caught a glimpse of MacKinnon pennants in the distance. His gaze traveled along the line of horsemen outlined against the dark wall of greenery behind them.

"Stay here," Craeg murmured to Gunn, his gaze never leaving the riders. "I'm going out to talk to him ... alone."

"I should come with ye." Gunn's voice held a warning, yet Craeg ignored it. Before the end came, he'd speak to Duncan MacKinnon face-to-face.

"Stay here," he replied, still not glancing at his friend.

With that, Craeg stepped out of the line and walked down the scrubby slope to where the horse and rider had halted at the bottom of the valley.

The sun warmed the crown of his head as he walked, and he was aware that after what seemed like weeks of grey, misty weather, the sky had cleared and summer had returned to the Isle of Skye.

Craeg walked easily, despite the heavy pine shield he wore slung across his back and the claidheamh-mor that hung at his side. Unlike many of his men, he didn't carry a quiver of arrows and longbow, for he preferred to lead the charge of warriors into battle. However, he'd strapped a long-bladed dirk to his right thigh for fighting at close-quarters, should the need arise. And it most likely would.

MacKinnon cut an imposing figure astride the magnificent warhorse. He sat easily in the saddle, and Craeg remembered what a skilled horseman his half-brother was. He'd heard about his prowess as a hunter too—Duncan would be a formidable adversary, mounted or not.

And as he drew near, Craeg finally made out the features of the MacKinnon clan-chief's face.

His breathing quickened.

So many years had passed since the pair of them had met face-to-face, since they'd looked each other squarely in the eye.

He'd heard many folk pass comment on the physical resemblance between them, but since the times were few and far between when Craeg ever glimpsed his own reflection, he would have to take them at their word.

Duncan hadn't changed much over the years, although there were perhaps lines of severity upon his handsome face that made him look sterner, older. Those iron-grey eyes were the same though: cold and shrewd.

But as Craeg came to a halt around eight yards back from the destrier, he realized that something wasn't quite right. Those lines upon his face weren't from age but strain. His skin had a grey tinge, and sweat gleamed off his forehead.

"No horse for Craeg the Bastard, eh?"

Duncan MacKinnon's greeting slammed into Craeg like a fist to the belly. In an instant, he was transported back to that fateful day in Dunan. The last time he'd heard that voice, he'd been curled up fighting consciousness in an alley that reeked of stale piss.

That arrogant, drawling voice had echoed in his ears for months afterward.

But now all Craeg heard in his ears was the roar of his own breathing. His heart started to race, and he clenched his jaw as he resisted the urge to bare his teeth.

Hatred rose within him, clawing up from his gut like a beast that had been waiting far too long for reckoning.

Finally, after all these years, the time had come.

23

The Yoke Breaks

WHEN CRAEG DIDN'T answer, MacKinnon smiled. It was a cold expression, full of malice.

Of course, his half-brother had waited a long time for this day too.

"Still proud," MacKinnon drawled. "Still believe ye are my equal, don't ye?"

"We're not equals, Duncan," Craeg said finally. The calmness of his voice surprised him. No one would have suspected the turmoil that churned within. "I've always been yer superior … and ye and I both know it."

The response was inflammatory, designed to anger, and when MacKinnon's smile faded and his gaze narrowed, Craeg knew he'd hit his mark.

"Ye have been a burr up my arse for too long, Bastard," he murmured. "I shall enjoy watching ye die."

Craeg smiled back, showing his teeth this time. "Ye should have killed me that day. Ye have made many mistakes over the years, but that was yer most foolish."

MacKinnon's dark brows knotted together, something feral moving in his eyes. He shifted his attention from Craeg then, just for a few moments, his gaze sweeping the line of warriors upon the brow of the hill behind him. "Coira is with ye, I take it?"

Craeg went still, his fingers flexing as the urge to draw his sword surged within him.

Seeing his reaction, MacKinnon's eyes gleamed. "Enjoying my whore, are ye?"

A taut silence settled between them then. The cold knot of hatred in Craeg's gut drew tighter. The impulse to rush howling at MacKinnon was almost overwhelming, yet Craeg mastered it. Instead, he let those words hang between them, let battle fury kindle in his blood.

Long moments passed, and when MacKinnon realized that Craeg wasn't going to bite, his mouth twisted. "Coira will be mine again soon enough. Get ready to taste steel, Bastard."

Once again, Craeg didn't reply—he didn't trust himself to. Instead, he turned his back on his half-brother and walked away up the slope, back to where his men silently waited. All the way up, the skin between his shoulder blades itched. He almost expected his brother to throw a knife into his back.

Yet no such strike came.

Still, it was a long walk up the hill, and Craeg was sweating when he reached Gunn's side once more.

The big red-haired warrior met his eye and raised a ruddy eyebrow. "Well?"

"He's sick," Craeg replied.

"The pestilence?"

"Could be." Craeg drew his claidheamh-mor, the scrape of steel echoing over the hillside. "But that doesn't make him any less dangerous."

He shifted his attention from Gunn then, back down the valley. MacKinnon was riding away, cantering back to join his men.

Swiveling on his heel, Craeg's gaze swept over the ranks of men who'd joined him from all over the territory. He saw the fierceness on their faces, the glint in their eyes. They were ready to fight for him, to die for him. Craeg's pulse accelerated. He raised his claidheamh-mor high then, drawing their gazes to him.

"Long have we prepared for this day." His voice rang out across the hillside. "Ye all know what ye must do … I won't remind ye of it." He paused then, his chest swelling. "Ye know of the bad blood between MacKinnon and me … but remember this fight is about much more than just vengeance … it's about freedom. Long has MacKinnon's iron fist crushed ye all into the dust. His Guard came to yer villages, took all yer savings, and robbed ye of yer last sack of barley—the only thing between yer families and starvation. And then when ye fought back, he called ye criminals and put a price on yer heads."

Craeg broke off here, breathing hard as fire caught in his veins. He wasn't used to giving speeches like this. But his men needed to hear these words. His gaze swept the ranks then, and there, near the back, he glimpsed a lone woman.

Coira stood watching him, her eyes gleaming, her jaw set. He didn't want her to fight—didn't want her to risk her life. But she had her own score to settle with MacKinnon today, and he wouldn't take that from her.

His belly twisted all the same when he thought of her facing men swinging claidheamh-mors. Although he'd witnessed Lady Leanna with a longbow, he hadn't seen Coira fight. What if she'd overplayed her abilities to him? What if, in the heat of battle, her nerve failed her?

Craeg swallowed the lump that suddenly rose in his throat. He wouldn't be able to help her. Once the fighting began, Coira would be on her own, and she knew it.

Pushing the realization aside, Craeg forced his attention back to the ranks of warriors watching him.

"The yoke breaks today!" He shouted, thrusting his broadsword high into the air. "Today, we take back our lives!"

A cry went up among the outlaws, rippling out across the hillside.

Craeg's skin prickled at the sound. Turning, he looked back across the valley and saw that MacKinnon's warriors had urged their horses forward. They were now careening down the slope toward the bottom of the valley.

Craeg's heart leaped. "Archers!" he yelled. "Ready!"

And then, as he and his men had planned long before this day, Craeg dropped to one knee. Beside him, Gunn did the same—as did all the warriors in the first three lines.

But the row of men behind them—those bearing longbows—didn't crouch. Instead, they notched arrows and sighted their quarry.

Craeg held his breath, his gaze tracking the line of horses that thundered toward them, and then a shout tore from his throat. "Loose!"

I'm taking them all to their deaths.

Leading the way up a steep hill interspersed with wildling pines, Mother Shona tried to ignore the guilt that dogged every step, yet it hung over her like an oppressive shadow, darkening with each furlong they journeyed east.

She'd made her choice; there wasn't any point in regretting it now.

Although the women traveled fast—alternating between a brisk walk and a steady jog—worry had begun to form a hard knot in the pit of the abbess's belly.

They're on horseback ... we'll get there too late.

Indeed, the urgency that had driven her to call the Sisters of Kilbride to arms had faded, and in its place grew a gnawing worry.

Things hadn't started well at dawn. Once she'd gathered the sisters to her, it had become evident that three of the nuns were unwell: Sisters Anis, Fritha, and Morag had all come down with fevers and coughs overnight. A chill had settled over the abbess as she'd sent the nuns back to the dormitory to rest—she'd feared that MacKinnon had brought the sickness with him to Kilbride, and she'd been right. She'd left Sister Magda to tend them; 'Old Magda' wasn't agile or strong enough to join the others anyway.

Mother Shona frowned as she pushed aside a pine branch. She didn't want to leave the nuns behind with only an aged woman to tend them, yet she had no choice.

She had committed to this now.

Breathing hard, the abbess pushed herself up the last few yards toward the tree-lined brow of the hill. Like the other nuns, she'd adjusted her clothing for this journey. Under her skirts, she wore woolen leggings, and she had knotted her underskirts and habit, tying them around her hips with twine. It wasn't an ideal solution, yet it enabled the nuns far greater freedom of movement.

Although she was one of the oldest women in the group, she had deliberately led the way. The sisters depended upon her strength and guidance. She could not lag behind.

Fortunately, the hard, physical toil of a nun's life prepared the abbess for this journey. Even so, as she shouldered her way between two embracing fir trees, Mother Shona noted that her legs now ached and her lungs burned from exertion.

However, when she stepped out of the trees, and her gaze alighted upon the valley beyond, the abbess came to an abrupt halt.

Behind her, Sister Elspeth, who'd kept pace with her the whole morning, breathed a prayer.

A pitched battle was taking place in the valley below. Men on horseback—the Dunan Guard—had engaged a host of warriors on foot. The clang of metal, the meaty thud of weapons connecting with flesh, and the cries of the injured and dying rang out.

"The outlaws came out to meet them," Elspeth gasped.

"Aye." Mother Shona glanced over her shoulder at the nun. She knew an abbess shouldn't play favorites, but she'd warmed to Sister Elspeth far less than many of the other sisters over the years. She could be a trouble-maker and a gossip. And yet, this morning, she'd shown a different side to her character.

The moment Mother Shona had announced her plan, the nun had swung into action, ordering the younger sisters about and ensuring they were ready to depart as quickly as possible.

There had been no word of complaint from her on the journey east. She had not questioned Mother's Shona's decision—not once.

Meeting the nun's eye now, the abbess saw the trust, the utter conviction that whatever Mother Shona decided was right.

The abbess's breathing hitched. *Merciful Lord, I hope I have made the right decision.*

She'd fought in battles during her time with the outlaws. But the women who followed her had not. She only hoped she'd prepared them adequately for this.

One by one, the sisters emerged from the trees and halted upon the brow of the hill, their gazes sweeping to the fight unfolding beneath them.

Mother Shona searched their faces, her belly clenching when she saw some of the nuns pale, their eyes growing huge as they observed the violence. One or two even swayed a little on their feet as if they might faint.

What have I done?

"Mother Shona!" Sister Elspeth's voice rang out, drawing the abbess's attention once more. "Look ... it's Sister Coira!"

Following Sister Elspeth's pointing finger, the abbess turned and peered into the fray.

And there, at the heart of it, she spied a tall woman, fighting with a quarter-staff.

Mother Shona's breathing caught. Coira was no longer wearing her habit—her long dark braid flying as she whirled, ducked, swung, and jabbed. Yet she stood out amongst a crowd of men—and as the abbess watched, Coira brought a big man down with a deadly swing to the jaw.

Mother Shona's heart started to pound. *I taught her that move.* Indeed, she had—although she'd never been as deadly with a quarter-staff as Coira was.

"She's magnificent." The surprise in Sister Elspeth's voice jerked the abbess back to the present. Sisters Coira and Elspeth had never been friends, and yet the nun stared at Coira with awe upon her face.

The expression jolted the abbess into action. Heart pounding, she turned to the nuns following her. "MacKinnon has brought nothing but misery to the folk of this land." Her voice lifted above the roar of battle that echoed up from below. "Our own sisters have suffered at his hands. He hunted Sister Ella and abducted Sister Leanna. They would likely still be with us, if not for him."

Breaking off there, Mother Shona saw the gleam in the nuns' eyes, the determination in their faces. Then, inhaling deeply, she continued. "Sister Coira is down there fighting for her life. Are we going to let her do so alone?"

A few feet away, Sister Mina drew the knife at her waist. A slight tremble betrayed her nerves, yet her gaze was fierce. "No!"

"No!" The other nuns echoed, drawing their weapons.

"Those with longbows remain at a safe distance and pick off as many men wearing MacKinnon colors as ye can," Mother Shona instructed. Calmness descended upon her. "The rest of ye, with me."

Her gaze swept over the line of nuns once more. There were only twenty of them: women armed with dirks, longbows, and quarter-staffs. Mother Shona was the only one of their number who wielded a sword. It was a different weapon to the huge claidheamh-mors that the men below used. She'd had a smith in Torrin fashion her a lighter blade not long after she became abbess, one that she could wield one-handed.

Mother Shona drew her weapon. The double-edged blade glinted in the bright sunlight, and a tight smile curved her mouth.

If only Aaron could see me now.

Her lover had taught her how to wield a sword. He'd taught her that speed and agility mattered just as much as strength when it came to swordplay.

It was at the end of one of their long practice sessions that he'd kissed her for the first time.

Aaron and the life she'd once lived had seemed an age ago until now. The walls of Kilbride had sheltered her from her past and kept the memories at bay. Yet at that moment, she wasn't Mother Shona, Abbess of Kilbride—but Shona of Lismore. Wild, brave, and fearless.

With a howl, she fled down the hill and to battle.

24

Legacy

COIRA KNEW THAT Craeg wanted to be the one to kill MacKinnon—but that didn't stop her searching for the clan-chief all the same.

Craeg needed to have his reckoning, yet so did she. However, she couldn't get close to the front. The press of male bodies was too thick.

From early on in the battle, she was glad that the quarter-staff was her weapon of choice. Although tall and broad-shouldered compared to many women, she still lacked a man's brute strength. Those massive broad-swords that even a warrior had to wield two-handed would never have suited her.

Instead, the iron-tipped quarter-staff cut a path through the ranks of the Dunan Guard. She'd just knocked two men off their horses, when a warrior came at her, sword swinging.

Blood coursing down one cheek, he had a maddened look upon his face, an expression that warned her the man had passed the point where he cared about his own mortality. If he died bringing her down, so be it.

Coira spun the quarter-staff, using a two-handed under-arm spin. The weapon flew so fast that it became a blur. Leaping forward, she struck the warrior across the face with the staff, before his blade could reach her. He reeled back, kept his feet, and lunged for her.

She spun the staff once more and struck her opponent again, felling him this time, before stabbing him through the throat with the pointed end of her weapon.

Breathing hard, Coira turned quickly to face another warrior and blocked his attack. She then delivered a downward strike, hitting him hard across the ribs. The man hissed a curse and attacked once more, but this time Coira ducked and swept low, knocking the warrior's feet out from under him.

Sweat trickled down Coira's back, heat pulsing through her as she struck, swept, and thrust her way through the fray.

And then, through it all, she caught a glimpse of black and white on the hill above.

Three nuns, spaced around half a dozen yards apart, were firing arrows into the fray.

Coira gasped.

The Sisters of Kilbride were here, fighting alongside the outlaws.

A few feet away, a MacKinnon warrior went down, a feather-fletched arrow embedded in the back of his neck.

Coira's attention snapped back to the fighting then, as another man launched himself at her, dirk drawn. He was trying to get under her guard. Coira gritted her teeth and struck hard, bringing the staff down on his hand. She felt the bones crack under the impact. The warrior howled, the sound choking off when Coira swung her staff into his face.

Whirling away from the fallen man, Coira peered through the fracas and spied the abbess.

Mother Mary ... she can fight!

Coira had sparred with the abbess often over the years but had always known the woman was holding herself back.

She just hadn't realized how much.

The abbess moved like a woman half her age, striking like an adder and dancing away from any attack that came near her. She toyed with the big men who swung at her with their claidheamh-mors. She made them look like lumbering giants as she escaped the reach of their blades again and again.

Blood splattered across Mother Shona's face and her snow-white wimple. Her delicate features were set in hard lines, and her brown eyes gleamed. An instant later Coira recognized Sister Elspeth fighting at the abbess's side. The woman wielded a dirk, its long blade dripping with blood. Coira remembered that Sister Elspeth was as good with blades as Sister Ella had been. Nonetheless, it was a shock to see the nun fighting with such savagery. The left sleeve of her habit was torn, and blood oozed from a long cut to her upper arm, yet Sister Elspeth paid it no mind.

Coira's fingers tightened around the ash quarter-staff.

She wouldn't let them face the Dunan Guard alone.

She resumed her path through the press of MacKinnon warriors and horses. Eventually, her breathing coming in short gasps, she staggered from the press to join the nuns.

Mother Shona yanked her sword free of a fallen warrior and favored Coira with a savage smile. "Thought we would leave ye out here on yer own, did ye?"

Coira shook her head, too exhausted to answer. The battle was starting to drain her, and she realized this was where men held a distinct advantage. Their stronger, more muscular bodies withstood battle for longer. They had greater endurance. It was just as well she now stood with the Sisters of Kilbride, for her arms had developed a slight tremor as she spun her staff and readied herself to face a man on horseback who now charged at her.

This wasn't the time for her body to fail her.

She widened her stance, anchoring herself on the ground. And then, an instant before she swung her staff at the warrior bearing down upon her, she caught a glimpse of two men fighting with claidheamh-mors in the heart of the melee: Craeg and MacKinnon.

Craeg slashed his way through the fray, searching for his half-brother. It seemed that MacKinnon had done the same, for when they finally found each other, the two men paused amongst the chaos, frozen for a moment.

We share the same blood, Craeg thought, a strange heaviness settling within him, *and yet he's my mortal enemy.*

Craeg knew he shouldn't be surprised by the hatred between them. How many siblings had turned against each other over the centuries? There seemed to be no greater hate than that between brothers.

Half-brothers.

Aye, that was the root of it. Craeg was a bastard, spawned by a whore, while Duncan was the rightful heir and ruler of these lands. And yet it had never stopped him from being threatened by Craeg.

He circled MacKinnon, shrugging out the knots in his shoulders. Years of hiding, years of slowly whittling away at the man who'd nearly killed him—and here they finally were.

MacKinnon attacked first, with an aggressive lunge that nearly took Craeg unawares. His brother was ill—he could see it in the rictus of pain and effort in his face, the wild look in his eyes, the pallor of his skin, and the sweat that poured off him. But his sickness had turned him vicious.

Yet reckless behavior also made a man careless.

Craeg only had to bide his time.

"Bastard," MacKinnon hissed, repeating the word, again and again, as he attacked. "Baseborn. Son of a whore. Misbegotten. *Bastard.*"

"Save yer breath," Craeg grunted as he brought his sword up to counter a violent overhead swing. "I am who I am ... the whole world knows about it but only *ye* care."

MacKinnon's eyes burned with loathing. It had all begun that day Jock MacKinnon brought Duncan to *The Goat and Goose* so he could meet his half-brother. The clan-chief had known what he was doing—but it pleased him to sow the seeds of hate.

And that hate had grown into something monstrous, something that risked destroying both men. It didn't matter to Jock MacKinnon anymore. He was dead, nothing but bones in a crypt. Yet his legacy lived on.

MacKinnon's onslaught was growing wearing. He attacked relentlessly, not allowing Craeg to counter. Around and around they went, Craeg's teeth jarring with each blow.

Craeg bided his time, waiting for the opening that would surely come. MacKinnon was a formidable swordsman. Even sick, his brother was the best he'd ever fought.

And then as Craeg shifted backward to block another overhead swing, he slipped on a patch of gore.

His feet flew out from under him, and he reeled back.

MacKinnon was on him in an instant, slicing downward in an attack designed to split his skull asunder.

Only Craeg's quick reflexes saved him. He dropped his sword, rolled, and drew his dirk.

MacKinnon lunged again, the blade of his claidheamh-mor whistling through the air. Craeg rolled once more, a chill sweeping through him as he realized that his half-brother now had the advantage.

Craeg was down, and MacKinnon's relentless attack made it impossible for him to rise to his feet.

Duncan was going to kill him. He swung his sword toward Craeg, in a deadly arc.

And then MacKinnon froze, his blade stilling. Craeg stared up at him, raising his dirk in an attempt to deflect the blow.

Yet the strike never came.

Instead, his opponent staggered forward and then sank to his knees. MacKinnon grasped at his right armpit, his fingers coming away slick with blood. He gave a pained wheeze, color draining from his already pallid face, and slumped sideways onto the ground.

Behind MacKinnon stood a small figure swathed in black, an iron crucifix gleaming upon her breast: Mother Shona.

Breathing hard, the abbess lowered the sword she'd just plunged into him.

Duncan MacKinnon could no longer hear the fighting.

It was as if his ears were suddenly filled with wool. Lying upon the ground, he stared up at Craeg. The man's mouth was moving. He was speaking, saying something to him. But Duncan couldn't hear the words.

He was grateful for that.

He didn't want the last thing he ever heard to be Craeg the Bastard's voice.

Damn his half-brother to hell. He couldn't believe it had come to this. He couldn't believe someone had attacked him from behind, had stabbed him in the armpit while his arms were raised.

Despair clawed its way up his throat, yet he fought it. His body ached, and his throat felt as if it were on fire, as if he were lit up by a furnace within. Pain ripped through his chest. Duncan fought it all. For a few moments, he tried to convince himself that he could defeat everything: the sickness, his enemies, death itself.

And then he saw her.

His angel of mercy. His angel of death. The woman stepped up behind Craeg, those vibrant violent eyes fastening upon him.

Coira's face was flushed and blood-splattered, and her chest heaved from exertion. In one hand she held a quarter-staff, and in the other a dirk. She no longer wore a nun's habit. Instead, she was dressed as an outlaw.

She's one of them.

Outrage pulsed through Duncan, its heat puncturing the agony that dimmed his vision. His mouth moved, and he tried to speak. Yet he couldn't hear if any sound came out.

Suddenly, it hurt to breathe. It felt as if he were drowning.

Duncan reached up, stretching out for the woman, his fingers clawing the air as he imagined they were fastening around her neck. She was just like all the other women who'd disappointed him. His mother. His sister. Ella. Leanna. Traitorous bitches, the lot of them.

Coira stared down at him, a nerve ticking in her cheek. And then she knelt, bringing her face close to his.

Duncan sagged back, his hands lowering. Maybe she was sorry after all. Perhaps she would comfort him.

But there was no comfort for Duncan MacKinnon.

Another woman, her blood-splattered face taut with ruthless determination, knelt down and whipped the dirk from Coira.

The last thing he witnessed before his life ended was the flash of a knife blade.

25

In Yer Debt

"HE'S DEAD." CRAEG'S voice was flat, disappointed.

"And not before time," Mother Shona replied. She sat back on her heels, her gaze moving to where both Coira and Craeg stared at her. "The man was a scourge upon this earth."

Coira gaped at the older woman. She couldn't believe the abbess had killed MacKinnon. "Mother Shona," she finally gasped. "I wanted to be the one to slit his throat. Why did ye take that from me?"

The two women's gazes fused. Around them, the battle was dying. The outlaws had finally managed to overcome the Dunan Guard. The remaining MacKinnon men had wisely cast aside their weapons, dropped to their knees, and raised their hands in surrender.

Mother Shona cocked an eyebrow. "Ye think I've stolen yer reckoning?"

"Aye, ye have," Craeg rasped. He was still breathing hard from his fight with MacKinnon. He stared at the abbess, gaze narrowed. "I had a few more things to say to him before ye interrupted us."

The abbess huffed. "He couldn't hear ye anyway."

"What makes ye sure of that?"

"He had that look dying folk get sometimes. The glazed eyes, vacant expression ... I doubt he heard a word ye said."

A muscle bunched in Craeg's jaw. "All the same, they were things I needed to say before *I* cut his throat."

Coira clenched her jaw at his words. Curse them both, *she'd* intended to slay MacKinnon.

"And that's why I stepped in," Mother Shona replied, her voice soft yet with steel just underneath. Her gaze swept from Craeg back to Coira. "Revenge is a poison. I couldn't let it blacken yer souls. I know what ye have both suffered at his hands, but he's dead now. Be content with that."

Coira realized that Mother Shona wasn't going to apologize. She wasn't sorry in the slightest.

"This was personal to ye too," Coira pointed out, still fighting down anger. "Ye couldn't stand him either."

A bitter smile twisted the abbess's blood-splattered face. "No ... few could."

"Then surely, revenge drove ye as well?"

Mother Shona shook her head. "No ... for me his death was simply necessary."

Craeg heaved a deep breath, shattering the mounting tension between the two women. He raised a bloodied hand and raked it through his sweat-tousled hair before rising to his feet. "Well, it's done now," he said wearily. "Thank ye, Mother Shona ... ye saved my life."

The abbess's smile gentled, and she favored him with a nod, accepting his thanks.

Retrieving his claidheamh-mor, Craeg swept his gaze around the valley floor. Coira did likewise, her skin prickling at the sight of so many bodies littering the ground.

Not all of them belonged to the Dunan Guard.

Her breathing hitched when she spied a small crumpled form, swathed in black, lying a few yards away.

Picking her way through the carnage, Coira went to the nun. An ache flowered across her chest when she saw that it was Sister Mina.

"Lord, no," she whispered, hunkering down next to the novice.

Sister Mina didn't stir. Her grey eyes stared sightlessly up at the sky, and when Coira checked her for wounds, her hands came away bloody. Someone had stabbed her through the chest with a wide blade—a claidheamh-mor. Her end had been swift.

Coira's vision blurred then, the ache under her breastbone intensifying.

She couldn't believe that Mother Shona had brought the Sisters of Kilbride to the outlaws' aid.

Lifting her chin, she saw the abbess limping toward her. Now that the fighting had ended, Mother Shona's face was slack with exhaustion and sorrow.

The abbess halted before Sister Mina, and Coira saw that she was weeping, tears running silently down her face.

The sun made its lazy progress across the sky, slowly dipping toward the western horizon. Meanwhile, the survivors had the grisly task of clearing the battlefield.

MacKinnon and his dead men were placed upon a pyre and burned at the southern end of the valley, whereas the outlaws and the five nuns that had fallen were placed upon biers to be buried back at Kilbride. There were a number of injured, including Farlan, who'd taken a nasty gash to the thigh, and Sister Elspeth, who bore a cut to her arm. Gunn, however, had come through the battle relatively unscathed.

Despite that they were the victors, it was a somber party that made their way west to Kilbride, following the course of the sun. Few of the men or the nuns conversed. Instead, they trudged onward, their heads bowed and their steps wary. Once the madness of battle had faded, exhaustion set in.

Coira walked apart from her companions, her thoughts turning inward.

MacKinnon is dead.

The realization kept hitting her, so sharply at times that her breath would sometimes catch. It seemed strange, almost like having a limb amputated. Her loathing for that man had become part of her. Knowing that he was dead, and could no longer threaten her, was a relief. And yet, her belly still clenched as she recalled the abbess snatching the dirk from her hand and finishing the deed.

He was mine to kill.

"Coira." Craeg dropped back halfway through the journey and fell in step next to her. "Are ye well?"

She nodded before forcing herself to meet his eye. Craeg looked as exhausted as she felt, his mouth and nose bracketed with lines of tension. "Curse the abbess," she said softly. "I hate it when she's right."

His mouth quirked. "I take it that she often is?"

"Aye ... I lose count of how many times she's counseled me over the years. She's wiser than anyone I know."

"Then perhaps she did us both a favor," he murmured. "Revenge has a way of taking ye over, of making ye forget what really matters."

Coira glanced up, and their gazes fused. For the first time since before the battle, Coira became acutely aware of him—as she had in that shadowed corner of the ravine before he'd kissed her.

Warmth rose within her, smoothing out the nausea that still stung the back of her throat, the tension in her muscles, and the hard knot that clenched her belly. Mother Mary, the man had a gaze that could melt a frozen loch.

When he looked at her in that way, it was like she was the only woman alive.

Eventually, the tension got too much. Clearing her throat, Coira glanced away. "Mother Shona says that MacKinnon was sick."

"Aye ... I noticed it too."

"She also tells me that three nuns back in Kilbride have fallen ill ... and one of the men we've taken captive has a fever."

When she glanced back at Craeg, she saw he was frowning. "Aye ... the sickness is upon us. How long before the rest of us fall prey to it?"

The warmth his gaze had caused ebbed away at these words. Nonetheless, his question was valid. All of them could now be on borrowed time.

"I wonder how Fenella is faring?" Coira said, voicing her thoughts aloud.

"Gunn has ridden back to the ravine to fetch her and the others," Craeg replied. "They will join us in Kilbride ... we shall find out soon if she lives."

The shadows were long, the afternoon sun gilding the hills, when the bloodied band reached Kilbride Abbey at last. Old Magda opened the gates to admit them, her wrinkled face tensing when she saw that five of the nuns who had left that morning—Sister Mina among them—now returned as corpses.

The elderly nun's gaze filled with tears, and she made the sign of the cross before her. "Dear Lord have mercy, what happened?"

Mother Shona went to Sister Magda and placed a comforting arm around her shoulders. "There was a battle," she murmured, her voice brittle. "MacKinnon fell ... but so did some of those opposing him."

Watching the two women embrace, Coira's throat started to ache.

Kilbride was a tight-knit community. The sisters might not have been related, but they were as close as if united by blood.

Tears streamed down both Mother Shona and Sister Magda's faces when they drew apart.

"How are the others?" the abbess asked.

Sister Magda's mouth trembled. "They steadily worsen," she murmured. "Sister Morag has started vomiting blood."

This news brought gasps from the surrounding nuns.

"I shall go to her," Sister Elspeth announced. The woman's face was strained and pale, and she favored her injured arm. However, Coira knew that Sisters Morag and Elspeth were close friends.

"No, Sister." The abbess turned to Sister Elspeth and held up a hand, forestalling her. "Sister Magda and I will be the only ones to tend the sick. We can't risk the rest of ye falling prey to this plague."

Sister Elspeth's thin face went taut, and she opened her mouth to argue. But Coira spoke up, preventing her. "*I* will tend to them." All gazes swiveled to her, including Sister Elspeth's. Coira held the older nun's eye, before her mouth curved into a weary smile. "I am a healer and have already dealt with the sickness. Mother Shona is right ... the rest of ye should keep yer distance."

Her gaze fused with Sister Elspeth's then, a look of understanding passing between them. The irony of the moment wasn't lost upon Coira. For years, she and Sister Elspeth had barely tolerated each other. Coira had never been one of the circle of nuns who'd hung on Sister Elspeth's every word, and the nun had resented her for it.

But all of that was behind them now.

"Thank ye," Sister Elspeth replied, her voice unusually flat and heavy. "Peace be with ye ... Coira."

Coira. Not Sister Coira.

Coira was suddenly aware then that she was no longer one of them. For the first time, she felt as if she stood on the outside looking in. This abbey was no longer her home.

My time at Kilbride has truly come to an end.

Looking about her, Coira realized how quiet the abbey seemed, especially after all the visitors they'd had of late. Craeg's men were putting up tents outside the abbey walls, for the abbess had warned him that there were sick nuns inside. Only Craeg had entered the yard with the nuns, and now he stood silently at Coira's side, observing the exchange between the abbess and her flock.

Coira tensed then, realizing exactly why the abbey seemed so quiet. It wasn't just the absence of MacKinnon and his rowdy warriors—besides Craeg, there weren't *any* men here. Her gaze swept back to the abbess. "Where are Father Camron and his monks?"

Mother Shona released a weary sigh. The abbess then glanced over at the kirk, where Coira noted that the doors were barred shut.

26

There Will Be Consequences

THE ABBOT BURST from the kirk, purple-faced and seething.

"Ye will pay for this, Mother Shona!" he raged, rounding on the abbess. She stood at the foot of the steps, awaiting him. "How dare ye lock me up!"

Suddenly, he stopped short, taking in the abbess's appearance: her leggings, bunched-up skirts, and the sword she wore at her hip. "What. Is. This?" he demanded.

"It was for yer own good, Father," the abbess replied, ignoring the question. Looking on from a few yards distant, Coira was surprised at how calm Mother Shona sounded. "Things have gone ill ... I was trying to protect ye."

The abbot gaped at her, torn between rage and concern. Finally, he drew himself up, fisting his hands at his sides. Meanwhile, his monks exited the kirk and gathered in a frightened knot behind him. "Protect me? From what?"

"The plague has entered Kilbride," the abbess informed him, her tone flattening. "Three sisters are ill with it."

At this news, Father Camron took a few rapid steps back from Mother Shona, alarm flaring in his dark eyes.

"That's not all," the abbess pressed on. "The outlaws clashed with MacKinnon today ... the clan-chief is now dead."

The abbot's eyes widened at this news, his throat bobbing. "MacKinnon's dead?"

The abbess nodded.

Father Camron's attention shifted then to where Craeg still stood, a few yards back, at Coira's side. The abbot frowned, clearly trying to place him. "Who's this?"

"I'm Craeg the Bastard," Craeg replied as he observed the abbot with a cool stare. "Surely, ye have heard of me?"

Father Camron's gaze widened before his face went taut. "Ye have brought the outlaw leader here?"

"Aye ... we fought on his side, Father," the abbess continued. "We helped bring MacKinnon and his men down."

The abbot's mouth worked soundlessly at this news. Watching him, Coira forced down the urge to laugh. The words sounded ridiculous, and yet they were the truth.

When Father Camron finally crossed himself, she noted that his hand shook. His face, which had momentarily slackened in shock, twisted, his cheeks growing an even darker shade of purple.

"Unnatural, wicked ... godless!" he spluttered, barely able to form a coherent sentence, such was his rage. "This will be the end for ye, Mother Shona. The Pope will excommunicate ye. I will see to it personally."

A chill settled over the yard in the wake of these words. Coira glanced over at Craeg, to see that he was scowling. "The abbess doesn't deserve yer condemnation, Father," he said, his voice a low rumble in the ominous quiet. "She is a good woman."

"She is an abomination. She has sinned against God," the abbot rasped. His attention swiveled to Coira then, pinning her to the spot. "As ye all have."

It was an effort to hold the man's eye. The hate on his face made Coira want to avert her gaze. Yet, she'd faced sword-wielding warriors today. She'd not let one self-righteous bigot intimidate her.

"I was right about this woman too." He spat out the words. "Look at her ... dressed as a man with her hair uncovered. Ye have no right to wear that crucifix about yer neck."

Father Camron took a threatening step toward Coira. "Take it off, before I rip it from ye."

"Touch her, and ye shall lose yer hand, Father." Craeg's warning was uttered softly, yet there was no mistaking the menace in it. He rested his right hand upon the pommel of his claidheamh-mor, his fingers flexing.

The abbot's eyes bulged. "Bastard ... are ye threatening me?"

"No ... I'm making things clear. If ye touch this woman, there will be consequences."

Father Camron's heavyset body started to tremble then—not from fear but fury. Glaring at Craeg, the abbot raised a hand to the heavy iron crucifix around his neck, his knuckles whitening as he squeezed. His gaze flicked from Craeg to Coira then, his lip curling.

"Fornicators."

Coira tensed. The abbot was taking his insults too far now. If he didn't put away that forked tongue, she wouldn't be held responsible for her actions.

She took a step forward, her fingers flexing around the quarter-staff. In just one move, she could bring him to his knees. Outrage pulsed within her. Just one more word from the abbot and she'd strike.

Sensing how fragile the leash was on her self-control, Craeg reached out and placed a cautioning hand upon Coira's arm.

"Father Camron," he said, the calmness of his voice at odds with the steel that lay just beneath. "I do believe ye have somewhere to go?"

For a long moment, the abbot didn't move. He just glowered at Craeg, as if a black look could strike the man dead.

But if that were the case, the abbot would have been dead ten times over—for now, all the nuns surrounding them were glaring at Father Camron.

The abbot eventually drew in a deep, shuddering breath and twisted on his heel. "Ready my mule!" he snarled at one of the monks cowering behind him. "Now!"

Four of the monks broke off from the group and scurried away across the yard toward the stables to do his bidding. Then, gathering up the skirts of his robe with as much dignity as his offended pride allowed, the abbot followed, the rest of his flock trailing behind him.

Coira watched them go, as did Craeg. And when Father Camron had passed out of earshot, Craeg glanced over at Mother Shona. "That man has the power to ruin ye, Mother."

The abbess's shoulders slumped. "Aye ... assuming we haven't just given him the plague ... but I knew that when I locked him inside the kirk."

"Do ye want me and my men to go after him ... ensure he never sends word to Rome?"

The abbess huffed a bitter laugh. "No, Craeg. As much as I'd like ye to cut out that man's tongue, I won't allow it."

"I was actually thinking of slitting the shit-weasel's throat."

"Again ... tempting." Mother Shona drew herself up, her shoulders squaring. "But no." Her gaze swept around the yard, at where the nuns all watched her, worry etched upon their faces. "I'm sorry, Sisters ... but our time here has ended."

"No!" Sister Elspeth burst out, her face blanching. "Ye can't—"

The abbess raised a hand, cutting her off. "Father Camron will indeed write to the Pope, and I will be removed as abbess and excommunicated. There is nothing left at Kilbride for ye." Mother Shona's eyes glittered with unshed tears as she continued. "Return to yer quarters and pack yer bags. Ye must all leave with the dawn."

Coira stifled a gasp. "But where will they go?"

Mother Shona glanced her way, her expression bleak. "To Inishail Priory on the mainland. The prioress there ... Mother Iseabal ... will welcome them."

"But we don't want to go." One of the nuns spoke up. Sister Robena had only been at Kilbride two years and had just recently taken her vows of perpetuity. "We wish to stay here."

"Ye can't, Sister." Mother Shona met the younger woman's eye, her features hardening. "I made a mistake, thinking that teaching ye all how to wield weapons would aid ye. I was arrogant, and my hubris has brought this abbey to ruin." The abbess paused there, her gaze guttering. "It's too late for me, but not for the rest of ye. Tomorrow, ye will leave Kilbride and make a fresh start elsewhere ... that is my final word on the subject."

A solemn air settled over Kilbride Abbey with the dusk. Emerging from tending to the three sick nuns in the infirmary, Coira raised her face to the sky and whispered a prayer for them.

Sister Morag was close to death. She was older and weaker than Sisters Anis and Fritha. Coira had left Sister Magda to tend to the sick. Now, she'd bathe and join Mother Shona and Craeg for supper in the abbess's hall.

Frankly, Coira didn't feel up to it, but Mother Shona had insisted. It would be the last time they'd break bread together—it was goodbye.

Outdoors, the air was warm and scented with the sweetness of summer. The world didn't know of the turmoil of the current days. It didn't care.

Coira circuited the complex of buildings and went to her cell. A little of the day's tension ebbed from her when she saw that some kind soul had left her a bowl of water, soap, and drying cloths with which to bathe.

The water was still warm.

Stripping off her clothes—which was far easier now that she no longer dressed as a nun—Coira washed away the grime, sweat, and blood. She even washed her hair, teasing out the tangles with her fingertips.

The same individual who'd left her the soap and water had also given her clean clothes—not men's clothing but a faded blue kirtle and cream-colored léine to wear under it. The cloth was poor, the hems frayed in places, yet Coira sighed with relief as she slipped on the garments.

Lord, it felt good to be clean again.

As before, she placed her crucifix around her neck; somehow, she felt naked without it. No matter what happened in the future, she would take her faith with her.

Quickly braiding her damp hair into a single plait, Coira then left her cell and made her way to the abbess's hall.

Craeg was already there, seated in one of the high-backed chairs near the hearth, opposite Mother Shona. His shaggy hair was loose and looked damp—it seemed that he too had bathed before joining the abbess.

The outlaw leader—who'd been talking to the abbess in a low voice, his hands wrapped around a goblet of wine—glanced up at Coira's arrival. His gaze rested upon her, lingering for a heartbeat longer than was necessary, and heat rushed to Coira's cheeks in response. Fighting down the instinct to adjust her clothing or check her hair, she crossed the flagstone floor to the hearth and lowered herself onto a stool.

"Good eve, Coira," Mother Shona greeted her with a tired smile. She rose to her feet, placed her goblet on the mantelpiece above the fire, and poured a third goblet, passing it to Coira. "How are yer patients?"

"They all worsen," Coira replied. "I don't think Sister Morag will last the night." Her words were bald in their honesty, yet she was too weary to soften them. "The illness has attacked her lungs."

Coira's attention shifted to Craeg then, to find him watching her. The warmth in her cheeks intensified. She hadn't gotten used to being 'seen'. Indeed, her habit had provided a shield from men's eyes. "Have Gunn and Fenella arrived yet?"

He shook his head. "It's too soon ... they'll be here tomorrow morning at the earliest."

Coira glanced back at the abbess. "I tried out a new treatment with an outlaw woman ... if it was successful, I should like to try it here."

Mother Shona nodded. "We are lucky to have yer skills, Coira. The Lord has indeed blessed us."

Coira offered the abbess a weak smile in reply and lifted the goblet to her lips, taking a gulp of wine. It was rich and smooth, not at all what she expected. Her eyebrows raised. "This is good."

The abbess's mouth quirked. "Aye ... I was saving it for a special occasion. Now seems appropriate."

Coira's smile faded. "I can't believe ye are sending the nuns away ... it seems so ... drastic."

Mother Shona sighed. "Drastic ... but necessary. If there had been another path, I'd have taken it."

"But—"

"Enough talk of this." The abbess waved her silent. "I've already gone over and over this with Sister Elspeth. My mind is made up ... and it's for the best. Now, ye must focus upon yer own futures."

27

Undone

"KILBRIDE WILL CLOSE for the moment," Mother Shona continued. She crossed the hall to her desk, where a platter of food awaited. It was simple fare—bread, cheese, and boiled eggs—yet Coira's mouth watered at the sight of it.

She was starving, so hungry in fact that she couldn't summon the effort to argue with Mother Shona. It was clear the woman wouldn't be moved.

I'll speak to her alone tomorrow.

The abbess carried the platter across to them and set it on a low table within easy reach of them all. She then helped herself to some food and took her seat. Mother Shona ignored her companions as she began to peel an egg.

Wordlessly, seeing that the conversation had halted for the moment, Craeg and Coira helped themselves to supper. Coira took a large bite of bread and cheese, forcing herself to chew properly before swallowing. Likewise, Craeg ate with the appetite of a famished hound, inhaling two huge slices of bread and cheese, before he eventually broke the silence between the three of them.

"Someone will have to let MacKinnon's kin know he's dead," Craeg said, his voice heavy. "I suppose I should send word to his sister in Dunan."

The abbess glanced up, her gaze spearing him. "*Yer* sister. This land needs a new clan-chief, Craeg ... and ye are MacKinnon's closest surviving male relative."

Craeg's face went taut, his gaze shuttering. "What?"

"Don't pretend ye don't understand me or that ye haven't thought on the possibility before." The abbess lowered the slice of bread she'd been about to take a bite of. Her face developed that steely look Coira knew only too well. "Ye are a born leader ... and the people of the MacKinnon territory need someone to guide them, especially now when times are bleak."

"I can't become clan-chief." Craeg's voice turned rough, his green eyes hard.

However, the abbess wasn't a woman easily intimidated. "Why not ... ye are MacKinnon's brother?"

"I'm his *bastard* brother."

"It matters not. Blood is blood."

"It matters to me!"

Coira cleared her throat. She sensed an argument brewing, something she really didn't have the stomach for tonight. "Would the folk of Dunan ever accept Craeg as heir?" she asked the abbess.

Mother Shona met her eye. "The people of this land *hate* Duncan MacKinnon … but they love his brother. Craeg knows this, but for some reason he's afraid of taking on the role, afraid of facing his destiny." Her gaze swung back to Craeg. "Yer enemy is dead now. It's time for ye to take his place."

"Ye make me sound a lot nobler than I actually am," Craeg countered, his handsome face taut. "It was revenge, Mother Shona. I did it for me … no one else."

The abbess shook her head, a rueful smile curving her lips. "Aye, ye had a score to settle with MacKinnon … but ye also drew men from every corner of this territory to yer cause. Ye inspired them in a way yer brother never could."

A brittle silence fell. Craeg continued to glare at the abbess, a nerve flickering in his cheek. And when he didn't contradict her, Mother Shona added. "If ye don't take Duncan MacKinnon's place, someone less worthy will, I'm sure. Would ye put this land ye love in peril again? Would ye let yer pride override good sense?"

Craeg swallowed. Watching him, Coira sensed his turmoil, his conflict. With a jolt, she realized he wasn't being falsely modest; he really didn't want to take Duncan MacKinnon's place. He couldn't see past the name that had defined him his entire life.

Craeg the Bastard.

Coira's breathing quickened. She wasn't sure what she thought about the abbess's idea either. Frankly, the suggestion had come as a shock. However, as the moments slid by, she realized that Mother Shona was, indeed, an excellent judge of character.

"The abbess speaks wisely," she said finally, her voice subdued. "No one would make a better clan-chief than ye. Please consider it."

Craeg's gaze widened. Mouth flattening, he looked away, staring at the glowing lump of peat in the hearth. He was so tense, she expected him to leap up at any moment and stride from the hall.

Yet he didn't.

The abbess finished her supper and brushed crumbs off her lap. Her attention then focused upon Coira.

"Craeg isn't the only one who needs to consider their future," she said softly. "What will *ye* do?"

Coira swallowed her last mouthful of bread and cheese and stalled by taking a slow, deliberate gulp of wine to wash it down. "I don't know," she admitted.

She was aware then that Craeg had shifted his gaze from the fire. She could feel him looking at her, awaiting her answer.

"Ye aren't staying here," Mother Shona reminded her. "Will ye go to Inishail Priory with the others and take up the veil again?"

Coira shook her head. The definitiveness of her refusal surprised her. She'd been too occupied over the last few hours to give her future any thought. However, she knew she wouldn't be going to Inishail Priory.

"I'm not sure where my path will lead me," she murmured. "But one thing I do know is that I won't be returning to the order."

The abbess's gaze shadowed. She looked almost disappointed. "Why not?"

Coira sighed. She glanced over at Craeg then, her chest constricting. "For years I've sheltered behind the walls of Kilbride … have tried to erase my past with prayer and penitence, and shrouded my body in yards of black cloth so that no man would ever see me as a woman again," she admitted softly. "God will always remain in my heart, but I don't want to hide anymore. I want to live."

Coira slipped through the gates into the make-shift camp below, her heart pounding like a battle drum.

A full moon hung over Kilbride, its friendly face casting a hoary light over the world. A perimeter of torches flickered around the clusters of tents, and a man standing guard greeted Coira with a nod. Neither of them spoke. He allowed her to pass through into the outlaw camp without questioning where she was going.

Maybe he already knew.

There was only one person here she'd have any reason to seek out. Only one person who dominated her every waking thought.

Coira's breathing quickened, and she did her best to slow it, to calm her thudding pulse.

She'd tried to go to her cell, where she'd spend her last night at Kilbride. She attempted to stretch out upon her narrow pallet and let sleep claim her.

She was certainly tired enough.

But sleep hadn't come. All she'd been able to think of was that time was slipping like grains of sand through her fingers. And she didn't want to waste one more moment.

Eventually, she'd risen from her pallet, donned her clothing, and left the abbey. Her feet carried her toward her destination of their own accord. She moved on instinct now, not questioning her decision.

Craeg's tent was easy to find. It rose above the others surrounding it and sat at the heart of the camp.

Coira halted before the entrance, her heart racing so fast now that she felt sick.

This is it.

Until now, she and Craeg had danced around each other, but once she took this step, life was bound to get messy, complicated. She risked getting hurt, risked having her heart ripped to pieces.

But she hadn't lied at supper. She was done hiding from life.

It was now time to embrace it.

Coira pushed aside the tent flap, stooped low, and entered the tent.

To her surprise, Craeg was still awake. He sat propped up on a pile of furs, staring moodily up at where shadows danced upon the roof of his tent. A small brazier burned next to him, the orange light burnishing the planes of his chest.

Coira's mouth went dry when she realized that apart from a form-fitting pair of leather breeches, he was naked.

For a moment, she merely gazed at him, taking in the beauty of his tall, strong body, his broad chest.

And then his gaze flicked to her, and she struggled to catch her breath.

Suddenly, the impulse that had driven her here felt reckless and ill-advised. She'd deliberately avoided thinking on the consequences. After years of steering clear of men, she'd now walked straight into one's lair.

And yet, this man wasn't a predator. He'd only ever been gentle with her.

Craeg stared at her, surprise flickering over his face before he favored her with a slow smile that made her belly somersault. "Couldn't sleep either?"

Coira swallowed. "No."

"I should be exhausted," he said, giving a slow, languorous stretch. "I *am* exhausted."

"So am I," Coira admitted. She couldn't take her gaze from his brawny arms, from the play of muscles across his sculpted chest. He'd removed the bandage from around his torso, and despite that she stood a few feet away, Coira could see that the injury looked healthy enough. The battle hadn't split it open as she'd feared. "But I couldn't sleep … not without seeing ye."

Craeg pushed himself up into a sitting position upon the furs. His mouth quirked. "And what can I do for ye, Coira?"

Heaving in a deep breath, Coira reached up and began to unlace the bodice of her kirtle.

"I want to lie with ye, Craeg," she murmured.

His gaze widened, his lips parting as he stared at her.

"Our world's in turmoil," she continued, "and there's every chance either of us could succumb to the sickness. That being the case, I want to live for the moment. I want ye."

She pushed down the sleeves of the kirtle and shrugged it off; the garment fluttered into a pool around her ankles, and she stepped out of it. Underneath, she wore the long sleeveless léine.

"Are ye sure this is what ye desire?" he asked. His voice came out in a rasp, very different to the confident tone he'd used earlier. His naked chest now rose and fell quickly. "Some things can't be undone, mo chridhe."

Coira, who now reached for the hem of her léine, stilled a moment.

My heart.

Did he mean those words, or was it merely an endearment?

What did it matter? The fact remained that her legs now trembled from wanting him, the pulsing ache between her thighs too much to bear.

"I know that," she whispered. "But I want to be undone."

And with that, she grasped the hem of her léine and drew it up over her head.

Standing naked before him, she was aware of the warm air inside the tent feathering over her sensitive skin, of the rasp of both of their breathing—and of the searing heat of his gaze.

"Come here," he said softly, the catch in his voice betraying him.

Coira obeyed. She moved slowly toward the furs, noting the sudden flush across his cheekbones and the huge tent in his tight breeches.

Coira's breath caught. She couldn't believe she was actually doing this, that after so many years, she wanted this.

She'd never lusted after a man. Those years at *The Goat and Goose* hadn't been about pleasure for her. No encounter she'd had there ever left her breathless and aching. It had been a mere transaction: flesh for silver.

But with Craeg, everything was different. With this man, she was willing to give up her soul.

Coira lowered herself onto her knees beside Craeg, and then, gathering her courage, straddled him. She bowed her head, gazing deep into his eyes.

"Sweet Lord have mercy," he murmured. "Is this a dream?"

Coira's mouth curved. "If it is, then it is a good one."

And with that, she lowered her lips to his.

28

Tainted Blood

CRAEG FELT AS if he'd died and gone to heaven. Strange really, since after everything he'd done over the years, he was sure he'd have ended up with Satan and all his demons.

Coira's mouth, tentatively moving over his, was divine. The nearness of her luscious, naked body, made his groin ache. She was long-limbed and lean, yet with large, high breasts that begged to be touched.

He was going to go insane if he didn't.

And when her tongue parted his lips, he knew this woman was going to make him lose his wits altogether.

He'd longed for this, hadn't been able to sleep tonight for wanting her.

Craeg hadn't enjoyed taking supper with the abbess. Mother Shona had brought up subjects he'd have preferred to ignore. And every time he'd shifted his attention to Coira—clad in a simple blue kirtle that hugged her long, supple body—he'd found it difficult to keep his train of thought.

It had been awkward when they'd bid each other goodnight outside the abbess's hall. He'd watched her walk off toward the nun's lodgings, and had almost called out to her, almost asked her to spend the night with him.

But after everything Coira had been through, it seemed too aggressive.

Although it frustrated him, he had to let this woman come to him. If they lay together, he wanted it to be Coira's choice. She needed to leap the abyss between them and take the initiative—as she did now.

Coira cupped his face with her hands as she deepened the kiss. Their tongues danced and tangled, and when she gently bit his lower lip, the dull ache in his groin grew unbearable.

Reaching up, Craeg unfastened the heavy braid down her back, his fingers tangling in the waves, still damp from bathing. Then he stroked the curve of her back. Her skin was so smooth, so soft. He could hardly bear it. And when his hands moved to her breasts, his fingertips brushing across her nipples, Coira groaned low in her throat.

It was too much. Craeg tore his mouth from hers, took hold of her hips, and pulled her against him as he buried his face in her breasts.

His mouth fastened on a nipple, and he suckled, lust exploding through him when Coira gave a voluptuous moan. She arched back, pressing her breasts hard against him.

They were both breathing hard when she finally drew back and their gazes fused once more.

It was an intense moment, almost too much.

The want he saw in those violet eyes made an ache rise in Craeg's chest. This woman completely unraveled him, stripped away the mask he'd worn his whole life. Aye, since becoming an outlaw he'd amassed a loyal band of followers. Craeg knew folk were drawn to him, that they looked to him as if he was their savior. For years, he'd played the role and enjoyed it even.

But Coira saw past all that. She saw into his heart, understood his loneliness, the belief he held deep down that he was as worthless as Duncan MacKinnon had told him.

He didn't need to explain himself to her, for when she looked into his eyes, she saw it all.

Coira's hands explored the planes of his face before sliding down his neck to his shoulders and then his chest. She traced the lines of his body with rapt attention as if she was committing them to memory.

The turmoil of the world they lived in made this moment even more intense.

Coira was right—all of them now possibly lived on borrowed time.

But for one night, death wouldn't touch them. This night belonged to them.

Leaning back against the furs, Craeg let Coira explore his body, let her take control. He sensed that was what she wanted, and although he longed to reach for her, roll her under him, and plow her senseless, he knew that this union was a gateway for her.

He gazed up into her face, his throat tightening when he saw the wonder there.

Desire was something new for this woman, despite her past. Having grown up in a brothel, Craeg knew why. He'd seen the men who'd visited *The Goat and Goose* on a regular basis, he'd witnessed how they'd treated the whores—treated his mother.

Tonight, he'd let Coira take the lead, take what she wished from him.

Nonetheless, when her fingertips trailed down his belly to the waistband of his breeches, Craeg wondered how much longer he'd be able to bear it.

Her slow exploration was driving him mad.

He watched Coira unlace his breeches and heard her sharp intake of breath when his shaft sprang free to greet her. Swollen and quivering, its tip slick with want, his rod was making his need for her clear.

A sultry smile curved her lips as her slender fingers curved around him, stroking him.

A strangled cry escaped Craeg, and his hands clenched at his sides. He wasn't sure how much longer he could restrain himself.

And then when she rose up on her knees and shifted so that his rod pressed up into the damp flesh between her thighs, Craeg caught his breath.

He'd thought she'd lower herself onto him, but instead, Coira began to stroke herself with the tip of his shaft, taking her pleasure. He watched wonder suffuse her face, watched her head fall back while soft gasps escaped her.

"Coira." His voice sounded strangled as if someone were choking him. "Ple—ease."

She ignored him, continuing to slide herself against the length of him now, her body quivering as she lost herself in the sensation.

Craeg was enraptured. He'd never seen a woman act like this before. Coira had no idea how lovely she was when she let herself go and followed her instincts. And when she finally lowered herself onto his engorged rod, her head snapped forward, her gaze widening.

Taking hold of her hips, Craeg guided her down so that she was fully seated upon him. He could feel the tremors that wracked her, the trembling that increased when he took hold of her hips and moved them in a slow, sensual circle.

"This is wonderful," she whispered, her voice full of awe. "Why is it … oh … Craeg!"

He felt her core tighten around him, sweat beading upon her naked skin. Craeg favored her with a slow smile as he continued to move her hips while he arched up, grinding against her. He loved that this was all new to her, loved watching her discover the pleasure that coupling could bring.

He started to rock Coira her back and forth, in a sensual rhythm that made her gasp. Craeg groaned, arching up once more as he sought to drive deeper. She was so slick now, so hot, that it was stretching his self-control to the limit.

Leaning forward, Coira grasped hold of the furs, the tips of her lush breasts brushing his face. This altering of position allowed him to thrust deeper, allowed her to push back harder against him.

Coira started to cry out, soft mewing sounds that excited Craeg beyond measure. His belly muscles tightened, and the world darkened. His release now charged toward him; there was no stopping it—not when this beautiful woman rode him, writhing and shuddering as she lost herself in her pleasure.

Breathing hard, her body damp with sweat, her core still pulsing in the aftermath of their lovemaking, Coira lay against Craeg, her face buried in his chest.

She could feel the thunder of his heart against her cheek. Like her, his skin was wet with sweat and his chest rose and fell sharply.

"God's bones," he rasped finally. "Where have ye been all my life, woman?"

Coira huffed an exhausted laugh, tracing her fingers down his breast bone. "I wish I'd met ye years ago," she answered honestly.

"Aye." His voice was soft when he answered. "Although ye might not have liked me then … I was insufferably arrogant."

Grinning, Coira propped herself onto an elbow. "Even more so than now?"

His mouth quirked. "Aye … if ye can believe it."

Their gazes held, and warmth spread through Coira's chest. Did this man have any idea how devastating he was? Arrogant or not, she'd have fallen under his spell.

The moment drew out, and, reaching up, Craeg stroked Coira's cheek. "I've been thinking," he said eventually, "about what the abbess said tonight."

Coira cocked her head. "About ye taking MacKinnon's place?"

"Aye." His gaze shadowed as the outside world intruded once more. "The abbess was right. I'm not going to pretend that I've never entertained the thought ... that those who follow me haven't mentioned it before."

"So why the reticence?"

Craeg's mouth twisted. "I don't rightly know ... maybe the fear I have tainted blood?"

"What?"

He gave a bitter laugh. "I'm not proud of the man who sired me ... nor of my half-brother. What if I end up like them?"

Coira stared at him, surprise filtering through her. He was serious. "Ye are as different to Duncan MacKinnon as the sun is to the moon," she said, vehement now. "The fact that ye even worry about such a thing shows just how different ye are. Ye would make a wonderful clan-chief. Ye would rule these lands justly, and ye would treat those who live here with the same respect ye show those who already follow ye."

Craeg's eyes widened. Her intensity had taken him aback, she realized. Yet she couldn't let him think for a moment that he was like MacKinnon.

"So ye think I should go to Dunan and take his seat in the Great Hall?" he asked finally.

Coira's breathing slowed. Not trusting herself to answer without betraying her sudden nervousness, she nodded.

"But what if I don't want to rule alone?" Craeg's mouth lifted at the corners, and his hand cupped her cheek. "It's not power I crave, Coira. None of it matters without ye."

Coira stilled. What was he saying?

"I'll go to Dunan tomorrow," he continued softly, his gaze never straying from hers. "But only if ye agree to come with me."

29

Together

"COME WITH YE?" Coira breathed, her pulse accelerating.

"Aye," he replied, his expression growing serious. "And when we get there … will ye become my wife?"

Coira's mouth fell open. She knew it wasn't an attractive look, yet his words had completely taken her by surprise. Her mind spun at the enormity of what he was asking.

"Life is short, mo ghràdh," Craeg murmured, his mouth curving into a half-smile that made something twist deep within Coira's chest. "We must take it by the horns while we have it."

"This is so sudden," Coira replied, finally finding her tongue. Her voice was higher than usual, brittle. "Are ye sure?"

"Surer than I've been about anything in my life." Doubt shadowed his green eyes then. "I love ye, Coira … but do ye feel the same way about me?"

The sudden vulnerability on his face, the fear that he'd just exposed himself only to risk being pushed away, made a lump rise in Coira's throat.

"Aye," she whispered, her vision blurring. The realization barreled into her with such force that she struggled to draw breath. "I love ye so much that it frightens me."

Indeed it did. She'd learned years earlier what it was to lose those she loved. After her parents had died, she'd been utterly alone in the world. She'd missed them so much that a permanent ache had lodged itself in her chest for many years afterward. She wasn't sure she could bear such heartbreak again.

"It scares me too," he admitted. There was a rough edge to Craeg's voice, and his eyes now gleamed. He reached down to where her hand still lay upon his chest, his fingers wrapping around hers. "But isn't it time we both faced our fears?"

"Good morn, fair Coira," Farlan greeted Coira with a cocky smile. She'd just ducked under the awning, where he and three other badly injured men were laid up. Coira was pleased to see that all of them looked better than they had the night before. Farlan was sitting up, eating a wedge of bannock.

"Morning." Coira stopped before him and raised an eyebrow. "How's the leg?"

"Burns like the devil."

"Let's take a look at it then."

Hunkering down, Coira unwrapped the bandages, her gaze taking in the wound that slashed down his right thigh. She'd hastily sewn it shut the day before. Despite her exhaustion, she'd done a surprisingly neat job of it. She'd cleaned the wound first with vinegar and then packed it with woundwort. This morning, although it was red and angry-looking, there wasn't any sign of souring.

"It's going to take a while before ye can walk," she warned him, sitting back on her heels and meeting Farlan's eye. "But ye were lucky … the blade just missed a large vein."

Farlan nodded, his throat bobbing as a little of his earlier arrogance dimmed. "So I'll keep the leg?"

Coira smiled. "Aye … I'd say so."

Voices, raised in excitement, drifted through the encampment then, drawing their attention. Stepping out from under the awning, Coira spied a stocky horse approaching from the east. A big man with wild red hair rode it, and a woman wrapped in a fur cloak perched side-saddle before him.

Coira's heart started to pound. *Fenella.*

Picking up her skirts, she hurried through the camp, skirting around smoking fire pits and men packing up tents, to greet the newcomers.

And she knew, the moment she saw Gunn's face clearly, that the warrior brought good news.

Reining in the horse, he smiled. "Yer treatment worked," he rumbled. "Fen is on the mend. God bless ye."

Gently, he drew back the hood of his companion's fur mantle, revealing a pale face. Fenella peered out and even managed a wan smile of her own when she spied Coira.

Excited chatter went up around them, joy rippling through the camp. Many of the folk here hadn't expected to see Fenella alive again.

A wide smile split Coira's face. The relief that flooded over her made her legs wobble. So much so, that she was grateful when a strong male arm fastened around her waist.

"It's so good to see ye back, Fen. I was wondering when ye two would get here," Craeg greeted them. "Lucky for ye, there are still some bannocks left. I know ye have the appetite of a half-starved hound, Gunn."

Laughter rose up into the balmy morning air. Coira joined in, the tension she'd been carrying around all morning, as she'd waited for Gunn's arrival, releasing.

Gunn grinned. "Speak for yerself, man." His gaze then lit up as he took in the sight of Coira and Craeg standing together.

Meanwhile, Coira leaned into Craeg, her arm snaking around his chest. She was aware of the curious looks, the stares, around them. If any of them had suspected the developing relationship between their leader and the woman who'd recently joined them, they were now vindicated.

Warmth suffused Coira as she realized she didn't care who knew. Nothing in the world felt as right as Craeg's arm around her.

"I don't want to leave ye here alone, Mother." Sister Elspeth's voice cracked as she spoke, betraying just how upset she was.

The nun faced the abbess at the foot of the steps to the kirk. Like the group of nuns behind her, she wore a leather pack upon her back. However, Sister Elspeth's right arm was in a sling.

"I won't be alone, Sister Elspeth," the abbess replied, favoring the nun with a tired smile. "Sister Magda is with me ... and so will be Sisters Anis and Fritha ... if they live." She paused then. Sadly, Sister Morag had passed away during the night. Earlier that morning, Coira had shown the abbess how to lance plague boils, a vile task but a potentially life-saving one. "We won't tarry here for much longer either. As soon as we can, we too shall move on."

Hope flared in Sister Elspeth's eyes. "Will ye join us at Inishail Priory?"

The abbess shook her head.

Sister Elspeth's gaze guttered. "Why not?"

"I don't know where I shall go after this ... perhaps Sister Magda and the others will join ye, but I will seek solitude."

A brittle silence followed these words.

Looking on, Coira saw that Sister Elspeth was now close to tears. She was an odd woman, Coira reflected. Watching her now, Coira realized just how much Kilbride meant to Sister Elspeth. It tore her up inside to leave it.

The nuns filed out of the abbey, solemn black-garbed figures. They carried a defeated aura about them—so different from the fierce women of a day earlier. They wielded no weapons now and probably would never do so again.

A dull sensation settled in the center of Coira's chest. She glanced across at where Craeg stood, watching the nuns leave. She was happy to stand at this man's side, to go with him to Dunan. But at the same time, the situation here at Kilbride filled her with regret.

Not for herself, but for the Sisters, for Mother Shona.

Turning to the abbess, she met her eye. "None of this is yer fault, Mother," she said softly. "Please don't blame yerself."

Mother Shona's mouth pursed, her gaze narrowing. "Isn't it? There's a reason why men go to war and women keep the home fires burning. For years I fought against the natural order of things ... I wanted to make ye all strong. Ye put yer trust in me, but I put yer futures all in jeopardy. I should never have taught ye all how to fight."

Coira drew back. "Ye did a good thing."

The abbess shook her head, her jaw tightening. "Father Camron wouldn't have returned here to investigate me if I'd run the abbey as I should have."

Coira tensed. "That bigot? He—"

"Hush, Coira. I like the man no more than ye do, yet he's an emissary of the Pope. For years I thought myself above following the rules. I can play games with my own life, but not with the lives of others."

Coira heaved in a deep breath. The abbess seemed intent on shouldering the responsibility for Father Camron's meddling. Although Coira didn't share her view, she could see that there was little point in arguing with her.

One thing she'd learned over the years was just how stubborn Mother Shona could be. The harder you pushed, the more she dug her heels in.

"So ye will go off to some forgotten isle and find yourself a hermit's hut?" she asked finally.

Mother Shona snorted. "Perhaps." She gave Coira a shrewd look then. "And what of ye, lass?"

Coira's cheeks warmed at the question. Although she hadn't minded standing with Craeg in front of his outlaws, being so bold with Mother Shona wasn't as easy. Embarrassed, she lowered her gaze.

"There's no need to look ashamed," the abbess murmured, a note of chagrin in her voice. "Do ye think I'm in a position to pass judgment upon yer choices?"

Coira lifted her chin, aware that Craeg had stepped close, his hand taking hers. The warmth and strength of his fingers made the awkwardness ebb a little. Even so, it was difficult to meet Mother Shona's eye.

"I took vows," she replied softly. "And I have broken them."

"Aye … but none of that matters now," the abbess replied. Her expression turned wistful then. "Ye never belonged here, not really. Like Sisters Ella and Leanna, ye used these walls as a refuge. But like it or not, our past catches up with us eventually, just as mine has. The Lord has other plans for ye, as it had for yer friends."

Mother Shona's attention shifted to Craeg then, and a soft smile curved her mouth. "Plus, love is hard to fight. I once gave my heart to a man like ye, Craeg MacKinnon … I know how difficult ye are to resist."

30

Ghosts

THE BULK OF Dunan appeared in the distance, lit up in red and gold by the setting sun.

The sight of it, rearing up against a backdrop of dark pine forest, made a host of unwelcome memories slam into Coira. The skin of her forearms prickled, and her breathing quickened.

This was going to be harder than she'd thought.

Glancing left, she saw that Craeg was staring at the fortress, his handsome face strained.

The pair of them walked at the front of the column of warriors, alongside the gurgling River An. However, when they were around four furlongs from the walls, Craeg halted and turned back to his men, his gaze sweeping over them. "Watch yer backs," he called out, his voice carrying down the line. "They will be expecting Duncan MacKinnon to return to them. Not us."

"He will have left a few of the Dunan Guard behind to guard the broch," Gunn pointed out. The warrior had put Fenella on one of the wagons and ridden forward to join Craeg. "They might put up a fight."

Craeg nodded. "Aye ... draw yer weapons, but don't use them unless I say so," he ordered. "Enough blood has been spilled of late ... but if we have to use force, we will."

Coira's gaze shifted over the faces of the outlaws before them. They were weary, their eyes hollowed with fatigue, yet their faces were set in determination.

The gates of Dunan would only hold them for so long.

The column moved on. They skirted the locked South Gate, taking the road to Dunan's main entrance, the North Gate. On the way, Coira saw the blackened embers of what looked like funeral pyres.

A chill stole over her.

The sickness.

The gates were open, and the arable fields before them were empty, the rows of vegetables left untended.

"Where is everyone?" Craeg breathed, looking around.

"They've fled," Coira replied. "For fear of getting sick." She met Craeg's eye then. "Ye may find that only ghosts now inhabit Dunan."

A lone guard met them before the archway leading into the broch's bailey. He was a broad, brawny warrior with short blond hair and a face that might have been handsome if it hadn't been set in such a severe expression.

A heavy claidheamh-mor hung from the man's waist, but he hadn't yet drawn it.

Craeg, who'd led the way up the cobbled street from the North Gate, halted a few feet from the guard.

The men's gazes fused for a few instants before Craeg spoke. "Do ye know me?"

The guard's mouth thinned. "The family resemblance is uncanny … Craeg MacKinnon I take it?"

The note of grudging respect in the man's voice surprised Coira. He'd not addressed him as 'Craeg the Bastard' as they'd all expected.

Another heavy silence stretched between the two men before the guard spoke once more. "MacKinnon is dead, then?"

"Aye," Craeg answered, his voice flat. "As are his men, save the survivors we bring with us. If ye'd like confirmation that he's gone … ye can ask them if ye wish?"

The guard swallowed, the only sign that this news moved him at all.

"And ye are?" Craeg asked when the man didn't answer.

"Carr Broderick," the man replied gruffly, "Captain of what's left of the Dunan Guard."

Craeg inclined his head, taking the man's measure. "So, what will ye do now, captain? Deny me access?"

Broderick's mouth twisted into a humorless smile. "I could … but we both know how that would end."

"How many of ye are left?"

"Twenty … three of whom are sick."

Craeg glanced over at Coira, and they shared a long look. They both knew surrender when they saw it. However, it was also clear that this was costing Carr Broderick dearly.

"Ye were loyal to my brother?" Craeg asked, his attention swinging back to Captain Broderick.

To Coira's surprise, the man's mouth pursed, as if Craeg had just said something distasteful.

"Aye," he replied after a pause, bitterness lacing his voice. "Like a hound."

"And can a man change loyalties?"

Broderick frowned, his jaw tensing as he sensed a trap. Tension rippled between them, and when the warrior finally replied, his voice was rough with suppressed anger. "I didn't like yer brother," he admitted. "But I still served him … not like Ross Campbell, who took a stand."

Craeg's gaze narrowed. "Ye knew Campbell well?"

"Aye … and I was sent to track him down. I caught up with him too, just before he and Lady Leanna escaped from Skye … yer brother never learned about that meeting though. I'd have swung for it if he had."

Craeg raised an eyebrow. "Ye let Campbell and Lady Leanna go?"

Broderick nodded, his features tightening.

"Then ye weren't MacKinnon's hound after all," Craeg replied. "Ye are glad he's dead. I see it in yer eyes."

The captain dropped his gaze, his hands, which hung by his sides, clenching into fists. He then shifted to one side, making it clear that Craeg and his men could pass.

Craeg moved forward, drawing parallel with Broderick. "Is Lady MacKinnon at home?" he asked coolly.

The captain's chin snapped up, and Coira, who'd stopped just behind Craeg, drew in a sharp breath when she spied the anguish in Broderick's grey-blue eyes. "Aye," he rasped. "Although ye won't want to see her ... Lady Drew is gravely ill."

Coira followed Captain Broderick up the stairwell to the uppermost level of the broch. The emptiness they'd seen in the narrow streets and alleyways of 'The Warren' had continued within the broch itself. Apart from the odd scurrying servant or skulking guard, the fortress was deserted.

"Surely, not all the servants fell ill?" she asked, hurrying to keep pace with the warrior's long strides as he led her along a hallway. There were no windows in the corridor; instead, a row of flickering cressets illuminated the cool space.

"A few did," the warrior replied, his tone as gruff as it had been at the entrance to the bailey. "The rest fled like rats ahead of a flood."

Coira took this news in, her mouth thinning. His words didn't surprise her, although it was concerning. How many of those who'd fled had been ill already, and had merely taken the sickness with them and passed it on to others?

Broderick led her halfway down the hallway, and into a dimly-lit bedchamber.

The first thing Coira did—before even going to the figure lying on the bed—was walk to the window and unlatch the shutters. She then pushed them wide, breathing in the pine-scented evening air with relief.

Turning back to Broderick, she saw that he was glowering at her. "Don't look so worried," she chided him. "I told ye that I'm a healer."

"The last one told us to close the shutters," he replied, his voice edged with suspicion.

"And where's he?"

Deep grooves bracketed Broderick's mouth then. "He fled with the others."

Coira sighed. "Well then ... it's just as well I'm here." She gestured to the open window. "Fresh air clears out the ill humors. Plus, it'll help me to see." Placing the basket she'd brought on a desk, she pulled out her scarf and gloves and put them on.

When she shifted her attention back to the captain, he was staring at her as if she'd just sprouted horns.

"It's for my own protection," she told him, moving toward the bed. "I'm not much good to the sick if the plague gets me, am I?"

Approaching the bed, her gaze fixed upon the woman reclining there. One glance told her that she was possibly too late.

The woman, around five years her elder, lay there, dressed in a sweat-soaked léine. Her dark hair fanned across the pillow, although her delicate features were gaunt with sickness and pain. The eyes that watched her were eerily familiar—iron-grey—marking her as Duncan MacKinnon's kin. Her clammy-looking skin was ashen and marked with dark spots, huge swellings visible under the arms.

Despite her scarf, Coira took in a shallow, measured breath. *The Lord have mercy on us all.*

"Can ye help her?"

The desperate edge to Captain Broderick's voice drew Coira's attention. Her gaze swiveled to him. She wondered why the man was so obviously upset before realization dawned.

He's in love with her.

Coira's throat tightened, and she shifted her attention back to Lady Drew. Even if the woman had been well, anyone could see that such a love match would be impossible. She was a lady and he a guard. Society would not allow it.

And would society allow a union between ye and Craeg? A voice needled her.

Underneath her scarf, Coira's mouth curved. A woman who'd lived as both a whore and nun, and an outlaw with a price on his head—they were a perfect match indeed.

"She is in the latter stages of the illness," Coira said softly. "But I will do all I can … even if the shock of the treatment may be too much for her." It was true, Lady Drew's weakened state made this procedure a risky one. Coira then reached for the knife she carried at her waist. "Can ye get me a bowl?"

31

Make Ye Mine

IT WAS AFTER dark when Coira joined Craeg in the clan-chief's solar.

He stood by the window, a lonely figure looking out at where a dark line of trees met an indigo sky. Even from the doorway, she could see the tension in his broad shoulders. He wasn't comfortable here.

She didn't blame him. Neither was she. However, she'd had plenty to occupy her since her arrival at Dunan. It had taken her a while to tend to Lady Drew and adequately clean the lanced boils. But after seeing to her patient, Coira hadn't gone to Craeg directly. First, she had gone down to the kitchens and found a bucket of water and lye soap to bathe with.

Tending the sick left a taint behind it. She wanted to scrub it off before she spent time with her love.

Hearing the thud of the door closing behind her, and the light pad of her footsteps, Craeg turned. His gaze was shadowed. "How's my sister?"

"In a bad way," Coira replied softly. "But I have treated her like the others ... if she survives the night, there may be hope for her."

Craeg watched Coira, his throat bobbing. "I never met Drew, ye know," he said after a pause. "Our father thought it fitting to bring Duncan to the brothel to meet me ... but it would have been unseemly to bring the bastard into the broch itself."

"So ye have never set foot in here before today?"

He shook his head.

Coira reached Craeg's side and linked her arm through his, leaning against him. "And how does it feel?"

"Odd," he huffed. "Like I'm trespassing."

"Well, ye aren't."

Craeg drew Coira close, his hand sliding up her back. "I feel as if the moment I step outside this room, a servant is going to appear, point at me, and shriek '*Bastard* ... what are ye doing here'?"

Despite herself, Coira laughed, burying her face against the warmth of his neck. "No need to worry ... there are no servants left to heckle ye."

"Ye mean we shall need to fix our own supper?"

"Aye ... if we can find any food."

Coira drew back from him then, lifting her chin to meet his gaze. The look on his face—both tender and fierce—made her heart leap, her breathing quicken. When he looked at her in that way, her limbs melted like butter in the noon sun.

"Mother Shona was right, Craeg," she said softly. "This is yer destiny. Ye might feel like an imposter right now, but no one could rule these lands better than ye. I am proud to stand by yer side."

Craeg gazed down at her, his expression suddenly vulnerable. "I'm glad ye are here with me, Coira," he murmured. "This broch is a tomb. I feel as if my brother's ghost is breathing down my neck."

Coira huffed. "Yer brother will be too busy trying to outrun the devil and his pitchfork in the depths of hell," she replied.

Craeg's mouth quirked at the image. "Aye." He reached out, his fingers tracing the line of her jaw, to her cheekbone. "Long may he burn there." He lowered his head then, his mouth slanting over hers.

His kiss was hungry, demanding, and Coira answered in kind. Reaching up, she linked her arms around his neck. Her mouth opened beneath his, heat rising in the pit of her belly.

She couldn't get enough of Craeg. His taste, his touch, swamped her senses.

It only took moments for the kiss to spiral out of control, for all thought to dissolve from Coira's mind.

Nothing else but this man mattered.

She reached down and unlaced his léine, her fingers sliding against the warm flesh beneath. Frustrated, she unbuckled the belt that prevented her from ripping the tunic off him.

Breathing hard, Craeg broke off the kiss, stepped back, and pulled off his léine. A soft sigh escaped Coira then, as she leaned forward and tasted the skin where his neck met his shoulder, her fingers sliding over the breadth of his chest and the crisp, dark hair there.

She'd been aching to do this all day. Last night had been but a taste of what she hungered for. Had circumstances permitted, she'd have locked them away together for a week so she could feast on him. Her lustiness shocked her. After years of numbness, yearning like this was unexplored territory.

Craeg groaned as she worked her way down his chest, her fingers plucking at the waistband of his braies.

"No, mo ghràdh," he growled. "Tonight is my turn to take the lead. Tonight, I will make ye mine."

Excitement fluttered low in Coira's belly, and delicious anticipation shivered through her.

Craeg undressed her swiftly, stripping off her kirtle and léine. He then gathered her to him, pressing Coira up against the wall next to the open window. A cool breeze feathered in, caressing her naked skin. Outside, it was completely dark now, and a moth fluttered by, seeking the flames of the fire burning in the hearth and the cressets upon the walls.

Bracing his hands on either side of her head, boxing her in, Craeg's mouth ravaged Coira's once more. His presence overwhelmed her, yet she gave into it. Her eyes fluttered shut as his lips shifted from hers, and he trailed kisses down her jaw and neck.

Mother Mary have mercy.

His mouth was hot, seeking, and when he reached her breasts, she let out a shuddering groan. Her hands fastened upon his shoulders, holding him fast as he stroked and suckled.

And then when he slipped farther down her body—and lifted one of her legs over his shoulder as he went down on his knees before her—Coira let out a soft cry.

Never had a man touched her like this.

During her time at *The Goat and Goose*, the men never took time to pleasure her—they risked catching the pox from a whore after all. As such, the intimacy of what Craeg was doing to her now made tears sting Coira's eyelids, made her chest tighten in a strange blend of tenderness and abandon.

Pleasure crested swiftly, making her cry out again, yet he didn't halt his ministrations. Coira's thighs started to tremble, and if he hadn't been holding her up, she'd have slid down the wall and ended up in a quaking heap upon the floor.

Coira was aware then that she was moaning his name, her fingers tangling in his hair.

Eventually, Craeg rose to his feet—the movement so swift that Coira's eyes flew open and she smothered a gasp.

Their gazes met. Craeg's face was all taut angles, and his eyes had deepened to dark green. Not shifting his attention from her, he reached down and unlaced his breeches. Then, almost roughly now, he took hold of her hips and raised her up against the wall, kneeing her thighs wide.

An instant later he entered her, in a slow, deep thrust that made Coira buck against him. The sensation of him sliding into her, of how she stretched to accommodate his girth, caused an aching pleasure to ripple through the cradle of her hips.

Last night, she'd reached her peak with a man for the first time—had marveled at how pleasure had set her loins on fire.

But this was even more intense. It was a pleasure that throbbed deep inside, radiating out like ripples in a pool, suffusing her whole body with a languor that made her feel reckless and wild.

Nothing in the world mattered except this. Nothing.

Craeg's body trembled, while he held himself leashed. He moved slowly, holding her pinned against the wall as he took her.

And all the while, his gaze held hers.

It was almost too much, too intense, too intimate. Coira felt stripped bare as if all she was—her heart and soul—was displayed before him. But she didn't look away. Instead, her hands clung to his shoulders, her fingernails biting into his flesh as wave after wave of aching pleasure rippled through her.

And when Craeg finally exploded inside her—his groan shuddering through the cool night air—tears flowed down Coira's cheeks.

A grey dawn rose over Dunan. Curtains of fine rain swept across the valley, obscuring the surroundings. It made the broch a grim place indeed, yet there was a lightness to Craeg's stride as he descended the steps into the bailey.

Gunn was there, checking over one of the horses from Duncan MacKinnon's stable. It was a fine beast, a huge bay stallion.

"His name is Curaidh," Gunn greeted Craeg. "Apparently, he belonged to yer brother."

Craeg smiled. *Curaidh—Warrior—a mighty name indeed.*

"He's recovering from a foot abscess," Gunn continued. "The old man who looks after the stables—one of the few folk left in this place—tells me that's why MacKinnon left him behind."

MacKinnon.

Soon folk would start referring to *him* by that name. For years now, the clan-chief's name had brought sneers and grimaces to the faces of the people of this land.

"He's a beauty," Craeg murmured. He stepped close and stroked the stallion's neck.

"Well, he's yers now," Gunn replied with a grin. He leaned down then and ran practiced hands over the stallion's hindquarters, checking for any lameness.

Craeg was observing him when suddenly, something cold and wet pushed against his hand.

Startling, Craeg glanced down to see a large charcoal grey wolfhound sitting at his feet. The hound stared up at him with soft, dark eyes, its tail beating out a tempo on the flagstones.

"What's this?" Craeg said, addressing the dog. "No use looking at me like that ... I'm not yer master."

"The hound's been pestering me all morning too," Gunn replied, glancing up. "The old stable hand tells me that the dog's name is Bran. He too belonged to MacKinnon ... so that means he's yers as well."

Craeg sighed before he reached out and ruffled the dog's soft ears. The hound looked a bit lost. A pang went through him then. Duncan MacKinnon had been such a vile individual—the only one who'd truly mourn him was his dog.

"How is Fen this morning?" Craeg asked.

Gunn straightened up and slapped the stallion on the rump. "Much better. She's starting to get her appetite back." The relief on his friend's face was evident. His eyes gleamed, and his throat bobbed. "And we have Coira to thank."

Craeg smiled. Stepping forward, he placed a hand on Gunn's shoulder. "Ye are the first to know that as soon as we can find a priest ... I'm going to make Coira my wife."

A grin stretched across Gunn's rugged face. "That is good news indeed."

"How is she?"

The rawness in Carr Broderick's voice made Coira tense. His face looked as if it were hewn from stone, yet he betrayed himself when he spoke.

"A little better, I believe," she replied cautiously. Coira's gaze narrowed as she examined the boils she'd lanced the day before. Although they had a raw appearance, she was pleased to see that they were clear of pus and blood. It also seemed that Drew's fever had lowered a little.

Indeed, the lady herself was awake and now observed Coira, her grey eyes clouded with pain and confusion. "Who are ye?" she croaked.

"My name's Coira. I'm a healer."

"And why do ye wear a scarf over yer face?"

"Ye have the plague, Lady Drew ... as ye know, the illness passes quickly from person to person."

Drew licked her dry lips. "I'm so thirsty."

"Here." Coira picked up a wooden cup of water, not an easy task when wearing leather gloves, and held it to her patient's lips. "Just take a few sips mind ... yer belly is still tender."

Drew did as bid before settling back against the mound of pillows. Her gaze shifted then, over Coira's shoulder, to where Captain Broderick stood, still and silent now that his mistress had awoken.

"Did ye fetch this healer, Broderick?" she asked weakly.

He shook his head. "She arrived here with Craeg, milady."

Drew's gaze widened. "The outlaw ... he's here?"

Coira stilled. Was that how Lady Drew saw Craeg? *The outlaw ... he's yer brother.*

Straightening up, Coira met Drew's eye. "I am Craeg MacKinnon's woman," she informed her softly, her breath catching a little as she said the words out loud. "Ye should know that there was a battle between the Dunan Guard and the outlaw band two days ago. Duncan MacKinnon is dead."

Drew stared at her for a long moment. Watching her, Coira's throat tightened. She wasn't going to apologize. When it came to MacKinnon's demise, she couldn't bring herself to show any regret. Not only that but, despite her weak state, she sensed that the woman before her was no whimpering maid. There was strength in the set of the lady's jaw and the steely glint in her eyes.

Silence stretched out, and then Lady Drew let out a long sigh. "It's over then," she whispered weakly.

"Aye, milady," Broderick spoke up. "Worry not, Craeg MacKinnon will allow ye to remain here."

Drew's mouth thinned. "That's generous of him." Her eyes fluttered shut then, the tension going out of her. "Well ... he can't be any worse a clan-chief than Duncan was I suppose," she rasped.

"He won't be." The vehemence in Coira's voice surprised her. "Craeg is a thousand times the man Duncan MacKinnon was."

Drew MacKinnon's eyes opened and then, surprisingly, she favored Coira with a tremulous smile. "That is a relief to hear."

32

Destined

Two weeks later ...

STANDING IN FRONT of the slender mirror, Coira surveyed her appearance. She'd never seen her reflection like this before—having only ever caught glimpses in a still pool or the polished sheen of metal.

She barely recognized the woman before her.

Dressed in a sky-blue kirtle with a violet over-gown, meadow flowers entwined through her hair, she looked like a princess.

It was hard to believe she'd once been a fallen woman, and then a Bride of Christ. Both those identities were behind her now.

Coira's throat thickened then, and she glanced down at the ring she now wore upon her left hand—soon she would wear Craeg's ring upon her right. How she wished her parents were still alive to witness this day.

"That shade is perfect," a woman's voice intruded. "It matches yer eyes."

Coira smiled and turned from the mirror, her gaze settling upon Fenella. Once her fever had abated, the outlaw woman had recovered swiftly. Now, only the thinness in her face hinted that she'd recently been ill. Usually, Fenella favored a more masculine style of dress, striding about the broch in braies and a form-fitting leather vest. Yet today she'd donned a dark-blue kirtle. Her wild mane of blonde hair, which usually tumbled over her shoulders, had been tamed and piled above her head.

Inhaling a shaky breath, Coira then smoothed out the silken material of her over-gown. "I'm nervous, Fen ... what a goose I am."

Fenella's mouth curved, her blue eyes twinkling. "As all brides are. Come on ... everyone's waiting in the kirk. Craeg will soon think ye have changed yer mind."

Coira's breathing hitched. *Never.*

Ever since Craeg had sent out men in search of a priest, she'd been looking forward to this day. The plague had ravaged parts of the isle while leaving some areas untouched, yet men of the cloth were hard to find. However, finally one of the men had returned with a priest from Dunvegan in MacLeod territory. He had arrived with the carcass of a prize stag and Malcolm MacLeod's best wishes.

It appeared that the folk of these lands weren't the only ones pleased by the news of Duncan MacKinnon's passing.

"Let us go to him then," Coira replied. She retrieved a posy of flowers from the sideboard—aromatic sprays of purple heather—and led the way out of the women's solar.

Outdoors, the sun bathed Dunan in warmth. The bailey was still quiet. Although the sickness had passed, folk were slow to return to the fortress. Even so, Dunan no longer had the desolate air of when they'd arrived here.

It still didn't feel like home, although Coira could now envision a time when it might. These days, she was just happy that the sickness had spared her and those she loved. Each night, she knelt by the foot of the bed and thanked the Lord for it.

The two women skirted the base of the broch and headed toward the South Gate.

Two men wearing MacKinnon sashes stood guard there. They both bowed to the women, smiles stretching their faces. Those of the Dunan Guard who'd not wished to serve Duncan MacKinnon's bastard brother had been let go—only those who willingly followed Craeg remained.

Passing under the archway, Coira and Fenella made their way through the kirkyard. The path led between haphazard clusters of gravestones. Ahead loomed the open door of the kirk.

Coira swallowed hard, sweat suddenly beading upon her back.

This was real. She was about to become Craeg MacKinnon's wife.

Only a handful of people awaited them inside. With the threat of sickness still lurking in Dunan, Craeg preferred to keep the gathering small. Still, those who mattered most to them both were there—even Lady Drew.

Seated by the doors, Craeg's half-sister turned to look at Coira as she stepped inside.

The two women's gazes fused for an instant, and Coira noted how much better Drew was looking. Color had returned to her cheeks, although she was still painfully thin. Behind Drew stood Carr Broderick.

The man had barely left the lady's side over the past two weeks. With Craeg's arrival, he'd become her shadow. Gunn was now Captain of the Dunan Guard and Broderick had taken on the role of Lady Drew's personal guard.

The moment drew out, and then Drew MacKinnon's mouth lifted at the corners, warmth showing in her grey eyes. It had been a strange time for Drew. When she was strong enough, Craeg had gone to her solar, and the pair of them had spoken for a whole afternoon.

Coira wasn't sure what had passed between them, but in the days that followed, when Drew joined them at mealtimes, she noted that brother and sister got on well, and even laughed together on occasion.

The family Craeg had never known wasn't completely lost to him after all.

However, Drew only occupied Coira's attention for a few instants. She shifted her gaze then to the tall dark-haired man who awaited her before the altar.

A squat individual with ruddy cheeks, garbed in priestly robes, stood next to him.

Both of them watched her approach.

Gunn sat upon a bench a few yards away from the altar, Farlan next to him. The latter favored her with a grin and a wink. A walking stick sat next to him; the outlaw's leg had recovered well, although he would be lame for a while yet.

Both men shuffled to one side, making room on the low bench for Fenella.

Craeg ignored them all. His attention never shifted from Coira, not for a moment. Dressed in a charcoal pair of braies and a snowy-white léine, with a sash of pine green and red across his chest, he'd never looked more handsome. His hair, although long still, had been trimmed. The striking green of his eyes stood out against his lightly tanned skin.

Coira couldn't stop smiling. With every passing day, she loved this man more—his strength, warmth, kindness, and courage. He was constantly surprising her. Since taking control of Dunan, Craeg had swung into action, clearing up the mess created by the plague and his half-brother's poor management. Crops had been tended, and the broch's stores of grain were now being used to bake bread for the locals. Folk were returning to 'The Warren' in a steady trickle now word had spread that Craeg MacKinnon was clan-chief.

Looking at him, it dawned on Coira that this had always been Craeg's destiny. Mother Shona had told her once that the Lord had a plan for everyone, and although he'd spent many years as an outcast, Coira now believed that Craeg was always meant to end up here.

Which meant that she was also destined to be his wife.

Coira's throat constricted. The joy within her brimmed so full it risked spilling over. She didn't know it was possible to feel this happy, to shine like the sun. She'd heard folk say that there were few as radiant as a woman on her wedding day, but she hadn't believed the tales till today. Now, she understood—if the match was between two people who loved each other, there was no happier moment.

Coira's step slowed as she approached the altar. She wanted to draw this moment out, wanted to imprint it forever upon her mind.

Smiling, Craeg held out a hand to her, his gaze shining.

And reaching out, Coira entwined her fingers through his and squeezed tight.

Epilogue

Belonging

Dunan broch
MacKinnon Territory

Yuletide
Four months later ...

"THE DRUIDS OF old used to swear by mistletoe, ye know?" Coira said as she hung the garland above a doorway. "It was seen as sacred ... a symbol of life in the dark winter months."

"I've always thought mistletoe a dull-looking plant," Leanna answered from across the room. "I prefer holly—the red berries are so cheerful."

Coira frowned, examining the sprig with dark green leaves and tiny white berries she'd just hung up. She disagreed. There was something timeless and wise about mistletoe—maybe it was the fact she was a healer, but she loved the plant.

"It's the scent of pine I look forward to every year," Ella spoke up then. "The Great Hall at Scorrybreac resembles a forest glade this time of year."

"Duncan never liked me to make a fuss over Yuletide decorations," Drew said, her voice oddly subdued. "It feels strange to see this broch so ... festive."

Coira turned then, her gaze traveling to where the three women sat near the fire in the chieftain's solar. Together, they'd decorated this chamber with all three of the seasonal plants. The only thing missing was the Yule log—the massive oaken log that they would try to keep burning for all twelve days of Yuletide—that burned downstairs in the hearth of the Great Hall.

A warm aura of contentment spread over Coira as she looked upon Drew and her two friends. Drew had recovered swiftly over the past months. She now had a bloom in her cheeks and a gleam in her eye as she peeked under the lid of the pot of mulled wine that sat keeping warm by the edge of the hearth.

A few feet from Drew, Ella looked well, although a little tired, for she held a swaddled infant in her arms. Wee Anice was three months old and had arrived just as the plague swept through the north of the isle. Fortunately, Scorrybreac had been only lightly touched by the sickness.

Coira's belly tensed as her attention shifted to the bairn's thatch of thick copper-blonde hair and rosy cheeks. They were so lucky that the illness had spared her and Ella.

All of us here today are fortunate.

Indeed, they were, for many upon the isle had died. Word had reached Dunan that whole villages had perished. Those who survived emerged into a much more subdued world. Whenever she went into 'The Warren', Coira was struck by just how quiet it was these days.

The Goat and Goose had shut its doors permanently. It appeared the sickness had torn through the brothel, and once Old Maude succumbed to it, the few whores still alive fled Dunan.

Coira's thoughts returned to the present, and she glanced over to where Leanna sat making a large holly wreath. It would be the centerpiece on the table for tonight's Yuletide feast. Coira noted how well Leanna looked. Her eyes were bright, her smooth cheeks pink with excitement.

Leanna had always loved Yule, even at Kilbride, where the celebrations had been considerably limited. Coira was glad she and Ross had made the trip from Barra to spend Yule with them.

After word of Duncan MacKinnon's death spread, a missive had arrived in Dunan around a month later. Coira had been sharing her morning bannocks with Craeg in this solar when Carr Broderick brought up a message.

It was from Leanna.

She and Ross were wed and farming a tract of land upon the Isle of Barra, where they raised sheep. Leanna had never been happier but admitted that she missed her old friends terribly.

Afterward, Coira had decided that she would invite both Leanna and Ella to stay. Now that the ravages of the plague were behind them, it was safe to travel again. While Duncan MacKinnon ruled, Ella and Gavin weren't welcome in Dunan either. In fact, he'd longed to have a chance to get his revenge against them.

Now, they no longer had to worry about him.

The rumble of male voices, punctuated by a burst of laughter out in the hallway beyond, drew Coira's attention then. Smiling, she met Leanna's eye. "Sounds like the men are back from hunting."

Leanna gave a squeal of excitement, cast aside her half-finished wreath, and leaped to her feet.

At that moment, the door to the solar flew open and three men entered.

The first was tall and broad-shouldered, a grey brindled wolfhound loping at his heel. Around his shoulders, the MacKinnon clan-chief wore a heavy fur cloak. Snowflakes dusted his shoulders and peat-brown hair.

Behind him another dark-haired man strode into the solar, his piercing blue eyes sweeping around as he took in the decorations. "Good grief ... ye have all been busy."

"Do ye like it?" Leanna rushed to her husband and launched herself at him. With a laugh, Ross caught her before lowering his lips to his wife's for a kiss. "Aye ... it's bonny."

"I don't suppose there's any mulled wine, is there?" A blond man entered behind Ross. Gavin MacNichol blew on his chilled hands. The clan-chief had warm blue-grey eyes and a boyish grin that Ella responded to with a smile of her own. "Aye ... the servants have just brought up some. It's still hot ... help yerself."

Gavin went to the cast iron pot sitting at Drew's feet and lifted off the lid. The heady scent of plum wine and costly spice—cinnamon and clove—wafted through the solar.

Coira breathed in the rich aroma with pleasure. This was her first experience of such a drink. She had grown up relatively poor, and her life in the brothel and then at the abbey had never given her the opportunity to try mulled wine.

Gavin ladled cups for everyone and handed them out. Coira took hers gratefully, wrapping her fingers around the cup as she took a sip.

Glancing up, she saw Craeg approach her. The pair of them shared a smile.

"Did ye enjoy the hunt?" she asked. Behind them, Bran had settled down in front of the fire and was licking his wet paws.

"Aye ... we brought down two red deer," he replied. He took a sip from his own cup, his gaze widening. "Lord, this is good."

"Mulled wine is as new to me as it is to ye then?" Coira asked.

"Of course ... outlaws don't live like lairds."

Coira laughed, stepping close to him. Around them, the chatter of conversation punctuated with bursts of laughter filled the solar. Ross was teasing Leanna over her messy wreath, Gavin had picked up his daughter and was tickling her, while Ella and Drew debated whether or not it was too early to bring out plum and apple cakes to feast on. It was a happy scene, one that gave Coira a true sense of belonging.

A feeling that eluded her until recently.

She was happier too since she'd received word from Shona. A message had arrived just a few days earlier. The former abbess of Kibride had found a new home far to the north of Scotland, upon one of the Isles of Orkney, where she lived as a hermit. And although it saddened Coira that Shona blamed herself for the events that had torn their lives at Kilbride apart, she was relieved to know that the woman was well. Maybe, one day, she'd realize the good she'd done them all. Coira knew she had much to thank Shona for.

"Ye have a smile to light up the world this afternoon, mo ghràdh," Craeg murmured, moving nearer still. "I love to see ye so content."

"I am," she admitted, her smile fading just a little. "I only wish I could make this moment freeze in time ... that all of us could remain exactly as we are ... that nothing could ever touch us."

"Aye, but it's the very fact that these moments are fleeting that makes them so precious," he replied, favoring Coira with that soft smile he reserved only for her. He reached out then and gently cupped her chin, raising it so that their gazes met. "Just remember that we will have other days like this in the years to come. I plan to spend many more Yuletides with ye, Coira. Many, many more."

The End

From the author

FALLEN was a real adventure to tell. I tend to plan my entire series before I write it, but there were still elements about this novel that surprised me. Coira and Craeg's relationship was less angsty than I'd expected. He ended up being far more of a gentleman with a real soft side. Despite his rough upbringing, Craeg is a guy of true class—just what Coira needed after everything she'd been through!

Of course, this novel does have a few heavy themes in it. Coira's past experiences had really damaged her, and the Black Death—which I'd been building up to in the previous two books—features prominently in this tale.

I planned FALLEN nearly a year before I wrote it, although it was an eerie feeling to be writing about the ravages caused by the Black Death when, in March 2020, a pandemic threw our world into chaos. History, indeed, has much to teach us.

The Bubonic Plague devastated Europe in the mid-14th Century, although the Scottish Highlands weren't as badly hit as more densely populated areas. The plague arrived in Scotland in late 1349 and reached its full, devastating heights in 1350. However, I tweaked the time frame by a couple of months as it hits the Isle of Skye earlier in 1349 when my story takes place.

We now know that the Black Death was caused by the spread of deadly bacteria from fleas—and from person-to-person through bodily contact and fluids—but at the time everyone was mystified by it. Healers had no idea how to deal with the plague, and some of the treatments such as bleeding and rubbing excrement on lanced 'plague boils' just quickened the patients' demise! As such, I had to be careful with just how much knowledge I gave Coira. In many ways, thanks to her very wise mother, she is 'ahead of her time'.

Later, healers did discover that people could recover from the illness if the buboes (enlarged lymph nodes), commonly known as 'plague boils', were successfully lanced. However, some patients went into shock after such a procedure and died anyway. Coira's discovery of this practice helps her save a few lives!

I hope you enjoyed this emotional trilogy, and the happy endings for Ella, Leanna, and Coira. I teared up as I wrote the last lines of FALLEN, as I really didn't want to leave this world behind. I hope too that you love CLAIMED, the wee extra where you'll find out what happens with Drew and Carr!

Jayne x

Claimed

Epilogue Novella
The Sisters of Kilbride

JAYNE CASTEL

Map

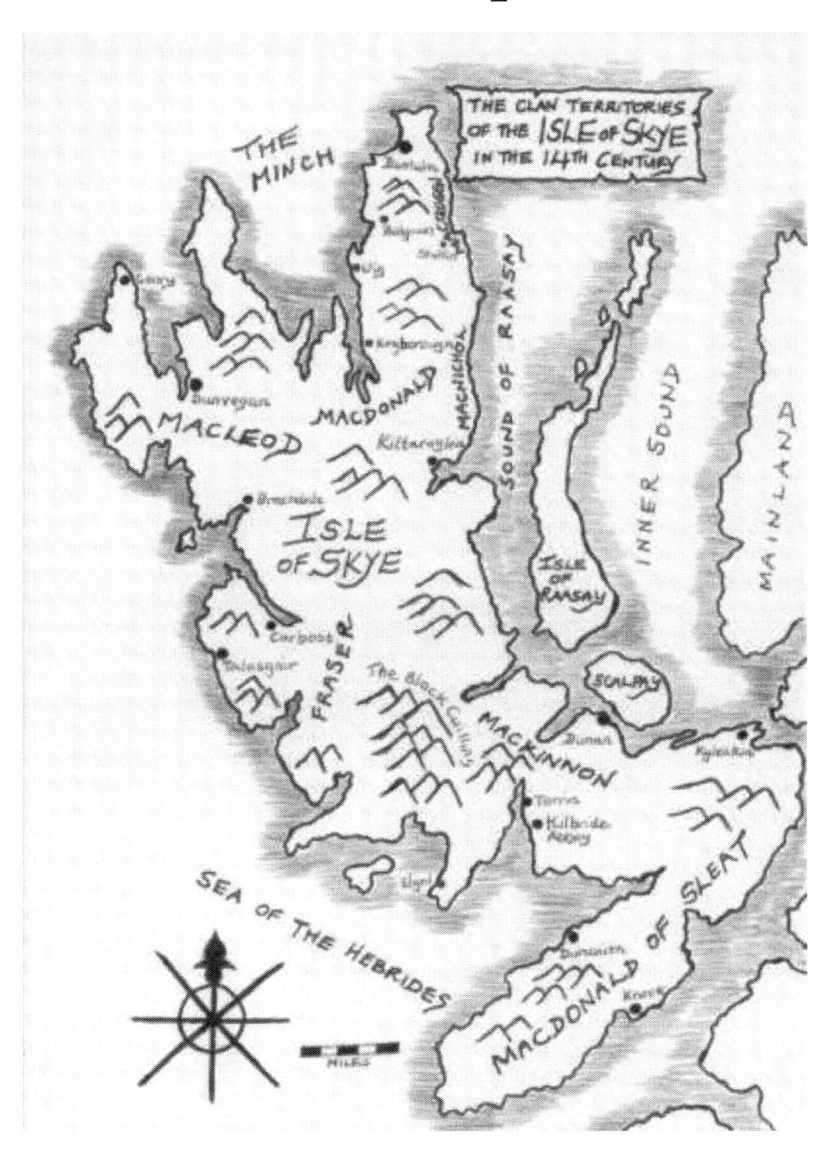

*It is never too late to be
what you might have been.*
—George Eliot

1

Bad Days

*Dunan broch
MacKinnon Territory
Isle of Skye, Scotland*

Winter, 1350 AD

SOME DAYS, IT was better to stay abed.

From the moment Lady Drew awoke in her frigid chamber to find that the hearth had gone out in the night, she resisted the urge to pull the blankets over her head and go back to sleep.

But retreating wasn't Drew's way—and so she gritted her teeth and climbed out of bed, wincing as her bare feet hit the ice-cold flagstones. She called for her maid—a sullen-faced lass named Cadha—thrice, before the young woman deigned to present herself. The lass's face was even sourer than usual when she finally appeared and helped Drew dress. She was so rough as she started to braid her mistress's hair that eventually Drew sent the lass scurrying away with a sharp reprimand.

Drew finished her hair herself—a task which took her an age, for her fingers were clumsy with cold.

By the time she joined her brother and his wife in the clan-chief's solar, they'd almost finished breaking their fast.

"We thought ye weren't joining us this morning, Drew," Craeg greeted her with a grin. He and Lady Coira sat together at the far end of the table. Her arrival had interrupted a passionate kiss.

"I slept in," Drew muttered, taking a seat at the table. She had the urge to complain about Cadha and yet held her tongue. Craeg was very good to her. She didn't want to appear ungrateful.

Instead, she reached for the last wedge of bannock. "I see ye left me plenty."

The tart edge to her voice made Craeg's grin widen. "Worry not, sister … I'll have Kenzie bring up some more."

Sister.

Drew stilled for a heartbeat before dropping her gaze to the wedge of bannock she'd just placed on the dish before her.

By rights, Craeg shouldn't even want her here. Although he welcomed her continued presence in the broch, Drew felt like an interloper. She was part of the old guard, from a time when their elder brother had ruled this broch.

When Craeg had bested Duncan MacKinnon and his men in battle and ridden to Dunan to take his place, Drew had been too ill to care. But afterward, she'd braced herself for his hate, his vengeance.

There had been none.

Drew's mouth thinned as she started to butter her wedge of bannock. Craeg deserved a better family than the one he'd been born into.

For years, she'd known of his existence—the bastard Duncan had loathed. Their father had sired him off a local whore, and many years earlier, Duncan had run him out of Dunan, although not before he'd nearly beaten his younger brother to death. He'd thought never to hear from Craeg again, but instead, the Bastard had risen up against him as the leader of an outlaw band that had caused the MacKinnon clan-chief no end of trouble over the years.

Drew stifled a sigh and reached for the pot of heather honey. She was glad that Craeg now ruled the MacKinnon clan, but his presence here was also a painful reminder that she was powerless in this world. Although Drew was clever and capable, she'd never have been allowed to become clan-chief. She was a woman—and as such was destined to forever sit in a man's shadow.

Drew clenched her jaw, before her attention returned to the far end of the table. She shouldn't dwell on such things—she risked turning bitter.

Oblivious to her brooding, the clan-chief and his wife had forgotten that she was present.

Craeg gazed at Coira as he fed her a morsel of bannock, while she leaned toward him, her proud face soft with love. They made a beautiful pair, both dark-haired and tall. Craeg's moss-green eyes hooded then when Coira licked honey off his fingers. Her violet gaze darkened with sensual promise.

Drew's jaw tightened. *God's teeth, can't they keep their hands off each other when others are present?* She tore her gaze from the couple and glared down at her plate.

Every morning, she had to endure this. Usually, she just ignored them, but this morning, their behavior grated upon her. Once, it would have pleased her to see two people so in love; once, she'd have happily entered into the spirit and flirted with the nearest handsome man.

But these days, it just made her feel jaded.

Drew's chest tightened. Craeg and his love, Coira, certainly deserved the joy they'd found in each other. They'd passed through fire to reach this point—had braved war and plague—battling against the odds that had been stacked against them.

But here they were, seated in the clan-chief's solar, a pale winter sun filtering in through the open window while a fire roared in the hearth—healthy, content, and in love.

It was no good. Try as she might to deny it, Drew envied them.

She forced herself to take a bite of bannock and chewed it with grim determination. She'd been hungry when she'd taken a seat at the table, yet her appetite had vanished.

A dry crumb stuck in her throat then, and she coughed. Reaching for a cup of milk, she attempted to wash it down.

However, the crumb had irritated the back of her throat, and she suffered a coughing fit.

Eyes watering, Drew shifted her attention once more to her companions. Coira and Craeg were laughing over something one of them had just said. She may as well have been invisible. Would they have noticed if she'd choked to death in front of them?

With a huff, Drew pushed herself up from the table.

Aye, she should have stayed abed. This morning wasn't improving.

Drew strode from the solar and nearly collided with the man standing guard outside.

"Good morning, Lady Drew." Broad-shouldered and well-built with close-cropped blond hair, Carr Broderick stepped to one side to avoid Drew, his grey-blue gaze settling upon her. "Is something amiss?"

"No, Broderick," she snapped. "I just need to get outside and stretch my legs. I'm going mad cooped up in here."

Days of freezing, stormy weather had prevented her from taking her daily strolls, but in her present mood, she'd not be thwarted.

Drew strode along the hallway, heading back to her bed-chamber to fetch her fur cloak.

Broderick fell in step behind her.

Irritation surged, and Drew clenched her jaw. *Damn the man.* He followed her around like a hound. When Craeg had taken control of Dunan, Broderick had stepped down from his former role as Captain of the Dunan Guard to become her personal guard.

Wherever she went, there was Broderick a few paces back—her second shadow.

The urge to tell the man to go away rose within Drew, yet she swallowed it. The warrior was impervious to her sharp tongue. He'd made it clear months earlier that there were still plenty of folk—both within the broch, and in the village and lands surrounding it—who bitterly resented Duncan MacKinnon.

They saw her as his supporter, and according to Broderick, many folk still wished to have their revenge. Drew had scoffed at his concerns, yet she'd been unable to get him to cease shadowing her.

Doing her best to ignore her guard, she threw open the door to her bed-chamber and stalked inside.

Outdoors, the winter wind gusted across the bailey, tugging at Drew's cloak and slapping her exposed cheeks. She squinted up at the sky; it was filled with racing clouds, many of which were leaden and ominous.

"We shouldn't go far, Lady Drew," Broderick murmured behind her. "Rain is on its way."

"A few turns around the kirkyard won't hurt," she replied. Not waiting for his reply, she headed left, circuiting the base of the broch toward the South Gate. The guards there greeted her before allowing Drew and her guard to pass through into the windswept kirkyard beyond.

Drew entered the wide yard studded with mossy gravestones, just as thunder rumbled across the sky. Halting, she viewed the dark sky with a jaundiced eye.

"We should really go inside, milady," Broderick said, stopping at her side. "It's going to pelt down in a moment."

Drew cast him a sharp look. "Ye go back if a little rain bothers ye, Broderick," she snapped. "But I'm going for a walk."

With that, she picked up her skirts and strode down the path.

Drew had just turned off the gravel, intent on weaving her way through the gravestones, when she stepped upon something slippery.

There wasn't even time to cry out in alarm. Her feet flew out from under her, and she fell, arms cartwheeling—straight into Carr Broderick's waiting embrace.

It was like hitting a wall. Drew's breath gusted out of her as his brawny arms fastened about her torso. A heartbeat later, he set her upon her feet.

Shaken, Drew looked down to see that she'd stepped into an enormous cowpat.

Broderick snorted. "Looks like someone's *coos* have gotten free again."

Drew's mouth twisted, and she hiked up her skirts, peering down at her leather boots that were now covered in dung. "These were new," she muttered.

"A bit of soap and water will see them right again, milady," he replied.

Drew glanced up sharply, her gaze meeting his. Was she imagining it, or was that amusement she saw there? His mouth was turning up at the corners.

"Laugh and I shall slap ye," she warned, her gaze narrowing. His mouth quirked into a rare smile at her threat, incensing her. "I'm warning ye, Broderick."

At that moment, thunder clapped directly overhead, so loudly that Drew cringed against Broderick's broad chest.

They both waited, breaths indrawn, and then cold rain started to patter down.

Boom. Thunder crashed again, and a sheet of lightning illuminated the western sky.

And then, as if God had just upturned a bucket of icy water, rain poured down from the heavens, drenching them both.

There hadn't even been time for Drew to pull up her hood. Not that it mattered—for the rain was so heavy it would have soaked the fur in instants.

Water ran down Drew's face, blinding her. Wiping it out of her eyes, she pulled back from Broderick and met his gaze once more. "Don't say a word," she growled.

Back in her bed-chamber, Drew removed her sodden cloak and hung it up next to the hearth. Cadha had relit the fire while her mistress had been out, and now a large lump of peat burned.

She'd done her best to clean her boots downstairs but had eventually left them for the servants to deal with.

Drew stretched her chilled fingers out before the fire, sighing as the heat soaked through her flesh. As much as she hated to admit it, Broderick had been right. She should have taken notice of those dark clouds before going out for a walk. However, she'd never confess such to him. The rain now lashed against the closed shutters of the bed-chamber's single small window, thunder booming so loudly that the broch's stone walls shook from the force of the storm.

Listening to it, Drew's eyes flickered closed. Today was a sign. Finally, after months of wavering, she had to take action. Dunan didn't feel like her home any longer—it hadn't in a while. She felt utterly superfluous here.

Alone in her chamber, she made the decision she'd put off for too long.

With another sigh, Drew opened her eyes and moved away from the hearth, before taking a seat at the nearby desk. A single stubby candle flickered there, casting a soft light across a neatly stacked pile of parchment, the wax tablets she used for sealing letters, and her inkpot and quill.

Lighting another candle, Drew helped herself to a leaf of parchment. However, before she reached for her quill, she hesitated. She'd delayed this moment deliberately. To write this letter felt so *final*. Once she sent it off, her days at Dunan would be numbered, for she doubted the request she was about to make would be refused.

That's the point, isn't it?

Jaw firming in resolution, she dipped the quill into the inkwell and began to write.

2
Welcome News

"LADY DREW ... A message has arrived for ye."

Drew glanced up from her bowl of porridge to see that Carr Broderick had joined them in the solar. Cheeks ruddy with cold, his grey-blue eyes serious with purpose, he held out a roll of parchment.

Taking the scroll with a nod, Drew's pulse quickened. She received few missives these days—and as nearly three weeks had passed since she'd sent her letter away, she knew that this was the reply she'd been awaiting.

Broderick cast her a questioning look, before he stepped back, to take up his position near the door. She saw from his expression that he'd sensed her nervousness, and the realization made her tense.

I've been spending too much time in his company, she thought, breaking the wax seal on the scroll. *The man reads me too well these days.*

She and Broderick had lived under the same roof for many years, but before Duncan's downfall, they'd had little contact. The warrior—who'd come to foster at Dunan as a lad and then remained to serve her brother—was still largely an enigma to Drew. She wondered how he felt about his demotion from Captain to lowly guard. Surely it must gall him to spend his days at her beck and call?

It was a considerable drop in rank, yet if Broderick minded, he never let it show.

Glancing away from her guard, Drew unfurled the parchment and scanned the missive within. It was brief, just a few lines, but as she read them, Drew's breathing slowed.

"What is it, Drew?" At the end of the table, Craeg put down the wedge of bannock he'd been about to take a bite from, his handsome face tightening.

Not for the first time, Drew marveled at just how much he looked like their dead brother. The same wavy peat-dark hair, arrogant bearing, and chiseled jaw. Yet unlike Duncan, who'd had iron-grey eyes like Drew—a legacy from their mother—Craeg's eyes were a warm moss-green. He also bore a long, thin scar that stretched down from temple to cheek, narrowly missing his left eye. Duncan had given him that.

His mother must have been a kind woman, for a great sense of humanity tempered the MacKinnon arrogance in Craeg.

No wonder the folk of this land love him.

"It's a message from my mother," Drew replied, lowering the parchment.

"Ill tidings?" Coira asked softly.

Drew shook her head and forced a smile. "No, actually … welcome news. She has spoken to the Prioress of Inishail Priory in Argyll … as I've asked. And they will admit me as a novice."

Craeg's gaze drew wide. "Ye are taking the veil?"

The incredulity in his voice made Drew stiffen. It didn't surprise her that found the idea preposterous; most folk who knew her well would.

Lady Drew MacKinnon wasn't the sort of woman one would expect to find in a convent.

"Aye," she replied calmly.

"But why?" Coira asked. Meeting the woman's eye, Drew saw the consternation there. Of course, Coira knew what it was to live as a nun—for she'd resided at Kilbride Abbey for a decade—before war and pestilence uprooted her life forever.

Drew inhaled slowly. She was aware then that Craeg and Coira weren't the only people present staring at her—she could feel Carr Broderick's gaze boring into her too. Glancing his way, she saw that he wore a stunned expression as if she'd just slapped him.

Drew's lips parted. She was about to offer some lie about how much she missed her mother and how the woman had begged her to come join her at Inishail. The words rose within her, but then they choked in her throat.

She cared for these people—the realization jolted through her—and they deserved honesty.

"I never expected to be welcome here after Duncan's demise," she said finally. "I thought that ye would cast me out for being his sister."

"But ye are *my* sister too," Craeg reminded her, frowning. "And I am glad of it."

Drew's throat thickened as she shook her head. Craeg's kindness made this harder than she'd expected. "Dunan is *yer* home now," she said, her throat aching, "but I no longer belong in this broch … I haven't for a while. The truth is that I feel useless here."

"Of course ye belong here." Craeg's frown deepened. "Dunan was yers long before it was mine."

"Aye, once. But every chamber, every corner, is a reminder of the past," Drew replied. It was true. She had grown up within these walls, the daughter of a callous father and shrewish mother—and then had lived under her cruel elder brother's rule for far too long. Duncan MacKinnon's presence still lingered here, a stain on her conscience.

She had to make a new start elsewhere. As a nun, she could do some good perhaps. Here in Dunan, she felt like an encumbrance, even if Craeg and Coira would never admit as much.

"The last few months have changed me," Drew admitted with a half-smile. "I feel a stranger within these walls."

"Give it time," Craeg said after a pause. Her brother was no longer frowning; he just looked worried. "It might just be the winter's gloom getting to ye ... ye'll feel different once the weather warms."

Next to him, Coira watched Drew, a thoughtful expression upon her face. She'd said little since her sister-by-marriage's news, yet Drew knew that Coira understood how she felt.

Sometimes folk just didn't fit into their old life anymore.

"Time won't change how I feel ... or my decision," Drew answered, stubbornness setting in. "The decision has been made. Space has been made for me at Inishail, and I will leave as soon as I'm able."

Coira's gaze widened. "So soon ... can't ye wait till the spring thaw at least?"

Drew shook her head. "I'm not fond of farewells ... I'd rather not prolong this one."

Silence fell in the solar. It was another chill morning, and a fire roared in the hearth as the wind whistled against the walls of the broch.

"I will organize an escort for ye," Craeg said finally, his voice heavy, his gaze shuttered. "I can't have ye traveling to Argyll alone."

"I will lead it, if I may." A low voice interrupted.

Drew's attention shifted to Broderick. The surprise she'd glimpsed upon his face had gone, and now he wore a somber expression as if they were organizing a burial.

"Thank ye, Broderick," Craeg replied with a nod before Drew had the chance to speak up. "Gather a party of six warriors. My sister must be well-guarded on her journey."

"Are ye sure ye have thought this through?"

Drew had been awaiting Coira's question. The silence in the women's solar had grown deafening as the morning stretched on. The pair of them sat near the hearth. Drew was embroidering the hem of a summer kirtle, while Coira wound wool onto a spindle.

Glancing up, Drew saw that her sister-by-marriage was frowning, her fine dark brows knitted together.

"Aye, I have," Drew replied. "Why? Do ye question my choice?"

"Taking the veil isn't a decision to be taken lightly," Coira replied, her voice low and firm. "It's not an easy life for many. I've known women who've regretted it."

Drew shrugged. "Ye enjoyed the life of a nun well enough, didn't ye?"

Coira sighed and lowered the spindle to her lap. "Aye ... although for me it was an escape. At Kilbride, I was free of male attention, free from brutality."

The words hung between them, and Drew tensed. Her initial reaction to Coira's concerns had been flippant, yet she couldn't continue to act that way now. Not when she knew that the brutality Coira spoke of had been suffered at the hands of Duncan MacKinnon.

Drew had so much to thank Coira for. Months earlier, she'd appeared at Drew's bedside like an angel of mercy at her darkest hour. She'd brought her back from the edge. In the moons that had passed since Drew had recovered from the sickness, Coira had treated her like a sister.

"I remember ye telling me that ye weren't pious before going to Kilbride," Drew said after a pause. "Yer life at the abbey gave ye purpose. I want to find such meaning for my own life."

Coira held her gaze, her expression shadowed. "Ye don't need to take the veil to find purpose."

Drew frowned, her irritation rising. "Ye think I'm ill-suited, don't ye?"

Coira's mouth quirked. "Aye. Ye are strong-willed to a fault. I hope the prioress knows what she's in for."

"Well then," Drew sniffed. "Perhaps Inishail will be good for me."

A heavy silence fell between them. When Coira broke it, her gaze was probing. "All those times I've asked ye to join me in prayer at the kirk, and ye refused. Ye can understand why I'm surprised by yer decision to become a nun. It seems so ... out of character."

Drew stuck her needle into her embroidery and leaned back in her chair. Of course Coira found her behavior odd; her sister-by-marriage deserved an explanation she supposed. "Dunan kirk holds ill memories for me," Drew admitted after a pause. "When I was a lass, Ma used to make me kneel for hours there before the altar after I'd misbehaved. I grew to hate the place. And these days, whenever I enter the kirk, all I can see is Father Athol crumpled before the altar after Duncan stabbed him."

Coira's violet eyes shadowed at these words, and when she replied, she deliberately avoided speaking of the man who'd driven her to take the veil many years earlier. "Do ye really want to live under the same roof as yer mother again?" she asked.

A sigh escaped Drew. She hadn't missed Lorna MacKinnon in the time since she'd departed Dunan, yet she decided against admitting that to Coira. She wasn't going to Inishail for her mother's sake anyway, but for her own. "Folk can change," she said crisply, picking up her embroidery once more. "Perhaps all the years at Inishail have softened her."

3
I'll Never Know Now

THEY RODE OUT of Dunan on a grey, wet dawn, headed southeast toward the coastal village of Kyleakin. The journey would take them the better part of the day, and so Broderick had insisted upon an early start.

The good-byes were awkward, difficult, as Drew knew they would be.

Craeg and Coira came out into the bailey to see her off. Their faces were pale with sleep and drawn from the chill damp that rose off the slick cobblestones. Wrapped in fur cloaks, the couple watched Drew lead her palfrey from the stables before Craeg stepped forward and approached her.

"There's still time to change yer mind," he murmured. "No one will think less of ye for it, Drew."

Throat constricting, Drew shook her head. She should have known her brother would make this hard for her.

My brother.

Aye, although she'd never set eyes on the man before last summer, Craeg MacKinnon was the brother she'd always wanted, the brother she'd wished Duncan could have been. He was younger than her by nearly three winters, her baby brother, yet he towered over her now as he reached out and took her hands with his.

Her fingers were chilled already, yet his hands were warm and dry. Why was it that men always had such warm hands? Winters were a trial for Drew, for she spent months with numb fingers and toes, and chilblains that rose in red, itchy welts on her hands and feet.

"I know ye wouldn't, Craeg," she said softly. "But the fact remains that I'd leave sooner or later … it would only prolong the inevitable."

"Please send word when ye reach Inishail," Coira said, stepping up to her husband's side. "It's not safe for travelers these days."

Drew tensed. She'd heard that in the wake of the sickness that had swept over Scotland, there had been a rise in lawlessness upon the mainland. Merchants had brought word that brigands patrolled many highways and preyed upon travelers.

Forcing a smile, Drew met Coira's warm gaze. "Aye ... but I should be safe enough with Broderick and yer men as my escort." She glanced back at Craeg. "Are ye sure ye can spare them?"

"Of course I can," he replied with a snort. "Coira's right. Let us know ye have arrived safely at the priory." Craeg shifted his gaze over Drew's shoulder then, at where Carr Broderick had just led his horse out into the yard. Drew noted how the men's gazes fused for a long moment. They had an odd relationship, Craeg and Broderick. Craeg had allowed the guard to remain on in Dunan and was cordial with him, yet there was a reserve between the two men. The shadow of Broderick's past allegiances hung over them.

He's not that different to me, Drew thought, casting a glance over her shoulder to see that her guard was holding Craeg's eye. *He doesn't belong here either.* What would happen to him once he delivered her to Inishail Priory?

"Look after her, Broderick," Craeg rumbled.

The guard nodded curtly. "With my life, MacKinnon."

Pushing back her hood, Drew peered up at the sky, hoping to see the pale glimmer of the sun. However, the clouds had sunk low, obscuring the soaring mountains that etched the sky to the west and the south. A misty rain continued to fall, although fortunately, there was no wind this morning.

It was going to be a wet ride to Kyleakin.

Drew inhaled slowly, drawing the fresh, damp air into her lungs. It was a relief to be away from Dunan. Her vision had blurred dangerously when Craeg had pulled her into a fierce hug and then Coira had done the same.

She'd stumbled, half-blind, over to where her grey palfrey sat patiently awaiting her and had allowed Broderick to boost her up side-saddle. It had taken all her will not to dig her heel into her mount's flank and send it careening out of the bailey.

Emotional displays weren't something that Drew favored. She hated the sensation of losing control.

Clattering out of Dunan's North Gate a short while later, she'd actually scrubbed away a tear that had treacherously escaped. However, her dignity was intact, even if her chest felt as if a boulder sat upon it.

Fortunately, the farther they traveled from Dunan, the more the pressure upon her chest lightened. Drew realized that whatever the outcome, she'd made the right decision to leave. The past, and all its memories, was behind her now.

A new start lay in Argyll. She wasn't going to pretend that adjusting to a life of prayer and solitude would be easy, but it would be a refreshing change from an existence that had been stifling her for a long while now.

Drew rode near the head of the column, just behind Carr Broderick and one other, while the remaining guards traveled behind her. They rode in companionable silence, something Drew was grateful for; not that Broderick was ever one to indulge in idle chatter.

Her gaze rested upon him now.

Like her, Broderick had pushed back his hood, letting the misty rain fall upon his head. Unlike many men, who grew their hair long, he wore his pale blond hair short. The rain had darkened it, and as she watched, he raked a hand through his hair, leaving it in spiky disarray.

The cloak highlighted the breadth of his shoulders, the strength of his muscular body. How old was Broderick? Around thirty winters perhaps—five or six years younger than her. A man in his prime, a warrior, who'd given his loyalty to the wrong man and was now paying for it.

He'd been a constant overbearing presence over the past months, yet a part of her was glad he'd offered to lead her escort.

Carr Broderick made her feel safe, protected.

Strangely, few other men—besides her half-brother—had made her feel that way. In truth, she struggled to understand males at all. Most of them seemed rough-mannered and limited in understanding compared to women. Perhaps that was why she'd remained a widow after Egan's passing.

Her husband had been over twenty-five years her elder, but that wouldn't have mattered if she'd desired him. Even now, she suppressed a shudder when she remembered being bedded by him. Egan had been a tall, thin man with watery pale blue eyes and a weak chin. An insipid, perfunctory lover, he was the sort to climb on, do the deed, and then roll off and go to sleep.

She might have overlooked the fact he was a disappointing lover if they'd been friends, yet Egan had little time for her. He was a 'man's man', who preferred to be out hawking or in the Great Hall drinking with the other warriors.

It had been shocking, the day he'd died, choking on a trout bone, but she hadn't grieved for him.

They'd been wed for years, although her womb had never quickened. A bairn might have given her a focus, might have made him warmer toward her. A decade of marriage, and she felt like she hardly knew him.

Drew's mouth compressed at her husband's memory, and she focused her attention on her palfrey's pricked ears.

She tried not to dwell on the past much these days. But seeing Craeg and Coira so obviously happy together, so in love, had just highlighted the emptiness of her own marriage. The attraction between them crackled in the air, like the heavy sultry atmosphere before a summer squall.

What was it like to feel like that?

Drew gnawed at her lower lip and urged her mount into a brisk trot as the company crested a hill.

I'll never know now.

She'd once had dreams. After Egan died, she'd looked around for a suitable husband, for a man she desired. She thought she'd found it in Gavin MacNichol. The MacNichol clan-chief was only a few years her elder. Blond and blue-eyed, with a boyish smile, and a tall, muscular build that drew a woman's eye, Gavin, unfortunately, hadn't been interested in her at all. A widower, Gavin had eventually remarried, to his dead wife's sister, but he'd never once encouraged Drew's affections.

Drew's cheeks warmed then as she remembered how she'd thrown herself at him on more than one occasion. The last time, she'd let herself into his bed-chamber during a visit to Dunan—and he'd rebuffed her.

I deserved that.

Aye, she had—but that hadn't taken the sting out of it. She was much warier around men these days. And soon, once she reached Inishail Priory, she wouldn't have to deal with them at all.

Carr slowed his horse so that he rode shoulder to shoulder with Lady Drew's palfrey. The weather had worsened as the day progressed, the veil of rain closing in around them.

"How are ye faring, milady?" he asked. "Do ye need to rest?"

Drew shook her head, her pert features set in a dogged look he knew well. "We rested at noon," she pointed out. "I'd prefer to press on for Kyleakin … how much farther is it?"

"Not much … the rain has slowed us, but we should reach the port before dusk."

She inclined her head, fixing him with that mesmerizing iron-grey gaze of hers. "Will we be able to find passage tomorrow?"

He nodded, taking in the loveliness of her face. She had an impish quality to her beauty, which gave her a youthful air. Her hair, coiled in its tight braids, clung to her scalp, while the mist coated her creamy skin. "There's a boat at dawn bound for Kyle of Lochalsh … if the weather doesn't take a turn for the worse, we shall be taking that."

Sometimes it was difficult for Carr to concentrate when talking to Drew. He'd made a point of riding ahead, of keeping his gaze upon the highway before them and scanning the roadside for any sign of danger. However, when they'd stopped at noon, his attention kept returning to her.

Now he knew that their time together was coming to an end, his gaze wanted to feast upon this woman, to memorize every line upon her face.

But even as he gazed at her, his heart felt as if it were slowly shrinking. Lady Drew was leaving, shutting herself forever in a priory—a place where he'd never set eyes on her again. A familiar heaviness pressed down upon him at the thought. Never again would he hear the velvet timbre of her voice, the music of her laughter. Never again would he inhale the scent of lily as she walked by, or meet that knowing iron-grey gaze. Ever since she'd announced her news, a dark shadow had settled over his world.

Holding his gaze, Drew's mouth pursed. "What is it, Broderick?" She reached up and touched her cheek. "Do I have mud on my face?"

Satan's cods, he was staring.

This was his chance. He could tell her how he felt, could lay himself bare before her and beg her not to take the veil. Yet the words wouldn't come—they never had.

Carr shook his head and ripped his gaze from hers. "No, milady," he mumbled.

An instant later, he urged his horse forward, leaving Drew to ride by herself once more.

4

Taking Supper Together

DREW WAS SHIVERING when they reached their destination at last—*The King's Arms* in Kyleakin. The port village, a cluster of white-washed cottages huddled against a brown hillside studded with dark pines, sat facing a grey expanse of water. The mainland lay to the north, just in front of Kyleakin, but this afternoon, a bank of dense cloud obscured it.

In the stables behind the inn, the company dismounted their tired horses.

"I'll see to yer palfrey, milady," Broderick said brusquely, addressing her for the first time since their awkward exchange earlier that afternoon. "Ye had best get indoors before ye catch cold."

Teeth chattering, Drew obliged. Her fur mantle dragged down at her as she crossed the straw-strewn yard and entered the inn through a narrow doorway. Warmth embraced her when she stepped inside, as did an array of smells: the fug of peat-smoke, the greasy odor of roasting mutton, the scent of sawdust, and the hoppy tang of freshly brewed ale.

Drew sighed and paused for a moment, taking in the crowded common room before her.

She hadn't been inside an inn or tavern for years now, not since before she'd wed. She'd forgotten how cozy they were, especially when the weather outdoors was so gloomy.

A huge hearth roared at one end of the room, and low beams crisscrossed the space. A number of oaken tables dotted the floor, although Drew's gaze went to the comfortable-looking booths that lined the walls.

She was aware then of the patrons—most of them men—turning their heads to look at the newcomer. Curiosity flowered on their faces, although Drew ignored them. Instead, her gaze went to the portly young man who hurried toward her.

"Lady Drew MacKinnon?" he asked, breathless, his eyes bright.

Drew nodded, glad that Broderick had sent word ahead of their arrival the day before. He'd wanted to make sure the inn could accommodate them all.

"Did ye have a good journey from Dunan, milady?"

"It was wet and cold," Drew answered honestly. She was aware then that everyone in the common room was now gawking at her. The innkeeper's excited greeting hadn't escaped any of them. "I'm looking forward to a hot bath and a meal."

"And I will ensure ye receive both, milady," the innkeeper assured her. "Come ... I shall escort ye to yer chamber. I will have hot water brought up for ye immediately." He ushered her across the crowded floor toward the wooden stairs that led to the upper level of the inn, his manner suddenly nervous. At first Drew wondered at his urgency, and then, when she felt intent male gazes follow her to the stairs, her spine stiffened.

Suddenly, she wished that Broderick had accompanied her in here. She remembered his warnings about the ill-will many folk still bore her dead brother.

She hoped no one inside *The King's Arms* had a score to settle with Duncan MacKinnon.

With a sigh, Drew sank down into the hot water. Her eyes fluttered shut, and she inhaled deeply. Lavender and rosemary—the innkeeper's wife had added a special oil to the water, one which created a scent that now floated like a cloud above the steaming bath.

Lord, this feels good.

The day's journey had chilled Drew to the marrow. Her hands and feet had felt like lumps of ice as she entered her bed-chamber. When she'd peeled off her clothing, she noted that even her léine, the long ankle-length tunic she wore under her kirtle, was wet.

Broderick was right—she risked catching a chill.

However, the hot, scented water was a balm, and as she lay there, she could literally feel the heat seeping through her chilled limbs and restoring them once more.

Eventually, Drew opened her eyes and took in her surroundings. Although much smaller than her bed-chamber back in Dunan, the room was very pleasant. White-washed with dark wooden beams overhead, it had a tiny shuttered window and a large bed with soft cushions filled with goose-down. Deerskins covered the wooden floors, and a hearth burned in one corner.

This chamber made the one she'd left behind seem cold and austere in comparison.

Don't get too used to it, she reminded herself. *Soon ye shall be sleeping in a nun's cell.*

It was a sobering reminder. A nun's life would be very different to the one she'd known until now. She had to prepare herself for the lack of comfort.

Drew's belly tightened as she allowed herself to think ahead, to imagine how she'd soon spend her days. There wasn't any point in shying away from it. Drew had always prided herself on being a realist. Entering the priory would be far less of a shock if she mentally prepared herself first.

During their last morning in the women's solar together, Coira had spelled out the realities of a nun's life for her. No longer would she have a large, soft bed; no longer would she wear brightly-colored kirtles. The rich meals at Dunan would be nothing more than a pleasant memory. She would likely have to cut her hair off and would wear a black habit for the rest of her life. She would also have to pray several times a day.

The heaviness in her stomach increased. Perhaps imagining the life before her wasn't a wise idea after all.

Drew sank further into the steaming water.

Glancing down, she let her gaze travel over her naked body. She'd regained flesh again after being sick last summer. Even so, the illness that had nearly claimed her life had left its mark upon her; pink scars remained from the boils that Coira had lanced. They were fading, but in the hot water still looked evident.

Drew suppressed a shudder. She'd been so weak after that sickness, so thin, that she couldn't sit down without putting a soft cushion under her backside.

She wasn't bony these days though. Her body had a pleasant softness to it; not that its appearance mattered much. Apart from Egan, no man had ever looked upon her nakedness.

And now no one would. Once she took the veil, men wouldn't see her as a woman any longer.

Just as well, for life in the priory will turn me into a stringy fowl, Drew thought ruefully. Coira had also told her how physically demanding the life of a nun was.

Drew sighed. Her thoughts were going around in circles and ruining her enjoyment of the bath. If this was her last soak in a tub, with scented oils and the sound of the rain pattering against the wooden shutters, then she wanted it to be a pleasant memory.

With that, Drew slid down, and, holding her breath, sank completely under the water, letting the liquid heat chase all thought away.

She bathed until the water cooled. Then, reluctantly, Drew climbed out and dried herself off as she listened to the storm rattle the shutters. She was glad to be indoors on a night such as this.

She was seated on the edge of the bed, clad in just a léine, teasing out the knots in her long dark hair with a wooden comb, when a soft knock sounded on the door.

"Lady Drew ... it's Broderick."

Drew paused in combing her hair. "Aye ... what is it?"

"The innkeeper wants to know if ye'd like any supper?"

Drew's belly growled in response. She had eaten a quick meal of bread and cheese at noon and didn't intend to miss supper. "Of course," she called back.

"Very well, milady ... I shall bring it up now."

Drew was about to thank him when she hesitated. She could dine here alone, but the common room had looked so warm and inviting. Soon, all her meals would take place in a grim priory refectory.

"Wait," she replied, casting aside her comb and rising to her feet. "Give me a few moments, and I shall join ye downstairs."

Carr took a draft of ale, savoring the sharp, hoppy taste on his tongue. *The King's Arms* in Kyleakin was known throughout the isle for its fine drink.

Sighing, Carr leaned back against the upholstered back of the booth he'd taken. The innkeeper had cleared a booth near the hearth as well as two tables on the floor for Carr's men. However, Carr had noted a tension in the air when he stepped into the common room. Unsurprisingly, most of the patrons in here were male—save two women, merchants' wives most likely, who were enjoying supper with their husbands across the room.

Carr's gaze traveled around the smoky space, noting the cool glances he and his men were receiving. Of course, they all wore sashes of MacKinnon plaid: pine green crisscrossed with red.

Kyleakin was a crossroads, a port that sat on the borders of two lands—MacKinnon and MacDonald—but a village that allied itself with neither clan. As such, it attracted those who didn't belong anywhere.

The King's Arms was a good establishment and served excellent ale, yet Carr knew it was wise not to let his guard down here.

He'd just finished observing a group of men playing knucklebones at a table a few yards away—noting that they seemed to be showing more attention to him and his men than to their game—when a flash of emerald green on the stairs across the room caught his eye.

As promised, Lady Drew had joined them.

Carr wasn't sure how he felt about her decision to take supper downstairs. It wasn't something a 'lady' did. And yet, Drew was soon to leave her old life behind her, so what did it matter?

On a purely selfish level, it would mean he got to share a meal with her—something he rarely did. The only time he'd sat at the same table as her to eat was that morning he'd discovered she was ill with the plague. Dunan had been largely deserted that day, as most of its inhabitants were either dead, sick, or had fled. He'd brought up a tray of bannocks to her solar before realizing that she had a fever.

Clad in a becoming green kirtle, her peat-brown hair twisted into a soft knot upon her head, Drew glided across the sawdust-strewn floor like a queen.

Carr's gaze tracked her as she walked—and so did every man in the place. Drew ignored them all. She'd grown up in a broch of rowdy men; she was used to being stared at and knew just how to quell a lecherous look with an icy glance.

"Good eve, Broderick," she slid into the booth and favored him with a smile that made Carr's pulse accelerate. "What's for supper?"

"Roast mutton, braised onions, and bread," he replied, pushing a full tankard of ale across to her. "Apologies ... it won't be the fare ye are used to."

Drew huffed a laugh. "It'll be better than what awaits me in Inishail ... Coira's filled me in on what to expect. I hear nuns exist on coarse bread, overcooked vegetables, and gruel."

5
A Confession to Make

CARR BRODERICK SMILED, and Drew stilled a moment. The man hardly ever let his mouth curve in mirth. He usually wore an austere expression, his gaze watchful and guarded.

But seated in the booth, his hand curled around a tankard of ale, he looked the most at ease Drew had ever seen him.

The smile erased years from his face. He was younger than her, yet she often forgot that, for severity had carved lines into his forehead and caused grooves to bracket his mouth.

And yet when he smiled, she noticed that he had handsome features and a sensual mouth.

"I'm sure the food won't be that bad at Inishail," he said, still smiling.

The arrival of the innkeeper at their table with plates of food forestalled Drew's response. The rich aroma of roast mutton and braised onions wafted across the table, and Drew's mouth filled with saliva.

"I hope ye are right, Broderick," she said once the innkeeper had departed with the assurance that he was at her disposition if she needed the slightest thing. "But I've gotten quite spoiled over the years. I fear the abbess might find me a bit haughty."

"Haughty, aye," he replied, his mouth quirking. "However, I wouldn't call ye spoiled, milady. When toil is necessary, ye have never turned yer back on it. Folk will remember how ye regularly brought baskets of food to them so they didn't starve over the winter."

Drew sucked in a surprised breath. That had to be the longest discourse she'd ever heard from her taciturn guard. His frankness unbalanced her. The urge to gently chide him for his words rose within Drew, yet she prevented herself.

They were away from Dunan, and the new setting had loosened both their tongues. She liked seeing this new side to Broderick. If she mocked him, he'd just retreat into his shell and they'd pass their meal in tense silence.

"Will they?" she murmured after a pause. "I fear many of them can't see past the fact that I am Duncan MacKinnon's sister. They still look for someone to blame … and tar me with the same brush."

"And yet they saw ye welcome Craeg as clan-chief. A loyal sister wouldn't have done so."

Drew snorted. "They probably judge me for that too," she replied, reaching for the half-loaf of bread the innkeeper had given her and ripping off a chunk. "Not everyone has such a rosy view of me, as ye well know." Drew paused there, suddenly aware of how bitter she sounded. "But ye are right. I did welcome Craeg. The MacKinnons needed a clan-chief. Bastard or not, he was heir."

"Ye were relieved ... we all were," Carr replied, his gaze never wavering from hers. "Ye didn't want Duncan to return."

The half-smile Drew had been wearing slipped. "Ye are right, I didn't." She motioned to the untouched plate of food before him. "Go on ... dig in, before it gets cold."

They started on their meals. It was simple yet delicious fare. The mutton had been slow-roasted—for most of the day, it seemed—as it fell apart in tender chunks. The onions were sweet, and the bread tasty and fresh. Washed down with the cool ale, it was the perfect meal.

Drew savored every mouthful, and she noted that Broderick did the same.

Around them, the rumble of conversation rose and fell in the common room. The noise grew increasingly raucous as the inn's patrons consumed tankard after tankard of ale. A harpist had set himself up upon a stool to one side of the fire. The lad was playing a jaunty tune, yet the melody was lost in the roar of surrounding voices.

Eventually, as her belly started to signal that it was full, Drew leaned back in her seat and observed her supper companion. Broderick was wiping up the gravy off his plate with the last of his bread. Like most men, he had an impressive appetite.

It was pleasant sitting here, lulled by the warmth of the fire and good food and ale. If she could freeze a moment in time from the past years, it would be this one.

"I planned to turn against Duncan, ye know?" she said finally, breaking the companionable silence between them. "I even asked Ross Campbell if he'd stand with me."

Broderick's eyes widened at this admission. "Ye did?"

Drew nodded. It was a treacherous thing she was revealing, yet what did it matter? Craeg was the MacKinnon clan-chief now. "It was just before Campbell ran away with Leanna ... so it wasn't much help to me." She observed his facial expression before she continued. "That's not the only betrayal against Duncan I committed ... later, when Campbell freed Leanna from my brother's bed-chamber, I helped them get out of the broch."

Broderick let out a slow exhale and leaned back. "That was a risk indeed, milady. If he'd ever found out, things would have gone ill for ye."

"I know ... but my conscience was bothering me." Her mouth curved at the arch look he now favored her with. "Aye ... maybe I'm not as cold-hearted as everyone believes."

He smiled. His right cheek dimpled slightly when he did that, something she'd not noticed until now. "Since we are speaking honestly tonight, milady ... I also have a confession to make." He lifted his tankard to his lips and took a deep draft before continuing. "Two days after their escape from Dunan, I caught up with Lady Leanna and Campbell."

Drew inclined her head at this news. "I'd wager that Campbell wasn't happy to see ye."

Broderick's mouth quirked. "Things were tense initially ... but in the end, I let them go."

Drew smiled. "Of course ye did."

His gaze widened. "Ye aren't surprised? I was yer brother's faithful hound after all."

The self-recrimination in his tone was hard to miss, and Drew's smile faded. "So was Campbell, once. But he changed his allegiances." She studied him, her hands now cupped around her tankard. "I'm glad ye told me this, Broderick," she said softly. "I wish I'd confided in ye the way I did in Campbell, but ye are so hard to read I couldn't be sure that ye wouldn't betray me."

His face tightened, a glimmer of the usual severity returning to his features. "I'd never betray ye, Lady Drew," he murmured. "I'd take my own life first."

The words were softly uttered, barely inaudible, and yet they made Drew's breathing hitch. Broderick's loyalty to her was surprising and humbling. She couldn't imagine what she'd done to merit it.

She was just about to say as much when a shadow fell across their booth.

Drew tore her gaze from Broderick, to see that a huge man with close-cropped dark hair and a short beard loomed over her. He'd been one of those playing knucklebones at the nearby table. She'd barely paid him any attention earlier, yet it was impossible to ignore him now when he stood so close.

An odorous wave of stale sweat and rank ale-breath washed over her.

"Lady Drew," the stranger greeted her. His voice, a low growl, made the fine hair on the back of her neck stand up.

Spine stiffening, Drew met his gaze. "Do we know each other?"

"No," he drawled. "Ye don't know me ... but I know ye well enough. I used to watch ye riding out on hunts with yer brother, with yer nose stuck in the air like ye were too good for the rest of us."

Cold washed over Drew. The hostility in the man's voice was impossible to miss. The urge to flick a pleading glance in Broderick's direction rose within her, but she forced it down. She wasn't the sort of woman to let a man intimidate her. She'd stood up to Duncan enough times over the years—even knowing he'd strike her for voicing her opinion. She wouldn't let this man cow her.

However, she didn't answer him. She merely held his gaze, waiting for him to back away from the booth.

He didn't.

"The lady is occupied," Broderick spoke up then, his voice cool and dispassionate. "I suggest now that ye have made yer greetings ye leave her to finish her supper in peace."

The stranger ignored the guard, his gaze never straying from Drew.

"Duncan MacKinnon wronged me and my kin," he growled. "He hanged my brother for poaching his deer, and he emptied our stores of grain so that we all nearly starved two winters ago."

Drew swallowed. She was sorry to hear that, yet voicing such sympathies wasn't appropriate here. This man hadn't come for an apology.

"My Da got so thin after the lean winter that he sickened and died," the stranger continued. "With his dying breath, he begged me to make MacKinnon pay for what he did to us."

Drew's breathing slowed, foreboding feathering down her spine. Indeed, this man had good reason to bear a grudge.

The man leaned toward her, his odor almost overpowering. "I always swore I'd have my reckoning upon him," he growled, "but the weasel went and got himself killed before I had the chance."

Drew still didn't say a word. There was nothing she could say that wouldn't make her look insincere. She could feel this man's hostility emanating off him in waves now. Behind him, she saw his friends at the table rise to their feet and move toward him. All eyes in the common room now seemed fixed upon Lady Drew and her guard.

Likewise though, Broderick's six warriors abandoned the remains of their suppers and tankards of ale and stood up.

Even the harpist had stopped playing.

Drew's heart began to thud against her ribs. *Lord, no ... they're going to start a brawl.*

"No fighting in here," the innkeeper called out from across the room. There was a shrill edge to his voice. "Take it outside."

"Nothing to say, eh, Lady Drew?" The stranger's mouth twisted. He ignored the innkeeper, ignored everyone except Drew. The intensity of his stare made a lump form in the pit of her belly. "I thought ye would be feistier ... but ye will react soon enough."

With that, a meaty hand shot out, grabbed her by the upper arm, and hauled her out of the booth. "Duncan MacKinnon is out of my reach now, but ye aren't. Tonight ye shall be my whore ... upstairs with ye!"

6

An Enigma

CHAOS ERUPTED WITHIN *The King's Arms*.

Carr Broderick launched himself from his seat, and his men pounced too. Fists flew and rough shouts boomed up into the rafters. The harpist let out a shriek and cowered against the wall.

"No fighting in here! No fighting!" The innkeeper yelled, his voice barely audible above the din.

A wave of dizziness crashed over Drew, her breathing coming in panicked gulps. Her attacker's grip on her arm was bruising as he towed her across the floor. However, a moment later he released her, for Broderick barreled into him, knocking him back across the nearby table. Knucklebones and tankards of ale scattered, yet Broderick was oblivious.

He went straight for Drew's assailant's throat.

Drew staggered, fear turning her limbs to porridge. She lurched toward the booth, crawling back into it in an effort to get out of the fracas. Her fingers curled around the knife she'd been using to cut up her supper. If that man came at her again, she'd use it on him.

But it appeared that Broderick had the situation under control.

She'd never seen her guard in a real fight before. She had watched him spar with the other warriors in the bailey a few times over the years and knew he was quick on his feet, but his savagery now shocked her.

Despite that the man who'd attacked her was well over six-foot, dwarfing most men in the room, Broderick had him pinned to the table and was slamming his fist repeatedly into his face. Around him, the rest of her escort were grappling with the man's friends.

One of them grabbed a knife and went for a MacKinnon guard with it. However, the warrior—a young guard named Aidan—side-stepped him, grabbed him by the wrist, and hauled him close before head-butting him.

The man went down like a sack of barley, sprawling upon the sawdust.

Moments later it was over.

Breathing hard, Broderick pushed himself up off the table and hauled the now unconscious man with him by the scruff. Meanwhile, the rest of Drew's escort had downed the other trouble-makers.

"Apologies for the brawl," Broderick panted, meeting the innkeeper's eye. The man had gone red in the face and wore a frantic expression. "But as ye saw, we didn't start it." He made for the door, hauling the unconscious man across the sawdust behind him. "Everyone can go back to their ales ... the lads and I will clear this up."

Drew watched him and the rest of her escort gather up the band who'd attacked them before they dragged them outside.

The shocked looks on the faces of the other patrons were almost comical—or they would have been if Drew could see the humorous side of all of this.

She couldn't.

Heart pounding like a battle drum, she relaxed her death-grip on the knife.

She knew that her brother had been hated, but she hadn't realized till this evening just how much ill-will some of the people of this land bore him—and her.

Just another reason why I have to leave Skye, she told herself. *Craeg needs to make a fresh start, one without my presence tainting everything.* As her attacker had so candidly pointed out, most folk associated her with Duncan MacKinnon, and they always would.

Gaze scanning the common room, Drew saw that the innkeeper and a serving lass were righting tables and chairs and scooping up broken tankards.

Drew met the innkeeper's eye. She could tell from his red face and pinched mouth that he was fuming, and likely blamed her for the brawl. "I really am sorry about this," she said, her voice unnaturally loud in the now silent common room. Surveying the curious faces and probing stares, Drew offered them all a weak smile.

"Another round of ale for everyone, please," she said, catching the innkeeper's eye once more as she dug into her purse and held up a silver penny. "And a jug of yer best wine at this table too when ye have a moment."

"This wine's got a kick like a pony," Broderick said, setting his empty goblet down on the table. He then favored Drew with a lopsided smile. "I don't suppose there's any left?"

"I think so." Drew picked up the jug and filled his goblet before topping up her own. "It's bramble ... delicious."

Drew was aware then that she'd almost slurred that last word. The wine—dark and spicy—was indeed strong. Despite that she had a belly full of food, it had made her woozy. Her head spun, and her limbs felt weak and languorous. A warm glow lit her from within.

The evening hadn't started well, admittedly. But now that the troublemakers had been turfed out, and Broderick had returned to her booth, things had improved.

The common room had emptied as the evening wore on. Two of Broderick's men were playing Ard-ri by the fire, moving carven pieces across a board, while the other guards had retired for the evening. The innkeeper was washing tankards in sudsy water at the far end of the room, and the serving lass was now starting to wipe down tables—a signal that it was getting late.

However, Drew didn't feel like vacating this booth just yet.

She was enjoying sitting in comfort, chatting to Broderick like he was an old friend.

When he'd returned from outdoors, he'd worn a formidable expression—one so severe that she'd thought the worst.

"Did ye kill him?" she asked, dreading the answer.

Broderick had shaken his head. "Why ... did ye want me to?"

"No," Drew had replied quickly. "It's just that the look on yer face is murderous."

"I *wanted* to end him," he'd answered, his voice soft yet with an underlying note of steel that had made her suppress a shudder. "If he'd harmed ye, I would have."

The answer had been brutally direct, and for a moment, Drew had fallen silent, not sure how to respond.

Broderick's protectiveness over her made her both feel flustered and flattered. Finally, instead of answering him, she'd gestured to the jug that sat at her right elbow. "Wine?"

Two jugs of wine later, Drew knew she was reaching her limits. If she drank much more, she'd likely sprawl on her face the moment she tried to get up from the booth. Not lady-like at all.

Broderick, however, seemed unaffected. Only the relaxed lines of his face, the slight gleam to his blue-grey eyes, betrayed him.

As the evening wore on, and they chatted amicably about the events of the last few months, Drew found herself observing the man seated across from her.

Broderick wore a cream-colored léine, open at the neck, and Drew's attention kept straying to that opening, where dark gold curls peeked over the top of the garment.

Dreamily, she wondered what the rest of his chest looked like, under the tunic.

Good Lord, ye really have over-indulged on the wine, Drew checked herself. Even so, her gaze still lingered upon him.

"Carr," she said finally, enjoying the sound of his first name on her lips. She usually addressed him by his family name, but this evening the wine had relaxed her formality around him. "All these years ye have served my family ... and I know very little about ye."

He reclined back in his seat, watching her. "What would ye like to know, milady?"

"Yer kin ... where are they?"

His mouth lifted at the corners. "All over Scotland these days ... but my kin hail from Cork, in Éire. I was born there."

"And do yer parents still live? Do ye have any siblings?"

He lifted the goblet to his lips and took a measured sip. "My parents died years ago. I'm the youngest of six sons. My father was once a wealthy man, a land-owner in Cork, but he spent every last bit of silver he possessed on finery, rich food ... and women. He died a pauper."

Drew raised her eyebrows. This tale was getting more interesting by the moment. "So ye set off to seek yer own fortune?"

He nodded, meeting her eye. His expression was veiled. Carr Broderick was definitely a hard man to read.

"No wonder ye and Campbell became friends," she said after a pause. "Ye are both the youngest sons of big families, forced to make yer own way in the world."

Broderick huffed a soft laugh. "We've always had that in common, aye."

Drew took a sip from her goblet, still holding his gaze. It was strange really, but the more she learned about Broderick this evening, the more he fascinated her.

Why haven't we ever spoken like this before?

The answer was simple enough, she supposed. Their positions at Dunan had been vastly different. While they'd lived there, she'd seen him only as one of her brother's warriors.

"Ye are quite an enigma, Carr Broderick," she admitted. "A man who never lets the world see what he's thinking."

He laughed once more, although his gaze turned watchful. "Aye ... but there's wisdom in that, Lady Drew."

Her mouth quirked. "But haven't ye ever wanted to take a wife ... to have a family? It seems a lonely life ye have chosen."

As soon as the words were out, she wished she could have chased them back into her mouth. Even for her, the question was too bold, too personal.

Broderick leaned back, his fingers sliding up and down the stem of his goblet. Breaking eye contact with him, Drew stared down at his hands. They were big but surprisingly graceful for a man of his broad build.

Blinking hard, Drew forced her gaze back up to his face. The wine was loosening her up far too much.

"Ye are right, milady," he said finally. His tone was measured, neutral, giving no clue as to whether she'd offended him or not. "There have been times when I have questioned the road I've taken ... but my life in The Dunan Guard was important to me. Until a few months ago, my loyalty to yer brother was unshakable."

"But ye appear to live like a monk. Why?"

Once again, the words were too bold, and the moment they slid off her tongue, Drew clamped her jaw shut.

That's it, she vowed. *No more wine for me.*

This time, Broderick smiled—and it was a slow, sensual expression that made Drew grow still. "What makes ye think I live like a monk?"

7

Stolen Moments

"WELL, I'VE NEVER seen ye with a woman," Drew replied. She deliberately injected a teasing edge to her voice, even as heat crept up her neck. "I assumed that—"

"I'm discreet," he replied, still smiling.

Drew could see the challenge in his eye now. He was daring her to push on.

"Who then?" she asked casually. She leaned back and took a sip of wine as if his answer mattered not to her.

"Kenzie."

Drew's lips parted in surprise. "The kitchen maid?"

"Aye ... there is none other of that name in the broch."

Kenzie was one of the few kitchen servants who'd remained after the sickness had swept through Dunan. Small, with hair the color of ripe wheat, and warm blue eyes, Drew could see why Broderick might like her.

Even so, Drew favored her guard with an amused smile. "Really?"

He raised an eyebrow. "Ye are surprised?"

"No," Drew scoffed. "It's just that Kenzie appears such a shy lass."

His eyes twinkled. "Not as timid as she appears. A few months ago, she knocked on my bed-chamber door wearing a cloak and nothing under it."

Drew's breathing caught. For the first time during their conversation, he'd succeeded in unsettling her. She couldn't believe that Kenzie, the kitchen lass, had the courage to do something so bold.

For all her flirting, Drew had never acted so recklessly. Something deep inside her chest drew tight as she wished she had. She'd lived such a dull life in many ways.

Drew lifted her goblet and held it up to Broderick in a toast. "Well, here's to a happy union between ye both ... have ye set a wedding date yet?"

Her guard shook his head. He was observing her now with an odd look on his face as if he was trying to gauge her mood. "Kenzie and I aren't together, milady. It was one night ... and stopped there."

Drew inclined her head. "Why is that?"

As she held his gaze, Drew saw a veil fall over Broderick's eyes. "Some encounters are best left to just one occasion," he replied, his tone guarded. "Kenzie and I both decided that it was for the best."

Carr followed Drew up the stairs, his steps heavy.

What had been one of the memorable evenings of his life had ended uncomfortably.

I can't believe I told Lady Drew about Kenzie.

The wine had lowered his guard, loosened his tongue. He was lucky he hadn't said anything else.

Just as well he hadn't told Lady Drew that he loved her.

Carr's lips pressed together into a hard, thin line as he imagined just how humiliating such a confession would have been.

His thoughts returned then to that eve, a few months earlier, when Kenzie had knocked upon his door. She'd stood in the corridor, her blue eyes gleaming, and had parted the cloak to show her nudity underneath. "Just once, Carr," she'd purred. "I know ye and I can never be ... but tonight let us forget that."

After they'd coupled, Kenzie had admitted she knew Carr's heart was already spoken for.

"It's Lady Drew, isn't it?" she asked, propping herself up onto one elbow and observing him frankly. "I've seen the way ye gaze upon her."

A chill had crept over Carr's body at her comment. Satan's cods, was he that obvious?

Kenzie had smiled at the panic that had obviously shown upon his face. "Worry not ... I doubt anyone else has noticed. Lady Coira perhaps ... although Lady Drew herself is oblivious to it."

Those words had stung, yet they were true. Lady Drew didn't see him as a man. To her, he was 'Broderick': the reserved guard who dogged her steps and curtailed her freedom.

They reached the landing at the top of the stairs, and Lady Drew tripped. She would have fallen against the wall if Carr hadn't leaped forward and caught her around the hips, hauling her back against him.

For the briefest of instants, their bodies were pressed flush together. He felt the slender length of her back against his chest, the curve of her buttocks against his groin.

Heat surged through his lower body, and Carr pushed her away from him, panic clamping around his chest.

The last thing he needed was to humiliate himself right now.

However, Lady Drew hadn't noticed. She gave an embarrassed laugh and tottered away from him.

"Apologies, Broderick ... I think I may have over imbibed tonight."

Aye, he thought grimly. She had—they both had.

And yet the words that had passed between them, the lingering looks, were an unexpected gift, stolen moments that Carr couldn't bring himself to regret. He'd treasure them till the end of his days.

Lady Drew stumbled along the hallway and reached a door, her fingers curling around the handle.

"Milady." Carr stepped quickly to her side and drew her back. "That isn't yer bed-chamber."

Drew glanced up, turning her face fully to him, her eyes widening. "It isn't?"

For a long moment, their gazes fused. Carr was aware then of just how close they were standing. They were so near that he could see the fine texture of her skin, the darker flecks of slate against the smoke grey in her eyes. She smelt of rosemary and lavender.

Carr could hear the 'thud' of his heart against his ribs. He was acutely aware too of the fact that his fingers now tingled, for he ached to touch her.

He swallowed. This wasn't good—not at all.

The moment lengthened, and Drew's eyes darkened, the pupils growing large, her Cupid's bow lips parting.

The Lord have mercy. He wasn't made out of stone. This woman's nearness was heady; it had far more effect upon him than bramble wine. A dull ache throbbed under his breastbone, the pain reminding him of just how impossible his yearning for this woman was.

Tonight had been both pleasure and pain, yet he had to put an end to things now before he did something he would seriously regret in the morning.

Lady Drew's senses were addled with wine, her defenses lowered. He wouldn't take advantage of her.

"That room is mine, milady," he said softly, taking a deliberate step back and gently pushing her in the right direction. "Sleep well."

Drew stepped into her bed-chamber and pushed the door closed behind her. Leaning her back against it, she took a deep, steadying breath. Around her, the shadowy room had started to spin. She needed to get to her bed before she fell over.

Lord, that wine has addled my brains.

Had she imagined it, outside in the hallway, or had Carr Broderick almost kissed her?

She'd gazed up into his face and seen hunger in his eyes. Standing so close to him had turned her breathless. His closeness, the warmth of his body, and the scent of leather and musky, virile male had overwhelmed her. She'd leaned into him then, wanting him to lower his lips to hers—yet he hadn't.

Drew raised a trembling hand and touched her mouth. She wished he had kissed her.

This trip from Dunan to Inishail hadn't begun as she'd expected. They hadn't even left Skye, and it had already turned into an adventure. A brawl and a revealing conversation that made her see the man who'd been charged with her protection in a completely different light—tonight was memorable, to say the least.

"I'm feeling unwell."

Lady Drew's comment, muttered between clenched teeth, made Carr glance over at her. He perched at the bow of the barge that was taking them across the water to the mainland.

Carr frowned, taking in her pale face and the lines of tension around her mouth. "It's not long now till we dock, milady," he murmured.

"I'm not sure I can wait till then." As if to make her point, Drew clutched at her belly, her pallor increasing.

Kyle of Lochalsh loomed before them, a cluster of stone cottages with thatched roofs rising out of the mist. Around them, the waters of Loch Carron were dark and still this morning. The crossing wasn't rough at all, although Carr knew that wasn't the reason why the lady was unwell.

Last night's excesses were catching up with her.

The rhythmic splash of the oars was the only sound this morning, for the rest of the escort were silent, huddled into their fur cloaks, and bleary-eyed after such an early start. They'd left their horses, including Lady Drew's palfrey, stabled at *The King's Arms*, and would collect them on their way home.

Their first task upon disembarking at Lochalsh would be to find new mounts in order to continue their journey.

Although he was keeping a wary eye on Lady Drew, Carr didn't make any further comment. Nothing he said was going to ease her roiling belly.

However, the moment the barge docked against the rickety wooden pier, Drew scrambled off the boat and fled a few yards up the dock, before falling to her knees and throwing up over the side.

The sight of her retching, huddled form, made concern well up within Carr.

Thanking the ferryman, and handing him a coin for his trouble, Carr disembarked onto the dock and made his way up to Drew.

"Milady," he began hesitantly. "Are ye well?"

"No," she gasped. "Remind me, Broderick, never to touch wine. Ever. Again."

His mouth curved. "Worry not, milady. Where ye are going, ye will be forced to exercise more temperance."

Drew muttered an unladylike curse under her breath and pushed herself to her feet. She then turned to Carr, fixing him in a gimlet stare he knew well; it was one she usually gave him when he thwarted her.

"Ye should have stopped me from drinking so much," she challenged.

He snorted at that. "I'm yer guard, Lady Drew," he said, his mouth twitching from the effort it was taking not to laugh. "Not yer nurse."

Seeing Drew's gaze narrow, he moved past her and motioned to the other men, who had gathered at the end of the dock. They were yawning and stretching and looked as unmotivated as Drew for the day's journey.

"Come on, ye lazy lot," he called out. "Time to go."

8

I Haven't Lived

DREW HADN'T REALIZED that a headache could pulse in time with her heartbeat, in time with each jolting stride her horse took—yet this one did.

She hadn't lied earlier. She never intended to touch wine again.

Unlike her elder brother, she'd been moderate with strong drink her whole life. She didn't like to have her senses impaired in any way, or to lower her guard. When Duncan was alive, it would have been dangerous to do so—for she always needed to be wary of him.

But last night she'd felt a bit wild. She'd been away from Dunan for the first time in years, and although she'd been scared when that brute had grabbed her, the brawl that had followed had been oddly exciting.

However, in the cold light of a grey winter's morning, with her mouth sour, her belly churning, and her temples pounding, the novelty had faded.

She was back in control, and reality had returned to her world.

She was a widow well past her prime, journeying to a new life as a nun. She shouldn't be downing jugs of wine with her guards.

The company rode east now, following the northern edge of the loch.

Slowly, as the morning drew out, the nausea that bit at the back of Drew's throat and the pain in her head eased. Thirsty, she drained the contents of her water bladder, which the innkeeper had graciously filled with cooled boiled water for her that morning.

She'd been unable to face her bannocks—just the sight and smell of them had nearly made her heave—but as the pale winter sun broke through the heavy canopy of cloud overhead and warmed her face, she felt the stirring of hunger in her belly.

At noon they stopped off upon the shores of the loch at the village of Dornie, where Carr bought bread, cheese, and dried blood sausage. It was market day in Dornie, and the large cobbled square in the heart of the village bustled with life. The bleating, honking, and clucking of livestock rose high into the damp air, vying with the call of vendors.

Seated upon a crate on the edge of the square, Drew took in the busy crowd. Women, with baskets under their arms and plaid cloaks about their shoulders, chatted together as they shopped.

A hollow feeling lodged itself under Drew's ribs as she watched them. She suddenly wished she was one of those women, buying a mutton pie, cheese, and eggs to bring home for her family. The ritual that these farmers' wives took for granted was something Drew longed to experience. A lady didn't take a basket to market—she had servants to do such things for her.

I won't be attending any markets at Inishail either. Coira had told her that abbeys and priories tended to be largely self-sufficient. Even if there was a village nearby, the nuns would likely have little to do with it.

This would possibly be the last market she'd attend.

Brushing crumbs off her skirts, Drew glanced up and caught her guard's eye. "I'd like to take a turn around the square, Broderick."

His mouth compressed. "We should really be on our way, milady."

"I'm sure we have time for this," she replied airily. Rising to her feet, she adjusted her fur mantle about her shoulders. "Stay here, if ye wish. I won't be long."

Of course he didn't stay with the others. Broderick never let her out of his sight back in Dunan, and he certainly wouldn't now that they were traveling together.

Usually, his presence irritated her. But today, now that she was feeling herself again, she found she didn't mind the fact that he walked two steps behind her as she wove her way through the jostling crowd.

Drew stopped before a stall selling cakes and pies. The aroma of the baking made her mouth water, especially when her gaze alighted on a tray of honey cakes. "How many days' journey is it to Inishail?" she asked Broderick, casting a glance over her shoulder.

"Another three at most," he replied, his expression as unreadable as ever. "Once we reach the eastern edge of this loch, we shall head directly south into more mountainous lands."

Three more days.

Drew turned from him, her attention returning to the honey cakes. Suddenly, Inishail loomed on the horizon, more of a dungeon than a sanctuary. Back in Dunan, her destination had seemed far off. "I wish it were farther," she murmured.

"Milady?" Broderick stepped up to her shoulder.

"I've seen so little of the world," she said softly, meeting his eye once more. "Three days isn't long enough. Three weeks would be better."

Breaking eye contact with her guard, she motioned to the woman at the stall that she'd like some cakes.

"How many, *milady*?" the woman asked, a smile stretching her face. Of course, dressed in her fine furs, rings sparkling upon her fingers, Drew stood out in this crowd.

"Eight please," Drew replied.

"Eight?" Broderick rumbled. "Ye have quite an appetite today, Lady Drew."

Drew gave an unladylike snort. "Clod-head, these aren't all for me. I take it ye and the others like honey-cakes?"

"I can't speak for the others, but I'm very partial to them," Broderick replied. His grey-blue eyes crinkling at the corners as his mouth curved.

The expression made Drew's gaze linger upon his face. Carr Broderick was actually quite handsome when he smiled.

Thunder rumbled overhead. The first droplets of rain pattered onto the ground as the company clattered into the tiny white-washed hamlet of Invershiel at dusk. The village sat on the farthest edge of the loch.

Finding lodgings at the only establishment, *The Shiel Inn*, the travelers saw to their horses before going directly to their rooms. After the excitement of the night before, Broderick had insisted they all get an early night.

Drew noted that none of his men objected. They were all as weary as she was.

Seated at a small table in her bed-chamber, listening to the rain drumming against the shutters, Drew ate her supper of venison stew and oaten dumplings alone.

A hollow sensation settled within her as she ate, despite her rapidly filling belly.

She knew that the night before couldn't be repeated; she and Broderick had been far too frank with each other. But, all the same, she missed his company.

Goose, she chided herself, putting down her spoon and pushing away the remains of her supper. *Ye and Broderick will soon part ways ... ye need to get used to not having him nearby.*

Her breathing slowed as she dwelled on that thought. For months now, she'd been irritated by his constant presence. But now the thought of saying goodbye to Broderick saddened her.

She wanted to travel with him for a while, chat with him long into the night at smoky inns, tease him until he smiled, and look on while he and his men dealt with troublemakers again.

All of a sudden, she wanted a little unpredictability, a little danger, in her life. Soon she'd be in a place where every moment of her day would adhere to a strict routine. But she wasn't there yet. There was still time for some excitement.

Drew rose from the stool and started to pace the scrubbed wooden floor of her bed-chamber. However, the act soon made her dizzy, for the room was tiny. There was nowhere to go.

I haven't lived.

Until now, she'd lived a restricted life. But out here on the road, she'd tasted what freedom might feel like. The last two days had awakened something in her, a longing that refused to be quietened. She was like a bird loosed from its cage—she wanted some adventure before she entered a new prison.

A heaviness settled within Drew then. She sank down upon the bed and listened to the howling wind and rain outdoors. Inishail inched ever closer. It was too late now to wish for excitement.

Drew was unusually silent when they set off the next morning. She noted that Broderick, and one or two of the other men, kept glancing her way while they saddled their horses. Although not a woman given to prattle, Lady Drew usually embraced the morning.

She liked to greet her escort and comment on what the weather might hold for the day's journey.

Yet this morning, she kept her own counsel.

"Are ye well, milady?" Aidan asked. "Ye are very pale this morning."

Drew pursed her lips and allowed the young warrior to help her up onto her mount, a leggy courser they'd hired at Lochalsh. The beast was spirited and a far less comfortable ride than the sweet-tempered palfrey she'd left behind at Kyleakin.

"I'm well, thank ye."

It was a lie. She felt tense and tired. She'd barely slept overnight. Instead, she'd lain for hours, staring up at the darkness, wondering at how she'd managed to reach thirty-six winters without truly living.

Long, hard years stretched before her, and yet she had few memories to sustain her.

Adjusting her skirts, Drew glanced up to find Broderick watching her. He'd mounted his horse and waited in the center of the dirt yard behind the inn. "If ye wish, we can take more rests today, milady," he said after a pause. "I don't want to deliver ye to Inishail Priory unwell."

Drew cast him an imperious look, her spine stiffening as she squared her shoulders. "I'm not made of silk," she reminded him. "I don't need to take more rests."

Broderick raised a dark-blond eyebrow. "Ready to ride out then, milady?"

Drew nodded. Despite that she was already weary, she welcomed being out in the fresh air and on the road. There was a restlessness within her this morning that made her want to give her horse its head. She wanted to gallop into the wilds and never return.

Urging the courser forward, she rode past Broderick and out into Invershiel's only street: an unpaved way with deep ruts. It was a blustery winter's morning, with a wind howling in from the north. The village folk she passed had red cheeks from the wind's stinging chill, but the rainclouds of the day before had cleared. This morning, white clouds chased each other across a pale blue sky.

Not bothering to glance behind her to see if her escort was following, Drew nudged the courser into a brisk trot. Then, turning onto the highway, she urged her spirited mount forward. The courser kicked up its heels and sprang forward into a fast canter.

Moments later another horse pulled up alongside.

Drew glanced over to see that Broderick now rode shoulder-to-shoulder with her. "In a hurry this morning?" he asked, raising his voice to be heard over the thunder of their horses' hooves.

Drew grinned at him. Just this brief spurt of speed had lightened her mood. "Aye ... this gelding chafed at the bit yesterday, so I thought I'd let him stretch his legs."

To her surprise, Broderick grinned back, a gleam in his eye. "And there was me thinking ye were trying to outrun us all."

Their gazes held for an instant, and then Drew swung her attention back to the open road before them.

An idea rose within her then—a thought so outrageous that her breathing stalled, her fingers clenching around the reins. Her already racing heart started to pound in her ears.

Heat flooded through her lower belly as the idea grew, taking shape fully in her mind.

No, she couldn't be so bold. She was about to enter a priory; she shouldn't even be entertaining such thoughts. She'd never behaved recklessly with men. Now certainly wasn't the time to begin.

And yet now that the idea had seeded in her mind, it would not die.

She remembered then the desire she'd seen darken Carr Broderick's gaze as he'd stood with her outside his room in *The King's Arms*. If she bade him, would he kiss her?

If I asked him, would he lie with me?

9
Tonight

WHEN THEY STOPPED at noon, Drew felt sick with nerves and excitement.

After the initial burst of speed, both she and Broderick had slowed their mounts, pacing themselves for the long day's journey. The highway had taken them south. They traveled across wild moor for a spell before entering a highland region. Bulky pine-clad mountains rose above them, etched against a windswept sky. These peaks were different to those of Skye, Drew reflected. The mountains of her home isle were craggier, almost brutal in appearance. The landscape upon the mainland had a softer edge to it.

Loosening her horse's girth, and letting it take a brief drink from a highland burn, Drew leaned against the courser's sweaty neck and attempted to draw strength from the beast.

It has to be now, she told herself, gathering her courage as anticipation churned in her belly. *Ye have to ask him.*

Drawing in a deep breath, she turned, her gaze going to where Broderick was handing out bread and cheese to his men. He then approached her.

"It's simple fare again, I'm afraid," he said, "although two of the men will ride ahead and see if they can hunt some game for tonight's meal."

Drew's gaze widened. "We'll be sleeping outdoors?"

"Aye ... there aren't any inns until our destination, so for the next two nights we'll be pitching tents."

Drew frowned. That complicated her plans a little, and for a moment, her resolve faltered. Her courage balanced upon a knife-edge.

"Carr," she said softly, taking the bread and cheese he offered. Her fingers deliberately brushed against his as she did so, and she heard his breathing catch. No, she hadn't imagined it. It was desire she'd seen in his eyes that night. She would press on. "Can I speak to ye alone for a moment?"

He frowned at the question. The others were standing a few feet behind them. The men weren't paying them much attention, for they'd already begun to eat and were bickering gently about what game would be the best to hunt for later in the day.

"This won't take long," Drew continued, moving back from him. She needed to make sure they were safely out of earshot of the others before she said anything.

Wordlessly, Broderick followed her, although his brow was furrowed now. He could sense her tension, and it concerned him.

Leading him over to where a single spruce rose high above them, its blue-green needles bathed in wintry sunlight, Drew turned to Broderick and took in another steadying breath.

God's bones, this was harder than she'd expected. Where was her usual brazen self-confidence?

She'd spent most of the morning going over and over in her head what she'd say to him, how she'd phrase things, and all the ways he could possibly respond. Only, now that Carr Broderick stood before her, and the heady scent of pine enveloped them, she felt flustered and tongue-tied.

"Is something amiss, milady?" he asked, his gaze searching her face.

"No ... aye ... well, not really," she replied, stumbling over her answer. Heat crept into her cheeks. She wasn't doing a good job of this. "The thing is ... this journey has made me reflect on things ... reflect on my life thus far. Quite frankly, it's been dull. I will go to Inishail and follow my mother's example ... but before I do ... I ..." she halted there, struggling to get the words out in a coherent fashion. "Before I do that, I want to live. I wish to enjoy carnal pleasure and ... well ... will ye lie with me?"

Broderick went still at that, his face freezing. An awkward silence stretched out between them, and when he eventually spoke, his voice sounded strangled. "Lady Drew ... I don't think—"

"I've thought this through," she cut him off. He was going to refuse her, and she couldn't let him. "It would only be once ... tonight ... and then we could just pretend it never happened. When we reach Inishail, ye and I will go our separate ways."

"This is folly, milady," he replied, his voice roughening now. "A woman's womb can quicken with a bairn after just one coupling. How would ye explain that to the nuns ... to yer mother?"

A laugh rose within Drew, yet she choked it back. "There's no need to worry about that," she replied with a shake of her head. "Ye forget that I was wed for years and Egan never managed to get me with bairn. I'm barren."

It was an ugly word, one that made Drew's throat close up. How often had Duncan mocked her over her failure to produce children; he'd angered Egan over it too when he'd brought up the subject at mealtimes in the Great Hall.

Silence settled between them once more. The shock on Broderick's face would have made her smile in other circumstances, but not now. She felt as if she'd just handed him a weapon he could so easily wield against her.

"I'm yer guard, Lady Drew," Broderick said finally. There was a pleading note in his voice now, blending with its usual gruffness. "Ye shouldn't be asking this of me."

"Why not?" Heat kindled in Drew's belly as her anger rose. In her head, this conversation had gone quite differently. She'd imagined his initial surprise and then ready agreement. He was staring at her as if she'd just sprouted devil's horns. "Am I distasteful to ye, Carr?"

Carr stared at Lady Drew and resisted the urge to take a step back from her—anything to ease the tension of this moment. He felt light-headed, his chest so tight that it hurt to breathe.

"Don't ask me that, milady," he rasped. "Ye shouldn't—"

"Is that it?" she countered, high spots of color appearing upon her pale cheeks. "Ye can bed a kitchen wench, but the thought of touching me turns yer stomach?"

"Stop it, Drew." He forced the words out. He had to prevent this exchange from escalating. She'd already gone too far. "Ye are wrong ... it's not that I don't desire ye ... it's that I'm yer guard. Craeg charged me with yer protection."

"And Craeg will never know," she replied. Drew's heart-shaped face had gone taut with determination. She wasn't a woman used to being thwarted. "This is between ye and me ... no one else."

Satan strike me down, why is she asking this of me?

Carr felt as if he were hanging off the edge of a cliff, clinging to a rope that was slowly fraying. In just a few moments, he'd be plummeting to the rocks below, and there was nothing he could do about it.

For years he'd dreamed of Lady Drew wanting him. How many times had he taken himself in hand in the quiet of his cramped bed-chamber, alone in the darkness, and brought himself to climax while thinking about her?

But those fantasies had been safe, private.

The things that Lady Drew was saying to him now were dangerous for them both—even more so for him, for this woman had his heart.

And she had no idea.

Lady Drew was asking him to service her like he was a prize stallion she'd chosen to put over her best mare. To her, it was nothing more than an exchange, yet to him, it would be everything.

Did she think he could just plow her and forget?

Drew stepped toward him, closing the gap he'd deliberately created. "I know that I am asking ye to break vows ye take very seriously," she said, her voice soft now, her gaze imploring. "But I will ask no more of ye than this. Lie with me just once, Carr ... please."

Carr swallowed, hard. He hated that she was on the verge of begging him. This wasn't how he wanted to remember Lady Drew. And yet, her nearness was intoxicating. The utter lack of guile upon her face, the way her lips parted, transfixed him. Her breast rose and fell sharply, and she clutched the bread and cheese he'd given her as if her life depended on it.

It was taking everything she had to ask this of him.

Yet she didn't realize what it would cost Carr. That wasn't her fault though—he'd been careful to keep his feelings hidden from her.

Letting out a slow exhale, Carr resisted the urge to reach out, to trace the determined line of her jaw with his fingertips. His gut twisted then. It would already be hard enough to leave her at Inishail and ride away, knowing their paths would never cross again.

After this, he'd be broken—inside where no one would see. But, he'd have one memory to treasure, to hold close as the years passed.

"Very well," he murmured, his voice barely audible over the roar of the wind through the overhanging spruce. "Tonight?"

Drew's eyes darkened, her pupils dilating so wide that her irises turned completely black. She then bit her plump lower lip.

Lust jolted through Carr's groin, a sensation so sharp that his breath caught. Heat spread through his limbs, making him feel feverish. God, how he wanted to take hold of her, then and there, pull her behind this spruce, lay her down upon the mossy ground, and give her the servicing she so desperately wanted.

Instead, he clenched his jaw, suffering the ache in his groin, and watched as she nodded and took an unsteady step back from him. "Tonight," Drew agreed softly, before she turned and walked back to the horses.

10

The Waiting

DREW HAD NEVER known a day to pass so slowly.

She'd barely been able to eat her bread and cheese. Her belly had closed in excitement—and as the sun traveled across the sky, that anticipation grew.

She'd done it. She asked him, and now Carr Broderick would lie with her. She was relieved he'd agreed. There had been a point in their conversation when she'd been sure he'd refuse her.

But now that he hadn't, she felt as giddy as a lass at her first dance.

It was silly really, yet she liked the recklessness that had caught fire in her veins since leaving Skye. If she was going to become a nun, she might as well know what she was giving up.

All her life she'd flirted with men, danced around them like a colorful butterfly, enjoying the game. She'd lived as if she had a hundred years to waste. But time was running out now, and she'd not let this opportunity slip through her fingers.

She and Carr barely spoke for the whole afternoon. She let him and Aidan ride ahead, and kept her own counsel. However, she was now acutely aware of him, and her gaze kept returning to his broad shoulders.

It would happen tonight. Her belly flip-flopped at the thought. When and where, she didn't know—but he'd agreed, and that was all that mattered.

Finally, the gloaming arrived. Two of the men who'd ridden ahead to hunt returned with a brace of grouse, which they plucked and roasted over hot coals while the others made camp for the night.

They set up their tents upon a hillside, next to a stand of old oaks. A creek bubbled its way over mossy stones at the bottom of the hill, and Drew collected a pot of water to boil over the fire. They'd need to refill their water bladders at some point.

The semi-circle of tents sat above the fire pit, with Drew's tent—the biggest of the group—sitting at the back.

While the grouse were cooking, Drew found herself growing agitated. Nerves danced in her belly like a party of over-excited brownies. She needed to keep busy, needed to keep her mind focused on other matters. Deciding she would sort through her belongings, she carried her saddlebags into the tent.

Carr was there already, rolling out a fur onto the ground. He glanced up when she entered, and their gazes fused for an instant.

"Will ye come to me here later?" she asked, favoring him with a coy smile.

Carr shook his head, a muscle flexing in his jaw. "It's too near the others ... they might hear something." He paused then, his throat bobbing. "I'll be taking the first watch after supper. When I finish it, I will fetch ye, and we will go to the oak wood together."

Drew's breathing quickened. "But ... how will we—"

"I've removed the pegs behind me." He motioned to the far edge of the tent, the side nearest the woods. "I'll lift the hide ... there will be enough space for ye to squeeze through."

Drew nodded, her heart galloping now. This calm explanation of how they would get time alone together was causing her already churning belly to somersault. They were whispering together like conspirators; the excitement of it was dizzying.

Carr moved toward the exit behind Drew but stopped when he was level with her. He'd stooped, to avoid hitting his head on the roof of the tent, and as such their faces were much closer than they'd have been usually.

Drew's breath hitched in her chest when she saw the gleam in his eyes, the look of rapt attention as he gazed upon her face. She'd never had a man look upon her so intently; it made her feel dizzy.

Heart pounding, she swallowed. "I shall see ye later then?"

"Aye," he murmured. "Are ye sure about this, Lady Drew?"

She nodded, smiling once more. "Please dispense with formalities, Carr," she whispered back. "This eve, just call me 'Drew'."

His eyes hooded, and Drew realized that, like her, he was breathing faster than normal. Like her, he could feel the charge between them. It was like the air was heavy with the promise of rain, and at any moment a storm would explode.

Warmth spread through Drew's belly, and the sensitive skin between her thighs began to ache.

The waiting was going to kill her.

Carr ate his supper without tasting a morsel. Under normal circumstances, he quite liked grouse, enjoyed the gamey flavor and the char of the meat cooked over hot coals. But this evening, his hunger had waned.

A cold, windy dusk settled over the hillside, making the flames in the small fire pit flare and gutter. The party huddled around it, picking flesh off the grouses they'd cooked.

Wiping the grease off his fingers, Carr glanced across the fire pit at where Lady Drew—Drew—sat. He couldn't get used to even thinking of her by her first name only, let alone hailing her by it.

But since they were about to get as intimate as it was possible for a man and woman, he needed to practice.

Drew looked lovely tonight, bonnier than he'd ever seen her.

Perhaps it was excitement, anticipation of the night ahead, but there was a healthy rouge to her cheeks and her grey eyes were bright and alive as she licked her fingers clean.

Carr swallowed at the sight. She had no idea how sensual that gesture was, especially after the conversations they'd had today.

Shrouded in a fur mantle, Drew perched upon a log and shared a funny story with the two men seated to her right. Her finely boned, yet expressive, hands danced while she told the tale, which had both warriors guffawing loudly at the end of it.

Grinning, Drew sat back, and then, as if feeling his gaze upon her, she looked across the fire at Carr. Her smile faded, although her eyes still danced.

Their gazes locked, and an ache rose under Carr's breastbone.

The Lord strike him down, how was he supposed to resist her when she looked at him like that; those grey eyes promised him the world. This woman would be his ruin.

Alone in her tent, Drew felt the urge to pace—but the tent wasn't large enough to allow it. The restlessness inside her was almost unbearable now.

Instead, she sat upon the furs, listening to the whine of the wind and the rumble of men's voices that punctured the night.

They should be all going to bed soon.

She certainly hoped so, for impatience thrummed through her.

Although the wind was up, the night was mild for this time of year. As such, the warriors who'd accompanied Carr were, unfortunately, in no hurry to retreat from the fireside.

Drew clenched her jaw and forced herself to breathe. *Patience ... the time will come soon enough.*

Glancing down, she took in the clothing she'd chosen for this occasion. She'd removed her heavy fur mantle, as it would only hinder her when she slipped out of the tent later. Instead, she wore a cream-colored léine with a pine-green kirtle atop it.

Drew's mouth curved into a half-smile as she reached out and traced her fingers over the soft fabric.

Foolish vanity ... he won't even notice what ye are wearing in the dark. Even more foolish too, for soon these fine clothes would be nothing but a memory.

Life at Inishail would strip all her finery from her. At the priory, she'd be the same as everyone else. However, it was something she actually welcomed.

She knew that many of the poor who lived upon MacKinnon lands had viewed her with resentment and jealousy, yet a life of privilege hadn't brought her any more happiness.

She'd never felt as alive as she did in this very moment. Maybe it was because she knew everything was going to change for her soon. The realization had slowed time down, had made her take notice of things she'd only ever taken for granted—like the softness of the finely made léine against her sensitive skin and the luxuriousness of the fur she sat upon.

Swallowing, Drew reached up and unpinned her hair. It tumbled down over her shoulders in soft waves. She usually wore it up, tightly coiled upon the crown of her head. But tonight such a style was too prim, too controlled.

Tonight she was a different woman.

11

In the Moonlight

IT WAS LATE when Carr finally fetched her. So late that Drew had actually lain down upon the furs and fallen into a light doze.

At the sound of someone whispering her name, she sat up, blinking.

The tiny fire pit in the center of the tent had burned down to glowing coals, yet she could just make out Carr's face as he lifted up the edge of the weather-stained hide.

Heart pounding, Drew moved.

Wordlessly, she went to him, took the hand he offered, and squeezed under.

As she rose to her feet, Drew felt nervousness flutter up under her ribcage. This was finally happening; it almost seemed surreal.

Outdoors, the wind buffeted against her, and she glanced up at the sky. There was a full moon tonight. It appeared as the racing clouds parted, allowing hoary light to filter over the world below.

Shifting her attention back to Carr, she saw that the moonlight now kissed the strong lines of his face. However, his eyes were cast into shadow.

He squeezed her hand then and turned, leading her into the oak wood. His hand was warm and strong in hers.

Drew didn't dare glance back at their camp. She knew one of the men would be still awake, keeping watch by the fire. But if they were quiet, he'd never know that they'd crept away.

Moonlight now frosted the trees. Carr didn't speak as he led her deep into the woods, and when they were at least five furlongs distant from the camp, he halted.

Drew's heart was now beating so hard that she could feel it pulsing in her ears. Earlier she'd been all aflutter with excitement. But now she felt sick with nerves. In her head, this encounter had been much less *real*. But now that she and Carr were finally alone together—now that he stared down at her with hunger etched across his features—she suddenly felt out of her depth.

And when Carr dipped his head to kiss her, she took a step back.

"What is it?" he murmured, the rough edge of need in his voice turning her knees weak.

Drew stared at him, her body going taut as a bowstring. Aye, she was in deep water here and floundering badly.

She wasn't sure she could bear it.

And so she turned from him, bracing her hands against the trunk of the massive oak that now towered above them. Moonlight shone down through its supplicating branches, making Drew's fingers, splayed across the rough bark, look so pale they appeared ethereal.

"Take me, Carr," she gasped. "Like this."

Carr didn't know how to react.

For a few moments, he merely stood there, staring at the back of Drew's head. He could hear the soft pant of her breathing and the rasp of his own.

His ribs tightened, his belly clenching in disappointment.

Was this what she wanted … to be taken like a whore? Drew deserved better than that. He ached to kiss her, longed to trace her lips with the tip of his tongue, to taste the sweetness of her hot mouth—but she was denying him that.

He wouldn't force the issue though, for he could feel her nervousness. It rippled off her body in waves, and that surprised him.

Stepping close to her, he let the length of his body press flush against hers. The soft, plaint feel of her made his breathing catch. He couldn't believe that after all these years, he was allowed to touch her.

He reached up then, his fingers delving into her hair. He loved seeing it like this, loose and wild. Tangling his fingers through it, he leaned forward, inhaling its scent. Then, he lifted her hair up, his lips tracing the long line of her neck.

Drew gasped.

Carr stifled a groan; her reaction set his blood aflame.

His lips left a trail, up her neck, to where his tongue traced the shell of her ear.

Drew moaned, arching back against him. He felt the quiver in her body as his hands closed over her slender shoulders, pulling her hard against him.

He might not be able to kiss her mouth, but he'd not make this coupling cold and passionless. He'd show her how her body could sing.

Nestling his erection into the cleft of her buttocks, he slid his hands down from her shoulders to her breasts, cupping them.

The layers of material between them frustrated Carr. He wouldn't be able to have Drew completely naked, yet he needed to get closer to her. His fingers went to the bodice of her kirtle, to the laces there. He loosened them, and the front of the garment sagged open. Underneath, only a léine separated her breasts from him.

Once again, he cupped the soft mounds, grinding himself against her as he did so.

Drew pushed back against him, her breathing coming in short, desperate pants.

Carr brushed his thumbs over the hard buds of her nipples, his breathing hitching when she gave a soft mewing cry. Carr adored that sound. They were far from the camp now; she could make a little noise.

"Carr," she groaned his name in a plea. "Please … I need ye."

Stifling a groan of his own, Carr continued to stroke her nipples with the pad of his thumbs. He then gently tweaked them, his shaft aching as she arched back against him, her supple body shuddering.

He then slid his hands down the length of her torso, over her belly to her hips, where he grabbed handfuls of her skirts and pulled them up. Nudging her legs apart with a knee, he slid his fingers between her thighs.

He then groaned.

She was so wet, so ready for him.

Slowly, he stroked her there, his heart thundering in his ears when she started to gasp and rotate her hips against his groin.

He couldn't stand it. He'd planned to take this slow, to pleasure her for a while yet before he took her, but the fire in his blood was raging out of control now.

All he could think about was being inside her.

With his free hand, he reached down and unlaced his braies, releasing his engorged shaft. And then, he stepped back from her, raising her skirts high so that they bunched around her waist.

The twin globes of her buttocks gleamed in the moonlight, and he stroked them, marveling at the smoothness of her skin.

It was as if his lustiest dreams had suddenly come to life. Drew was heart-stoppingly sensual. She was panting loudly now, pushing her exposed rear toward him.

A low growl rose in Carr's throat. How did she expect him to go slowly when she did that?

Taking hold of her hips, he raised her up, placing the tip of his shaft at her core's entrance—and then he entered her in one slow, deep movement.

Drew's hoarse cry echoed through the trees.

They shouldn't really make too much noise, for, despite their distance from camp, sounds carried in the night, but Carr was past caring at this point.

She was so hot, so tight, he almost lost control, then and there.

Drew bucked against him, yet he gripped her hips tightly, holding her still as he withdrew almost completely and then plunged into her once more.

He took her like that—in long, hard thrusts—while she writhed and shuddered. Her heat contracted around him, and he felt a rush of wetness as his shaft stroked deep within her.

"Carr," she gasped, when he thrust deep once more, her voice raw, beseeching. "It's too much … please stop!"

12

Not Enough

TO DREW'S SURPRISE, he halted.

She'd thought him too far gone to listen to her, thought that he'd just continue to plow her until he found his own release—but Carr had heard Drew's plea, and he stilled, still buried deep inside her.

Suddenly, the only noise in the oak wood, besides the whistling of the wind and the creak of branches, was their rough breathing.

An ache rose in Drew's breast then, as disappointment filtered through her. It had been too intense; she'd been on the brink of losing control. But now that he'd stilled, she wanted him to ignore her—to plow her until she fainted.

He didn't say a word, slowly withdrawing from her.

Drew's throat thickened at the feeling of loss. How she loved having him inside her. When he'd first entered her, his size had been a shock. Her husband had never stretched her like that, had never turned her loins molten.

Drew closed her eyes, tears stinging her eyelids.

Goose, she chided herself. *Yer one chance to let go and ye have ruined it.*

Yet, Carr didn't release her and step away, as she'd expected. Instead, he gently turned her around to face him.

Moments slid by, and then he took hold of her chin and lifted it so that their gazes met. Drew's breathing caught; the fierce look of tenderness and desire that played across his shadowed features was almost too much to bear.

"Do ye trust me, Drew?" he asked, his voice husky now.

"Aye," she whispered.

"Tell me what ye want, and I'll do as ye wish."

Drew swallowed, her heart galloping as the pad of his thumb softly traced her lower lip. He was giving her the chance to end this if that was what she truly wanted. He was letting her choose.

"Carr," she breathed his name, reaching up and tracing his jaw with a trembling hand. For one night she needed to be wild and reckless—to let go. "Claim me," she whispered.

Carr's breathing caught, and for an instant, he went still. And then he moved.

He gathered her up and took two steps forward, bringing her hard up against the oak trunk. He then kneed her trembling thighs apart and drove into her.

And this time, as he did so, his mouth claimed hers.

He kissed her wildly; his lips and tongue ravaging, demanding.

Drew didn't think, didn't analyze. Instead, she responded with a hunger equal to his. Somehow facing him, kissing him, made her fear ebb. She felt reassured. Reaching up, she wound her arms around his neck, pulling him closer still, the aching tips of her breasts rubbing against the leather of his vest.

He took Drew slowly, purposefully, grinding his hips against hers in a sensual dance that had her clinging to him.

Trembling like a leaf in the wind, Drew held on. She'd thought the last position had been wonderful, but this one was even better. The intimacy of it made her ache for him unbearable. He filled her. The taste and smell of him overwhelmed her senses.

The sensual slide of Carr's tongue against hers as he thrust into her was too much, and Drew spun out of control. She clutched at him and cried out against his mouth, yet this time he didn't stop. This time he plowed her hard until his body shuddered and arched against Drew, his mouth bruising hers.

Drew clung to him in the aftermath, gasping while the pleasure ebbed and a melting sensation suffused her body. She'd never felt so relaxed, so at peace in the moment. Nestling her face into his neck, she breathed in his warm, musky male scent. She placed a hand upon Carr's chest then, her fingers spreading out over his racing heart.

Awe swept over her, the sensation so powerful that tears pricked her eyelids and a lump rose in her throat. He was still buried inside her, and she never wanted him to leave.

"That was wonderful," she whispered, tracing feather-light kisses over the hollow of his throat. "Can we do it again?"

Laughter rumbled through Carr's chest, and she felt his grip around her tighten. "Aye," he rasped. "Just give me a few moments."

Stretching languorously, Drew opened her eyes before rolling over onto her back. The first glimmers of dawn peeked through the smoke hole in the roof above her.

A dull ache pulsed between her thighs, yet her body had never felt so good. A smile spread across her face. She now understood why Coira gazed at Craeg with that secret, soft look—why she blushed when he lowered his mouth to her ear and whispered to her.

Until last night she'd always believed coupling to be an uncomfortable, animalistic urge. She'd never known that it could strip away the rest of the world, make all her worries and cares meaningless.

For a short time, she and Carr had been the only two people alive. And she'd wanted him like she needed air.

Drew's eyes flickered open, and she pushed herself up. The murmur of men's voices warned her that she couldn't lie here any longer. Carr and his warriors were packing up, and shortly they would continue on their journey south.

Inishail Priory was only two days' ride away.

The veil of contentment that had shrouded Drew for hours fell away, and her smile faded.

That was it. Carr has given ye a memory to treasure, but it ends here.

A heaviness settled over her then, as the full force of the realization hit her. She was greedy for more of him. She wanted to have days and days alone with Carr Broderick. She wanted to undress that strong body, to explore his skin with her lips, tongue, and fingertips.

Last night wasn't enough.

Drew's mouth compressed then.

It will have to be.

Getting to her feet, she grabbed the edge of the fur and started rolling it up. Sometimes she tired of herself—of her selfish will that railed against the confines of the life she'd been given. She had to quash it.

Last night had been a gift. However, Carr wasn't hers and soon they'd part ways forever. She needed to remember that.

Fool.

Carr swallowed a mouthful of twice-baked oatcake and glared at the smoking remains of last night's fire.

He should have known this would happen; it would have been obvious to anyone else. He was already sick with love for Drew MacKinnon, and last night had turned that sickness into a raging fever that now consumed him.

Being inside her, touching her, kissing her—it had unleashed a part of him that could no longer be caged.

I can't let her take the veil.

Yet Lady Drew didn't belong to him. He'd agreed to last night, knowing that it wouldn't be repeated. But having a taste of the woman he loved, the woman who dominated his every waking thought, had broken through his usual self-control and reserve.

He couldn't bear it.

A flash of movement to his left caught Carr's eye. Glancing up, he watched Drew emerge from her tent, and try as he might to prevent his physical reaction, his breathing caught.

Unlike the night before, her peat-brown hair was now braided and coiled tightly upon her crown. However, the style exposed her swanlike neck—a neck that he'd kissed and tasted.

Carr's pulse quickened, and he tore his gaze away, looking down at the half-eaten oatcake.

Suddenly, he had no appetite for it.

"Lady Drew." He tossed away the oatcake and rose to his feet as she neared the smoldering fire pit. Around them, the other men were taking down the tents. He should be helping, but this morning, all he could do was stare at this woman like a lackwit. "Can I speak to ye for a moment ... alone?"

His jaw clenched when he finished speaking, for his question reminded him of the one she'd asked him the day before at noon.

How much had changed since then.

Drew halted, her grey eyes widening as their gazes fused. She stared at him, her lovely face tensing. Then, warily, she nodded.

He led her over to where the horses waited, tied to trees on the edge of the oak wood. Even being near this place, the secret spot where he'd taken Drew up against a tree, made Carr's pulse accelerate.

Not thinking, not allowing himself to dwell on what he was about to do—lest his courage fail him—Carr turned to Drew.

She stopped, around three feet away from him. Close enough that he could have reached for her if he'd wanted, could have hauled her into his arms and kissed her for all the world to see.

The need to do so was a dull ache in his chest.

"Drew," he whispered.

Her eyes widened. "Isn't it Lady Drew now, Broderick?" she asked, favoring him with a smile. However, the expression was wobbly, forced. He could see by the sharp rise and fall of her breast that she was as affected by his nearness as he was by hers.

"I don't want it to be," he murmured. He was aware of the desperate rasp in his voice, yet he couldn't stop it. He couldn't hold back how he felt anymore. He'd ached to tell her the night before, but instead, he'd led Drew back to her tent, kissed her in the darkness, and then let her return to her bed.

He was running out of chances. Inishail Priory loomed before them, a specter on the horizon. He had to say this now.

"I'm in love with ye, Drew."

13

Tell Me Ye Don't Care

IF CARR BRODERICK had just struck her across the face, Drew would have been less surprised. As it was, she merely stared at him, aware that her lips had parted in shock.

I'm in love with ye.

What was the man saying? Yet he hadn't finished.

"I have been for years," Carr continued, taking a step toward her. "Don't take the veil at Inishail. Come away with me instead."

Drew stared at him, her lips parting. "Carr," she finally managed. "I don't think—"

"Last night meant much to me," he pressed on, his voice raw. Those blue-grey eyes, which she'd once thought so dispassionate, gleamed from the force of the emotions now roiling within him. "It was a claiming. Ye are mine and I am yers."

Drew's mouth clamped shut, and she swallowed. "It was a *coupling*, Carr … an enjoyable one … but it can never be more than that."

"Why not?" His gaze narrowed, his throat bobbing.

"I'm a widow about to take the veil, and ye are my guard … it wouldn't—"

"What does it matter?" he cut in, a nerve flickering in his jaw. "What I feel for ye, transcends everything."

A wave of dizziness swept over Drew. She couldn't believe she was hearing these words. Taciturn, stoic Broderick who'd shadowed her for the past six months, and who'd served her brother loyally for years before that, had just laid his heart bare before her.

"Carr … please don't say such things, I can't—" she began, but he interrupted her once more.

"Why? Because I'm a lowly guard and ye are a high-born lady?"

Drew sucked in a sharp breath. "No, but I … d—don't …," she stuttered, before her voice choked off. Her chest ached and her heart fluttered. Did he really think her so shallow?

"Ye would make a poor nun," he pressed on before she could continue, his face all taut angles now. "Ye can't follow rules … ye will make an enemy of the prioress within days."

Drew gave a sharp laugh. He was likely right, but she wasn't going to admit that. "All my life I've been willful and selfish," she said, recovering her equilibrium. She then folded her arms across her chest. "It's time I learned to follow the rules."

He stepped closer still, the male scent of his skin enveloping her. The sensation of dizziness increased, as did her ache for him. She needed him to move away, she needed some distance between them.

And yet she couldn't move. Her feet felt as if they'd just grown roots.

"Coming away with me wouldn't be selfish," he said softly.

"It would," she replied, stubbornness rising now. "I've already sent word ahead to the priory. Both the prioress and my mother are expecting me."

"Then send word that ye have changed yer mind."

"I can't do that," Drew shot back, frustration rising within her. Why wasn't he listening to her?

"Look me in the eye, and tell me ye feel nothing for me." He ground out the words as he stared deep into her eyes. "Tell me ye don't care … and I will leave ye be."

Drew went still. She really wished he hadn't cornered her like this. She didn't want to be cruel. Why would he make himself so vulnerable before her? He'd just handed her a dirk before baring his chest.

It was as if he wanted her to plunge the knife into his heart.

Reckless fool.

He knew who she was, that she could be ruthless if needed.

Pain lanced through Drew's ears as she clenched her jaw. Her chest started to ache. Suddenly, she hated him for making her do this, for forcing her hand.

She didn't want to part ways with him under a storm cloud, but he'd left her no choice. Why did her life always have to be so hard?

Drew breathed in sharply, her pulse thudding in her ears. Each word hurt her throat, yet she forced them out. "I feel nothing for ye, Broderick."

Carr rode ahead of the company, his gaze scanning the road before him. The sun was shining, basking the pine-clad mountains in unexpected warmth. The wind had died to a brisk breeze that ruffled the horses' manes. Wispy clouds flitted across the sky, and despite that winter was upon them, it seemed as if spring might come early this year.

And yet, Carr paid the sunshine and beautiful surroundings no mind at all. Inside, he felt hollow. His heart was so empty it ached.

He'd taken a great risk—he'd known it the moment he'd demanded the truth from her.

Drew MacKinnon didn't like being pushed into a corner, but he'd done it all the same. He was sick of waiting in the shadows, tired of hiding how he felt.

But the moment he'd said those words, a chill had settled over him.

He'd seen how those expressive grey eyes had shadowed, how her features had tightened. And when she'd told him she felt nothing, that she didn't care from him, it felt as if she'd just punched him in the belly.

At least she didn't lie to ye, he told himself as he urged his courser into a brisk canter up a hill. The breeze whistled against his cheeks, bringing a welcoming sting.

But the thought was no consolation at all, not when it hurt to breathe, hurt to exist.

He'd been wanting to stretch this journey out so that he could savor every last moment he spent with Drew—but now he wished that their destination was in sight. They were making good time, especially while the weather was good. With any luck, they would reach Inishail before dusk the following day.

But that meant he and Drew would still have to spend another evening in each other's company.

A heavy weight settled upon Carr's chest at the thought. He wasn't sure how he was going to endure it.

Drew picked the last piece of meat off the bone—grouse again—and ate it. She had little appetite tonight. Each mouthful was a trial, yet seated at the fire with her escort, she didn't want any of them to fuss over her.

Least of all, Carr Broderick.

Drew swallowed, fighting a wave of nausea before wiping her fingers on the cloth that Aidan passed her.

There was little chance of Carr bothering her. He'd barely glanced her way all day.

Steeling herself, Drew looked across the fire at where he sat, talking to one of the other men. They were discussing the last stretch of the journey. One more day's ride and they'd reach their destination.

At first glance, Carr seemed relaxed this evening, but when she looked closer, Drew saw that wasn't the case. Lines of tension bracketed his mouth and furrowed his forehead. His broad shoulders—shoulders she'd clung to as he'd taken her up against that old oak—were rounded, betraying the unhappiness he hid from the world.

I've hurt him.

The knowledge made Drew feel even queasier. Over the years, after she'd been widowed, she'd spurned the attention of many men. Some had deserved it, and yet there had been one or two who hadn't. Yet she'd barely cared at the time.

She did now.

Tell me ye don't care.

Carr's words from that morning mocked her. He'd now think her a cold, heartless bitch. But the truth of it was that she did care for him. Every time she remembered the hurt in his eyes when she'd rebuffed him, when she'd lied to his face, her belly twisted painfully.

"I think I shall get an early night," she announced to the group, rising to her feet. "Since we have another long day ahead tomorrow."

The rest of the party nodded or smiled, wishing her a good rest. All except Carr. He merely glanced up, his gaze resting upon her for the first time all evening.

And for a moment, they stared at each other.

The raw look in his eyes, the tension in that ruggedly handsome face, made Drew's belly twist once more. The supper she'd eaten churned uneasily in her belly.

I'm sorry. The words whispered through the air between them, unsaid, and yet Drew felt them keenly. She'd never felt sorrier about anything in her life, and yet the stubborn core of resolve within her wouldn't be shifted.

The idea that she'd run away with Carr Broderick—a man who'd served her family for years now—was ridiculous.

Drew tore her gaze from Carr's and stepped away from the fire. She made her way back to her tent, to where someone—most likely Carr—had lit a brazier.

Vision blurring, Drew reached out and warmed her fingers over the low flames.

He's always been so kind to me ... even now.

And yet here she was, reminding herself that a match between them was impossible. They were too different, the gulf between them too wide.

It shouldn't matter and yet it did.

A secret tryst in the dark was one thing, but riding off into the sunset with him was another. The very idea was ridiculous. Carr should realize that too. However, after their night together, he'd been seized by a recklessness that was entirely out of character.

He hadn't been lying. All this time he'd been in love with her, and she'd been too blind to notice.

Drew squeezed her eyes shut. The lump in her throat made it difficult to swallow.

Looking back, she saw it now.

The way his gaze would linger upon her.

How he'd volunteered to become her personal guard and hadn't been unhappy in the slightest that someone else would lead The Dunan Guard.

His loyalty to her, even as she lay in a fever, her body covered in plague boils. He'd barely left her side for days; when the other servants fled the broch for fear of catching the plague, Carr had remained.

And all the while she'd told herself it was because he'd sworn fealty to her family.

But he'd done it for love.

Tears escaped then, trickling down Drew's cheeks. Usually, she hated to weep and would scrub away any treacherous tear. But tonight, she cried silently, her eyes squeezed shut, her chest aching.

14

Beyond Repair

DREW SLEPT BADLY. She passed most of the night staring up at the smoke hole in the tent roof, at a patch of star-strewn sky.

She'd wept at intervals too when the pain in her chest got too much—whenever her thoughts turned to Carr.

Moments from their tryst in the oak woods haunted her. The feel of his mouth on her neck. The way he'd kissed her as if she was a feast he'd been hungering for his whole life.

He was right—it had been a claiming. As she recalled the intensity of their passion, Drew broke out into a cold sweat.

It wasn't the fevered images of their joining that reduced her to tears, but all the kindnesses he'd shown her over the years. Unlike every other man close to her—except for her half-brother, Craeg—he'd never tried to change her. He'd never once implied that she was too aggressive, too mouthy, or too self-centered.

Carr loved her exactly how she was.

And she knew she'd never be accepted by anyone like that again.

An ill mood plagued her when she emerged from her tent. It was a chill, misty dawn. The warmer weather and brighter days had disappeared, and winter's gloom settled over the world once more—almost as if it sensed Drew's dark humor this morning.

Aidan was bent over a small griddle, frying up oatcakes.

"Morning, milady," the young warrior greeted her with a smile. "No butter or honey to go with these I'm afraid ... but they're fresh at least."

Drew favored him with a wan smile and took the two cakes he passed her. They smelled wonderful, yet she had little appetite this morning.

"Thank ye, Aidan," she murmured, before biting into a cake and forcing down a mouthful. As she ate, Drew glanced around. Without even realizing it, she was looking for Carr.

He'd plagued her thoughts all night, had made sleep near to impossible. And when she caught sight of him saddling the horses behind the tents, her chest constricted. Carr had his back to her, yet she could see by the rigidity of his shoulders and back, his jerky movements as he swung a saddle onto a horse's back and did up the girth, that he was unhappy.

She was the cause.

Drew's fingers tightened around the oatcake. If she was a braver person, she'd approach him now and make a proper apology. The man deserved that at least.

I am brave, she reminded herself, setting her jaw. *This needs to be done.*

Leaving the fireside, she circuited the edge of the tents that two men were starting to take down and marched up to Carr.

Hearing someone approach behind him, he turned.

Drew's breathing caught when she saw his face; she was sure she looked pale and strained this morning, but he looked worse.

Dark shadows smudged under his eyes. He almost appeared unwell.

Drew stopped a few feet back from him, aware that she was still clutching her uneaten oatcakes. Holding out the one she hadn't taken a bite from, she smiled. "Here ... I don't imagine ye have eaten yet."

Carr shook his head, his expression stony. "Keep them for yerself, milady ... I shall break my fast when I'm done here."

The cool formality of his tone cut her deeply. Gone was the man who favored her with slow smiles, who'd shared two jugs of wine with her, and who'd spoken of his past. This morning, he was 'Broderick', the aloof guard. He was virtually a stranger.

And yet Drew wasn't that easily put off. Lowering her hand, she kept the weak smile plastered to her face. It was her armor; without it, she'd crumble. "Carr," she began, her voice catching. "I have to say this ... for I might not get a chance later ... I'm sorry. I had no idea ye felt the way ye do. If I had, I wouldn't have asked that favor of ye."

His gaze shadowed, and a chill prickled Drew's skin.

I've just made things worse, she thought dully. *He's angry now.*

"I'm not sorry," he replied roughly. "And I won't be ... ever."

"But this has only hurt ye," she whispered. "I don't want that."

He shook his head. "Leaving ye at Inishail would still have hurt," he said, his voice clipped now. "But this way, ye know how I feel."

The boulder in Drew's belly grew heavier then. "It doesn't change anything, Carr," she whispered, her voice barely audible now. "It just makes our farewell harder ... for us both."

His mouth pinched. He then turned away from her and resumed saddling the horse. "Aye ... it does."

Carr wasn't proud of himself.

He kept his gaze on the buckle he was fastening as he listened to Drew walk away. He'd been cold and harsh—something he never was with her. But her apology—even well-meant as it was—was like a dirk blade to the gut.

Didn't the woman realize? He didn't want her to say sorry, he wanted her to acknowledge that what lay between them was rare and beautiful and that she'd be a fool to turn her back upon it.

Drew MacKinnon wasn't as hard as the world believed. He didn't like how pale and frail she looked this morning. The tremor in her voice made him ache to reach for her. Standing a few feet from Drew and not being able to touch her was torture. Her grey eyes were red-rimmed.

Had she been crying?

He'd never seen the woman he served weep. Surely, he'd been mistaken.

And yet the ache under his breastbone intensified as he let her walk away. She'd wanted to mend things between them. She'd wanted them to be friends again before he dropped her at Inishail Priory, and part of him wanted that too. But the baser part of him wanted to lash out at her.

Dolt, he chided himself. *She told ye she doesn't feel for ye, as ye do for her. Ye must accept it.*

Misery churned in his gut, and for an instant, Carr's eyes flickered shut. He'd always been stoic; he'd always been strong. He'd never been one to fight against fate, or against the hand life had dealt him.

But that was until today.

Despite that Drew had made the nature of their relationship clear the morning before, part of him still fought it.

I can't give up ... I won't give up.

Carr reached up and dragged a hand down his face. It seemed he was intent on wounding his heart beyond repair, on driving that dirk blade in to the hilt.

At the day's end, they'd reach Inishail, and there he'd watch Drew ride through the gates and out of his life forever.

But before she did, he had to try to change her mind—one last time.

The day that followed sped by with frightening speed. Despite the cloak of low cloud that obscured the mountains, and the light veil of rain that settled over everything, the company made excellent time.

This last stretch of the journey to Inishail was upon a surprisingly well-kept road. As noon approached, they forded a river and rode alongside a dark loch framed by lush green mountains wreathed in mist.

Loch Awe. Drew's mother, in her rare missives, had mentioned that the priory sat near the shores of a long, thin loch that stretched for leagues northeast and southwest.

If she hadn't felt so wretched, Drew would have found the landscape pretty; even with the bad weather, she could see that it was a lovely spot. Forest stretched down to the loch-edge in places, and the air was rich with the scent of pine. Two red deer sprinted across the road ahead of them before disappearing like wraiths into the trees.

But Drew could feel nothing except a hard kernel of unhappiness in her gut—a sensation that seemed to grow tighter with every furlong they traveled toward their destination.

They rested briefly at noon, and Drew made sure she avoided looking at Carr. Instead, she forced down cold oatcakes and cheese and listened to the rumble of male conversation around her.

After the morning's humiliation, she couldn't bear to look at him.

She'd tried to apologize, and he'd thrown her words back in her face. Not that she could entirely blame him. As Drew ate her noon meal, she tried not to relive those last few moments.

How bleak his gaze had looked.

They finished their meal quickly and were soon on the road again. Drew rode next to Aidan, while Carr and another took the lead.

"Ye have been quiet today, milady," the warrior observed, and when Drew glanced his way, she saw that the young man was observing her. "Is something amiss?"

Drew inhaled slowly and forced a gentle smile, before shaking her head. She was used to providing a façade to the world; she could do so now too. "The journey has just wearied me, that's all."

"Ye will be looking forward to reaching Inishail then?"

Drew nodded, not trusting herself to speak, lest her voice betray her.

Now that she focused upon it, she was dreading her arrival at the priory—a cold dread that clawed at her belly.

"I'm looking forward to returning to Dunan, milady," the warrior continued, unprompted. Studying his face, she saw the gleam of excitement in his blue eyes. "My love waits for me there."

Drew forced herself to keep breathing steadily, even if an iron band was now tightening around her ribs. "Really … what's her name?" Her voice was higher than usual, forced, yet Aidan didn't appear to notice.

"Brenna," he replied, grinning widely. "We have been promised to each other for years now … but as soon as spring arrives, we shall wed. I feel like the most fortunate man alive."

Drew saw the way the young man's face softened as he spoke of his love, how his eyes darkened as he'd said her name.

Swallowing hard, she forced herself to keep smiling, even if her face ached from the effort. However, her next words, when she managed them, were heartfelt. "Brenna is also very fortunate. I wish ye both happiness, Aidan."

15

Parting Ways

INISHAIL PRIORY CAME upon them too soon.

Drew wasn't ready for the sight of the high grey walls, etched against an emerald carpet behind them. As her mother had mentioned, the priory sat near the shores of the loch, less than a furlong back from the pebbly shore. A blanket of milky-white mist crept in from the loch, curling around the base of the priory walls.

And as they approached, an iron bell clanged, tolling through the mist.

Drew tensed. *Vespers*.

From this day forward, her day would be ruled by the clanging of that bell. It would tell her when to rise, when to pray, when to eat, and when to go to bed.

The thought made the queasiness she'd been fighting all day rise in the back of her throat.

The farewells to the men who'd accompanied them were brief, yet Drew held each of their gazes for an instant and wished them a safe return to Dunan.

"Make sure Brenna carries a posy of heather with her when ye wed in the spring," she told Aidan with a conspirator's smile. "It brings good luck."

Her comment made Aidan grin, while around him the other warriors laughed, ribbing the love-struck young man. Only Carr remained still and silent. Waiting while she said her goodbyes to the others. He alone would escort her the last two furlongs to the gate.

Turning her horse, she urged it up next to Carr's, and the pair of them rode in silence up to the arched gateway. When they were a few yards distant, they drew up their horses and dismounted, leading them the rest of the way.

The heavy iron knocker loomed before Drew. That knocker represented safety to so many. A fugitive could claim sanctuary just by touching it, and yet Drew was loath to reach out and curl her fingers around the cold iron.

Instead, she turned to Carr.

He was watching her with that same intense, focused look he'd given her when he'd revealed his feelings.

Please don't gaze upon me like that, she thought, something twisting deep within her chest. His expression made her long to throw herself into his arms, to dig her fingers into his short blond hair, and to ravage his mouth with her own.

But instead, she squared her shoulders and forced herself to remain in the present—to not think about what they'd done together or the things he'd said to her. It was the only way she was going to get through this.

"This is where we part ways," she said softly.

"It doesn't have to be," he replied, stepping close. Suddenly, he was towering above her. "It's not too late. Ye can take my hand now and go. No one but us will know."

Drew stared at him, her pulse thundering in her ears. The Lord give her strength, was he trying to reduce her to a pathetic wreck? It was hard enough as it was to bid him farewell, without him saying these things.

"Yer men will know," she said, her voice hoarse now. "How will ye explain this to them?"

He shook his head, gesturing to where they'd left the others. "They have ridden off, Drew ... there's only me and ye here."

A glance to the left revealed that he'd spoken true. Her escort had gone.

"I won't be returning to Dunan with them," Carr continued, his voice roughening now. "I will travel to the coast and take a boat to Éire, where I will seek out what remains of my kin. I wish for ye to join me ... as my wife."

Drew stared up at him. Her heart was beating so hard that she felt sick. "I've already told ye why I can't do that," she replied, hating the tremor in her voice.

"I don't believe that ye don't care for me," he cut in, a nerve flickering under one eye. "I think ye are lying ... to me and to yerself."

Drew stiffened. "Excuse me?"

"Ye tell me ye must do this ... ye tell me it's because we are too different, that ye have made yer mother a promise, that ye somehow deserve a life of penance." His voice was strained now, each word an effort, and yet he pushed himself on. "But all of it is a weak excuse. The truth, Drew MacKinnon, is that ye are afraid."

Drew's jaw tightened. "I am not."

"Aye, ye are terrified," he countered. "Ye are scared of taking a risk, scared of letting anyone see who ye really are. Ye are afraid of *love*."

His words hung between them, while Drew struggled to breathe. She didn't know what was stronger—the urge to slap his face or to weep.

Before she could do either, Carr continued. "I know ye have been hurt, but ye can trust me, Drew. Ye know that I have only ever cared for ye. I'm offering ye a new life ... I'm offering ye *hope*, and yet ye would throw it all away for certainty. Ye have made yerself a prisoner of yer own fears. If ye do this ... if ye throw this chance away ... ye are nothing more than a coward."

Drew took a shaky step back from him, and then another. A sob welled up in her throat, yet she choked it back. She was crumbling inside, but she couldn't let him see her pain. "Then I am a coward," she whispered.

Carr continued to watch her, his blue-grey eyes narrowing. "I will make camp near the priory ... five furlongs northeast of these walls," he said, his tone harsh with the grief and disappointment that vibrated from him now. "If ye do not come to me by morning, I shall ride away." He paused then, letting his words sink in. "Please don't throw this chance of happiness aside so lightly."

Drew didn't answer. She physically couldn't. Her throat had closed. Her pulse thundered in her ears, and her eyes burned from the urge to cry. But she wouldn't. Not here, not now.

She turned her back on him then. Gathering the last of her self-control, Drew stepped toward the gates. She reached out, her fingers grasping around cold iron, and she knocked.

Coward. Coward. Coward.

With each breath, those words mocked her.

Alone in the prioress's hall, Drew started to pace. As she'd entered the priory during Vespers, she was being made to wait.

The nun who'd met her at the gate hadn't been overly welcoming. She'd cast a jaundiced look at Carr before beckoning Drew inside.

The dull thud of the gate closing behind her had made Drew start to sweat, even as her legs began to tremble. With a huge effort, she'd managed to shove the panic down, and had followed the nun to the stables, where she'd seen to her horse before waiting for the prioress.

Completing another circuit of the narrow hall, her boots whispering upon the flagstones, Drew twisted her fingers together.

Fury now pulsed through her, hot and galvanizing, as she inwardly raged at Carr. *How dare he call me a coward? Who does he think he is?*

And yet, part of her loved that he'd stood up to her. He always had.

But she hadn't been able to look at his face as she'd entered the priory. She hadn't the strength.

The click of a door opening roused Drew from her tormented thoughts. Relieved that she was no longer alone to torture herself, she glanced toward the entrance and saw two women enter.

One was small, with a sharp-featured face that might have once been pretty if sourness hadn't withered it; while the other woman was heavy-set and jowly, a large iron cross resting upon her ample breast.

Drew's gaze immediately went to the first woman. Lorna MacKinnon—now Sister Lorna of Inishail—met her daughter's eye and favored her with a cool smile. "Ye have come sooner than we expected," she greeted her.

Years apart, Ma and that's the best ye can manage?

Her mother had never been the warmest of women, but her years in the priory had made her even colder than Drew remembered.

Drew forced an answering smile. "Aye ... we made good time on the road south."

"I am Mother Iseabal of Inishail," the second woman spoke up. She had a thin, sharp voice that immediately made Drew's irritation rise. "Kneel before me, so I may bless ye."

Drew did as bid, lowering herself on one knee before the prioress, while Mother Iseabal made the sign of the cross above her.

"Ye can rise now," the prioress said, her tone commanding.

Getting to her feet, Drew met the woman's eye and watched the prioress's gaze narrow at her boldness. She obviously wasn't used to others holding her gaze like an equal.

Ye will make an enemy of the prioress within days.

Carr's words came back to her then, and Drew tensed her jaw. Of course the man knew her well; he understood how difficult she'd find it to take orders from anyone, let alone another woman. At the time, Drew had dismissed his comment—he'd been trying to convince her not to take the veil after all.

But now that she stood before the prioress, a chill feathered down her nape.

This woman wasn't like Mother Shona, the former Abbess of Kilbride. Although Drew had never met her, Coira had told her of Mother Shona's warmth, her bravery, and her kindness.

Mother Iseabal dragged a disapproving eye down Drew, taking in her damp clothing and the muddy hems of her kirtle and cloak. "Ye shall enter Inishail as a novice," she informed Drew. "Sister Lorna will take ye to the dormitory so that ye might change into yer habit."

Drew's gaze flicked from the prioress to her mother. Both garbed in black habits and veils, their faces were framed by crisp white wimples.

"What will I do with my clothes?" Drew asked.

"They will be burned," Mother Iseabal replied, her gaze dropping to the rings that Drew wore upon her fingers. "Ye must give me those … no nun is allowed to wear adornment of any kind."

Drew did as bid, removing the gem-studded gold and silver rings from her fingers and handing them over to the prioress. She'd expected this, yet now that she was about to be admitted into the order, her chest felt tight and sweat trickled between her shoulder blades. How would she feel when she actually donned that crow's garb?

As the prioress took the rings, Drew noted how her fingers tightened possessively over them. Was that an avaricious gleam she'd just seen in the woman's eye?

"I take it, ye shall use the rings to feed the poor, Mother?" Drew asked sweetly. "I'd hate to think that the priory hoards its riches."

"Of course we don't," the prioress snapped, her gaze gleaming with outrage. "We live in poverty here. Go now and change into yer habit. We shall meet again in the kirk for prayers."

16

Ye Have My Heart

"MOTHER ISEABAL SEEMS a ... humorless woman."

Drew's comment broke the uncomfortable hush between mother and daughter as they crossed the yard to the dormitory. It was dark outside now, much later than Drew had thought. They had kept her waiting inside the prioress's hall for longer than she'd realized. Braziers illuminated their path.

Sister Lorna cut her a sharp glance. "She is a god-fearing woman," her mother sniffed. "Which is more than can be said for ye."

Drew arched a brow. "I'm here, aren't I?"

"Aye ... no doubt in penance for the wicked life ye have led."

Drew let her mother's comment lie between them for a few moments, before she answered. "I have flaws, Ma ... but I'm not wicked."

Sister Lorna snorted. "Our Lord will be the judge of that." Her grey eyes narrowed when they focused upon Drew. "Never again address me as yer mother. Here, we are not related ... we are bonded merely in service to God."

Drew held her mother's gaze, unflinching. For years she'd lived in fear of Lorna MacKinnon. When she'd been a bairn, she'd been terrified of her, and of the willow rod she'd used to administer beatings. Their mother had thrashed Duncan the hardest—until he'd grown big and strong enough to fight back—but Drew would never forget the sting of the rod upon her back or the screech of her mother's voice.

An icy sensation settled in the center of Drew's chest as she realized just how much she disliked this woman.

She'd given her life, yet she'd never given her love.

No wonder I'm as I am, Drew thought bitterly. *No wonder I'm afraid of giving my heart to anyone.*

Coward.

Drew's throat thickened then. Aye, Carr was right. But with this woman as her mother, was it any surprise? Part of her had hoped that she'd arrive at Inishial to find her mother changed, that life in the priory might have softened her somehow. But it had not. If anything, it had made her even bitterer.

"Does that *bastard* still rule Dunan?" Her mother said then, her mouth pursing.

Drew inclined her head. "Craeg?"

"Who else do ye think I'd be referring to?"

"Aye ... he's now the MacKinnon clan-chief."

Sister Lorna's face went taut at this admission, and she hurriedly crossed herself. "Ill news, indeed," she muttered. "Yer father would turn in his grave to see such a day."

Drew held her tongue, although she had the urge to point out that Craeg MacKinnon wouldn't exist if it hadn't been for her father's dalliances. Instead, she favored her mother with a wintry smile. "Craeg is an able clan-chief ... a far better one than Duncan ever was. The people love him."

The nun's step faltered at this, her grey eyes turning hard. "How dare ye?" she hissed, and her hand actually raised as if she wished to strike Drew across the face. Drew didn't flinch away. If her mother dared hit her, she'd return the gesture. "Yer brother was the rightful ruler of Dunan," Sister Lorna snarled. "Not this ... this *whoreson*."

"Duncan made a poor clan-chief ... and don't pretend that ye liked him," Drew countered. "We all knew why ye left. Once Da died, ye were afraid of what Duncan might do ... for ye knew he hated ye. And ye were right, he did."

Sister Lorna's head jerked back as if Drew had indeed just slapped her. She moved back a few paces, her shoulders rounded, her face a mask of fury.

"Ye will learn to curb that viper's tongue here," she hissed, her gaze gleaming with spite. "I have told the prioress of yer wickedness, and she's promised me that she will make ye penitent by the year's end."

With that, Sister Lorna spun on her heel and stalked toward the dark bulk of the dormitories, her spine as stiff as an outraged cat.

Drew watched her go, suddenly rooted to the spot.

Her mother was wrong; she already regretted her sins. She didn't know what had possessed her to throw Duncan's hate in her mother's face. Perhaps she too had a latent need for vengeance, for a chance to get even with this cold, cruel woman.

A sickly sensation rose in Drew's throat. The problem with revenge though, was that the pleasure it brought was short-lived.

I'm turning into her. The thought made her shudder. This was what bitterness did. It poisoned. *In a few years, that will be me.*

Even now, the warmth that Carr Broderick had brought her during this journey, the joy, was starting to fade. Once again, he was right. She was a prisoner of her own fears. For a few short days, she had seen what life could be like if she had the courage to leave the past behind—yet she'd turned her back on it, on him.

Her mother had almost reached the door to the dormitory, and Drew knew that she should go after her, should bend her head and ask forgiveness for her angry words.

But, once again, she couldn't summon the will. It was as if her limbs had turned to stone.

Carr poked the embers with a stick, watching as a spray of sparks shot up into the night. He'd found a dry birch branch for his fire, but it wasn't throwing out much heat. The air was damp and cold tonight—although it was nothing like the chill in his heart.

It felt as if a lump of ice had settled there and would never dislodge.

She's not coming.

Carr didn't want to admit it to himself, and he'd tried to cling onto hope ever since riding away from the priory, but as the night wore on, the truth was becoming clear.

She's not coming, and I'm a fool.

Aye, he was a fool all right, but he'd been a hopeful one. Carr shoved the stick into the embers again, sending more sparks shooting into the heavens. He'd had to take the risk. He'd had to know that all hope was lost.

And now he did.

Muttering a curse, Carr scrubbed a fist over his face. His chest, belly, and head all hurt. He'd ripped himself open before Drew, and he'd been brutally honest with her out there before the gates of the priory.

She probably hates me now.

He couldn't believe how roughly he'd spoken to her. He'd told her she was a coward, for pity's sake. Did he really think that was going to win her over?

If it wasn't the middle of the night, he'd pack up right now and ride away.

She definitely wasn't coming.

Squeezing his eyes shut, Carr leaned his head forward, resting his brow on his clasped hands. His eyelids burned. He hadn't wept in years, but he was on the verge of doing so now. He'd given his heart to a woman who didn't want it; he'd wasted years and years pining after Drew, knowing it was impossible. And yet there had always been a kernel of hope within him.

Until tonight.

How he wished to drown himself in a barrel of ale. The first thing he'd do tomorrow would be to ride to the nearest tavern and drink himself into oblivion.

The pain in his heart couldn't be borne. He needed to escape it; he needed to escape himself.

"Carr!"

A woman's voice cut through his pain, his darkness. He glanced up, blinking as if waking from a dream. Had he been imagining things?

"Carr."

Instinctively, his hand went to his dirk, and he swiveled around to face the figure standing behind him. He'd been so lost in misery, he hadn't even heard her approach. His horse, tethered a few yards away under a tree, snorted nervously.

Before him stood a slight figure, wrapped in a heavy fur mantle. The firelight played across her pale, heart-shaped face and eyes the color of storm clouds.

"Drew," he breathed, stunned. "Ye came?"

A smile curved her lips as she stared down at him. "Aye."

Carr blinked. He'd been so far gone in his despair, he wondered if he'd lost his mind. Maybe he was imagining things. "Is this a dream?"

Her smile widened, her cheeks dimpling. "No ... it's real, Carr."

He leaped to his feet and closed the gap between them in a heartbeat, pulling Drew into his arms. She *was* real—warm and plaint in his arms, her body trembling, her mouth eager under his as he kissed her.

When Carr finally broke off the kiss, they were both gasping for breath. Gazing down at Drew's face, he saw that her cheeks were wet with tears.

"I thought I'd lost ye," he admitted hoarsely, his hands cupping her cheeks as he kissed away her tears. "I imagined it was the end."

"I couldn't do it," she gasped out the words. "Ye were right. I was afraid ... terrified in fact."

Leaning down, he kissed her again. This time it was gentle, tender. "*I* was terrified I'd never set eyes on ye again," he murmured against her lips. "Ye have my heart, Drew ... ye have for a long time."

Her eyes glittered and tears spilled over once more. He realized then that she was too overcome with emotion to speak.

"What happened?" he whispered. "Did something occur inside the priory ... something to make ye change yer mind?"

Her mouth curved at the edges. "Aye ... let's say things became clear to me," she murmured, her voice catching. "Things that should have been evident before. Seeing my mother was like having my own future laid out before me. I don't want to become that woman." Drew inhaled a deep, shuddering breath then, trying to regain her shattered composure.

"How did ye get away?" he asked softly. "Surely, they didn't want ye to leave?"

"I didn't ask the prioress's permission if that's what ye mean," she replied, her lips quirking. "I just left." She paused then, her hand rising to his face. There, she traced the lines of his cheek, jaw, and chin with her fingertips, as if committing them to memory. "All these years, Carr, ye have only ever treated me well," she whispered. "Ye have seen the worst of me, and ye still want me. I'd be the most dull-witted woman alive if I turned my back on ye ... on us. And if ye will still have me, I am yers."

Carr's breathing caught. Had he heard that right? "Ye are?"

"Aye," she whispered. Her eyes were luminous in the firelight, tears sparkling on her eyelashes. "I love ye, Carr ... but I was such a fool that I didn't realize what that actually means." She offered him a watery smile. "Ye have taught me."

Epilogue

I Only Have Eyes for Ye

Belvelly Castle
Cork, Éire (Ireland)

Six months later ...

ROUGH MALE SHOUTS made Drew glance up from her weaving. In the solar, high in the tower keep, she was at work near the chamber's tiny window. Leaving her loom, she peered out, her gaze alighting upon the bailey below.

"What are they doing?" Clara called from behind her.

Drew glanced over her shoulder, her gaze settling upon Clara De La Roche, wife of the man who ruled this castle. Small and red-haired with jade-green eyes, Clara wore an impish expression as she glanced up from her embroidery. "They aren't brawling again, are they?"

"No," Drew replied with an answering grin. "Carr's got them wrestling each other in the dirt."

Clara laughed, cast aside her embroidery, and joined Drew at the window. "This I have to see."

"We're too far away to catch much," Drew replied. However, both women could see that the men had stripped down to their braies, gathered in a semi-circle around two wrestlers locked together.

Clara gave a huff of annoyance. "This won't do." She stepped back from the window and picked up her skirts. "Come ... Drew. Our weaving and embroidery can wait."

With that, Clara turned and hurried from the solar. Still grinning, Drew followed her. They'd been living at Belvelly Castle for over three months now after Carr had taken the position as Captain of The Belvelly Guard. They'd originally gone in search of Carr's kin, only to discover that few of his family now resided in the area. And those who did lived in poverty.

Carr decided to strike out on his own, and shortly after, he'd found this position.

It had taken Drew barely a day to realize that she and Clara would become good friends; the women shared the same wicked sense of humor, the same sharp wit.

Life had been good ever since she and Carr made Belvelly their home. As soon as they'd gotten settled, Drew sent word to Dunan. She'd known that Craeg and Coira would be worrying about her. In her missive, she let them know she was safe and well—and living in Éire with Carr Broderick.

The women descended the narrow stone steps, wending their way to the bottom of the tower keep and into the Great Hall that made up most of that level. The noon meal approached, and the servants were busy setting the long tables that lined the chamber. The aroma of mutton stew and baking bread wafted through the keep.

Outdoors in the bailey, the wrestling continued. And as she approached the group of warriors, Drew realized that one of the wrestlers was her husband.

Husband. She got a warm glow in the pit of her belly whenever she thought of Carr that way. It was ridiculous really, for they'd been wed nearly six moons now, yet she still felt as giddy as a blushing sixteen-year-old maid around him.

Her gaze feasted upon him now, naked to the waist. His muscular torso gleamed with sweat. Years ago, Drew had thought of Carr as 'stocky', yet the first time she'd seen him naked, she'd realized there wasn't any fat on him. His body was pure muscle.

"This is entertaining, is it not?" Clara whispered to Drew, linking arms with her. "I must say, yer husband is a fine specimen."

Drew smiled, although she never took her gaze off Carr. As they watched, he hooked his leg through his opponent's and brought him crashing to the ground. The onlookers cheered and clapped, as did Drew and Clara.

Breathing hard, Carr straightened up. He wiped the sweat off his brow and exchanged a few words with the man next to him before he realized they had a female audience. His gaze widened. "Drew … Lady Clara. This is hardly a place for ladies."

Clara gave a delicate snort. "I must ask ye to practice wrestling with Conor sometime … now that's a sight I'd enjoy."

This comment brought guffaws of laughter from the surrounding warriors. Conor De La Roche, Baron of Belvelly, was a huge bull of a man. One that few would want to wrestle with.

However, Carr grinned at this. The sight made Drew's heart flutter. It was so good to see him smile. It made Drew realize how much happier he was these days. Dunan had cast a shadow over him as much as it did her.

Here in Éire, they were both lighter, freer, as if a heavy mantle had been lifted from their shoulders.

Taking a drying cloth that one of his men handed him, Carr approached Drew. Perhaps realizing she was intruding, Clara moved away to talk to one of the guards, giving them a few moments alone.

"I enjoyed that," Drew greeted him with a pert grin. "I hadn't realized how much I love watching half-naked men fight."

Carr smiled, a slow, sultry expression that made her belly melt like hot tallow. "I aim to please, wife," he said softly, before bowing his head to kiss her. Oblivious to the fact that they stood in the midst of the bailey, surrounded by men and horses, he deepened the kiss.

Drew stood on tip-toe, her lips parting under his. Pulling back, she realized her pulse was racing. "The noon meal is almost ready," she murmured, breathless now. "Will ye come inside with me?"

He nodded. "Just let me get my léine." He turned and retrieved his tunic from one of the guards. He then pulled it over his head and took Drew by the hand, leading her back toward the keep.

"I'm not sure I want ye coming out here to watch me wrestle," he said with a wink. "The other warriors stare too much at my pretty wife for my liking."

Drew laughed, the sound carrying over the bailey as she squeezed his hand. "Let them stare. I only have eyes for ye."

She meant it too. The connection she and Carr shared was powerful and grew stronger with each passing moon. She'd almost lost him once, through her own blindness, and she'd never let that happen again.

Carr smiled down at her, his gaze soft now. He drew her hand up, placing it over his heart, letting her feel its strong, steady beat. "And I for ye, mo chridhe," he whispered.

The End

From the author

Some stories just have to be written! I don't know about you, but Drew and Carr intrigued me right from Book #1. During the first draft of UNFORGOTTEN, I realized that I wanted to tell their story … I just wasn't sure in what format. It wasn't going to be a full-length novel, and it certainly merited more than a short story.

So instead, it ended up being a kind of 'epilogue novella' for THE SISTERS OF KILBRIDE series. At 30,000 words, I'd like to think I have done their romance justice.

Characters like Drew and Carr are so easy to write about. She's feisty and willful, a woman that would scare many men off. But Carr sees past all that. I must admit, I'm a sucker for 'unrequited love' stories. I love writing about the longing, the frustration, and then the moment the balance of power between the two characters starts to shift. CLAIMED ended up being more angsty and sexy than I'd anticipated. As always, writing a romance between two more 'mature' characters, especially where the heroine is a few years older than the hero, gives me more scope during sex scenes. This wasn't a story about a blushing virgin!

I hope you found CLAIMED as fun to read as I did to write. Sadly, we now come to the end of THE SISTERS OF KILBRIDE. But fear not, dear reader, I have plenty more stories in store for you … including a special bonus to complete this series. Keep scrolling to find out more!

Jayne x

About the Author

Award-winning author Jayne Castel writes epic Historical and Fantasy Romance. Her vibrant characters, richly researched historical settings, and action-packed adventure romance transport readers to forgotten times and imaginary worlds.

Jayne has published a number of bestselling series. In love with all things Scottish, Jayne also writes romances set in Dark Ages Scotland ... sexy Pict warriors anyone?

When she's not writing, Jayne is reading (and re-reading) her favorite authors, cooking Italian feasts, and going for long walks with her husband. She lives in New Zealand's beautiful South Island.

Connect with Jayne online:
www.jaynecastel.com
www.facebook.com/JayneCastelRomance/
https://www.instagram.com/jaynecastelauthor/
Email: **contact@jaynecastel.com**